ALSO BY KIRA SHELL

KISS ME LIKE YOU LOVE ME
Let the Game Begin
A Dangerous Game

Game OVER

KIRA SHELL

Copyright © 2020, 2026 by Mondadori Libri S.p.A
Cover and internal design © 2026 by Sourcebooks
Cover design by Silver Grace/Bitter Sage Designs
Cover images © liliya/Deposit Photos, LilsRaven/Deposit Photos, alexroz/Deposit Photos

Sourcebooks and the colophon are registered trademarks of Sourcebooks.

All rights reserved. No part of this book may be reproduced in any form or by any electronic or mechanical means, including information storage and retrieval systems—except in the case of brief quotations embodied in critical articles or reviews—without permission in writing from its publisher, Sourcebooks.

No part of this book may be used or reproduced in any manner for the purpose of training artificial intelligence technologies or systems.

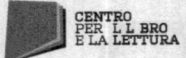

This work has been translated with the contribution of the Center for Books and Reading of the Italian Ministry of Culture.

Originally published as *Kiss Me Like You Love Me Vol. 3: Game Over* © 2020 Mondadori Libri S.p.A. Published by Mondadori Libri for the imprint Sperling & Kupfer. Translated from Italian by Nicole M. Taylor.

The characters and events portrayed in this book are fictitious or are used fictitiously. Any similarity to real persons, living or dead, is purely coincidental and not intended by the author.

All brand names and product names used in this book are trademarks, registered trademarks, or trade names of their respective holders. Sourcebooks is not associated with any product or vendor in this book.

Published by Sourcebooks Casablanca, an imprint of Sourcebooks
1935 Brookdale RD, Naperville, IL 60563-2773
(630) 961-3900
sourcebooks.com

Originally published as *Kiss Me Like You Love Me Vol. 3: Game Over* in 2020 in Italy by Sperling & Kupfer, an imprint of Mondadori Libri S.p.A. This edition issued based on the paperback edition published in 2019 in Italy by Sperling & Kupfer, an imprint of Mondadori Libri S.p.A.

Cataloging-in-Publication Data is on file with the Library of Congress.

The authorized representative in the EEA is Dorling Kindersley Verlag GmbH. Arnulfstr. 124, 80636 Munich, Germany

Manufactured in the UK by Clays and distributed
by Dorling Kindersley Limited, London
001-358649-Apr/26
10 9 8 7 6 5 4 3 2 1

CONTENT WARNING

This is a dark romance series. It includes some sensitive themes as well as explicit content. It contains scenes of nonconsensual and dubiously consensual sexual activity as well as depictions of violence and child sexual abuse. It is recommended for a mature and aware audience.

Love sometimes makes you live out a fairy tale.
Other times, it drops you into the darkest reality.
But it is still love.

PROLOGUE

> "Nothing can save you from the monsters.
> Not love, not the power of the stars, not even
> fairy dust."

NEIL

It was the twenty-fifth of November.

Rain pattered on the windows.

Mom still hadn't come back from work, and she'd called to let Kimberly know she'd be late.

My babysitter had then decided to take a shower and left me alone for a few moments. As soon as she left, I thought, *It's all up to me.* I had to save myself and stop the woman who had been hurting me for a year at that point. So, naked and covered in sweat, I got up off the couch. The irritation around my genitals made me grimace in pain. But I tried not to dwell on it because I had a concrete goal: Get to the phone. The sound of running water from the bathroom meant I still had some time left in which to act. I screwed up all my courage and grabbed the phone to call 911.

Trembling in fear, I felt tears building up in the corners of my eyes. I swiped them rapidly with the backs of my hands and waited for the operator to pick up.

"Nine-one-one, what is your emergency?"

I sucked in a breath at the sound of the man's stern voice and spoke, despite my fear.

"I'm at home alone. My parents aren't here. There's a woman here with me. She's hurting me... She does things to me that she's not supposed to do. I-I... Please help me..." It all came out in one terrified breath, and then I heard Kimberly calling for me. My eyes bulged, and I immediately hung up, running back to the couch so she wouldn't get suspicious.

She wanted to play with me again. This time, though, would be the last time.

"Neil." Kim strode toward me wrapped in a white bathrobe. "Go wait for me down in the basement with Megan," she ordered, and I hesitated. For a moment, I'd forgotten entirely about the little girl downstairs. "What are you waiting for? Get a move on!" I flinched when she yelled at me but got up from the couch and crouched down to pick up my underwear. She came closer to me, though, and I froze. "No, don't get your clothes back on." She gave me an impish grin and stepped aside, gesturing for me to go past her. I just nodded and, shaking, went down to the basement.

It was cold down there, and the cold seemed to sink inside my skin. The light was dim, and there wasn't a lot of furniture down there. Immediately, my attention was caught by Megan's sobs. She was naked as well, standing in front of a camera.

I was just a boy, but I had known for a while what Kim had in mind.

"Neil..." Megan moved cautiously toward me, one arm clasped over her chest, though I wasn't looking at her naked body. "What is she going to make us do?" She wiped away a tear with the back of her hand and stroked her long black hair compulsively.

"I don't know." I lied so as not to scare her. "But I called the police. All we have to do is pretend for a little while," I whispered to her as I cast a furtive glance back up the stairs to see if Kim was coming down.

"The police?" Megan managed. "Do you think they'll...come here?" She blinked in bewilderment.

"Of course." But I wasn't sure, actually. I hadn't even had time to tell them my address. I prayed, though, that somehow the man on the phone would be able to get here and rescue us.

"I think they're ready, but I'll try it and see." I heard Kimberly's voice and then the sound of the door shutting. She was on the phone. Megan hid behind me, and I tried to be strong for her. "I understand that the buyers are getting impatient, Ryan, but Neil is still too unruly..."

Kim began to walk down the stairs. Her shadow crept ominously along the dimly lit wall. As she advanced on us, her shadowy silhouette looked more and more like some skulking monster. "Yeah, okay. I'll remember. I have to go now. I'll call you back later," she said testily before hanging up the phone.

When she got down to the last steps, I could see she'd gotten dressed in a basic pair of jeans and a sweater. She tucked her phone into her back pocket and approached us before sitting down in a wooden chair. Never once did she take her eyes off our bodies.

"Christ, look how pathetic you are. Why are you shaking?" Kim crossed one leg over the other and sighed in irritation. "Megan, stand over there next to Neil and stop blubbering. Ryan's coming to pick you up in an hour, and he'll be very angry if he finds out you weren't minding me," she snapped.

The little girl came over by my side, her eyes downcast and her legs clenched tightly together. Kimberly was silent for a few moments before bursting into laughter, flinging her blond hair over one shoulder. I could never predict her mood swings, and I suspected that she was crazy as well as evil.

"I don't know what to do with you two. Each of you is worse than the other one." She shook her head, pinching the bridge of her nose. "Ryan and I taught you all of this for one specific purpose," she continued. "And today is the day you're going to put it all into practice. So quit wasting my time," she barked irritably before stretching out an arm to turn on the camcorder. The bright light blinded me immediately. I covered my eye with one hand, the other still between my legs. Megan hid herself behind me and started crying again, which annoyed Kimberly. She got up with a huff.

"All we're doing is making a movie," she explained, putting her hands on her hips. "And you two are going to be the main characters. You'll play Peter and Wendy. It's nothing to be afraid of." She waved a lazy hand through the air before sitting back down.

"Now, Neil," she called out again, her voice so hard that it made me flinch. "Show Megan how you love a woman," she ordered.

I turned to look at the little girl then, and she shied away from me, afraid.

I knew what my babysitter wanted me to do to Megan, but I couldn't bring myself to act like Kimberly.

"Do it or I go to Logan's room. Your choice," she added severely. I swallowed hard. Just the idea of her abusing my brother the way she had done to me was horrifying. But I turned to look into her glacial eyes and shook my head slowly, showing her clearly that I wasn't going to do as she said.

"What the fuck is your problem, you little shit? Give her a kiss! Now!" Kim leaped to her feet but then frowned when she heard rapid footsteps on the floor above us. It sounded like someone was running through the kitchen. "Be quiet!" she whispered to me. Freezing in place as I approached the stairs, my eyes locked on the closed door at the top of them. My heart began to pound in my chest; I staggered back a few steps when someone kicked the door down. Kimberly gasped as two police officers came barreling down the stairs, weapons pointed right at her.

"Hands up!" The first one yelled while the other looked uncomprehendingly at the camcorder and then at Megan and me.

I felt an instinctive shame and a need to hide, so I backed into the corner and tucked my knees up against my chest to cover my body. Megan took refuge behind an old sofa, bursting into full-on sobs.

"Christ..." one of the officers muttered, running a hand over his shocked face.

"You have the right to remain silent. Anything you say can and will be used against you in a court of law. You have the right to an attorney. If you cannot afford an attorney, one will be provided for you," one officer recited, handcuffing an unresisting Kimberly, who just smiled mockingly in return.

Then she turned to look at me and appeared to realize in that moment that I had been the one who called the police. Her bright eyes went stormy, her lips curled into a sly, plastic grin, and her blond hair tumbled back over her shoulders as the officer forced her to walk.

All at once, her expression shifted, and her face became such a twisted mask of rage that I froze, staring at her, unable to react.

I felt nothing. I didn't cry.

I couldn't understand that it was truly over.

The child-eating witch was walking away from me wearing handcuffs, cloaked in her sins and perversions.

She was going to pay for the things she'd done, and I would never see her again.

The memory of her, however, would stay on me, indelible as a tattoo.

No one was going to be able to give my destroyed childhood back to me.

I'd ended the war that Kimberly started, but nothing would ever be like it had been before.

I wasn't a child anymore.

I was a monster, made by another human's wrongs.

A monster made by Kimberly Bennett's wrongs.

1

"I felt a wave of heaviness, like my body had been transformed into lead."

NEIL

"In exactly five minutes and...ten seconds, that's going to explode," the maniac on the end of the phone informed me. I was frozen in shock.

"So, still having fun playing with me, Neil?"

I considered the question.

My sister's life hung in the balance, so I knew I had to be smart if I wanted to avoid the worst possible outcome.

"Clock's ticking. Good luck." Player ended the call.

I stood back up, staring vacantly in front of me in shock. For a second, I hoped this was just another nightmare. Anguish and fear that I wouldn't be able to save Chloe swept over me, rendering me speechless. I had no idea what to do.

"Neil," Logan called, moving toward me. I didn't look at him.

"Hey, man. What's happening? What'd he say to you?" Xavier clapped a hand on my shoulder and gave me the mildest shake, but it did nothing.

"Five minutes. We only have five minutes before the bomb goes off." I spoke like a robot and moved my eyes slowly over to Logan, whose face was drained of color.

"The *bomb*?" Xavier echoed, looking bewildered for a few moments longer. "Then we need to move our asses now!" He brushed past me and picked up the baseball bat I'd thrown to the ground. "He doesn't get to win," he said, looking determinedly back at me. In one blow, he smashed through what was left of the car's window and stuck his arm in to unlock the doors.

Meanwhile, I just kept standing there silently, still in shock. I felt a wave of heaviness, like my body had been transformed into lead.

"I'll check if there's a trunk release up here. Cars are always supposed to fucking have them. The rest of you look under the floor mats and see if there's anything that might pop the trunk," Xavier ordered. He sat down in the driver's seat and bent over, searching for the lever in question. I continued to watch all of it, listen to all of it, and do nothing.

I could feel the sweat running down my forehead, the powerful beats of my heart, the tremor in my right hand...

"I..." I tried to speak, but I couldn't get out an intelligible sentence.

"Neil, time's running out!" Logan grabbed me by the shoulders and shook me, trying to get me to move, and my breathing got heavier. "Come back to me. Please. We'll get her in time, you'll see," he said shakily. I didn't even blink, so my brother took my face in his hands and forced me to look at him. "I'm going to go into the motel and ask for help. I know that you're thinking this is your fault, but it's not. We're going to save Chloe. We just have to stay calm and keep a clear head." He clapped my back twice before rushing away with Alyssa in tow.

"Neil, get over here!" I was prodded to alertness only when I heard Xavier's shout. I jumped. I wasn't going to let myself be disheartened. I wasn't going to let Player win this war.

I hurried over to my friend and looked at him, still not speaking.

I must have looked like a total asshole, incapable of making myself useful in an emergency. It wasn't at all like me to be so passive.

"I found a trunk release cable under the floor mat," Xavier said, showing it to me. "Except it's stuck or something. You're going to have to give me a hand," he told me, sounding agitated. I just nodded and knelt down.

He called out to me again, and I turned to look at him, terror in my eyes.

"Listen, man, I've never seen you shell-shocked like this, and you need to get your shit together and quick, okay?" he said urgently. He was right.

I stared into his dark eyes, and I could see how worried he was. I wasn't going to fix shit by just standing there and letting the dark thoughts overwhelm me, so I forced myself to act instead of just thinking out worst-case scenarios.

"Yeah... I know," I mumbled, trying to cut the exchange short as I focused on the trunk release, pulling it hard.

"What we need is a pair of pliers," Xavier murmured, wiping his forehead with the back of his hand.

"We don't have the time, Xavier," I said shortly.

"Okay, so let's try this. I'll see if I can fold the back seats up and shift them forward and check underneath for another lever or something. You stay here and keep putting pressure on the release," he said, quickly moving to the back of the car. I stayed in the driver's seat and bent over, trying desperately to get the damned lever to move. Periodically, I cast quick glances at the motel entrance, hoping I might see what the hell was going on with Logan, but I couldn't spot him there.

"There's no fucking lever back here!" Xavier raged suddenly, and I turned to look at him. He drove a hand through his black hair, sweating.

"Kick it in," I suggested, and his eyes lit up. Xavier had a violent streak a mile wide, and, more than that, he was completely unable to moderate his strength. "Pretend it's your father," I continued, well aware of the kind of sick rage Xavier felt whenever he thought of the man. Xavier didn't say anything and just breathed heavily in response. Then he positioned himself against the back seats, albeit with some difficulty. The car was too small for two people of our size, but we weren't letting that small detail stop us.

Moments later, he started pummeling the back of the car with one leg while I returned to the stuck cable.

"How much time do we have left?" he asked quickly, pausing to catch his breath.

"Not much." I had been keeping track of every minute that passed. Three more were gone by then.

"Guys!" My brother raced over to us and leaned in the open door to reveal an iron crowbar.

"Well, that's fucking handy," Xavier commented, and we both crawled out of the car.

We had to go fast.

I snatched the bar out of Logan's hand and walked around to the back of the car. Then, with all the strength I could muster, I began to force the trunk open.

After three failed attempts, I succeeded.

With one more sharp strike, the trunk sprang open, and my eyes went wide when I saw Chloe's huddled form.

Her wrists and ankles were bound with ropes, a strip of duct tape covered her mouth, her blond hair was disheveled, and her eyes were closed. I didn't waste any more time, hurrying to scoop her up and pull her out of the trunk. I crouched down, clutching her body to me, and pulled the tape from her lips.

"Kiddo, can you hear me?" I touched her cold cheek while Logan, on the verge of tears, got down next to me and stroked her hair.

"It's us, Chloe," he said in a pleading whisper while Alyssa and Xavier stood and watched us silently.

"Come on, sis. Come back to us," Logan added, tortured. Chloe's breathing was so shallow that it was nearly imperceptible.

She had to come back and smile again, to look at me with those impish gray eyes.

She had to come back to my room to get into my closet and take all the sweatshirts she wanted.

She had to come back and tell me what an asshole I was with girls.

She had to come back to lecture me about smoking too much, like she did all the time.

She had to come back to snuggle against my chest and whisper to me how much she loved me and how she'd always be there for me.

She had to come back to give me compliments only when she wanted something in return.

She had to come back to make her sassy faces and sulk when we fought and flip me the bird when I said something insulting.

She had to come back because, if my siblings weren't there, I wouldn't be there either.

Because if they were done, I'd be done too.

"I'm right here, kiddo," I whispered, hugging her tightly. I didn't cry. I never did, in fact. I felt so drained, so exhausted, that I didn't have any tears left to express my internal state. I just held her tight to me and squeezed my eyes shut, hoping that when I opened them again, I would wake from my nightmare.

But, unfortunately, that wasn't what happened. As soon as I opened my eyes, reality stared me in the face again.

Just this fucked reality.

"Neil..." Chloe's weak voice moved across my skin, raising goosebumps. She clutched my leather jacket with one hand and looked up at me, her gray eyes hitting me like a blow.

"Good morning, kiddo." I smiled, feeling my heart soften and melt like ice in the sun's heat.

"Thank God, Chloe." Logan kissed all over her head the way he used to when she was little: her head, her cheeks, her forehead, and her nose.

It was these two, the only good things that came from my childhood.

We had just seconds to get away from the car—seconds that would mean the difference between life and death.

"We need to run, now!" Xavier shouted, urging us to move. I scooped up Chloe in my arms, and we all began to run with all the energy we had left, lungs burning as we sucked in air.

It was a matter of a moment.

A moment in which we managed to get as far as we could from that doomed car.

A moment in which our lives hung in the balance.

A moment in which I realized that, if I didn't free my sister in time, there would be nothing left of her but ashes.

We quickly made it to my Maserati, and I deposited Chloe in the back seat with Logan and Alyssa. Xavier threw himself into the passenger seat, and I got behind the wheel.

And, just then, the other car exploded.

It was blown sky-high, causing a thick cloud of smoke to rise into the air. The shock wave from the blast was so intense that the windows of my car vibrated. I started the car and hit the gas. The tires screeched noisily as we peeled out of the parking lot. In the rearview mirror, I watched as the flames climbed higher into the sky.

"I win, you son of a bitch," I murmured in satisfaction.

....

When we got back home, my sobbing mother tackled Chloe just before Matt gave her a long, loving hug. My sister was still very shaken up, even though Logan had untied all the ropes and comforted her all the way home.

"Daddy!" she exclaimed, embracing our father, William, who was, surprisingly, there as well. He looked unsettled but still impeccably dressed in a designer suit. He kissed her forehead and gazed at her, his eyes so bright and clear they looked like blue glass. He looked at her the way I had always wanted him to look at me, especially when I was a kid. Though I never would have admitted that to anyone else.

"I've been so worried..." he said in a tortured murmur. He who had always been such a cold, unflappable man now looked fragile and vulnerable.

"I'm okay," Chloe answered with a weak smile before turning her attention back to our mother and Matt.

"Can anyone tell me how this happened?" William shifted his withering gaze from Logan to me, waiting for me to say something. As usual, the only thing I could muster up for him was complete indifference. He was fully aware of how much I hated him, but it didn't seem to bother him.

He'd certainly never made any efforts to patch up our relationship.

He had never been there for me.

Annoyed by my silence, he stalked over to me and gave me an evaluating look before turning slightly to do the same thing to Xavier, who was standing next to me.

"So, you're letting your sister hang around these thugs now..." he noted with a superior air. He looked at the piercings in Xavier's eyebrow and lower lip, his face a rictus of displeasure, before his eyes slid down to take in Xavier's clothes.

William knew all the members of the Krew and had repeatedly ordered me to stay away from them, but I'd never paid him any mind. No one was going to tell me what to do—or not to do—least of all him. The man meant nothing to me; he had no right to dictate anything about my life.

"So, Hudson, how's your father faring in prison?" He gave Xavier a mocking grin, and the boy next to me went rigid. William didn't give two shits about Xavier or his family; he just wanted to get in a shot at me, reminding me that I spent my time with what he called "the dregs of society"—troubled, dangerous kids who would inevitably land me in jail, thus ruining the Miller family's good name.

Xavier took a step forward, ready to get into it with him because he hated it whenever anyone who wasn't a close friend brought up his father's incarceration for his mother's murder. I stretched my arm out across his chest, silently telling him to let it go.

"You should go," I said, giving him a speaking look. His jaw tightened, and he rubbed his eyebrow in agitation. Knowing him, he was going to ignore my warning completely.

"You know what, Bill?" Xavier shot back predictably with a devious little half-smile. "You talk about my father one more time, and I'll do a whole lot more than bring your kid home late from a party..." Xavier tried to step closer to him, but I automatically grabbed his arm to keep him from attacking. I yanked him back as he stared wrathfully at William. After a moment, he peered down his nose at the older man, as though repulsed by the signifiers of wealth that dripped off his person. Xavier turned abruptly and left, slamming the door behind him.

I kept silent, but my father could sense my satisfaction. Another son might have sprung to his parent's defense in that kind of situation. I, on the other hand, had just basked in it like a pig in shit.

"You and I need to talk," he told me in his usual autocratic tone.

"I have nothing to say to you." I tried to push past him, but he blocked me. He was as tall as I was, and he seemed to have more muscle than I remembered. He'd always taken great care of his physical condition, and that had only ramped up since his divorce from my mother. He was now an inveterate middle-aged bachelor, constantly sleeping with much younger women but incapable of committing to anything serious with anyone.

He was a man who knew next to nothing about me, but I undoubtedly knew everything about him.

"Neil, your father's right," my mother put in. "Logan, Alyssa, please take Chloe up to her room and stay there with her," she told them to remove their buffering presence. My brother gave me a concerned look, and I gestured for him to go with a jerk of my chin.

I wasn't afraid of anything or anyone, and definitely not my asshole father.

When we were all alone in the spacious living room, my mother sighed, rubbing her forehead, and Matt patted her shoulder comfortingly. William, on the other hand, just turned to me, hands on his hips.

"Do you have any idea what could have happened to your sister?" he exclaimed with an inquisitorial expression that I longed to punch right off his face.

"And don't try to lie to me. I called Logan to see if you'd found Chloe, and he told me everything," he added firmly.

I remembered that conversation. I was driving, but Logan nimbly answered our father's questions, quickly spinning out a story about Chloe sneaking out to a party she heard about from the Krew (that part was mostly true), drinking too much, and losing her phone before passing out. I could hear William's indistinct outrage through the phone, but I knew it was better than telling them anything about Player or his deadly games.

"I didn't take her to the party." I hated pretending to be so cavalier, but I couldn't tell them the truth.

"No, that was just your degenerate friends." He sighed, fixing me with a stare full of the distaste he could never fully hide from me.

"I don't see how this is my problem," I answered simply and

began feeling around in the pockets of my sweatshirt for my pack of Winstons.

"No?" he said in a mocking echo. "So you think it's just fine if your underage sister is exposed to the kind of cesspools you spend your time in? Or maybe you don't care if your sister gets assaulted by one of the punks you hang out with?" He went on the attack, baring his teeth so ferociously that my mother moved toward him in alarm.

"William!" my mother chided him.

"What, Mia?" He turned on her, enraged. "You know as well as I do that this is his fault. How many times has he brought trouble down on this family?" He raised his voice, and my mother retreated. She never could stand up to her ex-husband. She was incapable of taking my side or even of trying to put in a good word for me. She hadn't been able to manage it even when I was a child and he was visiting his awful punishments on me in the name of "education."

"There's no point dredging up all the things I've done wrong. I know what I did," I said loudly to draw his attention. "But Chloe's not me. She screwed up like any other teenager, but she's okay, and she's home safe now. Trust me, she won't do it again," I continued.

"Did you hear that?" William said sharply, turning to Matt and Mia. "She's learned her lesson, he says. Because he's such an expert on normal teenage behavior," he laughed mirthlessly. "Are you even hearing yourself? How do you know she's not going to get hooked on something and end up just like you, out there running wild for everyone to see?" Ah, of course, his priority was the same as it always was—protecting his fucking reputation.

"What's the matter, William? Are you worried about your bottom line? Or maybe about the reporters who are always circling?" I taunted him with a cold smile. "I can see the headlines now: 'Children of CEO William Miller, embroiled in yet another scandal.'" I let out a laugh and pulled a cigarette from the pack, tucking it between my lips before I continued. "I still remember the army of overpaid lawyers you needed to make everything disappear so quick after the cops arrested my babysitter..." I lit my cigarette and advanced on him until our razor-sharp stares aligned perfectly. "You remember my babysitter, right? The woman who abused me. The one you got so *friendly* with." I blew a cloud of smoke into his face, but he remained impassive.

"You're talking crap," he said, shaking his head as though amused. "Your mother never believed that particular story, and do you know why?" He cut his eyes at his ex-wife before looking back at me. "Because, back then, she knew better than to listen to a disturbed child, just like she isn't going to listen to a raving lunatic now," he sneered. I continued smoking, unmoved, as I stared into his eyes.

I'd never look away. He was lucky I hadn't already kicked his ass.

"She was the reason I was 'a disturbed child.' And you were fucking her while your wife was pregnant with Chloe," I shot back tauntingly.

Go on, William, let your monster out, I thought.

I wanted him to expose his worst side so I'd have a valid reason to hit him.

"You've always had such an imagination, ever since you were a boy," he taunted me, licking his lower lip. He was getting antsy; I could see it in his tense muscles and tight jaw.

"Oh, yeah. Guess I imagined these, too..." I pushed the sleeve of my sweatshirt up roughly and exposed the three small scars on my left forearm. William creased up his forehead and took a step back, speechless. There was nothing more to say.

I shoved my way past him and crossed the living room. Then, without so much as a glance at my mother or that asshole Matt, I raced up the stairs. Despite the powerful urge to shower that I was feeling, I instead headed for Chloe's room and went in without knocking. I spotted Alyssa on the end of the bed first and then Logan, stretched out beside our sister.

"Hey, there you are." My brother grinned at me and threw a stuffed animal in my direction, which I dodged easily. I gave him a thin, sad smile and moved closer, my eyes locked on Chloe, who still seemed subdued. Alyssa abruptly cleared her throat and got up awkwardly, fixing her dress.

"I'll let you all have a minute," she said, correctly sensing that she was one person too many in that room. I lay down on the bed next to my siblings and let out a long sigh.

"Are you mad at me?" Chloe whispered as she cuddled closer to my chest, under her pink covers with the weird bunny-shaped pattern.

"I'm not mad, no. Blackout pissed? Yes." I stroked her blond hair. She was sandwiched between me and Logan, and she looked back and forth at us. "But we'll talk about all that tomorrow," I continued wearily.

"That's right. You'll have to tell us everything," Logan put in, propping himself up on his elbow.

"I shouldn't have gone to the party. I don't remember much. I drank something, and then I passed out, and when I woke up I was in that trunk, and..." Chloe began to sob, shaking like a leaf. Seeing the pain she was in only fueled my rage.

No one was ever supposed to lay a hand on my siblings.

"Shh... It's over now." I pressed a kiss to her hair. I could feel her tears wetting my neck and her fingers digging into my sweatshirt. I knew exactly what she was trying to say: *"Stay here. With me."*

And I would.

For them, I would always stay.

I waited a while longer, stroking her hair until she had fallen into a deep sleep. I disentangled myself and got up, antsy with the intense need to wash myself. As if everything that had gone down in the past few hours wasn't enough, my tics were flaring up again as if to remind me just how far I was from being a normal human being. I left Chloe to Logan and shut myself up in my room. I took a long shower and then put on a pair of black jeans with a black hoodie. As I did so, I reflected on the encounter I'd just had with my father; his cruel words, my impenetrability...and I smiled. I had grown accustomed to that treatment, his lack of care, and the intense disdain he reserved just for me for years and years now with no particular cause. I had never understood what made him hate me so much. I had been a pigheaded and rebellious child, sure, but certainly not enough to justify the level of animosity he had toward me.

I couldn't remember getting so much as a hug from him nor the last time he'd acted like a father with me.

I hadn't called him that since Kimberly was taken away.

The sound of my phone ringing cut through my musings. I quickly fixed my hoodie and walked over to the bed to grab the phone. I looked at the screen, dumbstruck—it was Selene.

For a second, I thought about rejecting the call or answering just to tell her not to fuck with me. I couldn't decide which of the two options would be worse.

"Missing me already, Tinkerbell?" I answered finally with my characteristic cockiness, stuffing my pack of Winstons into my pocket.

I listened to her sigh on the other end of the phone, and it occurred to me that just hours had passed since I'd returned to New York. Yet she'd still felt the need to call me.

"You were pretty upset when you left. I wanted to know if everything was okay out there." All I had to do was hear the delicate tone of her voice, and I felt a powerful shiver in my lower stomach.

"Yes, everything's good." I decided not to tell her about Player because I didn't want to worry her. When I told her, I'd be looking in her eyes. I'd be able to reassure her. "And I already told you: I never call a woman after spending the night with her," I pointed out.

Though we'd had outstanding sex in Detroit, and I'd had a phenomenal orgasm thanks to her, I didn't want her to have any illusions. Truthfully, I had immediately regretted telling her about my sexual dysfunction because I wasn't used to trusting people or confiding in them things about my life that I considered personal.

With Selene, I was starting to open up too much, and that was unsettling for me.

"I'm not 'a woman.' I'm Selene Anderson," she answered with a hint of humor that made me smile. She wanted to hear me say that she was important, that she was the only one for me, but that was never going to happen. Yes, I'd had experienced things with her that I'd probably never have with anyone else, but that didn't mean anything to me.

"And you are my Disaster," she added in an indulgent tone, and something rumbled in my chest.

Shit—what was this new feeling I was having?

For a second, I actually liked what she'd told me, then my rational mind took over and swept away any positive feelings I might have had.

"Seriously...yours?" I grimaced in irritation. I considered possessiveness an even worse sign than jealousy. It was a symptom of a deeper emotional entanglement, and that bothered me. I didn't belong to her—I didn't belong to anyone—and Selene had to understand that.

"I told you I wanted to be exclusive. You said you'd think about it," Selene reminded me confidently. Fuck, I'd completely forgotten that conversation. It had just been a tossed-off answer. I vividly recalled the moment: We were lying in bed together, and I was exhausted. All I wanted to do was sleep, and I needed her to stop asking me pointless questions, so I told her the first thing that popped into my head. In reality, I thought it would be too difficult to actually quit fucking the blonds because they were as much a compulsion for me as the showers were. I could have a serious meltdown if I wasn't allowed to vent in the ways I'd learned.

"Do you know why this drama of ours is deathless?" I asked her, all in a rush, skipping over everything she'd just said. Selene didn't say anything for so long that I had to check the phone's display to make sure she hadn't hung up on me.

"No, why?" she asked finally; her voice at least sounded curious.

"Because it's me and the Boy. If I choose you, I'm abandoning him. There's never going to be a way out." It was my circuitous way of telling her that I didn't think I could do without my other lovers because so much more than sex was at stake. "But...you could become a part of my madness, and we could be deathless together. What do you think?" I taunted her. I was expecting a sarcastic comeback, but Selene's long silence instead made me furrow my brow. I imagined her, deeply reflective, her crystalline eyes pointed into the middle distance, her plush mouth pursed into a skeptical expression.

I would have kissed it—bitten it—if she were standing there in front of me.

"I think I entered into your madness a long time ago, and if that can make what we are together deathless, then I'm in," she said eventually with all the determination that made her a woman. A real woman.

Babygirl was gentle and understanding, loving, and patient, but she was also stubborn and brave. She knew how messed up I was, and yet she still tried to banish her fears so she could stay by my side.

Feeling thoughtful, I walked out onto my room's balcony and leaned my elbows against the railing, staring out over the backyard.

The freezing air stung my skin, but I didn't care. I needed the cold to keep my head clear.

"After how I fucked you that last time, you should want nothing to do with me," I told her harshly.

That's what I would have done in her position. I would have gotten as far away from me as possible and tried to forget about the whole insane scenario.

"But I..." She cleared her throat. "...liked it."

I could hear how embarrassed she was.

Despite the fact that I'd probably spent more time with her naked than dressed, Babygirl still retained her sense of modesty and shyness.

"I believe it; you came more than once," I said just to needle her a little bit more and was rewarded with her response.

"Neil!" she shrieked, and I broke into laughter. I'd never stop finding her adorable. She was so honest, so genuine, and, at times, so funny that she made all my worries disappear. At least for a moment.

"I still remember your first time, you know," I told her abruptly, sinking into the memory. "You telling me to be gentle, and me not knowing how to do that. I just kept thinking, *You and I shouldn't have a fucking thing to do with each other.*" Those words were supposed to remain inside my head—be just for me—but, to my surprise, I had blurted them out without a second thought. I scrubbed a hand over my face, realizing that this whole situation had gotten out of hand and was edging into disaster territory. I was faced with just two options: I could let Selene go, or I could be a selfish bastard and continue taking pleasure in her.

I knew that the first choice was the right choice, but I kept leaning toward the second, much worse option.

"Fate is unpredictable," Babygirl answered, drawing me back to our conversation.

"And cruel, sometimes," I added, knowing that she deserved more than me and that I was never going to change. I couldn't predict the future, but I strongly suspected that if we let this madness go on between us, neither of us was going to end up happy. Especially not her.

With that realization, my mood shifted, and I stood up straight before walking back into my room.

"I have to go now," I concluded coldly, making it clear to her that I didn't want to talk anymore.

"Okay. I hope..." She sighed. "I hope I hear from you or see you soon," she said, almost sounding afraid of how I might react. I also longed not just to see her but to kiss her, to touch her, and to take her to bed again. I yearned to breathe in her coconut scent, to stroke her soft skin, to feel her legs wrapped around me, and to lose myself in her heat, in the only place where I felt truly good.

My Neverland.

"Good night, Tigress." I ended the call without another word and walked out of my bedroom.

I ruffled the long hair on top of my head and went down the stairs, heading for the kitchen. Though hearing Babygirl's voice had given me a momentary peace, I still called up Xavier because I needed William to know just why I'd seemed so calm with him.

"Talk, asshole," my friend answered on the second ring.

"I'm going to text you the code to my father's garage. You can take out your rage on his car," I chuckled.

He burst into laughter. "Are you fucking with me?"

"Do I ever joke about shit like that?" I cocked an eyebrow as I entered the kitchen.

"I guess not," he admitted.

"So go on, knock yourself out." I ended the call and sent Xavier the text just as I said I would. Then I opened the fridge to fish out a bottle of pineapple juice.

"I'd have thought you were more of a beer guy."

I sucked in a breath when I heard Alyssa's voice from behind me. I spun around to find her sitting on a stool at the kitchen island, drinking a glass of something amber-colored. Did she get into the liquor while she was waiting? I hadn't expected to find her there, but, then again, Alyssa had been spending more and more time with Logan, so I shouldn't have been surprised that she hadn't just gone home.

"I don't drink much." I got out a glass to pour my juice into and went back to ignoring her. The fact that she was Megan's little sister bothered me.

"I see," she murmured thoughtfully. I turned away from her then and leaned against the counter. I slid my phone into my pocket and lifted the glass of pineapple juice to my lips. I gave her an assessing look, not bothering to appear anything but cold. It was the kind of look I frequently offered to women and girls I found unattractive to make sure that they knew not to try it on with me. "You always have such a strong scent. Did you know? I can smell it from here." She gave me a sliver of a smile, and I cocked my head to one side, unsure what exactly she was trying to tell me. I continued to stare flatly at her until she stiffened up and quickly turned her gaze elsewhere.

Clumsy flirtation did nothing for me, especially not when it came from her. I loved my independence, and I was always the one who made the decision to get with a woman. Besides, there was no way in hell I was going to make a pass at my brother's girlfriend.

"Where's Logan?" I asked her quickly, taking a sip of juice. The sweet pineapple taste hit my tongue, and I instinctively licked my lower lip. Alyssa watched this completely involuntary movement and looked embarrassed. I kept my face blank. Her discomfort was not my problem.

"Still upstairs with Chloe. So I came down here for a drink." She gestured toward her glass, and I said nothing in response. Instead, I rifled through one of the cupboards looking for a bag of pistachios. I was craving them, and I'd been forced to leave behind the ones I bought in Detroit when Selene forced me to go grocery shopping with her.

I smiled slightly at the memory.

Sometimes, just thinking of my Babygirl's ocean eyes let a little light into the darkness that surrounded me.

"Shit," I hissed when I couldn't find a single bag. I should have reminded Anna to get some more.

My shoulders slumped, and I let out a disappointed huff like a little kid. I'd never been a big eater, and I'd trade just about any fancy meal for a bag of pistachios.

"We're going to eat soon. Did you come here looking for a snack?" Alyssa asked teasingly, reminding me that she was still there. I turned to see that she'd gotten off her stool. Her high-heeled boots elevated her slim figure, and her short woolen dress highlighted her curves. *Logan has good taste*, I thought. We both appreciated a certain harmony in the female form.

"Yeah, but apparently I'll have to wait for dinner," I answered in a bored tone as I gulped down what was left of the juice before putting the glass in the sink. I was about to leave when Alyssa, in a single impulsive movement, grabbed me by the hips and pinned me against the kitchen counter.

I looked at her in bewilderment.

I didn't even have time to process what she meant to do before she was up on her tiptoes, kissing me. She pressed her hot lips to mine and teased me with her tongue, coaxing my mouth to open reflexively. I could taste her lipstick as she laid claim to me, bold and aggressive. I reciprocated her deranged show of desire but only for a few seconds. She panted against my mouth with a strange gleam in her eyes. Her arms held me tight until I managed to wriggle free from her and push her away.

"All the girls at school say your kisses are addictive. I wanted to see for myself," she shrugged. I was frozen, staring at her. Typically, I had full control in any situation with a woman. I was almost always the one making advances and coaxing them to give in to me. In that moment, however, I was literally rendered speechless with shock. I knew women wanted me; there was nothing I could do about that, but I'd never expected this kind of move from my brother's girlfriend of all people...

My brother's girl...

"What the—" I wiped my lips off disgustedly with the back of my hand.

"Fuck!" Logan shouted from the kitchen doorway. I whirled around to look at him, and the reality of the situation finally dawned on me—the knowledge of what he must have just witnessed. My brother's eyes were wide, his breathing rapid, and he stared in horror at both Alyssa and me. "What are you doing? What the hell is going on?" he shouted so loudly that his girlfriend flinched.

No, no, no, goddamnit!

I didn't want Logan to misconstrue what had just happened. I also wanted to know what the fuck his girlfriend had been thinking and why she'd done it, but I turned away from her and went to him instead.

"Logan..." I began, horrified, but he just backed away from me, shaking his head.

"Don't make excuses, you asshole!" He stabbed a finger at me, and I sucked in a breath. "I stood right here and watched you stick your tongue down my girlfriend's throat!" he accused, enraged, before turning his attention to Alyssa, who ducked her head in shame. "And what about you? You're pathetic!" He gave her a glacial look. I moved toward him again, though I knew how impossible it was to get through to him when he was this angry. I needed to tell him what had actually happened.

"Logan, I had nothing to do with this. You have to believe me; your girlfriend owes me an explanation too!" I gestured furiously at her, and my brother arched a skeptical eyebrow at me before chuckling mirthlessly as he rubbed his face.

No, he didn't believe me.

He thought I was lying to him, but even worse...
How could he believe I'd do something like that to him?

"Don't start with that shit!" he said, rounding on me. "You want Alyssa now too? You already hurt Matt by fucking his daughter. Are you going to do the same to me?" he lashed out at me, a betrayed look on his face. I tried to chalk these dark thoughts up to his anger in the moment. He probably wasn't thinking clearly; maybe his wounded pride was doing the talking. Anything to avoid believing that he had so little faith in me.

"What are you talking about?" I murmured incredulously.

"How would you feel if you caught me making out with Selene, huh? How?" he insisted venomously, and I gave him a tortured look.

"I wasn't the one who kissed her. It was her! Fuck's sake!" I shouted back. It wasn't like me to put the blame on other people. I always took full responsibility when I fucked up, but in this case, I wasn't about to lose my brother over some fucking girl's raging hormones. "I would lay down my life for you or Chloe," I continued as he stared at me, his face screwed up in a grimace. "I would do anything to keep you from feeling any kind of pain, and you know that better than anyone. You *know* what I went through to keep you safe. Do you seriously think I'd betray your trust in such a disgusting way?" I asked him, without yelling this time. I didn't need to; he understood me well enough.

All at once, the feeling of guilt melted away, giving way to the understanding that I hadn't done anything wrong. I pulled myself together and returned to my usual unbothered demeanor.

I turned to Alyssa and leveled a glare at her.

"You need to get shit straight with your girlfriend. Because apparently she's the one who's confused." I turned to look at Logan. His hazel eyes stared into mine as, slowly, his anger receded. In that moment, my brother seemed to see me clearly once again, and, slowly, he moved to stand next to me.

"Alyssa," he said to his girlfriend. "You want to explain yourself? After that, you can leave this house, and I will never see you again, but, right now, I think I deserve a fucking explanation!" he said with a raised voice, and Alyssa looked like she was really struggling. I folded my arms over my chest and leaned on the counter, scrutinizing her. I, too, wanted to know what she had to say for herself, but, at the same time, I almost felt a little pity for her.

"You've always been interested in Neil, haven't you?" Logan murmured, sounding disillusioned. She said nothing in response. "That's why you were always asking me if he was at home or how things were going with him and Selene." He shook his head like all the clues were finally coming together for him. "That's why I caught you staring at him all the time. That's why you had such a hate-on for him and said you couldn't stand him." He smiled thinly and gave her a sneering look. "Because my brother always just ignored you. Because he was never attracted to you. And you wanted him to be." He rubbed his face, chewing his lip as he came to that awful conclusion. Logan's guesses troubled me as well—I didn't want to think about how much he must have been hurting just then.

"I didn't see it until it was too goddamn late," he whispered, overwrought.

"Logan, I…" Alyssa tried to speak, but my brother lifted a hand immediately to silence her.

"Get out!" He pointed at the door in a way that brooked no arguments. Logan didn't even want to listen to her try to explain. After all, he knew why she kissed me, didn't he? She wanted me.

The girl had been concealing a little crush on me all this time.

I still couldn't really believe it.

It made total sense that Logan no longer had any trust in her. He was a good man but definitely not a stupid one.

There was nothing for Alyssa to do but obey him. She turned and headed for the door, not having the guts to look either of us in the eye.

And then we were alone. The silence that fell over the kitchen made me feel awkward.

I was so torn up that I didn't even know how to face my brother. I glanced at him, trying to get a bead on how he was doing. He was undoubtedly devastated, but I wanted to say something to him to make sure that things were still going to be okay between the two of us. I started to open my mouth, but he just shook his head, still looking shell-shocked, and walked out into the backyard without giving me so much as another glance.

I felt like a piece of shit.

After all, I had briefly returned the kiss, albeit unintentionally. My body reacted automatically to contact with Alyssa because she was a woman. Though my brain had no intention of kissing her, my lips had opened to admit her, if only for a few moments.

Shit.

I wanted to go after Logan, to beg him to forgive me and to please not hate me, but I forced myself to let him have some time alone.

He needed to cool down—God only knew what I would have done in his position.

I pinched the bridge of my nose between my fingers and squeezed my eyes shut.

I couldn't do anything right.

It seemed like women were my worst nightmare, and, at the same time, I couldn't survive without them. Not for the first time, I put the blame on the way I looked. Kimberly had been right all along: Women thought they loved me because I was physically attractive and made them think lewd thoughts. The fact that it had been Logan's girlfriend who had fallen for the deadly honey trap this time made me feel wracked with guilt.

Half an hour later, we sat down to dinner, and I didn't touch my meal. I spent the whole time staring at my brother, who was seated across from me.

He couldn't even bring himself to look at me.

I kept trying to catch Logan's eyes because the blank indifference he showed me was worse than any "fuck you," but he just kept ignoring me. Then, I shifted my attention to Matt, who was eating his chicken, and watched Chloe nibble at a piece of bread, lost in her own thoughts. The only sounds in the room were the clink of cutlery and Anna's soft footsteps as she moved around the dining room, making sure that nothing was missing from the table. The tension between my brother and me was so biting it was almost tangible.

"Okay, that's enough. What's going on, kids?" my mother broke the silence with a vexed tone and stopped eating. I leaned back in my chair then and gave her a flat stare, drumming my fingers on my plate. "Logan?" Obviously, she'd decided not to waste time trying to pry anything out of me, knowing how seldom I talked, and started with my brother instead.

"Nothing, Mom. It's fine," Logan answered with a sigh of irritation.

"Is it? I'm your mother. I know when something is wrong," she answered, dabbing her mouth with a napkin. I managed to keep from laughing aloud and instead just cleared my throat sarcastically to get her attention. Her eyes moved to me, and she frowned.

"And what are you scoffing at, then?" she asked me sternly.

"Do you really consider yourself the kind of mother who is good at knowing when something's wrong with her kids?" I asked sardonically. "I don't, but, you know, we can pretend for tonight." I waved a hand through the air like I was shooing away a gnat.

I stared at her, daring her to argue with me, and, fortunately for her, she decided to pretend I hadn't spoken.

"As I was saying, Logan..." She turned back to my brother. "What's up? Also, where did Alyssa go? Wasn't she going to have dinner with us?" she continued, glancing at the empty chair where

Alyssa often sat. A tic in Logan's jaw demonstrated his discomfort, and a new surge of guilt hit me, crushing my chest like a boulder.

"Apparently she wanted to fuck someone else," he answered decisively. He shrugged, and suddenly everyone, even Matt, turned their attention to him.

"What?" Matt asked.

"For real?" Chloe cut in, and I went rigid, staring down at the fork abandoned on my plate.

"Yeah. She cheated on me just like Amber did," Logan said sharply, referring to his ex-girlfriend. Before Alyssa, she was the most serious relationship he'd had. I didn't know what to say or what to do. I didn't even have the balls to tell the rest of the family that I was the other man involved. Instead, I just silently reflected upon everything that had happened recently. Everything was going tits up: Matt hated me ever since he found out I was sleeping with his daughter. Chloe almost died because of me, because Player was using the people around me to get revenge on me. And now I'd let my brother down as well. I was the sole reason that each one of them was suffering. I was the one who was always causing pain and frustration, fear, and worry.

I was the cause of everything.

"I'm going to leave after graduation," I blurted out, still staring at an indeterminate spot in the middle of the table. I figured I had all eyes on me by that point because I'd said somethin g so unexpected and caught them all off guard. But there was nothing else to do at that point. Walking away was the best choice for everyone. I could keep my family out of the shitshow that was my life and protect them from whoever wanted to kill me.

"What are you talking about, Neil?" my mother asked, and I almost laughed at her crestfallen tone. I chewed my lower lip anxiously and looked up at her so she could see that I was serious.

"My architecture professor put me forward for this internship in Chicago. It's for the most deserving students in his class, and apparently I'm one of them. I hadn't decided whether to accept it or not, but I think I'm going to go. The distance will be good for all of us," I told her, affirming for myself that it was the right call.

Shit, the thought of spending that much time with Megan made me wince, though. But that would have to be a problem for another time. I could find out something to keep her away from me. Besides, graduation was still a few months off, so there was no point in getting myself tied up in knots about the situation right away.

"You didn't tell me anything about that," my mother answered, sounding confused.

"I haven't told you anything about me or my life for years now. This shouldn't come as a surprise." I got up, unwilling to keep sitting with them and enduring this unpleasant atmosphere that only made me sick to my stomach. Then I walked out of the room without waiting for her reply. I had no interest in stumbling through some faux-maternal conversation with her.

I knew that, inside, they were all celebrating my decision. I felt like a stranger in my house, someone who was only ever a complication in the lives of others. Unsurprisingly, everyone was looking at me like it was an inquisition, like they were ready to judge and condemn me.

I went out to the backyard and, ignoring the cold, sat down on a lounge chair. I gazed into the pool and took note of how my breath condensed in the freezing air.

I felt like I'd been drained of all emotion.

I had a void inside me, and I knew that empty place would never be filled.

I turned my face up to the sky, a mantle of black serving as a backdrop for the full moon, high and bright. I wondered what Babygirl was doing just then. Was she wearing those horrible pajamas or those boner-killing fluffy slippers? It was only then that it occurred to me that my decision to leave would actually take me closer to Detroit.

I smiled bitterly at myself.

There was no future for us, just like I'd thought. Our paths were fated to diverge. Selene still needed to finish undergrad and achieve all her dreams. Plus, there was no way she was going to leave her mother and move to God knows where with a man who didn't love her and was incapable of giving her anything like security.

Disheartened, I gave up on trying to find something positive about my life and recognized that it was nothing but negative.

All fucking negative.

I didn't have anything to hope for; even the idea of leaving for Chicago didn't engender much enthusiasm.

I shook my head and scrubbed a hand over my face, feeling inundated with thoughts.

Then, my phone rang, and I was roused from my funk. I fished it out of my jeans pocket and, after a brief glance at the screen, answered it.

"What do you want?" I snapped at Megan, my back already up.

That girl had the uncanny ability to show up at the most inopportune moments just to bust my balls.

"What is this about Logan kicking Alyssa out of the house after you kissed her?" she asked me angrily. She'd even raised her voice like she was going to intimidate me somehow.

"Tell your bitch sister to quit lying to you. She's the one who kissed me," I said truculently, not caring in the least if I sounded aggressive. The girl had blatantly lied about me.

"What?" she murmured, sounding unconvinced.

"Yeah, you heard me right. Be pissed at her, not at me." I sighed as I considered, yet again, how ridiculous all of this was. And the irreparable consequences were all falling on me.

"My sister wouldn't do something like that," Megan insisted, sounding surprised.

"Yet, she did. But you know what? I don't give a flying fuck what you believe. I don't need to keep wasting my breath on you, Head Case." I leaped to my feet and felt rage spreading throughout my body.

"Try to relax, Miller," she answered flippantly.

"Relax? Because of her, I don't know if my brother is ever going to look me in the eye again!" Terror clenched my chest tight at the idea of Logan hating me. I couldn't get a breath, though I inhaled deeply and squeezed my eyes shut. I had to get myself under control, or I was going to break something.

"Your brother loves you. And, if what you're saying is true, I don't get why Alyssa would do something like that. That's not her." Megan tried to defend her sister, though she sounded as shocked as I had been. I had many flaws. I was far from perfect, but I wasn't a liar, and Head Case knew that about me. "Were you able to straighten things out with Logan?" she added almost immediately, and a sneering laugh burbled up from deep in my throat.

"That's none of your business. You and your sister just need to stay the hell away from us," I said menacingly, only getting angrier. I had started to think that the Wayne sisters might be bad luck for us.

"Mmm... That might be a difficult request to accommodate, Miller. Did you think some more about the Chicago internship? If you take it, you'll be putting up with a lot of me." I listened to her laugh and rubbed my forehead uncomfortably.

"I'll figure out some method for keeping you away from me, rest assured," I retorted firmly. In reality, I had no idea how I was going to keep our paths from crossing.

"Wait, wait—does that mean you've accepted the internship?" she asked, and I sighed impatiently.

"What's it to you?" I dodged her question. I hadn't emailed Professor Robinson yet; I still had time to rethink my decision and maybe change my mind...

"I need to know so I'm prepared to bow to the king of the

assholes when I see him in person," she teased me in her most irritating voice, but I remained as unmoved as ever.

"Listen, Head Case, I gotta go now. Try to never call me again, okay?" I said, scowling. "In fact, lose my number. Pretend you never knew it." There, now I had made myself perfectly clear, and my authoritative tone would surely have the desired effect.

"Is that an order?" she asked with a sneer in her voice, and I wanted nothing more than to slap her.

"Exactly. It's an order, and you need to listen to me!" I said, raising my voice. Why couldn't she understand that she had to just leave me in peace? Why did she insist on pushing me over the edge?

"I don't enjoy an overbearing man. I believe I've already told you that," she continued.

"Fuck off. I'm not wasting any more time on this shit." And then I hung up before she could answer, an expression of self-satisfaction on my face.

I smiled a sly, victorious smile. If Megan thought she was going to fuck with me, she was grossly mistaken.

I'd known for a while that she got off on getting a rise out of me, so I played along.

Her arrogance bothered me, and her pushiness was even worse.

I played the part of the thin-skinned guy to make her feel like she had some power over me.

Oh... they were my favorite kind of adversaries.

Soon enough Head Case was going to realize that's exactly what she was to me: an adversary. And that there was only going to be one outcome with an opponent like me...

A crushing defeat.

2

"And there's no Prince Charming coming to give you that fateful kiss that will wake you from your curse."

SELENE

The last time we were together, I asked Neil to be exclusive.

I still couldn't believe it. I must have experienced a temporary bout of insanity after he'd given me another little piece of himself. He had actually admitted to me that he suffered from a sexual dysfunction that kept him from achieving orgasm with a woman. Despite that, when he was in my bed, he surrendered himself completely to a passionate climax.

How stupid could I get? For goodness' sake!

I knew that backing him into a corner and putting pressure on him definitely wasn't the right move, and yet I'd let my gut feelings lead me astray. Right before he fell asleep beside me, Neil had told me that he'd think about it, but I had a suspicion that wasn't the truth and was instead just his way of shutting me up and putting an end to my interrogation.

By then, I knew him well enough to recognize his moves.

We'd talked on the phone the night before, and, like usual, I could tell that Neil was giving in to the dark thoughts that constantly inundated his mind. He told me that I should hate him for the way he'd been with me, but all I could do was remember everything we'd done together the next morning. When I got the wild idea in my head that I needed to taste him.

I turned bright red every time I thought about that moment, but, despite my embarrassment, I couldn't bring myself to regret any of it.

It had been magnificent, seeing him so aroused for me.

I had to smile when I recalled the way he clenched his fist around my hair and how his golden eyes stared into mine reassuringly. And I pressed my thighs together as I thought about my lips sliding along him.

He was still fighting with himself, but, with me, he felt more than just the physical pleasure a man with his specific kinks usually felt. He also managed to shatter every psychological barrier, even that of his own ironclad self-control. Ever since he'd left, I had to admit that a strange desire had been kindled within me: I thought about him constantly and longed for a repeat.

I wanted to make love to him again and pleasure him with my mouth. I was even wondering why I'd waited so long to explore his perfect body in such an intense and earth-shaking fashion. My thoughts had me off kilter. Sometimes, I even thought it was wrong to want a man so much and that it might be bad for me. Other times, I thought my brain was just becoming more lustful as I discovered the true beauty of sexuality.

"Did you know you have to massage your boobs every day if you want them to grow?" Janel managed through a mouthful of chips. Janel, Bailey, and I were all on my couch watching an episode of *Sex Education* on Netflix. Every so often, my friend would come out with some kind of nonsense like that, making me smile.

"What are you talking about? That's an old wives' tale. There's no scientific support for it," Bailey answered, not looking away from the TV because she was intent on understanding the sexual issue discussed in that particular episode.

"Now people just get surgery. I like my boobs the way they are, though. Little but firm," I put in. I had a slight frame, but I had no complaints about my body.

"Of course, you can't complain; you're very proportionate. You were even a ballerina when you were a kid," Janel shot back.

"True, but I only danced until I was twelve. Then I started on Pop Rocks and Cheetos," I answered.

"Selene, you're going to make me hungry if you keep talking like that," Bailey grumbled with a noisy huff. "Have you ever tried a Goo Goo Cluster?" she added, licking her lips.

"I have. They're so good," Janel said.

"I've never had one. What is it?" I creased up my forehead and inched closer to the fireplace to warm up a little bit.

"It's a round candy bar with a chocolate covering and peanuts, marshmallows, and caramel inside. You should try one." As Bailey rhapsodized about the characteristics of a Goo Goo Cluster, I began to feel too warm. The air was suddenly sweltering, so I pulled off my woolly sweater, leaving just my short-sleeved T-shirt.

My friends shot me weird looks, and I gave them a nonchalant shrug.

"I'm too warm," I explained quickly and turned my full attention back to Bailey. I frowned, however, when I noticed her eyes were fixed on a spot on my arm.

"What is that?"

My first thought was that I had some sort of bug on me, so I turned to look where she was staring in alarm. Instead, I saw faint but undeniable bruises on my skin. I had more of them on my hips and my neck, so I could guess pretty quickly what they had to be thinking.

"Selene...what happened to you?" Janelle asked softly. She

reached out to touch me, but I ducked away from her. I knew perfectly well where those bruises came from; the problem was figuring out how to explain them to my friends.

"Nothing. I'm... This... I'm..." I didn't know what the hell to say. A fall? That didn't sound credible. I'd worn my hair down to cover the ones on my neck, but I hadn't even thought about how taking off my sweater would expose more of them.

"God, it looks like someone beat you up," Bailey declared, just as I'd feared she might.

"No!" I answered hurriedly. "Oh my God, no! Nothing like that," I tried to be very firm to reassure her at least a little bit. Except, I still had that irritating yearning sensation between my thighs that wouldn't go away ever since Neil had gone back to New York. No, he definitely hadn't been gentle the last time we were together, but he hadn't crossed any lines or done anything without my consent. In fact, I'd been the one urging him not to stop, to keep pushing through until he got his long-awaited orgasm.

By that point, I had accepted him in his totality, even when that meant accommodating him when he was at his wildest.

"Selene, you need to tell us right now what the hell happened to you!" ordered Janel, who, despite not actually knowing him, despised Neil.

"Nothing. Truly, nothing major. We just... I mean..." I had no idea how to define what we'd done with each other. I was in real trouble now. "He's just very passionate. And I don't mind," I admitted, rendering them both speechless. They exchanged blank looks before going back to staring at me.

"So...you're saying he's a sadist?" Janel cocked a skeptical eyebrow.

"Or he's pushing you into unusual sexual practices like bondage or—" Bailey cut in, and I shook my head until she stopped talking.

"No, absolutely not. Neil isn't doing any of that. He once told me flat out that he's not into that kind of...thing." I waved a hand vaguely in the air, and they both sighed with relief.

"So how'd you get all marked up then?" Janel pressed, still not convinced. I chewed my lip uncomfortably.

"I told you, Neil is kind of—" I didn't even get all of my sentence out before Janel was finishing it for me.

"A brute? A barbarian?" she offered contemptuously. "That dude is an animal, and not in a good way," she declared with finality, and I grimaced.

"Janel!" Bailey chided her, but she just kept going.

"No. I don't like that guy, and I'm not going to change my mind. And these bruises only confirm my theory." She gestured to my arm, and I immediately tried to cover it with my hand.

"It's not what you think," I squeaked out, embarrassed.

"Oh no? That dude *fucks* you. That's what he does. And don't try to tell me he makes love to you and cares about you or any of that bullshit. It is one hundred percent not normal the way he uses your body. You are not a sex toy." She moved an agitated hand over her black bob, clearly upset. I wasn't sure how to make her see that her understanding of Neil was only partially correct.

But I didn't know how to explain this thing between us.

"No, Janel," I murmured, tracking her with my eyes as she leaped to her feet, furious. "I promise you, he hasn't done anything against my will. And I like the way he..." I turned my face down, incredibly uncomfortable.

"The way he...?" Bailey prompted, and I took a deep breath.

"The way he dominates me, basically." I cleared my throat and rubbed my hands against my jeans. I couldn't fully explain that bizarre idea nor the reason for the changes that seemed to be happening inside me. Who knew what my friends would think of this confession?

"Hold on... Explain more," Janel demanded.

"The last time we..." I glanced at both of them before continuing, with difficulty. "Okay, so, the last time he was here, I had this very intense experience..." I bit the inside of my cheek and prayed that this time they would understand, but, if anything, they just looked even more bewildered and confused.

"You mean...you got turned on because it was rough?" Bailey tilted her head to one side, and I blushed violently. All I wanted to do was end this conversation as quickly as possible.

"Maybe. Probably. I mean...yes?" I admitted breathlessly. My face felt like it was on fire. "The sex is always great with Neil. He thinks about my pleasure every time; he's not selfish at all. And I've gotten used to the way he is. He's never been gentle, except for that first time. The first time that I remember, I mean," I specified, thinking of what I considered to be our first "official" time, in my bedroom. Neil had been passionate but also respectful and extremely controlled.

"So you're saying that it's never been sweet, never been kind, and that..." Bailey paused and looked at Janel.

"That you like it rough, basically?" Janel continued.

Hearing it said aloud gave me pause. I had always been so sure that, someday, I would fall in love with my soulmate Prince Charming and that I'd give my virginity to him on a bed strewn with rose petals, surrounded by scented candles. Instead, I'd fallen for the allure of the dark knight and had only just recently realized how much I liked it when he mastered me.

"Oh my God." Bailey burst into laughter while Janel remained stone-faced. She even put her hands on her hips and gave me a stern look. "Oh come on, it's funny!" Bailey chucked a pillow at her, but Janel didn't even flinch. "The boy knows how to lay pipe. Congrats, Selene," she added, winking at me. I barely restrained my own laughter, pleased that she at least understood.

"I don't think you understand how serious this is," Janel replied, shaking her head.

"What are you talking about? What's wrong with enjoying a little aggression in bed?" Bailey shot back.

"You have to be kidding me right now," Janel said.

"There are plenty of guys who can't seem to understand that a woman likes a little spanking or biting every now and then. Neil seems to have a handle on what his lovers like and don't like." Bailey shrugged, twining a lock of red hair around her index finger.

"You've never even met this man, and you're stanning him. You're like some screaming girl at a Shawn Mendes concert," Janel grumped, rolling her eyes toward the ceiling. "The point is that this is a violent guy. What happened to protecting women?"

I made a face; Janel always thought she knew best, and she could get overly dramatic.

"You're seriously making this a gender thing? We're talking specifically about men taking a position of power *in the sexual sphere*. It's okay to let a man take the lead in bed sometimes!" Bailey grumped, and I nodded in complete agreement.

"You are truly ridiculous!" Janel snapped, increasingly certain in her convictions.

"Selene shouldn't have to be afraid to cop to the things she enjoys. She hasn't had any other sexual experiences, and she's figuring out her likes and dislikes. She shouldn't have to worry about us judging her. People can do whatever they want in bed, so long as everyone consents." Bailey had begun to lose her patience, her face taking on a severe cast. I followed their discussion closely, my eyes bouncing from one to the other as I got increasingly annoyed.

"Neil is very experienced; he understands my boundaries, and he'd never do anything I didn't want," I said in an impatient rush, and both of them fell silent immediately. "He watches me for a long time, trying to figure out what I'm thinking, what turns me on, and what my body is trying to tell him. The intensity creeps up, little by little. He intuits what I want. He can sense it. I don't know how he does it, but it's like he can feel everything, and I can never hide what I really want from him. It's... it's unnerving," I finished, looking down.

Neil took free rein in bed. He was fully in command, and he knew just what to do, how to make me give in to his every whim.

"There, see? If the sex was so awful, would she be talking about Neil like that? Try to lighten up a bit. Our little Selene is growing up," Bailey said stoutly, and I gave her a smile. Janel raised her eyebrows and gave us both a doubtful look before rolling her eyes.

"Okay, fine. Whatever you want." She surrendered at last, flopping down on the couch as though drained. She was never going to change her mind; I knew perfectly well how stubborn she could be. And if she did meet Neil someday, she'd probably only be more concerned.

I was about to say something more to her when the doorbell distracted me.

"I'll get it," I said, getting up off the sofa. I opened the door curiously, and my eyes went wide when I found Alyssa standing before me with a small overnight bag. For a moment, I just stood there, perplexed. I was happy to see her but also pretty surprised.

"Alyssa," I said, my voice barely audible, and she managed a shaky smile as she met my gaze.

I wasn't imagining it: Her face really was a portrait of sadness. She had dark circles under her eyes and no makeup on. She was dressed down in just a pair of jeans, a basic sweater, and a sandy-colored coat. Rarely had I seen my friend without her colorful clothes, bold lipstick, and perfectly done hair.

"Hi, Selene. I hope I'm not bothering you." Her voice shook, and I immediately stepped to the side, gesturing for her to come in.

"Of course not. What are you doing here? Not that I'm not happy to see you," I answered enthusiastically. I took her coat after she slowly shrugged it off and hung it up on the coatrack. Looking spacey and worried, Alyssa glanced around the living room blankly.

"Alyssa, this is Janel and Bailey." I motioned at the two of them, and they turned to face me.

"Girls, this is Alyssa. Neil's brother Logan is her boyfriend," I informed them as welcoming smiles appeared on my friends' faces.

"It's nice to meet you, Alyssa," Janel began.

Bailey, by contrast, was focused on her appearance: "Wow, you're gorgeous," she added. Alyssa gave a small, embarrassed laugh, and I silently thanked Bailey for putting her at ease so quickly.

"Get used to that, Alyssa. That's Bailey's whole deal. She showers people with compliments and is constantly on the lookout for Prince Charming when she isn't listening to Ed Sheeran all day long." Janel jerked her thumb at the redhead, her face taking on a wearied expression.

"What are you talking about?" Bailey shot back before turning to Alyssa, who was still standing next to me. "Don't pay her any mind. Janel is really a nice girl underneath it all. But she has been demonstrating a weird amount of negativity toward life and human beings generally lately. I think it's some kind of developmental phase she's going through. Selene and I are both truly hoping she realizes just how wonderful the world is someday," Bailey said with a dreamy sigh, and I cocked an eyebrow. Alyssa glanced at me in total confusion, undoubtedly wondering what was up with these two crazy girls in my living room, and I could do nothing but shrug.

"I think you all will get along very well," I told her dryly, and she smiled at me.

After that round of introductions, I decided to make hot chocolate for everyone. Alyssa chatted pleasantly with my friends while I did so. She found she had a lot in common with them and sounded cheerful, but I could tell from her subdued affect that something wasn't right. I wanted to figure out why she'd come all the way to Detroit to see me, unannounced. Various theories swirled around in my head, including a fight with Logan or her parents, but I felt like it would be impolite to ask about that kind of thing in front of the other girls.

"Here, hot chocolate for everyone," I proclaimed as I came back into the living room. I set down a tray with four steaming mugs on the coffee table and then took a seat next to Janel. Alyssa had picked a spot next to Bailey, who was grilling her for tips on how to make her hair shiny.

"She is a hopeless case," Janel muttered into my ear, gesturing to Bailey, who just continued talking without pausing for breath.

"Leave her alone; she's socializing," I answered. The two of them had a very odd rapport. People who didn't know them as well as I did might assume they disliked or even hated each other, but they were actually very close despite being total opposites.

"She's going to give that poor girl a headache," Janel insisted, watching the two of them. Bailey was gesticulating excitedly while Alyssa nodded along, trying to follow her speech.

"Well, it looks like you two are becoming fast friends," I cut in, pleased with the way everyone seemed to be vibing.

"Yeah, we've discovered that we both like basketball players," Bailey answered. "And we both think Instagram is the optimal tool to keep tabs on dudes, we're both obsessed with hair care, and—"

"Does Alyssa also still watch animated Disney movies as well?" Janel asked with a sardonic arched eyebrow. Bailey made a face and huffed in annoyance.

"Um...I actually prefer live-action movies and TV series," Alyssa answered sincerely, not yet comprehending the ongoing war between the other two girls, who ignored her and continued bickering.

"So I love *Cinderella*, *Snow White*, and *Sleeping Beauty*. What's so wrong with that?" Bailey folded her arms over her chest challengingly.

"Oh my God! You're twenty-one years old!" Janel shot back derisively.

"And?"

"And there's no Prince Charming coming to give you that fateful kiss that will wake you from your curse," Janel teased her, and my eyes flew to Alyssa, who was now staring down at her knees and chewing her lip. She looked so tense and uncomfortable. I looked at her, my brow furrowing, and all at once, she leaped to her feet and raced into the kitchen.

Bailey and Janel ceased their back and forth, and I went after Alyssa to see what was going on with her. Walking into the kitchen, I found her leaning against the counter with her face in her hands.

Was she crying?

Alarmed, I went over to her and rested a hand on her shoulder.

"What's going on, Alyssa?" I had held back on that question for too long. Now was the time to talk and figure out just what the hell had happened.

Bailey and Janel appeared behind me, both focused on Alyssa, who had started fully sobbing. When she pulled her hands away from her face, I could see that her eyes were filled with sadness.

She wept, her shoulders shaking with uncontrollable sobs... She was distraught.

"Oh my God... Are you okay?" Bailey cut in, just as worried as I was.

"N-no," Alyssa stammered and wiped one cheek with the back of her hand as she tried to take deep breaths.

"Talk to me, Alyssa. Tell me what's wrong," I said encouragingly, rubbing her shoulder.

She let out another sob but then seemed to gird her loins and looked up to meet my eyes.

"He..." she began, and I assumed she was talking about Logan. "He did it..." She squeezed her eyes shut, unable to go on.

"He who? Your boyfriend?" Janel asked, and Alyssa shook her head.

"Who, then? Who are you talking about, Alyssa?" I pressed, nervous. A bad feeling had crept into my chest, and I tried in vain to push it away. Alyssa stared at me, looking mortified at what she had to say, and my body went stiff.

"Neil," she said, her voice barely a whisper, and her eyes did not leave mine. My friends looked to me, worry all over their faces.

"Neil?" I echoed, confused, and Alyssa nodded. "What does he have to do with anything?" I continued, though I had a sick feeling that whatever I was about to hear wouldn't make me happy at all.

"He..." she sobbed as I silently waited for her to explain. "He kissed me," she cried, and it felt like she'd punched me in the stomach. My eyebrows shot up in shock, and I staggered back, shaken by this shocking revelation.

"He kissed you?" I repeated in a whisper, like I hadn't heard her correctly.

"Yes," she affirmed. "I was in the kitchen, just drinking a glass of water..." she said haltingly, but I still managed to understand her clearly. "I could feel his gaze lingering on me, and I wanted to get out of there, but when I tried to walk past him, he grabbed me by the waist and..." She began to move her hands animatedly as I watched her, increasingly disconcerted. I didn't want to believe what I was hearing. I thought about stopping her, about dismissing it as crazy talk, but I was determined to make myself hurt. I was determined to know what kind of man I had fallen in love with.

"Go on," I prompted her, my voice breaking. I barely recognized the sound of it.

"He held me still, and then he kissed me really hard out of nowhere." She burst into tears again, and I staggered back. My legs felt like jelly, and my head was spinning. My heart pounded in my temples. I rubbed my breastbone, trying to keep breathing.

"It can't be true..." I murmured incredulously. At the same time, Alyssa's gaze collided violently with my own to erase any doubts I might have had.

"It is," she answered, with difficulty.

"What did I tell you? The guy is a beast," Janel said loudly, rubbing a hand over her face.

"Does your boyfriend know?" Bailey asked.

Alyssa nodded and dropped her gaze.

"Logan walked in on us, but, of course, he believed Neil over me." She looked up at me again and inched closer. "Selene, Logan kicked me out of the house because he's too tight with his brother to accept what actually happened." She rested her hands on my shoulders and gave them a gentle squeeze. I stared blankly at her. My brain apparently wasn't going to cooperate with me. It was too busy short-circuiting. My lips fell slightly open, though I said nothing.

"Neil knows he did wrong," she continued, "but he'll never admit it because he's too afraid he might lose Logan. The truth is, he couldn't control himself. I really believe that Neil has an actual psychological problem with sex and women," she trailed off sadly.

Other doubts crept into my mind: *Has Neil really been lusting after Alyssa right behind his brother's back?*

I felt a sick, instinctive jealousy toward my friend, but I forced myself to pause and reflect. Neil was the one who had kissed her. He was the one who had betrayed Logan's trust and done such a disrespectful thing. Despite knowing how erratic that walking disaster could be, I never would have expected him to do something like that, something so vile and reprehensible to one of the most important people in his life.

Not so much because Alyssa was my friend but because she was his brother's girlfriend.

His brother's girlfriend, for God's sake!

"Bet this is making you rethink some things, huh?" Janel said softly, looking at me. She looked sorry for me but also satisfied that her dislike of Neil had been borne out.

All at once, a wave of nausea washed over me. I pressed a hand to my stomach and winced slightly.

My mind drifted back to a few days before. I went through everything we'd shared: his hands on my body, his lips that traversed every part of me, his quiet, masculine moans, my fingers gliding down his powerful back, my legs clenching around his hips, and...

And the nausea came back, making me suck in breath.

Maybe he was thinking of someone else during that moment. Maybe Alyssa or Jennifer or Alexia and Jennifer together, or Britney from the pool house, or Professor Cooper, or...

No. Enough!

I tried to force myself to stop this self-harm, but apparently my body didn't get the memo.

I ran for the bathroom with a hand clamped over my mouth and knelt in front of the toilet.

An intense burning sensation spread from my stomach all the way up to my throat, and I vomited out all the suffering, all the disappointment, and all the pain I was experiencing. I spat out the time I'd spent with Neil, his golden eyes, his clean smell, and his intense voice. I spat out dashed hopes until only my feelings for him remained, clinging stubbornly to my heart.

I'd never be able to stop loving him; that love wasn't going to evaporate or go away. But that love would only ever mock me and make me acutely aware of the colossal mistake I'd made, bonding myself to a man like him.

I had started to believe that I deserved to suffer, that I had gotten myself into this mess, and now I was reaping what I'd sown. I'd been reaping it, actually, ever since Jennifer beat me up months ago. Except, I had been convinced back then that I could handle a complicated person like Neil, that I could cope with his mood swings and heal wounds even as deep as the ones he had. Unfortunately, that was not the case.

In an act of desperation, my mind had conjured up another world, making me dream of something that was impossible to realize and long for things that I could never have. And that's exactly what Neil was.

He was unobtainable. A wistful memory was probably the most I would ever have of him. Even he had made that clear the last time we were together: I deserved a different ending, an ending that didn't include him by my side.

I coughed miserably and had the strange sensation of acid burning in my throat. I got back to my feet, trying to clear my head once again. I washed my face and brushed my teeth, holding tight to the rim of the sink like my legs weren't strong enough to bear up under all the wretched things I was feeling. I looked into the mirror and examined my reflection, standing there motionless. My eyes moved over the evidence of Neil's passion speckling the curve of my throat. I touched them lightly with an index finger and felt my breath catch in my chest. Neil's lips had been on my skin right there.

I still felt like I belonged to him. That this boy had taken ownership of my soul, and he could do as he liked with it.

I was his, and, despite everything he said to the contrary, there had been several moments when I felt like the same was true for him.

So why had he done such a thing? Why had he kissed Alyssa? Why had he stabbed both Logan and me in the back?

I resisted the urge to cry and tried to recover some composure. Then I walked out of the bathroom and headed for the living room, where my friends were still trying to comfort Alyssa.

I approached them on shaky legs and narrowed my eyes as I observed her for what felt like an endless moment. Alyssa was beautiful, extremely beautiful, but she wasn't blond. She wasn't the type of woman who typically would drive Neil wild and make him act on impulse.

I knew his behavioral patterns well: He had a fixation on blonds. Or, rather, on having sex with blonds, as he himself had once specified.

What if Alyssa was lying to me?

For a moment, I considered the possibility that it might be completely made up, but I quickly discarded that idea, shaking my head. I mean, why would my friend do that?

But all the unanswered questions were driving me crazy.

I was too shaken up to think clearly.

"Selene, are you okay?" Bailey asked me, sounding concerned.

I just gave her a weak nod and then sat down next to her.

"I'm sorry," Alyssa whispered.

"It's not your fault. You're welcome to stay here tonight," I told her. It was the right thing to do. My mother would have no problem accommodating one of my friends.

"Thank you. You're an angel," she answered, wiping away her tears with the back of her hand.

"Well, now that everyone's calmed down a bit, I need to bounce. It's getting late," Janel declared, standing up. "Ivan needs the car back that I stole from him." She chuckled and fished the keys out of her jeans pocket and gave us a wicked grin.

"So petty," I teased her.

"He's gonna be piiiissed," Bailey noted, following Janel to the door.

"Oh, I know exactly how to threaten him into silence," Janel answered craftily. "By the way, he's having a party tomorrow night. You should come," she suggested, looking at all of us, even Alyssa, who would probably be back in New York by then.

I snorted. "You know parties aren't my thing," I pointed out.

Plus, by that point I was even less in the mood to spend my Friday night with a bunch of drunk, high college students.

"Oh come on, don't be a wet blanket. Ivan's throwing it at the Delta Psi house, and you know how only the privileged few get to step foot in there." She winked at me, and I made a face.

"What? Are you for real?" Bailey cut in.

Janel nodded enthusiastically. "Of course, I am," she answered, fixing her black bob.

The Delta Psi house was less like a frat and more like a sacred temple for athletes at school. It was near the basketball facility on campus, and a lot of players were brothers, so it was a popular hangout spot for the sporty crowd. No one was allowed inside without express permission from a brother, and their parties were legendary. I had often heard about it but had never seen it in person.

Girls were always angling for an invite, but I'd never been particularly drawn to the place, only mildly curious.

"Oh my God! I can finally see my Tyler again!" Bailey clapped her hands in joy as I rolled my eyes.

"You haven't stopped creeping on his Instagram, have you?" Janel asked, taking on a stern tone while Bailey bit her lip awkwardly, making the answer obvious. "Jesus, Bailey! When are you going to give it up? That guy just used you, plus he's totally up his own ass and has zero respect for women. Move on already!" she lectured Bailey sternly, and Alyssa giggled, drawing my attention back to her. I was happy to see that she seemed more peaceful, but that feeling of relief vanished almost immediately, obliterated by the memory of what Neil had done to upset her in the first place.

I kept going back and forth between trying not to think about it at all and vividly imagining their kiss.

"All I said was that I'd see him at the party," Bailey said defensively, distracting me from my miserable thoughts.

"For you, 'seeing him' means 'drooling over him again.' But you're just holding me up here; let's go," Janel said impatiently as she walked over to the door and grabbed her coat, which she quickly shrugged on.

"Text me when you get there," I called out to my friends without getting up from the sofa.

"Yeah, okay, Mom," Janel teased. "I'll see you tomorrow night. Pick you up at eight," she decreed, not even giving me a chance to argue. She waved goodbye to both Alyssa and me before opening the door to leave. Bailey dashed back to give both of us a kiss on the cheek, proving again that she was the sweet one.

"Move your butt!" Janel yelled, and Bailey obeyed her, cursing under her breath.

"Your friends are awesome," Alyssa said.

"Yeah. I'm really fortunate to have found them," I answered before getting up and looking around for her bag, which I found sitting on the floor. "I'll show you the guest room. You can get yourself settled in there, and then we can have dinner," I informed her, picking up the bag.

"Actually, I think I'll just take a shower and go to bed. I'm kind of wiped out," she answered uneasily. All at once, the atmosphere was unbearably awkward. Usually, Alyssa and I laughed and joked together, but, just then, we both seemed to be struggling. Her eyes constantly avoided mine, and there was an uncontrollable hint of chill in my voice. I was upset. And I didn't know whether it was because of the insane thing Neil had done or because Alyssa had told me about it and cratered my mood.

I tried to stifle yet another irrational idea.

I had to quit it with the doubts: My friend told me the truth. She wanted to warn me about that walking disaster and make sure I knew not to trust him. It was unfair for me to be angry with her for doing me a favor. Even if it did hurt.

"Selene, I... I'm so sorry about all of this. I know how much you care about him," Alyssa said in a weak voice as she followed me down the hallway. All the self-assurance she typically displayed had deserted her and left just the fragile, sensitive part of her behind. I sighed as I opened the guest room door, hesitating for a few moments before I answered her. I wanted to not speak rashly and wind up venting all my inner turmoil on her.

"I don't want to talk about it," I admitted simply.

Alyssa seemed to understand my need to push that conversation off to another time and walked into the guest room, glancing around.

"All the essentials are in here. Make yourself at home." I turned to leave, but she called me back.

"Selene..." She stared at me, looking like she might burst into tears again. I waited motionless in the doorway. "I hope you're not angry with me." She dropped her gaze as she took a seat on the edge of the bed and rubbed her palms against her pants.

I considered the statement for a few moments. Could I really be angry at her for telling me the truth?

It hurt to think of Neil wanting her, wanting her so much that he'd go against his brother that way, but I couldn't take that hurt out on her.

Alyssa wasn't the one at fault.

"No, I'm not mad. If you need anything, I'm just over there." I jerked my thumb toward the living room and shut her door, more than ready to be alone.

An hour later, I was sitting out on the porch steps in the cold.

I'd taken a shower and gotten into my pajamas before draping a blanket over my shoulders and heading outside. Even I couldn't say why I was sitting there, staring up into the dark sky speckled with the occasional bright star.

Alyssa hadn't come out of her room, and I'd also tried to lie down in bed to no avail. I'd even put in my earbuds and listened to some Coldplay songs in a desperate attempt to wind down, but even that hadn't made me feel the slightest bit better.

Sighing, I shut one eye and held up my index finger to do something silly I used to do when I was a kid: trace imaginary lines between the stars to see if I could uncover some hidden symbol or letter there.

I drew a line between four points, four luminous stars, and the letter that emerged was an...N.

I froze with my arm suspended in midair, grimacing as I continued to stare up at the stars over my head where the giant N loomed.

What the hell?

"Perfect," I groused, lowering my arm. "Now you're showing up in the sky as well?" I muttered, as though I were actually talking to Neil.

No matter where he actually was, I always felt like he was somewhere nearby. Or maybe that was just my brain conjuring up unreal visions. Maybe I was just losing my mind. "I'm the hopeless case," I muttered to myself, trying to think of some way out of this insane situation.

It was clear, however, that there was no real solution except to fully detox from the man.

Neil had infected me with his golden eyes, his domineering personality, and his sly smile, and there was probably no fix for a problem that size.

I rubbed my forehead with one hand, feeling my scar from the accident under my fingers. I sighed heavily.

I wanted Neil to get out of my head. I wanted to forget all about him and about what Alyssa had told me, but that human disaster continued to occupy all my thoughts.

He simply refused to leave.

"What symbol did you find?" I gasped at the sound of my mother's voice.

She stood in front of me with Anton Coleman at her side. She observed me with her usual affectionate expression—she knew me well enough to know exactly what I had been doing—while Anton frowned. He was probably wondering what I was doing sitting out on the porch in the cold in a pair of pink pajamas at least two sizes too big and a yellow comforter around my shoulders.

"I found a letter. Doesn't matter which one..." I answered flatly, waving my hand. Mom didn't like Neil, or, rather, she didn't trust him, and so I tried not to bring him up with her. She would undoubtedly have forbidden me to see him if she found out all the things I'd gone out of my way not to tell her.

"Hi, Selene." Anton smiled at me and pulled back the arm that he'd had wrapped around my mother's waist. It was a quick, hesitant movement, like he was afraid of how I might react.

I'd known for a while that they were seeing each other, though my mother hadn't made anything official. She kept telling me they were just getting to know each other, so I didn't push her too much on it.

Though I'd felt otherwise when she'd first told me about him, I was becoming less enthusiastic now that they were actually starting a relationship. I felt like I'd already lost Matt, and I was afraid I was about to lose my mother as well. I was afraid that Anton—or some other guy—might take her away from me, and I felt like I couldn't let that happen.

She was all that I had left. Without her, I was alone.

That was why I'd stopped asking her questions about her love life—I wasn't sure I really wanted to hear the answers.

"Hi, Anton," I said, smiling politely at him. His gray eyes dipped down to examine my clothing, and he lingered on my fuzzy slippers that Neil thought were so hideous, along with the rest of my wardrobe.

"Cute slippers," he noted in a dry way that made me blush. If I had thought it at all likely that I was going to run into my mother and her *friend,* I would have tried harder not to look like a twelve-year-old with her first broken heart.

"Thanks," I answered, clearing my throat. He was obviously trying to make a good impression upon me, but since I admitted to myself that I was still possessive of my mother, no amount of charm from Anton was going to banish my fears of losing her.

"You should probably head out," my mother told him, looping her purse over one shoulder. "I'll see you tomorrow at the university," she added with a little smile.

He moved toward her confidently, putting his hand on her hip and tilting his head like he was about to kiss her. In an instant, I was frozen, fearing the worst. I relaxed, though, when Anton pressed a brief kiss to her cheek and said simply, "Okay. See you tomorrow, Judith."

I breathed a sigh of relief and nodded to him when he waved before walking back down the driveway to his car. I studied him as he walked away, his trim frame, elegant black coat, neat hair, and broad shoulders. He was definitely an appealing sort of man—perfect for my mother—but that didn't mean it wasn't still difficult to welcome him into my life.

Into *our* lives, actually.

"Selene, come inside. You're going to catch a cold," my mother chided me, searching my face for whatever it was that I didn't want to tell her. My mother had an innate gift for knowing when I was hiding something from her.

"Alyssa's in the guest room; she came for a surprise visit," I told her blandly. Typically, I would be more enthusiastic about that kind of thing, but, at that moment, I didn't have it in me to fake anything more than absolutely required.

"Oh, that's nice. How long is she staying?" she asked.

"I think she's going back to New York tomorrow," I answered, shrugging. My mother frowned slightly, probably at my indifference. I didn't mind spending time with Alyssa, and I would have hosted her for days if that's what she wanted, but I just couldn't get past that kiss with Neil. I had barely been able to look at her mouth. I was bothered by the thought that her lips had made contact with my Disaster's.

Mine.

It was delusional to think of Neil as mine, but the immature dreamer in me was clinging to that delusion.

"Okay. That's fine. Now get inside," she said sternly, and I shook my head.

"I'm going to stay out there for a little bit. I need to..." I fumbled for some plausible reason to remain outside. "I need to make a call," I added hastily. She looked skeptically at the watch on her wrist and then back to me.

"At midnight?" she pressed, sounding concerned.

"Yup." I nodded. "But if you keep giving me the third degree, I'm going to miss the call time and..."

"Okay, okay. I'll wait inside for you." She shook her head and went in the house, flipping on the porch light as she did.

It was a lie. I had no one to call.

My phone rested on the step between my legs. I stared at it. The idea of reaching out to Neil had crossed my mind more than once, but I had been the one to reach out last time. Like always, I set aside my own pride and accepted his disrespectful behavior. Because I was trying to make myself understand him and not judge him, especially after Logan told me a bit about his brother's history.

I couldn't always be the one to give in, though. I couldn't just let him win and walk all over me.

I raised my index finger to my mouth and chewed on the fingernail. I felt unsettled and angry. I had a deep internal need to express my thoughts and feelings to him. I wanted to tell him how profoundly he had let me down with what he'd done. I wanted to give him a piece of my mind so I could expel those thoughts forever. I wanted to tell him to stop chasing me, to forget about me, and to try to make things right with Logan.

I wanted, wanted, wanted... and all the while I sat motionless, staring at my phone's display, lacking the guts to pick it up and make the call.

I also confirmed the time. It was late, and Neil was probably asleep or, even worse, out with the Krew. He might have even been in bed with Jennifer.

I snorted as I kept casting insistent glances at my phone.

There was one voice inside me that said I ought to call him up and ream him out and another voice that said I should just let it all go and make a clean break at last. I began to jog my knee up and down and anxiously adjusted the comforter around my shoulders until, with a heavy sigh, I snatched up my phone. Quickly, before I had time to change my mind, I scrolled through my recent calls for his number. He was one of the last people I'd called, so he was right near the top. I found his name and touched that ominous green call symbol, raising the phone to my ear.

I bitterly regretted my decision as soon as I made it, but I also couldn't help but feel that getting this boulder off my chest might make me feel better. Lighter or more satisfied, maybe.

After two rings, I squeezed my eyes shut in apprehension.

Two more, and I opened them again, worrying my lower lip relentlessly.

Another ring, and still nothing.

I was just about to hang up when I was stopped by the sound of his voice.

"Hello," he answered.

I gulped, and it felt like my heart rose up in my throat only to sink back down into my chest. I concentrated on what I had to say to him, trying not to babble even though the sound of his labored breathing was distracting.

I pressed the phone against my ear more tightly to be sure I wasn't hearing things, but no—Neil's breathing was erratic and too fast.

What was he doing? Had he been...

"Don't tell me you're with a woman right now. I swear, I will fly to New York and kill you myself!" I leaped to my feet, allowing the comforter to fall to the porch floor. I didn't even care that I was getting loud. It wasn't jealousy that I was feeling but rage. Pure rage, because Neil thought he could just walk over everyone without sparing a single thought for their feelings, and it needed to stop. Alyssa was crushed, Logan was probably even worse off, and what was he worried about? Making time with some random blond?

His guttural laugh brought me back to the moment.

Was he seriously laughing at me? The balls on this man!

"Why the hell are you laughing? Dick!" I snarled, not caring if my neighbors, the Kampers or the Burns, could hear me.

"What is it, Tinkerbell? And hurry it up; I've got things to do," he answered, sounding amused. I could even picture the smug little smirk on his too-perfect face.

"Hurry it up? Tell whoever you're screwing that I need to talk to you and require your full attention!" I demanded furiously, and he chuckled again.

Since when did Neil laugh so much?

"Hold on, give me a minute to notify her," he said with faux courtesy. So he really was with a woman, then? Just the thought of it made my stomach clench. In that moment, I felt like bringing out the worst insults I could conjure up, but instead I tried to control myself and project a certain aura.

"I won't even give you thirty goddamn seconds!" I raged.

"Love the aggression, Babygirl. You're going to spoil me if you keep going this way..." Neil lowered his voice to a sensual whisper, and, for a brief but intense moment, a shiver moved through me with the power of an electrical shock. I rested a hand on the porch railing next to me and breathed in deep, trying not to be seduced by him no matter how difficult that was.

"I'm not remotely in the mood for jokes, Neil. I have Alyssa here in tears because of you. Because of what you did to her—what you did to her and Logan both, actually. Aren't you the least bit ashamed?" I demanded accusingly, and, on the other end of the phone, I finally heard the silence that I'd wanted all along. "How dare you just kiss her like that? Like she's one of your blonds? You've hurt her and your brother and me too! Yeah, me too, because Alyssa is my friend, goddamn it!" I was getting louder again. I had never been so angry, not even when the Krew insulted and mocked me.

"You've created this deep rift between me and Alyssa and between Alyssa and Logan. Sometimes I have to wonder who you even are and if it's right for me to continue to try to accept you the way you are. I wonder how far you'd actually go, how much harm you might do to other people. And, probably, to me as well. I wonder if it's even possible for you to understand the way I feel about you or reciprocate in any way and if it wouldn't be better just to let you go and live your life your way.

"I'm always asking myself these questions, Neil. I've gone against my principles for you, against my self-interest, my father, and anyone else who told me to stay away from you. I've never judged you, and I never will, but sometimes I think I need to stop trying to figure you out. Stop chasing you. You can't save someone who doesn't want to be saved. They have to save themselves. You should go on alone, and maybe...maybe that's for the best. Sorry I wasn't as strong as I thought." The last words came out in a broken murmur, and I was honestly surprised I was able to finish my speech at all. I held my tears back in the hopes of convincing first myself and then him that I was making the right decision.

On the other end of the phone, there was nothing.

No sound, no breath, not a word or even so much as a syllable.

I immediately looked to see if Neil had hung up on me and saw that the call was still active. I hoped in that moment that he wouldn't hang up. That he would say something—anything—to me and chase away the misery I felt inside.

This call was the lone, thin thread that still connected the two of us, one that I couldn't bring myself to sever yet. I was really contradicting myself: My words didn't remotely reflect my actual desires. Putting more distance between us wasn't going to make me happier. I knew, though, that putting a stop to this pseudo-relationship was the right thing to do. I needed to let my Disaster go, even if it might mean losing him…maybe forever.

"N-Neil?" I stammered at him when the prolonged silence began to alarm me.

I made a face, and suddenly, the call ended.

The thread was snapped.

Neil hung up on me without even offering me the dignity of a response.

Had I hurt him? Or maybe he didn't give a rat's ass and had decided to run back to the one-night stand waiting for his attention?

As I slowly came back to myself, I began to wonder if I'd gone too far. It was difficult for Neil to communicate with words, and he unsurprisingly preferred a silent language of signs and actions that I had to interpret. I should have expected his silence.

I had gone hard on him, attacking him with no warning when he'd answered my call with the intention of teasing and laughing with me.

What if I'd gotten it all backward? What if I should have been questioning Alyssa and trusting Neil?

Wouldn't it have been better to at least hear his side of the story as well?

I'd treated him the way everyone else always did—like I was some tyrannical judge handing down sentences without even giving him a chance to defend himself.

Me, the one who was always making such a big deal about how important it was to talk about things. I had made a huge mistake.

"Selene, come inside."

I startled when my mother rested a hand on my shoulder. I whirled around, phone still clenched in my frozen fingers, and stared into her eyes. She looked solemn and stern.

It occurred to me that she had likely overheard my whole conversation, and I suspected it had only given her a worse impression of Neil.

I didn't have the strength to argue with her, though. I didn't want to have a conversation about Neil or what had happened, so I just gave in with a nod and followed her inside, bearing all my misery along with me.

I'd been choosing to walk a perilous path for months now, trying to follow a deeply troubled man, and only now was I starting to come to terms with the harsh reality of my choices...

3

> "I wasn't going to let myself be hurt by her or anyone else."

NEIL

On edge.
　　That's how I was feeling.

I hadn't gotten a wink of sleep because of that fucking girl.

Selene had an incredible capacity for changing my mood. Not that it was particularly difficult, but she had become an expert at it.

I hung up on her the night before because she didn't deserve any explanations from me. From what I could decipher, Alyssa had told her a completely false version of what happened with the kiss, and Selene had believed her immediately without even hearing me out.

Wasn't she the one who was always saying how important it was to communicate verbally? But what had she done instead?

She hadn't let me get a word in edgewise.

Feeling disillusioned, I continued to stare into the smoke from my cigarette as it dissolved into the sex-saturated air.

"Mmh..." Jennifer mumbled next to me, one leg hooked over my waist.

I clamped the cigarette between my lips and looked up at the ceiling, my head propped up with one arm underneath it. Blondie was plastered against me, naked and sleepy, while I felt like I was wrapped in chains. A prisoner of the sick coping mechanisms that I'd likely never be able to completely banish from my life.

"How can you smoke like that first thing in the morning?" It was Alexia who spoke that time, lying on my other side. I turned my gaze to her and found her also still half-asleep. She was naked as well, and her hair was mussed, and her eyelids were barely cracked open. Her breasts were pressed against me, and her hand was resting on my stomach. She moved her fingers, stroking me, and I moaned in appreciation. Usually, those kinds of obscene theatrics pleased me, but, in that moment, the idea that I'd fucked the both of them was repellent to me. I could smell them, their skin, and their saliva on me, and a rictus of pure disgust twisted my face.

I shouldn't have done it.

When Selene called me the night before, she wasn't interrupting anything except one of my practice sessions with the heavy bag. I wasn't with a woman the way I'd led her to believe because I wanted to get under her skin.

I hadn't slept with anyone else since I'd gotten back to New York, but after her unexpected little speech, I couldn't deal with the miserable feeling in my chest.

I felt like I needed to get back to the place I belonged, back to my world. So I called up the Krew girls to remind myself of exactly who I was and that I didn't belong to anyone, least of all to Babygirl.

I wasn't going to let myself be hurt by her or anyone else. Never again would some girl be able to wound and shatter me the way that Kim had done.

Selene didn't want me in her life anymore, and she hadn't been shy about telling me that.

So I wouldn't chase after her. Instead, I would respect her choice. After all, that was exactly what I'd wanted all along.

I used her; she used me... We were using each other, and we both knew that we had an expiration date.

"How come you look so perfect even first thing in the morning?" Jennifer's drowsy voice brought me back to the moment. She, like many of my lovers, insisted on elevating me above other men, despite the fact that I'd never put her on a similar pedestal.

I took a long drag from my Winston and gave Jennifer a frosty look. She responded by licking my bicep, tracing the lines of the toki with her tongue. Then she grinned impishly up at me, perhaps convinced that I'd be turned on by her bold overture.

I looked her right in the eyes, squinting ever so slightly. Her eyes were blue and bright, but they were not limpid. There was no ocean in them.

They did not make me think of a field of cornflowers at dawn; they were neither shy nor sweet.

They weren't my Tinkerbell's eyes.

And there I was thinking about her again.

I moved Jennifer's leg off me with a growl of irritation and sat up. This turmoil inside me was impossible to soothe, and I didn't understand why.

That girl was not supposed to have that kind of power over me.

No one fucking was.

I ran one hand through my disheveled hair. The other held a cigarette that wasn't remotely calming me down. My mood was decidedly bleak.

Alexia dug her elbow into the mattress and rested her chin on her palm, looking at me with an arched eyebrow. I was sweaty; I didn't smell like bath gel. I wasn't clean in the way I usually was.

I felt dirty both inside and out.

"Shit," I muttered to myself.

Feeling antsy, I clambered over Alexia's slim body and got out of the bed. I clamped my cigarette between my lips as I pulled off the condom I still wore.

I was clean underneath: no climax, no cum.

Damn it, that was another reason why I'd returned to my old habits: I wanted to see if I was truly cured, if I'd really gotten over my inability to orgasm. I wanted to test myself, to prove that I could reach just as strong a sexual climax with other people as I had with Babygirl, but the experiment had been a total failure. I'd been able to do it with Selene, though it had been difficult, and yet with two hot and skilled women in my bed, I hadn't managed it.

My body had tensed up, had gotten right up to the pinnacle of arousal, and then it refused to release the tension.

What is my fucking problem?

"I'm going to take a shower. Get dressed and leave. I want you gone when I get back." Was all I said as I stubbed out my Winston. My right hand had started to shake, and I tried to hide it. Neither of them knew anything about my problems, and they weren't going to either.

I turned around only to find them giving me the usual fawning looks that I couldn't stand.

I hated being watched with heart eyes, like I was the very best sex toy on the market, like I'd put on the best performance they'd ever had between their legs. Or like I was some dream lover who could fulfill all their fantasies.

I was just another bastard, nothing more and nothing less.

"Well, good morning to you too, you little ray of sunshine," Alexia teased. I ignored her.

I went to the bathroom immediately. I couldn't breathe the air in that room anymore. It reeked of a mixture of sex and the kind of fruity, too-fucking-girlie perfumes that I could also detect on my own body.

"Nice ass, Miller!" Jennifer called out with a laugh.

I shook my head as I slammed the door behind me, heading straight for the shower. Then, I halted and turned around, determined to make the situation clear for them.

"Jen, I'm serious. I want you out of here in five minutes!" I raised my voice and pounded my fist on the closed door to emphasize my point. "Do you hear me? Five fucking minutes!" I repeated angrily. I forced myself to keep my distance because I knew I didn't have any self-control when I was too agitated, and the only thing to do then was to either stand way back or lock myself up somewhere like a rabid beast.

"Go fuck yourself!" Jennifer shouted back challengingly.

So I abruptly threw the door open and took a few steps out.

I could feel the fury burning along the tendons of my throat and in the raised veins on my arms. I must have looked frightening because they both went pale when they saw me, naked and enraged.

Jennifer was putting her barely there thong back on, while Alexia was already half-dressed. Of the two of them, I preferred Alexia because at least she knew when to quit pushing. Blondie, on the other hand...

She was either stupid or pathologically attention-seeking. She knew how attractive she was, and she thought that meant she should be able to have me any time. She was like a cat in heat, willing to do anything, no matter how wrong, to get my attention.

"What?" she snapped. She bent down with an impish shimmy, picking up her bra from the floor and putting it on. She gave me a heated glance as she closed the front hooks in a slow, seductive fashion, a move carefully calculated to ensnare me. But I wasn't going to fall for it.

I wasn't the easy kind; she couldn't win me over with a few banal little tricks.

I stared darkly into her eyes. Her face changed, suddenly growing worried as though she had finally realized I wasn't kidding around at all. Still, my anger didn't want to dissipate; it kept me bound, completely subject to its unstoppable power. My body was tense, my muscles were tight, and my jaw hurt from how hard I'd tightened it.

I passed a hand through my hair and then snatched a shitty nearby lamp and chucked it at the wall with all my strength. The girls both jumped, backing up.

I wasn't remotely satisfied.

I was still so worked up; I wanted to smash everything.

I was on the brink of reducing the pool house to a pile of debris, just as I had done before.

"Piss off. Silently. I don't want to even hear you breathing," I said in a low, menacing voice, alternating my gaze between the two of them. Alexia was frozen with her fingers still resting on the elastic of her skirt. Jennifer, however, had inched closer to the door, terrified.

When I was satisfied that they both knew enough not to argue with me, I turned on my heel and went back into the bathroom. I kicked the door closed behind me. My heart felt like it was going to burst from my chest, and my head was spinning. I rubbed my forehead. I stepped into the shower and took refuge under the warmth of the spray. I put my hands up on the smooth tiled wall and tried to relax each one of my muscles.

I didn't know why I was feeling like that... except maybe I did.

It was that fucking girl's fault.

My beautiful but perilous Tinkerbell.

There was no other explanation.

Selene was right: You couldn't save someone who didn't want to be saved.

I had no interest in changing my life, my character, or my whole way of being just to be accepted by her. But, despite my obstinacy and her decision to cut me loose, I still had to have her.

I craved her. I wanted her more than my Maserati, more than

all the women I'd had put together, more than any other thing in the world.

I had felt that need to possess her since the moment we met, and it had never faded.

At the same time, I needed to respect her decision. I also knew that letting her go was the right thing to do. The problem, though, was that I couldn't seem to stay away from her.

Life really was a cunt: First it gave me a glimpse of a future that I'd never be able to realize, then it gave me a bitter taste of the lingering past, and, finally, it wouldn't stop showing me exactly what kind of monster I had become.

These insane thoughts only worsened my mood.

I soaped up my hair, my body. Everything.

I scrubbed urgently until I smelled like the shampoo aisle. The scent of musk replaced the fruity odor of the two women. I washed away their lingering kisses, their voracious tongues, and their possessive touches. I shut my brain down and focused on how clean my skin felt, and, eventually, I began to calm down.

After spending an interminable amount of time under the boiling water, I got out of the shower and wrapped a towel around my waist. Steam had fogged up the mirror and hung in the air. I took a few steps forward, trailing water everywhere, and rested my hands on the rim of the sink.

I was about to swipe a hand over the mirror to look at my reflection when a feeble sigh from behind me forced me to turn. I immediately went rigid when I saw the Boy with his familiar basketball under his arm, his wrinkled Oklahoma City basketball jersey, and his dirt-stained shorts... He looked bedraggled and exhausted.

"The game's almost over. You know that, right?" he murmured in his reedy little voice. I examined his golden eyes, his wild brown hair, and his face that was already masculine but still immature. I wasn't at all surprised to find him there; I was used to it by then. I was more interested to know what he was talking about. "Time's running out, Neil," he added before I even had a chance to answer him. I nodded my head ever so slightly, and he came closer to me. I held still and waited to see what he would do, and, eventually, he took my hand. He lifted it up and guided it toward the mirror. Then, like my body had stopped obeying me, I began to sketch something with my index finger. The finger moved little by little, revealing a five-pointed star enclosed in a circle.

The symbol was unmistakable: a pentacle.

I stood there slack-jawed and stared at it.

I had vague memories of having reproduced that same symbol at other times as well, never knowing why my brain had memorized it or what it was related to.

"What does it mean?" I asked softly, shifting my gaze to the Boy beside me, who was smiling.

But he just repeated, "Time's running out," and dribbled the ball on the tile floor a few times before making for the door.

"Hold on, kid. You can't just do that, okay? You have to explain!" I shouted, reaching the end of my patience.

The day was already off to a rocky start; this was the last thing I needed. The Boy turned and shot me a mischievous look over his shoulder before giggling and running away. I forced myself from the trancelike state I'd lapsed into and went after him into the now-empty bedroom.

Alexia and Jennifer had gone, just like I'd told them to do.

The lamp I'd thrown at the wall lay in pieces on the floor. The sheets were still rucked up, and my phone and pack of Winstons were exactly where I'd left them. The Boy seemed to have vanished into thin air without disturbing a single thing. I passed a hand through my damp hair; with a frustrated grunt, I let my towel hit the floor and went over to the dresser for a pair of boxers. After I'd gotten them on and inspected the room thoroughly, I admitted to myself that I was alone in the room and that I'd had another hallucination.

Like always, the Boy had just been a symptom of my dissociative personality disorder. Or, at least, that's what Dr. Lively called it.

I knew he was right, but I still refused to acknowledge it to myself. I wasn't ready to admit that there were these *alters*—other personalities—that existed inside of me.

The day after my sixteenth birthday, Dr. Lively had discovered that two personalities coexisted in my mind. He hadn't ruled out, however, the possibility that more could have emerged in the years since then.

I was afraid that exact thing might be happening to me at that moment. Sometimes, it felt like my head was crowded with people and voices; other times, it was just me and the Boy. On several occasions, I had no memory of things that I had done, like some other part of me had erased them.

It was still me—my body—doing those things, but my entire psyche was being piloted by a different person.

I often got the strange sensation that my brain was like a cell, always splitting and multiplying.

All of it was a result of dissociative identity disorder: a defense mechanism that the mind develops to protect someone who has experienced severe trauma.

In my case, I wasn't sure who was the defense mechanism: the adult me or the child me. I had no idea who was trying to protect whom or, more importantly, which of the personalities was better.

The only real solution would have been to integrate into one personality, breaking down the fragile parts and drawing forth the stronger ones. But, to achieve this, I would have had to start treatment again and maybe check myself into a psychiatric facility. That was something I was never going to do voluntarily.

With all those thoughts swirling around in my head, I pulled on a pair of dark jeans, a white sweater, and my leather jacket. Fortunately, I always keep a spare set of clothes in the pool house; otherwise, I would have been forced to walk naked back into the house. Not that I would have been bothered—after all, I was pretty uninhibited—but Matt would have torn me a new one. He'd been giving me the cold shoulder ever since he found out I'd been screwing his daughter, so even the smallest infraction was enough to whip him into a fury.

I sighed as I gathered up all my stuff and left the pool house. I let Anna know that she should just throw away the broken lamp when she went in to clean, and then I got into my car. I noticed that Logan's Audi wasn't in the garage. He'd probably already headed over to campus, which was exactly where I was going as well. He hadn't asked me for a lift, though. Clearly he still hadn't gotten over what had gone down between me and Alyssa. He barely spoke to me and was still upset with me because I'd reciprocated that fucking kiss, if only for a few seconds. I should have shoved her away automatically; I never should have let her tongue touch mine. Instead, I allowed shock and disbelief to turn me into a slack-jawed idiot and made my fateful mistake.

I parked my Maserati in the student lot and got out, ignoring the hungry looks from the scattering of girls who had just noticed my arrival as well as the enthralled looks from a few guys checking out my panther. Most people my age couldn't afford that kind of treasure, so seeing a car like that roll up to the university parking lot was almost like a dream come true for them.

"There's my favorite asshole." Xavier threw an arm around my shoulders as I tucked the key fob into my pocket.

"What do you want? And quit touching me!" I snarled at him, shaking off his arm. He gave me a sardonic grin and glanced at Luke, who was finishing up his cigarette a few paces away.

"You in another bad mood today?" Luke asked, strolling toward the university's entrance. Xavier and I fell into step behind him, Xavier looking way too cheerful.

"Like every day," I answered dourly. I couldn't remember the last time I'd had a few carefree hours. Probably the happiest I'd been recently was when I was in Detroit with Babygirl. And not just because of the incredible sex we'd had or the timid way she'd sucked my cock the next morning. It was the feeling of lightness, the peace that her presence seemed to always give me.

When I was with her, I wanted more than a fuck. I wanted to experience everything that she could give me.

My personal hell seemed a little more bearable when the Tigress was also walking through it with her ocean eyes and dizzying smile.

She made a racket inside my head.

She was becoming a pleasurable sort of madness.

"So, did you hear?" Xavier turned his attention back to me, draping his arm over my shoulders again. I shot him a dirty look but didn't otherwise object.

"Hear what?" I asked, patting my jacket to make sure I'd remembered to bring my cigarettes from the pool house. I needed regular smoke breaks to keep calm.

"About your dad's car. The pictures are in all the papers," he informed me in tones of delight, and I stopped mid-stride.

"What?" I asked, bewildered.

"This dumbass fully set fire to William's car. *Boom.* It exploded, and the resulting fireball has been immortalized in every newspaper and tabloid in the city," Luke explained, flicking his cigarette butt in an outdoor ashtray. I followed the movement before looking back at Xavier, trying to understand. Sure, I had been the one who gave him the green light to get his revenge on William, but not in such an egregious way that a flock of reporters was drawn down on him.

"Why do you always have to be such a dick, huh?" I shoved him away from me, and he broke into laughter, completely unintimidated. I didn't give a shit if the other students saw us or heard us; he'd crossed a line this time.

He was allowed to get his own back, yes, but within reason.

"You were the one who told me I could do it," he said defensively. I advanced on him furiously and stared him down with a threatening look on my face.

"Yes, but you weren't supposed to blow up his car. Jesus Christ! You were supposed to do something that would piss him off...not something that would draw media attention," I hissed through gritted teeth, and his eyebrows shot up in surprise.

What was he expecting? A round of applause? Or maybe I was supposed to bullshit him and compliment him on his great job?

"Neil has a point about that. I did warn you." We both ignored Luke's contribution to the conversation.

"Come on. Don't be melodramatic. What's the big deal? That prick got what he deserved," Xavier insisted, apparently not realizing that he had also exposed himself to serious risk and that was my fault too.

"That is not the point. Everyone in New York knows my father; he's the CEO of a major corporation. Do you understand what I'm telling you?" I rubbed my face, hoping William wouldn't send one of his goons to figure out what had happened. If he really wanted to, he could have gotten to Xavier and had him behind bars in a matter of hours. Scratches in the paint job, a few flat tires, or a broken window—those could have been dismissed as simple vandalism from some local gang of kids, but setting the entire car on fire? That was a threat, and it was going to put him on high alert.

"Relax. He's got no evidence. I made sure there weren't any cameras around. It's not like I did it right outside his building, so unclench." Xavier continued to dismiss the situation, and I shook my head in frustration. Trying to reason with him or even get through to him really was pointless. Of the entire Krew, he was the one most likely to do irreparable damage. I was just as crazy as he was, but the difference between us was that Xavier enjoyed tempting fate; he always wanted to go over the edge.

I gave up trying to explain it to him more clearly and decided that if my father came to me with questions, I'd just deny everything. He was a shrewd man, though, and he surely recalled that he'd just gotten into it with Xavier and me and that we were the two people most likely to have beef with him.

I stalked furiously toward the school's entrance. I was already late for my meeting with Professor Robinson.

He wasn't in his office when I arrived, but the door was open, so I walked in and took a seat in front of his large, messy desk.

"Welcome to the neighborhood, Miller."

I turned to see Megan slouched sensually in the chair next to me. Could I really not have noticed her there? Apparently so, because, in addition to being on edge, I was eternally lost in my own thoughts.

"Fuck," I said in a frustrated whisper. I hadn't realized this was anything other than a one-on-one meeting with Robinson, and I definitely wouldn't have shown up if I'd known otherwise. I had an unmistakable trapped feeling as I leaned back against my seat.

"Relax, unlike the rest of the girls on campus, I have no interest in your genitals," she replied, sounding amused. I rolled my eyes skyward and turned my attention to Professor Robinson's still-vacant desk.

"Just as well. He's out of your league," I muttered with a hint of masculine self-satisfaction. I usually tried not to get vulgar with women I wasn't interested in, and Megan certainly fell into that category. She was perhaps the last woman in the world I would have fucked, and I wanted to make it clear that she'd never get the opportunity to assess my skills in the sack.

"Oh, for sure. I am well aware of your tremendous physical gifts. Rumors run wild amongst the female student body. But you know me; I'm a skeptical woman. I have to see it to believe it," she whispered into my ear, giving me a whiff of that orange blossom smell that I remembered so vividly.

I wrinkled my nose slightly. It was a nice scent, but I couldn't stand it because it belonged to her.

"Didn't you just say you had no interest in my genitals?" I repeated her own words mockingly as I fidgeted in my seat, already wishing I could light up in here.

"Maybe I lied," she shrugged.

I gave her a flat look. "Head Case, today is not the day. Knock it off," I said as my knee bounced up and down with nervous energy.

"Or what? Are you going to put me over your knee and give me a spanking?" she asked challengingly, and I turned and gave her a good, long look, lingering on her large tits concealed by a basic black sweater. She wasn't dressed to impress, and I felt no attraction toward her, yet she still had a feral beauty that was unmistakable even in understated, unappealing clothing.

"Not a terrible idea," I shot back and stared into her green eyes. "I love having a woman's ass in the air. Any woman..." I paused. "Except you," I finished with a cheeky smirk. Megan's eyes dropped to my lips, and, for a second, she looked pensive, but then she cleared her throat and took on her familiar confident posture.

"Is that the only position you know, Miller? I'd have thought you had more imagination," she needled, and I narrowed my eyes in challenge. Had she been just another girl, I would have dragged her straight into a bathroom or empty classroom and demonstrated exactly how wrong she was, but when it came to Head Case, I could not give in.

I knew what she was trying to do.

She enjoyed toying with me, knowing that I would never cross the line with her. A line that I had drawn myself ever since we were kids. I wouldn't touch her when we were children and standing in front of that camera in the basement, and I wasn't going to do it now that we were both grown up.

All at once, the memories hit me like a tsunami: the movie about Peter and Wendy, Kim's voice, the freezing cold that got into my bones, the musty smell coming off the walls that enclosed us...

"That's enough. Don't fuck with me," I warned her loudly, making it clear that I was no longer willing to joke around or have a conversation. At the same time, I suddenly became aware of Professor Robinson, standing awkwardly in the doorway. He cleared his throat, and I tried to pull myself together and make my face look indifferent. The professor just sighed and circled around to sit behind his desk.

Megan, finally, had stopped needling me.

It was all her fault. She and Alyssa—all they did was give us grief. Me and Logan and even...

My mind careened over to Selene, to my Tinkerbell, who was in Detroit at that very moment doing God knew what with God knew who.

I still couldn't accept what she'd said, and I was still angry about it, but it was obvious to me that Alyssa had fed her some bullshit to freak her out. She probably told her I was the one who initiated the kiss or that I tried something else. Whatever else she needed to say to paint me as the monster that I definitely hadn't been—at least, not with her.

I pulled my phone out of my jeans pocket then and thought about texting Selene, about asking her what the fuck was going on in her head and if she was still sure about what she'd told me.

It was my pride, my goddamned pride that I could never put aside, that won out and ensured that I didn't go after her.

I never chased a woman.

She was just like all the others.

I repeated that to myself for the umpteenth time, slipping my phone back in my pocket.

"Okay," Professor Robinson said when I looked back at him. "Let's talk internship logistics."

....

After nearly three exhausting hours, I walked out of Robinson's office with an intense urge to have a smoke.

I needed one because not only had my agitation not eased in the slightest, but also because the thought of trying to prepare for the internship amidst all these distractions was stressing me out.

I sighed, wondering when it was all going to let up and when I might get back to some semblance of peace, when I'd finally be able to actually solve these problems.

What if that day never came? I hoped it would, but I feared it wouldn't.

I took the sidewalk to the parking lot, my forehead wrinkling up when I spotted a cluster of students gathered in the area where I'd left my Maserati.

What the hell are they doing?

I drew closer, cigarette trapped between my lips. A few guys noticed my presence and blanched, immediately making a hole for me to pass through.

What I saw left me literally in shock, and I immediately understood why all those people were crowded around my car.

I stood motionless, and I felt my heartbeat slow.

I blew the smoke out through my nose, tossing the still-mostly-unsmoked cigarette to the ground before moving forward at a sedate pace. I crunched across shards of glass on the pavement, and I thought for a moment that I might be dreaming or having another hallucination, but then I blinked several times and realized it was all real.

Someone had smashed in my window with a giant rock.

"Who did this?" I demanded, staring uninterrupted at the damaged glass. I couldn't even recognize my own voice, the harsh tone making it obvious that I could not be reasoned with. "Who the fuck did this?" I asked again in a rasp. I glared into the shocked faces of the other students, who backed away fearfully.

They didn't say a word; they were all just silently shitting bricks.

But I knew perfectly well about the code of silence the students had. They minded their own business and didn't give a shit about what happened to other people, not even in the most serious cases. One of them could have seen the culprit; maybe they even saw more than one of them. Maybe the person was standing right there enjoying my enraged face, but none of those assholes would have said a fucking word if he was.

"Goddammit! Answer me, motherfuckers!" I stabbed a finger at a random group of people and narrowed my eyes. Sensing my intentions, they all took a few steps back.

Their fear didn't give me pause, far from it: It gave me a thrill. I was like an animal that had caught the scent of prey.

I advanced on them quickly, my right hand beginning to tremble, and my heart battered in my chest like it wanted to force its way out. I felt like bashing someone's face in, and I didn't care who it was.

"Hey, hey, pump the brakes, man." Luke moved in front of me and forced me to halt.

Where the hell had he come from?

"Don't touch me." I shook off his hand and continued staring in a fugue at the unfortunate kids behind him.

"Calm down. We don't know who did this." I stared at him. Was this man trying to reason with me? "You can't just beat up these random people. You've gotta keep your nose clean," he chided me.

Since when did Luke dispense advice or try to give me pep talks?

"What the fuck do you know about it?" I exploded on him. "It's my car, not yours, and some asshole bashed in the window. Get out of my way." I tried to shove him aside, but Luke planted his feet.

"Neil..." he said sharply.

"Luke, I told you to move," I repeated insistently. He didn't listen. Then Xavier appeared to back him up and took me by the arm to drag me away.

"Come on, man. Don't do this shit. It was probably some punk kid who picked the wrong car to fuck with." He managed to pull me away, but I didn't stop glowering at the little group behind Luke or even at Luke himself, who stood there motionless with a pitying look on his face.

I couldn't stand being looked at that way by my friends any more than I could stand these random assholes sticking their heads in the sand.

And I definitely wasn't used to not responding to a clear challenge.

"There's nothing to see here, you assholes. Piss off!" I yelled at the rest of the students. Xavier's hand was still clamped around my bicep to keep me from falling on someone like a wild animal. "Did you hear me? Get fucking gone. Now!" I was raging so loudly that everyone flinched.

"Come on, chill out." Xavier kept tugging me back. I tried to recover some composure before finally breaking free from him and passing a hand through my hair. Instinctively, I went to the Maserati and opened the door to assess the damage. I made a face, however, when I saw there was a piece of paper attached to the rock in the front seat, tied down with crisscrossing red thread. I immediately picked it up and read the words on it: *Hard Candy. Player 2511.*

Why had this not occurred to me before?

Sure, I had a lot of enemies, but the only person who'd gone after me lately was him.

"Shit," I whispered, holding the paper tightly in my fingers. I got out of my car and shut the door behind me. There was no point in rereading the note; it wasn't going to help me come to any conclusions. His messages were typically indecipherable, but this one wasn't even a riddle, so it would be more impossible than usual to figure out what he planned to do with just two miserable words.

"Hey, what happened?" Xavier asked, trying to read the sheet of paper in my hand. I glanced around and realized that I didn't want to have that conversation in the student parking lot. So I pushed the threatening note into my pocket and jerked my chin at the both of them.

"Let's get out of here," I ordered firmly.

A few minutes later, we hit up a restaurant near the campus, a place we typically came after class. The smell of coffee and freshly baked pastries was in the air as soon as we walked in, along with the irritating cacophony of voices from other patrons.

We walked through the restaurant with our heads held high, not sparing a glance for anyone else. Everyone knew how prone to aggression we were; it didn't take much to provoke any of us into a brawl. Ignoring the alarmed stares we received, we sat down at our usual table right next to the big window. My friends both looked at me, waiting for me to speak.

"You want to tell us what's going on?" Luke asked first, but before I could answer him, a waitress materialized to take our orders. I shot her an irritated look and saw that it was the same one that Xavier had mocked and humiliated in the past.

"Don't be stupid," I warned Xavier, already knowing what he was going to do, and he gave me a lopsided grin.

"What can I get for you?" the girl—I'd never caught her name—said haltingly. She kept her eyes on the little notebook she had clenched in one trembling hand. She was obviously less than thrilled about our presence.

"Hey, Babydoll. Nice to see you again..." Xavier leaned sideways to get a better look at her ass in her short uniform skirt. Luke immediately elbowed him in the gut.

"Three coffees," Luke said, deciding for everyone and allowing the girl to get away as soon as possible. Xavier made a huff of annoyance, but I silently thanked Luke for intervening. All we needed was for the owner to boot us for indecency or harassment.

"So?" Luke turned his attention back to me, and I rested my elbows on the table. My leather jacket tugged at my tensed biceps. I was so on edge it felt like I was suffocating.

I didn't bother with words, instead just digging around inside my pocket until I grabbed the paper and slammed it down on the table. Both of them sucked in a breath.

"Hard Candy. Player 2511," Xavier read. "This nutjob again?"

"What are you talking about? Who the fuck is Player 2511?" Luke asked.

"This asshole in a mask who's been sending riddles and notes to Neil and his family for a while," Xavier responded, summarizing the situation pretty clearly.

"Xavier's got it. I don't know who he really is. He's shown up on multiple occasions with a white mask and a black Jeep," I explained.

Luke looked from Xavier to me. "On which occasions?" he pressed, increasingly bewildered.

"The first time, he caused my brother's accident, and then he crashed into Selene when she was trying to go back to Detroit. He's also the one who attacked Chloe at the masquerade party she went to with Madison." I stared into his eyes. "You were the one who told Madison to come to the party, weren't you?" I still needed to have a conversation with Chloe about the whole thing.

"Yeah," he admitted.

I shook my head, rubbing my temples. I held him partially responsible for what had happened to my sister, but I had to keep my cool.

"You know she's just a girl, right? What the hell is a guy like you doing with a girl that young? I'd feel like I was fucking my little sister if it were me," Xavier observed, sounding horrified. For once, I actually agreed with him. I had no interest in how my friends chose to live their lives, but sleeping with a seventeen-year-old was depraved, even by mine and Xavier's standards.

"She's not a little girl. And she knows what she's doing in bed," Luke said defensively.

"Just because she knows how to act like a woman doesn't mean she is one," I interjected, and both of them gave me thoughtful looks. It was a simple enough concept: Some women were women, while others were just girls imitating them. The difference could be subtle, even invisible, to someone who was less observant or less experienced with the phenomenon.

I, unfortunately, had plenty of experience, courtesy of Kim.

"My sex life is none of your concern. Why don't you focus on sharing women, playing heads or tails, and all the other twisted shit you guys get up to?" Luke said dismissively, waving a presumptuous hand in the air.

"Shall I remind you that you've done all that same 'twisted shit' yourself? Don't play the white knight now, because you're not," Xavier shot back in irritation, and, once again, I agreed with him completely. I could vividly recall how Luke had talked about Selene and how he'd kissed and touched her in the pool house.

Just the thought of it made my chest shudder and my stomach clench.

Luke was absolutely no better than the rest of us.

"Let's get back to the broken window on my fucking Maserati," I snapped. I didn't enjoy talking about my problems with them, but Player had attacked me in broad daylight this time, right in front of the school and countless students. I couldn't just pretend nothing happened; I couldn't ignore it, and I needed to use the Krew to my advantage.

"Right," Luke agreed. "Why not call the police?"

The main obstacle there was that if Player was an enemy or someone I'd hurt, the police could very well wind up investigating things I did in the past and tossing me in jail instead of him.

"Are you a moron?" Xavier put in. "He can't do that. Did you forget about Roger Scott and the whole thing with Scarlett?" he continued, just as the waitress arrived with our coffees. Xavier clammed up, and the girl set the mugs down in front of us, hurrying around the table like she owed somebody money. Xavier watched her with amusement, thrilled at the idea that his mere presence was putting the waitress into such a panic. When she turned to leave, he gave her one last lingering look, turning back to pick up the interrupted conversation.

"Her father wants us dead. Me most of all," I noted, leaning back against my chair. Sleeping with Scarlett Scott was the biggest fuckup of my entire life. I wasn't proud of what had gone down three years ago on spring break. It was a week every American college kid looked forward to, one where you were supposed to go overboard and drink, fuck, and party to your heart's content. People flocked to tourist destinations and let themselves become total animals. Everyone turned their brains off and allowed themselves to be whatever they wanted to be, indulging in whatever kinks or sick fantasies they had.

It was a week without boundaries or inhibitions or morality or sense of shame or any fucking thing like that.

And, three years ago, I had been acting like a beast along with the rest of them, and I'd made the fatal error of underestimating Scarlett's obsession with me. I'd handled the whole thing entirely wrong.

And something irreparable had happened...

"Neil?" I heard Luke's voice calling to me, and I blinked several times, pulling myself away from those thoughts. Once again, I had gotten lost, indulging myself in the still-painful memories.

"Yeah...I'm listening," I muttered, though I hadn't heard a single word. Luke and Xavier exchanged knowing looks, because they knew exactly where my head was at.

They'd both been there on that fateful day with my ex.

"It wasn't your fault. Scarlett was obsessed with you. She was unhinged and desperate for your attention; you couldn't possibly have predicted how far she'd go..." Luke went on, and I squeezed my eyes shut briefly. The air felt thin around me, and the feeling of remorse rose up like a ghost from the depths of my soul. I opened my eyes again and tried to suck some air back into my lungs.

I wasn't that same person who trampled recklessly over all limits; I was done with that kind of excess.

I still had to live with the cursed part of me that emerged now only when I was extremely frustrated, disappointed, or enraged, but I'd locked up that old Neil three years ago and thrown away the key. I had no intention of releasing him ever again.

"I could have been clearer, though. I could have told her—" I said tentatively, but Xavier shut me down immediately.

"Fuck that, Neil. You did all that. You've always done it. She was the one who refused to get it through her head. She was the one who dreamed up this whole fairy tale with you," he reminded me earnestly. It was the truth.

Though I'd often felt like I'd been stripped of my humanity, there was still a hidden part of me—all but imperceptible to anyone else—that had been holding on to a very human sort of guilt for three years. It was impossible to completely erase.

"Okay, but back to the other thing... If you're not going to call the police, how are you going to get rid of this psycho?" Luke asked, lifting his coffee cup to his mouth.

"No idea," I answered, drumming my fingers on the table.

"Do you know if it's a man or woman?" he asked.

"No. The few times I've spoken to them on the phone, they used a voice modifier, so I couldn't tell," I answered, and Luke's eyebrows arched up in surprise. I knew what he was thinking about—that time I'd asked him to trace one of Player's calls.

"The Brooklyn Bagel..." he said softly, and I gave him a speaking look, letting him know with a glance that yes, this had been going on for a while, and yes, he had actually been the first person to whom I had gone for help.

"What the hell are you talking about?" grumped Xavier, who didn't know any of that.

"A while ago, Neil came to me asking me to trace an anonymous call. He didn't tell me much, so I just did what he asked. All we could find out was that the call had been made from a public restaurant, so it was impossible to pin down who made the call," Luke explained.

Xavier stared at us, openmouthed.

"Fuck, this kind of thing gets me hyped. This is some James Bond shit!" he enthused while both Luke and I remained stone-faced as we looked at him. This wasn't a joke. It was an enormous problem that I needed to solve as soon as possible.

"Player usually sends riddles. Hard candy doesn't mean anything to me." I returned my gaze to the sheet of paper that lay beside my now-cold cup of coffee. Again, it had been typed and printed to make sure there was no handwriting to recognize.

But this message was even more challenging than the ones that had come before.

"Yeah. A puzzle, however difficult, at least has a solution. But with just two words...how the hell do you figure out what he's trying to tell you?" Luke mused.

"What if it's some girl you fucked in the past? I mean, there have been a lot of them, and it ended badly with pretty much all of them," Xavier speculated.

I lifted my gaze from the note to his dark eyes and gave them an impenetrable stare. I should have ignored his inane question, but instead, I gave in.

"All of them were well aware of how I was and how it worked," I argued. None of my partners had been shocked when, after a single fuck, I'd dropped them and made it clear that I had no desire for an ongoing relationship.

"Sure, but a good eighty percent of them still fell for you anyway. I wouldn't be surprised if some of them wanted you dead to this day," Luke chuckled, and I heaved a sigh. It wasn't my fault that women were drawn to me despite my awful temperament. I always approached them honestly and bluntly. I never changed how I acted with anyone; I was always myself. But even when I made it clear that I wasn't looking for anything serious, their heads got turned by the dominant role I took on in our coupling. I acted with bold self-assurance to get what I wanted from them, and they often deluded themselves into thinking that meant something more. That *they* meant something more. They tried to fit themselves into the role of savior and began to believe that they had the power to conquer my heart as well as my body.

It never came as a shock.

"You know how I am. I always had everything under control, and I take responsibility for everything I say. Why would some ex of mine hate me that much?" I asked, looking between the two of them. "Because I fucked her consensually and she liked it?" I smiled at the direction our conversation had taken.

I could see how someone might get hung up on something like that, but the idea of someone harboring that much hatred toward me just because we'd fucked once or twice was beyond the pale.

"Well, the whole experience with Scarlett should have taught you that women can do things you never would have imagined when their hopes are dashed," Luke noted, as he finished his coffee. I shook my head and took a sip of my own as well. As I did, I noticed a couple sitting across from us.

The man was wearing a sleek blue suit, and his chiseled face was wrinkled in a frown as he stared persistently at me, not even sparing a glance at the woman with him who was trying to talk to him about something inaudible. I shifted my focus to look more closely at her. Pearl earrings, blond hair, and a tightly stretched blouse rang an immediate bell: I had seen those firm breasts somewhere before. Felt them up and sucked them, too.

It was her... Amanda Cooper, the art history professor.

I sat motionless, coffee mug in midair, just staring at her until Luke gave me a gentle nudge to bring me back to earth.

"Are you still doing Ms. Cooper?" he teased. I put the mug down on the table with my usual unflappable expression.

"No, it was a one-time thing," I answered blandly. I didn't give a flying fuck about the woman, and I didn't understand why the man with her was watching me like that.

"Once is probably enough. She looks like she'd drain a man dry," Xavier chuckled, giving her a lascivious glance.

"Who's the guy with her?" I asked, shifting my focus to the man who occasionally nodded at Amanda but regularly looked back at our table.

"Oh... is Neil Miller jealous?" Luke asked mockingly.

"No, dumbass. I want to know who he is before I beat his face in. He won't stop staring at us," I answered and then began returning the dude's stare with the same intensity. I was used to men feeling competitive with me or the specific possessiveness that my presence triggered in them when they had a beautiful woman on their arm. Other men saw me as a threat, as a hunter who might be looking to draw the attention of their women to himself. I figured that was what was happening in the moment. What this guy didn't know, however, was that I had already sampled the seductive Miss Cooper's sexual talents. I vividly remembered the delightful butterflies she had tattooed around the base of her spine. How could I forget them? I caressed them with my thumbs the whole time I had her bent over in front of me.

"That's her husband," Luke informed me.

"For real? The blond bimbo's married?" Xavier asked, more incredulous than me. I wasn't surprised in the least. She was a beautiful woman in her thirties. Hell, she was probably already tired of marriage.

"Yeah. He's an entrepreneur or something like that. I don't know his name, though," Luke went on. The three of us watched him get to his feet and hand a coat to his beloved unfaithful wife. It always made me want to laugh, seeing a couple like this, pretending to adore each other.

The more I saw of society, the more certain I became of my own ideas.

I would never get married.

Love was an illusion that got dispelled sooner or later, and marriage was a useless institution.

Man was sinful by nature; we were inclined to do wrong, and none of us was worthy of wearing that ring on our fingers.

Picking one woman and pretending to declare eternal love to her was just a convention, just a fashion that society followed. Normal people thought that a marriage helped stabilize a relationship by adding obligations and commitments. In reality, though, nothing changed.

Women picked up men and left them behind like they were toys. They fell in love every day because what they really loved was the *idea* of love. They loved the attention, the fawning, and the idea of being with someone. They loved thinking of themselves as necessary to another person, and they loved hearing "I love you."

They loved jealousy.

They also loved the sex; they practically worshipped it.

And if they could find a man who gave them all of that, it was enough to call it love.

Whether it was me or some other man, it was all the same.

And Babygirl would understand that one day as well.

She'd forget about me in no time. She would come to understand that I was interchangeable, just like she was for me.

She would demonstrate how she could "love" anyone and that she said those meaningful words as lightly as I expelled smoke from a cigarette.

And I would know that I couldn't trust Selene because she'd been sold a bunch of feelings by a society that didn't understand how to feel anything at all.

Rejecting love was my only constant.

It was the only ending I could believe in.

"Hmm…" I grunted, taking a brazen look at Amanda's ass as she put on her black coat. "Interesting." I glanced back at the man who looked like he was trying to read my lecherous mind. He stared me down until he finally rested a hand on the base of his wife's spine and followed her toward the exit.

"Can you imagine if he found out his blond bimbo had cheated on him with a student?" Xavier commented, and it brought a sly smile to my lips.

"I could give him some tips on how to keep her happy so she doesn't need to go looking for other men. After all, that little butterfly deserves to be appreciated…" I answered amused, and Xavier and Luke laughed aloud at the insinuation.

That moment of levity, however, was interrupted by a pair of long legs wrapped in leather. I followed them up to a matching leather jacket and a white sweater concealing firm tits and clinging like a second skin to a wasp waist. I considered the combustible combination of curves and savage femininity wrapped in black leather for a second before lifting my gaze to meet Megan Wayne's emerald eyes. Head Case was headed right for me, proud and self-confident. Trailing behind was Logan. That was a combo I hadn't been expecting.

"Oh, there you are, Miller. Your brother's looking for you." Megan halted in front of our table, drawing wicked glances from my friends. Like me, they had also noticed that, no matter how insufferable and obnoxious she might be, the woman oozed sex from every pore.

Megan was so goddamned similar to me. We both acted and thought in the same ways. We had both been made strong by the traumatic things that happened to us. It was that trauma that kept me from ever making a move on her. If she were any other woman, I'd wonder how hard she applied herself when it came to pleasing a man. I'd wonder if she…

Shit.

I cleared my throat, coming to my senses.

"Why do you always feel the need to be where I am?" I snapped in annoyance.

"Think of me as a guardian angel." Megan gave me a wink, but I ignored her, turning my attention to Logan, who was obviously agitated.

"God, Neil, are you okay? I saw what happened to your car. Who did it? Where were you when it happened?" He looked me up and down, checking to make sure there wasn't a scratch on me.

"I was in a meeting with Robinson. And yeah, I'm fine," I said reassuringly, giving him a pat on the back.

Logan sighed in relief and readjusted the heavy bag full of books on his shoulder. He still looked upset and afraid. I would wait until we got home to tell him about Player.

"It's so touching, the way you care about him, princess," Xavier sneered, but a look of warning from me was enough to shut him up.

"He was looking for you all over campus, and when I saw you leave with—" Megan spared a glance for Xavier and Luke, her lips twisted in disgust. "With these thugs you call friends..." She waved a dismissive hand. "I said I'd come with him. He was really freaking out," she explained, and Logan gave her a grateful smile. This easiness between them was more than a little irritating for me. Had my brother forgotten how dangerous the Wayne sisters could be? I couldn't even say which of the two was the worst.

"Fine. But we have to go now, and you have to give me a lift," I ordered Logan, cutting Megan off. I didn't feel like giving her any more of my attention.

Just her being that close to me was irritating.

"Well, as you can see, Neil is safe and sound. And a prick, but that's nothing new," Head Case continued anyway. When I walked past her, I paused just inches from her pretty face. She had to tilt her head back to look me in the eye, and I watched her inhale. I knew what she was smelling: the scent of the excess bath gel I'd used just a few hours before.

"Knock it off. You are trying my patience," I warned her seriously, though I had lost count by then of how many times I had given her a similar warning. Still, Megan just gave me a knowing grin and inched fearlessly closer.

"If you say it in that sexy voice, I'll do whatever you bid me, my liege." She mock-bowed and cocked an eyebrow at me. She was truly off her rocker. She just couldn't stop provoking me even when I was explicitly telling her to stop. It was why I hated her so much—she always did the opposite of whatever I told her to do, and she enjoyed winding me up until I lost control.

"I'm out of here," I said, unwilling to continue that little scene. I was a man, not a boy consumed with pointless games. Logan followed me, but before we got too far, Xavier called me back.

"You going out with us tonight?" he asked. He and the rest of the

Krew were going to Blanco. I, however, had no desire to get with a woman or to get drunk while club music slowly deafened me. But, as I looked back at him, a wild idea occurred to me.

"No, I think I have somewhere to be," I said, sounding slightly uncertain. I didn't even understand myself this time.

I swore under my breath and headed for the door, certain that I was headed straight into another major fuckup.

4

"I had to stop wondering if, one day, he might be able to love me."

SELENE

Alyssa left Detroit the following morning.

I hadn't asked her any more questions about the kiss with Neil, but I hadn't gotten a wink of sleep either. I couldn't stop thinking about what I'd said to him on the phone. I'd told him I was going to stop chasing him, that I was afraid of him and the pain he might bring to the people around him, including me.

But Neil didn't care about the people around him. And he'd hung up on me, which surely meant that he agreed with my decision and didn't feel I even deserved a verbal answer.

At the moment, however, I had a different problem: my mother.

She'd overheard my late-night phone call—or, rather, my outburst of suffering—and she seemed determined not to talk to me about it.

"Mom…" I called out to her while she poured herself a cup of coffee.

We were both standing in the kitchen, me still in my pajamas. Mom had to go into the university in about an hour.

"What is it?" she answered shortly. I frowned; it was out of character for her to snap at me like that.

"You want to tell me what's wrong?" I asked, taking a bite of yesterday's cherry pie.

"You know what's wrong, Selene. That boy is no good for you," she said, like it was an indisputable fact. I just knew that she was going to get the wrong idea about him after last night. Neil was an asshole—I certainly thought so—but he wasn't all bad.

"Mom, you shouldn't make too much of what you overheard last night," I told her, preparing my defense of Neil, no matter how ridiculous it was of me to do that, considering how I'd just told him where he could get off the night before. I should have been agreeing with everything she said, but, once again, I was setting myself against everything and everyone to protect him.

"Oh, I shouldn't, should I? He kissed his brother's girlfriend. That is not a normal thing to do. If he's willing to hurt someone who is so dear to him, I can't imagine what he would be willing to do to you!" she insisted in a rush of worry. I understood where she was coming from. She was my mother, and she was afraid for me, but the irrational part of me stubbornly insisted that I could bring out Neil's human side.

"He didn't do it to hurt Logan on purpose. Or me. He wouldn't do that," I answered. And it was true, in a way. He wouldn't hurt me; he'd just touch me in that savage way of his and make me want him to the point of madness.

"Are you sure about that?" she asked skeptically. No, I wasn't at all sure.

After all, I'd been through a lot because of Neil, and I'd never even told her about most of the things that had happened in New York: his little performance with Britney in the pool house and his insane proposition of a three-way with him and Jennifer on Halloween night... Neil had an incredible capacity for doing me harm.

"Yes," I answered, but only to reassure her.

My mother shook her head and pinched the bridge of her nose in irritation. "You have completely lost the plot over this guy. You aren't seeing him clearly, and that's a major problem," she scolded me. She was right about that too: I was completely gone for Neil. I'd fallen victim to his shadowy charm, just like all the others.

"Relax, I know what I'm doing," I insisted, pretending at a certainty I didn't feel. In reality, I had no idea what I was doing.

Just last night, I had convinced myself that I was done with him for good, that I was going to be rational and see Neil for what he was: a bad risk. Yet, I still thought about him all the time, missed him, and was already regretting tearing into him before hearing him out.

"No, I don't think you do," my mother argued, but I had already decided the conversation was over. I stood up and headed for the stairs. I needed to shower and get dressed for the day.

"Selene Anderson, I'm not done with you! Get back here right now!" she called after my retreating back.

I ignored her.

....

That evening was the fabled party at the Delta Psi house. Janel and Bailey were in my room, much more enthusiastic about that fact than I was. I really didn't feel like getting ready and going out, but I understood that it was a rare and exclusive opportunity: It wasn't every day that one got to step foot in the basketball team's holy temple.

"Imagine Tyler's face when he sees me," Bailey said, lying on her stomach on my bed, ankles crossed behind her and her chin propped up on her hands. She had put her red hair up in a high ponytail and had more makeup on than usual, highlighting her mouth in particular with cherry red lipstick. The vibe of the party was casual, so she had gone with a pretty simple outfit: a pair of light-wash jeans and a sweatshirt with…

"Was it really necessary to wear the team's merch to the party?" Janel asked, making me laugh. She was wearing blue pants and a thin black sweater with shiny beading along the neck and sleeves.

"Of course, it is. I need Tyler to notice me," Bailey answered, with eyes on the prize as always.

"He's going to sleep with someone at this party, and it's for sure not going to be you," Janel shot back in yet another attempt to make our mutual friend open her eyes to Tyler Traborn's terrible reputation. But Bailey seemed unwilling to accept the reality that the most she could ever expect from him was to be used like a sex toy before being replaced by the next girl who came along.

"I know for a fact that he wants me. Deep down, he loves me," Bailey answered dreamily, and Janel shook her head in resignation.

I, meanwhile, sat down at my vanity to finish putting on my makeup. Usually, I only put it on when I knew I'd be seeing Neil, but I had recently decided that it wasn't right for me to neglect my appearance just because he wasn't around. I was a woman, and I was about to go to a party, so I needed to hide the dark circles under my eyes as well as the hickeys on my neck. I touched them gently with my index finger, and an odd, warm sensation made me squirm in my seat. I could still feel his kisses on my skin, his hands clutching me possessively. My desire for him was damaging.

I felt truly pathetic.

"Your eyes look like two shining beacons," Bailey joked, and I looked at her reflection in the mirror. All I'd done was apply volumizing mascara and some soft eyeshadow, but I was pleased with the result: It was delicate yet eye-catching.

"Yeah, you look good," Janel put in, taking stock of my outfit: a thin white sweater with a black, high-waisted skirt, black thigh-highs, and tall boots with a modest heel. My hair fell in soft waves down my back, and my bangs were artfully arranged to hide the scar on my forehead.

All in all, I thought I was looking sensual without being tacky, which was just how I liked it.

"You too," I answered, getting to my feet. I got my winter coat and my purse out of the closet before dabbing some perfume on my neck with a sigh. I was ready for a fun night out. The conversation with my mother that morning had brought down the mood, and I hoped going out might do me some good.

About fifteen minutes later, we were headed for the Delta Psi house. We rode in Janel's car because Ivan was apparently already there with the rest of the basketball team. As usual, Bailey was by far the most excited. "God! I'm so psyched!" she exclaimed from her spot in the back seat. I glanced at Janel as she threw our companion a flat look.

"Girl, get a hold of yourself," she chided Bailey as she parked on the side of the street behind a series of expensive cars.

We got out of the car, and all at once, I got the same uncomfortable, on-edge feeling that I always had before a party or a night out. Before us sprawled the Delta Psi house, with its large front lawn and music pumping out through the closed windows and doors. It was a grand old place—historic, but much larger and flashier than my mother's house. We passed a cluster of guys smoking on the front porch, and they gave us appraising looks before greeting Janel, whom, of course, they all knew.

When we got inside, I finally got why everyone was slavering to get into the place. There was a large atrium that was shockingly clean and well-appointed for a frat house. The decor was club-lite—a mix of luxury with a little bit of flash. There were leather sofas and armchairs scattered around the main room along with a few small tables here and there. There was a built-in bar with several bottles of alcohol on display beneath a big flat screen that was currently playing one of the team's old games. There was even a DJ at a booth playing pop songs. Through an open door, I glimpsed a pool table in the next room with a few people gathered around it for a game.

"Well, what do you think?" Janel muttered into my ear, and for a moment, I didn't know what to say. There were athletes everywhere in their signature team sweatshirts and hoodies. Clusters of guys chatted with female students in the atrium as well as the other rooms. The girls, in turn, laughed at the merest suggestion of any joke and batted their eyelashes, trying to make themselves more desirable to the basketball stars.

"It's...something," I managed.

"It's incredible. You smell that in the air? That's all the excess testosterone," Bailey jumped in, and we all laughed. She was so into the tall, powerful athletes. They left me cold, however, and not because I couldn't appreciate a well-formed man, but because my mind was still stuck on someone who could have put them all to shame. Neil had the kind of physique that was made to be admired, all the muscles perfectly proportioned on his six-three frame.

He was simply perfect.

"Hey, it's Charlie's Angels." Ivan approached us with a red cup in one hand and his arms spread wide in a welcoming gesture. Janel rolled her eyes as he snaked an arm around her shoulder and pulled her against his chest. "Sister, I must thank you properly for bringing these two treasures to my party," he told her, glancing first at Bailey and then at me. He looked me from top to bottom before inching closer with a cheeky grin that made a dimple appear on his right cheek.

"Captain," I greeted him with a mock salute, and he cocked an eyebrow at me.

"Selene Anderson, what brings you to our humble celebration?" he asked drily.

"You sound like a doofus," I scoffed, and he burst into laughter, immediately transforming back into his normal, low-key self. The same guy who gave me class recommendations and never missed a chance to mess up my bangs.

"Make yourself at home. If anyone gives you shit, let me know," he finished hurriedly as some six-foot-plus maniac hooked an arm around him and dragged him over to the bar. I tucked my hands into my coat pocket as my friends and I moved through the room. I didn't know most of the players, but I did recognize a lot of the students who were there.

"You want to get a drink?" Janel asked, pointing at the bar, and we followed her lead.

"Have you seen Tyler around anywhere?" Bailey whispered into my ear.

I automatically glanced around, searching for the guy's distinctive head of curls. Tyler was a good-looking guy, but I'd never liked him. He struck me as conceited and self-absorbed. The few times I'd ever actually heard him open his mouth, it was exclusively to brag about his sexual performance.

It was just one of the many reasons I wasn't into the trifling little boys who surrounded me at school. I was attracted to strong, self-assured men. Men who took what they wanted without worrying about getting approval from other people. The kind of man who proved his manhood with his actions and didn't need words.

Every time Neil and I were together, I felt like a child again, too inexperienced to fight with an unmanageable and devilishly complicated person. A girl, whose lack of experience was not enough to heal her inner wounds.

Deep down, I knew that Neil needed a stronger woman than me. Someone who could stand up to him and face down the beast that lived within him.

And whenever that awareness resurfaced, anguish shook my body.

"You're thinking too much," Janel said, handing me a strawberry vodka cocktail. I let out a little gasp; I'd just been staring blankly at the bar with no idea what was going on around me.

"Are you still thinking about Alyssa and what she told you?" Bailey added, taking small sips from her own cocktail.

"No. I'm fine," I reassured them, sniffing the contents of my cup. I didn't really like alcohol, but I wasn't the teetotaler I used to be either. I decided I could probably use a distraction; maybe a drink would be a good place to start.

"Having fun?" Ivan appeared behind us not even five minutes after he'd been dragged away. His cheeks were a little flushed, and his green eyes looked brighter than I remembered.

"Correct me if I'm wrong, but aren't athletes supposed to avoid getting drunk?" I asked skeptically.

"I'm not drunk," he said with the look of a wayward child who'd just heard something insulting.

"Of course, you're not. And how many fingers am I holding up?" Bailey raised four fingers, and Ivan narrowed his eyes at her.

"Four. And knock it off, I'm perfectly sober," he insisted before looking back at me with a strange sort of half-smile on his face. "A couple friends of mine would like to meet you." He jerked his chin back the way he'd come, and I leaned slightly to get a better look. They were two of his basketball teammates.

Tall, strapping, and wearing sickly matching grins.

"Ivan... No, I'm not interested." I shook my head and set my drink down on the bar. All of a sudden, I didn't feel like drinking anymore.

"Oh, come on. I'll be right there with you. You know, it's kind of an honor for us to have you here. My friends noticed you back in freshman year, and this is the perfect opportunity for them to finally talk to you." He took my elbow gently, coaxing me to go along with him while my own friends watched, saying nothing. I wove through the crowd with Ivan at my back until I made it to the couch where the two players in question had sat down next to some girls.

"Here she is. Fellas, meet Selene," Ivan announced, his hand still resting on my arm. I discreetly pulled away from his touch and registered the gazes of the two other players, which were gliding along my body. They looked first at my chest before dipping down to my thighs highlighted by my tight skirt. It was on the shorter side, but not so short that it should be provoking perverted thoughts in anyone who looked at me.

"Damn...you're even prettier than I remembered," one of the two guys noted. He was blond with deep hazel eyes. He looked wholesome enough, but I was very familiar with the reputation that athletes had on campus. "I mean, nice to meet you. I'm Cameron," he added, with a little wave.

Then it was his friend's turn.

"I'm Alexander, but you can call me Alex." The other boy had black hair and jet-black eyes to match. I smiled politely at the two of them, and Ivan gestured for me to sit down with them all. Instead of taking a spot next to one of the boys, however, I chose to perch on the armrest, away from everyone. Ivan chuckled and flopped down next to me, passing a hand through his dark hair.

"So, Captain, have you told Selene about the kind of games we like to play here?" Cameron asked, giving Ivan an inscrutable look. My forehead creased as I turned to look at the three girls who were also lounging around. Each one of them was dressed to impress, and they looked at ease amongst the athletes. They all watched me, however, like I was some new challenger they needed to chase out of their territory.

"Cam, what the fuck are you talking about?" Ivan answered, suddenly sounding annoyed.

"Doesn't she know about how we entertain ourselves here at the Delta Psi house?" Alex continued, turning his attention to Ivan, who had begun to sprawl out comfortably on the sofa next to me.

"She's my sister's friend, you dick," he snapped irritably, and it sounded like a warning.

"So?" Alex shot back.

"We were talking about power hour," Cameron cut in, nudging Alex with his elbow. He was pretty transparent; no one believed they'd actually been referencing some banal drinking game.

"I'm familiar with power hour, but I don't really drink. Plus, that kind of thing is idiotic. Grow up," I said in a burst of annoyance before standing up and preparing to walk away. A smug chorus of "oooohs" came from behind me, but I ignored them. That was exactly why I couldn't stand student athletes. They all thought their minor celebrity was enough to get any girl, and maybe that was true for a large part of the student body, but it wasn't for me.

"Jackasses," I muttered to myself as I moved through the throng of people. I was well aware that they'd actually been trying to allude to some sex game, and I was happy Ivan had shut them down on my behalf, but I still felt extremely uncomfortable about the whole thing. It was embarrassing even thinking about sharing that kind of intimacy with someone else.

How did Neil do it with all his women? I'd never be able to understand it. The way I was with him was unique, and even though I lost all my inhibitions with him, I couldn't imagine letting someone else touch me like that.

I looked around for my friends and found Bailey flirting with Tyler beside one of the large picture windows, so I decided to concentrate on finding Janel, but she appeared to have vanished into thin air.

What the hell? Did she ditch me?

I snorted as I thought about what to do next. There were too many people in the room and not enough air. So I made my way outside and sat down on a wooden swing on the porch. I huddled into my coat and tried to ignore the stares from the boys outside who looked at me like I was fresh meat to be devoured. I heaved a sigh as I began absently tracing a shape on my thigh with one finger. A shell with a pearl inside.

"Every time you feel alone, draw a pearl inside a shell," Neil had told me in one of the loveliest moments we'd shared. He'd drawn that same thing on my hip with a marker just after he'd allowed himself to climax inside me, unprotected. The first time he'd done that with anyone.

I bit my lip at the profane memories that ran through my mind: his sculpted body, the satiny amber skin that could make anyone dream of running their tongue all over it, and his stifled masculine moans—the ones I would have recognized anywhere.

And, most of all, his touch that can make me tremble from my fingertips to my toes...right down to my bones.

My Disaster wasn't the kind of man to be easily forgotten. Even at a distance, he could knock me for a loop, could make me think the wickedest thoughts despite how erratic he was, despite the terrible things he could do.

It was too late; he was in me.

In my heart and in my soul.

"Hey, Selene. I'm sorry about those dumbasses."

I startled when I heard Ivan's voice. He'd joined me outside and sat down next to me without saying a word. He looked at me shamefacedly.

"Don't worry about it. I know how you boys are. You're used to girls drooling and rolling over at a snap of your fingers." I shook my head, and a bitter smile spread across my face as I thought about how, deep down, all men were like Neil. They all valued physical attraction over the beginnings of a real relationship.

"Yeah... I mean, not really. It doesn't always happen like that," he said defensively.

"Don't bullshit me, Captain," I said, looking at him askance.

"I know you're a good girl, Selene. I'm sorry my friends got the wrong idea." He bit his lower lip, looking sincerely worried, and I took the opportunity to study him. Ivan was handsome, the kind of young man to whom God had granted every blessing: a brilliant future in sports, model good looks, money, success, and a completely normal existence, free from trauma or a bad childhood or any obvious behavioral disorders.

Why hadn't I fallen in love with someone like him?

"Okay, apology accepted so long as you keep both Cameron and Alex away from me," I said warningly. Ivan laughed and stared at me for a moment that seemed to last forever. His eyes lingered on my lips before moving to my eyes, coaxing a blush from me. I never liked it when a guy stared at me so insistently, and the certainty in his gaze only made it more discomforting.

"Can I tell you a secret?" he murmured in a low voice.

"Sure," I answered hesitantly.

"I really thought that after you ended things with Jared, you would have come to me," he revealed, surprising me.

"What? You barely notice I'm alive most of the time." I gave him a wry smile and shrugged. I was certain that, with Neil still in my head, there was no way I was going to develop an attraction to anyone else. My Disaster had demanded all of me right from the start, and I had given him what he wanted.

"Is there someone new in your life?" he asked, giving me a shrewd look.

"No. I'm not dating anyone right now," I answered.

"But?" he prompted.

"But...there is a guy I like, yes," I admitted, my cheeks burning.

"Do I know this guy? Does he go here?" Ivan had never struck me as particularly curious, and certainly not about my personal life, so his inquisition surprised me.

"No, he's not in Detroit," I clarified while he looked thoughtfully at me. He was probably wondering how I knew someone not from the city. "I met him in New York when I went to stay with my father," I continued, and he raised his eyebrows in understanding.

"Oh, so he's from there?"

"Yeah, he is." I nodded, thinking unavoidably of Neil. I wondered what he was doing at that moment. Was he by himself or with one of his women? The idea of someone else touching him or kissing him the way I had done made me sick to my stomach. I hated knowing that he was incapable of being exclusive with me. His need to seek out other girls, even after being with me, got under my skin. It hurt my pride, making me feel like I wasn't enough, like I wasn't worth anything at all.

"So what? What's wrong with him?" Ivan continued. I was disquieted and said nothing. "Oh, come on, Selene. It's just me. You know me. You don't have to be afraid to tell me anything," he added in a coaxing tone. Despite his reputation for being something of a fuckboy, he seemed sincerely interested in understanding what was happening inside my head.

"There's not much to tell." I sighed. "He's not interested in a relationship, he doesn't have feelings, and he's cold and distant. It's not worth talking about..." I bowed my head, and Ivan inched closer, tipping my chin upward with one finger. I looked at him then—really looked at him the way I probably should have been doing from the start—and I finally understood what all those girls saw in him. His green eyes were threaded through with luminous, tawny streaks that drew one in deeper and invited a closer scrutiny of the rest of him. But I was too dumb, too bamboozled by a pair of golden eyes, that I just couldn't seem to quit, so I couldn't accept that invitation.

"May I kiss you?" he asked me earnestly, a hairsbreadth from my face. His breath was fresh and warm against my skin. I swallowed hard as I looked at his lips, not because I was drawn to them, but because I was imagining another pair—a pair more lush and insistent. "Someone once told me that a man never asks for a kiss," I said softly. Echoing Neil's words felt like a stab to the heart.

Ivan gave me a small smile.

"I was really just asking to be polite," he murmured, trying to move in closer again, but I pulled back away from him.

"Only those who know me well...shouldn't ask me that," I said, pulling away from his touch entirely and getting to my feet. Ivan looked up at me, surprised and bewildered. He probably didn't get rejected very often.

"Sorry," he mumbled. "I mean... I... I wasn't..." He looked increasingly confused and uncomfortable. He rubbed his hands along his pants and cleared his throat awkwardly.

I hadn't been sure if I could call what I felt for Neil "love," but after turning Ivan down, I suspected it might really be. It was a true, pure feeling that would not fade, not even if I met the world's most perfect man. Still, I had to accept the fact that Neil and I weren't anything. I had to commit to not chasing after him anymore and to just let him go the way I'd promised him on the phone.

I had to stop wondering if he was thinking of me or if one day he might be able to love me. But it wasn't going to be easy.

Because, clearly, I couldn't just run into someone else's open arms. Love wasn't a fleeting thing for me; it wasn't a game or a hobby.

Neither was it an illusion, the way Neil clearly believed. He was so convinced that the only things I really "loved" were the way he looked and the passionate way he touched me.

But that couldn't be further from the truth.

I loved the way he always fell asleep on his side.

I loved his enigmatic smile, alluring and sexy as hell.

I loved his clean smell and how it clouded my mind.

I loved the way his eyes looked when they caught the sun. They became, somehow, even more golden until they could rival the sun itself for beauty and brightness.

I loved the delighted look on his face when he found a package of pistachios, like a little boy presented with his favorite treat.

I loved the way his forehead creased up when he was trying to understand something I told him, and I loved the powerful, stubborn, sexual, troubled, and uncontrollable side of him as well.

I loved the heart that he kept locked behind glass where it could never be touched.

I loved his unfathomable behavior that concealed the fragile soul underneath.

I loved his intelligence and his erudition, though he only ever displayed them quietly.

I loved everything about him: the chaos, the mess, even his fear of staying with me.

I loved the things that made him easy to hate, but to my misfortune, I'd found even more things that made him easy to love.

And if that wasn't real love, then I had no other name for it.

Half an hour later, Ivan and I stood in the driveway of my little house.

He'd offered to give me a lift home, and I couldn't find either of my friends, so I sent them a text letting them know I was ducking out early. Bailey had almost certainly gone off to some bedroom with Tyler, and as for Janel… Well, I'd have to track her down later to get the whole story.

"Thanks again, but I could have gotten an Uber or something," I told Ivan as he walked me up to the porch. His foreign scent still lingered around me. The awkwardness over the kiss that wasn't had mostly faded, and Ivan was back to being funny and charming, like nothing had ever happened.

"It's cool; you have no idea how jealous my friends are right now," he said, winking at me, and I grinned back at him.

"Well, just imagine how many girls are currently seething at me, Captain," I said teasingly as he strolled easily alongside me, hands tucked into the pouch of his basketball hoodie.

"Yeah, there's probably a few of them wondering where I went," he said with a strange grimace.

"But you are going back, right? Night's still young," I said knowingly. Surely his night was going to end like all his friends'—in bed with someone or other.

"Well, since you shot me down so hard, I'll have to console myself somehow, won't I?"

We stopped a few feet from the porch steps and looked at each other.

"Fair warning: Next time I want to kiss you, I'll know better than to ask for permission," he said archly, his gaze drifting to my mouth. His green eyes lingered on me longer than they should have, and all at once, I got the feeling that we were being watched. It was probably just paranoia, but it was uncomfortable.

"What's wrong?" he asked, tracking my gaze as I glanced around at the darkness that surrounded us.

"Nothing," I said reassuringly, giving my head a shake.

"Well, I'll head out then. See you around." Ivan leaned toward me, and I immediately turned to give him my cheek. He bent down—he had to bend quite a ways—and kissed my cheek, his lips warm against my skin. I had once made the mistake of jumping into something while I was still entangled with Jared, and I refused to do the same thing with Neil. Even though we weren't together and I didn't owe him anything, I valued my feelings for him too highly to pursue anyone else. Despite the unrelenting disappointment about how things were going between us, the things I felt for him hadn't changed, and they weren't going to change. Because, when you really love someone, they become a part of you, and there's no replacing them.

I wasn't sure exactly when Neil had become a part of me. Maybe he had been from the start.

From the moment I looked into his dazzling eyes on that city sidewalk.

And no matter how sad or frustrated I was, I would jealously guard that part of him that lived inside me.

Because I could still dream, and in my dreams, he could love me.

"I think I'd better go inside." I half-turned, and Ivan's jaw tensed up before he arranged his lips into a tight smile. He was just about to say something more when someone else beat him to it.

"Yeah, I think you should."

That voice—intense and rough—obviously did not belong to Ivan.

For a second, I thought I had hallucinated it, but that was impossible. The shivers that moved over my body could only have been caused by one person: Neil.

I went very still before turning slowly, searching the darkness for him. A moment later, I picked out a dark silhouette on the porch steps, barely outlined by the distant lights from the front walk. My arms fell slack against my sides, and I stood there in shock. I squinted to make sure it was indeed him, and as I did so, he lit a cigarette. I saw his face in the glow of the lighter, a stormy glower making his perfect face look ominous.

Even cloaked in that diabolical aura, he was breathtakingly beautiful. I blushed like a schoolgirl and struggled to draw in a full breath.

"Hey, Tinkerbell," he said softly.

5

"If you want me, it has to be just me!"

SELENE

I blinked rapidly, trying to clear my head.

After greeting me, Neil stared into the middle distance, looking lost in his own thoughts. He kept taking long drags from his cigarette and then blowing out the smoke in a methodical, automatic fashion. It felt like he wasn't really present.

His body was, but his mind was far away.

"Who's this guy?" Ivan asked with an edge of concern in his voice. I had no idea how to describe—let alone explain—Neil and what he was to me.

A friend? A...family member? Just some guy I knew?

"He's..." I trailed off, still staring at Neil as he continued to sit unmoving on the porch steps, his legs splayed, elbows balanced on his knees, and his leather jacket straining against his crooked arms. Dressed all in black, he looked like damnation in the flesh. "This is Neil," I managed finally. "Miller," I added, sounding awkward.

My whole mood had shifted again, and I was back to being that overawed little girl who was hooked on the golden gaze that had now locked on me. I shivered; it felt as though those eyes could see straight through my clothes and examine the goosebumps that covered my skin underneath. I gave a strangled gasp.

"Oh...and why is he just sitting there motionless? He looks like a crazy person," Ivan noted. He wasn't wrong; Neil looked far from lucid. I'd seen him lose control on a few occasions, and that had been enough to show me that there was a dangerous part of him that he usually tried to hide.

"It's fine, Ivan. You can go," I reassured him, trying to sound calm. He moved closer to me, shaking his head.

"I'm not leaving you here alone with...that person." He gestured to Neil like he was some sort of unwanted pest, and I hoped my Disaster wouldn't take exception. But I didn't even have time to urge Ivan to get out of there before Neil was getting to his feet and taking a final drag from his Winston. He flicked it to the ground, stepped on it, picked up the butt, and very deliberately put it in his cigarette pack. Then he cocked his head to one side, carefully scrutinizing the guy who had driven me home.

"Seriously, Ivan, I think you need to leave." Something stirred within me, and I began to get afraid. I could see the tension in Neil's body, the deep, slow breaths he was taking, and the agitation that swam in his veins. It was extremely inadvisable for Ivan to stay there with me any longer.

"Are you kidding?" Ivan insisted. "Look at him. The dude looks high or something. Who the fuck is this guy?" he asked again.

The situation was deteriorating. When Neil went quiet like that, it meant something bad was about to happen.

I took Ivan by the arm and tugged him back.

"You need to go! Now!" I insisted, raising my voice, and his eyes widened in surprise. He tried to shake me off, not yet realizing that I was only trying to save him. He grabbed my wrist to pull my hand away, and I heard a furious exhalation behind me. Neil had leaped into motion and came at Ivan, shoving him until he staggered backward. Neil followed that up with an immediate right hook to Ivan's jaw, and I leaped to my friend's defense, putting myself between the two of them.

"Oh my God! Ivan, are you okay?" I drew closer to him in horror, but he recoiled from me, terrified. He touched the place where he'd been hit and wiped away the thin line of blood that leaked from the corner of his mouth. He stared wide-eyed at Neil, panting heavily behind me.

"What the fuck?" He stared at the blood smeared on his hand before looking back up at Neil and me. "This dude's fucking psycho. What is his problem?" he shouted wrathfully, and I didn't have the guts to turn around and check Neil's expression. I knew that if Ivan kept provoking him, Neil was going to give in to the untamable beast that he became when he fell into a rage.

"Please just go." I was on the verge of tears as I pleaded with Ivan. I couldn't have forgiven myself if anything else happened to him because of me. Ivan seemed to read the sincerity in my eyes; he could see that this wasn't a joke or game for me.

"Am I seriously going to have to leave you here with this guy?" He gestured to Neil again, and I heard a growl of irritation from behind my back. I could smell his familiar scent of musk whenever the wind changed. Which meant that he was very close to me as well as being in a dangerous headspace.

"Yes," I said finally. Ivan backed up a few steps, massaging his injured jaw where a large bruise was forming already. A few moments later, he left, albeit with visible reluctance. I squeezed my eyes shut and breathed in and out slowly.

I knew the worst was still to come.

Hesitantly, I turned to face Neil, who had been standing motionless behind me that whole time. There was already a wicked expression plastered across his face: He was pleased to have hurt Ivan.

I moved past him and walked up to the front door. My hands shook as I attempted to get my key into the lock, and that gave Neil enough time to catch up with me.

Is he planning to come inside too?

I wasn't brave enough to ask him, so I just unlocked the door and walked inside, the devil himself hot on my heels. Fortunately, Mom was out to dinner with Anton again. She wouldn't have let him step foot in the house if she were there. I tossed my coat and purse onto the living room couch and went into the kitchen to grab an ice pack from the freezer for his hand.

"So...have you completely lost your mind or what?" I demanded with a shaky voice, but there was no hiding the anger in it. I tossed the ice pack onto the kitchen counter nearest to Neil, keeping my distance from him. Neil just stood there looking entirely shut down. The rage that lit up his eyes was alarming, to say the least. His right hand shook occasionally, and his knuckles were red from where he'd hit Ivan's face, but he didn't seem to be feeling any pain. He was still restless with dark energy that he needed to vent.

"Your hand is swelling up. Put some ice on it," I said, swallowing thickly, but he just continued to stare at me, not saying or doing anything else. Then, his eyes squinted fractionally and flicked to the ice pack before returning to me.

Nothing. No reaction on his face.

This was abnormal behavior, even for him, and I didn't know what to do with it.

"Are you going to tell me what's going on with you? How long have you been in Detroit? Also, why did you come to Detroit?" The more I tried to communicate with him, the more Neil seemed to retreat into his own chaotic inner world.

"Because..." He clenched his jaw and scrubbed a hand over his face. "Because I'm a dumb motherfucker, that's why," he continued confusingly, the fury in his voice making me wince. I stepped back until I was pressed against the counter, prepared to defend myself against whatever insanity he had for me. Neil glanced around, spotting a glass vase that my mother had recently finished painting, and snatched it up with one hand. He shot me a pitiless looked and then hurled the vase against the wall as hard as he could. I gasped and covered my ears automatically as it shattered.

"I came all the way out here to work things out with you after that bullshit phone call of yours, and what do I find, Selene?" he shouted, turning around to face me. I thought that after obliterating that vase, his anger might have been placated slightly, but instead his chest continued to heave, his hands were still clenched into fists, and a furious look still twisted his face. "You don't give a shit!" he went on, and I felt tears welling up. I was completely overwhelmed, and he was completely over the line. Maybe I had gotten too heated on that call, but why couldn't we talk about it like reasonable adults? Why couldn't we just sit down and talk things through until we saw eye to eye? Instead, Neil seemed determined to make me afraid of him, to shock me with this demonstration of who he really was inside.

"Alyssa told me what you did and—" I muttered, keeping myself pressed against the counter and far away from him.

"I don't give a fuck what that girl told you. You should have listened to me. You should have trusted me!" His voice was getting louder again, and I felt completely helpless. I certainly wasn't going to say or do anything that would match his unhinged energy.

"How am I supposed to trust you when you never let me really know you?" My calm tone contrasted sharply with his violent movements. Rarely had we seemed more like opposites, as we each coped with this so differently.

Neil visibly tried to calm down at that point, breathing deeply. There were beads of sweat on his forehead, his hair was in more disarray than usual, and his lips looked chapped. My head began to spin, and I tightened my grip on the counter to keep from stumbling as I briefly shut my eyes.

"I let you have a look inside me. And there's nothing beautiful there, nothing good for a person like you."

I opened my eyes again at the ragged sound of his voice, quieter and hoarser, probably because he'd done so much yelling.

"And I don't know what to make of you," I murmured, letting out a sob of frustration. I covered my face with my hands, barely managing to stay on my feet.

My head felt like it was bursting; my whole body was trembling. I...

I couldn't understand Neil, and I couldn't deal with him either.

I managed to calm myself slightly, though I was still wracked with occasional sobs as I looked at him again. His eyes scrutinized my entire body, and just for a moment, I caught a glimpse of want, which he immediately suppressed, running a hand over his face. Neil was trying to get himself together, and it looked like he was forcing himself to keep his distance from me. I just kept quiet. I was afraid that anything I might say would only reignite his rage.

Suddenly, Neil began to stalk back and forth in front of me, visibly fighting against his demons. Then he turned and walked quickly over to the kitchen island and took a seat on one of the stools, cradling his head in his hands.

Instinct told me to go to him and try to comfort him. Reason, however, said I should stay right where I was.

"Why?" he asked himself, staring unseeingly at the kitchen island. "Why? For fuck's sake!" He tore a hand through his hair again, his movements fidgety.

Was I crazy for loving him even like that? Out of his mind, enraged, and bewildered?

Yes, he was all those things.

Something was wrong with me. Even I couldn't figure out how Neil had burrowed so deeply into my head.

After a long silence, I finally ventured in a soft tone, "Why what?" But he just stayed slumped forward, his hands digging into his hair as he breathed laboriously.

"Shut the fuck up!" he told me, and I flinched.

I had gotten used to his anger, his profanity, and his rough manner, less so to this obvious incoherence that made his behavior impossible to decipher.

Tension rose up between us, and I didn't allow myself to utter a single word. Still in shock, I began collecting the shards of glass from the smashed vase and putting them in the trash. My hands were shaking, and my heart was pounding so hard that I could feel it in my stomach, but I couldn't give in to apprehension and dread if I wanted to keep a clear head.

Meanwhile, Neil had put the ice pack over his swollen knuckles and stared off into space. He looked worn-down and vacant.

I cared more for him than any other man in the world, but that didn't mean I could make excuses for him. I couldn't believe he'd come into my home and treated me so disrespectfully.

"Tell me what you want from me," I said, if only to break the silence that enveloped us. He didn't answer, only raising his head to give me a furious glare. I could see the mess of emotions he was experiencing in his golden eyes. I took a step back, cowed by his hard expression, and Neil noticed.

The small amount of confidence I'd had was snuffed out then, like a candle before a gust of wind.

He got to his feet, dominating the small kitchen with his bruiser physique. He tossed the ice pack onto the kitchen island and then stepped around it.

It seemed that every step he took shook the earth until even the devil below felt the trembling.

I backed up until my back was against the wall. He halted.

He studied me for a long moment, though I had no idea what,

if anything, he was trying to figure out. He was too well concealed behind his psychological walls of silence and remove.

"Take your shoes off," he ordered while he shed his own leather jacket at a disarmingly leisurely pace. He tossed it aside without ever breaking his stare, and my eyes tracked the motion as I panicked internally.

Now in just his dark jeans and sweatshirt, he leveled his stormy, impenetrable gaze at me, urging me to do as he said. But I hesitated.

"Take off the fucking shoes. Now," he repeated impatiently, and I sucked in a breath at the intensity in his voice.

I tightened my lips in disdain at his high-handed attitude, but I did as he said. I pulled off one boot and then the other, letting them fall to the floor with a brief thud. I wore only my thin white sweater, skirt, and thigh-highs. He looked me up and down, lingering on my bottom half, and from the flare of lust that illuminated his eyes, I could tell he was thinking about how easy it would be to slip a hand up that skirt.

Was he seriously going to try something right after an outburst like that?

I found myself wondering what I should do if he did make a move. I could go along with it and let him make me feel good, or I could yell at him for being a psycho and kick him out. In either case, I knew Neil would somehow end up getting what he wanted. After all, he never stopped until he did.

He had something to tell me, and he wanted to communicate it through the only language he really understood—sex.

He began to approach me again, taking slow but decisive steps, and I held still, waiting for him. My breath came faster and faster as the air itself seemed to grow stormy in his presence.

Then, finally, he was right in front of me, my nose level with his chest. Neil towered over me, and I felt terribly small before him. He wasn't trying to highlight our size difference or how powerful his body was compared to my much more petite one, but rather he was demonstrating his ability to always win over me, to dominate me, and to exert a masculine authority over me at will. No matter how much I tried to resist him.

"What do you want to do now? Use me?" I sneered at him, and he gave a soft, cruel little laugh.

Was it amusing for him how helpless I was?

"Quiet now," he snapped, and my lip curled in disgust.

"If you want me, it has to be *just* me!" I spat, and his eyes went wide. He looked unrecognizable.

His mind was somewhere far away, and his body was not saying "desire," instead it was all intimidation and dominance.

In one firm motion, he grabbed my hair in his fist and pulled my neck back. It didn't hurt, but he was holding me tightly. Then, he spun me around with a hard yank, and I found myself with my cheek plastered against the cold surface of the wall. My breasts were crushed painfully against it. All at once, I could feel his chest pressing against my back and his nose grazing the curve of my neck. He sniffed deeply, like an animal, and moved up to nibble on my earlobe. I moved slightly against him, trying to wriggle free, and Neil put his hand on my hip, squeezing my ass so possessively that I could feel his fingers sinking into my flesh.

"Are we back to this again? Is it going to be like when you took me hard on that desk to show me who was boss?" I asked drily.

My question went unanswered, though.

I could feel his breathing get ragged, and a pleased groan came from deep in his throat. Apparently, that memory really did it for him because he pressed his hips against my ass until I was completely flush with the wall. There was no longer the least bit of space between us.

I gave a faint moan of pain before going rigid when I felt his fingers gliding along the outside of my thigh, heading up under my skirt. His touch was delicate but also intractable and menacing. I should have pushed him away; I should have hated him for the totally unreasonable way he was acting, but instead my nipples stiffened and a devouring heat rose from the bottom of my stomach all the way up to my chest.

"You're wearing makeup. You put on a skirt...for him?" he whispered darkly.

Just what was he suggesting? That I was interested in Ivan or had maybe started something with him?

"So what if I did?" I jeered back at him. At the same time, I felt his finger slip underneath the edge of my panties.

"Hmm...lace..." he observed, close to my ear, feeling out the fabric with his fingers. I had skipped the cotton panties for once and dared to wear something a bit more sensual. But I'd had no idea what was about to happen to me. "I suppose you also wore this for your...captain, right?" he sneered, and I ground my teeth, insulted.

"You know what? Maybe I did. Maybe I was about to find out what he thought of them when you interrupted us." It was a lie, of course. I couldn't have brought myself to do anything like that. I just said it to provoke him, and I succeeded marvelously because Neil slapped my ass. Hard. I was propelled forward, my backside burning from the strike, but I didn't have time to dwell on the pain because Neil was spinning me around to face him, tightening his fist around my hair. My shoulders banged painfully off the wall, but I didn't care. His smell surrounded me, and I was forced to lift my eyes up to meet his.

Small as I was, I felt enveloped by his aura of darkness.

"Don't play games with me, little girl," he warned, sounding severe, and I continued staring into his eyes, trying to hide my fear. I would not allow him to ride roughshod over me again.

"Or what?" I challenged him, and something flared to life in his honey-colored eyes. Neil hated anything that felt like a slight, especially such an obvious one. He bent, perhaps to kiss me, but instead I bit down on his lower lip and pulled it, trapped between my teeth. He emitted a growl of irritation and tightened his grip on my hair.

And so the fight began.

When I finally released him, he winced and licked his wounded lip, which had started to bleed.

He didn't look like he was in pain, however. He looked even more aroused than before.

"You really are a wild tigress," he said in a seductive whisper, and the sound of his deep baritone only stoked my desire. All my insides lit up, burning like an unquenchable flame. "And I'll bet you're getting all hot and bothered as well," he added with an insolent smile. I swallowed hard and didn't answer. I *was* hot and bothered, and Neil seemed determined to see proof of it.

He released my hair and used one hand to trap my wrists over my head. He snuck the other under my tight skirt and pulled the lace panties aside so he could stroke me. I blushed as his fingertips met my wet arousal. I forced myself to keep meeting his eyes steadily. I was determined to show him that no matter how pliable my body became for him, I was still capable of thinking clearly.

"Such a wicked Babygirl, getting soaked over so little…" he brought his fingers up to his mouth and licked them, staring at me all the while. He gave a groan of masculine relish, like the taste of me was driving him out of his head. He was trying to discomfit me, but I was determined not to let him take the upper hand. I wiggled my legs, trying to shake him off me, but he didn't budge an inch.

He was too strong; I had to give up.

"Like you're much better off," I shot back at him, because I could feel his enormous erection pressing into my crotch. We were both struggling to catch our breath, and our chests grazed one another with every inhalation. We were barely holding back from leaping upon each other like maniacs and giving in to our mutual desire.

"I'm a man. My body reacts to all the girls," Neil said dismissively. So I inched closer to his throat and pressed my lips to it before lightly biting down. I could taste his clean skin against my tongue. He shivered only slightly, so I gave him another bite, this one closer to his jaw. The friction of his stubble against my mouth was as dizzying as his delicious scent.

"But you can't come with *all the girls*." The last time we were together, he had told me about his anorgasmia, but he'd had no problem climaxing with me that night. I still wore the marks of our passionate evening.

I definitely hadn't imagined that encounter.

"That's beside the point," he answered cautiously, but he did nothing to halt my ministrations.

"It's very much the point. What's the use in screwing if you can't get off? With me, you can," I taunted. His fingers clenched around my wrists until I was breathless. With his other hand, he took my face and tugged me forward until I was perhaps a hand's length away from him.

"Shut up," he said again, low and blunt. I could feel his hot breath against my lips. Like always, he didn't want to have a real conversation with me.

"You're such a coward. You can't even admit the truth to yourself," I went on as his gaze alternated between my mouth and my eyes. Then, in one wild movement, he took my mouth and released my body from his iron grip. My arms tightened around his neck, and he slipped his hands under my thighs to lift me. Instinctively, I wrapped my legs around his waist as his tongue moved hungrily against mine, demanding my complete submission. I ran my hand through his soft hair, clutching the longer strands on top of his head, and even through my haze of lust I managed to meet his kiss with a violence of my own. It was still a struggle, keeping up with him, but I had learned to push past my inexperience to bring him pleasure.

"Get ready, Babygirl, because this is going to be hard and fast," he whispered against my lips, his forehead pressed to mine.

He had me truly trapped up against the wall as he used one hand to hold me there while the other slipped between our bodies. He unbuttoned and unzipped his jeans to free his erection, which I looked at only briefly before tugging my panties to one side. With nothing in the way of delicacy or foreplay, he positioned himself between my thighs and entered me in one smooth thrust.

There was no mercy.

In that moment, I was nothing but a body to be used. Just like his blonds.

I tossed my head back against the wall and clung to his shoulders, producing a groan of commingled pain and pleasure. I wanted Neil with everything I was, but I had to admit that his aggressive approach was uncomfortable for me. He was large, and he knew that, but rather than making allowances for his size, he was just pounding away.

He began to move more skillfully, his fingers digging into my thighs, which were still wrapped around him.

His strokes were short and deep, firm and rough.

I cinched my arms around his neck and gave myself over to his power, knowing that there was nothing else for me to do.

He was going to take what he wanted, like always.

No asking. No waiting.

"You hated seeing me with Ivan, didn't you?" I needled him, wincing as I hit the wall with each one of his unstoppable thrusts.

"You think I care about you and that kid?" His hardened voice was somehow even sexier. He sounded like he was in complete control of himself while I was starting to struggle for breath.

"Y-yeah..." I managed, tightening my hold on the nape of his neck, and Neil thrust harder to shut me up. I jerked as I felt pain shooting down my spine. I moaned in pain and rested my forehead against his shoulder.

"Wrong. I don't give a shit," he answered shortly. He was on edge, angry, and confused. He continued to move inside me without so much as a kiss. He gave me nothing but the relentless, pistonlike movement of his hips.

"Then why are you acting like a maniac?" I whispered breathlessly, my pulse throbbing in my head. Neil had lit a fire inside me that only he—and he alone—could quench. My legs trembled with every thrust, my stomach tightening against his powerful movements. I ground my heel into the firm muscle of his ass, clenching with every movement of his pelvis, and wrapped myself tightly around him to hold on.

"You're the one who makes me crazy." I felt his breath graze my throat and shivered. When he began to move with even more furious intensity, I arched my back and took it all.

My heart was pounding wildly, and my body felt storm-tossed.

I thought about how bizarre this relationship was—if a "relationship" was even what I should call it.

Neil was different. His issues were obvious and particularly difficult to resolve.

There was nothing I could do for him if he couldn't learn how to love himself.

He was cold and impersonal in that moment. He was only using me, and he wanted me to know it. He didn't kiss me; he didn't touch me lovingly. He wouldn't even look me in the eye. All he wanted was my submission.

Then, abruptly, I squeezed my eyes shut and bit down on his neck as my body tightened around his erection. I groaned, feeling his hands slide down over my ass to get a better grip on me. As I came, I heard his proud chuckle in my ear.

In that moment, I saw Neil as a beast in every way, shape, and form: devastating, unstoppable, and dangerous.

He didn't even pause, continuing to take me, undaunted, trying to drive my pleasure to new heights.

I clutched his back, trying to hold on any way I could, and he let out an angry "fuck" when he felt my fingernails poking through the fabric of his sweatshirt.

It was insane, the way I wanted him but was terrified of him at the same time, along with all the other irrational feelings he brought out in me. My head pounded with those thoughts even as my body continued to yield to him and demonstrate the full power he had over me.

Neil stared at me with animal lust, but once again, he made no attempt to emotionally connect with me. He was driven, twisted, and vacant—a slave to his own want.

When his movements increased in intensity, I embarrassed myself, coming again with a cry.

It seemed impossible that I was reacting in such a way to his mad frenzy.

I hoped he was going to stop soon; it felt like the fury with which he penetrated me was unstoppable.

Or was he once again struggling to orgasm?

I would have taken him in whatever way he wanted to give himself to me because he showed me a world of such loveliness no matter how abrasive he got. The only problem was my physical weakness and perhaps my inability to satisfy a man of his appetites.

"Enough…" I pleaded in a stupefied whisper.

I was very familiar with his staying power, and I knew he could have gone on a lot longer. But I needed to catch my breath, to give myself a little break. I was too sensitive—aroused but exhausted.

Neil went rigid, pressing even harder into me like he was trying to break me in half. His fingers clutched my thighs with untempered strength, and then he froze with a masculine growl.

Finally, he had reached his peak, and he couldn't escape the involuntary shudders that totally overwhelmed him. They were so violent that I shook with him. His shoulders were trembling; his breath came out almost as a sob. I waited for him to completely savor the moment of pleasure, which lasted even longer than usual. And, when it finally faded, he released me.

I felt the absence of his hands on me, and my legs were too exhausted by that point to hold me up. I slid down the wall to land on the floor, still sweating, living proof of what his unbridled power could do. I trembled with aftershocks of the pleasure that he'd given me exclusively to satisfy his male ego. He'd proved to both of us that he could have me whenever he wanted me, and neither Ivan nor any other man could replace him.

He knew how addicted I was to him.

And I knew that I was trapped in a dark void, the place his shadows had drawn me down into.

I rested a hand over my wildly pounding heart and then looked up at him from the ground.

Neil staggered back, disoriented.

For a moment, he looked dazed, but he came back to himself, taking on his familiar glower. He pushed his still-stiff cock back into his boxers, pulled his jeans back up, and was once again just as unruffled as ever. The only evidence of the moment we had just shared was his reddened neck, the mess that was his hair, and his wet, red lips, which wore the imprint of my teeth.

He looked a little shaky, but it was only from the jolt of erotic energy still circulating throughout his body. Emotionally, he was gone. He hadn't felt anything except the simplest physical pleasure, the way it hadn't been between us since our earliest days together. I felt like I had traveled back in time to my stay in New York.

"Satisfied?" I asked him sharply to keep from bursting into tears. All the feelings were still there; they had a stranglehold on my heart, but I didn't want to make myself look even weaker in his eyes.

"Get up," he demanded, ignoring my question. He ran a hand through the disheveled hair on the top of his head, and it occurred to me that, even immediately after sex, he was still just as hot as he was an asshole.

"What do you think you've achieved here?" My head spun, and I felt completely discombobulated. Despite the fact that I'd been able to climax—something that was inexplicable even to me—there had been no feeling in the act. Neil had just imposed himself upon my body.

"The same thing you achieved." He cast the space between my legs a speaking look, telling me without words that we'd both enjoyed ourselves, though we had very different feelings about that fact. His cold expression made me just as much of an object as his blonds, the ones he used to pleasure himself. I tried to stand up, but physical weakness sent me back down to my knees. I shook my head, frustrated with myself and with the condition that I was in. Finally, I pulled myself to my feet using the nearest thing I could grab, the kitchen counter. I certainly wasn't about to ask for Neil's help.

"Did he kiss you?" he asked abruptly, confirming my theory that this whole incident had been an extreme manifestation of the jealousy he felt over Ivan.

A sick sense of satisfaction spread through my chest at the idea that he might be a bit addicted to me. He never would have admitted it to me, though, as proud as he was.

"And quit smiling. Jesus!" he scolded me.

"And what if he did?" I asked archly, and his eyes narrowed in challenge.

"Don't push me, Selene," he warned.

"You're nuts," I muttered, trying to claw back some control over myself even as my hot skin and the feeling of his seed between my thighs continued to remind me of what had just happened.

"You're the one who makes me nuts; you fucking know it!" he shouted again. I couldn't handle fighting with him again; it was too much for me. He had sapped all the energy from me, and I was exhausted.

Once again, Neil had won.

"Get out," I said, well aware of how difficult it was to reason with him. A sudden band of pain tightened around my head right around where my scar was, and I touched it, squeezing my eyes shut. I was barely keeping myself upright, and now I was having another one of the dizzy spells that had occasionally bothered me ever since the car crash.

"What's your problem now?" Neil moved closer and tried to take my elbow, but I dodged away from him.

"Don't touch me," I said urgently. "You need to quit thinking I'm like those other women; quit using me to vent your frustrations, and quit treating me like this. Get out of my house, and don't come back!" I pointed at the door, glaring up at him. The gesture felt impotent; it wouldn't have intimidated a child. A tear slipped from my eye. I was letting him go, once again.

Neil stared intensely at me, his eyes gleaming bright as gold. Then, something softened in his gaze, and he took a step toward me. I cursed myself for the shiver of electricity that passed through my body when he cupped my face in his hand. He wrapped one palm around the back of my neck and pressed my head into his chest.

Then, he enveloped me in a consoling hug that I never in a million years would have expected from him. He balanced his chin on the top of my head, and I was gobsmacked. I breathed in his good smell and nuzzled against the fabric of his sweater, trying to make sure I wasn't dreaming.

"I know I'm not the right person for you. But you…" He paused, sighing. "You make me feel things that I haven't felt before. Often they're uncomfortable or negative things, and I… I don't know how to handle them." He stared into my eyes as he gathered up my tears on his thumb. Then he gave me a faint, sad smile and delicately kissed the tip of my nose.

How could he go from being so unfeeling and domineering to gentle and even kind of sweet?

My forehead creased up as I allowed his touches, too torn up inside to push him away.

I would never understand him: Neil's nature was unfathomable and extremely unstable. I was in love with him, and I was attracted to him, though, and that wasn't going to change. No matter how good he was at inflicting mental wounds on me, I would remain his prisoner. Even if it meant being devoured by his madness.

He was my eternal punishment, and I would allow him to torture my soul until the end of time.

That was what it meant to accept him.

"Do you still want me to go?" He rested his forehead against mine and shut his eyes, waiting for my answer. No, I didn't want him to go and maybe even seek solace in some other woman. But I was afraid his mood toward me might shift once again.

He couldn't help himself.

"I…" I attempted to answer him, but Neil stroked my waist and then my breast. His hand tightened over it, and I shivered, my head spinning. Like always, Neil excelled at seduction.

"Talk to me, Selene. What do you want?" His lips traced the curve of my throat before landing just below my ear, where he gave me a warm kiss.

I blinked rapidly, trying to clear my head. "Right now, the best thing for us to do is get some space," I managed finally while he nibbled my earlobe and his hands drifted down to the globes of my ass, groping them impulsively. He pulled me tighter against him, and I let out a gasp, caught fast by a desire that once again burned through every part of me.

Even though I was still sore, my body was apparently ready to submit to him again.

And I had to admit that I liked Neil taking charge. I liked being at the mercy of his chaos.

"That's the best thing to do. But what do you *want* to do right now?" he asked, and I struggled to resist the urge to kiss him. I stared at his full lips, the kind of mouth that would make any woman crave the most delightful sins, and took a deep breath.

"I want to be with you," I admitted.

This relationship was destroying the both of us. We were all flame and ash, and neither of us knew how to handle the draw we both felt nor the mismatch of our natures and the intense emotions that bonded us together.

Neil appeared to be lost in his own thoughts as he tucked my hair over my shoulder and examined my neck, fully checked out of our conversation.

"Who gave you these marks?" he asked, sounding annoyed again. Had he seriously forgotten those were his handiwork?

"You, the last time you were here. And now I'm going to have more on my back and thighs," I said with a weak smile. I was worn-out, and he must have realized that because he stared back into my eyes with his marvelous golden ones and gently stroked my cheek.

"They're a sign of passion," he observed in his lovely deep, lulling voice, but I wasn't ready to concede just then.

"No, they're a sign of you being an animal. That's different," I said in a contrary grumble, and he bent his head ever so slightly to graze my lips with his own.

"Leave the lovemaking to the romance movies, Babygirl. I'm my own kind of romantic. And you like me that way." He licked the seam of my lips, and I opened them, waiting for him to venture further. But Neil had no intention of kissing me; he just wanted to get me drunk on him.

"Not true," I whispered, holding tight to his waist.

"Liar. I can feel how badly you want me, Tinkerbell," he said, a bare inch from my mouth. Then he leaned forward and took my lower lip in his teeth, biting down. The metallic taste of blood hit my tongue, and I was sure he was going to leave a scar. Then he licked the small wound he'd given me and gave me a look of deep satisfaction. It was as though he wanted to carve his name into me, to leave some obvious claiming mark on me.

You are mine, his eyes proclaimed.

You are nothing to me, his words told me.

And I would probably never know for certain which sentiment won out, though I was sure he thought he was making it clear to me.

"I don't like it, though. I don't like it when you don't kiss me and won't let me connect emotionally with you at all. It's all too cold like that; I prefer you engaged," I said softly. I slid my hand beneath his sweater to rub the base of his spine. His muscles tightened when my fingers touched them, and I delighted in the smooth warmth of his skin.

Even just touching his muscles gave me a hard jolt in the bottom of my stomach.

"And I prefer you naked, Tinkerbell. Naked and needy underneath me. But only when you're not driving me crazy," he whispered into my ear, and I flushed.

How did he have such an insane talent for planting the obscenest images in my mind? If someone had told me in the past that I would one day become so thoroughly wicked, I never would have believed them. Still, I tried to demonstrate a little self-control and put my hands against his hips to push him away from me.

"I need to shower and eat," I told him. Just then, my stomach let out a growl as if to confirm my words. Neil gave me a tiny, cryptic smile and a long, scrutinizing look. He was probably pleased to see how thoroughly he'd exhausted me. "You can take a shower in the guest bathroom, if you want," I said, putting a little stress on "guest bathroom" to eliminate the possibility of him trying to worm his way into my shower. I didn't have his endurance. I was sore all over, and I couldn't let him get his hands on me again when my mother might walk in on us at any time.

"Okay," was his only response. Then he walked off down the hallway, and I could breathe again.

Once I was confident that I was alone, I tried to process exactly what had just happened.

Neil had steamrolled me, shifting moods on a dime and never explaining any of his feelings. I suspected he had gotten jealous, though he'd never straight out admitted it. I decided not to dig into that issue again, though. With Neil, the line between discussion and argument was very thin. Sometimes I found it so hard to understand him: His mind was terra incognita, his soul was impenetrable, and his character was a complete mystery.

I shook off those thoughts, however, and went up to my room to clean up. As I got undressed, I saw that marks on my fair skin had definitely multiplied. Fortunately, my clothing would cover enough of them that no one—most especially my mother—would get suspicious. They were bruises left by a man at the peak of pleasure, and for that reason I was glad I had them. It felt flattering, having something of Neil still on me.

After showering, I put my hair up in a ponytail and pulled on my leggings, covering them with a thin sweater that fell just below my butt. I stepped into my fuzzy slippers, well aware that they weren't remotely sexy, and walked back to the kitchen. Neil wasn't there yet; undoubtedly, he was still relaxing in the hot shower, so I decided to make us both something to eat. It was late, but I was starving, and I figured he'd probably skipped dinner too.

I grabbed a pan, deciding to make grilled cheese. Something easy and fast. I glanced at the kitchen doorway as I settled the pan on the burner.

There wasn't even a hint of Neil's presence.

What if he just ran away?

It wouldn't have shocked me; he was unpredictable, after all.

I chuckled at the thought as I opened the bread and put two buttered slices in the pan. I grabbed a couple of slices of cheese from the fridge and layered them on top of the bread, focused on my culinary efforts.

All at once, the air was thick with the strong scent of bath gel. I breathed it in, getting drunk on it, and like a moth determined to light herself aflame, I turned to face Neil. My eyes went wide and my lips drew tight when he sauntered into the kitchen shirtless, the toki on his right bicep fully visible, and the pikorua on his hip only partially hidden by his dark jeans. I could vividly recall where the design ended, right at the root of his...

I cleared my throat and scrutinized instead his damp amber skin, his wet, tousled hair... I could not help but appreciate the sheer magnificence of his body. His magnetic eyes met my gaze with identical desire, and I shivered from a wave of heat that I could not control. Neil sat down on a stool, his abdominal muscles contracting with the movement. Once again, I thought about what a profoundly masculine form he had. He seemed to me like some otherworldly creature with an untamed appeal sent by God to make women—me included—fall at his feet.

None of us could escape his lure.

He furrowed his brow at me until he noticed the way my eyes were locked on his pecs, then he gave me a self-satisfied smile.

Suddenly, I felt a wave of sadness come over me as I thought about how it would feel on that inevitable day when I lost him for good. I knew it was coming.

Neil was far from perfect. He wasn't some prince you'd be happy to introduce to your friends or take home to your parents. Being with him meant walking through hell, but somehow, it felt better than heaven when he was with me.

I might have done anything, even lost my mind completely, if he were actually gone from my life. Yet, I was the one who kept saying that we needed to stay away from each other even if I didn't have the guts to actually put any distance between us.

"I think it's burning." His voice shocked me awake, and for a moment, I didn't know what he was talking about, but I figured it out almost immediately—the grilled cheese!

I immediately turned back to the frying pan, where the sandwiches had turned from nicely golden to almost charcoal.

"Dammit," I muttered awkwardly. I scooped the sandwiches up with the spatula and transferred them to the plates, burning my thumb in the process.

Well, that was a wash.

I brought my thumb to my mouth, trying to soothe the burning sensation with my tongue before turning to look at Neil, who was gleefully watching the show with a smirk of amusement on his face.

I turned violently red before regaining my composure enough to pick up both plates. I moved over to the kitchen island, placing one in front of him as I sat down on the other stool with the second plate.

Neil cocked an eyebrow down at the charred sandwich. He stared at it as though trying to decide whether it was edible or not.

"It has to taste better than it looks," I grumbled in annoyance, and he turned those gorgeous eyes on me. I chewed my lip in the exact spot where he had bitten me, and for a moment, I felt just like I had when he was devouring my mouth with his sinful one.

"Hmm...then I'll give it a try," Neil said, and I focused on the sandwich. It wasn't difficult; I just had to keep from looking at his naked chest or ripped biceps, and those unruly desires of mine would take a hike. "If I get food poisoning, it'll be your fault," he teased before taking a bite of the hot sandwich. He chewed slowly, evaluating the taste.

Did he like it? Was it disgusting?

"Not bad," he confirmed flatly, continuing to eat. Well, that was a somewhat ambiguous verdict but not a completely negative one, as I'd feared. I breathed a sigh of relief and took a bite as well. The silence that descended upon us was both tense and embarrassing at the same time. Neil didn't look at me. He seemed thoughtful and not entirely calm. Meanwhile, I was squirming constantly in my seat.

"Are you still on the pill?" he asked abruptly after finishing the last bite of his sandwich. He'd devoured the whole thing in just a few bites, and I was happy because it meant I was taking care of him in some small way. I sometimes suspected that he skipped meals and ate more irregularly than he should.

I took a beat and then lifted my eyes from my plate to his face and frowned.

What did he just ask me? Why?

"Yes, of course," I confirmed, though I was a bit confused.

"You've never skipped a day?" he pressed, licking a few scattered crumbs from his lips.

"No, why would I have? I'm meticulous about that sort of thing," I reiterated, though I didn't see what he was getting at.

"You know you have to tell me if you ever decide to go off it or forget a day, don't you?" he went on, staring deep into my eyes as though searching for some uncertainty there.

"Yes, I know that," I said in a perplexed murmur, and then he did something I wasn't expecting. After rubbing his hands together to get rid of the crumbs, he lifted his hips slightly and retrieved his wallet from the back pocket of his jeans. My eyes dropped to the V leading down to his pelvic area and his abs, which popped as his core contracted. Once again, I willed myself to put aside the lewd desire coursing through my body and tried to focus on what Neil was doing.

He unfolded his wallet and stuck his middle and index fingers inside. He emerged with a small silver packet between his fingers, and I reddened when I realized it was a condom.

"I always have one of these on me. Do you know what that means?" he asked, staring right into my flushed, embarrassed face.

"That you're sleeping with other girls?" It was the first answer that came to mind, and Neil must not have liked it because he gave me a warning look.

"It means that I choose not to use one with you, so you have to tell me about everything. If you go off the pill, if your period's late—you have to tell me about any accidents that might happen." He slid the little packet back into his wallet and tucked it into his jeans again. I noticed that he did not deny what I'd said before. Obviously, he was still having sexual encounters—albeit protected ones—with other women, and the idea did not thrill me. I looked down uncomfortably at my half-eaten grilled cheese. "There's no need to be embarrassed. This is the kind of conversation that people who are fucking have to have sooner or later—" I didn't let him finish and interrupted him instead.

"I already told you, Neil. I want to be exclusive. I can't take it anymore, sharing you with other people," I burst out, reaching the limits of my patience. I could deal with the way he dominated me; I could deal with his angry outbursts and his general instability. I could deal with him using me however and whenever he wanted, but I absolutely could not deal with other women touching him and taking pleasure from him the way that I did.

Neil hadn't been expecting such a confession and looked bewildered. He obviously wasn't ready for that conversation, and maybe he never would be, but the time had come for him to make a choice.

"Selene," he snapped back irritably, pounding a fist on the countertop. No, he wasn't remotely pleased with my stated position or the way I'd cornered him with the issue. I was glad to see him looking troubled, though, because that meant he was actually thinking about my proposition.

"Choose, Neil," I went on, my fear giving way to determination. "Me or everyone else," I told him starkly. I had accepted that he would not occupy the position of boyfriend or partner in my life because I knew he'd never abandon his beliefs about relationships, but if he wanted me, even if only to satisfy his carnal instincts and indulge in the physical draw that we both shared, he would have to prove to me that he could choose me.

Choose me above all others.

6

*"We had both known what my answer was
always going to be."*

NEIL

I rested my chin on my hand and stared at Selene while the fingers on my other hand began drumming on the surface of the kitchen island.

I didn't need to stand up to loom over her; I could overpower her just as well sitting down. Instead of shouting and allowing my craziness to show like I had been doing since the moment I set foot in Detroit, I decided I was going to stay calm and give her an assessing stare.

As I'd expected, the girl couldn't meet the challenge for long, and she lowered her eyes, bowing to my innate charisma.

Did she seriously think that I was going to choose her and stop fucking other people?

Impossible.

Unfortunately, Selene couldn't understand the pressing reasons that kept me from changing, the ones that kept me in my own personal limbo.

The Boy needed it from me.

He needed to feel strong, to know that no one would ever

subjugate him or tear at his soul or hurt him ever again. For me, choosing Selene wasn't just about setting aside the blonds; it meant abandoning the Boy.

Which was something else entirely.

If casual sex with many partners had just been about pure physical pleasure, entertaining myself, or even indulging a kink, maybe I could have gone without it. In my case, though, there was much more at stake.

My mental health, for one.

And the other part of me that I kept locked away.

"I can't do that," I told her without a hint of uncertainty, and her shoulders slumped in disappointment. We had both known what my answer was always going to be. Though I could appreciate her attempts to accept me as I was, my problems were too deep and too glaring. Just from the way I'd railed her up against that wall, anyone could tell I was absolutely not a normal person.

If I were in her position, I'd run far away from someone like me.

"Why?" she insisted, injecting some strength into her voice. Her tenacity was admirable, but, alas, it would not be enough to change the reality of the situation.

"Again with all your whys?" The only way I could destroy her hopes—whichever ones she had—was to make her hate me. I had to behave in such an unacceptable, disrespectful, and downright mean way. I needed to unleash the full fury of the animal that lived inside me.

"I deserve to know," she shot back, and I gave her an amused smile.

And just who had given her the right to poke around in my life?

I had allowed her to have the smallest glimpse into my world and to learn a bit about my doomed soul; she shouldn't have dared to demand more.

"It doesn't matter who else I take to bed. What matters is that I am, in some way..." I paused, rubbing my lip with my index finger before echoing a word she had said to me recently on one of our calls: "Yours," I said softly. Selene started, as though she hadn't expected to hear something like that.

We had two very different ideas of what ownership was: I belonged to the world, and the only time I was hers alone was when we were together. She, however, only ever belonged to me, and, somehow, this made sense in my head.

Nothing else mattered.

"Mine? You'll never belong to me so long as other people get to touch you," she answered obstinately.

It was typical female logic: Babygirl believed, just like all the others did, that if I committed to her, it would be a victory on her part and that I would fall for her. Maybe even fall in love with her. I wasn't stupid: Selene was the kind of girl who could coax genuine feelings from the most damned of souls. The problem was, as long as I had the Boy inside me, I would never really have my freedom and could never really form a relationship with anyone. The Boy would only ever allow me a few trips to my Neverland before I had to come back to reality. To my blonds and the trauma we both had and all the conditions I'd been suffering from since I was a child.

"Pretend I belong to you. Forget about what happens with the others," I suggested. It seemed like a reasonable solution to me, but Selene just shook her head scornfully.

No, she wouldn't be satisfied with having me for an hour or even a day. She wanted me always. She demanded all of me, not just my body. I had known that she would from the very start.

My Tinkerbell couldn't imagine, though, what I'd actually been through. She had no way of knowing how different the sex I had with her was from what I did with other people. It was just domination with them. I dominated Selene as well, but at the same time, I allowed her to touch my soul.

My Babygirl was too naive to understand the gravity of that gift.

"Come here," I demanded, sliding back a little on the stool. I patted my knee so she would understand that I wanted her on my lap. Selene hesitated for a moment, unsure whether to do what I said. I gave her a look, however, that clearly told her I was not willing to be disobeyed. And so she assented, moving around the kitchen island with notable elegance. She perched on my knee, and her coconut scent wafted over me, reawakening all my desire for her. And that desire only grew stronger from one day to the next. I was afraid that it would never go away, that I would never be sated no matter how many times I feasted on her.

"I've learned something tonight—you really can't cook," I teased her, resting my hand on her quivering thigh. Selene pretended to be unmoved by the low tones of my voice, though I knew she enjoyed it thoroughly. I examined her finely drawn profile. I adored her huge, expressive eyes as well as her plush lips and the small, upturned nose that made her look like a cheeky little imp. Without conscious thought, I had slipped my hand under the hideous, oversized, and generally sorry blue T-shirt she wore until I reached her breast. I was well aware she didn't have a bra on; I'd seen her peaked nipples pushing against the fabric of her shirt, and I couldn't wait any longer to touch them.

I squeezed one breast in my hand, and it occurred to me how perfectly it fit into my hand. It was a little larger than Alexia's and lightly fragranced with a coconut scent that was more delicate than Jennifer's heady perfume. It was as though it had been crafted especially for an asshole like me.

I found myself closing my eyes and nuzzling into her neck like I couldn't help myself.

My strong grip coaxed a shy little moan out of her, and I had to resist the urge to bend her over the counter next to us.

I hadn't been remotely gentle when I was impulsively fucking her earlier, and I didn't want to unsettle her again.

It was still imprinted upon my mind, the sound of her back hitting the wall, her ragged breathing with each one of my energetic thrusts. I'd fallen on her like an animal, driving in and out of her ceaselessly, not stopping even when she went rigid against me as she tried to accustom herself to my rough invasion. I had to admit that I enjoyed pulling her over the line with me because, each time I did, I learned something new about her and uncovered more of what excited her.

I knew now that she liked rough, dominating sex more than the merely passionate variety, and we were of the same mind about that.

It had been a huge struggle during her first official time when I had to force myself to touch her gently and temper my aggression. I wasn't me; the real me was very far away from the sweet, tender man I had shown her on that one occasion.

"You took something from me, so you should give me something of yourself. Our compromise is still in effect." Selene tried not to stammer, but I could tell from her reddened face and the silken sound of her voice that she was struggling to hold on to the prudish distance that she tried to use as a shield against me.

"What do you want to know?" I asked, trying and failing to suppress a smile.

Our compromise...how could I forget about that? The girl knew how to get what she wanted even if she did use very different methods than I did.

"The truth. What happened with Alyssa?" she blurted out, turning to the topic that had infuriated me more than anything else for the past few hours.

"She was the one who kissed me," I began with palpable anger in my voice. "I have no idea what she was thinking. She jumped me, and I instinctively reciprocated for a second. Logan walked in on us and blew up." My hand slipped down slightly from her breast to her downy stomach, which tightened just from the touch of my fingertips. Selene stared at me with her ocean eyes, and I wanted to kiss her.

Goddamnit.

"That's really how it happened?" she whispered uncertainly, as I stroked her flank with my other hand, pulling her closer to me. I could feel myself being drawn toward her full lips, worse than a teenage boy with his first crush.

"I've got a lot of flaws, but I don't lie," I answered seriously, holding her gaze to show her that I wasn't trying to hide anything.

"Alyssa told me that you came on to her. And she described the way you kiss, the intensity, and it seemed...accurate." She grew sad, looking down at the hands she was wringing to vent her nervousness. So I grazed my nose along her cheek and pressed a kiss to her throat, making her shiver. Sometimes, I didn't understand myself at all. I couldn't figure out why I felt the need to constantly be feeling her or breathing her in.

"She made it all up. She knows me, Selene, and she knows how I am." I wasn't trying to convince her, only to make her realize that she couldn't trust just anyone and that it was particularly easy to make up wild stories about me that still had a ring of truth.

"How am I supposed to trust you?"

She still didn't believe me, and I couldn't fucking stand it. I would never hurt my brother with a reprehensible move like that. Nor would I lie about it to my Babygirl who was, at that very moment, still looking at me with suspicion in her eyes.

"You just have to. I've got no reason to bullshit you about this," I said, growing irritated, and her gaze drifted down over my chest. She wanted to touch me again. I could feel her desires and read her thoughts. I gave her a sly little smirk, and her eyes snapped up to my face, pulling me from my own twisted fantasies.

"You have to do something to earn my trust," she said positively, a new firmness in her voice.

"Like what?" I asked skeptically.

"I'm not asking you to start a relationship with me, just to be faithful…" She paused. "Sexually," she suggested, chewing her lower lip uneasily. Nothing had changed; the substance of her request was the same: She was asking me to choose her, even if she was asking in a slightly different way.

"Babygirl," I said in a soft, wry voice. "Do you think I'm as green as the little boy you were out with tonight?" I needled her, referencing that Ivan dude, who looked all of twenty. A cute kid, sure, but he had nothing on me. I recalled Selene telling me that he was her friend's twin brother and that he played basketball. He was your standard issue college-aged guy; he probably did okay with women and generally led a charmed life.

I went on the offensive then and began stroking her beneath her shirt again. No one could resist when I went into virile seducer mode, but somehow Selene tried to squirm away from my touch.

"Quit it… Stop it, now!" she shouted, trying in vain to break out of my hold, though the goosebumps all over her skin told a different story.

"Being faithful to you would be the same as getting into a relationship with you, and it wouldn't be like how it was with Jared. I'm different, Selene. A freak," I told her gravely, tightening my grip around her to keep her in place.

"You aren't a freak to me. You're special, and I could accept you as you are. I feel like I've already shown you that," she answered, stung. She was undoubtedly referring to the last time we fucked in a bed when I'd told her about my anorgasmia. And then, the very next time we were together, I had punished her because… Well, I didn't really know why myself.

I'd felt this uncontrollable rage in my chest when I'd caught her with someone else while I was so anxious to get to her and explain what happened back in New York with her little friend Alyssa.

She'd pissed me off during that phone call, and I wanted to talk to her about it face-to-face. But when I found her smiling at that guy, it made me think that she hadn't attached the same importance to the call. And now she was acting like nothing had happened, telling me again that she could accept me as I was.

How could she possibly be so sure about that?

She didn't know that I had been raped, had no idea that my innocence had been torn from me against my will, and that I'd been molested for a year. If I could turn back time, though, I would have made the same choice: I would always let Kimberly violate me to keep her from taking her twisted perversions to my brother.

That was my reality, and this sweet girl could not possibly accept it. She couldn't walk through hell with me.

I wanted better for her.

"I don't think so. And it's not just about sex, though I do see how hard you're trying to keep up with me in that," I murmured. I had known for a while that Selene was working hard to act like a woman with me, despite the fact that she still had a lot of inner growth and life experience to catch up on before she got there. She was searching for justifications for my addiction to sex, trying to convince herself that it was all normal when it was anything but. It wasn't normal that I needed to vent my misery on a woman's body or risk falling into the void. It wasn't normal how I got pleasure from reenacting my abuse, subjugating anyone who happened to succumb to the temptation I presented. It wasn't normal for the Boy to control so much of my current life.

None of it was normal.

"So try me, then," Tinkerbell went on, and my right hand trembled as I raised it to adjust my hair. Selene tracked my movement with a heavy sigh before slowly inching closer to me. She took my hand in her own and shot a glance at me before pressing a kiss to the back of it. I remained motionless, stupefied by this display of profound sweetness. Babygirl smiled and pressed her head against me, this time leaning forward enough to sniff my throat. She deposited another gentle kiss there, and when I felt her warm, moist lips against my skin, I closed my eyes in sheer bliss over the contact between us. I hated being touched without my permission, but when it was her... she had long since taken liberties I'd never allow anyone else.

Touch me.

Touch me all the time.

Because when you touch me, you touch my soul, was what I wanted to say. But I remained silent.

"Get up, please," I whispered into her ear. She got off my lap and tugged gently on my hand, urging me to stand up with her. I did as she asked, and the first thing I saw was my Babygirl, looking up at me with irrational admiration.

She should have looked at me like the monster that I was, not like some god.

She stroked my shoulders with her slender, elegant hands, trailing them gently down my arms. I looked at her in confusion, not understanding what she was after. When her lips came to rest on my chest, I stiffened as though it was a foreign sensation. I even briefly considered pushing her away, but then I recognized her gentle touch, and I relaxed.

There was nothing to be afraid of—this was Selene, not some random woman.

All at once, I felt sapped of all strength, afloat in a paradise of the senses like I had never felt before. Her lips, so delicate, traced the lines of my body. She slowly made her way to my chest, barely grazing a nipple, and then moving along further still to my abdomen.

And I did not feel at all dirty.

There was nothing nasty or perverse in her actions, and still I began to long for her head to sink below my waist, for her to pleasure me there with her unpracticed tongue.

It felt like an angel was touching me, intent on enfolding me in her feathery wings until the demon in me was mollified.

The sweet, feminine scent of Selene filled my nose, blocking out the smell of Kim or of any other woman.

Babygirl continued to drift even lower, hitting the waistband of my jeans before getting on her knees to continue touching my tensed legs. Her hands moved over the heavy fabric, seeming to transmit some divine energy to me.

I shut my eyes, my heart beginning to ache as I imagined all the things that I could never have.

I imagined a happy future. I imagined joining her in her ethereal light. I imagined the door to her world, so pure and uncontaminated, opening to allow me inside. I didn't envision a castle nor anything else out of a fairy tale, just an unadorned path where Selene waited for me. She wore a dress as blue as her eyes, and she had one hand outstretched for me.

She was as radiant and beautiful as any fairy creature.

My fairy.

All I had to do was step forward, just take one step out of the enveloping darkness at my back, and I could reach her. I could clearly see the line dividing light from dark, and I could see where I was—standing firmly on that line. And then, all at once, the cry of a child from behind me forced me to glance back. Little Neil stood there, fearfully clutching his basketball as he shook his head in disappointment at me.

His Oklahoma City jersey was wrinkled, as were his shorts.

He didn't want me to leave him behind because that would mean he'd suffer once more. He'd live through all the evils of the past.

All over again.

Alone, without anyone beside him.

On his narrow shoulder, there rested a woman's hand. The fingers were long, the nails painted a fiery red that recalled the very flames of hell. I couldn't see her face, but even in the shadows, I could make out her long blond hair and the white shirt that clung to her large breasts. The Boy tried to squirm out from under her hand, but whenever he struggled, the woman's fingers only pressed in harder.

Possessive and violent.

He cried for me. When he called for help, it was my name that he screamed. I swallowed hard, horrified.

What kind of coward would I be if I left him in the clutches of the child-eating witch?

Could I really stand by and watch a little soul like him be destroyed?

No, I wasn't capable of it.

He and I would have to face the monster together.

Then, my eyes shot open.

The vision evaporated into nothingness, and with a fierce movement, I shoved Selene away from me.

"Don't touch me!" I threw out a hand to keep her from approaching me again. She staggered back in fright, a shocked look on her face. She had done nothing to provoke my fury; it was my own brain that had put that distorted reality in front of my eyes. None of it was her fault. "Don't touch me again, for fuck's sake..." I murmured in a low voice.

I felt fuzzy-headed, and I leaned back on the kitchen counter bonelessly.

Babygirl tried to move closer to me, and I shot her a forbidding look to keep her away.

I could still feel her lips on my skin and her hands on my body.

What did she want from me?

To seduce me? To stagger me? To make me forget who I was?

"I am not afraid of you or of anyone who lives inside you." Selene, stubborn as always, took one step forward and then another, eating up the distance between us. "When you were here last time, when you marked yourself with the pen, you told me about the Boy..." she began, and I was immediately uncomfortable. I hated words, especially when they were used like weapons against me. "You told me that he let himself be raped, that he couldn't stop the person from committing such an atrocity." The more she talked, the more I retreated, pulling back into my shell, a place where I felt safe and protected, and there was no need to expose myself.

"Enough," I snapped, afraid.

There was an unknowable struggle going on inside of me.

"I told you that it wasn't his fault, Neil. That it wasn't *your* fault. And when I said we were both stained, do you remember that? I'd never judge you, Neil. You don't have to be afraid of me. You aren't the monster; whoever did that to you was the real mon—"

I covered my ears, making her words sound far away, and I sank back down on the kitchen stool in a daze. My body was weak; my legs could no longer bear the weight I had been carrying for so long.

"Enough," I whispered weakly, but Selene advanced on me and reached out to hold my wrists in her little hands. Now I was the one looking up from below as she insinuated herself between my knees to get even closer to me.

"Stop hiding. I...I figured it out. I've known about what happened to you for a while," she admitted tragically, leaving me shocked.

My world was crumbling around me; it felt like I was on stage in front of a crowd, naked.

The curtain had opened without warning, and I was not prepared.

I had no script to study, no lines memorized, and no scene to perform. The crowd just stared at me—at the cluster of scars on my left arm, at the rash around my genitals, and at my shattered heart, which I had tried to piece back together in any way that I could, just to keep on surviving.

I felt exposed, too exposed.

What was I supposed to say to her now?

I stared into the middle distance, incapable of speech, and Selene stroked first my face and then my hair.

"I know what happened to you, and I still accept you. There is no one in this world who is better for me than you. I wish you could see yourself through my eyes. I admire your strength so much; not everyone survives such intense trauma," she murmured in that tooth-achingly sweet way of hers, and I surrendered, resting my head between her breasts. Something ruptured inside me, and my walls began to crumble, little by little, until the urge to share some small part of me grew too strong to be denied.

She deserved that much.

After everything I'd put her through, she deserved to know me at least a little bit.

Then, she put her arms around me, and it seemed that I could feel her heart beating all over me.

Was she ready to know the truth?

Maybe.

"Her..." I said, wincing into the blue fabric of her shirt. "Her name was Kimberly Bennett, and she was about twenty. She was our neighbor's daughter and a babysitter. My mother was pregnant with Chloe, and she didn't have much time to devote to Logan and me. We couldn't stay home by ourselves. My mother saw an opportunity and asked Kim to come work for us." I lifted my anguished face and looked at her. Selene looked back with an unspoken comprehension in her ocean eyes as well as a hint of compassion. And all at once, I turned back into my old self. My walls sprung up again, unscalable and too strong to let anyone through them to reach me.

I got to my feet, making her gasp, and shook her hands off me.

"Right from the beginning, I knew that there was something off about her. She was too friendly, sort of sly, and she was always trying to touch me in ways that felt inappropriate at my age. I didn't like her frosty eyes or her overbearing attitude or the kind of games she started offering to play with me. They usually involved fondling, other forms of foreplay, and 'sex education,' which I had to pay the closest attention to or else I'd be punished. She hadn't been there a month before she started taking it even further. One afternoon, while I was sitting on the couch watching cartoons, it happened: She raped me, like she done to several other kids. That...that was the start of all my issues." My head was spinning as I confessed the truth to her, but I refused to let my state of mind show in my voice. I appreciated the bravery Babygirl had shown in hearing me out, but there was no way I was going to lose my composure.

I was the master of keeping my emotions inside.

At that point, Selene pressed a hand to her lips as if to stop herself from weeping. Me, I felt nothing. Just disgust for myself and for the whore who had used me.

"She threatened me," I continued pitilessly, not softening anything. "She kept saying she was going to hurt Logan. My brother was my whole life; I couldn't let her lay so much as a fucking finger on him! And so I went along with it. I did whatever she wanted. I couldn't escape her orders..." I inhaled hard and yielded slightly as I fought against the memories.

"Neil," she murmured, but I didn't let her continue.

It was my turn to talk.

"Kim had been violated in the same way by her own father. She was deeply disturbed, and she wanted to put other people through what had happened to her..." I locked eyes with Selene, hers as crystalline as the sea. She was on the verge of tears. I decided to cut my confession off there and spare her the most disgusting parts. It had been hard enough for me to tell her that much. I didn't want to scare her or rub her face in just how depraved and immoral people could be. I didn't tell her about my various trauma-induced disorders, the most serious fallout from what had happened to me.

I was afraid I'd lose her completely if I told her everything.

Not only had I not yet accepted them myself, but I was also deeply ashamed of them.

And the realization of that shame triggered a burst of rage.

"You should want nothing to do with me now. I should make you sick!" I shouted at her, coming at her like a lunatic. She backed up flat against the kitchen island and shook her head before throwing out her arm defensively in my direction. I looked down at my trembling hands and took a pause.

I couldn't figure out whether she was scared of me or simply felt bad for me and didn't want me to see it.

"I don't want your pity!" I accused anyway. "I hate women who try to get with me out of compassion. I don't need that shit." Telling her the truth had already dredged up my terror of being rejected by others, especially by her, and that turned me cold and remote. "I've made it this far on my own; I can keep going just fine." The harshness that crept into my voice made her falter. Finally, she started to understand that the situation was more dire than she could possibly imagine, that I had been broken so completely that there was no redemption available for me.

"I don't pity you. I just think you are…out of reach." She gave me a troubled smile and cautiously moved closer to me, afraid of how I might react. I watched her like a caged animal, drawn to her flesh yet at the same time wary of her touch.

Then she tilted her head to one side; what was she trying to do?

"Did you tell me everything?" Even before the sound of her voice, her perfume reached me, hitting me like a punch to the face. Babygirl stood right in front of me and brushed her thumb against my lower lip. Her touch was soothing but not soothing enough.

"I told you everything you need to know," I answered in an impenetrable tone.

What else did she want?

I had already laid myself too fucking bare for her, especially in the psychological sense.

She couldn't expect anything more.

"You know, Neil..." Selene watched me as though I were the most beautiful man in the world, like she couldn't wait to burn once more in the flames of my desires. "Now that I understand your past, or at least parts of it, I have some answers to all those questions I've had. And I won't deny that I'm disturbed by them, but I want you to know that I would do anything for you. Except let you go; that, I won't do." She smiled tenderly at me, and her fingers, which had continued to caress my jaw, gave me a strange, heated feeling. It was a sensation that I couldn't quite pinpoint, right there in the center of my chest.

"You don't understand. I have too many problems to deal with and you..." I was trying to argue with her, to destroy the false hopes she had undoubtedly developed under the delusion that she understood me. But then she shook her head and took a tiny step forward to press her lips to mine.

"You are the one who doesn't understand, Neil. I am addicted to you," she whispered slowly, and I felt almost afraid of the yearning that I glimpsed in her eyes. "Just let me be with you. All I'm asking is that you take my hand and walk beside me, whatever paths we go down or wherever our destiny leads us..." She stroked the nape of my neck, and I stood, dumbfounded, listening to her. Her hot breath was as much an irresistible temptation as the breasts that pressed against my torso. I trembled with the desire to strip her, to lose myself in her, to let myself be engulfed by her tight walls. I wanted to move between them without fear of being thought wrong or perverse instead of what I was—a normal man with a visceral desire for a particular woman.

"I can't, Selene." I was dead set against changing my outlook. "Kim damaged me, I... I'm not capable of love, not the way you think of it. Love, for me, is something bad. Something that destroyed me before..." I rested my hand on her hip and tried to push her away from me. Her shirt, however, lifted slightly with the movement, allowing me to touch her and ruining any chance I had of resisting.

My fingers seemed to burn as they moved over her hot skin.

"I don't want a love story, Neil." She pushed back, looping her arms around my neck and standing up on her tiptoes. "I want you to be able to talk to me and share whatever you want only with me. Even if it's wild, obscene sex... Whatever you want. I want to know you inside and out. I'm not asking you to love me or to be my man. I don't want to become a couple," she said clearly, and I was relieved. "I'm asking you for more. I want to be in the fight with you. I want to see you live and dream. I want to watch you destroy the gilded cage you're trapped inside and take to the sky. I want to watch you demolish the past and build your future. I want to see you find a new light. I want to see you find yourself and discover the thing inside you that is worth fighting for. It doesn't matter if there's no place for me in that future..." She cupped my face in her hands, not allowing me to look away from her sincere, anguished eyes. "I just want you to get better. Let me be with you and take whatever you can give to me. I won't ask any more of you than that," she pleaded, and the tears she'd been keeping back for so long finally slipped down her cheeks. I caught them with my thumbs. I hated it when a woman cried, and I hated it even more when that woman was her.

"You promised you wouldn't cry for me again," I said as her feet sank back down to the earth, just like I hoped her fantasies would. Babygirl was dreaming too big. But I couldn't just play the bastard again, no matter how strong the urge to drive her away might have been.

So I just sighed. "Okay. Be with me. That's it, nothing more." I gave in without really knowing myself what it would mean. I was uncertain because I'd never confined myself to a relationship before.

From what I could surmise, that's what our arrangement would be even if it was different from other relationships in many respects.

She had to at least understand that I couldn't be exclusive with her, right? Or was my fidelity also part of the package?

I chose not to ask her.

"Now get off my back and cut the cutesy shit. You're getting on my nerves." I nudged her gently aside to reclaim my space. Selene invaded it sometimes, stealing my breath and seeming to take up the room of a formidable giant rather than the Tinkerbell that she was...

"Thank you," she said, smiling like the happiest woman in the world. She gave a little bounce before frowning.

Did fairies bounce too?

"Can I touch you?" she asked immediately, like I hadn't just told her to get away from me.

"No," I answered brusquely.

"A kiss?" she pressed.

"I said no." I shook my head as I took a step back.

Air. I needed to get some air.

Too much had happened in the last few hours, and I needed to be alone with my thoughts for a while.

"A hug?" she asked again, and I patted my jeans pockets searching for my cigarettes. How long had it been since I'd had a smoke? This girl made me lose all track of time.

"No, Selene! For fuck's sake, no!" I shouted at her in exasperation.

I had no urge to hug her, but the urge to fuck her again...that was strong.

It was always strong, nearly uncontrollable.

I needed to get my shit together and get my carnal instincts in check, not pop an inopportune hard-on. First things first: I was going to go to that guest room and take another shower, and then I was going to have a cigarette and get into bed, where I could gather my thoughts. My mood had shifted too rapidly in too short a time;

my actions flirted with madness, and worst of all, I'd actually told her about Kim.

Shit.

I absolutely had to regain control of myself, my life, and all that chaos that inevitably gravitated to me.

I didn't want to take out my frustration on her and treat her like a mere object again.

I'd railed her up against that wall because I was out of my mind with anger, and now that I could think clearly again, I regretted letting my impulses control me.

"I'm going to the room. Try to stay away from me at least until morning. I need to be alone," I told her with conviction. I had flown in from New York with no warning just to be with her, and now I wanted nothing more than to get as far away from her as possible.

Selene just nodded, her cheeks rosy and her eyes bright. She fingered her long ponytail, looking anxious but elated at the same time. I had no idea what had put her in such a mood, and I didn't investigate further.

Instead, I examined her sinuous form, covered too completely by clothing, and lingered on her fuzzy slippers, which could put a damper on any sexual fantasy. She noticed my downcast gaze and blushed harder. I, on the other hand, just peered down my nose at her with a grimace of distaste before walking off down the hallway, away from her and her decidedly horrible footwear...

I passed a sleepless night.

I took another shower and smoked almost an entire pack of Winstons.

I couldn't get a wink of sleep with the knowledge that I'd given Babygirl such an important piece of me.

I had a strange feeling, like my privacy had been violated, even though I was the one who had told her what really happened.

I was a walking contradiction at that point: I was constantly telling Selene that we couldn't be together, but on the other hand, I never rejected her attentions or her attempts to keep up with me, to move at my pace into the kind of darkness that would have scared off any other woman.

Even worse, I seemed to be developing a fear that Babygirl was going to figure out that I was all wrong for her and get tired of chasing after me. I had realized that I didn't want her to abandon me. Drifting through the noxious inner workings of my own mind, I stood frozen in front of the open window, naked and still wet from the shower. My skin gave off the scent of the shower gel I'd used... It wasn't my usual kind, but the smell was not unpleasant, and most importantly, it was clean.

I waited for the sunrise, like I so often did. I believed that, by doing so, I could anticipate my fate for the day and change it, even if nothing actually fucking happened.

The world remained the same, just like people remained the same and my life and even me.

The days crawled by, childhood memories pressing down on my soul, and sooner or later, I was going to have to let go of my last hopes for a better future.

I took one last drag from my cigarette and released a plume of smoke into the air. I soaked in the cold that was all around me. The room was almost completely dark, and so were my eyes as I stared into the void, trying to see myself there. A self that I was never going to find.

I passed a hand through my soft, disheveled hair.

The sides were short, just the way I liked them, but the quiff on top was getting long. I'd have to get it cut; it was always falling over my forehead.

Did Selene like it that way?

I smiled at the thought of me caring about her opinion on the matter.

I didn't usually give a shit what women thought. I knew that I was attractive to them, that I exerted a certain allure for them, and that was enough for me, except when it came to my Tinkerbell.

I wanted to be perfect in her eyes.

I wanted my looks to be peerless as far as she was concerned.

I wanted to bind her to me, to show her that she would never find anyone else who could make her feel what I made her feel. Again, the enormous selfishness and ridiculousness of those thoughts occurred to me.

I was supposed to be letting her go, and instead I was trying to strategize some way to set her off balance before I went back to New York so she would be thinking of me even when I was far away. The same way I thought of her when I was trying to soothe myself in bed with other women.

Bored, I glanced at the clock on the dresser.

There were two hours and forty minutes before my flight; I had no more time to waste.

Reluctantly, I pulled on my clothes from the night before. I was used to changing clothes several times a day, usually after a shower, but at least the clean smell of them offset some of the urge to scrub the filth from my body.

I got myself in order and gathered up my things before slipping on my leather jacket and leaving the room. I walked down the hallway and tossed a glance at the stairs that led to the upper floor, specifically to Selene's room. I had held back on bothering her in the night, but I wouldn't have been at all disappointed to spend those hours with her—and certainly not "talking." But she had, after all, complied with my wishes and had not sought me out, so I did the same and gave her time to process what had happened, both my insane reaction to seeing the basketball player and the deeply personal confession that had followed.

Feeling thoughtful, and as usual a little annoyed, I went into the kitchen just to get a quick drink of water before I left. Instead, I was confronted with the sight of Ms. Martin, who appeared to have been waiting to deliver a dressing-down. I froze, surprised to find her there, fully dressed, at that hour of the morning. She stared back at me with her penetrating blue eyes, not at all surprised to see me in her kitchen.

"Good morning, Neil," she greeted me calmly, leaning against the kitchen counter. She was drinking coffee; I could smell it in the air.

"Hey," I answered, unenthused, taking a few steps into the confined space. The woman gave me a faint smile but never stopped evaluating me with her eyes.

"Selene texted me last night to let me know that you were here," she told me, clearing the sleepiness from her throat. "What are you doing awake so early?" she went on curiously.

I remained where I was, motionless, while her eyes swept down my body in analysis.

It was one of the rare times when a woman looked at me not with admiration but with caution and perhaps a little bit of anxiety.

"I always get up at dawn," I answered, glancing down at the stool before looking back at her.

Ms. Martin furrowed her brow. "Make yourself at home. Would you like something for breakfast?" she asked courteously. I sat down on the stool, crooking one knee and letting the other leg stretch out.

"Just a coffee, no sugar," I answered.

"You're not having anything to eat?" She grabbed a clean cup and poured some coffee into it, settling it on a little porcelain saucer. Then she approached and handed it gently to me.

"No," I answered flatly. I was a man of few words.

Actually, I was uncomfortable. It wasn't my habit to spend the night in strange places or to sleep in a bed other than my own. But my compulsion to see Babygirl was forcing me to do the craziest things.

"Somebody told me you really like cherry pie, though. Would you like a piece?" she offered, and I knew there was only one person who could have reported that information to her: Selene.

I smiled at the thought.

So she talked about me to her mother, then.

What the hell kind of situation had I gotten myself into?

Not waiting for an answer, Ms. Martin started cutting the pie into slices and gave one to me. I thanked her quietly and just drank the coffee, ignoring the sweet treat.

I was a creature of habit, and if my breakfast didn't typically include any fucking pie, I wasn't going to eat it then.

She clocked my resistance but said nothing.

I was positive she could see how agitated I was.

I had never crossed so many boundaries with a woman before, never entered into her life or eaten breakfast with her mother.

I had broken too many rules with Selene; I was absolutely fucked.

"At least try a bite," Ms. Martin insisted, with a knowing smile, but I just took another sip of coffee.

"No, thank you. I'm good with this," I answered frostily, and only then did I dwell on her the way she had on me: She was standing far away from me and nervously tapping her own porcelain cup with one finger.

"How's school going?" she asked me abruptly, and there seemed to be a certain disquiet in the tone of her voice. After all, I had always been good at feeling out a woman's emotions, understanding her intentions, and intuiting her thoughts; Judith Martin would be no exception to my sixth sense.

"Good. I'm getting ready to graduate," I answered without breaking her cold gaze. She just continued to sip her coffee with both an innate elegance and a hint of agitation.

Wary, I continued to stare intensely at her.

"And after graduation? What are your plans then?" she volleyed back, and again, I got the feeling that I was being carefully assessed. I could feel the pressure, not so much from the questions she was asking but from the detached way in which she asked them. I recalled that I'd already told her about my desire to be an architect, so it felt pointless to have that conversation again, but I felt compelled to do so, nevertheless.

"Like I told you a while ago, I'm studying architecture. Recently, I was offered an internship in Chicago, and I think I'm going to take it," I answered, almost testily. I wasn't hiding how uncomfortable I was, and she could no doubt see my changing mood.

Talking about the future brought back all the fears I tried so hard to chase away. I knew perfectly well that society at large would not accept a person like me with a shitty character and a disturbed personality. How was I supposed to work with other people when I was still trying to find an equilibrium within myself? How could I attempt to be a normal man when I couldn't even accept myself?

"I'm glad to hear that. You should chase your dreams," she commented, putting her cup down on the counter. Then, she looked at me, letting out a heavy sigh. "On that note, Neil..." she began, sounding a bit more certain. "I want my daughter to finish college as well. I want her to achieve her goals and start her teaching career, which is something she's dreamed about since she was just a little girl," she continued firmly, walking over to the kitchen island. I looked down and forced myself to stay seated, though I didn't like her tone one bit. "Every woman falls for a guy like you when she's in her twenties," she added, watching me carefully. "And you know, don't you, that this kind of story—the kind of story you two are living right now—is a short story, right?" she asked sharply, but she didn't wait for me to answer. "Selene has always been a smart, principled, and, most of all, level-headed girl. But I don't recognize that girl now. She's lost her mind over you, and it's not good for her." She gave me a long, severe look.

I had sensed right away that Selene's mother wanted to have this talk with me face-to-face, to bore me in person with some fucking harangue that felt completely unacceptable.

"What are you trying to say?" I tried to cut to the chase because I couldn't stand all the pussyfooting around.

"Take a look at yourself, Neil. You could get any woman you want. You think I don't know what happens here when the two of you are alone?" She shook her head. I did not feel the need to confirm that I was fucking her daughter. "Lately, Selene seems sad, lost in thought, or distracted all the time. I've seen marks on her body…" She shot a frosty glance at me and went on. "I have no doubt that the things you do together are consensual, but on your part at least, I don't see any respect toward her," she said with an accusing frown.

Was she seriously trying to tell me how I ought to be fucking her daughter?

I managed not to laugh right in her face, but it was a close thing.

Ms. Martin picked up on that and seemed even more unsettled than before. Maybe she thought of her daughter as young, but she couldn't have thought of me like that. In terms of experience alone, I was far ahead of my peers and surpassed even some much older men.

"Are you telling me that I should take a more…timid approach with your daughter?" I tried not to use more vulgar terms to avoid upsetting her even more. She reddened slightly, displaying the same discomfort that Selene showed whenever we had similar conversations. The difference was, she stood firm in that moment and tried to push back at me.

"No, I'm sure you know best how to handle those situations. I'm only asking you to try to show a little respect," she clarified.

What Ms. Martin didn't understand, though, was that the way I handled myself with women was an essential part of me, of my personality. Every man had his habits and preferences, and he couldn't simply alter them to please someone else.

I was no different.

"I don't want to get into details, Ms. Martin, so let's suffice it to say that what you are calling a lack of respect is something your daughter enjoys quite a bit," I told her evenly.

I didn't feel remotely guilty about the shocked expression that appeared on her face. She'd been the one who decided to stick her nose where it didn't belong; it was only right that she found this stuff out. "She's not a little girl anymore..." I went on, in a tone that made it clear that I knew sides of Selene that she could never even imagine.

I went back to drinking my coffee, which tasted somehow more bitter than before. Or maybe it was just this conversation that was bitter.

"I won't keep Selene from seeing you, but if you do care about her, you need to let her go, Neil. What's going to happen when you go away to Chicago? She won't be able to follow you. She won't be able to leave her school or..." Her lip trembled, and her gaze dropped. Then she looked back up at me and said, with an almost frightening strength, "Me."

She took a breath and went on: "Please don't hate me. I am her mother, and I have to protect her," she said in a placating tone, and I gave her a sideways smile that made her frown.

I understood Judith's little speech perfectly: She wanted what was best for her daughter, and the best was obviously not me. She had to protect Selene, yes. Protect her from me. I wasn't surprised by anything she had just said to me, and it was all completely understandable. She didn't like me; she had never liked me, in fact, and deep down, I'd always known it. The only thing I couldn't understand was why she'd waited so long to tell me.

Instead, she had lied to me. She'd put on a little performance last time when we talked about art in her living room, and that was something I couldn't stand in a person: lying and hypocrisy.

All at once, I got to my feet, and she tilted her head back to look up at me before taking a step back. I stared at her, serious and blank, determined to intimidate her and make it impossible for her to see what was going on inside my head.

Ms. Martin looked to me like she was having some trouble.

I rounded the kitchen island with my usual self-assured air and approached her. When I got close enough, I stopped and searched her face carefully. She didn't flinch, though.

Instead, she swallowed and waited for me to speak.

"You know, Ms. Martin," I said, leaning in toward her. She tensed up, her shoulders going rigid and her eyes blinking rapidly. I breathed in her pleasant, feminine scent and went on: "I could take your daughter away from you with a snap of my fingers. But I'm not going to do that because I have never seen a future with her," I said in a stormy whisper before stepping back slightly to look her in the eye.

Ms. Martin was not fooled by my appearance of tranquility.

She saw the storm raging inside me.

She saw my monster. She saw my torments.

And an indescribable fear spread over her face, which filled my entire body with a sick sense of satisfaction.

"I am not your enemy, Neil," she answered, screwing up her courage to face me. "But if you care even one tiny bit about my daughter, you will get far away from her and let her live in peace," she pleaded in an anguished tone.

I looked into her eyes and didn't feel a hint of compassion. "You don't need to tell me that, Ms. Martin," I said austerely. "I can promise you—there is no place in my life for your daughter."

"So promise me that you'll let her go when you leave for Chicago. You know it's the right thing to do. Don't pull her away from me; don't destroy her dreams," she pressed, just as stubborn as her baby girl. For a few seconds, I considered her words. I had already thought about how impossible it would be to date or even see Selene in the future.

I would have been the first person to say that Selene should not abandon her education, her friends, her mother, or the life she had waiting for her in order to be with me. Yes, I was selfish, but I wasn't incapable of understanding what was best for her. I gave myself a moment to think, and then, with a deep breath, I answered, "I'll let her go. I promise."

Ms. Martin pressed a hand to her heart, relieved. She knew as well as I did that the choice was all mine, all in my hands. I was stronger than Selene, and I was the only one who had the stomach to put a definitive end to our relationship.

Selene was in too deep with me, drawn to me and bound to me by a feeling that I refused to name.

She would accept my decision because I could manipulate her thinking and persuade her in my own unique way. I had already succeeded in getting her to give in to desire months before when I'd coaxed her into getting with me while she was still with Jared. It would have been no trouble at all to convince her to end things and give up on realizing her dream of a future together. A future in which I could only ever corrupt her.

And Ms. Martin knew it all.

She sensed the power that I had over her daughter.

In that moment, a war began inside me.

A war between my good sense, which knew that I should push Selene away, and my instinct, which said that I wasn't done with her yet.

Just a few hours earlier, I'd told her she could be with me, but now another detail would need to be added to our little compromise: our intimacy would have an expiration date.

In just a few months, our paths would diverge forever.

I would have to go on without her velvet lips, her glowing skin, and her ocean eyes.

I would have to renounce all urges to kiss or fuck her.

I would have to vanish from Babygirl's life, no matter how intensely I might continue to yearn for her.

In the meantime, I would have to wait and hope that the turmoil inside me died down, just like I waited every goddamned day for the blaze in my chest to be extinguished.

I waited, I waited... and nothing ever fucking happened.

I kept on burning for Tinkerbell and fighting fruitlessly against myself to keep away from her, trying to convince myself that she didn't matter at all to me when she did matter, a little bit.

Just a little bit, I told myself again and again, ad nauseam.

"Goodbye, Ms. Martin," I said, putting an abrupt end to our conversation as I stalked out of the kitchen. I couldn't stay there a moment longer. My wounded pride had begun to make itself known, driving my every action.

I knew now that Judith was just like Matt and that my presence in her house was not nearly so welcome as both Selene and I had been led to believe.

Shaking my head, I recalled what Babygirl had told me the night before: *"You aren't a freak. You're special."*

All of it is bullshit.

There was too much wrong with me—wrong in my head—for me to ever be special. I'd never be fit for a girl like her.

And now her mother understood that too.

"Go fuck yourself," I blurted out, and I myself didn't know who it was directed at. I was furious and disillusioned.

Every time Selene made me hope for something better, made me willing to stretch even a finger up toward the sky, reality dragged me right back down into the pit.

Tinkerbell wanted to sneak her illusions into my head.

She wanted me to believe that a more colorful world existed, a world that was fair, even for people like me.

But I was living in my own personal hell, in my dehumanized reality, and all I had to do was look into the eyes of those people who watched me to know where I really belonged.

In the shadows.

I was seated in the front row, watching the total disintegration of my life, and who could fucking say when the show would be over?

While I reasoned my way through all my shit, I went back into the guest room and beelined for the desk. I'd already seen a small notebook with a pen attached there for jotting down notes, so I opened it up and tore out a page to write a message for Tinkerbell. But then I thought twice. I immediately remembered the argument that had ensued the last time when I'd left her nothing but a Post-it Note stuck on one of her books.

No...a note was definitely not the way to go.

I crushed the paper in one hand and left the room, heading back down the hallway.

"Neil..." I heard Selene's voice calling out to me just as I'd nearly made it to the door. I ignored her. At the same time, I was cursing myself for smoking my last Winston because I really needed a cigarette at that point. "Neil, where are you going?" Babygirl pressed, and only then did I turn around to look at her.

She sucked in a breath when my eyes met hers. She looked worried, even afraid. I didn't care at all and just scrutinized her outfit. She wasn't wearing anything hot, just a pair of pj's that was at least a size too big. Pink with insipid little rabbits on them.

What happened to the tigers?

"I need to catch my plane back to New York," I answered

brusquely, lifting my gaze to her still-sleepy face. A moment later, I caught a whiff of her coconut scent on the air all around me.

"What are you talking about? Why are you in such a hurry? Did something happen?" Selene hurried after me while I continued on without acknowledging her. "Neil. Please, talk to me." She grabbed my arm abruptly, and I stopped, turning to stare at her.

She was adorable, like always.

Her cheeks were pink, her lips were dry and still red from my nips, and her eyes were filled with hope.

"You seemed okay last night and..." She cleared her throat and did not go on. She was too embarrassed to talk about what we had done. If I'd been in the mood for it, I might have taunted her or whispered something filthy in her ear, but I was so out of my mind angry that I couldn't even stand to be near her.

She was the one who made me unrecognizable to myself.

"And what? You thought I was going to spend the day here with you? I have a life too, Selene. And it's in New York," I snapped. She jolted, taken aback by my churlish attitude. I ran a trembling right hand through my hair anxiously. She spotted it, but then I wasn't really trying to hide the symptom of one of my many conditions.

"I still don't see why you're so keyed up," she insisted. I really didn't want her poking around in my head; I was in no mood to talk or to waste more time there.

"There is no why," I answered irritably. "This...this...*thing* between us has to be dealt with in some way." I didn't even know how to define what we had together.

For me, it was just this fucking *thing* that was causing all manner of problems, now even with her mother.

Selene's shoulders slumped with obvious disappointment.

We'd had a significant talk the night before.

Not only had I bared my soul to her, but I had also led her to believe that I was going to let her be with me. That I was going to give her due importance and elevate her above all my other lovers. I knew how callous I was being with her, but for me it was difficult to be any other way. My body's instinct was to touch her—I needed to have some sort of contact with her again before I left for good. So I raised her chin with my index finger and saw myself reflected in her eyes, which were like two cornflowers so early in the morning.

That is to say, they were beautiful.

That detail, like all the others, would linger forever in my memories.

"Go to school, go out with your friends, have fun, and live your life, Babygirl…" I said softly, urging her to have interests outside of me. I did not want to be the center of her world.

As soon as that thought crystallized in my head, however, my selfishness overrode my good intentions. Abruptly, I reached out with my free hand and grabbed hers where it had been dangling alongside her hip. Then, like a secret just between the two of us, I pressed the now balled-up piece of paper I'd still been clutching into her hand.

I shouldn't have done it, but…

Selene frowned, and I gave her a faintly seductive smile before drawing near enough to plant a brief kiss on her lips.

"Read that note as soon as you can," I added in a velvety tone.

And then I walked out the door, leaving her behind me, enthralled and…confused.

7

*"The past was a terminal disease,
a cancer in its final stages."*

NEIL

I wondered what Babygirl's face looked like when she read that note.

She hadn't called or texted me, so I suspected she was still deciding what to do.

I knew in the moment that it was crazy of me to use such an unconventional mode of communication with her. A normal man would have just said everything directly to her, but I couldn't deal with words. I used them sparingly most of the time and even more so when I lost my patience or felt like my back was against the wall.

I'd returned to New York a few hours before, but I didn't want to hang around the house because Matt hadn't left for work yet for God knows what reason, and I had no desire to share space with him. Instead, I accepted Dr. Lively's invitation to attend a special patient meeting at the clinic as a guest. I hadn't gone to Lively's clinic for three years, and I still hadn't officially resumed treatment, but that didn't seem to matter to him.

"Where is he, then?" I snapped impatiently at Ms. Kate, who was stationed at the entrance. As usual, the secretary just rolled her eyes at me, as if my very presence was annoying, and unwrapped a caramel. She eyed me distrustfully as she ate it.

"He'll be here shortly. Calm down and wait in the waiting room." She gestured at the large space behind me littered with leather sofas and low tables.

I snorted, thinking that it was all business as usual here: the annoying classical Muzak, the big screen showing boring advertisements, and a few colorful prints on the white walls. The perfectly ordered and sterile environment had, counterintuitively, only increased my anxiety.

I turned away from the woman without giving her any further thought and headed for a sofa.

What the hell had possessed me to accept Lively's invitation?

Already, I regretted it bitterly. I could have been having a good time with the Krew or even just called up Jennifer and had her blow me at the pool house. Maybe I could get Alexia on all fours after that? But the thought of actually reaching out to them or anyone else I'd fucked only gave me the barest ghost of a thrill and only for a second, leaving me not particularly excited.

Which was very bizarre.

I was used to immediately indulging my worst perversions, but, just then, I was too on edge to think of sex as a solution to my dark mood. Plus, I still hadn't been able to achieve orgasm with other women, only with Selene. Trying and failing with them would only dredge up all my worries that something was really wrong with me. Before, I had followed my shrink's advice; I had abstained from sexual activity for a period of time; I had stopped violating my own body and putting myself through even more stress. But my enforced abstinence ended when I gave in to Babygirl in Detroit, and I could not figure out how to solve my problem.

Why could I let go enough to come with her but not with anyone else?

"Oh, hey Miller, this is an honor."

I quit my musing and looked up at Megan in front of me, staring fixedly at me with her usual sharp half-smile.

Her presence was not at all surprising.

I cocked an indifferent eyebrow and regarded her: She had her black hair up in a high ponytail, her legs swathed in the leather pants I'd often seen her wear, while up top she sported a white shirt so tight and translucent that I could see the fuchsia bra she wore underneath it. She completed the whole look with a black leather jacket, the shoulders adorned with silver studs.

I hated to admit it, but although she had an irreverent, even somewhat masculine style, Megan Wayne managed to look like every man's idea of sexy.

I received confirmation of that when a staff member walked by us and leered shamelessly at her ass.

"Take a seat somewhere else. Perhaps outside in the cold?" I snapped at her as though she were my worst enemy. And she was. She was the one who coaxed forth all the painful memories, the one who made me regret not killing Kim the day she took us down into that basement to play one of her psychopathic "games."

"I thought you weren't into me..." Head Case answered, screwing up her forehead.

What the fuck kind of response was that?

I gave her a confused look. I had no idea what she was talking about, and she just chuckled in response.

"Did I not just see you check out my tits?" She gestured to them, but I kept my eyes fixed on her face.

Sure, I did, but that didn't mean anything. I appreciated abundant curves on any woman.

"So what? That doesn't mean I like you," I said, clearly and without any hesitation. Her intense gaze, a dazzling green color, could have seduced anyone. Anyone except me, that is.

"Okay, I'll pretend to believe that." She sat down across from me and crossed one leg over the other. She picked up a motorcycle magazine and started flipping through it. Then she let out a low wolf whistle, and it occurred to me again how alike we were: She was acting like I did when I was trying to get under someone's skin.

"Knock it off," I demanded sternly, and she turned her gaze my way. Now, the object of her appreciative attention was not the magazine but me. She looked me up and down, from my splayed legs to the gray sweater under my leather jacket, which outlined my muscles. She made a "not bad" face before locking eyes with me again.

"This again? I told you the tyrant vibe does nothing for me." She shook her head for emphasis and went back to whistling, this time bouncing her crossed leg in the air. I tried to just breathe in and out, telling myself again and again that she was trying to get a reaction from me, and I didn't want to give her one. But my instincts got the better of me, and I leaped up off the sofa. I advanced on her, and in one savage moment, I tore the magazine out of her hands and threw it onto the coffee table behind me.

Megan was neither upset nor surprised. She just gazed sadly at the magazine, like a child who had just been denied her favorite flavor of ice cream, before letting her gaze drift down to my pelvic area. I looked down to see what he was staring at and realized the crotch of my pants was directly at eye level with her.

Head Case fanned herself with one hand and gave a sultry flutter of her eyelashes.

"Miller, half the city is always talking about how aggressive your game is, but don't you think this is pushing it a bit? We are in public, after all." She looked back up at my eyes, and for a moment, I imagined her on her knees before me, pleasuring me while the tubby receptionist summoned security guards to escort me out. Thinking about a pair of lips around my cock was arousing, but when I thought about those lips belonging to Megan, the tingle in the bottom of my stomach evaporated and was immediately replaced with revulsion.

Disturbed, I took a step back and actually felt shame, for once, at that obscene place my head had gone. I reminded myself to breathe.

"What the hell..." I ran a hand over my face as I reestablished the proper distance between the two of us. I shouldn't have even been thinking something like that.

Never.

I wouldn't touch her if she were the last woman on earth.

"Chill out, Miller. Try to rein in those fantasies." Head Case winked at me, and I shot her a glare.

"Who the fuck gave you permission to cross that line with me?" I roared, and, finally, Megan stiffened. Her self-assured smile faded little by little, and she uncrossed her legs, taking on a more guarded posture. "Stop acting like a stupid kid," I railed at her. "Always starting shit and fucking with me...because if I ever really did lose my cool, you'd see a side of me you would not enjoy," I continued decisively, my tone even more severe. Megan had no comeback. She knew that now was not the time to antagonize me further.

Was that what she wanted, to be put in her place? Well, if so, she'd found just the man for the job. The kind of man who wouldn't be subjugated by anyone, least of all her.

I touched my hair anxiously and growled like a wild animal. I felt trapped.

I pictured a wall in front of me, one so high that I couldn't see the top of it.

I had fought my demons, and just like always, I had lost.

I couldn't find a way out of my situation, and perhaps, for me, there wasn't a way out.

"Sorry, I didn't want to make you mad," she told me, and I rubbed my temple with one finger. I had developed a headache all of a sudden. I needed a smoke.

"Shut your trap," I snapped at her, and she looked away awkwardly. Agitated, I felt around in my jacket for my packet of Winstons. Finding it, I pulled out a cigarette with my teeth, clenching my lips around it to hold it in place. I wasn't going to light it—I knew the clinic's rules—but I needed to keep it there, inert, to soothe myself.

"Oh, I'm glad to see you, Neil. You've finally come to visit us." Dr. Krug Lively appeared before me wearing his usual business casual and a benevolent gaze. I figured from the small smile on his face that he hadn't picked up on the conversation Head Case and I had been having. I tucked my cigarette away and grunted. Beside him stood John Keller, his partner in the clinic, who was nattily dressed in a dark blue suit. Unlike Krug, John had an enviable aura of class, especially when he wore his high-end blazers and jackets. In a way, I appreciated his sartorial flair—it suggested an independent spirit, someone who didn't give a flying fuck what other people thought, like me.

"Hi, son," John greeted me, and I just gave him a chin dip in response. I hadn't seen him since he told me that story about the dolphin and the pearl, and I hoped he wasn't about to start that bullshit up again. That was also the time when I'd told him about Selene, about the "kiss me like you love me" fortune that I still secretly kept in my wallet, and how, right there in that Detroit diner, Babygirl had been ready to bare her soul to me with that word I hated most in all the world: *love*.

"How have you been?" he asked, moving closer.

"Not bad. And how are you doing, John?" I spoke to him with casual ease, the way he'd encouraged me to in the past. I saw Dr. Lively frown, though, like he was wondering when his partner and I had gotten to a first-name basis with one another.

"And since when are you two friends?" he asked.

"Neil and I had a conversation a little bit ago out by our lovely fountain in the garden. I got to know him a bit better, and I have to say, he's a great guy," John said, hyping me up, but I just watched him, indifferent. He was, after all, a shrink I'd spoken to a handful of times; I could hardly trust his assessment.

"And a terrible patient, considering he's never once listened to me," Dr. Lively cut in drily. If he'd been serious, I would have responded in kind, but because I could hear the irony in his voice, I said nothing.

"And Megan! Are you ready for today?" John asked Head Case, who had been sitting quietly on the sofa ever since my outburst. She nodded silently and got to her feet, moving toward us. For a moment, I thought I could smell her orange blossom perfume in the air, but that was probably just a sensory hallucination. There was another odor, however, that I recognized for sure: the smell of defeat. I'd won a battle here, and though it wasn't the war, after this the bitch would understand that she'd been playing with the wrong one.

"Of course, when do we start?" she said enthusiastically, pasting a plastic smile on her face. She didn't deign to acknowledge me at all, and that was just fine with me. I stared at her for a few moments, and when she noticed my gaze locked on her, she looked embarrassed, a faint blush appearing on her cheeks.

"Perfect. Alright, let's go." John gestured for us both to follow him, though there was no need for him to lead. I was familiar with the clinic and already had an idea where we were headed: the extra-large room they used for groups and meetings.

Everything was just how I remembered it: secure doors, a sterile environment, and an omnipresent security system. All of the common areas and some of the treatment spaces had cameras used to spy on patients so the doctors could see if the individual courses of therapy were having the desired effect.

I still remembered back when I was being treated there. I used to sneak into the bathroom to evade the cameras along with this chick who worked there so I could practice all of Kimberly's lessons on her.

"How does it feel to roam these halls once again?" Lively asked me, pulling me from my thoughts. He smiled slightly at me, and I shrugged.

"Boring. Same as always," I answered flatly, choosing not to tell him about the impromptu trip down memory lane my brain had taken me on, reminding me of everything I'd gotten up to during my teens and early twenties. "How many people are going to be at this thing?" I asked disinterestedly. I'd never really cared to know how many others had lived through what I'd lived through.

"Approximately twenty-one," John answered for him from in front of us, where he was walking beside Megan. Megan, who continued to ignore me. Maybe I'd put her nose out of joint, and she'd get right back to busting my balls when she got over it, or maybe she'd finally realized that she shouldn't be fucking with me in the first place.

I enjoyed imagining that it was the latter.

"We have eleven men and ten women who are regulars," Dr. Lively added as we approached a sliding door, which opened automatically to let us pass. "You remember where everything is, right? The library, the game room, the fitness center, a room for music therapy, and another for bibliotherapy. I created all of this in my attempt to improve outcomes. I wanted to make sure that every patient has a healthy, comfortable environment," Lively explained, like he was trying to sell me on coming back to resume therapy with him. But I was standing firm on my decision to quit.

"Your clinic bears a close resemblance to a luxury resort, Doctor Lively, I get it. Don't waste your time hyping it up to me because I'm not coming back here. The only reason I agreed to attend this meeting was because you insisted, and I wanted to get you off my fucking back. You should be content with me showing up today!" I blurted it out all in one breath, drawing John and Head Case's attention as well. I hadn't realized I was raising my voice. I got anxious and lost my cool very easily when I felt pressured, as I did in that moment. I scrubbed a hand over my face and tried to get my breathing back under control.

"Okay, I apologize, Neil. I was just making conversation." Dr. Lively's tone shifted dramatically. He sounded placid and even, just the way I liked him.

Finally, we reached a large room, half full of people.

The young men and women in the room, all about my age, were milling around and chatting. I observed them carefully, sniffing out details like a bloodhound. Immediately, a few stuck out from the crowd: a curly-haired girl who lingered in the back of the room hugging a teddy bear and a dude with a bandanna keeping his messy black hair off his forehead who strummed on a guitar, occasionally pausing to jot something down in a notebook. Then there was the tattooed guy smoking a cigarette out on a little veranda with a cute blond plastered against him.

She smiled constantly, and he watched her like he was starving—yes, truly starving—as he gazed at her slim, well-proportioned body clad in a delicately pretty, long-sleeved dress.

"Drew! Brenda!" Dr. Lively's attention was drawn to the couple I'd just been staring at, and they both jumped. Irritated, they looked first at me and then at Megan before turning their attention to the doctors as the whole room immediately fell silent. "Come here, everyone," he went on sternly, and everyone dropped what they were doing to come over to us. Except for the tattooed guy who whispered something into the blond's ear and gave her ass a squeeze before heading over.

"What's going on, Dr. Lively," asked the girl—Brenda—adjusting the exaggerated neckline of her dress. I took the opportunity to slowly run my gaze up and down her shapely body. I ended up lingering on her long blond hair, which extended well past her breasts, and then on her bright blue eyes, blue as the sea. For a moment, I lost myself, thinking of the ocean eyes I searched for everywhere, the ones I found again in every face. The ones that were so far away from me now.

"Be patient, Brenda, I'll explain everything," John answered gently.

All at once, I felt terribly exposed and disquieted with so many curious eyes boring into me. The women in particular were watching me closely, like it was the first time they'd ever seen a man in their fucking lives. The blond especially was checking me out carefully, letting me know right away that she very much liked what she was seeing. Liked it a bit too much for a girl who was, just moments before, making eyes at some other dude.

"Who's this guy, Dr. Keller?" The asshole with the tattoos walked over to us, having stubbed out his cigarette. Immediately, he wrapped his arm around the shoulders of the blond, who was, presumably, his girlfriend. He was obviously marking his territory. His stare was pointed, and he seemed annoyed by my very presence.

"He's Neil Miller. He's a former patient of Dr. Lively's. Consider him a guest for today. He'll be spending a few hours with us," John informed them, smiling.

"Interesting," the tattooed guy murmured, narrowing his eyes at me as though issuing a challenge. "We love new fish." His tone was sly and suggestive of something that I didn't like at all, threatening to awaken the less rational part of me.

But I forced myself to get a grip and stay calm.

Dr. Lively took a step toward me and cautiously inserted himself between us.

Not to protect me from the guy but to protect the guy from me.

He knew me very well.

"Drew, don't start," he reprimanded him, getting nothing in

return but an annoyed huff. "Everyone else, please welcome our guest," he added, trying to dispel some of the tension. Except I hated those kinds of pleasantries and rarely paid attention to them. In fact, as each person told me their name, I forgot the person immediately before them.

"Great. Neil, try to make yourself comfortable. John and I will be right back. We need to finish up a few things, and then we'll get started," he said, and I grimaced.

Where the hell were they going? Were they going to leave me there? Alone?

"Megan will stay here with you. She knows everyone already," John told me as if he'd sensed my panic. Likely he intended this information to soothe my agitation, but the thought of continuing to hang out with Head Case was far from comforting.

As both doctors walked away together, Megan came over to me, and I sighed in apprehension.

"See, I really am your guardian angel. And you need me," she said, going right back to busting my balls like she'd forgotten everything I said.

"I need a smoke," was all I said in response before turning to cross the room and head for the terrace. By that point, everyone had gone back to their activities with a shrug. Only the guy with the tattoos stared daggers at me while he made out fiercely with the blond.

I had no interest in his woman, but evidently the idiot thought I did.

I screwed up my courage to cross the big room in full view of everyone. I was wound so tight by that point that I was nothing but a bundle of nerves, waiting to explode.

I was being inundated with memories: my father, my prayers, Kimberly, the years of treatment...I needed to drive them away immediately.

I headed for the partially open glass door that led out onto the terrace. The cold hit me right away, but I didn't care. I pulled out my pack of Winstons and lit one. I couldn't help myself. Smoking was a kind of brain trap, one of the only ways I could relax and feel better.

"I know this is hard for you, Miller." Megan came out to join me, drawing in her shoulders against the cold. I pinched the bridge of my nose and rested my elbows on the railing, squeezing my eyes shut for a moment.

I felt like a fucking caged animal, ready to maul someone.

"I don't believe you do know. You're used to it now. I'm not anymore." I inhaled smoke into the bottom of my lungs, pinching the cigarette between my index and middle fingers while I examined everything I could see, vigilant and attentive to the most minor detail. I blew the smoke out into the air and turned to Megan. She kept her distance from me, still with that proud affect, that self-assurance that showed in her every move. The impenetrable armor under which only I could catch a glimpse of her fear.

Megan was not invincible, just like I was not invincible.

"It's just a few hours, and then you can go home," she attempted to reassure me, staring deeply into my eyes with her green ones, and just for that moment, I felt relieved that she was there with me. I couldn't stand her presence or her pushiness, but she was the only person I knew in that room.

"It's not easy hanging out with you and the other head cases. Trust me," I blurted out, continuing to smoke. What else was there to do? I alternated between moments of rational thinking and moments in which I turned rough and intractable. Keyed up, I looked behind her at the tattooed guy, sitting on the sofa and fully focused on flirting with the blond. I pinched the bridge of my nose again.

"His name is Drew, and that's Brenda with him," Megan said softly, anticipating my question. "She's cute, right?" She paused to give the other woman a look, folding her arms over her chest.

"You into girls this week?" I asked with my characteristic bluntness, oblivious to the fact that I was prying into her personal life. I'd known since our adolescence that Megan was bisexual, and I'd never judged her sexual preferences. I was mostly just curious.

"Man or woman, I like anyone who's got a soul. I thought you understood that, Miller." She gave me a small, amused smile.

"I don't understand anything about you, Head Case." I took another drag and blew the smoke through my nose, all while continuing to stare at Drew. I didn't give a shit about the little blond; he was the one that interested me.

"Tattoo guy, what's his deal?" I asked, jerking my chin at him.

"He's the alpha male of the group. One of the worst cases here, probably. He started coming to group about six months ago, but he hasn't shown much progress yet. I overheard Dr. Keller saying that he's got a hard road ahead of him..." Megan took on a look of chagrin and toyed with a lock of jet-black hair that had fallen over her shoulder.

"Is the blond his girl?" I pressed. I didn't really give a shit either way; I just wanted to know why he'd acted like I had a target on my back from the moment I first saw him.

"Yeah," she confirmed. "Brenda got here about a month after him, and there was an immediate spark between them," she said with a sly grin.

"Were they both abused?" I lifted my chin slightly to blow the smoke upward as Megan chewed on her lower lip. My eyes caught on her plush mouth.

I sometimes thought that, if she weren't the girl with whom I shared my traumatic history, I would have tried to get her into bed. I had always been extremely curious about how she experienced sexuality and sexual encounters. I wondered if she also tried to reclaim a controlling role in bed by pretending that the man was Ryan or if she simply gave herself over to the pleasure of a passionate moment.

I wanted to know if I was the only one for whom sex was such a sick experience or if everyone else who was like me had the same thing happen.

"Yeah. They both have pretty horrific backstories. They're kind of like you and me…" She took a pause, and I stared at her, unsure what she was implying. She sensed my confusion and went on, "They fight all the time, but they are really very similar, and sometimes it seems like they can't stand each other, but then…" She paused and gave me a cheeky little smirk, like she knew she was about to say something that would bother me.

"But then?" I prompted her, though I wasn't at all sure I wanted to hear any more.

"But then they have this intense emotional connection. Chemistry. They have a lot of sex and work out their problems between the sheets." She gave me a suggestive smile, but I just kept staring gravely at her.

Unexpectedly, I thought of Selene.

That was also the way we resolved our issues.

Babygirl would ask me to tell her something about myself, and in return I took what I wanted from her: on a bed, over a desk, or against a wall…wherever I felt like it. We didn't make love, and, in fact, the idea of that horrified me, and we weren't a couple because I had no idea what it meant to reciprocate affection. For me, sex was set apart from all human emotions. It was just an act of want and perversion. Though, with Selene, it had also become an irregular beat of my heart, warmth, kissing, holding, and a longing to learn more of her unblemished world.

Every time Tinkerbell sprinkled a little bit of her fairy dust on me, it set off a giant clusterfuck in my head.

"You're thinking about Selene." Megan's voice called me back to the present moment. She was not asking me a question but making a clear, precise statement. I realized that I had been standing there in a stupor with my cigarette dangling from my lips until it had accumulated a long worm of ash. Before it could fall onto my jacket, I pinched the filter between my fingers and tapped it away with my index finger.

"No," I lied.

Never would I admit to her that I was long dead but felt alive when I kissed my Babygirl, that I was caged up but felt free when I touched her soft skin. I would never tell her that I became a blazing fire when I moved between Selene's thighs or that, though I was broken, I felt a little more whole when I looked into her ocean eyes.

"She's very beautiful, very sweet. I only needed one night to see what kind of girl she is," Megan noted with a small smile.

"Sickeningly sweet," I corrected.

Sometimes her sweetness was too much, and it really got under my skin. On the subject of her loveliness, however, I agreed with Head Case. Selene was very different from my other women but no less beautiful. She was compelling in her own way, sensual and feminine without excess.

She was sexy as fuck, too…even when she was wearing her childish pj's.

Before Selene, I'd never fantasized about someone like her.

"But you enjoy it," Megan prompted me.

"Sure, I enjoy fucking her," I clarified. There was no way I was going to confess the strange things I sometimes felt about Selene. They were undefined and rare but intense, nonetheless.

Maybe my attraction to Selene was particularly powerful, and so my body allowed me to lose control more easily with her than with the others.

It was the only plausible explanation.

"She's not like the others, Miller."

"She's not like me, either," I agreed firmly. "Not like us…" I added, reminding her of the vile history we shared, the obvious scars, the deep problems to overcome, and the future full of nightmares instead of dreams.

Selene was my woman, my girl, and also my lover.

She was everything to me and nothing at the same time, because I could never really let her into my arid heart. I didn't want to condemn her to a disastrous life by my side. I was going to continue to savor what we had for as long as I could, right up until I left for Chicago. Then, I would let her go, just like I'd promised her mother.

"You should trust her, open up to her. I think she'd accept you. You do have a soul, Miller, and it's not as rotten as you'd like her to believe," she told me, her voice softening. "I mean, you're definitely a perv, and I wouldn't approve of the shit you get up to with the Krew either..." she added, looking into the middle distance.

"What do you know about that?" I asked her with a frown.

"People like to talk, and, tragically, lots of people know what you do with your blond poodle and the other one..." She waved a hand in the air, referring to Jennifer and Alexia. "If you let Selene get away, you'll go right back to fucking those two boring chicks who only tolerate your perversions because they want you to dom them," she finished, giving me a serious look.

Of course, I knew all that already. The Krew girls lusted after me just like all the others, drawn in by my looks and attracted to the way I was in bed, nothing more. They didn't know anything real about me because I myself had erected an impenetrable wall around myself to keep them out of my life.

"Selene couldn't handle me." I gave a thoughtful shake of my head.

I was positive that Babygirl would never be able to give me orders or domesticate me like a fucking dog. I wasn't like other men who fell in love and lost all authority in the relationship, letting women bewitch them.

I was different than all the rest, someone who eschewed convention, and I'd never change just to be accepted by the world at large.

"Selene already knows you've got a very strong personality. And I don't think she wants to control you, just to understand you." Megan shrugged and continued to stare me down. I began to think that it wasn't so bad, having her around. When she wasn't fucking with me, that is. She had the ability to look deep inside me without me even having to say anything.

There had always been a sense of shared empathy between the two of us ever since we were kids, and it was particularly intense in that moment.

"So, in your opinion, I should keep going on with this *thing* we have, Selene and I?" I asked, cocking my head slightly.

"Do you seriously call your relationship 'this thing'?" She laughed and smirked at me again.

"Yes, and we don't have a relationship," I chided her. "We have a *thing*. I prefer to call it that because it's undefined but still understandable, you know?" I explained haltingly, trying to make sense of the idea myself. Megan narrowed her eyes thoughtfully and rubbed her chin, not remotely convinced.

"Yeah, I get it. I remember how much you hate defining concepts," she answered.

"Hey, you two!" someone called out to us, halting the conversation before I could answer her. When the guy stuck his head out the door, I recognized him as a staff member at the clinic. He gestured for us to come inside, so, after one last drag, I put out my cigarette and headed back in.

"Come on, Head Case, time to go in," I told her roughly.

"Sir, yes, sir! You know, Miller, I've always thought you'd look very charming in uniform. You'd look like a dude who had his shit together; you'd get to order everyone around... Yeah, I think that'd be just the thing for you," Megan answered, going right back to teasing me.

Clearly our truce hadn't lasted long. For her, at least.

"Don't start," I shot back at her, proceeding forward without a glance. I knew she was following me; I could hear the irritating sound of her boots on the floor.

"Real talk—instead of architecture, you should consider the armed forces," she went on blithely.

I spun around abruptly, and she slammed right into my chest. She gave a little grunt of pain and rubbed her forehead as I stared down at her. I didn't give a shit that we were in a room full of people who might be watching us.

"You are getting on my nerves," I informed her. "You've earned a good spanking. One you'd remember for the rest of your life. So, if you want to keep me from losing my patience, don't keep needling me," I said in a menacing rasp. She cocked an eyebrow, unbothered as ever, and brushed past me with a shoulder-check that didn't budge me an inch.

"Let's get a move on, Miller." She gestured for me to follow her, and I did, but only because there was nothing else to do.

I didn't know exactly where we were going. The staff member talked to Megan and told her something, and after she nodded at him, he fucked off without saying anything else. As if the uncertainty wasn't sufficient, the sterile walls, warm air, and too-narrow halls were also affecting my mood. I sped up abruptly, grabbing Megan by the wrist. I tried not to show her the sudden state of agitation into which I had been plunged, but I must not have looked too good because Megan stared at me warily.

"Where are you going?" I demanded of her, and the troubled note in my voice told her how anxious I'd become. She examined first the fingers that I had wrapped tightly around her wrist and then my eyes. It occurred to me that I was probably hurting her, and I dropped her wrist.

"Relax and come with me." Megan rubbed her wrist and made

a face. Then, with a gentle smile, she continued walking down the hallway that led to some other room in the clinic.

I hated the place. And not for anything could I pretend that everything was fine. I knew that I had failed miserably in my attempts to take back control of my life—the same life that had been slipping through my fingers for a while now and that I needed to take back to keep the worst from happening. Instead, I would continue to deny the evidence and prevent myself from doing what I needed to do to get better, all because I'd already tried for years, and it had done fuck-all.

"Here we are. It's the music therapy room." Megan stopped abruptly, and I almost crashed into her. She gestured around the big room with lots of empty chairs arranged in a big circle. There was nothing grim or uncanny about it. There was a giant stereo system, a grand piano, a drum kit, and a guitar. Two large windows allowed the sunlight to filter in, but the shadows were present, nonetheless. I could see them all around me, and soon they'd be sitting in that circle, baring their very souls in the futile hope of getting a little bit better.

But that hope, like love, was just a story they told themselves. An illusion. The past was a terminal disease, a cancer in its final stages.

It could not be destroyed, and there was no escaping it.

Megan smiled and looked at the room in front of her, a peaceful brightness in her eyes. She was happy to be there. I was not.

"How long has it been since you participated in one of our meetings with the lovely music in the background?" she asked, and I sighed.

"About three years," I answered sharply.

"Well, today will be something different for you." Megan shrugged, like it was all very simple for her. I, however, had never approached my issues so casually.

"'Scuse me, I gotta get by…" A low, sensual voice pulled me from my thoughts.

I hadn't even realized I was blocking the doorway inertly until the little blond, Brenda, moved past me. Or, rather, rubbed herself up against me. She ground herself on me so extensively that I could feel her ass shifting my fly until she was rubbing directly on my zipper. Then she shot me a sly glance to confirm that she'd done it on purpose, and I didn't so much as twitch. It wasn't easy to lure someone like me, especially when I wasn't interested in the first place.

Sure, I liked women a hell of a lot, but not all of them.

I needed to make sure the little blond understood that.

"And you've already hooked Brenda. Incredible," Megan noted wryly.

I was neither pleased about that nor flattered in the slightest.

"Maybe she's on the lookout for a good, hard fuck because her boy's shit in the sack," I said loudly, heedless of the fact that anyone might hear me. Megan's eyebrows shot up in surprise while I, with an enigmatic half-smile, just walked into the room ahead of her.

My thoughts circled back again to my Babygirl.

I wished she was there with me.

If she had been the one to sidle past me with her ocean eyes, that coconut smell that had become my favorite scent, and her incredible body, I would have torn off her panties, pushed her up against the wall, and bitten her all over. I would have longed to hear my name like a prayer from her full lips, because her moans had the power to halt all the chaos inside my head.

Selene protected me like a helmet did a broken knight.

She was a warm blanket that shielded me from the cold of my memories.

She was the medicine that could not cure but eased my wounds, nevertheless.

She was the otherworldly voice that whispered into my ear not to give up because the real failure would be to stop fighting.

She was the compass that wanted only to show me the path to follow into a new life.

She was so much more than just another woman I could take for myself. With her, I felt all-powerful, like the kind of man that, on my own, I could not create.

Even hell seemed somehow different when she was lying naked by my side.

I, however, preferred to just die a little more each day.

Lost in thought, I leaned against one of the two windowsills, and Megan stood beside me, watching the others come in one at a time to take their places on those spindly chairs.

"Okay everyone, get into the circle. Let's take our seats..." Dr. Lively came into the room with John and began issuing orders, the same kind I always hated to receive. "Greg, if you would be so kind as to play us some of your songs..." He laid a hand on the shoulder of the guy in the bandanna, who was now carrying an acoustic guitar.

"Neil, why don't you sit down with us?" John asked, watching me attentively.

"I'm good here. You all go ahead." I waved a hand as though shooing away a fly, as though I was about to observe something that had no relation to me at all.

"Whatever you want. Krug, let's get started," he told his colleague, who nodded in reply.

Then they each took a seat amongst the patients, smiling and looking calm.

"Alright, now what is our mantra before we get started?" Dr. Lively looked at everyone present, his eyes lingering on Drew, who, seated next to Brenda, kept one hand resting on her bare thigh and continued to give me the stink eye. I ignored him, focusing on the meeting.

"Today is a new day..." they chorused together. Greg began playing his guitar and singing a melody in the background of the session. I heaved a sigh of boredom.

"Great, now who would like to begin?" Doctor Lively folded his arms over his chest and waited for someone to volunteer. My eyes moved over each scared, ashamed face, clouded with the darkest memories. I stopped on that tattooed man whose hand had begun to slide up and down the blond's thigh while his mind was somewhere else entirely.

"Me." A slim arm rose hesitantly into the air, drawing everyone's attention. I observed the girl in question: It was the curly-haired girl clutching a stuffed animal to her chest, the same one she'd been talking to before in the activities room.

"Excellent, Jenna. We're listening." Dr. Lively smiled and watched her attentively, waiting for her to speak. She gulped, stroked her hair again and again, and blinked convulsively. She was extremely nervous. Inexplicably, I could feel the same sense of dismay she must be feeling, the same emptiness, the same fear.

"Hi everyone, I'm Jenna. I'm nineteen years old, and when I was little, I was abused by a wonderful prince who quickly turned into my bogeyman. That prince was my father," she said, sounding disturbed already. "I was very shy as a little girl, and my father and I had this bond that was very close and pure. I can remember him reading me bedtime stories or letting me sleep in between him and my mom. Then, when I became an adolescent, everything changed. He started showing me the kind of attention a father should never give his daughter. I had no idea whether any of it was normal; I was just scared. My mother never realized. She didn't see the cries for help in the twisted drawings I did at school or when I wrote that I was wrong on the walls of my bedroom. She still didn't get it. She just kept leaving me there in the wolf's lair. Then I started to have interpersonal problems. My mom thought that I barely talked because I was just shy. She thought that I was alone all the time because I was too introverted. She thought I did weird things to get her attention."

She shook her head with a sad smile, breathing in deep before continuing her story. "Meanwhile, I was spending almost all day with my own personal monster, and he touched me every chance he got. He asked me to do all sorts of things to him or else to lie down on the bed and let him do things to me. He said I needed to be respectful, that I should be grateful to him because, over time, I would learn how to please him better…" She paused, her hand against her stomach like she was about to puke. "The abuse stopped when I was sixteen. My mother started believing me after he raped another girl: the daughter of our neighbor." Abruptly, her gaze dropped down to the stuffed animal she held. "The only witness to what I was going through was my teddy bear. His name is Fear. He is always with me, and he was the only one who believed me from the start." She breathed raggedly, tormented by the memories, by the pain that would not ease.

That pain fluttered over the melancholy notes of the guitar, the same pain that I also felt. It was like a wound that never healed, carved into the soul.

I felt it—I would always feel it.

I felt that guilt, the filth flowing through me, the kind of filth that I'd never be free from, that I would never be able to wash away, not even with my innumerable showers.

Kimberly and every other child-eater like her would remain inside of us… forever.

"Bravo, Jenna. You've shared a small portion of your experience with us, and for that, we thank you." Dr. Lively smiled at her and glanced around, waiting to see another brave soldier ready for battle. "Hmm… Nora?" He turned to a girl with a red bob, deep, dark eyes, and a tattoo along the curve of her throat. I looked at it until I could determine that it was a red-eyed snake that stood out starkly on her pale skin.

"This is the story of the snake girl…" The girl stroked the snake on her neck, staring into the middle distance, and then licked her lower lip where a small metal ring glistened before appearing to come back to herself. "I'm Nora, I'm twenty-two. I was raped by my uncle when I was nine years old. The man always looked at me like I was a grown woman instead of a child, like I was a whore instead of a niece who needed raising. One summer day, he decided he was going to destroy everything: my childhood, my dreams, but most of all, my smile." She worried her piercing insistently and squirmed around in her chair. All signs of the obvious jitteriness shared by anyone who had experienced these particular atrocities. "That day, he asked me to come into his room with him. I found him in there naked on the bed. I...didn't want to do it, but when I tried to say no, he started yelling at me for being stupid. Every time after that, he told me that there was a snake in my stomach, and if I ever told anyone our secret, it would eat me up from the inside. I believed him; I truly believed him. I kept that secret for months. He raped me twenty-one times, and now I've tattooed twenty-one snakes on my body..." She looked to Dr. Lively, wringing her hands. I felt a chill move through me.

No one in the room made a sound; the guitar's melody turned melancholy.

There was nothing there but dead souls, darkened souls, shadows without smiles.

This was hell.

A hell that stole all strength, stopped all breath, and sat in your chest like an ache.

The truth was, even in this room full of other people, each one of us felt alone, trapped in our own world, far away from reality.

We occupied a parallel universe in our minds, still living in our abusive pasts. Our abusers were the monsters who came to visit us every night. But instead of lurking in the closet or under our bed, they were inside us.

That was their favorite place to hide.

It was no use closing our eyes to the obscene things they did or covering our ears against the cruel things they said. The child-eaters were always there, ready to hurt us, to rape us, not just physically but mentally as well.

Behind every act of abuse you would find an unrelenting psychological violation. Our bodies inevitably remembered the disgusting things that had been done to us. Every time, your chest was shattered into a million pieces; the pain would clog your throat, and anything you did would be useless: weeping, fighting...even living.

Only the body survived.

The soul died every time.

"Thank you, Nora, for sharing your story." Dr. Lively was as calm as ever. He was used to listening to this sort of thing. Yes...he was used to sticking his nose all in our business and analyzing us like lab rats, but he could not truly feel what was going on inside of us.

In our heads. Under our skin. Inside our souls.

It was the kind of evil that no one could comprehend unless they themselves had experienced it. That was why I'd only been able to tell Selene about some of what Kimberly did and nothing about the havoc that was left in her wake. I hadn't been able to tell her about what had happened in that basement with Megan nor explain to her my current conditions.

Was this the future I wanted for Babygirl? A life lived alongside someone like me?

No, I never wanted to dirty her, to contaminate her.

She was the only one who could listen not only to my words but also to my silences, to my fears, and to the often conflicting emotions I felt.

She was a rare pearl.

All at once, the walls felt like they were closing in around me, I became short of breath, and the urge to flee—to get away from that room—became overwhelming. I snapped into action like I was spring-loaded and began striding toward the door. I blew past Megan, and she simply watched me go.

It had been a bad idea, coming to this group session.

It was obvious to me why Dr. Lively had been so insistent on my coming—it was his sneaky way of trying to bring me back into therapy.

But that wasn't happening; I wouldn't have made it.

I knew that there were others in the world who had gone through the same kind of abuse I had suffered, but I also knew that I wasn't as strong as I appeared. More likely than not, I would never escape my personal hell. I would never be free from the poison that flowed through me.

"Neil, wait!" I heard Megan calling after me as I strode rapidly toward the exit. I walked through the automatic doors, and as soon as I got outside, I took in a deep breath of fresh air.

I pulled the keys to my Maserati out of my jacket pocket and continued to stalk furiously toward the parking lot until Head Case grabbed my arm, trying to stop me.

"Wait," she said again, and only then did I turn to face her. Her green eyes bored into me immediately, lush lips parted to say something while her high ponytail swung in the slightest breeze.

"Wait for what?" I pulled away from her unwanted touch and loomed over her. "I want to forget about all this shit." I gestured to the clinic behind us, and she started. "Go back in. I'm out of here," I said firmly and continued walking, halting almost immediately when I saw her Ducati parked right next to my car.

What the...

"Why in the fuck do you gotta park your bike right next to my car every goddamn time?" I exploded in rage, longing to punch something if only to get some relief. I was on the verge of an unparalleled nervous breakdown.

Megan chuckled and arched an eyebrow with an air of superiority.

"Shouldn't two bombshells be together? Those two look like they should be on the cover of a motorsports magazine," she observed as though there wasn't a man at the breaking point standing right next to her. I squeezed my eyes shut for a moment and rubbed my eyes with my fingers, taking three long breaths so I didn't give in to the urge to strangle her and leave her lying there motionless on the sidewalk. There was a small part of me, however, that had to admit she had a point. Especially now that my Maserati was sporting a new windshield and a gleaming chassis after Player's attack.

"Listen, Head Case, in a few minutes here, I will not be responsible for my actions." I opened my eyes and approached her threateningly. "So you need to go get on your bike like a good girl..." I told her with a frosty calm. "Then you take it and yourself out of my sight. You disappear. You get the fuck away from me," I continued, feigning self-control. "Are we clear?" I truly hoped she wouldn't keep pushing it with her intolerable sarcasm, but apparently she had a different take on what was happening, because her lips turned up in a sharp smile. I narrowed my eyes at her warily.

"I know a way you can vent that anger of yours," she rhapsodized, obliterating any hopes I'd had of her knocking off the provocation.

"Me too. I can put you flat on your back on the hood of this car and pump it all into you. Sound good? Except you're not the right kind of woman, so I'm going to rule that one out," I said, making it explicit that I would never fuck her. The thought of calling Jennifer instead flitted through my head—she was the only one who could remedy the sickness I felt inside. With her, I could unleash the beast that I really was without any restraints, self-righteousness, or faux morality.

I could violate myself again to restore the natural order of things.

The Boy would have been assuaged.

"Don't talk shit. And don't do that, not with me and not with your other girls. If you're frustrated, take it to Selene," Megan bristled, and I pulled back because I hated it when people tried to get overbearing, even if it was only in the tone of their voices.

"It's not frustration I'm feeling, and you know it." I'd had it; I was over talking to her. Lately, everyone was trying to squeeze something out of me, to analyze me and make me use more words than I ever had in my life up until that point.

But she didn't give up and followed me instead. "I don't seek out men who look like Ryan to hurt me. What you're doing is totally insane!" she shouted at my back, unwittingly giving me the answer to a question I'd always wanted to ask her.

"Well, if you think I'm so crazy, then stay away from me," I answered without turning around. I could hear her heavy breathing behind me and her rapid footsteps trying to catch up to me, but by that point, I had reached my car. I opened the door, despite her motorcycle blocking my way, and started to get in. But she stopped me again.

"You are doing yourself an injustice," she said softly, her fingers digging into my arm. "Kim stopped raping you a long time ago; now you are the one who won't give yourself peace. You won't let yourself have a second chance." She shook her head, and, again, I threw her off roughly.

"It's the only way I have to keep from going crazy," I muttered without much heat, feeling exhausted. Megan should have been the first person to understand me, but instead there she was, ready to judge me.

"No, you'll go crazy if you keep doing what you're doing." She released me, slowly dropping her arm in surrender. I didn't want to keep having that conversation, but I didn't want to go on the attack against her either, so I let my instinct take the wheel and threw my honest thoughts in her face.

"It seems I'm surrounded by women who've got that Florence Nightingale syndrome. You all need to stop trying to save me and accept reality for what it is. You need to stop looking for some good in me. There isn't any. It does not exist. What you see is what you get." And it was in that moment that I realized the real reason why I'd left that infamous note for Selene: I was testing her. I was letting her know who I really was so I could see if she really would be able to stick by me the way she said she wanted to.

It was easy for Babygirl to say she would when she didn't know the other part of me, the vilest part, the tortured part that I still dragged along behind me. And if she did what Megan and the rest of them did and started thinking about how to fix me or save me, then I would have known she wasn't the right woman for me after all. Not even for the brief time before I left for Chicago.

I was afraid to discover that she wasn't right for someone like me, especially because I was beginning to trust her. Or maybe I already frustrated her because we'd crossed so many boundaries together, boundaries I'd never even approached with the others. With that, even the erotic daydream of calling Jennifer or some other lover evaporated into nothingness. It wouldn't help me get better.

I slid into the car without telling Megan goodbye and scrubbed a hand over my face, even more on edge than before.

The truth was, my body only wanted Babygirl, my Tinkerbell, because when I was with her, I wasn't thinking about Kimberly or feeling repulsed by the man that I'd become.

Still, I was afraid to find out what she'd think of me when my full past came to light, especially the part about Scarlett...

What if Selene also abandoned me one day?

I would have kept on struggling, running through a city of madness.
No one would turn on the lights.
No one would stop me.
No one would banish the voices that slithered around inside me.
What if I really did need her after all?
What if I needed her coconut-smelling hair?

What if I needed her soft skin, which was like lying on powdery sand?
What about her lips that had become my safe place?
What if I needed the freedom I felt when I looked into her eyes?
What if I needed the hope I experienced when I smelled her perfume?
Then I would have to fight for her as well because she was the only woman that I wanted.
She was the only one I couldn't stand to lose...

8

"Apparently, the idea of focusing on just one woman is too scary for you."

SELENE

Meet me in New York.
I'll be waiting.

That was what it said on the note Neil left me.

We hadn't spoken since then, though I suspected he was expecting me to respond or maybe even to show up outside of Matt's place with a big fake smile on my face.

How was I supposed to set foot in New York after what had happened there?

After the blow-up with my father, I had no intention of ever going back.

"You are aware he punched my brother in the face, right?" Janel had been saying the same thing over and over for the past half hour by then. She was pacing back and forth in my living room with one hand running through her hair while Bailey crunched her way through a bag of Cheetos, lost in thought.

"Ivan did provoke him. First, he implied that he was a druggie, and then he called him a psycho." I would have defended Neil, of course, even if he was completely in the wrong, but in this case, his reaction had been at least partially justified. He didn't tolerate any insults or slights, and Ivan really had crossed the line.

"Are you defending him? For real?" Janel shook her head, disappointed in my attitude.

What else was I supposed to do? Agree with her and insult the guy that I loved?

I wasn't condoning Neil's violent actions—I would never approve of that behavior—but I probably wasn't the right person to condemn him either. When it came to him, I was incapable of being impartial or rational. I simply felt compelled to take his side.

"Janel, guys get into fights all the time; don't make a federal case out of it," Bailey cut in, still continuing to munch.

"Have you lost your mind too?" Janel snapped.

Bailey just laughed and shot back, "I just think the two of us can't really talk about this. I get that Ivan is your brother, but we don't know how things really went down. We can't blindly defend either one of them because Selene is the only one of us who was actually there."

Sure, I was well aware of how things went down. I also felt guilty about it.

Neil had gone for Ivan right after the latter grabbed my wrist while I was trying to talk him into leaving. I couldn't say for sure what had triggered such a fury in my Disaster, but I strongly suspected that it was Ivan being there, and even more so, him having his hands on me.

That thought alone sent a shot of warmth through my chest.

Was he jealous over me?

He'd never admit it to me, but even the possibility was flattering.

"What are you smiling about now? And, more importantly, what happened to your lip?" Janel looked at me, scowling. I immediately turned serious again and instinctively raised a hand to my mouth. The mark from Neil's bite was still clearly visible there, to say nothing of my back, which was still recovering from the merciless way he'd taken me up against that wall.

Like always, he'd been rough and impetuous.

Someone else, perhaps, wouldn't have allowed him to impose himself like that, but I had enjoyed it.

Once again, it occurred to me what a deviant Neil had made of me.

I no longer believed in Prince Charmings or fairy tales. I'd even quit reading the romance novels I used to love so much. I had learned by then that there was no such thing as the perfect man, especially not Neil. He was like a dark knight with a heart swathed in shadows. His golden eyes glowed with a deceptive brightness, and his magnificent outer appearance enthralled everyone he met.

There was nothing of the fairy tale in him, nothing fantastical or noble.

He was a devotee of sex, an able seducer, and a lover of perversion.

My decision to be with him implied that I accepted him in his totality, the good and the bad. Even though I knew he'd never really allow me into his soul.

He'd been clear: He'd let me be with him but not as a partner or a girlfriend.

Did that mean I wouldn't get the exclusivity I wanted?

I didn't think so.

I sometimes believed that I meant something to him, like the night he told me about Kim. At other times, though, I felt completely insignificant. After all, if he really valued me in any way, he would have long ago given up the other women, and yet that hadn't happened, and it probably never would.

I sighed, upset.

I clung to the hope that I had finally earned some trust from him after all we had been through. I knew that it had been hard for Neil to tell me about himself and especially about Kimberly Bennett, though I got the sense that he'd left out a lot of information.

I still remembered the room full of hidden boxes I had found during my stay in New York. The newspapers I'd only caught a glimpse of had said something about a scandal, a dark figure, and the children of the shadows...

What if the truth about his babysitter was something even more terrifying?

Something even more dangerous?

Something that Neil was afraid to tell me?

Too many doubts were still swirling around in my head. His confession that he'd been abused hadn't come as a surprise to me, after all. I'd had my suspicions from the start, and then Logan himself had dropped some hints at the beach house about what had happened to his brother. I'd never told Neil that, though, because I didn't want them to get into some awful argument.

Still, I appreciated Neil's willingness to confide in me, even if it was the edited version.

I came back to the present moment and turned my eyes to Janel, who was arguing with Bailey about my appearance—the hickeys around my throat, the bite mark on my lip, the dark circles under my eyes, and my head-in-the-clouds attitude of late.

"Janel, I'm never going to turn on Neil, and I'm not looking for your blessing or anyone else's," I told her sharply, and she looked at me in shock. "That's enough for now. I need to get ready," I added, getting up off the sofa.

Bailey frowned at me, and Janel tilted her head to one side, still surprised by my outrage.

"Ready for what?" Bailey asked me, putting the bag of Cheetos down on the coffee table.

"To go to New York."

I had made the decision to go without thinking about what to tell my mother or how I could defend my choice to her.

She knew about my rancorous relationship with Matt, which had recently only gotten even worse, so telling her I wanted to visit my father for a little while wouldn't work. But I couldn't tell her that I wanted to be with Neil either. I had a suspicion that it had actually been my mother who had caused him to leave looking so disillusioned the last time. Maybe they'd had a conversation while I wasn't around. I felt trapped, and the only solution I could think of was to drag Bailey into my evil scheme, which I had only just devised that morning.

I was going to leave for New York that afternoon and come back the following evening, but I'd tell my mother that I was staying over at Bailey's during that time.

Bailey, after a few moments' hesitation, supported me. Unlike Janel, who thought my little white lie was a terrible idea. After the latter left, Bailey and I waited for my mother to get back from work. Then we told her our lie, and she bought it. She seemed pleased at the idea of me spending time with my friend, possibly because she wanted me to put Neil out of my mind and begin to think clearly again in a way I hadn't since I'd met him.

I myself couldn't believe I was about to do such a thing. I'd even considered not telling Neil I was coming and surprising him, but I needed someone to pick me up at the airport, so I had to abandon that idea and text him.

My plane lands at six o'clock.

Madness. It was pure madness. I kept telling myself that I hadn't lost my head over Neil, but my every thought and action suggested otherwise.

I mean, where was I even going to sleep? Obviously not at my father's house.

I brushed off my worries, though, and packed a couple of dresses, a pair of high-heeled shoes, and two sets of underwear (not the juvenile kind I usually wore) into my overnight bag. I'd bought them on a shopping trip to the mall with my friends, not knowing how soon I'd have a chance to wear them.

I had asked Neil to be exclusive with me, and he'd said no, right? So all that remained was for me to prove to him that my body was just as good as those belonging to his lovers and that I also knew how to be sexy and alluring. Once I was ready, Bailey and I headed out after I told my mother goodbye and gave her a kiss on the cheek.

....

The trip from Detroit to New York felt much longer than I had been expecting, perhaps because of my nerves.

Once I arrived at the airport, I headed for the passenger pickup area, where the air was heavy with smog and exhaust fumes. There were so many cars and taxis as well as people on foot walking every which way. I had a moment of déjà vu, recalling the day Matt Anderson, asshole father, had taken me to meet Mia and her children.

It felt like an eternity had passed since then.

I tossed my head, shaking off the memories, and looked around, afraid that I might not be able to find Neil or that he'd completely forgotten I was coming. I'd sent him another text as soon as we landed, but he still hadn't said anything back.

Where the hell was he? And, more important...what was he doing?

I dropped my bag on the ground and stretched, the bones in my sore back crackling. I was sore not from sitting so long on the plane but from the way my Disaster had taken me.

His hands, his kisses, his tongue...everything about him exuded this unstoppable energy and aggression that often transformed into pure passion.

Neil didn't just love sex; he was also really good at it, and...

"Knock it off, Selene," I snapped at myself, trying to derail my lusty train of thought, which was particularly inappropriate for that moment, and instead concentrate on watching the cars speed by ahead of me. I began to get truly afraid that I was going to have to take a cab back to the house by myself when a black Maserati pulled up with a roar, catching my attention. My gaze was immediately drawn to the gleaming paint job and the chrome trident that made it look so majestic. I couldn't tell if Neil was inside when it pulled up next to me, but then he lowered the window to greet me with a sensual smile. So I bent down to pick up my overnight bag and opened the door to get in the passenger seat. The leather smell of the interior, combined with the scent of clean musk, wrapped around me, and I turned to face Neil.

I regretted it immediately because every time he got near me, I ceased to be myself and became the inelegant, inane... in-love girl that he'd made me into.

"Hey, Tinkerbell," he said softly, eyeing my body at length. I wasn't wearing anything fancy. A wool hat, dark jeans, a heavy sweater, and a white coat with some low-heeled ankle boots. And why the hell hadn't I worn something with higher heels?

I looked like a high school student rather than a young woman. I turned red, imagining that he had to be thinking—not for the first time—about how basic and unfeminine I was.

"I thought you forgot that I was coming," I murmured, hoping to distract from the blush that I was sure had spread over my cheeks. The air around me felt blazing hot, and I wasn't sure whether to blame it on the car's heater or Neil's proximity.

The electricity between us was palpable, just like the powerful attraction that neither of us knew what to do with.

"I was only ten minutes late. I had a small hitch." He stepped on the gas, making the engine rumble, before pulling out into the airport's traffic.

"What does that mean?" I asked him, looking around the car's interior, which looked like it had just been detailed. There wasn't so much as a scratch or speck of dust on the dashboard, the numerous controls, or the multimedia display—signs of Neil's mania and fixation on cleanliness. I remembered how he'd once told me that he refused to have sex in the car.

"Nothing major. Had to wash my baby," he said lightly and patted the steering wheel. I turned my gaze to him as he focused on driving and thought he looked even more handsome than usual. He was wearing a leather jacket with a fur collar, a dark sweater, and jeans. He wasn't wearing anything fancy either, but he could still turn any woman's head.

"Don't start with the staring," he chided me roughly, like always.

"Wh-where are we going?" I asked, hoping it wasn't a stupid question.

I knew we were probably going to Matt's house, but I wanted him to say it so I could tell him that I'd rather go to a hotel than set foot inside that place. There were too many painful memories in that house, especially in the pool house. Maybe Neil wouldn't agree with my suggestion that we should find another place to stay, but I needed to at least try.

"To one of the apartments my mother keeps in the city," he answered, stunning me instead.

"In one of..." I muttered. "What?" I blinked in shock and reached up to adjust my hat anxiously.

Neil just smiled and kept driving.

"I lifted her keys. It's an apartment she bought last year. She only goes there when she needs to relax, so no one will bother us," he explained, turning onto an unfamiliar street. Of course, I'd only visited New York briefly, so I couldn't possibly know it as well as Neil did.

Wait a minute—did he say *us*? Did that mean he was staying with me?

"Bother *us*?" I repeated, getting agitated.

Oh God! No. No. No.

If Neil and I stayed together in the same apartment for several hours, I would come out completely obliterated, wrung-out, and consumed by his desires. I could already imagine the demands he'd make of me and the things he'd try to start when we were in bed together that night. I was never able to think rationally or make sensible decisions when I was with him, let alone try to resist him when he came on to me like he always did.

"You want me to leave you there alone?" he asked, shooting me a penetrating glance.

"No," I answered too quickly, obviously agitated. "I just thought that you'd go home and I'd be staying in the apartment, that's all," I explained, rubbing my hands together awkwardly. Neil pulled a pack of Winstons out of the jacket and extracted a cigarette with his teeth.

Did he seriously want to smoke in here with all the windows rolled up and the heater on? I would die of asphyxiation.

"Maybe don't—" I started to say, but he lifted up a hand to stop me.

"It's my car, and I'll smoke in it when I want," he cut me off. "Don't start busting my balls, Babygirl," he said calmly, as though he'd just given me some friendly advice.

Well, this was shaping up to be a fantastic evening!

I rolled my eyes and searched for the button that would roll down the window so some of the fog could dissipate.

"How long are you staying? Does your mother know you're here?"

His question unsettled me, and I felt a stab of angst in my chest. I had never lied to my mother before, and I knew, deep down, that it had been the wrong thing to do. But I also knew that I had to meet Neil in New York, no matter what the cost.

"No," I admitted. "She thinks I'm hanging out with my friend Bailey and that I'll be back tomorrow." I cleared my throat, glancing up at the skyscrapers towering all around us.

"I figured," he commented with a smug smile. I looked at him with a frown. I was about to ask him what made him so confident, but before I could demand to know, we pulled into a parking garage, and I was completely distracted. "Here we are, Tinkerbell," he told me, shutting off the engine, as the garage attendant stepped up to take the key and give Neil a ticket for the car.

He turned his bright gaze on me, maybe waiting for me to react. I offered him a shaky little smile. He stared at my mouth, and I was positive he could sense my uncertainty.

"Relax," he said in a low, seductive voice. "I don't bite." He winked at me and then got out of the car. I followed him, bag in hand. Neil didn't make a move to take it, choosing to let me carry it instead, something that didn't surprise me at all.

Neil Miller, not a gentleman—more news at eleven.

He led me to the elevator, and we stepped through the sliding doors. I forced myself not to look at him, even though his good smell was the flame to the fuse of my desire.

The ride up put me on edge.

I leaned back against the mirror behind me and observed Neil, intent on watching me in silence. The serious, intense expression on his face communicated a poorly concealed desire to make me his. Immediately.

The deadly draw that filled the air between us shocked me to the spirit.

I caught my breath at the devastating emotions that were ravaging my heart, and Neil gave me a satisfied little smile, knowing full well that every bat of his eyelashes had the power to shake my soul.

I cleared my throat, awkward as always, and turned my attention to the floor numbers above the door slowly lighting up one by one.

None of them, however, seemed to be our destination. When were we going to get there?

I rocked back on my heels and dropped my eyes, embarrassed.

How bizarre that the two of us, who were always on the brink of tearing off each other's clothes, couldn't manage to start a conversation. I gave a sigh of relief when, finally, the elevator opened on the fiftieth floor, allowing us access to the enormous apartment's door. The rare wood and gold fixtures on the door gave me a sneak peek at the luxury I would find inside.

After all, Mia wasn't the kind to spare any expense, just like Matt.

"I forgot to mention it, but it's the penthouse," Neil said as he opened the door and gestured for me to go inside.

Wow!

I had never been inside a place like that before. I moved forward unsteadily across the marble floors threaded with silver. I felt bad even walking on them because of how glossy they were. Then I turned my eyes to the furniture: sophisticated and refined yet extremely sumptuous. Two giant leather sofas were arranged in the middle of the living room with a glass table between them. I stepped in a bit further and admired the glowing ceiling peppered with small inset lights. It felt like I was standing under a starry sky.

I set my overnight bag down and continued peering around in astonishment. I moved over to the enormous windows, which offered a panoramic view of the skyline.

I was thoroughly dazzled.

The city looked like an architectural miniature, the people walking around on the sidewalks practically invisible, no bigger than ants. And the cars driving on the streets...

"The cars look like toys," I noted under my breath, smiling an enchanted smile. Neil came up beside me with a cigarette hanging from his lips. He exhaled smoke against the glass of the window, his eyes fixed on the skyscrapers laid out before us.

"People are so insignificant when you see them from up here..." he said softly in that baritone that always sent shivers of arousal down my arms. "When I think about how many monsters are walking around down there with them every day, all I can feel is disgust," he went on, taking another drag. He turned away from me, and I watched his austere frame.

His stride was sure, his back strong, and his shoulders broad... He gave every appearance of being an invincible man, and yet he was wounded inside just like any other person.

His soul was out of reach, but it wasn't unassailable.

The difference was subtle, but I had taken note of it.

"Why did you write that note asking me to meet you in New York?" I asked him, pulling off my hat. I tried to straighten my bangs with my fingers, despite the fact that there were more important things to be done in that moment. Namely, listening to Neil.

"Because you can't say that you're willing to accept me or be with me if you don't know everything about me," he answered shortly. He shrugged off his leather jacket and tossed it onto the sofa with a sigh.

He thought that I didn't know him? Was he kidding me?

"I know a lot about you, though," I replied, and he gave me a cynical smile.

"Oh, really?" he asked derisively. "What do you know, besides how I fuck and that I got raped?" he challenged me. He stood before me, hands clenched into fists and his stare sharper than any blade.

"I know you have a fixation on bodily hygiene and on blond women..." I stepped forward, and Neil watched me warily, like an animal preparing to attack, but I didn't back down. "I know you love to draw. That time I snuck into your room without permission, I took a peek at your notebook and saw that you are really into architectural drafting. You love The Neighbourhood; they're your favorite band. When we were living in the same house, I heard their music coming from your room all the time." I smiled and moved closer to him, just a little bit. "You're a reader, and you really, really like pistachios, but I've already told you that, just like I've told you about all the things I've noticed about you... and I won't deny that I am dying to learn even more," I finished, drawing close enough for his scent to invade my space. His golden eyes scrutinized me closely while giving away nothing themselves. Neil had shut me out again.

I couldn't enter his world; he only ever let me in when he chose.

All at once, Neil took a step back, staring at me as though he didn't know who I was.

Why did he do that? Why did he always seem to lose the thread whenever I tried to extend a hand to him?

Suddenly, a cell phone ringtone resounded in the air around us, breaking the tension. I quickly realized it wasn't mine as Neil reached into his jacket pocket for his phone and answered it.

"What do you want, Jen?" he snapped.

It occurred to me then that all his other lovers lived around here. I had no idea whether their number had decreased or increased since I'd left. One thing I did know, however, was that my homicidal urges would have spiked off the charts if I had to see Jennifer again. I hated her the most out of all of them.

"Okay, I'll be there tonight," he answered, undoubtedly because Jennifer had asked him to go out.

And what about me? Was I supposed to stay here by myself?

Neil ended the call without another word and heaved a sigh, putting his phone back in his pocket. Then he stepped back and watched me with a scornful look on his face.

"Put on something decent and ditch those terrible little boots," he ordered me firmly, and I winced at his tone. Then he walked toward the door, and I just stood there, stunned and confused.

"Why?" I asked him, bewildered.

Neil turned and gave me a flat look. "Because you're going out with me tonight. And the shitheads where we're going lose their minds over good girls like you, so put on something a little bit racy, something that makes you look more like a grown woman and less like a student." He turned the apartment key over and over in his hand while he assessed my outfit.

He wanted to go out with me? More importantly...would the whole Krew be there?

"Are Alexia and Jennifer going to be there?" I said their names with all the disdain I would have reserved for my arch nemeses.

"Yeah," he said, turning his back to me and moving toward the door again.

"Where...where are you going?" I asked again, only feeling more adrift.

Neil turned around, looking impatient. "I'll come get you again in a few hours. I need to shower and change. I don't have clothes here. Make yourself at home."

I looked down at the key he had clutched in one hand, and his apparent kindness took a back seat to my concern.

"So what are you going to do? Just leave me here?" I ventured, though I thought that was probably an absurd suggestion.

Instead, Neil grinned at me, pleased and proud. I couldn't believe it...

I moved to stop him, but Neil was faster than me, and he left before I could reach him. I heard the sound of the key turning and the lock clicking into place.

Dammit.

"Neil?" Anxiety began gnawing at me. I opened the door to see him waiting nonchalantly for the elevator.

"Don't go wandering around the city without my permission. See you later, Tinkerbell," he said, sounding amused.

"You dick!" I shouted at him. He started laughing like an asshole and stepped into the elevator, and the doors closed on his still-laughing face. My rage only grew, and I called after him one more time.

By that point, certain that I had been left alone with only my fear and panic to keep me company, I tried to breathe and turned around to face the enormous apartment before me.

I felt adrift in an unfamiliar environment, in a faraway city, removed from my mother and all my friends. For all I knew, Neil was going to leave me here all night. Maybe he'd just go out with the Krew instead and wouldn't show up again until the next morning.

I felt short of breath. I wasn't used to sleeping all alone and certainly not in some apartment I'd never been to before.

"Okay, calm down, Selene. Breathe." I tried to get centered while I took off my coat. I was sweating from all the agitation, so I tossed it on the sofa before sitting down myself to take in my luxurious surroundings. I could have gone snooping around the place, but I felt too much like an intruder. Even worse, guilt rose up in my chest. I regretted lying to my mother; she didn't deserve that. Most of all, I regretted this whole clusterfuck—going along with Neil and his goddamned note.

Why had he even asked me to come see him? Was it a game? Was he messing with me?

"Relax," I told myself, massaging my forehead. My fingers passed over my scar, and I thought about my accident, about the puzzles, and about Player.

What if he went after me again?

What if, somehow, he learned about my presence in New York?

I was getting paranoid.

"That's dumb, knock it off." I threw up my hands and got back to my feet. I had an extremely luxurious apartment at my disposal, and though I wasn't in the habit of sneaking into other people's spaces, I decided I was going to take advantage of it with a hot shower. To start.

Except, where was the bathroom? Big problem.

I picked up my bag and headed down the long hallway, which had various rooms branching off it. I opened a random door, and my mouth fell open.

The room inside could only be described as fit for a king. A huge bed lorded over the middle of the room with two modernist bedside tables flanking it. A bookcase stuffed with books stretched up to the ceiling, and a large window offered the same view as in the living room. The atmosphere was welcoming, and the bedspread smelled nice; there was the scent of vanilla in the air. There wasn't so much as a speck of dust on the furniture, and the windows gleamed. Mia must have hired someone to keep up the place. Maybe it was even Anna, the housekeeper at Matt's place. Who knew?

Either way, the apartment was clearly neither abandoned nor neglected.

I set my bag down next to the bed and got out a clean set of white lace lingerie, one I hadn't worn yet. It was bold but not vulgar. Once I determined that, unfortunately, there was no bathroom in that room, I started wandering around again until I found one just a little bit farther down the hall.

As soon as I entered, I saw that pomp and luxury were also the order of the day in here. The gilded marble with white finishing on the decor was particularly eye-catching. I undressed and laid my clothes neatly on the countertop next to the sink before glancing at my reflection. The bite mark on my lip was still visible, as were the various other marks on my body, having turned from a burnt umber to an awful shade of yellow. I wrinkled my nose in disgust as I stepped into the shower. I found various bath soaps located there and selected the one that smelled like almonds.

No coconut; not this time.

I soaped myself up in small circles and then rinsed carefully, trying to relax in the warm spray of the shower. When I was done, I found a fresh towel hanging nearby and wrapped it around myself. I stepped out, still dripping all over. I wrung the water out of my long hair with a huff. I needed to get it cut one of these days.

I spent an hour drying my hair and, miraculously, achieved the desired effect. It ended up looking soft and sleek. My bangs had migrated to one side of my head, but since they covered my scar completely, I decided to leave them there.

I didn't get dressed right away and instead explored the apartment in my underwear. I was alone, after all, and no one was going to bother me. Occasionally, I would stop to adjust the panties, which kept giving me wedgies. I wasn't used to wearing such a tiny pair, and I cursed myself for being an idiot when I had to admit that I'd worn them for Neil.

That asshole didn't deserve a single thing from me.

He was probably already hanging out with Jennifer, pregaming in the pool house before they met up with the other members of the Krew. Meanwhile, I just hung around here waiting for him.

What the hell had I been thinking?

I should have just stayed at home.

My period of solitary confinement was long and slow.

Eight o'clock came, and I was still in my underwear, lying on the sofa and staring up at the ceiling.

I hadn't gotten dressed or put on any makeup. That jackass might have been making fun of me, pretending we were going out when we weren't, so I had no intention of dressing up and becoming his punch line.

I wasn't going to get all glammed up for him just to be ghosted.

"Damn it all to hell. Go out alone with those Krew degenerates!" I spit, knowing that he couldn't have heard me, but I needed to ease some of the weight pressing down on my chest, and yelling at an imaginary Neil seemed to do the trick.

I sighed and rolled over into the fetal position. I was cold. I didn't know how to turn on the heater or where to find blankets. I didn't want to just steal them off the bed.

Despair welled up, and I heaved a defeated sigh.

Then my phone, which I had left on the glass coffee table, vibrated with a text alert.

It was from Neil. I'll be there at nine o'clock.

Nothing more, nothing less.

Bite me, asshole, I tapped out furiously.

It wasn't like me to be crude, but he deserved it.

Fairies must not swear, he answered after a couple of seconds.

"...must not?" I read, only getting more annoyed.

There he was—the insufferable tyrant.

He needed to take charge and not just in bed. Even in his daily life, he issued orders and demanded that everyone (me included) obey him.

You swear all the time, I wrote back irritably.

You don't need to do what I do. Again, his answer came back almost immediately. I considered what he'd written: He didn't want me to be like him; he wanted me to remain uncontaminated by his world. So why didn't he just stay away from me?

I'm not ready. I don't want to go out with your precious friends. I dug my heels in like a child.

Too bad for you. That means I get to fuck you...any way I want, he replied quickly.

I paled as I read the message. "Any way I want" meant just like all the other times: wild, overpowering, and passionate.

But I couldn't let him get his hands on me again, not after he'd disappeared for hours without a word and not when my body was still sore from what had happened at my house.

Fine. We'll go out, I wrote back in resignation.

I'd pick a night out over whatever crazy sex he was already planning in his warped head.

Then I remembered right before he left, when he'd told me to get rid of the boots and dress like a woman.

Okay, I'd oblige him.

I stalked into the room, more determined than ever, and pulled my two prettiest dresses out of my bag. One was blue, knee-length, and quite simple; the other was flaming red and sexy as hell. Of course I opted for the second one, determined that I was going to show him I too knew how to be attractive to men. I wasn't perfect, but people liked me. I'd had my share of admirers in the past, and some pretty cute ones, too. Plus, although Mother Nature had been stingy with my breasts, she'd made up for it with my butt. So I was going to flaunt it.

I slipped the dress on with a cheeky little smile, careful not to wrinkle it, and then zipped it up in back...not without some difficulty. Then I went over to the room's mirror to take a look at myself.

It was a long-sleeved dress, short and tight with a sensual boat neck. It wrapped perfectly around my delicate curves, and just as I'd expected, it really highlighted my backside.

Maybe it was a wee bit shorter than what I'd usually wear, but the occasion called for it.

"You wanted me to ditch the good girl? Well, here you go," I told the invisible Neil with a surprising amount of decisiveness. But my evil scheme was not yet complete. I arranged my hair over my shoulders before applying my makeup. I was usually the quintessential soap-and-water girl, but that night I coated my eyelashes with mascara and applied ruby red lipstick, a big departure from my usual pink gloss. It made my blue eyes sparkle and my lips look more sensuous.

My face looked completely different; I even looked more mature.

Then it was just the finishing touches that remained. I pulled on a pair of sheer thigh-highs, followed by my pair of black high heels.

I slipped into them and wobbled slightly, taking a moment to get used to my new elevated height. Then I glanced in the mirror one more time to assess my completed work.

I was pleased with the result: I looked seductive yet elegant.

"Alright, Selene. You're a woman." Confident in myself, I went back into the living room to get my phone and check the time—it was almost nine. I perched on the couch, one leg crossed over the other, and waited for my Disaster to come back. Exacting as he was, I had no doubt that he would be right on time, and I liked the idea of seeing the shocked look on his face when he walked in and saw the new Selene.

I drummed my fingers nervously on the couch's arm and waited.

My heart was beating like a wild thing in my chest, but I tried to ignore it.

Nerves weren't going to derail my plans.

Then, right at nine o'clock, the lock clicked, and my whole body went on alert.

Neil came into the apartment wearing a black winter coat and a white sweater that popped against his amber skin, and I forgot how to breathe.

I held my breath as my heart pounded out of control.

Calm... I had to stay calm.

Neil approached me with his typical proud posture, a severe expression on his face. His soft forelock fell over his forehead, and his beard looked shorter than when he'd left. I knew he'd neatened it up for me, and he looked like a god.

He was overwhelmingly beautiful; you couldn't find an aesthetic flaw on him, no matter how many character flaws he might have had.

Without so much as a hello or a single friendly word, he stopped just short of me and regarded me. I stood up to give him a better view, proud as the tigress he sometimes compared me to. From the little flares I saw in his golden eyes, I could tell he was neither pleased nor excited about my clothing. In fact, he looked almost frantic, and my confidence slipped away in a most cowardly fashion.

I swallowed hard, and my legs began to tremble.

Neil continued to check me out, looking at me from top to bottom, wrinkling his brow. He looked irritated and ill-humored.

"You wanted a woman, right? And now you don't like it?" I spoke first, my voice slashing derisively through the air even though I was still trembling. Neil didn't move a muscle. He just stood there, studying me, refusing to give me a clue as to what he was thinking. Why didn't he say anything?

I would have rather had him yell at me, to tell me he hated it; anything but that nerve-racking silence.

"Well?" I insisted, growing angry.

"You look like an enchanting fairy who somehow wound up wearing a slut's dress," he answered cynically.

I sucked in a breath and blushed violently, instantly uncomfortable.

Tears stung my eyes, but I refused to cry. I wouldn't give him the satisfaction, no matter how much his words had hurt me.

"But..." he continued as I stared resentfully at him. If he'd been any closer to me, I would have slapped him. "If your intent was to look hot, then yes, you've succeeded." He scrutinized me once again, and this time, I saw lust and excitement in his eyes along with the desire not to succumb to me, all of those feelings in conflict with one another.

"Is this you trying to fix things? Maybe with a compliment? It's not going so hot if it is." I shot him a glare full of ire, and he gave me a little half-smile in return.

"I'm just telling you the truth, Babygirl," he said nonchalantly.

"Don't call me that," I warned.

"Why not? Are you mad?" He provoked me with a smile, well aware that I was enraged.

I hated it when he thought his charm was enough to pacify me or when he talked to me in that oh-so-delighted tone, smug over having hurt me.

Was it another one of his kinks, needing to treat women with such condescension?

Was this too about Kimberly? I feared that it was.

Neil was a man who, since his early childhood, had been inculcated with a very negative, distorted view of women as a whole.

"What are you trying to prove? Why did you even ask me to come to New York?" I demanded, disappointed. Maybe this was all just a game for Neil. I now knew about the trauma he'd experienced, but that didn't excuse the constant disrespect he showed me. Yes, I had promised to accept him and not to judge him, but I couldn't allow him to keep treating me like a doormat.

"You'll understand why tomorrow, not tonight," he answered, growing gloomy and impenetrable again. "And we'll see if you want to stick with that being with me and accepting me thing..." he went on, and suddenly the thought occurred to me that maybe he was going to try to drag me into one of his little performances, like on Halloween when he cooked up that insane game with Jennifer to intimidate me and get me to leave town.

"You're nuts. I'm going to stay in a hotel." I grabbed my coat and put it on again, moving toward the door. Before I got there, however, Neil took me by the wrist and pulled me to him.

"You're not going anywhere," he told me, his eyes boring into mine.

And there he went, imposing himself again, like he felt real fear at the prospect of someone not doing what he'd ordered them to do. Maybe Neil had that strange habit of always refusing to bend to anyone else's will because he'd been forced to do too much of that when he was little?

Though I wanted to yell and rage at him, logic told me that there was a why behind his every attitude and that all of it, without fail, came back to the babysitter.

"Oh yeah? And who made that decision?" I pressed, breathing in his good smell of shower gel mixed with aftershave. It was a very nice smell, but I wasn't going to let it lead me astray.

"Me. You're staying until tomorrow," he said as though this had been decided upon, despite the fact that he'd never even asked me and I was visibly unhappy.

"You've got some nerve..." I answered with a shake of my head, and he grinned at me.

What the hell did he have to smile about?

"Maybe so, but you like my nerve." He tightened his hold around my arms, pulling me closer to him until his hard chest pressed against mine. My body reacted immediately to his touch. "Do you deny it?" he asked softly as he pressed his erection, stiff and ready, into my pelvis. He was showing me that he wanted a different sort of attention and that his mind had gone off in a completely different direction than mine. But I ignored his question; I had no desire to confirm just how much I liked him, even when he was being all rude and outlandish like that.

"I thought you didn't like my dress," I said in a spiteful mutter. He *had* insulted me. I hadn't hallucinated it.

"I told you I thought you were hot. Don't you know what that means in man language? Or should I show you?" He talked to me like I was immature, fickle, and inexperienced and couldn't hope to get the better of someone like him.

"I get it; it's not subtle," I answered pertly, feeling the tense way he held his body and how his hard member still pressed into me. "You should apologize to me," I continued.

"I'm never going to do that. You knew what I was like from the start." He released me and passed a hand through his hair in frustration. He looked like he wanted to jump me but was restraining the impulse. And a thought occurred to me. *Maybe this is all a test? Maybe he is trying to see what I will endure for him?*

"We'd better go." I pushed past it and ended the conversation, knowing that it wouldn't have changed anything anyway.

About a quarter of an hour later, we arrived at Chandelier, the club where we were meeting the Krew.

On the trip over, Neil and I had completely ignored each other. I was still mad about what he'd said, while he, on the other hand, seemed lost in his own twisted thoughts. He'd smoked in the car again without the least consideration for my presence, and when he turned on the radio, it was to play a song by his favorite band. The first notes of "Nervous" had floated out into the interior of the car, the lyrics seeming to mock me.

After Neil parked, we got out and went straight to the entrance of the club, bypassing the long line of people waiting to get inside. Apparently, Neil was familiar with the musclebound bouncer. All he had to do was say hello, and the guy let us in without any problem. Inside, the music was so loud it rendered me stunned, while the colored lights dazzled my eyes and the crush of people made it hard to breathe. Someone bumped into me out of nowhere, and I stumbled, but the walking Disaster I was with just kept going, not even bothering to check if I was following along behind him.

"Try not to get lost," he yelled over the music when he finally turned around to check on me. I automatically reached out for his hand, and the gesture made him glare at me. I could see right away from the look on his face that he wasn't pleased with my taking the initiative like that, and he stared at me in confusion.

"I can keep track of you better this way," I said into his ear, and after a brief hesitation, he sighed and entwined his fingers with mine. He gave them a firm squeeze before continuing to walk, pulling me along with him. My heart rate accelerated at the heat of his palm on mine, and I began to sweat.

I thought about how anyone watching us probably thought we were some happy couple holding hands, but in reality, we were nothing of the sort. However, I didn't want to ruin the mood with my paranoia, so instead of turning myself inside out over how I was being perceived, I decided to take a look around and get a better sense for what kind of club I'd wound up in. There was a DJ spinning a series of earth-shaking electronica tracks, numerous tall tables occupied by groups of men and women of all ages, and a series of black sofas arranged around the edge of the room. The dominating color scheme was black and deep scarlet, real hellfire vibes. A perfect place for the Krew.

I jolted when I felt the sudden absence of Neil's hand. I frowned, seeing that he'd stopped but not immediately realizing why. Then it became clear to me when I spotted his friends.

"Oh, there you are. We've been waiting for you." Xavier raised a glass in our direction with his usual devil-may-care attitude. He chuckled as he lay splayed out on a couch amongst the others.

"We thought you weren't coming," Luke, sitting next to him, put in.

"And apparently you brought your little brat with you too." It was Jennifer who spoke that time, in tones of the utmost bitchery. I stood back and looked at her challengingly. I could have shot something back at her, but I decided to ignore her instead. She wasn't worth my attention. Instead, I evaluated her outfit and that of her friend Alexia.

Both were dressed boldly to catch the eye.

But Jennifer was the clear winner.

She wore a white dress that, along with her long blond hair, gave her an almost angelic appearance.

She was as beautiful as she was evil.

"Holy fuck! Babydoll, I didn't even recognize you. How are you doing?" Xavier checked me out and lingered on my legs, exposed as they were in my short dress. Meanwhile, Neil sat down between Alexia and Jennifer, who immediately made space for him, and jealousy gnawed at my stomach.

"Well? Xavier asked you a question, princess," Jennifer prompted me nastily.

All at once she gave me a sly grin and got up only to sit down on Neil's lap, wrapping her arms around his neck. I went rigid as she crossed her legs, allowing her dress to rise up so high that I almost got an eyeful of her panties. I twisted my lips into a hard expression while Neil did nothing whatsoever to remove her, despite my obvious displeasure.

"Who told you that you could sit on me?" he asked her instead in a placid tone, not quite stern enough to get her moving. Had he wanted to, he could have pushed her away easily. We all knew what he was like.

But he didn't seem to mind having her on top of him. Far from it, apparently, because he rested a hand on her bare thigh.

My jealousy only increased. It coiled around me like a venomous snake, and I felt an awful emptiness in my chest, but I forced myself not to lash out.

"Sit here, Selene." Luke gestured to the place next to him, and I accepted his invitation. It wasn't like me to do things out of spite, but if Neil didn't mind Jennifer coming onto him right in front of me, then I didn't mind sitting next to a guy I'd once kissed in Neil's pool house. The Disaster, who had upended my entire life, noticed this and narrowed his eyes slightly at me in challenge. I grinned cheekily at him and took off my coat to give his buddies a better view of my seductive dress.

"So, where are you living now?" Jennifer continued to needle me as she stroked the back of Neil's neck with her sharp claws. She feigned interest in my answer, but the fight in her eyes left no room for doubt: She hated me.

"Detroit," I answered coldly, rubbing a hand over my knee. I forced myself to look into her bright eyes and tried to hide how much it hurt to watch her drape herself all over a man I considered... mine.

"Oh yeah, of course. And why'd you come back? A little vacation?" she asked arrogantly.

"Well, it certainly wasn't to see your whore face," I burst out.

Xavier burst into laughter. "Whore face? How classy, Babydoll," he commented, bringing his cocktail to his lips.

Jennifer just took the hit and dug her heels in, casting a glance at Neil, who had been watching our spat in silence. She moved closer to him until her breasts were pressed to his chest, then tossed her golden hair back to expose the generous cleavage that made it so obvious she wasn't wearing a bra. The message was clear: She was marking her territory.

"And yet... men still prefer someone like me to someone like you," she said with a superior air, as though she were up to the challenge of being with someone like Neil and I was not.

"Only the ones with a negative IQ," I snapped back, determined not to let her bitchiness get the better of me. She smiled and exchanged knowing looks with Alexia before giving me her undivided attention once again.

"But your man is no exception; just the other night he was hanging out with me and Alexia. He wanted to play heads or tails... Do you know what that means?" she asked insolently.

I didn't know, but I could take a guess.

Just the thought of Neil continuing to have sex with other people—even worse, with the two of them—disgusted me.

I couldn't seem to catch my breath.

"He wanted head from me and Alexia's tail." She gave me a sneering little wink, and that was the coup de grâce for me.

Suddenly, Neil sprang into action. He shoved her off him and slid her over onto the sofa before leaping to his feet.

"Why the fuck are you telling her that?" he barked reprovingly. My eyes sought out his; I wanted him to see just how hurt I was, but his gaze was locked on the blond.

"And you were with him too?" Xavier asked Alexia with the same look of dismay that I wore. Apparently he, too, was not aware that the three of them had spent a night together. When Alexia didn't answer him and just lowered her eyes, Xavier stood up and hurled his glass to the floor. "Guess you haven't stopped slutting around then!" he shouted at her, and in a flash, Luke was up and in between them, putting a hand on Xavier's chest to settle him down.

"Xavier, take a walk, man," he told him quietly.

"Go fuck yourselves, you assholes!" he lashed out at them, and then he left in a huff, vanishing into the crowd.

I'd known for a while that the men of the Krew liked to share women, especially Jennifer and Alexia, but Xavier had reacted with real jealousy. I probably should have been storming out like him, but instead my body remained motionless, frozen by the misery that spread all throughout me. I was afraid that if I tried to stand up, my legs wouldn't have held me.

"Are you okay, Selene?" Luke asked in concern, and it was then that something inside me shifted. I stood up and took in a deep breath, trying not to cry, trying not to give in to the weakness of emotions. Though I didn't show it as openly, I could completely understand what Xavier was going through. I had pinned a lot of my hopes on Neil. I had given him every part of me, and I knew that if he continued to withhold his soul from me, it would destroy me. Neil stepped toward me as though sensing that I intended to leave, but I ignored him. Then I turned my back on him and his little band of maniacs.

"Selene!" he called after me, but I didn't care. In that moment, the only thing I wanted to do was get away from him, spend the rest of the night in a hotel, and in the morning go home. Back to Detroit. I plowed angrily through the crowd, pushing people aside in my attempt to get to an exit.

I had put up with enough of his indifference, callousness, and cruelty for one night.

How could he act like that? How could he ask me to come spend time with him in New York and then be so completely dismissive?

I walked out of the club and pulled my coat around me to shield me from the cold.

I was a mess, but I needed to stand up for myself and get out of there.

But how? I'd have to take a taxi.

I walked over to the curb and leaned into the street in the hopes of seeing a passing cab that I might hail, but several minutes went by with no sign of one.

"Babydoll, you don't wanna hang out here for too long."

I whirled around with a gasp, only to find Xavier standing there. I looked him right in the eye, wary.

His cold stare now appeared to be hiding a silent pain that he worked hard to suppress. Was he actually in love with Alexia? I recalled how she had tried several times to get closer to him while he had turned his attention to other women.

Maybe she'd gotten sick of it? Had she turned the tables on him?

That still didn't excuse her sleeping with Neil, though. On the contrary, I was beginning to hate her as much as I did Jennifer.

"I'm about to leave right now." I made to turn away from him, but Xavier kept talking.

"We both have good reason to get out of here. I'll give you a lift, if you want." He threw the cigarette he'd been smoking onto the pavement as he waited for my answer. I stared at the piercing that stood out starkly against his lower lip and the other one in his eyebrow before looking him up and down. He was definitely not the kind of guy who screamed "safety."

He was the worst of the Krew; I knew that perfectly well.

"No," I blurted out. "I haven't forgotten all the times you were happy to humiliate me, Xavier. You're just like them..." I gestured at the club's entrance, referring to his friends inside. I had no idea why he was trying to be nice to me now. "So don't get any weird ideas," I told him bluntly. Xavier cocked an eyebrow and barely held himself back from laughing at me outright.

"Trust me, Babydoll, no matter how cute you are, you couldn't satisfy someone like me," he sneered before taking a step toward me. I stepped back automatically. "I do wonder how someone like you can be with someone like Neil, though." He frowned inquisitively at me.

I didn't understand it either. I didn't want to save Neil from his past or even change who he was; I wanted more than that: I wanted him to understand that the world wasn't just darkness, that it wasn't only full of monsters like Kimberly, that he didn't have to be ashamed of what he'd been through, and that I would never judge him.

Often, society marginalized people who demonstrated psychological problems as a result of trauma they'd experienced. But some people, like me, looked beyond that prejudice and tried to see the human inside.

I was certain that there was something good inside Neil; I knew he had the capacity for love. He could be soft with his siblings and even with me sometimes. A man without a heart or feelings wouldn't be able to treat others with that kind of care.

"Somehow, our differences unite us," I murmured.

What a fool I was! Despite what I'd just heard from Jennifer, I couldn't bring myself to run Neil down and give up my faith in him.

"And you can accept the...way he is?" Xavier tilted his head slightly. He looked like he was observing me, like a specimen from another planet.

"What do you mean?" I asked with a frown.

A faint smile moved over his face as he approached me. "I've seen how he fucks. Fucks for real, Selene, with all that rage he's got in him. When he shares a woman with me, he becomes an animal, and not just in the way he touches them. It's in the way he talks to them and looks at them..." His disturbed tone chilled me. I looked at him in shock. Why was he telling me something like this? "But I think that he's gotta be different with you, or else you wouldn't be here right now," he frowned thoughtfully, sticking a hand into the pocket of his black jeans.

"What...what are you trying to tell me?" I asked hoarsely.

I didn't trust Xavier, so I had no idea how to interpret his little speech.

"You don't know anything about Scarlett, do you?" he asked me like he already knew the answer.

I had actually tried several times to learn more about her, but I'd been unable to get any information out of anyone. The girl was like an omnipresent ghost, and everyone knew her story but me.

I shook my head slightly.

"Not even about her father, Officer Roger Scott?" he asked, and I thought about it. I had seen the man once before when he'd showed up at Matt's place investigating the attack on Carter Nelson, the guy who had ended up in a coma after a fight with Neil. Other than that one meeting, I didn't know much about him. So I shook my head again.

"Like I thought," Xavier noted sardonically. "Roger Scott is the person who hates Neil most in all the world. He's been after him for years now. One day, when you really want to know the man you're sleeping with, you'll find out what I'm talking about. I don't think Miller's the type to confess all to you, Babydoll." He rolled his shoulders and went on. "It's your life, and, quite frankly, you can do whatever you want. But just tell me one thing…" He paused for effect. "Why do you want to roll around in this shit with us pigs?"

I sucked in a breath at his rough words as my head began to spin from information overload.

What did Officer Scott want with Neil? How many more secrets from his past was I unaware of?

I'd had no idea he was Scarlett's father, though it was now much clearer to me why I'd gotten such a strong impression that he and Neil knew each other.

"Why does Officer Scott have it in for him?" I asked abruptly, ignoring his other question. He looked gravely at me and didn't say a word. "Has Neil had trouble with the law before?" I tried again, but still, Xavier kept silent. "Damn it, I need to know!" I raised my voice as I stepped toward him.

I'd had it with all these cryptic mysteries.

I had a right to know what Neil was hiding from me. I'd even begun to suspect that he might be a danger to me, but the feelings that kept me soul-bound to him took over and chased away all fear.

He was reckless and acted impulsively, but he was not a criminal.

"No, nothing like that," Xavier answered, and I breathed a sigh of relief. "But Neil did take his daughter away from him. That's enough to brew hatred and resentment in any man," he added seriously, and I let my arms fall to my sides, feeling suddenly weak.

What did that mean? In what way did Neil take her away?

I was just about to ask him when a grim, intimidating figure appeared over Xavier's shoulder. I didn't even need to take a good look; I knew exactly who it was. I could smell the scent of musk from where I stood.

Neil.

"Xavier." He addressed his friend immediately, and I could tell from his rigid tone that he was in a bad mood. "I know what you're trying to do. Don't use her to get at me." He moved closer as if to shield me with his powerful body, and I looked at him in consternation.

What the hell was he talking about?

"Why would I do that?" Xavier asked him, a derisive tone in his voice. Neil didn't so much as twitch; he remained completely blank. It wasn't surprising, though. It was difficult to make him lose control, except when someone pushed him beyond his limits.

"Alexia chose to join in that night. I certainly didn't force her," Neil said confidently, ignoring his friend's sarcastic question. The air had grown tense; the two of them had entered into a specifically masculine sort of competition. It was their own unhealthy habits that led to all this drama that was destroying their friendship. But, as far as I was concerned, this conversation was just making me nauseous.

"I don't care!" Xavier exploded. "I'm fucking pissed that she still keeps picking you!" he ground out through clenched teeth.

I looked at Neil to see if I could tell what he was going to do. I could see from his eyes that he was still clearheaded, at least.

"So you're throwing a jealous fit at me over a girl you didn't give a shit about yesterday? Do you hear yourself? You're pathetic, Hudson," Neil said bluntly.

Xavier shook his head, annoyed. "You're the pathetic one!" he shot back immediately. "Leading on all these little goody-goodies who come your way, using them for as long as you feel like, and then tossing them aside when you're tired of them. You should share some of those interesting anecdotes from your past with Babydoll here. Let her get a real look at who you are, and we'll see if she keeps on spreading for you then!" Xavier spat at him.

I cringed back instinctively at the violence in his tone. A few people clustered around the exterior of the club started throwing curious looks at us. Neil spotted them and glowered at Xavier, a look so grim that it even scared me.

"Go back inside, Xavier," he said in a low, measured, but nonetheless menacing voice. Xavier, not at all intimidated, appeared to be considering his next move.

It was a clash of the titans, and either one of them could have come out on top.

"And what are you gonna do if I don't? Hit me?" Xavier goaded him, and Neil quirked up a corner of his mouth, an arrogant smile.

"I don't want to hurt you. I wouldn't be able to recognize your face afterward, and I'd feel bad," he answered firmly. Then he moved over to me, and without any warning, took me by the wrist. "You come with me, though," he demanded.

Was he seriously expecting me to just follow him after what his blond said to me?

"Forget that!" I jerked away from him, and he shot me an annoyed look, like he was so put out by my disobedience. "Go see your sidepiece. She'll know how to keep you entertained." I gave him an insolent grin and tried to step away, but his strong, confining hand was locked around my arm, and he stopped me again. I glared first at those possessive fingers and then into the golden eyes that were watching my face with their usual cool aloofness.

"That wasn't what you think," he explained, and I burst out laughing.

Did he think I was stupid?

"Oh, for sure. You accidentally tripped and fell, first into one of them and then into the other." I continued laughing hysterically. In reality, I was trying to conceal the pain that carved up my heart behind a facade of insolence.

Neil remained serious, and I caught a brief flash of distress in his eyes as well. For the first time all night, he looked ashamed.

"It happened right after you called me," he said in a rush. "I was training with the heavy bag. I was alone and didn't feel like calling anyone. You said all that stuff to me and—" I cut him off furiously.

"Are you saying it was my fault? Seriously?" I scoffed. It felt like his fingers were burning into my skin. "You gave in because you're a pervert and vanilla sex isn't enough for you. We both know it. Apparently, the idea of focusing on just one woman is too scary for you," I burst out, electrified with rage.

"Quit it," he warned me in a threatening whisper. I could feel his hot breath against my lips. I could smell the smoke on his breath. But I would not allow myself to be distracted by the electricity that passed between our bodies, even in a moment like that, and I went on.

"Or what? You going to offer me another threesome with your blond like you did at the Halloween party? This time, invite Xavier along so I get something out of the experience too," I answered contemptuously.

There was no stopping me; it all burst out of me like a river flooding its banks. Memories, disappointments, suffering—it had made me reactive and irrational like I'd never been before.

Neil's eyes changed color; they appeared to grow less brilliant and duller. My breathing sped up as he moved so close to me that he grazed my nose with his own.

"You will come with me. Stop being a fucking brat," he ordered. He breathed in my scent, and his eyelashes fluttered. He gave me a small, crafty half-smile. "You don't want to piss me off, Tinkerbell." He took my chin with his other hand and held it tightly. Then, without any warning, he gave my cheek one languid lick, holding me still the whole time. "Be good," he concluded hypnotically after this show of possession, strange and animalistic as it was. I should have been irritated, offended, and disgusted, but instead his voice and actions had a lulling effect on me. My body relaxed, and my muscles stopped putting up a fight against him. The hitch in my breath told him exactly how a strange kind of need had replaced all the emotions I had just been feeling.

Lust had taken hold of me.

It was obvious from the blush that reddened my cheekbones and the way I was moving so sluggishly on my legs.

He looked at me, pleased with himself. He knew exactly what I was feeling.

Neil was hyperaware of my physical reactions, and when he was trying to seduce me, he made sure to hit all of them so he could bend me to his will.

With all his experience, it was easy for him to get the upper hand, and it all made me feel so helpless.

"Let's go." He pulled me along by the arm, passing Xavier, who had been standing there motionless, just watching our interaction. Then he led me out to his car and never let go of my arm, despite my complete surrender. Maybe he was still afraid I was going to make a run for it?

"You're a lunatic," I murmured, tripping along in my high heels. It was intended as an insult, but he just smiled.

"And you are my Tinkerbell," he said cheerfully before unlocking the Maserati, opening the passenger door, and ushering me inside.

Though I persisted in fighting this war against him, I couldn't help but follow him into his darkness, promising him my mute, sincere love.

Day after day, Neil wove his golden threads around me, imprisoning me.

He didn't just dominate my body; he dominated my mind and heart as well.

My soul belonged entirely to him.

It had belonged to him since the first time that I'd been caught in that enigmatic stare.

His looks bewitched me.

His mature voice awakened my most sinful carnal desires.

I was his.

It was an enormous problem for which there was no cure.

9

> "Even though he was a train wreck of a man,
> as grim as the abyss and as unpredictable
> as a storm at sea, I loved the bitter, savage,
> indomitable creature that lived within him."

SELENE

We'd been back at the penthouse apartment for about five minutes.

We hadn't even tried to talk in the car; I was too uncomfortable and disappointed, and Neil just didn't like to talk unless he had to.

I watched attentively as he peered into the refrigerator, searching for something to eat. The doorless arch between the two rooms gave me a view right into the kitchen and allowed me to watch his every movement. He'd already taken off his leather jacket and tossed it onto the couch a few moments before while I stood in the living room still wearing my own coat. I was furious about what Jennifer had told me and by the way Neil himself had behaved, but he seemed to be much more interested in getting a snack. Must be nice; my stomach was closed up tight.

"You hungry?" he asked, pulling out a bottle of water and setting it down on the kitchen counter.

"No," I answered tartly, letting him know I wanted his undivided attention.

But Neil still seemed uninterested. He grabbed a glass and poured himself some water, which he then sipped in an attitude of total calm. I watched his Adam's apple bob, his arm flexing, and his biceps contracting as he drank. I couldn't tell if the white sweater he wore was too tight on him or if he'd just been working out extra hard. I thought about how often I'd dismissed guys in the past for being too muscular or too polished. Neil didn't take it to excess, though.

His powerful physique was in good proportion with his height, his broad shoulders making him imposing from all angles.

Once again, I felt love constricting my heart as I admired him in a daze. He noticed, putting the glass down on the counter and giving me a smug look.

I was probably just standing there slack-jawed. Damn it!

"You shouldn't have let Jennifer sit on your lap!" I blurted out. I just couldn't keep holding back the jealousy I'd been fighting for so long. "And you shouldn't have had sex with her and Alexia, my God!" I passed a hand through my hair while Neil just furrowed his brow and looked at me in confusion. I usually tried to hide my anger and control the possessiveness I felt over him, but after everything we had been through, after he'd shared parts of his past and finally told me about Kimberly, I deserved a little more consideration from him. "How can you stand to touch other people the same way you touch me? How?" I lashed out at him, stabbing a finger in his direction. I felt like I was burning up, and the fabric of my coat suddenly seemed too tight for my body.

I felt like slapping Neil in the face and getting out of this penthouse.

From the way he was watching me, I knew he could see all the despair I was feeling in my eyes.

He was capable of reflection; he knew perfectly well why that despair was there.

He sighed and rested his hands on the kitchen island, rounding his shoulders slightly. It was going to be difficult for me to calm down, and he knew that. He could not continue to diminish what there was between us. Whatever the true nature of it was, it was clear to both of us that some sort of bond connected us, so he needed to give me a valid reason why he'd done the things he'd done.

"It's hard to explain," he answered, his tone flat.

"Try," I prompted him, trying to catch my breath after my outburst.

"I don't just have sex with anyone," he began, trying to clarify the issue for me. "I need to have sex with women who remind me of her..." He looked down at the counter to avoid looking me in the eye.

"Her?" I asked, confused.

"Kimberley. She was blond, shameless, bold, and... I always pick women who look like her..." His jaw clenched uncomfortably. It obviously wasn't easy for him to tell me this, but I needed to know all of it if I was going to understand him and the sides of himself that he'd kept hidden from the very beginning.

"Why? You should be trying to forget her, not forcing yourself to remember. It doesn't make sense," I said, trying to make my voice less accusatory and more nonconfrontational so he might feel a little more comfortable.

If he retreated into his shell again, he'd stop talking to me entirely.

"It makes sense to me," he answered, raising his eyes to my face. He stared bitterly at me, probably because he thought I was about to judge him. I knew how he couldn't stand that. "I need to reverse the roles, to squash that feeling of emptiness that presses down on me every day. I need to show myself that no one's ever going to be able to bend me to their will ever again. The violence I experienced wasn't just physical; it was psychological too. My dignity was ground down, my soul was violated, and my childhood was stolen from me, and I can never get it back. Kimberly is the monster that lives inside my head, and I'll never get rid of her," he said in a soft, resigned voice, allowing his head to hang down.

With each word, my heart bled for him. I didn't know what to say. All I wanted to do was go to him and wrap my arms around him to show him that I'd always be with him. I stayed right where I was, though, so he couldn't push me away.

He didn't like to be touched, especially when he was feeling emotionally exposed.

"Can I ask you a question?" I said, breaking the silence. There was something I'd been wondering about for a long time, and perhaps, finally, this was the moment to ask.

"Ask it," he said seriously. He rounded the kitchen island to get closer. My heart began to beat wildly against my chest; his sensuality beguiled me, and my knees went weak. He stopped right in front of me, waiting for my response.

"With me..." I cleared my throat, trying to banish my embarrassment. "Did you ever think about Kim...when we were..." I trailed off; it was obvious what I was talking about.

He furrowed his brow, and I hoped I hadn't been too invasive or indelicate. With Neil, I never knew when I might be hitting a sore spot or how to address it with him. His mood shifted so easily and shut down our conversations.

He watched me attentively in that moment. I should have been ashamed of myself for how weak he made me with just a look, but I couldn't resist him. Just like I couldn't truly get angry at him, hate him, or try to hurt him.

He was becoming everything to me.

"No. Not with you," he answered, after a few moments of reflection. "That never happened."

I heaved a sigh of relief and looked down, flushing. He could have told me something else, if only to hurt me, but he'd given me the truth. I knew in my heart he wasn't lying to me.

"This is going to sound nuts, but..." he went on, rubbing the slightly scruffy jaw that made him look so savagely appealing. "My brain is very complicated, especially after everything that happened to me. To understand what I mean, picture a line going up and down..." He raised a hand, tracing an imaginary line in the air in front of me. "On this line is making out, sex, carnal contact of any kind, pleasurable things, obscene things, everything that was done to me and what I like to do..." he told me coolly, staring intently at me to make sure I was following what he was saying.

"And, for me, that is normalcy," he told me nonchalantly. "Then there's this straight line." He drew another imaginary line through the air. "On this one, we have sweet kisses, gentle touches, compliments, attention, relationships, and love. All the regular stuff. The actually normal stuff. The stuff that, for me, doesn't exist," he explained, lowering his arm. My eyes stayed fixed on the empty space where he had sketched those two lines.

I furrowed my brow. "I don't understand, Neil. What is my role in all of this?" I asked softly as he looked at me, his eyes hooded in a pensive expression.

"You make my waving line less miserable." He drew closer to me, and I held my breath as he caressed my cheek. His touch was gentle, completely unlike the passionate, hard-driving touches he usually gave me. "When I'm with you, for a little while at least, Kim isn't in my head. You're a pleasurable distraction, Babygirl, like a pill that dulls the pain for a little while. But she's still there; she lives inside me. I can't pretend that I've gotten over what she did to me. I'm still just a pile of broken shards..." He smiled so sadly, and I wanted to cry. "My line is going to stay wavy; it's never going to straighten out...you understand that, right? I might have the...

wrong perspective on life, but I've had it since I was little. It's a part of me now..." His eyes bored into mine, waiting for me to say something—anything.

"So being with me is a need you have? I'm sorry. I'm not trying to insult you. I just want to understand..." I was being cautious, lest our conversation turn into an argument. Neil continued to stroke my cheek, his knuckles moving delicately over my skin, and I wanted to feel his warm touch on me forever.

"Yes. It's a distraction, a way to block out the memories and stifle the pain. You allow me to have a moment of relief; you let me soar to your Neverland, but that's not enough to cure me. The reality is something else, and we can't do anything to change it," he concluded, breaking off contact with me. "That's why I can't give you a relationship. I know I've got too many problems in here..." he tapped his index finger against his temple. "How can I care for someone else when I can't even take care of myself?" He turned away from me, shaking his head.

I was overwhelmed by emotion. Speechless, perhaps because there was nothing to say in the wake of a powerful confession like that. Neil pulled his pack of Winstons out of his discarded jacket and grabbed a cigarette. I just kept staring at him as he stood there by the coffee table, watching as he tried to control the tremor in his right hand that was keeping him from holding the lighter steadily against the end of the cigarette.

I'd noticed his hand shaking before, but I'd never dared to ask him about it.

I knew, deep down, that I was seeing the worst of him.

The disappointed part.

The worn-down part.

The part that everyone avoided.

The part that everyone feared.

The worst of him.

I was learning to love the worst of him.

Just like I would love the best of him.

I could wait for his sweetness.

I could wait for his sadness to fade.

I could wait for the sun to rise inside of him.

Everyone would see his worth, and I'd be right there beside him.

And maybe…one day…he might fall in love with me.

But, until then, I would fight. For me and for him.

I would love him in silence.

"What are you thinking about?" Neil asked, and I jumped. I hadn't realized he'd gotten so close to me again. His lit cigarette hung from his lips as he watched me with a frown. There was no way I could tell him what was actually going on in my head.

Silent love was all that I could give him until he was capable of accepting what I felt for him. Though I still thought it was crazy that he could be content without giving or receiving feelings.

"Just that I'm glad you talked to me. When I asked if I could be with you, that was exactly what I meant: I want you to communicate with me, tell me more about yourself, and put a little more of your trust in me. Thank you for doing that." I gave him a small, shaky smile. His eyes slipped down to my lips, and my reaction was immediate.

I went red all over again. His fresh scent mingled with the dissipating smoke in the air warmed me all over. I could never really be in control of myself when I was close to him because my very soul was caught in his stare. "I think I'd better get changed and go to bed now," I added quickly.

In reality, I wanted nothing more than for him to follow me to my room and make love to me, but I couldn't allow myself to give in to him after what happened with Jennifer.

He had to learn that he couldn't have me whenever he wanted and that I deserved to be shown some respect.

"Get undressed right here, in front of me," he ordered, making me shiver. "I know you're wearing different underwear than usual. Show them to me." He looked at me, his face full of expectation, and then leaned back on the kitchen island, waiting for me to obey him. How did he guess about the lingerie? Maybe he could tell because my dress was so tight?

"I'll undress, but you can't touch me," I said clearly, though the need to feel his hands on me was nearly overwhelming.

Neil looked annoyed at my peremptory tone, but I didn't care. I had my own dignity to defend, and I was going to do so, starting right now.

Did he really want me?

Then he'd have to give up all the rest of them.

"Okay," he agreed, stubbing out the cigarette in a nearby ashtray. He blew out the last of the smoke through his nose and folded his arms over his chest, adopting a casual stance. Obviously, he was ready to enjoy the show. I felt a little awkward because Neil knew so much about dazzling a woman, but I tried to get a hold on my feelings of inadequacy.

I had learned what he liked and how to make him feel good.

First, I slipped off my coat and tossed it on the sofa.

Then I bent one arm behind my back and unzipped the dress. Then I slowly let the sleeves fall, allowing the garment to slip down over my hips and legs until it was just a puddle of fabric around my ankles. Neil narrowed his eyes and looked me up and down, lingering over my breasts, squeezed into white lace. The deep breath that made his chest swell told me that my body was having the same effect on him that his muscles had on me, and I was pleased.

I lifted first one leg and then the other to step out of the dress, balancing on my high heels, sexy lingerie, and thigh-highs in full view just like he'd wanted.

As long as I wasn't completely naked, I could hold on to some self-confidence.

Neil rubbed his lower lip with his index finger while his other hand clutched his bicep.

What was he thinking? Did he like it? Or no?

Then, he focused in on some of the visible bruises on my skin, and his forehead wrinkled, giving him a more glowering expression. I had the vague suspicion that he was chastising himself for putting those bruises there.

Then, he rose and moved toward me.

Everything about him—his catlike stride, his magnetic stare, and his lips tipped up into an alluring smile—made me think he was about to do or say something that was going to embarrass me.

My knees went weak as he cut the distance between us.

When he stopped right in front of me, I stopped breathing.

Even with the heels, I wasn't at eye level with him, so I still had to tilt my head back to look him in the face.

Neil looked me over from head to toe and let out a groan.

"White lingerie…" he murmured. "I like it," he added.

A compliment; I could hardly believe it.

"Wow, I feel honored," I joked, trying to deflate some of the erotic tension that had arisen between us, but he ignored me, concentrating instead on my body.

Abruptly, he raised his hand, and with one index finger he traced the contour of my cheek. My breath caught at the motion.

He had broken his promise, but I wasn't mad about it.

Neil drew a trail down my throat, moving into the space between my breasts, and slowly descended to my abdomen, stopping just below the waistband of my panties. I tightened my abdominal muscles slightly at the seductive brush of his hand and shivered when he circled my navel with a finger.

"I know all your erogenous zones, Babygirl. Every time I've fucked you, I've paid close attention to what you like…" He drew his index finger back up to the place between my breasts and, this time, ventured further out to circle my nipple, which stiffened against the white fabric. Neil was good with his hands; he knew how to seduce a woman and make her want him. I had to hold myself back from begging him to continue touching me.

He leaned in close to my ear and breathed in my scent. "And how you like it...," he whispered, dragging his hand away from my breast.

He stared deep into my eyes, his blown pupils betraying the arousal that coursed through him, the same kind he had kindled in me.

The urge to fall upon each other was palpable as we stood there trading breaths. We just stared at each other's lips, tempted to kiss.

"Now I get to see another side of you, Tinkerbell," he told me with an insolent smile. "My favorite side," he went on wickedly, and finally it dawned on me what he was talking about.

It would be embarrassing to turn around to leave now, and Neil had realized that because he stepped around until he stood behind me. I couldn't see him looking, but I could feel his eyes burning a hole into my back and further down. He let out a small, guttural noise of satisfaction, and I blushed.

Fortunately, he wasn't in a position to see it.

"Your ass, Babygirl..." His voice deepened my arousal. "Is absolutely my weakness," he noted with approval before moving back to face me, scrutinizing me with those golden eyes as though he were a god prepared to judge some poor human subject.

"If you like it so much, I don't see why you go looking for other people's," I taunted him with a self-assurance that surprised me. He raised one eyebrow, and then he laughed cheerfully.

What was so funny about what I said?

"You've just made me a dangerous proposition..." He bit his lip and moved closer to me until he could actually put his hands on my ass. He cupped my cheeks and pulled me forward until I was plastered against him. The warm material of his sweater against my bare skin thrilled me, and I gasped when I felt his erection pressing into my lower abdomen. "Do you even know what you offered?" he asked me, and I blinked in confusion.

What was he talking about? By now, I had completely lost my train of thought due to his fingers kneading my buttocks.

I was telling him that if he liked my body, he should pick me and not anyone else, and then...

"Oh God, no!" I exclaimed. In a moment of clarity, I realized just what the hell he was thinking. "No... No, I didn't mean that... I mean... I..." I descended into total panic. I put my trembling hands against his pectorals and grabbed hold of his sweater in agitation. I flushed violently, and all my confidence vanished in the face of the knowledge that Neil was still using my naivete to mess with me.

"When you're ready, I'll take this too," he whispered against my lips, tightening his hold on my butt. "But not tonight..." He gave me a chaste kiss and released me. I gave him a disapproving look and smiled smugly back, perfectly aware that he'd one day coax me into even more indecent acts, things I'd never even thought about. Though maybe it was especially important for a man—a way to reach a greater level of intimacy with his woman.

With his woman...

I pondered this.

Neil did not think of me as his; he'd never said that he did. Therefore, I was not required to satisfy his every wish, even if it went against my own wants. If he'd been willing to give me exclusivity, he'd be able to take even more from me than I'd already given him.

"I want to go to sleep now. Preferably alone," I told him in a tone that brooked no argument. Neil watched me, unreadable as always, and I scooped up my dress from the floor. "Goodnight," I added seriously.

I turned and strode elegantly away on the high heels I couldn't wait to remove.

I knew that his eyes were locked on my backside. He might have been hurt by my refusal, but even if he was, his pride would never allow him to show it.

But I didn't care.

I left him there, alone and aroused.

And achieved, for once, a small victory.

....

I couldn't figure out why, when the night came, my mind felt the need to turn over everything that had happened during the day. But, as it did so, I saw things differently and came to conclusions I hadn't understood before. Neil had talked to me; he had explained his fixation on blond women, and I, like a sulky child, had held on to the Jennifer and Alexia issue and refused to touch him.

He had given me something of himself, and I had given him nothing in return.

Our deal...damn it!

Could I really have been so thoughtless?

Overcome, I rolled over on my side and pulled the blankets around me. The room was enormous, dark, and solitary. Not a single sound disrupted the silence, except for the rustling of the sheets whenever I moved. I was chilly under the vast comforter because I had forgotten to bring my pajamas from Detroit, so I was still in just my underwear. I sighed, staring out into the void before me. A small alarm clock on the bedside table read 1:20 a.m. in blinking blue lights.

Neil hadn't come to my room after our conversation. He knew that my door wasn't locked, so he could have come in at any time if he'd wanted. But he hadn't done that.

Did that make me feel happy? Relieved? Sad?

I wasn't sure. The only thing I knew for sure was that my head was too stuffed with negative thoughts to close my eyes.

What if he stopped wanting me? What if he sought out other people because he didn't think I was at his level?

"Will you shut up and let me sleep?" I murmured to my brain, rubbing my forehead. If I kept going like this, I was going to get a severe headache.

Before I went to bed, I called my mother to reassure her and make my big lie as believable as possible, telling her that I was having fun with Bailey.

But what was I even doing in New York?

I still didn't see why Neil had asked me to meet him, which only made me worry more. He told me that I didn't know enough about him, but what did he mean by that?

Enough! For God's sake!

I huffed and forced myself to shut my eyes.

I would think more tomorrow about how to talk with him—it wasn't a simple thing to do. I couldn't always figure out his strange reasoning, like the thing with the wavy line and the straight one. I made a skeptical face, having no idea whether I'd understood his reasoning correctly. He had likened the wavy line to all that was unstable, everything that regular people might think of as questionable: treating women like objects, sex without feelings, a hatred of love, a refusal to enter into relationships, and an unconventional approach to sex. Meanwhile, the straight line represented morality, restraint, modesty, love in the universal sense...basically everything that he couldn't tolerate and didn't fit into his life.

Yes...maybe that was the point of his speech, and it was just his way of telling me.

"You're so strange," I whispered, aware that he couldn't hear me. "But I'll never stop thinking you are special, Neil." I smiled as I felt my cheeks heat up. I really was falling for—or worse, was actually in love with—this mess of a man. With another insane mood shift, this time more positive, I closed my eyes and fell asleep.

I became restless several times in the night.

I would open my eyelids just a crack, just enough to see the silvery moonlight filtering into the dark of the room, and then go back to sleep. I didn't feel entirely at ease, maybe because I was by myself.

Far away from home in a giant penthouse apartment, in this impersonal room with an odd man, who could say where he'd ended up?

Suddenly, I felt something depress the mattress behind me and the blankets shifted.

I was too deep in an intense stupor to pay closer attention to my surroundings.

It wasn't cold anymore, and I had a nice feeling in my chest, like when I was a little girl and felt completely safe and protected.

There was something heavy lying across my side; it felt just like a strong, powerful arm, but I didn't investigate, just squirmed closer to the new heat source at my back.

It was probably a dream, but I liked the idea of Neil being there with me; it made me feel good. In dreams, anything could happen, and it always felt real while you were dreaming.

There, if nowhere else, I could pretend that I was his.

And there, Peter Pan could pick Tinkerbell.

Content, I drifted back into unconsciousness for an unknown amount of time until the body behind me shifted, startling me. My eyelids opened a sliver; my back was much warmer, as were my hands.

"Neil..." I said in a sleepy rumble. Immediately, my mind went to him, but I got no verbal response. I did, however, feel something hard poking into my back. Something stiff and enormous. "Neil," I said again, uncertain. I was still trying to figure out if I was awake or asleep, much less determine details about anything else.

"Tinkerbell," he answered, his voice intense, low, and rasping. I blinked in surprise and smiled as he gently pulled me closer to him. "You need to wake up," he whispered. He stroked my ribs and then moved slowly down my thigh. Once again, I lay motionless, welcoming his soft caress.

It was so nice...

A blazing heat began to spread from my heart to the place between my thighs, which I rubbed together.

"Still sleepy," I whispered. He chuckled, and his hot, voracious mouth grazed my neck. I raised my hand to shoo him away and heard another amused chuckle from behind me.

"So lazy..." he muttered cajolingly. Still half-asleep at that point, I turned over and peered at his face in the half-dark. Despite not being fully awake, I still had a sense of what his intentions were.

"What are you doing here?" I asked him, but he shushed me quickly.

"You know I get frequent carnal urges..." Neil kissed my cheek and stroked along my ribcage before moving on to the area between my breasts and then down...to my stomach. I opened my eyes wide then but was still unable to see what I was looking for: his face.

"What...what time is it?" I stuttered confusedly, and he nibbled my neck.

"About four thirty. And you've done nothing but grind that sweet little ass against me, Tinkerbell," he said in a sensual whisper, trying to defend his own state of arousal.

How long had he been in my bed?

I slid my fingers into his hair and stroked it while his lips meandered slowly down my throat.

I let him do it.

"And what if I don't want to indulge you?" I decided to needle him just a bit; it was never a bad idea for a woman to make herself a little more enticing.

"Have I ever fucked you or even touched you without your consent?" he whispered into my ear, biting down on the lobe, and my breath caught. Why did he always have to talk like that? But I loved his words, no matter how crude or rough.

"No, never," I answered unhesitatingly.

"Then I'm not going to start now," he clarified, continuing his languid caresses all over my body. "But the thing is, you want me every bit as much as I want you..." His hand drifted slowly down to my pelvis and slid beneath my panties, searching for confirmation of his words. I tensed up as he explored that intimate place with a wickedness calculated precisely to arouse my desire.

At the same time, I felt the rough skin of his cheek graze me as his lips sought out mine. He sucked hard, and I let out a gasp, my hips automatically moving against his hand. In the dark of the night our breaths chased one another. My muscles were tired and thick, but Neil was so firm yet delicate that he kept me suspended between dream and reality.

He could be less aggressive when he worked at it, but I knew that, soon enough, his savage side would emerge.

Abruptly, he brushed my mouth with his tongue and stole a kiss. His other hand, meanwhile, continued to stroke between my thighs. He pressed the heel of his hand against my mons to stimulate my clit before sliding two fingers inside me. It was a game of lust, slow and sensual, that had me kissing him back with passion, just as he wanted.

I groaned and strained in the darkness to catch his stormy golden eyes, but the shadows were too thick to see his face.

He abruptly stopped kissing me—though he didn't stop touching me—and sighed, rubbing the tip of my nose with his own.

"Should I go on, or do you want me to stop?" he asked mockingly, delighted by my physical reactions and well aware of how aroused I had become. I gave him a swat on the bicep that must have felt more like a caress to him.

"Keep going," I answered in a shy voice. Neil accepted my

invitation immediately and moved rapidly in the darkness. I felt his hands grope for my hips to pull off my panties. I raised my pelvis to help him and felt the fabric gliding down my thighs. Once he'd taken them off, he slowly traced a finger over the contours of me. He seemed to be studying me, like a sculptor might his masterpiece.

He meandered over the soft slopes of my body, searching for my bra clasp. He unfastened it deftly as soon as he found it, inviting me to take it off entirely. His every movement was certain and confident.

He didn't say a word, but with one abrupt movement, he flipped me over.

I let out a surprised cry at finding myself suddenly on my stomach, my breasts compressed against the mattress.

I had briefly hoped that he wouldn't choose this position again. It felt like he was still trying to overpower me, to bring me to heel and leave me no escape.

He forced my hips up, arranging me until my face was pressed to the pillow, my back arched, and my butt in the air. He maneuvered me easily, manipulating me the way he liked, and I lay there, completely exposed to him and his cock, which rested stiff and hot along the cleft of my ass. Then he began to move languidly, preparing us both for what was about to happen.

I tried to prop myself up on my elbows, but even with one hand, Neil pushed me back down easily. The message was clear: He wanted me to hold still.

"You are unbearable when you get like this," I grumbled against the softness of the pillow. When he decided that he wanted me, there was nothing I could do to turn him away.

He drew one finger down the curve of my spine, provoking a series of intoxicating chills. My muscles were all subject to his touch, tortured in his inferno. Neil leaned over me, his warm breath touching me, and he began to kiss down my body from the nape of my neck. He proceeded delicately down my back until he arrived at my butt cheek, which he bit. I flinched in shock, and he massaged the sore spot, not realizing the ferocious pleasure it had kindled in me.

"I've been thinking about this all night." His sultry voice diffused through the darkness, making everything feel surreal. "The men in that club were panting after you, wanting to touch you, but I'm the only one who can have you. Remember that, Tinkerbell," he told me forcefully.

I smiled slightly, and he grasped my hair in his fist, using it to tilt my neck back. I gasped at the ferocity of the movement. "You are *my* Neverland," he said with feral possessiveness. I felt his breath again, tickling my ear this time. "...never stop," he finished assertively, then I felt his penis nudging between my butt cheeks, right up against the spot that had never been breached by anyone. I held my breath and went rigid. I was nowhere near ready for that next step, and Neil seemed to sense that, moving down to my thighs to tease my pussy, which was waiting eagerly there for him.

I sighed with relief, and he laughed at me.

He was probably delighted to have alarmed me, like my heart wasn't pounding hard enough in my ears already.

When his laughter died down, I realized what was about to happen.

He thrust inside me with one decisive stroke, finally pulling me completely out of slumber. He demanded my full attention. My toes curled, and I screamed, but not in pain. I curved against him, and Neil emitted a raspy groan. He filled me completely and then held himself there motionless for a moment.

He stretched out over me, one hand still clasping my hair, and pulled back his hips to give me that first vigorous thrust.

So, caged beneath him, I was conquered and captured by his body, incapable of moving or fighting.

It was as though I had a god between my thighs.

A shiver passed through me. Neil knew that I was ready for him; he could feel how wet I was for him and how perfectly I reshaped myself around his powerful erection.

Then, he began to move.

It was marvelous to hear his panting breaths, his chest like marble gliding against my back, and the movements of his hips getting stronger and more relentless.

Pleasure, passionate and undeniable, spread from the middle of my chest out to my nipples.

I started sweating and tightening around him in an attempt to sate his endless hunger, his constant desire.

Feeling him in such an intense, enveloping way knocked me off kilter, just like it always did.

I bit my lip to keep from moaning aloud, though it was almost impossible to resist.

"Speak up, Tinkerbell. I want to hear the pleasure you get with me, but especially…from me," he murmured into my ear before slapping my ass, and it was impossible not to scream at that point. Neil laughed, proud of himself, and I pushed aside my prudish sensibilities to give myself over to him.

I felt so full of Neil, I even feared that I was already about to climax.

I knew how it was going to end: I would beg him for relief, and he would deny me until he'd completely worn me out. His movement wracked me like a wild tempest; each powerful stroke between my thighs was like a bolt of lightning.

Neil slipped a hand along my abdomen, moving up to my breast, and pinched one nipple between his fingers so hard that I couldn't breathe. I went stiff. My body accepted his thrusts, trying to stand up against the energetic assault. Only when he pulled out for a momentary pause was I able to catch another breath, but that was such a fleeting instant that I didn't really get time to enjoy it.

He slid back into me and moved into another brutal series of thrusts, determined to make me explode. I felt that my life was inextricably tied to his, the way light is tied to the stars.

Neil was a dark knight taking hold of my plumage; he pierced me like a lance, and he slashed me like a sword.

He sucked the soul from me like an insatiable beast, and my intoxicating orgasm broke over me without warning.

It was as devastating as it was unexpected.

I clamped around him again and again, enveloping him completely as I came. I shook all over as I tried to catch my breath.

I knew Neil wasn't going to stop, though—my response only made him more eager.

He kept fervently pounding me into the bed, taking advantage of my body's lassitude and my wetness to speed up his strokes and prolong the pleasure.

Annihilated by this lusty passion, I groaned and squeezed my eyes shut.

It was too much for me.

Neil could make me lose my mind and could make me rage, dream, and hope for an us that might never exist. I was aroused by the physical sensations and irrepressible feelings that he gave me, but I would have liked our contact to be more intimate. I wanted to kiss and touch him to really forge an emotional connection, but he seemed to be focused exclusively on branding me as his. I sometimes found his ferocity unnerving, but when I heard his quiet panting, I knew it was the sound of a man who was truly getting pleasure from me.

He was there with me, mind and soul.

I could sense the understanding between us.

His toned chest hovered over me, and I couldn't move a muscle. My heart was beating like a wild thing. For a moment, I had the urge to wriggle out of his hold, to push him off me, and to flee from his savage ardor, but I dismissed that idea quickly because I knew that I could not help *myself*.

Neil wasn't just a guy who knew what to do in bed, who could make himself and a woman feel good—he was so much more than that.

He was a universe of secrets, an unexplored landscape, a puzzle with no easy solution.

He was an abyss of chaos and disorder.

Of loneliness and strangeness.

Every time he gave himself to me, I realized all over again why so many others had fallen for him.

I called his name until, with a few final savage thrusts, he stopped.

He clutched the sheet in one hand, the other still clasping my messy hair, and then his body stiffened. His climax came with a guttural shout, and hot jets of cum shot deep inside me. His orgasm was so powerful and vivid that it shook the both of us. He slumped on top of me, exhausted. His chest heaved relentlessly, his breathing went wild, his body was tense and sweaty, and he weighed heavy on my back for a few seconds while his penis remained inside me, unmoving.

We both stayed silent, just basking in the union of our heated bodies.

Neil was satisfied to have fed his unhealthy appetite, while I was feeling pretty pleased with myself that such an attractive man wanted me enough to sneak into my bed in the middle of the night.

Even though he was a train wreck of a man, as grim as the abyss and as unpredictable as a storm at sea, I loved the bitter, savage, indomitable creature that lived within him.

How long was I to remain this incurable lunatic?

How long was I going to let him devour my flesh to sate his desires?

Was there some way to recover from love?

What if he was my cure?

After what felt like an eternity, I squirmed a little to let him know that he was crushing me with his weight. Neil propped himself up on one elbow and stroked my hair. I could barely make out his face from that position, while he must have been looking at my profile.

There could be no eye contact between us, and I was glad for it.

I was so twisted up inside that I would have been embarrassed to be analyzed by his devastating eyes.

"Everything okay, Tinkerbell?" he murmured with a hint of irony.

He was worried about me?

I just nodded, though I knew that I'd have more bruises when I woke up the next morning. I felt like I was on fire, and I was tired and sore, but I loved every part of him, even the aggressive, passionate parts.

Neil was a wild animal, impossible to domesticate.

He had a cold heart and an overpowering personality.

No one could contain such a rebellious creature.

"I like it when you can't speak," he chuckled, gathering my hair into a loose ponytail. My skin stung from the way he'd gripped it in his fist at the height of his climax, and not even his tenderness afterward was enough to soothe the ache.

He kissed the nape of my neck, trailing his moist lips down between my shoulder blades.

I sighed gently to let him know that I appreciated the unexpected cuddling, and Neil abruptly stopped his caresses.

He pushed himself up off me, and I could feel the absence of his body.

He'd barely moved, and already I was missing him.

"Neil." I sought him out in the darkness, using the faint moonlight to help. But my eyelids were heavy, and my head was spinning. When I sensed him next to me, however, I quieted.

He was still there.

I rolled over onto my side, wincing at a twinge of pain between my legs, and eased myself down onto his chest. I heard him suck in a breath, but I didn't care if he didn't want to be touched just then. I needed him, and the sooner he realized I was nothing to be afraid of, the better. I breathed in his smell and rested my hand on his tightened abdomen, feeling the defined muscles there. The back of my hand brushed against his member where it curved up from his groin. Then I wrapped my hand around it and gave it an impish stroke.

It was warm and wet to the touch.

I rotated my thumb around the glans, his most sensitive area, and he let out a moan.

"You want to give him a little more attention, Babygirl? Give him a half hour to recover, and he'll be looking just as perky as before. Your pussy is more of a lion, you know," he teased, and I let out a laugh.

At times, his unexpected quips would put me in a good mood.

I wished he could always be like that: calm and dryly funny.

I stopped stroking him and rested my hand a little higher up on his side, holding him as tightly as I could.

"For some reason, your sense of humor always surprises me. I guess I'll have to get used to it," I answered, amused, resting my head against his pecs. Neil wrapped his arm around my shoulders and pulled the covers up over us. I was trembling, and he probably thought I was cold, but it was actually just from the powerful feelings I got in proximity to him. My nose brushed against his skin, and I drew it along him, intoxicated. "How do you smell so good even when you're sweaty?" I asked, visibly surprised.

Neil laughed and slowly stroked my arm.

"I took a shower right before I came to see you. I'll have to take another one in a little bit," he murmured.

I occurred to me then that our skin-to-skin contact might be bothering him, and the thought made me sad.

"You can't stand to smell me on you?" I asked, hoping he would say that wasn't the case. I knew that people like Neil who had experienced severe trauma in their childhood often developed unusual behaviors in adulthood.

One very common one was a fixation on cleanliness.

"I can't stand to smell anything on me that's not me," he clarified. The darkness concealed the finer features of his face, but I was certain it had gotten grimmer as he thought about what had happened to him. I decided in that moment that I was going to pull him away from those thoughts and bring him back to the present with me. I raised a hand and felt for his face, rubbing his jaw, which I could feel was tense. The friction of his stubble against my palm raised goosebumps, and from the almost imperceptible motion of his cheek, I suspected he might be smiling. To make sure, I ran my fingers along the edges of his warm, full lips to confirm it. He had pulled one of his mysterious or wicked smiles.

"What is it, Babygirl?" he asked softly, before opening his mouth and trapping my index finger between his teeth playfully. I jumped at the sudden movement and laughed.

"Are you staying here?" I asked, enthralled. When he released my finger from captivity, I continued to trace the lines of his perfect face. I slid along his straight nose, which dominated a face full of firm, masculine features, and, fortunately, he didn't reject my touch. He let me do it.

"If it won't cause you to have delusions about our future relationship, then yes, I'll stay," he answered, blunt as ever.

I was always hopeful at heart for some sort of change in him. The only way he'd be able to truly understand that not all women were like Kimberly would be to actually share his soul with one. But his wounds ran too deep to be healed by an inexperienced girl like me. So I would have to content myself with what he could give me and love him in silence because he wouldn't accept any other sentiment from me.

Once before I had said to him, *"What if I love you?"* And I still hadn't forgotten how that had gone for me. I promised myself that I would never again be explicit about my feelings for him. "Love" was a word he simply did not want to hear, even if I struggled to really understand why.

"Then stay," I answered simply, making myself comfortable on his chest.

"Go to sleep, Babygirl. You have a busy day tomorrow; you're going to see what you're doing here." He stroked my hair, and I relaxed against him. My body was worn-out, and Neil's arms were the only ones that could warm my heart.

He was like a book with a dusty cover that had never been read.

He was a broken record, discarded without ever being heard.

He was a storm with a beautiful sunset on the horizon.

He was the art and imperfection.

He was a good soul trapped in the wrong life.

He was a man trapped in his own world of chaos, but it was also the most beautiful place I'd ever visited, though he couldn't imagine that.

By that point, there was no escape.

I would be his Neverland forever.

And he would be my rebellious Peter Pan.

10

"I wished I could just cling to him forever."

SELENE

I shifted on the fluffy bed.

Soft blankets warmed my body, and my eyelids refused to open up. I felt worn-out and sleepy. It was so nice there with my nose buried in Neil's pecs and one leg tucked between his, that I wished I could just cling to him forever. I opened my eyes slowly just to be really certain that I wasn't dreaming. When I saw that he was truly there, sleeping next to me, I smiled and breathed in his delicious smell.

Shower gel, smoke, and sex.

I exhaled gently, trying not to wake him, even as a shiver of lust went down my back when I saw his every sensual angle pressed against me.

Neil lay beside me, naked and with no protective barriers. I could have taken the opportunity to coax him into another round of lovemaking. The thought of it made me blush, and my nipples, stiffened by my lewd desires, poked into his chest.

He moved very slightly, and only then did I notice his arm slung over my side.

Neil was holding me prisoner, like a dark angel who wanted to trap me inside his eternal damnation. Delighted to have slept beside him, I tried to absorb all the heat that his body could transmit to mine.

He was breathing slowly, his plush mouth slightly swollen from our kisses.

I studied every part of his face: the masculine jaw, the symmetrical nose, and the catlike eyes. I also spotted a tiny mole right below his left eye, and I was proud of myself for having noticed it, despite how minuscule it was.

In sleep, his forehead relaxed. Gone was the little furrow that formed between his eyebrows and made his expression look so perpetually sullen.

I laughed, thinking about how innocent Neil looked in sleep, if nowhere else.

Then, his eyelids fluttered, and I gasped.

What would he have thought if he'd caught me staring slack-jawed at him? Fortunately, I didn't think he'd seen anything. I watched him yawn like a lion waking from a long nap, then he lifted his arms upward and stretched all his muscles. The sheet slipped all the way down to the V around his groin, and I tracked its movement carefully. Another inch and I would have seen him totally bare, because Neil wasn't wearing boxers as he stretched out next to me. I was highly anticipating that I'd see him au naturel in the next few moments.

"Hey, Tinkerbell." His voice was nothing short of incredible first thing in the morning—low and somehow even deeper, so weathered it sounded like it belonged to a much older man. I blushed like an idiot and felt my heart galloping in my chest. Impossible though it was, Neil always provoked the craziest feelings...

"Good morning, Mr. Disaster," I whispered shyly. I wanted to move closer to him for a kiss or maybe even a cuddle, but I forced myself to stay where I was.

With Neil, I was never quite sure where the line was.

He didn't want a relationship; that much was clear to me, but could I at least show him the kind of affection that a woman in love would show her man?

I didn't know, and I was afraid he'd feel pressured if I asked him.

I had to appreciate the little bits Neil was giving me without pushing him or trying to accelerate his timeline.

I should have been trying to be spontaneous, behaving freely, but instead...

There I sat, covering my breasts with a sheet, my head already too busy with thoughts.

I touched my hair, which felt tangled under my fingers, before my distracted gaze caught on something completely unexpected. My eyes went wide as I stared at Neil's crotch area, where a notable, extremely robust bulge was barely concealed by the sheet. I leaned in for a better look, and...yep.

That was a for-real giant erection.

"Ah, it's that time again. I like to call it the Morning Glory." He patted himself between the legs over the sheet to put himself back in order, but that just ended up highlighting his erect cock.

I could not breathe.

Neil was the kind of guy I could only have defined in one word: virile.

"Yeah... I would definitely describe that as a large, majestic..." I babbled awkwardly, "...glory." I cleared my throat and quickly looked away, already feeling my cheeks start to burn.

What the hell was I talking about? I was completely embarrassed, and he chuckled.

I tried to inch away to escape the awkwardness, but Neil grabbed my wrist and tugged me back onto the bed before nimbly hopping on top of me. Without so much as a good morning kiss or a measly little caress, he hit me with one of his provocative smiles. I had some idea of what his intentions were, but I hoped he didn't want a full repeat of the night before—I was still sore.

I closed my eyes and gulped.

He arched his back so I could really feel his stiff member against my crotch. He was trying to seduce me, to make me melt in his hands. I readied myself to take him again, to weather the ferocious thrusts, the hungry hands, and the kisses that stole my breath, but I didn't feel any of that. Slowly, I opened my eyes, and I found him propped up on his elbows, frowning intensely at my neck, then at my breasts, and finally at my hips.

"Have you ever felt like I don't respect your body?" he asked abruptly, his eyes suddenly boring into mine. He sounded unusually serious, and it seemed that I could even detect a hint of worry in his tone. It wasn't easy to parse his question with his body still on top of mine, but I answered him honestly.

"That you don't respect me as a woman? Yes. But my body specifically... no," I admitted. I hoped I was making sense: I felt belittled when he sought out other women while he was with me, but I had never felt like he'd physically violated me or touched me against my will. Even when I pretended to reject his touch, he knew my real desires; he could sense my arousal, and he knew what I wanted.

Every time, we played lion and gazelle, but we both knew how it was always going to turn out.

"So you like the way I am?" he insisted, and he appeared to be genuinely troubled and anxious to hear my response.

"Which part are you talking about?" I asked, and he sighed impatiently.

"In bed... how I am in bed," he specified, and I finally realized what he was trying to have a conversation about.

"Yes..." I managed, a little embarrassed. "Sometimes you can be a bit too..." I paused and tried to find the right word. "Carnal," I said finally. "But I like all of you," I admitted freely, heart on my sleeve. I had accepted him, all his virtues and all his flaws.

He looked skeptically at me for a few seconds before drawing closer to press a kiss to my throat. It was unexpected. The sweet gesture gave me chills, and I dug my hands into his hair as he bent down to kiss one of my breasts as well. He mouthed my nipple, and I moaned, pressing his head into my chest. I loved the passionate way he laid claim to me, even when he was giving me the most basic attentions in an apparently gentle fashion. He proceeded to mark me with his fiery mouth all the way down to my bellybutton, but he froze when he got to my right hip.

I frowned and raised myself up slightly to see what had caught his attention.

Neil was fixated on a bruise there similar to the one on my breast, which was probably similar to the one on my neck as well.

Then I understood the reason for his odd behavior, and he confirmed that thought when he kissed me right on that spot. I sat back comfortably again and waited for him to continue. By then, he was kneeling between my spread legs, rubbing my thighs. My remaining prudishness made me blush at the thought of him looking right into my most intimate place. I grew agitated when he leaned down to pass his tongue along my slit with a seemingly benevolent smile that concealed behind it the desire he felt for me. However, his intention wasn't to pleasure me; he was just stopping for a taste on his way to soothing the bruises on my thighs with more kisses.

His lips drifted down to my knees, and I shivered at the friction of his beard against my skin.

Then he turned his attention back to me, eye to eye.

"I'll give you more of them," he warned, referring to marks caused by his methods of owning me, always too passionate and too wild.

"I don't care. If it helps you express what you feel when you're with me, I can accept that." I caressed his jaw to communicate to him that there was nothing to be afraid of, and he didn't need to feel guilty. His expression darkened, and he sighed.

"You're crazier than me, Babygirl," he grumbled, and I couldn't tell if he was making a joke or earnestly scolding me.

"I'm just very pale with delicate skin." I tried to coax him with a smile, but he shook his head and knelt again, showing me his body in all its beauty. I admired him, wondering what I had done to deserve someone like him, and without meaning to I spoke my thoughts aloud.

"I don't think there are many men who can sense what a woman wants and pleasure her the way you do. You should be shouting it from the rooftops or at least be happy about it," I complimented him before sitting up and finding myself faced with his member, long, semi-hard, and right in front of me. It was catnip for my libido, so I bit my lower lip, trying to keep it under control. Instinctively, I touched his left hip, tracing the shape of the pikorua with my index finger. Neil gasped slightly and tightened his abdomen, but he didn't shake off my touch. I gazed deep into his eyes, trying to show him that I wanted to give him some of what he'd just given me, that I was wild for his body and for him. There was nothing wrong with sharing sexuality with the one you loved, even if that love wasn't necessarily requited. I knew for sure that I'd never let another man touch me because I was in love with Neil and that would never change.

But when I tried to cut to the chase and moved my mouth closer to his hard-on, Neil pulled away. Embarrassment washed over me, and I bent my legs to shield myself. I wrapped a forearm over my breasts and looked down, turning red. I never made the first move, and the one time I decided to give it a try, I got shot down.

Idiot!

"Tinkerbell." Neil tilted my chin up with his fingertip, forcing me to look at him.

He observed me with an indulgent smile, tracing the contours of my lips with his thumb in an attempt to dispel some of my embarrassment.

"I would love to let you do that, trust me...but, x you before, today's going to be a big day," he informed me, bending forward to drop a kiss on the end of my nose. "You will get your mouth on me another time, don't worry. I won't let you get away," he whispered wickedly before letting go of me and getting off the bed.

He gave me a full view of his tight butt as he walked toward the door.

Once alone, I hurled myself back against the pillow and stared up at the ceiling. The air was heavy with our smell, the sheet infused with his masculine odor.

I brought it up to my nose and breathed in his fresh, clean smell.

I had the same one on my skin, and if it were up to me, I wouldn't have washed it off.

It was the only thing I wanted to smell on my skin.

There were times when I feared what I felt for him. My emotions were so powerful and uncontrollable that they often had me doing the most irrational things.

Sighing heavily, I searched around in the bed for my bra and panties. After I slipped them back on, I left as well and headed for the living room.

The air was cool in the penthouse, so walking around half-dressed wasn't a great idea. When I spotted Neil's thick sweater abandoned on the sofa, I picked it up and shrugged it on. It was white, at least three times my size, and it went down all the way to my knees.

I rummaged briefly in the refrigerator, the pantry, and on the shelves in search of something to put in my stomach. I found a half gallon of milk and a few coffee pods that went in the coffee machine.

"Great, no breakfast," I muttered to myself and heard my stomach growl in protest.

What was there to do? After all, nobody was living in the apartment; obviously there wouldn't be any food there. What had I been expecting to find?

My mother's famous pancakes?

Or maybe some of her cherry pie?

I snorted at myself as I instead simply heated up the milk for myself and made a cup of plain black coffee for Neil.

I recalled that he didn't really eat breakfast.

When I was done, I sat down with my big cup of milk and blew on it so I wouldn't burn my mouth.

A few moments later, Neil appeared, wearing just his jeans. I looked him up and down in fascination, lingering over the toki on his bicep just as I'd done in bed with his pikorua. Those were the only two tattoos Neil had, but they both meant something to him and suited him perfectly.

"I made you black coffee, just the way you like it. There isn't anything else." I wrapped my fingers around my mug to warm them. He moved closer, passing a hand through his wet hair, and stared fixedly at me. I cocked my head to one side, trying to figure out what he was looking at when suddenly I remembered his sweater and gasped.

"Oh, I'm sorry. I was cold, and I just put it on without asking your permission; that's probably not cool with you, and that's reasonable... I can take it off right now if you want?" I said, all in one breath. After he'd rejected my advances earlier, all I needed was a good long dressing-down from him to complete my humiliation that morning. But Neil just gave a thoughtful blink, not looking angry at all, just confused and maybe surprised?

"Keep it. I just turned the heater on. All you had to do was ask," he answered shortly, sitting down across from me. He sipped his coffee and didn't thank me for making it or even pay me much attention at all as he got his phone out of his pocket and started texting with some mystery person.

Seriously?

I was there with him after dealing with a long flight and a nearly sleepless night, and he thought he could just ignore me?

I still felt like I'd been hit by a car after the night before and he was chatting with someone else? Worst-case scenario, chatting with another woman.

I tried to reel some of the paranoia back in—I was getting too jealous, too possessive of him. But with Neil, I lived in constant fear of losing him. I gulped my milk down quickly out of nerves and just kept staring at him. Meanwhile, he messed around on his phone, presumably waiting for whoever it was to respond and occasionally typing something in return.

Great...he was super interested in his conversation. "Neil," I called out, setting the cup down hard on the kitchen island. He didn't even dignify the gesture with a look, so I tried again. "Neil!" I was more assertive that time, and his lovely golden eyes shifted from the phone screen to me. Once I had his attention, I should have been firm and decisive. Instead, my mouth just fell silently open, unable to ask him the questions I really wanted to ask.

"Where are we going this morning?" I asked him finally, my voice uncertain. He creased up his forehead, and then, having decided my question was trivial, he went right back to his phone, sliding his thumb rapidly across the screen.

"To a place," was all he said as he finished his coffee.

The thought of just getting up and peering over his shoulder at the phone did cross my mind, but I discarded it.

I wasn't good at that kind of thing—I would have gotten busted immediately.

"Okay. Should I get ready now, then?" I went on.

"Yeah, the sooner you get a move on, the better," he said, terse and annoyed.

Oh, was I distracting him?

I got up and washed the mug out in the sink before drying it and putting it back in the cupboard. I turned around to see Neil looking at my ass, his phone still clutched in one hand.

"Could you tell your lovers to look you up some other time? Perhaps after I've gone back to Detroit? That way they'll have you all to themselves, and you can play your little games together." I waved a dismissive hand, and he raised his eyebrows in surprise. He hadn't expected that reaction out of me, but I was fed up, and his attitude needed to change, specifically the arrogant disregard. Neil's only answer was to raise the corner of his mouth before, unable to hold back any longer, he burst into laughter.

Was he making fun of me?

I stalked around the kitchen island, determined to get out of there, but he took me by the arm and stopped me. He stood up, looming over me. I looked up at him, daring him to say something. If he tried to seduce me with words or actions, he would have gotten a slap to the face that time.

One he'd always remember.

"Tinkerbell..." he said in a soft, singsong tone, mocking me. I glared at him. "You are absolutely right...about waiting until after you leave to see all my lovers." He tried to brush a strand of hair away from my eyes, but I moved to block him. All he did was laugh. "But the person I was texting just now was actually Logan. So you can relax..." He pinched my cheek before releasing me.

Oh, so he *was* going to see all his other women after I left? Well, two could play at that game.

"And I'll happily wait until I'm back in Detroit to ask Ivan out so we can get back to our...ah...unfinished business." I shot him a wink and watched his shoulders straighten. His golden eyes went hazy with unmistakable anger, and he began to breathe heavily.

Guess my aim was good because that shot *hit*.

I wouldn't have done anything with Ivan, whom I considered

just a friend. But just hearing his name was enough to provoke the human disaster in front of me and I hoped to make him feel some of what he made me feel.

That might be the only way to make him understand how much he was hurting me.

"I'm going to go get ready," I announced cheerfully, wearing a smile just as broad as it was fake, and then sashayed victoriously back to the bedroom. All the time, I could feel his glower on me.

"Fucking brat," I thought I heard him mutter in an irritable growl, but I didn't care in the slightest.

....

Half an hour later, we were driving in Neil's car.

Neither of us said a word about our little sparring match.

I wanted to ask him what this "place" he was taking me to actually was, but I didn't want to be the one who broke first. Maybe I was being childish, but my pride got the better of me, and I couldn't stand the idea of talking to him, not even just to get basic information.

I contented myself with giving him sideways looks while he focused on driving. He grasped the steering wheel firmly in one hand while leaning his head on the other, thinking who knew what kind of thoughts.

Neil often seemed to be lost in his own world, far away from everything...me included. It was like he retreated to some secret space in his head, and the door was barred to anyone else.

In his black jacket and jeans with the sweater I'd so recently used to keep myself warm, he looked every inch the enchanting beast.

His gaze was cold, his face perpetually frowning and unreadable, and his mouth lush and capable of biting, rousing me and stirring me up like none other. The lines of his face were firm, his jaw defined.

His clean smell hung around in the car's interior, which cut through the air like a dart.

All around him, an ominous aura of darkness hovered.

Neil provoked a dangerous and painful kind of love, an otherworldly torment.

An eternal punishment that was scarier than death itself.

His beauty struck me like a bolt of lightning—terror and electricity at the same time.

The feeling was like a thick cloak of fog that obscured my common sense, bewildered my soul, and annihilated my sense of self.

My want for him refused to give me a break as my feelings only grew and grew.

I reached over instinctively and squeezed his thigh. Neil reacted to my unexpected touch with a slight indrawn breath, but he didn't move. I, on the other hand, narrowed my eyes at the feeling of his powerful muscles underneath my fingers, with only a layer of jeans between me and his warm skin. I moved my hand up a bit higher, and Neil didn't stop me, allowing himself to be fondled. I was surprised at how calm he appeared, especially when I reached his groin and began to trace the curve of his penis. He continued to stare at the road, concentrating, but I knew he was very aware of my hand pressing on his visible bulge.

"I'm driving," he chided me before glancing quickly into the rearview mirror and grabbing my wrist to pull me off him. I gave him an impish grin—I had been expecting the rejection.

He had just confirmed my theory that Neil always needed to be the one who decided when to engage whenever someone showed any interest in him physically.

"So you are capable of rejecting a woman's advances, then. Why do you find it so difficult when it comes to Jennifer or one of the others?" I asked.

"Are you trying to start a fight?" he snapped, pushing the hair back off his forehead.

"No. I just want to tell you you're an asshole," I shot back at him.

"You want to dredge up the exclusivity thing again, is that it?" He sighed in frustration.

"No, please continue," I said sharply, waving a hand in the air. "I certainly wouldn't want to bother you with such a trivial issue."

"Good, that's settled, then," he answered flatly. I shook my head in resignation and leaned my head against the window, letting the unhappiness flow through me. More and more, I found myself flip-flopping between moments of wild joy and the utmost despair. My entire romantic experience consisted of one guy, and as far as I was concerned, I'd never be able to completely understand Neil. Sometimes it felt like he couldn't live without me, like when we were in bed and he claimed me with all this longing he had inside him and pleasured me until I fell apart. Other times, he was so distant and uninterested.

His behavior was erratic, possibly because he was afraid of exposing any weakness to me. Even when he'd told me about Kimberly, I still felt like he was putting up a huge, unscalable wall to hide himself from me.

Was he still afraid I was going to judge him?

I didn't know what else I could do to make him understand that I accepted him just as he was.

I sighed and was only distracted from my thoughts when he turned on the radio, probably to break the exhausting silence between the two of us.

Alex & Sierra's "Bumper Cars" came on, and I let the delicate notes of the song fill up my head as I focused on the lyrics, which seemed particularly apt for our situation.

"I hate romantic music," Neil grumbled and reached out to change the station, but I stopped him.

"You hate everything; that's not the same thing," I retorted. "Listen to the song."

He sighed and reluctantly put his hand back on the steering wheel.

He was humoring me for once, being surprisingly compliant, but I knew that to be a vanishingly rare occurrence. He never usually let me win so easily.

After just a few moments, in fact, he snorted.

"Fine, change it," I snapped. "Do whatever you want!" I raised my voice before putting my temple against the window again, trying to tamp down my irritation. Neil had a special talent for frustrating me, and I didn't know what to do about him anymore. We were two bumper cars, just like the song said.

It was pointless for either of us to chase after the other; we always ended up smashed into millions of pieces.

"I'm on edge today," he said, drawing my attention. He was trying to explain himself. I looked at him, so beautiful and tormented, and my heart seemed to vibrate in my chest.

Damn feelings!

"You're always on edge," I pointed out. It made me feel useless, knowing that my presence did nothing to improve his mood. Neil always seemed to make me happier, despite often also being intolerable. I had no idea how he did it.

"More so than usual today," he specified. He pulled his package of Winstons out of his jacket and tugged a cigarette out with his teeth.

"Could you not..." I was all ready to ask him not to smoke in the car, but instead I just let it go with a shake of my head. It wasn't like he was going to listen to me anyway. And, as if to confirm that thought, he lit the cigarette and took a long drag before cracking the window so he could blow out the smoke. I goggled at him.

Well, at least he'd learned to show the most basic consideration for a nonsmoker like me.

Since he'd explained that he was feeling edgy, I decided to change the subject to something lighter, like...

"Am I dressed okay for where we're going?" I asked him and looked down thoughtfully at the sweater and skirt I'd put on to leave the house. I hadn't brought much clothing from Detroit, and for whatever reason, I opted for the only outfit that wasn't part of my plan to dazzle Neil.

"Yeah, you look nice," Neil answered, his face completely unenthused.

"If you tell a woman she looks 'nice,' you might as well just liken her to hamster poop: small, neat, and not too smelly," I said in an offended grumble, and he remained stone-faced. In fact, he ignored me completely. "It's an aggravating adjective," I insisted. And still, nothing. No reaction. So I thought back on *Peter and Wendy*, which I'd been reading for a while now and had yet to finish.

"Every time a child says, 'I don't believe in fairies,' there is a fairy somewhere that falls down dead," I quoted. "By the same token, every time we describe something as 'nice,' something beautiful dies because we didn't have the courage to make an actual judgment or say what we really think, often due to completely unfounded fears. That's a Neverland rule," I explained, raising my index finger.

Neil just sighed.

"Spare me the wordplay. I think you look nice; that's it," he answered brusquely.

"Do you really understand what I'm talking about?" I asked, making a face. I didn't think he did.

"Of course," he said, his tone sardonic.

"Really?" I cocked a skeptical eyebrow.

"Yeah," he answered, just to get me to shut up.

"Neil, stop humoring me," I said irritably. I had figured out his little game.

"Okay." He shrugged and went on smoking, completely indifferent.

"Oh my God! Quit it!" I exclaimed in exasperation, rubbing my forehead. Trying to talk to him was useless. Now he was agreeing with everything I said just to annoy me.

We fell silent, and the song continued to accompany us for a couple more minutes until Neil pulled up in front of a large building I didn't recognize.

"Where are we?" I asked him.

"You'll see." With the cigarette clamped between his lips, he turned off the car and got out, gesturing for me to follow. Once outside, I shivered in the cold air and retreated into my coat. I shot a glance at Neil and saw that his right hand was shaking as he pulled the Winston, still only half-smoked, out of his mouth and flicked it onto the pavement. He ground it out with his shoe and then turned his golden eyes on me. From the dark expression that had fallen over his face, I knew he was about to tell me something I wouldn't like to hear, and I mentally prepared myself to face whatever new obstacle he was about to put in front of me.

"This is a private psychiatric clinic operated by Krug Lively and John Keller. It's the reason I asked you to meet me in New York," he said coolly. I felt unsettled and wrinkled my forehead in confusion.

"And why are we here?" It might have seemed like a silly question, but I couldn't figure out what he was trying to tell me.

"I pretty much grew up here. I was in behavioral therapy for twelve years," he answered starkly, and I couldn't hide my surprise. My head spun at the unexpected confession, and he must have seen it because the emotional distance between us seemed to grow.

"You…"

"Had behavioral disorders when I was a kid…" His eyes fled mine to instead observe the clinic. I was still in shock. I felt like the earth had opened up underneath me while he remained unruffled and motionless, his shoulders rigid. He wasn't letting me see his pain, but I could sense it. I could feel it under my own skin, like we were sharing one body. "Don't know what to say, do you? Just like I thought," he added scornfully, immediately jumping to the worst conclusion. In reality, I just needed a moment to process what he was telling me. I needed some time.

I had always tried to present myself as strong and willing to fight, but the reality of the situation was disconcerting, even for me.

I was beginning to understand why Neil always tried so hard to push me away, and I suspected that this was another attempt to get me out of his life.

"No, you're wrong. I'm just—" I started to say, but he took me by the wrist and pulled me closer to him abruptly.

"I have a lot more to show you. Don't say a fucking word yet. I'm not going to listen until you know everything," he whispered against my lips, furious. I forced myself to just nod, buckling under the weight of this truth that I may not have been ready to hear. Once again, I felt small and unsure. Unable to be with someone like him. I was the one who had asked to be part of his life, and now Neil wanted to show me just how foolish and reckless that had been. Because what did I really know about what had happened to him?

"Follow me." He released me and walked toward the entrance of the building with his usual upright bearing.

I did as he said, trying to banish the uneasy feeling I had, but after just a few steps, my gaze caught on a magnificent fountain that had pride of place inside a manicured garden. A dolphin with a luminous pearl in his mouth coaxed a shaky smile out of me. One that disappeared the moment we got to the automatic doors.

Neil and I walked through quickly, and he headed for a chubby woman sitting behind a reception desk. I hung back a few feet and waited for him, looking over the antiseptic atmosphere of the place, characterized by a maniacal attention to every detail. The smell of fresh paint told me the clinic was either new or recently renovated, and it had a lavish, regal look.

I peered around curiously for a few moments before I spotted a sharply dressed man heading right for us. As he approached, I got a better look at him: He wore a very elegant charcoal gray suit tailored perfectly to his slim frame and a white button-down that highlighted his lean chest. He was tall and carried himself proudly; he looked to be in his fifties, and he had the kind of powerful charisma that caught one's eye immediately.

He was a man of distinction.

"Son," he said to Neil, by way of greeting. Neil turned to face him and sighed.

"John," was his only answer.

"What are you doing here? Are you looking for Dr. Lively? I believe he's leading group right now in the music room," the man informed us with a friendly smile that Neil clearly wasn't going to return.

"Dr. Lively used to be my therapist," Neil explained gravely, seeing my confusion, and I nodded again, incapable of doing anything else. "This guy, on the other hand..." Neil attempted to introduce me to the man who was watching us, curious and attentive. Instead, the man got ahead of him and approached me himself.

"Oh, I didn't realize you brought company," he said archly, and I caught a whiff of his cologne, a fragrance that was bold yet delicate at the same time. He stuck his hand out at me: "I'm John Keller. Please, call me John," he said jovially.

"Pleased to meet you. I'm Selene." I shook his hand a bit uncertainly and curiously examined his face in detail. Fine lines bracketed his lips and crinkled the edges of his bright eyes. I dwelled for a moment on those unusual eyes. They were a strange color, like sand or sheaves of wheat in the sunlight. His nose was proportional, and his jaw balanced out the rest of his face. It was a good face, and along with his innate charisma, it probably drew women to him.

For a fleeting moment, I thought that John and Neil looked oddly alike, but I quickly dismissed that silly thought.

I was so obsessed with the human disaster next to me that I was starting to find his likeness even in men who had nothing to do with him.

"Oh, so you are the famous Selene. I've heard good things about you." John smiled slyly at me, and I frowned.

Neil had talked to him about me? Why?

"Don't be surprised if he starts telling you some legend or recites a paean to the sea or some other bullshit," Neil murmured, resting a hand on the base of my spine. I sucked in a breath at the gentle contact.

"Don't listen to a thing he says, Selene. It's an honor to have the Pearl Girl here with us." John watched me closely, a benevolent look on his face. Then he shot a knowing glance at Neil who just rolled his eyes in response.

Was he talking about the glass cube that Neil gave me right before my accident?

"If Dr. Lively is occupied, we can come back another time," Neil said, trying to put a damper on Dr. Keller's enthusiasm. But the other man was undeterred and turned to me.

"Selene, do you need to get out of here?" he asked me confidently, as if he already knew my answer.

"No, actually," I answered honestly, and he smiled.

"Good. Then let me buy you something at the café; they make a great herbal tea," he said, gesturing for us to follow him. Neil muttered something under his breath but didn't object. We followed the doctor down a hallway, past a large waiting room. It was too warm in there, so I took off my coat and draped it over my arm.

Neil and John walked ahead of me, having a conversation I

couldn't quite understand. I stared at them, trying to catch a few more of their words, when two guys came down the hall toward us. One was dark-haired, and the other was wearing a colorful bandanna, and both were smiling. I presumed they were also patients of the clinic. The dark-haired one, who also had an eye-catching series of tattoos all over his neck and the backs of his hands, waved hello to Dr. Keller before meeting my gaze.

Immediately uncomfortable, I pretended I hadn't seen them as they passed us. But, as they did so, I received an echoing slap on my butt cheek. I didn't even have time to process what happened; I jolted in fear and froze at the strong burning sensation.

What the hell?

"Nice ass, new girl," the dark-haired boy said, winking at me.

All conversation between Neil and John stopped abruptly, and a sudden silence fell over the sterile hallway. I glared furiously at the two idiots, and I was just about to respond when a hand clamped down hard on my shoulder and pulled me back away from them.

I knew right away that it was Neil. I was very familiar with his possessive touch.

"What did you say?" he asked the dark-haired boy threateningly. Undiluted anger flared in his eyes. I wouldn't have traded places with those other two guys for anything in the world.

John had caught up to him by then and took him by the arm. The two patients, looking like they'd just seen a ghost, abruptly stopped laughing.

"Let it go, son," John said, trying to hold back the mass of muscle and rage that Neil had become. Neil was intimidating, and it was difficult for most people to compete with his physical power, but Dr. Keller was proving himself to be surprisingly capable.

"'Nice ass' to who?" Neil demanded again, a slave to his anger. His voice thundered off the walls, and I flinched in fear. I had seen him lose control a few times, and it was always terrifying.

"Can't I compliment your girl, Miller?" The dark-haired boy laughed, trying to look brash. I sucked in a breath not just at the slight toward me but also at the way he had defined me: I was not Neil's *girl*.

"You don't touch a woman without her consent, asshole. Don't even look at her again or I'll beat your ass!" Neil burst out, still being restrained by John. "Do you hear me? I'll smash your face in!" Neil continued screaming at him, completely out of his head.

I appreciated that he was trying to defend me.

I had thought on occasion that he felt jealousy over me, like when he'd seen me talking with Ivan and had a similar reaction, but he'd never actually explained himself, so it was never clear to me.

My head was still too full of doubts.

"Drew, get back to the music therapy room," John told the tattooed one, who just ignored him.

"Last time you were here, you were eye-fucking my girl hard, Miller. Brenda told me all about it," Drew told Neil, a belligerent challenge in his tone. If he kept going on like that, he was going to irreparably blow the situation up.

"The two of you are both nuts. I want nothing to do with your bitch in heat. In fact, maybe tell her not to rub up on my cock next time," Neil snarled back with a malevolent sneer. John, without loosening his hold on Neil, tried to coax him into backing down. I had no idea who this Brenda was, but the simple fact that they were fighting over a woman bothered me. Thinking about Neil being with other women in any way bothered me, in fact. And, from what I could tell, this girl had tried to come on to him.

"Drew, Greg, I said go to the music room, now! Both of you!" John thundered, out of patience. The guys stared at the severe tone of his voice and did as he'd said without further objections. Though Drew didn't leave before tossing one last furious glance over his shoulder at Neil. After John had assured himself there was no more danger, he let Neil go with a deep sigh.

"Dick," Neil growled at the other guy, venting the remains of his anger. He straightened his leather jacket and turned to me. My first instinct was to look down because whenever he got dictatorial like that, it always made me feel embarrassed. When I heard the sound of his footsteps heading toward me down the hallway, I forced myself to keep silent until he was right in front of me. He cleared his throat to get my attention, and I lifted my head to look at him.

His magnetic eyes locked on me for a moment, icy cold.

They were heavily lidded and icy cold, so I couldn't figure out what he was trying to say to me.

All I knew was that I felt guilty about what had just happened and ridiculous for almost provoking a fight.

Who knows what would have happened if John hadn't been there?

"Put your coat back on. This is not the place to show off how..." He leaned in close and whispered into my ear, "*nice* you look."

I shivered at his hot breath passing over the curve of my neck, and the low tone of his voice turned deliberately velvety. He stepped back and took a long look at my body, simultaneously appreciating and despising my outfit. Still embarrassed, I did as he'd suggested—if, indeed, it could really be called a "suggestion"—and put my coat back on to avoid attracting more unwanted attention.

I was there to learn more about Neil because it finally seemed like he was willing to let me do that, not to catch anyone else's eye.

"Come on, let's go," John urged us to follow him, trying to defuse the tension that had sprung up between us.

A few minutes later, we made our way to the café, which was just as elegant and sophisticated as the rest of the clinic.

The decor was classy, with vibrant colors interspersed with white and silver. The lighting was soft, and the tables and chairs blended in perfectly with the rest of the atmosphere. John leaned an elbow on the counter and said hello to the uniformed woman there. She gave him a friendly smile in return.

"Hi, Dr. Keller," she answered with a curious glance at Neil and me. Though I was still a bit shook up from what had just happened, I did my best to look relaxed. I examined the array of fresh-baked pastries: croissants, brioche, and muffins. I hadn't eaten anything for breakfast, and my stomach had growled several times in the car on the way over. I wondered if my Disaster had noticed... I hoped not.

"Just my usual passionflower tea. What would you like?" John said.

"Coffee for me," Neil interjected before immediately shifting his gaze back to me. He was waiting for me to put in an order as well, but I just shook my head. He sighed impatiently and turned back to the woman. "And cut me a nice big slice of that cherry tart as well." He indicated the dessert, and I gave him a sideways look.

"What are you doing?" I asked him under my breath.

"That's your usual breakfast, right? The tart won't be exactly like your mom's cherry pie, but it has the flavor that you like," he said easily, coaxing a smile from me.

"So you do listen to me?" I asked him, flattered.

"Yeah. I do it often so I'll understand you, even if I don't always respond," he explained cryptically. "Plus, you burned a lot of energy last night, Tinkerbell. You need to refill the tank," he murmured impishly, making me blush. I shot an embarrassed look at John, who was watching us and looking amused.

"I'm studying a lot right now, and I've been a bit stressed..." I told the doctor, trying to sound remotely believable. "...so, I need to keep up my strength for that." I gave him a strained smile, and he looked thoughtfully at me. I was probably making a terrible first impression. Dr. Keller obviously wasn't the kind of guy to be easily fooled.

"Oh, of course. I'm sure studying really wipes you out." He winked at me before taking a sip of the tea the woman had just brought over for him. Then, Neil took a drink of his coffee, and I stared at the glass of orange juice accompanied by a small plate completely eclipsed by an enormous slice of tart.

Was I supposed to eat all of that myself?

Neil moved the plate until it was right under my nose and gave me a challenging look, daring me to refuse it. So I gave a little huff, and using a napkin, picked the slice up in both hands and took my first bite. I let out a groan as the sweetness hit my tongue. It wasn't as good as Grandma's or even my mother's cherry pie, but it was still delicious.

"It's incredible," I said thickly, through a mouthful of pie, which made both men laugh. I drained the juice in a few gulps and devoured the rest of the tart just as fast.

Neil watched me, luminous eyes filled with unusual tenderness, and smiled.

"But you weren't hungry... were you, Babygirl?" he teased me as I cleaned off my hands.

I knew I must be completely pink, but he just brushed his thumb across my lower lip to wipe away some crumbs. His touch was so gentle and so kind that my heart did not do one, not two, but *three* flips in my chest. In those incredibly rare moments, I felt like I must have mattered to him, at least a little bit.

"What school do you go to Selene?" John looked inquisitively at me, cup of tea still in his hand. Neil stood up next to me after finishing his coffee in just a few gulps.

"Wayne State in Detroit," I answered.

"And what are you hoping to do after graduation?" he asked with more interest.

"I want to teach literature, like my mother," I answered proudly. Mentioning my mom made me feel like I had a knot in my throat as I thought about how I'd lied to her. She had no clue where I really was nor who I was with, and she would have been so disappointed in me if she ever learned the truth. But ever since I met Neil, I'd become prone to making more irrational and even insane choices.

"You're a girl with a good head on her shoulders. That isn't true of everyone your age," John noted, unaware of the fact that I did not, in fact, have a good head on my shoulders. At least not when it came to love. I spent too much time drifting into fantasies that Neil was doing his best to thwart. This trip to the clinic, in fact, was intended to show me what a monster he was. Instead, I saw it as an incredibly brave act that, honestly, only made me like him more.

I couldn't ask for a relationship, and I couldn't tell him that I loved him, but I could continue to think he was something special.

"How long ago did Dr. Lively's group start?" Neil cut in.

"About a half hour ago. Why?" John answered.

"Because Selene and I are also going to participate," he answered with an unreadable smile. Dr. Keller didn't seem to be fully on board. His lips flattened into a doubtful expression, but Neil pressed on. "It's the whole reason I brought her here," he said. John turned and looked at me with perhaps a bit of dismay, but he didn't object, likely because he knew how pigheaded Neil was.

John led us down another hallway on the opposite side of the café, this one apparently leading to the music room.

I didn't know what the group was about or why Neil suggested that I attend as well, but I was sure that this was all part of an attempt to shock me.

"Are you trying to freak me out?" I asked him pointedly as we followed John down the hall. His proud posture, cynical bearing, and omnipresent grave frown made him look like a divine creature, both beautiful and damned.

"I just want you to watch and listen," he answered flatly, without so much as a glance in my direction.

"Like you wanted me to watch the blond in the pool house suck you off? Or like you wanted me to watch you and Jennifer on

Halloween?" I pressed, feeling unnerved. "You failed those times, and you'll fail this time, too," I told him clearly. Neil did things, abnormal things, often in a cynical or ruthless attempt to make me hate him and force me out of his life.

"Don't be a fucking brat. Now is not the time," he scolded me, an especially irritating note of condescension in his voice. He always used that tone when he wanted to quickly put me back in my place.

"Is this war of ours ever going to end?" I asked, still trying to find common ground with him, despite the fact that John—who was only a little bit ahead of us—was surely listening in on our entire conversation.

"It's not a war; it's just reality," Neil answered just as we stepped into a large room. In the middle of the room, a group of young people were sitting, talking, and laughing with another man who, to judge by his white coat, was probably the other doctor. He had a notepad and a pen in his hands as he moved amongst the others, looking at them one by one. He looked just like a psychologist, studying and analyzing his patients' every movement.

Was this the man who had been caring for Neil since he was a child?

"Let's try to take our seats quietly so we don't disturb Dr. Lively and the others," John suggested under his breath. He gestured at a series of chairs next to the wall.

I sat down next to Neil and automatically put my hand on his leg. He looked calm, but he wasn't actually comfortable. All he could do was give the appearance of being comfortable.

I had gotten a feel for his emotions, and I could sense how awfully tense he was.

"Each one of you is like an actor playing lots of roles." Dr. Lively took note of our presence, but he ignored us and continued with what he was saying. "You put on what I would consider to be masks to make yourself palatable to others, mostly to avoid their judgment," he went on. "In this room, though, all you need to do is be yourselves. You need to think of yourselves as insulated by the kind of normalcy that no one out there will give you. And do you know why?" he asked one girl rhetorically. I took a look at her—she had a stuffed animal clasped to her chest like it was a holy relic, and she stared intently at the doctor. "Because I am here to shed some light on the dark parts of you. I am here to give you an opportunity, not just to change your lives but to change your mental habits. I'm here to awaken your subconscious and allow it to be part of a better reality. Because, believe me—a better reality does exist for you," he said firmly with such engaging enthusiasm that he coaxed a smile from everyone present.

My fingers automatically tightened on Neil's leg. I wanted him to not just hear those words but really take them in, make them a part of him and use them like a compass as he set off on his path to rebirth. I shot him a brief glance and found him staring seriously at the doctor. His unflappable expression didn't allow the slightest emotion to peek through, and his golden eyes, cold as metal, took in everything and were surprised by nothing. He was aware of my hand on his leg, and he had not objected, but he hadn't moved to hold it in his own either.

Disheartened, I turned to look back at Dr. Lively, who was asking a very pretty blond if she'd be willing to do an exercise. I observed her carefully: She wore a short dress, her legs were crossed in a way that showed them to maximum effect, and she had long blond hair that fell past her breasts. I tried to keep my jealousy in check and didn't even glance at him to see if Neil was looking at her thighs in that hot, hungry way of his. Instead, I kept my gaze fixed on her.

"Brenda, tell me the first word that pops into your head right now," Dr. Lively instructed. She thought for a moment as she looked at the boy sitting beside her.

It was the same tattooed guy who had slapped my butt in the hallway—Drew.

"Ice cream," answered the girl.

"Why ice cream specifically?" the doctor pressed, scrutinizing his patient attentively.

"Because my brother and his friends treated me like a sweet thing, free to be taste-tested." Brenda swallowed hard and stroked a section of her hair nervously. "He told me that I was beautiful and that he was attracted to me. He was jealous and possessive, and at first, I thought that it was…brotherly. Part of his bond with me. Then he snuck into my room one night and took off his pants, and I realized I'd been wrong. He demanded we go all the way, no matter how many times I told him no." In her eyes and in her voice, I could sense all the pain that Neil surely felt because of Kimberly. My grip on his leg tightened, and he looked at me, narrowing his eyes slightly as though looking for any signs that I was crumbling.

But why?

Did he really think he'd get rid of me that easily?

Did he think I was going to run off with my tail between my legs and say goodbye to him forever?

Not going to happen.

"My brother was never satisfied," Brenda went on. "It wasn't enough to make me sleep with him whenever my parents went away for work; he started taking me with him to these parties and nights out organized by his friends. He'd make me lie down on a sofa or a table, and then he'd let them touch me, abuse me, and do whatever they wanted to me. I wasn't even a person to them; I was like a carton of ice cream they could just dip into however they liked." She finished speaking with obvious difficulty and then dissolved into sobs. I could feel the hurt those men had done to her; I felt like it was covering me, smothering my skin like a thick layer of slime. Her every word had stung like a slap.

I came back to the present moment when Brenda got abruptly

to her feet and ran out of the room, leaving only her suffering in her wake.

Neil suffered the same way. I was sure of it.

He felt lost, his head clouded with negative thoughts, unable to let himself feel human emotions, so he froze them instead, too afraid he might feel even more pain.

With his heart frozen like that, he reacted to the world in a highly individualized way that was different from other people. His responses to everything that happened around him had been conditioned by the trauma that had been visited upon him. It was a monster who had kept him prisoner for way too long.

"We all know how difficult it is to confront these topics. Revisiting the past, reopening those old wounds is a journey of introspection that you have to..." Dr. Lively started talking again, but I was still too unsettled to follow what he was saying. Neil had brought me here to upset me, and I had to admit that he was succeeding.

I gave him a sideways glance and caught him staring intently at me like he could sense all the tumult inside me. He didn't look surprised.

Too many times, I'd asked him to give me something of him in exchange for part of me, but I could not have imagined that he might give me a piece of himself in such a cruel way. He wanted to rub my face in the truth without adornment—totally transparent, clear, and rough, but above all else, honest.

It was just more confirmation of how foolish I had been at the beginning of our relationship when I imagined that I could save him. I believed that he was just overly passionate and impulsive, that he had some issues in relationships. Nothing—in short—that couldn't be fixed. Instead, I was now realizing that Neil was not a man who could be managed, and it was very likely there was no cure for what ailed him. Certainly love wasn't it.

It may have been one of the necessary components, but it wasn't enough by itself for him to learn how to accept himself.

"I will vanquish all your fears," I whispered into his ear, leaning into him.

I shivered as I smelled him, fresh and powerful. Neil narrowed his eyes, hiding the dominating stare that he so often used to bend me to his will. He was telling me in that moment that it really was war between us and that he was going to do everything he could to obliterate me.

Nothing was going to shake his conviction that I wasn't brave enough to stand beside him.

But I wasn't just going to let him win either.

I gave him a defiant smile and settled into my seat, turning my attention to Dr. Lively, who was now asking the guy with the tattoos to say the first word he thought of.

"Drew?" He prompted him as the young man paused for a moment to think, irritatingly chomping on his gum. Then he turned in his chair to look directly at Neil.

"The one word that's always in my head, Doctor, is *net*," he answered decisively, as though an entire world were concealed within those three letters. I felt Neil's leg tense under my hand, the fabric of his jeans stretching against his muscles.

"You know my story already, Dr. Lively. The woman in question was a lot older than me, around twenty... I was just eleven. She was our babysitter. My parents were working long hours so they decided to leave my sister and me with this girl. I noticed there was something off about her right away. She'd touch me and try to coax me into doing things I didn't want to do, all leading up to the first rape. It went on for months before culminating in her final sick act: She set up a camera and filmed what we were doing together. The video ended up on a website owned and operated by my rapist, Kimberly Bennett, and her boss. It was sold to other internet pedophiles..."

An insincere smile spread across his face, and he never once looked away from Neil.

"I'm one of the seven kids from the dark web scandal... I should be grateful to Neil Miller for calling the police and getting that monster Kim arrested, but I just can't do it." All at once, Drew jumped to his feet with so much force that the chair clattered to the ground behind him.

I was frozen at the revelation I'd just heard.

The scandal... The newspapers... The secret room... The dark web...

My head was spinning, and I automatically pressed a hand to my chest, trying to soothe the ache I felt there. It was like someone had kicked me.

"I can't be grateful because you're the reason everyone found out about what happened to me. I was bullied for years in school...all because one snot-nosed little brat couldn't keep his mouth shut!" Drew advanced on us like an enraged animal, sending the rest of the room into a panic. Neil stood up and stepped in front of me, shielding me.

Frightened, I hid behind his back and put my hands around his waist, holding him tightly. I could feel my heart pounding in my ears as I began to shake with fear. I hated violence; I hated witnessing it because then it would replay in my mind on an endless loop of awful memories. So I closed my eyes, trying to shut it out.

"Call security!" John shouted, probably holding Drew back from starting an actual altercation. Neil was still with me, standing protectively as I clung to his back.

I wasn't usually so easily frightened, but ever since the accident, I panicked at the first hint of danger.

"Stop shivering, Babygirl..."

My eyes were squeezed shut, and my fingers were digging into Neil's jacket. When I finally opened my eyes again, I saw that Neil had turned around to reassure me. His intense baritone cut straight to my heart, quieting me and making me feel like I was safe with him.

"Stop shivering," he said again. "Everything's okay. We're getting out of here," he continued, tilting my chin up with two fingers. I blinked confusedly, saying nothing. I didn't have the wherewithal to speak, nor to look around at anything other than his golden eyes, warm and all-encompassing. All I did was nod.

He grabbed my hand and pulled me along with him. Drew was panting while Dr. Lively and John tried to get through to him. His dark eyes tracked our movements all the way across the room, but Neil didn't hesitate for a second. He wasn't running away from the other man, though—he was trying to shield me from the truth I had just discovered. Neil probably hadn't expected it to turn out that way; he surely never thought I was going to find out to what, precisely, those headlines alluded.

Now I had one more piece of the puzzle.

"You need to go back home," he ordered as we hustled out of the clinic and toward his car. Neil grasped my hand with no intention of letting go while I tried to keep up with him, frequently stumbling and trying not to fall.

"Did she do that you too? Did she—" I was about to say "film you," but he stopped abruptly and whirled around to face me. I flinched. I didn't want to be too pushy or invade his privacy, but I did want him to open up to me, to stop hiding his past.

Why couldn't we just communicate? Why couldn't he trust me?

"It's none of your business," he said in a growl of rage. His eyes looked even brighter out in the natural light. I hesitated, staring into them, and I could see that he didn't want me to push his boundaries, to demand too much, but...

"I need to know, Neil. I need to know the whole truth. I would never judge you. I haven't ever judged you," I said, my voice getting louder in exasperation as I tried to pull free from his grasp. I fortified myself with all my patience and calm, trying to soothe him. From the sudden spark of terror I could see in his eyes, I knew that he was genuinely afraid to tell me about himself and about what that monster had done to him. "I won't judge you," I said again, trying to stroke his face, but he jerked away from me with an indignant look on his face.

"Don't touch me." He spun around, cold as ever, and continued walking away from me, but I wasn't about to give up. I ran after him, determined not to go back to Detroit without getting some answers out of him. Enough was enough. I needed to break down that psychological wall he kept putting up to keep me from ever getting a real look at his soul. "I'll drive you to the airport. You need to leave," he continued stormily, passing a hand through his messy hair. All I could see were his broad shoulders and twitching back muscles, but that was more than enough to see how anxious and tense he'd become. He was pulling back emotionally from me, tucking himself up in his protective shell.

"No. I'm not leaving this city until I know what the hell actually happened!" I reached out and snatched his forearm, forcing him to turn around. We were almost at the car; if Neil had gotten away from me, I wouldn't have been able to stop him from leaving entirely. I struggled to catch my breath as I thought about everything we'd face together, and I knew that I was more deserving of his trust than anyone else. "I have faced down all these obstacles for you. Your women, the Krew, Player..." I pled softly. "Don't you see that?" I gestured to the scar on my forehead, and he trembled.

"Every morning, I wake up remembering what happened that day when I left New York. But if I could go back in time, I'd do it all over again, Neil. All of it. Because it was my choice. It was what I wanted, right from the start. If I'd never met you, I never would have felt so alive," I confessed, watching as his full lips fell slightly open in surprise. I wasn't going to make the mistake of telling him I loved him. I still didn't fully understand why he hated to hear "I love you" so much, but I respected his wishes nonetheless.

I would stick with him in the darkness.

I would love him in silence.

I would go along with him and his madness.

Because he had saved me.

He had saved me from monotony.

From the "everything" I had that was actually nothing.

From what I thought life was.

Because, for me, my real life began with our first shared look.

"How?" Neil shook his head, stubborn and immovable, and I took a step back. "How in the fuck are you failing to see how wrong I am for you?" he said in a burst of rage. "I brought you here so you could see that I had mental problems, and I still do," he admitted. "Why aren't you running? Why can't you see me for what I really am?" he demanded. I shivered, and I didn't know if it was from the biting winter air or the callous way he was talking about himself.

"Because, for me, you and your damage are the fairy tale." I shrugged and gave him a sad smile as he stared at me in total confusion.

"When I was eleven, I was diagnosed with obsessive compulsive disorder. I wash myself constantly because I am always trying to wash away the feeling of Kim's hands and tongue on me," he burst out furiously. "When I was fourteen, I was diagnosed with intermittent explosive disorder, which causes me to have uncontrollable outbursts of anger. The tremor in my hand is one of the first signs an episode is coming on." He showed me his shaking hand. I had taken note of it before, particularly when he was keyed up or nervous. I held still and just stared into his face, shaken but not deterred. I was not afraid of him. Neil just narrowed his eyes and went on, determined to break me.

"When I was sixteen, I was diagnosed with dissociative identity disorder. Two souls exist within me at the same time. One is an adult, the other childlike. The latter forces me to relive my trauma by fucking women who remind me of the babysitter." He moved closer, each step more uncontrolled. I sucked in a breath, never moving my eyes away from his, though he was blind with rage. Neil grabbed my chin and forced me to hold still. "And now you, the innocent that you are... You need to go away, find a normal man, and get it through your head that my life is no place for you. For me, there are only two ways of being: one good and one bad, and the two of us are divided by the boundary between them. *You* are the boundary... and I... I can't get to you..." All at once, he began to struggle for breath and went white. He let me go like I'd scalded him and staggered back away from me.

Neil lived in his own world, a chaotic, fascinating place, and I had immediately needed to become part of it.

I approached him, slowly closing the distance between us while he stood there motionless, assessing me. I wanted to kiss him. I wanted to toss words out the window and ease that grave frown from his face with a gesture of love. I thought him even more fragile as he stood there with that guarded, powerful stance, the facade he showed the world to protect himself.

"I'm not giving up on you, Neil Miller," I declared, still moving toward him. "If anything, knowing more about your past has made me less afraid." I didn't know if I was trying to lull him or lure him. He cocked his head to one side and looked at me in shock. He probably thought that I'd lost my mind, and maybe I had. He parted his lips slightly as though to respond but shut them again, apparently preferring to remain indecipherably silent.

Abruptly, I wrapped my arms around his waist. I held him close to me, resting my head against his chest and breathing in the good smell of him. He was stiff, like a sheet of ice against me. He seemed confused by my approach—he marveled at it while also appearing afraid.

"Whatever it is that I feel for you, it makes it impossible not to accept you," I confessed, raising my head to look into his eyes, which, as usual, were magnetic and filled with a world that defied all logic. I wanted to show him that I wasn't lying, and I was positive that he could read the truth in my eyes. "I would never ask you to change. Nor would I try to make you love me." I gave him a smile filled with love. But Neil had turned gloomy again at my words. Maybe he thought he was protecting himself, retreating into his internal chaos so he didn't have to admit to himself that he'd failed to frighten me off.

The clinic? It had upset me, sure.

The stories of those people? They were disturbing, as was his confession that he was still struggling with serious mental health issues. I had no idea how to approach that kind of situation; it was far beyond me. However, there was one thing I was certain about: I wasn't afraid of it or of him.

"What am I supposed to do with you?" he muttered wearily. He sounded tired of fighting against me and the connection we had. But that didn't mean my words had convinced him, and he surely wasn't about to acknowledge the possibility of an *us*. He was probably going to regroup and think up some other strategy to drive me away.

"Accept me. It's your turn now," I told him, and I could feel it in my chest: that all-encompassing pull toward him, so powerful there was no point in fighting it.

The love I had for him had thoroughly invaded me and had contaminated every part of me.

That was when Neil moved. He tucked my hair behind my ear and leaned down to sigh against my lips. I wanted to ask him about the dark web, about how far Kim had taken her perversions with him, but I decided that could wait for another time. I didn't want to smother him or be rude.

It was hard enough for him just to deal with the fallout from such heinous abuse every day.

"You..." he began in a soft voice, "little fucking girl..." he went on, irritated by my tight hug. "You don't know the risk you're taking." The heat of his breath made me part my lips in the hopes that he might kiss me. Instead, Neil just smiled his enthralling smile and didn't move.

"So prepare me then," I answered, my eyes locked on his.

My Disaster grabbed my ass in response, pulling me flush with him. It was his own way of returning affection. "Why me? Why not pick that Ethan guy? The basketball captain with the perfect life?" he asked, an unsettled thread of possessiveness in his voice.

"Ivan. His name is Ivan," I corrected him, amused, and looped my arms around his neck. I grazed the nape of his neck with my fingernails and watched his face transform. His rigid features relaxed; he was enjoying my touch.

"I don't give a fuck what his name is," he shot back. "You never actually told me if you kissed him," he added, sounding bothered. Again with that? I couldn't believe he still wanted to talk about my non-date, but if he insisted, then I should take the chance to tease him a little.

"What's your goal here?" I asked him. "The clinic didn't do enough to scare me off, so now you want to push me into the arms of another man? It's not going to work." A challenging smile spread across my face, drawing his golden eyes to mine. He slid one hand from my butt to my waist to squeeze it compulsively. I loved those little instinctive touches.

"I can see how this is going to go, Selene," he said in a persuasive murmur. "I won't do anything but fuck you. Always. Every time I get a craving for you. I'll never give you a love story, though. And we both know why..." he finished, his masculine, sensual voice seeming to touch every single part of my body.

I knew exactly what he was trying to do.

"You've crossed lines with me that you wouldn't with anyone else." I felt his hard member pressing into my lower stomach—I could literally feel his desire. Neil was reacting to me exactly the same way I reacted to him.

"You're in Detroit, and you still don't really know what I get up to here when you're not around. I like to fuck. I still think you're too naive and too young." He licked his bottom lip—the lip that I wanted to seize and suck and bite and vent all my frustration upon. I wanted to kiss every inch of his skin, to caress every part of his body until I dug out his deepest fears and swept them all away.

"What if I told you that I did kiss Ivan?" I switched strategies, deciding to play dirty. I watched with satisfaction as his muscles tensed and his beautiful eyes scrutinized mine.

"Then I would tell you you'd made a major mistake," he answered with false, forced calm. Meanwhile, our bodies traded heat, sensation, and want as though they were now dependent upon the other. Our words floated away on the wind, and the truth was that we were bonded by something so strong, so toxic, and so intense that it amounted to complete insanity.

"What if I said that I'd gone to a party at his frat and that I shut myself up in a room with him alone?" I continued. His stare turned sly, his jaw tightened, and he put a hand around my throat, holding it in a firm clasp. I tensed as I felt his fingers tightening against me, but I didn't back down.

"Then I'd give you a swift kick in the ass and send you back to Detroit right now." His tone turned spiteful and dark, and his full lips flattened into a hard expression. My victory was close at hand.

"And what if I told you instead that he didn't kiss me? That I rejected him because I could only think of you and how you make all the others look like insignificant little boys?" I regarded him seriously, slowly moving my fingers from his waist to his defined chest like I was tracing the lines of a sculpture.

"I would say that you did the right thing." His voice softened, and the corners of his eyes crinkled up slightly.

I was so in love with him.

"What if I told you that I didn't let him touch me because there were no flaws in him? And because it is flaws that I adore most about you?" I hoped I didn't scare him—I didn't know any other way to explain how I felt. If a silent language was the only one that Neil could accept, then perhaps I could make him feel that there was nothing to be afraid of when it came to me.

"Then I would tell you that within every man there is a little boy in search of his Neverland. You're mine. You always have been," he whispered softly, a small but sincere smile bringing the light back into his eyes and into mine as well. I clung to him, infusing into my embrace all the fear I had of losing him at any moment. The dread that I would not turn out to be the one for him would go away, just as I knew his personal torments would always reemerge.

But I would not be afraid.

His world was rare and wondrous to behold, so I would enter it delicately, on tiptoes.

"Then lay down your weapons, Peter Pan. I win."

Not waiting a moment more, I pulled him to me and arrogantly seized his lips.

I took him.

I took his madness.

I took his taste of tobacco and man. I took his eager tongue, sliding along mine in a language just for the two of us. I took his raw power and rough manner because I loved the way his wild hands felt running through my hair. I loved the feel of his teeth on my lips and loved wearing his marks of possession so proudly. I took his sultry groans that mingled with my own, all under that clear blue sky outside a psychiatric clinic. An unusual place to indulge in one's passion, maybe, but we didn't care about the outside world because we were living in a Neverland of our own, messy and mythic.

And it was our place.

I would stand beside him forever.

Beside the boy whom no one trusted.

The one the world had backed into a corner.

I would wrap my arms around his fears.

I would make him indestructible.

I would give him a love that was mute but nevertheless knew how to speak to him.

I wouldn't seek to change him, only love him.

I would show him that there were other horizons, and he could look to them with his own eyes.

He'd always thought of me as his Tinkerbell, and so I would follow along with him…

Beyond all limits.

11

"What would our lives be like if we were always surrounded by the gloomiest darkness?"

SELENE

Colors...
I was firmly convinced that colors could meld with a human being, lending meaning to the world around them and making humans less sad.

What kind of life would a colorless one be?

What would our lives be like if we were always surrounded by the gloomiest darkness?

I watched my mother as she painted one of her vases.

She was outlining the petals of a rose with meticulous care, occasionally pausing to dip the fine tip of her brush in red paint.

"I hope I'm not screwing this up," she grumbled under her breath because it was not easy to paint realistic-looking flowers. They seemed like they'd be easy enough to reproduce, but that was not at all the case. Getting all the soft shapes and brilliant hues just right required a lot of focus, especially if one wanted to replicate their natural charm.

"You never screw it up, Mom," I said, peering down at her painting. She really was very good, just too modest to admit it.

"How was Bailey's? Did you two enjoy yourselves?" she asked suddenly, not looking at me, and I stiffened. I'd been back in Detroit for two days, and I hadn't heard a thing from Neil since the day he took me to the clinic. I had sent him a couple of texts, but he hadn't responded.

I'd thought about calling him, but I resisted the urge because I was hoping he would reach out to me.

"It was good. I needed some friend time. We had lots of fun. We did some school stuff, watched a horror movie, and ate way too much junk food," I told her, forcing a smile. My mother had an uncanny ability to determine whether or not I was lying just by my intonation alone, so I hoped I was able to sound convincing enough to avoid an argument. I'd dodged the subject of Bailey several times already since I'd gotten back, and Mom, busy with her work at the university, hadn't pursued the matter. Now, though, she was apparently ready to bring it up again.

"Hmm..." she murmured thoughtfully as she drew in the veins on a petal. "That's funny. I ran into Bailey's mom at the grocery store yesterday, and she told me she hasn't seen you in months."

My blood ran cold.

My mother abruptly stopped painting and raised her head to look directly at me.

I had been transformed into a wax statue. Except maybe paler.

Bailey's mom...

Damn it! I hadn't even thought of that loose end.

"You got a flight to New York and met up with Neil without me finding out. Congratulations." Her voice went hard. She had me dead to rights. I chewed on my lower lip like a kid who knew she'd once again broken the rules. She heaved a sorrowful sigh, pinching the bridge of her nose. "Forbidding you to see him won't do any good. We both know that," she reflected, sounding defeated. I'd never seen my mother look so dispirited.

"I can hardly recognize you these days, Selene. It's like you've completely lost your common sense." She stood up then, wiping her hands with a paint-smeared cloth. "You don't notice what's going on around you. You're just bewitched by that boy's looks. But beauty isn't everything in a man, and neither is..." She paused, looking pointedly at the visible bruises on my neck before taking a deep breath and shaking her head. "Neither is what he's offering you. And what, really, is he offering?" she continued sharply. "A spot in his bed? It seems to me that he offers that to everyone. Why do you think you'll be any different?" She raised her voice, and I blushed violently while my heart pounded in my chest. "The fact that your father is so devastated about this relationship should tell you something. I am telling you, that boy is no good for you. He's older; he's sly, calculating, and vicious. Neil is everything a parent doesn't want for their daughter!" she yelled.

I staggered back, incapable of responding. I had known that, sooner or later, we were going to have this fight and that my mother would tell me what she really thought. I'd been confident for a while that she didn't like Neil and didn't trust him either. Still, it made me sad to know we thought so differently about this. It had always been just the two of us, a tiny but indestructible family unit, but now she seemed so far away from me...

"Mom," I said, moving closer to her, and she stepped back to duck my attempted hug. "I don't know what's going on with me." I burst into tears, letting loose with all the feelings I'd kept inside for way too long. I was lost, and I constantly wondered if I was taking the right path. I had no doubts about the feelings that tied me to Neil, but I had many about what exactly awaited me at the end of my journey with him.

"It's like I'm trapped in this bubble. I can't think clearly; my chest aches whenever I see him. It's like... It's like he's holding me captive. The more I try to stay away from him, the more the chains around me tighten." I sobbed as she stared at me in shock. "I feel alive when I'm with him. The whole world just goes away. Neil has this ability to overpower every part of me and slip under my skin. It's like being locked in a cage and tossed into the deepest part of the ocean, and that sounds terrible, but it actually turns out to be the best place I've ever been," I admitted, all in one breath and confused all over again.

My mother looked frightened by what I was telling her, while I was just so bewildered by Neil that I didn't fully register what I was saying.

I knew that he was a wild creature and that he was a controversial, amoral man who loved making himself inscrutable and elusive. One who reveled in being contaminated and needed to contaminate others in return. Ever since I'd woven my life in with his, I wasn't the naive, pure-hearted girl that everyone remembered. I was not the same Selene who had believed that she could offer him salvation or redemption. I knew now that would be impossible. I had accepted Neil the moment I allowed him to weave threads of damnation all around me.

It was too late now.

"This won't last," my mother said after a few moments of hesitation, and she sounded more like she was trying to convince herself than me. "It's going to end, and you'll go back to being my daughter. The girl I raised, the one I instilled my values in. Don't give up on your education; don't lose sight of yourself. Have the experience of this kind of relationship, but always remember that he is not all that exists. I'm here too. I'm your mother, and I want what's best for you, starting with you achieving your goals. Don't throw your future away over one guy, a passing infatuation. You are so young, and you still have so much to learn about the world..." She rubbed her forehead, and I didn't appreciate the way she was talking to me. Neil was not some high school sweetheart, the dizzy thrill of a first kiss, or a momentary crush. He wasn't some idol whose poster I'd stuck up in my room or the cute boy in school everyone went nuts for.

Neil was just Neil.

Every part of me was with him, even when we were far apart.

And the name for that feeling was not "passing"...

It was forever.

Because he was...mine.

....

Days went by.

Slowly. Too slowly.

I kept texting Neil, asking him how he was doing and to just please check in with me but to no avail.

He never bothered answering, and my disillusionment only grew.

I began to think that he regretted taking me to the clinic and giving me a look at such a personal part of his history.

But by then, I had learned to read him: Whenever Neil took any kind of step forward, whenever he demonstrated his vulnerability in any way, he would immediately turn on his heel and run back to his walls. He had to protect himself from everyone, even me.

He pushed his feelings down, keeping a tight leash on them so no one could hurt him.

Kimberly had put that terror in him, teaching him that love could only be shown through lust and physical pleasure. It was why Neil couldn't deal with a real relationship and might never be able to do so.

Still, his absence had an irreparable impact upon my daily life.

I became increasingly annoyed by guys looking at me in the hallways at school. I avoided all the basketball players—Ivan in particular—after that party at their frat.

Janel was the same as she ever was, though now she never missed an opportunity to remind me how violent and dangerous she thought Neil was. Bailey, meanwhile, maintained that he wasn't as bad as everyone thought and that she'd like to meet him in person to prove that theory.

I spent long afternoons poring over my books, both to reassure my mother that I was not about to abandon my education and to distract myself from thoughts of that human tornado with the golden eyes.

Why couldn't he just take the time to tell me he was okay?

The ongoing silence was wearying, to say the least.

"I can't stand it when you act like this," I grumbled to myself as I lay in bed. I was wearing my prescription reading glasses, which I only used when I read books after a long day of classes and wanted to avoid straining my eyes. My hair was pulled up into a messy bun, and I was bundled up in warm clothes.

I glanced over at the clock: It was only four o'clock in the afternoon. I'd eaten a quick lunch at school with my friends, and now I was alone for the afternoon.

My mother wouldn't be home until dinnertime.

We hadn't spoken any more about my lying to her and going to see Neil, but her frosty looks were more than sufficient to tell me she was still upset with me.

Suddenly, the doorbell rang and pulled me out of my thoughts.

I reluctantly left *Peter and Wendy* on my bed and hurried downstairs to the door.

When I flung the door open, I found the object of my obsession standing on my front porch in all his glory. He looked like he'd come to haunt me with his stern frown and diabolical beauty. My breath caught at the sight of his nose, tip reddened in the cold, and his lush mouth cracked down the middle. That cut on his lower lip seemed like it might have been from someone biting him...the way I did.

"Hey, Tinkerbell," he said in his baritone, and I blinked in surprise. It felt like New York was no further than the next block for him—he just showed up here like it was nothing, completely disarming me with his enthralling appeal.

"What...what are you doing here?" I adjusted my glasses, and he took notice, smiling. It was the first time he'd ever caught me looking so dressed down. Good thing I had at least taken a shower because I was otherwise a hot mess.

"Are you alone?" he asked, not answering my question.

"Yeah, my mother won't be back until dinner." I shrugged as he walked proprietarily inside, shutting the door behind him. I took a step back and tilted my head to get a good look at him, feeling small and awkward.

As always, Neil was magnificent.

"I texted you these past few days, but you disappeared," I said, only after he'd spent a moment looking around without noting anything in particular. He made me wait before deigning to give me his attention. The smell of musky bath gel filled the air. It had only been a minute, and he was already invading my space with his essence.

"I've been working on my application for my internship," he explained, looking down at me. He lingered over the long sweater I wore before moving on to my light pants and fuzzy slippers. With an amused look on his face, he looked up into my eyes. "Since when do you wear glasses?" he asked, and I reddened. I knew he was going to say that.

"When I read," I answered, staring at the tiny cut on his lower lip.

"And how come I never noticed?" he asked, cutting the distance between us. The closer he got, the more I felt crushed, disintegrated, scattered to pieces, and absorbed into his soul.

"Maybe you were distracted," I whispered. Neil lifted up a hand to stroke my cheek and graze my chin with his thumb without ever taking his eyes off me.

"You think so?" he asked, smiling wickedly. "I bet you were reading one of your dull books. Maybe something by Nabokov?" he said in a sensual murmur.

"No, *Peter and Wendy* by J.M. Barrie." I blushed again, preparing myself for whatever snarky remark he had for me. Instead, he just furrowed his brow, and with a rough chuckle, he kept caressing my cheek.

"You really are a kid at heart." He leaned down and dropped a chaste kiss on my lips. I marveled at the delicate movement. He lingered a few more seconds against my mouth, but it was not one of his passionate, devouring kisses. It was a kiss hello, a show of affection.

As soft as it was powerful.

A few moments later, he pulled away and looked into my eyes, sensing the enveloping warmth there. He seemed pleased to see me. Still, I couldn't bring myself to just enjoy the moment.

How many days had he avoided me?

Neil wasn't capable of suppressing his urges for long, and the mark on his lip made me think he'd run straight into the arms of one of his other lovers.

"What happened to your lip?" I asked him suspiciously.

I felt like peeling off his clothes and examining every inch of him for marks that didn't belong to me. He came back to earth and turned serious, shutting himself back up in his darkness.

"It's from the cold. My lips get dry, and I get these little cracks," he explained with his usual cool. He seemed sincere enough, but I couldn't be entirely sure.

"Are you still sleeping with other people?" I blurted out, my possessive urges getting the better of me.

"Even if I did, it wouldn't mean anything to me," he answered honestly, a hint of shame in his voice. He looked up over my shoulder so I wouldn't see the hurt on his face.

It was useless, though, for him to try to hide from me: His brilliant eyes told me everything.

By that time, I had realized what sex was for him; it was like a chess game against himself, an addiction, a panacea that made him feel better, and a way to keep a hold on this world and to process, in his own way, what he'd gone through as a child.

But even though I understood the way he was and his reasons, I couldn't stand the thought of sharing him with anyone else.

"I know you can't understand that and—" he began, but I just shook my head, deciding not to ask him any more questions.

"I'm going to try." I smiled at him, inescapably drawn to the fragility that I could now glimpse behind the facade of the immovable and inflexible man. "How long are you here for?" I asked, deciding to show him kindness instead. After all, I was pleased to see him, and I wanted him to know it.

"A few hours. I'll be gone before your mother comes back," he said softly, as though already aware that she wouldn't approve of him being there.

"Okay. So what do you want to do?" I asked naively, and he shot me such a wicked look that I immediately realized what he intended to "do."

It was me. Obviously.

Was there any occasion when he didn't want to tear off all my clothes?

I gulped and cleared my throat in a way that made it obvious I was embarrassed.

"Go back to your reading; I won't bother you," he said instead, knocking me for a loop. I'd been expecting him to lead off with one of his dirty comments or a peremptory instruction like "get naked" or "get on your knees and suck me off, Babygirl." Instead, he seemed interested in actually spending time with me. I was surprised.

"Oh, okay," I said hesitatingly.

I led him up to my room, and once we got inside, I sat down on the bed and watched him wander inquisitively around. He still wore his black coat, his gloomy figure contrasting sharply with the soft, bright colors of my decor. He stopped abruptly in front of my desk and reached out to stroke the glass cube with the pearl inside, which was sitting next to a photo of me with my grandma. He appeared lost in thought for a few moments, staring vacantly at the precious object, and let his mind drift far away from me.

That happened to him regularly, and I usually tried to respect those moments when he turned inward.

"You kept it..." he noted, breaking the silence.

He turned around to look at me, and I just nodded.

Why would I throw out something I cared so much about?

Despite the fact that his very presence had been blowing up my life for months, I felt alive with him. I should have been thanking him every day for sparking emotions in me that I'd thought nonexistent, like love. Before I knew him, I had never realized how powerful and all-encompassing it could be between a man and a woman.

"You are important to me," I allowed myself to tell him, and he raised his eyebrows in shock.

I'd caught him by surprise.

I liked this disarmed version of Neil. I loved to see him without his defensive walls, though he only rarely allowed me to do so.

He cleared his throat, and I was satisfied.

Had I made Neil Miller uncomfortable? This was a one-time event.

He resumed his investigation of my desk, pausing on a book lying near the cube. It was a philosophy text by Nietzsche.

"*The Birth of Tragedy*..." he read in a thoughtful murmur, grazing the cover with one hand. "A subject that I also find very interesting," he told me, still not turning in my direction.

"You like philosophy?" I asked with obvious enthusiasm. He'd already demonstrated a love for Bukowski and a familiarity with the work of René Magritte; was Neil about to dazzle me with his understanding of philosophy?

"I find Freud and Schopenhauer a lot more compelling," he answered, picking up the book to page through it slowly.

"Is this a strategy for luring in women? Showing off how cultured you are?" I teased. I could feel a comfortable understanding between us, and it made me happy. I'd thought that he'd ignored my texts for days because he regretted telling me about the clinic and his conditions. Instead, he seemed placid and easy.

I felt gratified.

"No. Women, in general, can't tell you whether or not I am literate," he answered flatly, putting the book back down where it had been. He turned toward me, and the sadness I saw in his face made me want to put my arms around him.

Neil was all alone, after all. Just like me. He had built up a suit of armor to protect him from everyone; he had isolated himself and frozen all his feelings, and no one was able to look past his appearance.

His other lovers wanted to compel him, to strip him down and own him, if only for an hour.

But I wanted more.

"Talk to me about Schopenhauer. What about his work appeals to you?" I pulled off my reading glasses and arranged myself cross-legged, ready to listen. Neil frowned and leaned back against the desk, narrowing his eyes at me. He was trying to decide if I was messing with him, but I wasn't. Everything about him interested me. "Come on, I want to know. Seriously," I prompted him, and after a moment's hesitation, he agreed.

"The world is just a representation, a kind of stage on which we are all acting. In every situation, we act out a role," he began, gripping the wooden edge of the desk until his knuckles went white. "Even in sex, which is all deception, power, and seduction, there is a force that affirms the self and denies the other... It is a manifestation of man's will to life. Sexual desire allows us to achieve a kind of physical fulfillment that cannot be matched by anything else." He licked his lips, staring into the middle distance. "But sex never makes anyone happy. After fucking, man recedes into his limited existence, into an emotional crash, and all the original pain returns. Everything slips away like a dream in favor of a tortured reality," he finished, still just standing there and staring at me. Even in a philosophical theory, Neil saw Kimberly and the sick species of love he'd experienced with her.

He was trapped in a repetitive suffering machine.

He lived and relived what was happening again like it was the only way he had to keep from losing his mind.

What could have possessed that woman to so completely destroy the psyche of a little boy?

I didn't know if I should question him or how to get him to open up if I did, but I still had so many questions: Did he take any medication? Was he still in therapy? If not, should he be in therapy?

I wrung my hands and looked down at my folded legs, plucking up my courage. "When Drew mentioned the..." I cut myself off, looking up at Neil to find him staring at me, waiting for me to keep talking. "He talked about the dark web and how Kimberly was associated with it...and..." I said in an anxious babble.

"Kimberly molested the kids to get them ready for it. When she thought they were prepared, when they were sufficiently 'educated' and didn't have normal inhibitions, she would film them," he admitted, surprising me. I had never expected him to tell me about it so readily. I scooched down to the end of the bed and gave him my undivided attention. "The dark web is a shadow internet that requires certain software to access. It's part of the deep web, and it's very dangerous," he explained, his tone cool. He was still determined not to show any vulnerability.

"Everything's on the dark web—arms dealing, drugs, hackers for hire, terrorists. It's just like a black market in real life. Kimberly, along with her boss, dealt in child pornography videos. Together, they sold digital files full of heinous content to dark web users depraved enough to want them. They paid for the downloads with untraceable transactions. Kim accidentally admitted to the police that she was an administrator on one of those sites. She regretted that right away. Usually, the admins remain anonymous," he explained baldly. He was rubbing my face in this reality, such as it was, so that I could feel the gravity of it. Not just an isolated case of abuse but a full criminal enterprise. "I was lucky. I stopped her in time, but there were other kids, victims like me, and they were filmed, and those videos were sold to pedophiles online. When I called the police to keep Kim from filming me, it blew up into this huge scandal that involved my whole family. We ended up in all the newspapers. New York was talking about it for a long time." Neil swallowed hard and looked down.

I could see the awful memories weighing down on him again.

Now it all made sense: He was afraid of being photographed. That was why there were no pictures of him as an adult in his mother's house. Only ones up to the age of ten...

"Did the police catch the sickos?" I asked, disturbed. The reality of what had happened to him was so much worse than I'd ever imagined.

"They arrested Kim, but trafficking in child pornography is still a widespread crime. There are lots of sites that exist specifically to host files temporarily. The material will be available for a day or so and then get taken down. That severely narrows down the window in which authorities can act, and most online pedophiles work hard to stay anonymous and never reveal their IP addresses," he said, sighing, his miserable face illuminated slightly by the light from my desk lamp. His lips were twisted in a bitter expression. Instinctively,

I stretched out an arm and offered my hand to him, trying to banish some of that anguish.

"Come here." I gave him an understanding smile. He looked down at my hand and then back up at me, uncertain.

"I don't want your pity," he answered tartly and stayed where he was.

"And I'll give you anything but," I answered, and he narrowed his eyes at me. A flare of naughtiness flickered in his golden eyes, and I blushed. As usual, he had willfully misunderstood me, but I also knew that sex was a tool he used to keep himself under control.

"Actually, we have some unfinished business, Tinkerbell. Enough about ancient history." He pushed off from the desk and strode toward me, rendering me breathless. He had given me another piece of himself, a very painful one, and now he wanted something in return. I hoped he didn't want to have sex because we wouldn't have had enough time. My mother would be back before dinner, and Neil's stamina was unreal.

It took a long time for him to be able to relax and...

He met my eyes when he got to the side of the bed, trying to figure out what was happening in my head. I chewed anxiously on the inside of my cheek.

"Get closer," he ordered, staring at me with a devouring passion. He'd probably already used someone else back in New York, or else he would have pounced on me much earlier. Still, he cleared his throat, waiting for me to make a move.

I moved slowly over to the edge of the bed, sitting back on my heels. He watched me, pleased.

"I liked the glasses on you. Why'd you ditch them?" he said softly as he touched my cheek. His thumb traced the contours of lips, and they parted for him. He leaned closer to me, and I leaned into him, seeking more physical contact to block out the cruel reality that always sought to break us down.

"I only wear them when I'm reading," I whispered against his mouth, which quirked up into a clever smile.

"Someday, I'm going to fuck you while you wear nothing but those glasses," he said, a lewd promise, and I closed the distance between us with a kiss. I clutched his neck, pulling his head down to me to show him just how much I wanted him. His tongue slid past my teeth, demanding my kiss. I complied ferociously, and Neil responded with passion. He still seemed a bit worked up about our conversation—I could feel it in his tightened shoulders—but I wanted to show him that I was there for him. He could trust me, and I would give him whatever he wanted. When he broke our kiss and pulled away, I let out an irritated groan.

He smiled at my visible disappointment, and then, with one hand, he unbuttoned his jeans and pulled down the zipper.

"Let me feel those lips where I want them most, Tinkerbell—around my cock," he told me, tugging his jeans and underwear down slightly to release his sizable hard-on.

I blinked hazily for a few seconds, appreciating how thick and stiff it was for me.

Seeing him completely bare like that was always a shock; I couldn't seem to get used to it.

Neil never seemed to be bothered, though. His body was a tool for him, and he knew how attractive it was.

I, on the other hand, was still a little anxious about my lack of experience. I wasn't bold enough yet when it came to foreplay, and every time I got started, the fear of not being able to make him happy rose up again, and I worried I was going to drive him away again.

"You did great the first time, Babygirl. You'll learn more with practice. I like this because...you're the one doing it." He stroked my face, running his fingers through my hair and freeing it from the hairband until it fell gently around my shoulders. The scent of my shampoo hit us both, and he inhaled deeply, grinning. He closed his fist around my hair and tugged me closer to his pelvis.

Sure, powerful, wild—just like always.

I swallowed awkwardly and let him position me. I looked up into eyes one last time to soothe my nerves, and the unspoken understanding I read there comforted me. It was incredible how Neil could banish all my fear and make room for determination.

Determination to give him every bit as much pleasure as he gave me. I was the one who had asked to know him in every way, and his taste, from the very first, acted like an aphrodisiac on me.

The clean smell of his skin urged me not to back down. I stroked his hard thighs through his jeans and felt the powerful muscles under my fingers.

Every part of him was perfect and deserved my attention.

I parted my lips and let him inside, feeling him shiver ever so slightly. I didn't want to disappoint him. I wanted to not just live up to his other lovers who had also done this but erase even the possibility of them doing it again.

His gentle strokes along the back of my neck relaxed me and kept me in the moment. Neil didn't groan or pant, so I wasn't sure if it was going well or not. All I could do was go with my instincts and try to remember the things Neil had already taught me.

When I couldn't take the full length of him, he gave me a fond look and didn't demand more from me. In exchange, I focused more intensely on his most sensitive places and was hyperaware of his every physical reaction. The moment I saw the first abdominal tensing, I laved his glans more enthusiastically. Then I looked up, blushing to find his eyes looking back into mine, golden and aroused, focused completely on me. His serious expression only made him more alluring, and his slightly parted lips, plush and inviting, only made me want to kiss him passionately. I used my free hand to cup his contracted testicles, and he gave the slightest gasp, tightening his hold on my hair. He was so stubborn about not allowing himself to lose control and stretching the moment out as long as possible, even though I was already getting tired.

Still no moans, not even another gasp, and my insecurity reared its head again.

Was I doing something wrong? Was I not on the other girls' level?

If I couldn't do this for him, he would definitely regret choosing me.

No...I couldn't let that happen, so I pushed aside my worries and went on, shy but determined to rock his world.

I pulled back for just a second to give myself a breather, but Neil grunted in annoyance and pressed on the back of my head, urging me to continue where I'd left off.

Neil would show his disappointment if I did the opposite of what he wanted, and knowing that he was in control gave me a feeling of total stupefaction. So I went back to blowing him devotedly to show him that I was enjoying it just as much as he was. I hoped he wouldn't hold himself back for too long and would allow himself to let go. Neil stared lustily at me, and I was hypnotized by the flames of desire burning in his eyes. When, after what felt like an endless number of minutes, I finally heard that rough, uncontrolled moan from out of his throat, I knew I was about to achieve my goal.

"Yes...good job, Tinkerbell. Faster..." he broke the silence, and his roughened voice gave me intense shivers all along my spine. I moved my hands from his firm thighs around to his marble ass. I squeezed his butt cheeks and stroked the defined musculature of them, thrilled by the idea that this body was all mine. That surge of possessiveness had me moving my tongue faster, and Neil moaned, captivated.

But I wasn't satisfied. Soon, I would have his soul as well.

"Fuck, yes," he whispered at the same moment he moved against me in one untamed thrust, his hand digging into my hair.

He caught my eye, wondering whether or not to pull back but I gestured for him to give me all of him. Then, with a powerful contraction, he exploded in my mouth. He gasped, an extremely masculine sound that seemed to have released all of his accumulated tension.

I was instantly aroused, pressing my thighs together to tamp down on my growing lust.

The taste of him was incredible.

I took it all and delighted in it.

I had no other men to compare him to, but all it took was knowing that it was his, that I had something inside me that belonged to him, and I felt enveloped and consecrated by him.

I pulled back from his body, which was still slightly trembling, and stared at him, bewitched. His muscles were all tensed, and his breath came in pants. His golden eyes watched me with satisfaction, and he gave me the kind of mysterious smile that always enchanted me. Unable to stop myself, I moved closer to him again to finish what I'd started. I licked his member clean, drawing out the lingering sensations from the orgasm he'd just experienced.

Neil trembled again when he felt my tongue wrapping around him, tracing the throbbing veins beneath his thin skin, and he gasped for breath. I just looked up at him adoringly.

Then, like a good little girlfriend, I pulled up his boxers and his jeans and did them up again.

It made me feel powerful, seeing this man who was wanted by so many other women seek out my attention all the time, like he couldn't help himself.

"You are becoming quite the fairy seductress," he said in an amused mutter. I sat up on my knees and looped my arms around his neck. I licked my lips and tasted him, slightly sour on my tongue. Neil's skin was hot to the touch; his cheekbones reddened slightly, and his eyes were glassy with arousal. His chest heaved rapidly, and whenever he breathed in, his hard pecs grazed my breasts, making my nipples stiffen. I tried not to focus on the pleasurable shivers running down my back and focused on him.

Neil stroked my hair with a fiery rapture.

"If we had more time, I'd lick you all over," he said softly, grabbing my butt. He gave it a firm squeeze, and I plastered myself against his quivering, breathless body. He bit my lip, and I moaned in pain. Involuntarily, I became aroused once more. How he managed to turn me to jelly with a butt grab, I had no idea. It seemed my body was happy to accept whatever kind of touch he offered me, tender or savage. Which was crazy, even for me.

"You have no idea how much I want to fuck you right now, Babygirl," he went on crudely, and the more he talked like that to me the harder I had to clench my thighs together to keep from giving into the urge to shove him back down on the bed. I squeezed my eyes shut, pressing my forehead to his, and he smiled, licking my freshly bitten lip. He saw the storm going on inside me, and it pleased him. I sometimes wondered if Neil knew how I really felt about him. He was an unpredictable man, one to whom I could never openly admit my love, but the need I had to be near him and to know him inside and out had to be obvious.

I couldn't say it with words, but I shouted it with every inch of my heart.

"I'm glad you came to see me today. Thank you for giving me another little piece of your past," I said with all the enthusiasm of a little girl at a theme park. But he just looked seriously at me before turning away. I sat up on the edge of the bed, thinking that I must have done something wrong. Maybe I'd gone too far, telling him too much of what I thought? I watched uneasily as he felt around in his coat pocket for something, presuming it was his pack of Winstons. Instead, I furrowed my brow when he pulled out a small box and offered it to me. I looked back and forth between his eyes and his open palm in confusion. His eyes were locked on me, waiting to see what I would do. So I took the little box and studied it: It was a rectangle made of decorative wood about the same size as my palm; it had a metal crank on the right side and...

My name. Engraved in the wood next to a little moon.

The moment I saw it, I felt my breath catch in my chest.

He brought me a gift?

I raised my head to look at the giant man standing a short distance away, fretting over my reaction. He ran a nervous hand through his hair and then jerked his chin, urging me to open it, which I did. Immediately, I saw a miniature set of pipes like on an organ, but I had no idea what they were for.

"It's a serinette. If you turn the crank, it plays a song," Neil explained before clearing his throat. He clearly wasn't used to doing this kind of thing, and I was still dumbstruck. I slowly turned the crank clockwise, and a tiny tune began to float in the air.

I recognized it: "The Scientist" by Coldplay.

I felt my eyes prickle, and a knot of joy swelled in my throat.

"Did you get it specially made for me?" I asked, looking up at his face, but he looked away and chewed his lip.

"It's...it's not a big deal. When I saw it, I thought of you," he said vaguely as though to assure me that I shouldn't assign too much importance to it, and I instinctively jumped on him, clinging to him like a koala. Neil caught me on the fly, cradling my thighs and marveling as I wrapped my legs around his hips.

"Thank you, Mr. Disaster. You never cease to surprise me. I am absolutely right when I tell you you're special." I kissed first his lips and then his jaw, rubbing my nose against his scruff while he grumbled under his breath.

It was adorable.

"Okay, Tinkerbell. Don't push it. Sit back down, come on now." He tried to pry me off, but I clung to him like a little kid. Neil rolled his eyes and snorted. "Why do you have to be so sickly sweet? Fuck...a thank-you would have sufficed," he groused. I smiled and nodded just so he would shut up. "Now get off me. Release. Come on." Another peremptory order. I gave him another delighted nod and didn't obey. "Don't just nod like you're humoring me, Selene. I'm starting to get mad," he warned me roughly. My only response was to stroke down the straight line of his nose, and he frowned, ceasing, at least for a moment, to object to my embrace. So I moved on to his lips like one enthralled, like I was trying to memorize every detail of his face. And, with a cheeky little smile, I gave him a chaste kiss. And then another and then another.

I looked impishly at him, and he cocked a skeptical eyebrow. Then he mumbled something about knocking it off.

We continued that silly tussle for a few minutes with me trying to kiss him all over, all the way to his soul, while he cursed and tried to squirm away from me.

Eventually, he put me back down on the bed and straightened his sweater, shooting a look of mock reproof at me. I cheekily stuck my tongue out at him and sat back as he put his coat on again.

Already it was time to tell him goodbye, and I had a ridiculous empty feeling inside.

"Do you really have to leave right now?" I asked him, tucking my hair behind my ears. He turned to face me, fixing his collar. I stared at him with frank admiration, totally consumed by the irresistible, almost magical hold he had over me.

"Yeah," he answered. "But now I have to go to the bathroom before I leave. I have another giant hard-on to deal with," he went on, gesturing toward his groin. I looked right there and went red. I had inadvertently rubbed myself on him when I leaped on him, creating another wave of lust in the both of us.

"Okay, I'll just wait here for you," I told him awkwardly, and Neil left. I breathed a sigh of relief, but his presence had a way of transporting me to another world from which there was no escape. I shivered at the simple memory of having pleasured him with my mouth like that and wondered when I got so uninhibited. Or maybe I was simply in love, and that crazy feeling was what encouraged me to abandon all modesty?

At least when it came to him.

I patted my burning cheeks and looked at the little serinette. He'd never honestly tell me why he made such a thoughtful gesture, but I appreciated it all the same. That box was worth more to me than any verbal declaration of love.

I understood that it was all imperfect.

That we were imperfect, but at the same time we were a perfect mess.

I wanted his chaos.

Because that's how Neil was.

He could show me the sunset without the sky.

He could give me a love poem without writing a line.

He could play me a song with no instrument.

He could make me fly without wings.

He held me without touching me.

He crawled inside me without asking for permission.

He asked me to stay with him without saying a word.

Mute love.

That was what he'd get from me.

That was what he could accept.

And that was what I would give to him.

Today.

Tomorrow.

And every day after that.

I clasped the music box to my heart and heaved a dreamy sigh before getting up off the bed to go put it next to the glass cube. I would undoubtedly glance at it every night before I fell asleep and every morning before I left my room, just like I did with the pearl. Just to make sure it was still real.

Just then, my open laptop screen lit up with an email notification. I glanced over at the closed bathroom, and while I waited for Neil to come back, I sat down to read it. Lately, I'd been getting a lot of correspondence about my upcoming classes, and I presumed it was more of that.

I opened my email account and checked the latest message:

Hey, Selene, or rather, Target #2,

So pleased to see you made it out of your wreck with only a measly scar on your forehead.

That wasn't how it was supposed to go. I've been thinking about you ever since.

So I hacked your computer to gain access to all your correspondence, social media, chats...

Everything. Absolutely everything.

I watched you every day through your laptop's camera, thanks to some malware that allows me to control it remotely.

It also allowed me to record what you just did to your man.

My compliments, I didn't think you were so...forward.

A real full-service whore!

It'll only take me one click to send that video to everyone you know and forever ruin your life as well as the life of that asshole with you.

Don't bother alerting the cops, Selene.

I am in control. I am watching. I am following.

> Any mistakes will be met with one little click.
> Think about it: How much do you value your life?
>
> Player 2511

I stood motionless in front of my laptop, staring frozen at the contents of the email.

My eyes were wide, my heart throbbing in every part of my body. Still in shock, I reread the email three more times. A wave of nausea made my lips purse and my head spin.

I was in genuine danger of having a heart attack.

For a second, I thought it had to be a joke, but when I saw the signature, I knew it was no joke at all. I heard Neil's footfalls behind me while I still stared in shock at my laptop.

"Selene?" he called.

I didn't answer, and Neil moved closer to me, troubled by my silence. Finally, he looked at the still-open email on the screen. He bent slightly to read, and it was only a few more seconds before he grabbed my laptop with both hands and brought it close to his face.

"What the..." He narrowed his eyes, rereading the message again while I stared at him. He seemed shocked at first, and then such fury welled up in his eyes that it made my blood run cold. His right hand began to tremble, and with a growl of rage, he hurled the laptop against the wall, making me flinch.

My laptop lay ruined on the ground, completely destroyed.

I leaped to my feet and moved away from him.

His ragged pants grated in the silence, and his features were twisted in blind fury, his golden eyes storm-tossed. Slowly, his gaze shifted to me, standing terrified by the bed, and I felt like I couldn't even recognize him.

He seemed completely out of his mind.

All at once, he marched rapidly toward me. Afraid, I tightened my shoulders and squeezed my eyes shut. He had never really injured or physically hurt me, but he wasn't in his right mind in that moment, and he could be capable of anything. I opened my eyes when I heard a strange rustling sound only to find Neil hunting around in the room. I held myself stiffly, trying to figure out what the hell he was doing, and then I realized he'd picked up my iPhone, which I had previously left on the bed.

He shoved it wrathfully into his pocket, and I looked at him in bewilderment.

"Delete your socials. Change your phone number. I am taking your phone with me. The son of a bitch has control of everything." He sounded like a robot as he scrubbed a hand over his face. He was in shock and disoriented. His eyes roved around, looking lost before, finally, his eyes landed on me once again. "Don't go out by yourself. Ever. I'll buy you a new laptop. Right now, though, I have to figure out how to fucking fix this mess," he went on, sounding like he'd been programmed to say those exact words. His voice was firm and alarmed but unshaken. I nodded dazedly, and he moved closer to me, taking my face in his hands. I sucked in a breath at his warm palms against my skin. "Do you understand me?" He gave me the slightest shake to make sure that I was hearing him, and I nodded again, trying to hold back tears.

"Don't make me worry about you," he went on gravely. His expression was tender, displaying a humanity that he usually tried to hide. "I'm so fucking angry, Selene. So angry," he repeated, holding my face tightly in his hands. I grunted at his intense grip and clutched at his wrists to let him know that he was hurting me. He breathed in sharply and regained his self-control, stroking my cheeks delicately with his thumbs. "But I can't be distracted now. I need to act right away," he said in a menacing whisper. "He's been spying on you. I..." he muttered through his clenched jaw. "I might actually lose it for good if I think about something happening to you." He bit down on his lower lip, and my gaze got stuck there. He did it so violently that a few crimson drops beaded up along the small cut he already had. His face didn't change. He remained cold and furious, like he didn't feel pain. Instinctively, I touched his lips to stop him, and Neil growled like a wild animal in full frenzy.

I needed to kiss him, but when I leaned in, he shook his head. No... that wasn't what he wanted.

"I have to go. I'll be in touch," he said quickly and pulled away. I immediately felt the absence of his warmth. I stared after him, wondering how he planned to deal with this situation and a little surprised at how unintimidated he was by Player. Instead, he seemed to have known that it was going to come to this sooner or later. "I'll also get you a new phone," he added.

I didn't give a shit about the things he'd broken, but I didn't have time to tell him that. Neil headed for the door immediately. Hurried footsteps echoed around the room until I saw his big, magnetic body pausing in the doorframe. He turned back to give me one last miserable look and then he left, taking my soul along with him.

I was left alone, frightened and disturbed, with a depthless emptiness inside me.

12

"They knew from the frosty expression on my
face that something serious was going on…"

NEIL

I'd been back in New York for one day, and I hadn't gotten a wink of sleep.

Before I left Detroit, I'd destroyed Babygirl's laptop in a fit of uncontrollable rage, and then I'd taken her phone, positive that son of a bitch had gotten access to every device she had.

I was losing my mind.

I was truly going nuts at the thought of Player daring to invade Selene's privacy by spying on her through her webcam.

Fucking *spying* on her.

That meant he had watched her reading her books, getting undressed, prancing around the room in her childish pj's, and—goddammit—even sucking me off.

After the attack on Chloe, the damage to my car's windshield, and the note with Hard Candy written on it, I was expecting him to make another move. But not like this.

Not doing something so vile as to invade a woman's personal space just to watch her like a pervert.

I thought again that it had to be a man, and I dismissed Xavier's suggestion that it could be one of my exes.

I didn't know for sure, though; maybe Player was revealing themselves little by little. The only person who could help me was Luke, who was much better with computers than I was. After sitting (barely) through another meeting at the university, I went outside for a smoke break and to check my phone. I had already sent Luke three texts, and the dickhead still hadn't answered me.

What about the "a Krew member responds promptly in an emergency" rule was unclear to him?

Irritated, I stood outside a campus building and lit up another cigarette, continually glancing up the main thoroughfare, hoping to see my friend show up.

"Get a move on!" I grumbled to myself, taking a long drag off my Winston. I packed my lungs with nicotine like a desperate man and blew the smoke out through my nose, trying and failing to get a grip. As I waited endlessly for Luke to appear, I spotted Bryan Nelson, Carter's older brother, surrounded by four of his basketball teammates. They were his faithful hounds, following him wherever he went, even to the John.

Then again, he was a basketball star and king of the school, especially because his uncle was the dean.

Dean Nelson covered constantly for his nephew, and Bryan took every advantage of his privileged position, passing all his classes with a snap of his fingers. As soon as he saw me staring at him, he shot me a cocky half-smile, whispering something to his sidekick next to him and then wrapped his arm around the shoulders of a grinning blond girl who had just approached. I looked at her, thinking I'd seen her before. She fit squarely into my usual type.

As the girl got on her tiptoes to reach Bryan's lips, the cropped sweater she wore rose up over her abdomen, and something shiny glinted in her bellybutton.

A piercing.

It was then that my mind rewound to a point in the recent past when I'd lured some girl into the pool house so I could fuck her and Alexia at the same time. Then, I had her blow me in front of Selene because I wanted to scare Selene off and get her away from me. I could now vividly recall just who Bryan's new girl was—Britney Porter.

I didn't give a shit about either of them, but as they passed, his glare swept over me and he gave his companions a knowing look. They, in turn, grinned back at him.

And I could have said nothing and remained peaceable, especially as we were still on campus, but...

"The fuck do you want, Nelson?" I snapped, blowing smoke out into the air.

He halted, arm still draped over the girl's shoulders, and turned to look at me, cocking an eyebrow.

"Chill out, Miller," he answered carelessly, glancing behind me. "I'll leave you in the company of your kind. People like me, we prefer not to get down in the gutter. Some of us have reputations to uphold." Then he winked at me and continued on his way, trailed by the four assholes. His little blond, though, kept staring bewitchingly at me until Bryan nudged her to leave.

I hadn't seen him since I beat his brother Carter's whereabouts out of him. Nor had I bothered asking any questions about what sort of state the kid was in now. All I knew was that he got out of his coma and probably wasn't in the hospital anymore. I'd warned him not to mention my name, showing him videos I'd pulled off his phone of him doing and dealing drugs, the kind that could definitely compromise his family.

Ever since then, there'd been nothing between me and the brothers Nelson.

Chloe never mentioned Carter, and I didn't question her about him because I didn't want to hurt her any more than she'd been hurt.

"What'd Bryan, Lex, Gregory, and the rest of them want?" Xavier appeared from behind me, watching the basketball guys walk away. I turned and looked between him and Luke, saying nothing.

"Yeah, I know. You're mad. I should have replied faster," Luke began to hastily explain. Xavier just laughed.

"You look fucking stupid, acting like a bitch just so Miller won't hit you," he teased Luke. "We oughta start calling you Fido, rolling over to show your belly like that..." he went on, sneering. Luke glared at him and gave him a shove; Xavier staggered back, laughing.

"Say that again, and I'll break your face, dipshit," Luke threatened him. I just watched the two of them, silent and bored. Sometimes, I looked at them and saw a pair of little boys. I took one last drag off my cigarette and stubbed out the end before clearing my throat. Both immediately stopped screwing around and looked to me, getting serious all at once. They knew from the frosty expression on my face that something serious was going on and that they needed to give me their attention.

"Talk to us." Luke was the first to speak. Xavier stood beside him, waiting for me to answer.

"What do you know about hacking?" I asked him. His forehead creased up in confusion at my question, and he thought for a few seconds.

"Enough. Why?" He asked in return.

"Because it seems that, in addition to being a skilled puzzle designer, Player is also a fucking hacker," I told him, passing a hand through my hair. I was no computer expert, but I knew that seizing control of someone's webcam and making them the unwitting star of a twisted reality show wasn't exactly child's play.

"What are you talking about? Did he hack your computer?" Xavier asked.

"Not mine. Selene's," I admitted, and they both looked surprised. Luke immediately realized the gravity of the problem and blanched.

He rubbed his chin, thinking about what to do.

"Okay. So...do you have the computer with you?"

"No. I broke it," I said. "I do have her phone, though, with all her passwords for socials and email." My first instinct had been to save her from being part of that depraved show and protect her from the spying eyes of a lunatic. But I hadn't thought through the wrathful gesture. I'd cut off her connection to the digital world to protect her, but I'd also left her alone with no ability to text or even call me. And I was worried about her.

Not hearing from her was making me antsy.

"Alright, see you tonight at six at my place, then," Luke said.

....

When I got back home, I did nothing but dwell on what had happened.

My head was spinning with dark, paranoid thoughts.

It was my fault, mine alone.

I had done everything possible to push Selene away from me, and at first, it appeared to be working. Then, like an absolute dumbfuck, I relapsed.

Thoughts of her tormented me every day. The women I passed time with meant nothing; I needed them exclusively to maintain some psychological balance. But no matter who was underneath me, I was always having sex with my Babygirl.

My body only responded normally to physical stimuli when I was with her, and not just when it came to arousal. It was about urges, cravings, wants, and hungers—feelings I couldn't contain— and that was what made me climax exclusively with her. It was as though she could reach into my soul and calm it with a touch.

When I was with Selene, I was a different...me.

And Player had realized that; along with my siblings, she was one of the most important people in my life. That was why he'd singled her out for attack again. I passed my tongue over my bottom lip, the one I'd bitten into to vent my stifled rage, and recalled her kiss, the sweet taste of her on my tongue.

Even when we were far apart, I could sense Selene all around me. I could smell her coconut scent on the air and feel her slim hands trying to soothe the worst of me, to render it tame and lead it back into its cage.

I saw her ocean eyes washing over my body with longing and her slender fingers tracing the lines of my muscles as if they were erasers that could banish every single wound.

I felt her everywhere, but most of all, I felt her inside of me.

And I, selfish as I was, wanted more.

I wanted to tear her clothes off with my teeth.

Leave more bruises on her pale skin.

Sink deep inside her and feel her heart beating in sync with mine.

I was firmly convinced that sex without love was a more powerful force than love itself.

It was an alchemy of the mind, understanding, consuming passion, and union.

I had been subjected to a distorted version of love when I was ten years old.

It was impossible now for me to love.

Those who had never known rape or abuse didn't know shit about it.

I chuckled at the irony.

I liked using Selene, and I liked being used by her in return.

I thought back on that moment when I'd slid in between her full lips, how she serviced me with innocent boldness, and I trembled.

I was disgusted with myself.

How big a bastard did you have to be to put a woman in mortal peril and not even have the decency to be in love with her?

How much of a bastard was I?

A huge one…gigantic.

Because if I'd just been a little more sensible, more cautious, and less selfish, Player wouldn't have gone after her.

When did I become so callous? When did I lose track of who I was?

My heart was paralyzed.

I couldn't feel anything except hate and shame.

I didn't know who the real me was anymore.

Had there ever even been a *real* me?

My brain worked differently: It was like being caught in a spiral from which there was no escape. I was in a constant state of alertness, inundated all the time with sick thoughts. I was always wondering if I was properly understanding human relationships, and my confusion only deepened when I tried to process the experience of being abused by fleeing deeper into my own mind instead of disassociating from it like many survivors did.

My mind, then, became the real prison that I lived inside.

The only time I could escape my cursed reality was when I was with Selene. With her, I felt free.

Different.

That was why I couldn't stay away from her. It was a constant struggle not to give in to the temptation to go back to her. On one hand, I needed to be with her to escape myself. On the other hand, I needed to protect the Boy from the monsters inside me.

So which was the right path? There was no easy answer.

I grumbled in frustration as I took off my clothes, preparing to take another one of my many showers.

Maybe it would help me calm down and ease some of my constant worries about Player.

The lunatic was on the loose, completely free to hurt the people

I cared about, especially my Tinkerbell, who was far away from me. The distance between us made me uneasy because I knew that, without my protection, Selene was a sitting duck.

I was trapped in New York; she was trapped in Detroit.

What if the son of a bitch was there right now?

Maybe creeping around underneath her bedroom window?

I lathered up my body, swearing furiously before allowing the warm water to massage my overworked muscles. If I'd left her phone with her, I could have just called her, but now I had no means of getting in contact with her. Misery washed over me, and I saw my past stretched out before me on the wet tile floor. It was vast and black, ready to suck me in. I opened and shut my eyes, trying to banish the mocking visions. I got out of the shower and dried myself off quickly.

Clearheaded. I needed to stay clearheaded.

Shit.

It wasn't six o'clock yet, but I was very anxious to meet up with Luke to get some answers about the hacking.

Agitated, I rubbed my hair dry and pulled on a black sweater as well as my usual dark jeans. I grabbed my packet of Winstons, car keys, and my phone and Selene's and tucked everything into my coat pocket.

"Where are you going?"

I jumped a little at the sound of my brother's voice. I turned to find him leaning against the doorframe. We hadn't talked much since we had that fight over Alyssa. That bitch had driven a wedge between Logan and me.

"Out," I answered shortly. I didn't enjoy acting that way with him; it wasn't like me to put up my impenetrable walls with my siblings, but my pride often made me act aloof, especially after receiving any sort of slight. In the few human relationships I did have, my inherent nature did nothing but cause problems and conflict.

"I don't like this tension between us. You don't talk to me like you did before," he went on, just as unyielding as I was. I didn't like it either, but he knew how I was. I still couldn't accept that he'd doubted me, even if only for a moment.

"If you hadn't believed your little fucking girlfriend, then none of that would have happened." I moved toward him on my way out of the room. Logan moved in front of me, however, halting me where I stood. I could see the sadness in his eyes, but I remained unmoved.

I was very good at pretending not to care about people. Even when the people in question were my whole life.

"You know how much you mean to me. I was angry." He pushed a hand through his hair with a heavy sigh. I remained cold, considering his words without conceding anything.

"You believed I would betray your trust. That's pretty serious to me," I said sharply. Never had I imagined something like that could happen between the two of us. Never. I let myself be violated by a psycho to keep her from acting out her perversions on my brother, and still, he believed the fantasies of some chick over me?

No... he really shouldn't have let me down like that.

And here I was, acting like an insolent child about it.

Perched up there on my wall of pride, kicking my feet and laughing as I raked my brother over the coals.

"Please, Neil. I don't know what's going on with you at all anymore. You shut me out completely. You don't tell me things, and you don't ask for advice..." he said in a rush of frustration. "I don't even know how things are going between you and Selene or if you've started therapy back up with Dr. Lively or how you're dealing with Player attacking our sister..." His voice shook as though he were about to cry. He wouldn't, but I could tell from his tone of voice just how much pain he was in. I shook my head and tried to push past him; he shoved me back furiously, and my guard immediately went up.

"Yeah, do it! Hit me! I'd prefer it to this fucking indifference!" he shouted in a show of defiance, and I clenched my hand into a fist. I wasn't going to lose control; I wasn't going to hit Logan.

I was a monster, sure, but not that much of a monster.

My siblings were like precious gems, like holy relics as far as I was concerned.

I would have done anything—no matter how insane—for them.

"Move. I need to leave," I said again, and he didn't so much as flinch, let alone let me pass.

"Whatever blond is waiting to get railed by you can wait. I'm more important," he said, echoing something I'd once said to him. He motioned to himself, and I screwed up my face for a moment before letting slip a genuine smile.

Goddammit!

I could never manage to be a complete bastard with my siblings. Logan sensed that and tried to hide a cheeky grin.

The two of us had always been more important to each other than any woman who occupied our time. That was the rule.

I huffed an irritated sigh, and Logan took advantage of my moment of weakness to wrap his arms around me.

He held me tightly and gave me a couple pats on the back as I stood there, completely rigid. Instead of repaying the gesture in kind, I immediately trapped him in a headlock and mercilessly rucked up his hair.

He struggled to break free, and when I finally let him, he staggered back grumpily.

"What the fuck! I just styled that!" he spat at me as he tried to fix his hair with his fingers, and I smiled at him.

"That's what you get when you attach yourself to me like a baby koala," I chided him mockingly.

"Chloe's the koala," he said, still attempting to straighten up his hair. In less than an instant, the tension between us had been obliterated. I was foul-tempered, and I was stubborn and touchy, but Logan could bring out my more indulgent side.

He loved me.

He knew everything about me: fears, anxieties, nightmares. And he knew that I wouldn't make it without him.

"You asshole. You'll never change. You really hurt me, not talking to me and ignoring me as much as possible," he grumbled, and the more I looked at him, the more of me I saw in his eyes.

That was how it had always been: My brother was the better version of me.

"I have to go to Luke's to sort something out," I said shortly. I didn't want to alarm him about Player, though he did look askance at me.

"What happened to your lip?" he asked, looking at my mouth.

"Why the fuck is everyone asking me that?" I snapped. "It's from the cold," I explained. Sure, I had also chomped on it in a rage, but it was also true that the freezing cold air had been causing small cracks in my lips since I was a kid. Logan should have remembered that.

"Sorry, I thought one of your girls decided to take a chunk out of you," he laughed, and I rolled my eyes. I brushed past him, but he reached out and grabbed my arm. "Can I go with you?" he asked. It had been a while since we spent any time together, and I did still need to tell him about everything that had gone down. Still, I didn't want to freak him out with Player's latest moves. I was torn.

"Come on, we haven't hung out in a while. I'm your little bro, your shadow, your—"

"My irritating, pain-in-the-ass Jiminy Cricket?" I finished for him, and he grinned cheerfully, like I had just paid him the nicest compliment. I hesitated for a few more seconds before finally deciding to just give in.

"Fine. Come with me," I said, realizing I was going to need to tell him the whole story.

From beginning to end.

Thirty minutes later, I was bitterly regretting agreeing to take Logan along.

On the long drive to Luke's place, I told him everything that had happened with Selene. Starting with Alyssa's lie all the way to the night at our mother's apartment. My brother said I was crazy and over the top and needed to control my impulses, but I shrugged off his criticisms and continued my tale. Then I told him all about how Ms. Martin wanted me to let Babygirl go and how I had promised her I'd do so as soon as I left for my internship because I couldn't see a future with her daughter. Logan managed to resist the urge to smack me, but I think that was only because he didn't want the car to go off the road.

"That's total bullshit. Does Selene even know that you're planning to take the Chicago internship? And now you've also promised her mother you'll dump her, and you've done all of this behind her back?" he said in outrage, making me suddenly swerve. "What is wrong with you? You are going to hurt her so bad," he went on, and I felt a stab of pain in my heart.

Of course I knew that I was playing dirty, but I was determined to enjoy my Tinkerbell for as long as I could, even if it was selfish.

After I left New York, our paths would fork, and that was how it should be. It made me uncomfortable, thinking about how to break that news to her, because I knew that, while it was the best choice for both of us, it wasn't going to make either of us happy.

But I was the strong one, the only one actually capable of putting a stop to our tumultuous relationship.

To avoid that discomfort, I switched off that topic and moved on to Player.

About him, I spared no detail.

I told Logan everything, particularly why I was asking for Luke's help.

When we got to Luke's apartment, Logan greeted the doorman politely while I ignored him. Then we got into the elevator.

"This is nuts. Player seriously hacked Selene's computer?" Logan asked, troubled. I didn't answer him, just stepping out onto the landing when the automatic doors opened. I walked down the long hallway, and upon reaching the correct door, I rang the bell repeatedly.

We waited a few seconds before the door opened to reveal Luke wearing a lopsided grin.

"You're ten minutes early," he said, looking appraisingly at Logan and me. I gave him a blank look, and he stepped aside to let us in. "Brought the kid brother along, eh?" he said sneeringly to Logan. I shot him a dirty look to shut him up and he backed off.

"We've been waiting for you, boss."

I stepped into the living room to find Xavier sitting on a leather sofa with Alexia. Standing nearby with her arms folded was Jennifer. She looked bored and lost in thought. Then she spotted me, and her blue eyes lit up. She gave me a provocative smile, which I did not return.

"What are they doing here?" I asked Luke. This was supposed to be a low-key, private meeting, but now...

"We're the Krew. You got a problem; we got a problem," Xavier answered, resting a hand on Alexia's bare thigh. Apparently they had been able to mend fences after he found out I'd fucked Alexia again in an attempt to vent my emotions and shut down my thoughts. I was different, though, and I wasn't about to forgive Jennifer for telling Selene everything we'd done, all to win some feminine game of one-upsmanship.

She'd deliberately made Babygirl uncomfortable all to try to prove that Selene was different from the other girls I spent time with. I hated those kinds of theatrics.

Plus, Jennifer could not get it through her head that I was not hers. I wasn't anyone's.

"So...do you have Selene's cell? What exactly did Player do?"

Luke asked, drawing my attention. So I fished Selene's phone out of my pocket, accessed her email on the app, and handed it to Luke.

He carefully read the incriminating email and shook his head in obvious concern.

"Selene's account sent it to herself; did you see that?" he asked, pointing out a detail that had completely escaped me. I leaned over to look at the screen. Sure enough, the message had been sent from Babygirl's email address, irrefutable proof that Player had indeed taken control of it. I went rigid, giving Luke a speaking look. "This kind of thing is called *sextortion*. The technique is always the same: The blackmailer threatens to release some private video or photos of the victim if they don't do what he asks. He mentions an intimate moment between you two caught by her webcam here, but since he's not asking for money or making any demands other than not going to police, I think he's mostly just trying to scare you," Luke offered thoughtfully.

"Now that's the good shit. What intimate moments were you filming?" Xavier cut in, his eyebrows raised in surprise. I gave him a furious look and ignored the question. I had no intention of telling the Krew, of all people, about what Selene and I did together. The things I shared with Babygirl belonged to us alone, though now Player could show them off to the world if he felt like it.

Just the thought of Selene's reputation being forever ruined made me feel furious and impotent.

"How did he get control of the webcam?" I turned back to Luke, who sat down on the armrest of one of the living room couches, Selene's phone in hand.

"It's tricky but not impossible. Hackers often use sophisticated malware to get access to a webcam, and once they have it, they can access it whenever they like. Sometimes all a person has to do is open an infected email, click on the wrong ad, or visit some virus-ridden site, and that's it. The victim doesn't necessarily know they're being watched because the indicator light on the camera can be turned off," he explained with a shrug. He was clearly a lot calmer about this than I was. But then, no one had touched anything of *his*. My hands shook with the suppressed desire to beat down whoever had been spying on Selene.

I didn't care if I did end up in jail; I was going to give him exactly what he deserved.

"So now there's also the risk that he might release this private video of yours or maybe pictures of the doll in her underwear if you go to the cops?" Xavier asked.

Fuck...someone had seen her in her underwear, had seen her in a way that, up until recently, only I ever had.

The idea tormented me, overwhelmed me.

Then the monster grabbed me by the neck and began throttling me, cutting off my breath.

I began to beg my rational mind to stay with me, to not abandon me.

To help me, to stay awake.

But a powerful force contracted all my muscles.

Rage put all my senses on alert.

A little voice in my head urged me to pour everything out.

It spoke to me. It was named IED.

And there was nothing I could do to keep it from slithering around inside me.

"Shit," I blurted out, messing up my hair. My right hand was shaking. I had started to sweat, and I could feel my heartbeat throbbing in my temples. I was so anxious; I wanted to smash something. Logan tried to put a comforting hand on my shoulder, but I flinched away from him because I couldn't stand to be touched by anyone just then, not even him.

"Hey, Neil, you've gotta calm down," Luke suggested. "This situation is already very delicate."

"Agreed. Also, you keep saying 'he' when you're talking about Player, but what makes you so sure it's a guy?" Xavier asked.

"My instincts are never wrong," I answered angrily.

I hoped to high heaven that it was a woman, some bitch who wanted to ruin me, to destroy me. I could have accepted any kind of blackmail or deal with her as long as she kept Selene and my family out of it.

"What if it's one of your exes? Scarlett, maybe?" Jennifer interjected, speaking for the first time since I'd gotten there. I stopped pacing and turned to look at her. Her blue eyes were locked on me, cool and wicked as ever. It irritated me, being stared at in that hungry way, like she wanted me to tear off her clothes and fuck her right there in front of everyone.

I shook my head, making a face.

"No... I don't think so. The spying, this sextortion thing... It just feels more like something a man would do," I answered shortly. She screwed up her forehead and chewed on her lower lip, considering my words.

"Protecting you and her is the most important thing. She shouldn't be alone in Detroit. Whoever Player is, he knows where she lives and is blatantly targeting the two of you. He struck out with Chloe and Logan, so..." Luke shot a glance at my brother, who had remained silent as the rest of us spoke, troubled by the insane turn things had taken. "You should bring her back here where you can keep a closer eye on her until this is dealt with," he finished, getting up off the couch. He walked over to me and handed me my Babygirl's phone, which I stared at blankly.

I stroked the dusty rose cover of it and tried to swallow the bitterness that was lodged in my throat like a handful of nails.

I felt drained.

This was why I didn't want her becoming a part of my life.

My problems were inexorably sucking her in.

I had always meant trouble for anyone around me; now I was trouble for her as well.

"Bullshit. I think she'd be safer there than right by Neil. He's the one Player's after," Jennifer commented tartly. I looked over at her and could clearly see how irritated she was at the idea of Selene coming back to New York. Instead of thinking rationally about the problem, she was worrying that Babygirl was going to come and snatch her favorite toy right out of her hands.

At the end of the day, that's what I was to her: a sex toy.

"Put aside your fucking jealousy for once. A girl's life is at stake, Jen. Do you get that?" Luke raged at her, and she flinched.

"It was just something to consider, Parker; don't get your panties in a wad," she said defensively, flicking her long blond hair over her shoulder. Her high-pitched voice was bugging the hell out of me. I tucked the phone into my pocket and signaled to Logan that we were going to leave.

I didn't have a lot of choices.

Keeping Selene far away from me didn't seem to be the smart move.

She was now a part of the web that Player was weaving around me, and I couldn't protect her if I wasn't with her.

And I had to protect her from the world's cruelty because she was more than just my Tinkerbell.

She wasn't just a fairy who had alighted upon the undeserving hands of a man like me.

She wasn't just my Neverland, the most beautiful refuge I had ever explored.

She was something more precious than that.

She was my Pearl.

And I was her Shell.

That's why I had to take care of her.

13

*"I had left my heart with her,
Even though it was broken."*

NEIL

Again.
   I sank back into my abyss once again.

Swallowed up by the darkness, condemned to eternal torment.

After talking with the Krew, I'd gone straight out to the pool house.

Alone and far away from everyone else.

It was cold in there, and I sat naked, huddled up in a corner rocking myself.

I had just taken another shower. Water dripped from my hair down the length of my body. Once again, I felt beaten down by the other who lived inside me.

"What did you do!" The Boy standing beside my bed regarded me disdainfully, disappointed in my behavior. Instead of letting me think and try to figure out the goddamned Player situation, he instead needed to rake me over the coals for spending too much time with Selene and revealing too much of our past.

"You told Selene everything! You shouldn't have done that!" he accused.

His childish voice was irate, almost unrecognizable.

"I only wanted to push her away," I said defensively, my hands on my endlessly throbbing temples.

I wished he would just go away, that he would vanish from my life, but I knew that would never happen. I knew that he would continue to hang on tightly to me because I was incapable of really dealing with the abuse I'd experienced.

"But you didn't! You let her into our world instead! You're giving her permission," he scolded me furiously. "How could you? I trusted you. You can't abandon me for her!"

He was on the verge of tears. I could see it in his eyes, glistening and full of suffering. And he was right.

I couldn't pick Selene; I couldn't make that kind of mistake.

I couldn't condemn her to a disastrous life alongside me.

My brain didn't work like other brains. I was a different kind of man, and not in a good way.

"That won't happen," I answered, looking at the mattress. My pack of Winstons was lying there, and I really wanted to light one up and exhale all my tension with the smoke, but I was too weak. My body barely reacted to stimuli. My muscles were shot, and my head was spinning.

If I'd tried to stand up, I would have ended up right back on the floor.

"It can't happen. You can't forget about what Kim did to us." These words were followed by an action I hadn't expected at all: The Boy pinched the waistband of his shorts in his fingers and pulled them down his slim legs. I frowned in confusion. He just kept going, though, hooking his thumbs into his boxers and taking them down as well, exposing his naked body to me.

The differences between us were immediately obvious: His little body was undeveloped and skinny, while I had the body of a grown man who had been wounded too deeply inside.

"Look at me," he ordered, pulling my attention back to him. "Remember how it hurt when I ran to the bathroom and scrubbed myself and the skin wouldn't stop burning?" he asked. I stared at the reddened area around his genitals and felt like the air had been sucked out of my lungs.

I remembered it all too well.

That skin irritation was one of the first signs something was wrong. It was something my mother should have noticed. She should have helped me, taken me to a doctor right away, but instead, the only treatment I had available was washing myself. It soothed the pain that I felt inside and out.

"What about these? Remember these?" The Boy continued tormenting me, lifting up his jersey. He had red scratches across his abdomen, caused by an adult woman's fingernails clawing at his skin and at his soul. I could still feel her long nails on me, and when my lovers also had them, it gave me the exact same soiled feeling.

By that point, I had lost all control over myself, and the Boy was proof of that.

He used our shared victimhood to keep us bound together, and in this way, he made it impossible to maintain a stable relationship. Because of him, I couldn't give myself over to anything except sex.

The Boy wanted me all to himself.

He wanted me totally socially isolated so he could force me to give up on the idea of ever having a better life. He suppressed my emotions, making me cold and often apathetic. He erected a defensive barrier all around me, cutting me off from anyone who wasn't him.

"You're selfish," I told him with a bitter smile. I was struggling to keep a lid on my anger.

I could feel the tension in my nerves, and that was never a good sign. My patience had limits, and beyond them, I knew no reason. I did realize, though, that it wouldn't do me any good to go at the pool house like it was my heavy bag.

It wasn't going to make the Boy leave.

"We both know what you need..." He slowly got dressed again, never taking his golden eyes off mine.

Sex.

I needed sex. Not for pleasure but to violate myself.

I got to my feet, still damp from my recent shower. The smell of shower gel enveloped me, but it offered me no relief. I still felt so dirty.

I began pacing around the room like a maniac, trying to decide if I should get in touch with Jennifer or one of the others.

My contacts were full of blonds ready to fall at my feet, if that was what I wanted.

The problem was that while I did feel some arousal at the thought, it was minimal.

If I thought of Selene, by contrast, a devouring, unmanageable passion burst to life inside me.

"You lost control a long time ago." The Boy read my mind, tracking my every move with his eyes.

"You shut up and piss off," I exploded, glaring at him. He just laughed insolently.

"I live in your head. Where can I go?" He shrugged and remained right where he was.

Damn, he was right.

Where was I expecting him to go when my body was his home?

"Go fuck yourself!" I snapped in a burst of frustration.

In a fog of confusion, I made my way over to the bed to retrieve my pack of Winstons and got myself a cigarette, bringing it shakily to my lips with my trembling right hand. It had been shaking for a while now.

What time was it? I had no idea.

The only thing I knew for certain was how profoundly unstable I was. With Selene, everything was way too difficult, way too demanding, and way too much for me.

Why the fuck hadn't the clinic freaked her out? Why hadn't she yelled in my face about how disturbed I was? Why hadn't she been disgusted and vanished from my life for good?

If she had turned around and walked away from me right from the start, she wouldn't be in Player's crosshairs now.

She wouldn't be a part of his game.

We'd had some good times in Detroit and even here in New York, but that didn't mean...

What if she was just too softhearted to abandon me?

Fuck.

That's what I hated more than anything: the pity...what a noxious feeling.

"Stop thinking about her," the Boy advised me, as I paced around nude like a lonely beast in his empty cage. "Call Jennifer," he went on coaxingly, determined to make me give in. I didn't want to hurt myself; I didn't want to violate myself again. I didn't want to suffer as I behaved like a man with no morals. "But you are a man with no morals, Neil. Why else wouldn't you stop Kim sooner? You're a sick, twisted person," he said challengingly. That was how he always acted when I wasn't listening to him: He turned to strong-arm tactics, dredging up memories of the past to make me feel guilty.

"Today, you abuse yourself. What if, one day, you abuse your daughter?" he demanded archly.

I froze with my cigarette between my lips and stared at him. I felt cold down to my blood and bones. That was one of the reasons I never wanted children, especially daughters.

"Maybe I ought to get my revenge; what do you think? If you abandon me, I'll just come back and hurt *her*. I'll turn big and strong like you, and then I'll show you who's boss," he challenged me.

By then, I was blind with rage. I stalked toward him and took him by the throat. I slammed him back against the wall before sliding him up to eye level with me. At first he kicked and struggled against me, but then he realized that was useless and just smiled smugly because he understood that, really, he was the powerful one.

He manipulated my mind and contaminated me again and again.

"If you keep living in my head…" I whispered to him a hairsbreadth from his face, staring hard into his eyes, "I will kill myself," I finished resolutely. Finally, just doing it would be the only real way to free myself from him.

Never… never would I put another person through what I had been through.

Least of all some hypothetical daughter whom I never even wanted to have.

"Your mind is torn in two, Neil," he replied. "Today, you think of yourself as the hero, trying to save everyone from yourself. Tomorrow, you might become the villain. You might hurt someone and not even remember it because…" He paused to laugh again before continuing, slowly and clearly so I could read every word on his lips. "I am the monster, and you are my victim."

I released him and turned away in shock.

The Boy was a part of me that I had to kill or suppress completely if I ever wanted to be free.

If I didn't succeed, I would have to follow him and die along with him.

"Get out…" I murmured, staggering back again. "Get out!" I yelled, and he walked through the bathroom doorway, vanishing into thin air.

"Neil…" It was Logan's voice this time that called out to me. I whirled around to face him and caught him staring slack-jawed at me. "What are you doing?" He was probably trying to figure out why I was chain-smoking buck naked while talking intensely with…

"Having an argument," I answered, taking another drag like this whole shit situation was completely unremarkable.

"With...with whom?" Logan asked, looking through the clear glass window in front of me.

"With myself," I admitted.

There was no use making something up; Logan was well aware of my...quirks.

"And...are you done now?" he said, playing along like I was a crazy person, which I was not.

Or was I?

"I think so. For the moment." I shrugged as he blinked in bewilderment. An odd silence fell over us as the Boy's voice still vibrated in my head.

"Do you want something to eat?" My brother swallowed hard, standing motionless. He knew that I wasn't in my right mind and that one false move could trigger me in ways I wouldn't be able to control.

"No," I answered rapidly, ignoring my hunger. How long had it been since I'd last eaten?

Maybe that was why I felt lightheaded and so worn-out?

"You're really pale and—" he began.

"And I need a good fuck," I finished for him, and he gasped like I'd taken the lord's name in vain.

Logan knew me very well and knew what I meant: I needed to relive my trauma to take possession of myself again.

I felt uneasy and profoundly troubled.

My eyes screamed my suffering at him.

"It's not the solution, you know," he murmured wretchedly.

I wasn't having sex with the blonds as often as I'd used to. I'd been focusing on Selene lately, and now I was starting to lose the thread. I was really starting to feel the weight of everything pressing down on me: Player, his email to Selene, the webcam...

I couldn't deal with all of that, let alone the Boy on top of it.

Whenever he showed up, he defeated me, and I sank back into the depths.

The only way to survive, the only way to reaffirm my value, was to seduce an ever-shifting roster of women and hurl myself into degrading sexual situations. I used my masculine appeal to overpower them and then observed, cold and detached, their erotic dependence on me, the same kind that I, as a child, had developed upon Kim.

Even though I knew better intellectually, I still couldn't help the feeling sometimes that it was my fault.

I couldn't stop telling myself that maybe I just wasn't as good as the other kids, maybe I deserved what I got.

"Do you want me to go, then?" Logan didn't take a step. He remained on alert, watching my every move. That was the emotion I inspired in my brother: fear.

"Yes," I confirmed. *No.* I didn't want him to go.

I didn't want to be alone in my misery. I didn't want to give in to the twisted compulsion to which I had been enslaved for so long.

When Logan finally shut the door behind him, I angrily stubbed out my cigarette in the ashtray and threw myself down on the bed. It was still cold in there, and I wouldn't have minded getting a woman to warm me up. But that woman shouldn't be Jennifer nor any of my other blonds.

It should be...Tinkerbell.

Fuck.

I wanted my Neverland and no one else. I wanted her silken skin, her clear eyes, and her coconut smell.

I'd left her all alone in Detroit, and I yearned to see her again, to make sure she was alright.

I wanted her. I was crazy, yes. Crazy for her.

I rubbed my forehead, which felt overstuffed with thoughts and fears. I needed to turn my brain off.

I was too tense, too anxious, too tightly wound.

How could she accept a person like me?

Just then, I heard a knock at the door.

I stood up, alert, but didn't otherwise move.

It obviously wasn't Logan because he would have just walked in. After two more firm knocks, I got up with an animal growl of irritation.

I didn't bother putting on a pair of boxers; whoever was at my door could get a look at my cock in all its glory.

I dragged myself over to the door, fully irritated, and when I opened it...

It was a vision or maybe a hallucination.

"I know. I should have waited for you to reach out to me, but..." That soft, feminine voice could belong to no one but Babygirl.

My Babygirl.

I furrowed my brow and shivered at the cold air against my exposed body. Then, when I had finally accepted that my mind wasn't playing tricks on me, I snatched her by the waist and pulled her inside, slamming the door behind us. I pulled her to me in a headlong rush. The need to fuse with her, to drug myself with her smell, became overpowering, and she moaned as my arms wrapped around her slim body.

"Well, this is quite a welcome. I'm glad to see you too," she chuckled.

The last time we saw each other, I'd smashed her computer and left her alone in her room...

Nothing... I couldn't catch my breath; I couldn't form a thought.

"Shut up, Tinkerbell." I cupped her face in my hands and stared into her eyes. The blue ocean of them washed over me, leaving me stunned. The tip of her nose was rosy. I pressed a chaste kiss against it to warm it up, and then I did the same to her chapped and swollen lips before licking and biting them wildly. She groaned, clutching my back.

I felt her nails poking into my flesh, but her touch didn't trouble me. It was the only one I accepted.

Instinctively, I lifted her up. She let out a little yelp and clung to my neck as she scrambled to wrap her legs around my hips.

"I'm glad you're here..." I murmured, carrying her across the room to the bed.

There were so many questions I wanted to ask her: Had her mother known she was coming to New York to see me? Was she planning to stay and clear things up with her father?

But I wasn't capable of having a conversation just then—I'd get to it later.

I wanted her hot and naked underneath me. Immediately. No waiting.

All I wanted was to bury myself in her and forget about all my problems.

I threw her down on the mattress and straddled her.

Selene, whose breathing had already sped up, seemed surprised. I began eagerly undressing her like I was unwrapping a Christmas present. I didn't give a shit about her clothes; I just needed to access her body—a body that was, little by little, becoming my newest addiction.

She let me do it without any hesitation.

"You were so freaked out when you left, and I..." she paused as I continued to peel layers off her with shaking fingers. "I was afraid... I wanted to see you." A gasp.

Me too...

I wanted to see her too.

Because I needed her.

I needed her to help me forget my history and remember that there was more to this world than just nightmares.

I needed her to help me forget the slaps and punches I'd taken and learn that kisses and gentle touches also existed.

I needed her to exorcise my demons and draw me into her light.

I needed her to help me forget the woman who had consumed me and to collect the pile of ash I had become.

I needed her to help me forget the scars on my body and her kisses to soothe the hurt from them.

I needed her to help stop dying every day and perhaps come back to life, little by little.

I needed her because I had left my heart with her.

Even though it was broken, even though it was a defective old clunker, rotten and in pieces.

Even though it was soiled.

I had left it with her anyway.

Because I wanted it to be hers.

Maybe it always had been.

In the midst of this utter confusion, I confessed something impossible to her. "I'm yours," I whispered, incapable of controlling myself. Then I bent to kiss her. I was frenzied; I wasn't myself, and I could no longer hold back what I felt inside.

I wasn't going to talk about feelings with Selene. I wasn't going to change my ideas about love, but she knew me, she accepted me, and...and she'd been doing it for a while.

I knew perfectly well that I'd acted like a real bastard. If Selene had the guts to seek me out even after hearing about all the things that were wrong with me, after being threatened by a murderous hacker because of me, then she deserved to truly be with me.

At least until I left for Chicago, which I was going to tell her about very soon.

Once she was nude and free of any encumbering clothing, I quit kissing her and just looked her all over. That perfectly proportioned body that made me feel like I'd just shotgunned a bottle of whiskey. Those small, firm breasts—just the way I liked them—rising and falling with each breath. Her lean torso, dotted with the occasional beauty mark, and her soft pubis, where I lingered hungrily.

She blushed even though I'd already done everything to her and knew her every curve by heart.

Then, I gave her a wicked smile as I prepared to devour her whole.

I went back to kissing her, insinuating my hips between her thighs. She moved underneath me, eager to have me. She caressed my biceps and my back, trailing down my pecs, and she deepened the kiss, moving her tongue forcefully against mine. She was just as aroused as I was. I proved that to her, rubbing my erection between her outer lips, which I could feel were already wet and ready to envelop me.

"The way you smell…" she observed, sliding her mouth along my jaw. She bit me gently before sucking on the curve of my throat, making me moan slightly. I didn't like to waste time on fumbling juvenile foreplay, but Babygirl enjoyed it and I could be patient.

I looked into her ocean eyes, gleaming with arousal, as I propped myself up on my elbows on either side of her head. Her auburn hair spread out across the pillow, and her cheeks grew redder and redder.

With a tentative smile, she began to trace my pecs with her tongue, embarrassed, even now, by her desire. In a brief moment of clarity, I thought that perhaps I shouldn't fuck her after all. I wasn't gentle, and I wouldn't take it easy on her this time either.

"Selene…" My breath caught as I felt her hot, wet tongue laving my collarbone. "I'm too wound up today…" I whispered apprehensively, though the uncertainty in my voice was belied by the throbbing between my legs. "I don't want to hurt you…" And I couldn't figure out what was holding me back. I typically never cared to explain myself, and I didn't try to have a chat before fucking, didn't feel the need to forge an emotional connection…but, with her, it was different.

I didn't want to just use her as an object. I didn't want to vent my frustration on my body anymore.

"You never hurt me. Never. All you have to be is yourself. That's how I like you." Selene groped my abs gleefully. Then she moved on to my hips and ass. She palmed it and ground herself against me, like she wanted to trap me in her enchanted world.

"I want to feel you, Neil. Give me all of you. I won't share you with anyone," she said sensually, trying to cast her spell like the deadly fairy that she was. Her tongue drew a burning line down my neck, sending jolts of electricity all through me.

I closed my eyes, trying to get a grip.

Her mouth was everywhere.

Her hands were everywhere.

Her breath was everywhere.

Her kisses were everywhere.

Not Kimberly.

My Babygirl.

Impatient, I grasped my erection in one hand and dragged the head along her outer lips, already puffy with arousal. She pressed herself against me subtly, delicately, tempered by that lingering prudery that I wanted to strip away from her. Then I licked her cheek like an animal and hovered around her pussy without pressing inside because I wanted to test her; I wanted to feel that first resistance as she stared up at me, ethereal like an angel and fully aware of my little game. I began to grind against her, driving us both crazy, and when Selene arched her back and tilted her pelvis to hasten me, I shut down all rational thought, ignored all the problems all around us, and unleashed the savage, morally bereft part of me that had just been waiting to exorcise all his suppressed cravings with her.

Only with her.

I seized her mouth roughly.

I touched her body with greedy hands—she was so soft and

warm that I felt drunk on her. I couldn't withstand the desire to sink into her or the frustrated tension in my muscles for a minute longer, so I spread her thighs wide and thrust wildly into her. She yielded instantly to me.

She was so drenched, I slid inside without any resistance.

She let out a scream, and I paused in her enveloping heat, squeezing my eyes shut. I licked my lower lip and, like a beast in rut, kept her impaled upon me, savoring the moment when I felt her hot, tight walls closing all around me. I could feel her heartbeat, but the only thing throbbing in me was the need to pound her, taking full advantage of whatever time we had left together.

Because she held insane sway over me, obliterating me, making me lose all control, and bringing every part of me to life.

The good and the damned.

Selene shivered and went rigid at my vehemence.

I receded slowly, drawing out the friction between us before sinking back into her like the worst kind of beast.

In and out I went, wrenchingly possessive, and Selene was jolted against the bed with every stroke, struggling to keep pace with me, to not deny me, and to take what she wanted: me.

I wanted to get into her soul, deeper and deeper, because she was getting into mine, and I had no idea how to stop her.

She was taking up her rightful place.

Not just for a visit but to stay. Forever.

I started biting her then.

I started at her shoulder and moved down to her stiff nipples, compressing them between my teeth, leaving my mark on her.

Another one. One of many.

Because she was trying to bamboozle me with her fairy dust, and that made me furious.

She cried out but didn't deny me; she trusted me. I gave myself over to my instincts, breathing heavily.

I focused on the sight of my hard cock vanishing between her thighs like I was trying to split her in two. I could feel her pelvic muscles putting up desperate resistance, but Babygirl wanted me; she whispered it into my ear. So I continued to move against her, undeterred.

When I saw her face grow cloudy from who knew what kinds of thoughts, I captured her mouth with mine and kissed her, teasing her with my tongue. I wanted to make sure she was getting as much pleasure from this as me, but above all else, that I was right there, uppermost in her mind.

She didn't need to think about anything else. Only me.

I closed my eyes and pressed my forehead to hers, glorying in the devastating feeling of being inside her. With each deep thrust, her knees clenched tighter around my waist and her heels dug into my ass, urging me not to stop, to give her all of me, despite how difficult it must have been to withstand my ferocious assault. A moan of pleasure-pain fell unexpectedly from her parted lips. I stifled it with a carnal kiss as I continued to pound into her with untamed force.

I was struggling to keep her hope from rekindling mine.

Her feelings could only drag me into a world that was as enchanted as it was false.

The only sounds echoing around the room were the wrought iron of the bed slamming into the wall and our ragged breathing.

We panted, sweated, burned, and fought.

Selene had the ability to sweep away my fear.

And then I would try to break down her persistent delusion of an "ever after."

She and I were nothing until we came together. Then, we destroyed each other and remade ourselves.

And I would fight it for as long as I could, the two of us becoming one.

"Are you okay?" I asked in a moment of clarity.

She nodded, slipping her hands into my hair. She was lying; her body shouted it at me every time she went stiff, though she still tried to keep up with my mania.

I eagerly refocused on our clinch and pushed deeper inside her because I wanted to feel her completely enveloping my cock.

Selene cried out, and I got even harder, even more tense, even lustier, even crazier.

I wanted her to enclose me, to suck me in, to drag me down.

I wanted her to beat me—to win.

Babygirl swallowed and let her head fall back on the pillow, her eyelids drooping.

She was hot, drenched, and worn-out, but I was dead set on making her combust once more. I wanted to ruin her.

My stamina would demolish her, and she would be left wrung-out but satiated.

"You're..." she panted, short of breath. "My Disaster...Peter Pan." She tried to smile even as her slim, luscious body writhed beneath me while I continued my fervent strokes.

Her nails dug into my sides, her scratches pulling a guttural cry from me.

It hurt, but she could have been actively murdering me and I still would have kept flying toward my Neverland.

"You're close," I warned her as I felt her pussy spasm rhythmically around me. She arched her back, and her cheeks blazed. At the same time, I rubbed her clit with my thumb to ratchet up her pleasure and kissed her, tearing the breath from her again and again and again...

She climaxed beneath me as I continued to invade her, to shatter her, to bend her to my will.

Every bit of her was full of me.

Her fingers tightened around my waist, cutting into my skin.

Up she rose like a moth, beating her delicate wings, drawn to the light that only I could show her before plunging back down again. Back to earth, back to me, where she seized my lip with her teeth.

The metallic taste of blood spread across my tongue, and when she let me go, she collapsed in exhaustion on the bed.

A grin of purely male satisfaction spread across my face.

After a few more brutal strokes—short but intense—I couldn't hold back anymore.

I grabbed on to the headboard with one hand and clutched the iron rail like I was falling off a cliff. The headboard stopped banging, and the mattress springs stopped squeaking. An unstoppable fire erupted from my lower legs, spreading along my spine before finally reaching my brain.

I tucked my head into the curve of her throat, my muscles seizing, veins pulsing. My back was on fire, and my eyes were fogged over as I exploded into a violent, breathtaking orgasm that inundated both her and me.

All the tension I'd built up evaporated.

Completely out of breath, I collapsed on Babygirl, exhausted and bewildered. Sex with Selene was satisfying yet agonizing at the same time.

She was a lethal weapon.

A cursed poem.

A surreal dream.

Whatever she was...she was dangerous.

I held still inside her, my head cradled between her sweat-slicked breasts as I stared off into the middle distance. Babygirl's long, tapering fingers stroked my still-trembling back.

In that moment, I could feel each beat of her heart, her breathing slowing, little by little.

I was really feeling it for the first time.

It was real, no hallucination.

I turned my head toward her and found her staring at me. Those weary blue eyes were locked right on me. I didn't even want to think about the pathetic state I was in, but she was watching me worshipfully, completely enthralled. I took advantage of my position to nibble delicately on her stiffened nipples.

With her eyes boring into mine, I licked her pale areola and the little mole shaped like an upside-down heart that drove me so wild. Then I gave her a sly grin.

Once that sweet torture was done, I drew myself up on my elbows until I was level with her face. I pressed my groin against her clit, fully aware of how much it would turn her on.

My cock twitched inside her and Tinkerbell let out a gasp.

The thought that it was my cum making her so hot and slick was exhilarating.

"Neil…" She squeezed my biceps with her little hands, and I chuckled.

"What is it?" I said in a leonine grumble. I was aware of the effect my voice had on her, and I had no problems using it as another tool of seduction.

"Stop that," she demanded, throwing her arms around my neck.

She was drained, had red marks all over, and her lips were puffy from my kisses. If I looked at her too much, I would get lost in the kind of emotion that I usually kept controlled and repressed.

So I moved away from her.

I felt the chill as I withdrew from her body, and Selene sucked in a breath at the abrupt distance.

I laid back on the bed next to her, and Babygirl curled into the fetal position, hot and sweaty.

I could smell it on her: She smelled just like me. I had fully contaminated her now.

And what about me? Had she contaminated me?

I stared up at the ceiling and began to wonder if Tinkerbell hadn't been created to become my madness.

To push past all my limits.

To kiss my soul.

To free me from my prison.

I didn't know... I was confused.

I sat up and felt around on the nightstand for my Winstons. I held one between my lips and lit it.

I had a sensation of unfamiliar feelings creeping up on me, and I had no idea what to do about them.

"Is everything...okay?" Selene whispered, but I didn't reassure her or even look at her. She needed to get used to my abrupt mood swings; that was just the way I was. I was broken.

I stroked my still-stiff cock with one hand. It was slick with our shared fluids.

I knew I should bathe, but I didn't feel the immediate need to do so like I did with the others.

I growled abruptly in frustration at the inexplicable warmth I felt spreading through my chest and continued taking long, deep drags off my cigarette.

Maybe smoking could bring me back to myself.

I needed to be that cold man again: the cynical, apathetic one who thought about Kimberly when he fucked and nothing else.

"Neil..." Babygirl called, drawing my attention, and I shot her a hard look to put her back in her place. She could tell that I was on edge, so she receded back into herself, breathing shallowly. I saw it all. She was so slight and fragile that I felt like taking her in my arms and kissing every red mark I'd made on her body, but my pride wouldn't allow it.

I was not the kind of guy who indulged in cuddling, displays of affection, or other mushy crap.

I just wanted Selene to stay with me for a finite period of time because it was easier to protect her that way. That was it.

"Can you give me a minute? Or is it too hard for you to keep quiet for even that long?" I snapped angrily. She breathed in sharply at the harsh scolding and sat up.

Shit... if I were in her shoes, I would have slapped me. I needed to dig deep and get myself straight.

Selene touched her messy hair, pushing aside her sweaty bangs. Meanwhile, I made myself comfortable, leaning back against the headboard and stretching my legs out in front of me.

"I want to leave," she said wrathfully.

I almost laughed at the expression that had sprung up on her face.

First she was blissed out of her mind, and then she was infuriated. Truly, she was adorable.

"Not gonna happen. You're staying here with me, Babygirl," I answered mirthfully, arrogantly continuing to smoke. I blew the smoke out into the air and narrowed my eyes at her exposed breasts, lewdly imagining them back in my mouth.

"Why the hell do you always have to act like this?" She covered them with her forearm, purposefully depriving me of that extremely erotic image until I was forced to look back at her face. Those blue eyes, so full of light, of life, of dreams, were aimed at me like deadly projectiles. Once again, I put up my thick walls to protect me from her.

"I don't *act* like this; I *am* like this. There's a difference," I corrected her.

"Oh, for sure. You're inherently moody? Rude and unstable?" she teased me before bursting into hysterical laughter.

Babygirl was losing her mind, just like me.

"I'm eccentric, but more importantly, I'm very romantic," I doubled down.

"Yup, romantic..." she echoed sardonically. "If by 'romantic' you mean 'insufferable,' sure," she went on, shifting on her bottom like it was uncomfortable for her to sit. I looked down between her legs and felt a spark of concern.

I hadn't been gentle with her just then, and I was afraid I might have gone too far and finally driven her away from me—though I'd never admit that to her. Once again, I thought about how counterintuitively I was acting, doing everything I could think of to make her hate me but refusing to accept the idea of her actually leaving.

I shook my head, laughing at myself.

My internal confusion was putting me on edge.

I was typically hesitant with people, but I could never hesitate with her.

Because Selene shone in my solitude.

Shone in my darkness.

She shone, and she smelled like freedom.

And I was afraid.

She had the power to piece me back together or to shatter me at will, and she didn't even realize it.

"We should sleep," I said, grinding out the cigarette in the ashtray on the nightstand.

I laid down on my side, showing her my back, and tried to calm down, though my head felt swollen with thoughts like a balloon full of water.

I shivered from the cold, but I didn't bother covering my body.

I would sleep like that, naked in my little corner of secure solitude.

I was just shutting my eyes when I felt her small, cold hand wrapping around my abdomen.

Selene plastered herself against me, her breasts pressed against my back.

My cock perked up at this feminine touch, ready to get some more of Babygirl's attentions.

I wanted to push her away, to shrug her off, but she felt strangely good there.

Secure.

She would never take advantage of my sleeping state to hurt me the way that Kim had done.

"Goodnight," she whispered, pressing a warm kiss to my shoulder. I breathed in raggedly at the sweet gesture.

I wanted to reciprocate, but I didn't. Instead, I rested my head down on the soft pillow and shut my eyes.

Selene was a refuge for a restless soul like me. That was why I called her my Neverland.

Then, at last, I fell asleep. Feeling no fear.

....

I got up with the sun and fled to the shower.

Cleaning myself was my favorite part of the day because it allowed me to purge my body of sweat, sex, torments...all the things I carried inside as well as on my skin.

Once I was finished, I went back into the bedroom with just a towel wrapped around my hips, careful not to make any noise.

Tinkerbell rested on her side in the middle of the enormous bed, gloriously nude.

Her auburn hair spilled out around her, and one hand was clenched into a fist and pressed to her lips. She'd hooked one arm over my pillow and held it tightly, like she needed me or something of mine even in her sleep.

I knew the pillow was permeated with my smell; it seemed she wanted to breathe it in even when she was unconscious.

I smiled. It was very sweet.

I wanted to go over and kiss her, but something inside held me back. An open display of affection like that was too far out of the norm for me.

I shook my head to clear it and went into the kitchen.

I needed a black coffee.

I had seriously just fucked her without even bringing up the issue of Player and how he was targeting her again. Like the giant bastard that I was, I'd thought only of my own pleasure.

While I made the coffee, I tried to think of some way to excuse my actions.

I wasn't bound to her—at least not in the way she thought.

I could no longer tell whether I was denying an inner truth that I nevertheless knew was there or if I was fully acknowledging that truth and acting indifferent to keep it compartmentalized.

I rucked up my hair.

There was one thing I was entirely certain about, though. Whatever feelings I did have for Selene were in direct opposition to the reality I'd built around myself.

She had become an obstacle, a burden, a return to the past, because love had already wounded me. Had destroyed me.

At the end of the day, my existence was about survival, and I was too fragile to be bound to any woman, even if I ached for her. My soul would have sunk into the depths and never resurfaced.

I didn't know exactly what kept me connected to Selene, what made me miss her, want her, or need to protect her.

I would just have to keep cheating at this crazy game of ours, telling a half-truth that was more comfortable for the both of us: I did care about her... at least a little bit.

And that was how it was always going to be.

Firmly convinced, I picked up the coffee pot and poured some into a mug.

I leaned back against the counter and sipped it. The warm liquid slid down my throat and straight into my hollow stomach. I hadn't eaten dinner the night before, compensating with a couple packages of pistachios. I couldn't go on like that.

I was still working out just as much, but I was eating very little. I knew that if I didn't start eating right, I wouldn't have the energy I needed to face my days.

I was focused on the aesthetic element, though.

I looked down at my torso, which had leaned down enough to show the clear lines of my muscles. My pubic area was bracketed by two lateral lines only partially concealed by the low waist of the sweatpants I wore, ties dangling over the bulge between my legs.

I had long ago learned how to use my looks as yet another tool of seduction, just the way Kim taught me. The strapping, powerful physique was a crucial part of my strategy. I sighed miserably before looking up at the sound of light footfalls coming into the kitchen.

Still holding my mug in midair, I looked at Selene, who was shambling toward me with clumsy, sleepy motions.

She really was cute.

She looked exactly like a disgruntled kid who'd been woken up too early, her long hair tumbling wildly to the base of her spine and her disheveled bangs covering her scar.

"Good morning," she muttered, holding back a yawn. Then, all at once, she froze like it had just then occurred to her that she'd spent the night with me. She looked me up and down with her big ocean eyes. She lingered a bit on my bare chest and licked her lower lip before dragging her eyes back up to my face.

"Good morning to you," I answered after a beat, watching as she sat down on a stool at the kitchen island. Selene looked thoughtful, staring off into space, and the idea that she was actually a million miles away in her head irked me. "What are you thinking about?" I asked her abruptly, making her jump.

For a second, I was afraid that she regretted coming to see me or even that she thought I'd finally gone too far with the previous night's fuck. I had been wild and uncontrolled, but I didn't want her condemning me for it—or herself.

Then Babygirl turned her face my way, and once again, gave me a look so unsettlingly worshipful that it almost made me embarrassed.

I read an emotion in her eyes that I didn't like at all, something I refused to name.

I made a scornful face, and she got off her stool to sashay over to me. I stared at her in confusion.

I never allowed a woman this kind of intimacy: sharing a bed with her all night, letting her invade my space, seeing her first thing in the morning, and even sharing breakfast with her like some happy couple.

It just didn't belong in my daily life.

Lost in my own thoughts, I failed to notice that Selene had reached me until I saw her looking me up and down like a deadly tigress. She was particularly focused on my waist, and I frowned as I tried to figure out what the hell had caught her attention there. I got it when she delicately brushed her fingers along the raised, reddish scratches that had been left there by her fingernails.

"Are those from me?" she asked, staring at them fixedly.

Was she for real?

She was the only other person there; the answer seemed fairly obvious, so I didn't say anything.

"Meaning, whoever touches you next is going to see them and know that you are mine," she continued, staring piercingly into my eyes.

"Yours?" I repeated, like she was speaking another language.

"Yes...you told me you were last night. While we were..." She trailed off, embarrassed.

"Well, I wasn't exactly thinking clearly then, was I?" I said defensively, thinking back to being naked and on top of her, eager to get inside her. I might have said anything to her then; my brain was not plugged in.

Babygirl stopped touching my waist, looking briefly hurt before regrouping and turning determined, like she didn't want to show any vulnerability in front of me.

"Have you ever said that to anyone else?" she asked probingly.

No, I had never felt any desire to belong to someone or, on the other hand, to demand that a woman belong to me.

That kind of possessiveness and need for ownership were alien to me. So much so, I wasn't sure I could identify those sensations if I was feeling them.

"No," I admitted, taking another drink of coffee—I really needed it.

"So sex clearly doesn't muddle your thinking that much, then. You're calculating by nature, Neil. We both know that. You don't just spout off," Selene pointed out.

I didn't break any of my many rules, except when it came to Selene where I broke them all.

Still, I was positive that I had been talking total bullshit the night before. I often got unbalanced and confused, but those moments would inevitably give way to reason and clear thinking. Like I was doing right then.

Without sparing her a glance, I went to drinking my coffee while her fingers began to move over my abs. Typically, I hated that kind of physical contact and had no problem making that clear to anyone, but in that moment, her delicate yet sensual touch pleased me.

She grinned impishly, her cheeks slightly coloring in minor embarrassment before moving closer until her breasts were pressing against my torso.

My breath caught like it was the first time I'd ever felt a woman's body against my own, and every part of me was on alert as Selene stood up on her tiptoes to drop a kiss along the curve of my throat.

My eyelids grew heavy as I got drunk on those delightful touches. I let out a moan when I felt her hand slip between my legs. She rubbed the hardness in my pants with her open palm, tracing its length with a smug smile.

She could feel my body reacting to her provocation. I stared seriously at her to let her know that I was down to satisfy her—that I'd fuck her right there on that kitchen island behind her—but I was keeping myself in check.

"Where'd you get that bad habit?" Her lips grazed my beard stubble, and I was hit with the hot wave of her breath.

Where had my shy Tinkerbell gone?

"Which of my many bad habits are you talking about?" I asked irreverently, refusing to let down my guard.

"The one where you go on the defensive like I'm the enemy," she answered softly, stretching to reach my mouth and kiss me.

Oh... what an adorable girl.

I moved away, so she missed my mouth, and Selene lowered herself back down with a look of surprise. "Does your mother know you're here?" I asked her. "Did you two have an argument over me?" I asked her baldly, and Selene went stiff. She nodded, and I scrubbed a hand over my face, trying to restrain my urge to yell at her.

Everything was going to shit. I'd already blown up her relationship with Matt, and now I was destroying the one she had with Judith.

"She's accepted my decision. I want to be with you," she admitted, like it was a normal thing to tell me. I couldn't suppress my rage, and my right hand began to tremble as I pushed it anxiously through my hair.

"This is not a fucking love story. Do you understand? How long am I going to be yours? A month, two? Not forever," I spat. "Besides, the only reason I'm keeping you here is because I have to protect you from a psychopath, not because you're going to be my girlfriend or my partner or whatever else..."

"Oh, so I can date whoever I want, then? Take them to bed and just..." Selene made a very articulate gesture while grinning slyly at me. I could feel the blood draining from my face.

Shit, no way! For a moment, I went weak at the knees, but I recovered and advanced furiously on her before grabbing her and pulling her roughly to me. Babygirl shut her mouth and held her breath.

"You will continue to do all of that with me. I'm the only one who can have you," I murmured in a possessive tone I'd never used with anyone else before.

I was blind with rage, my thinking obscured by the mental image of her with someone else. I was getting nauseous, and I was afraid I was going to vomit up the small amount of coffee I'd managed to drink.

What the hell was happening to me?

I didn't release her from my grip, not even when she clenched her teeth and I could tell I was hurting her.

"If I don't matter to you, then why are you jealous?" she whispered, staring deeply into my eyes. Something in my chest shook loose at the sound of that word.

I was... jealous?

I never had been before. I wasn't even sure if I could recognize jealousy in myself. But maybe with her...

"I don't..." I started to say, but the words were trapped on the tip of my tongue. Selene smiled victoriously and stretched up again to give me a kiss. In shock, I allowed it.

She didn't retreat when she felt my body's resistance—I had tensed up, unsure about returning her affections. She rubbed herself boldly against me, and I let out a groan, letting go of her waist to cup her ass and bring her more tightly against me.

"You're trying to destroy me. You're dangerous. You're a wicked witch. A formidable enemy. You're no Tinkerbell... You're really just a little bitch," I hissed, pulling back slightly, but she just rubbed the nape of my neck and kissed me again, even more passionately this time, like she was trying to get me to take her right there on the kitchen counter. I opened my mouth, indulging her and merging our desires.

Who had told her she could kiss me like that?

No one. And yet, here she was, boldly laying claim to me as if she had every right to do so.

I couldn't bring myself to push her away, though, and kept succumbing to the frustrating urge to taste her, to steal her breath, to invade her with my tongue and leave her stunned.

I reciprocated her gesture with violent desperation, and she began to struggle for breath. She tightened her hand on my shoulder, signaling that I should slow down a bit, but like the huge bastard I was, I refused to stop.

This was what she wanted—me—and I was going to do it my way.

"Good God!"

I pulled away from Selene when I heard a masculine voice bouncing off the pool house's walls. Reluctantly, I turned to see who our heckler was, only to find Matt Anderson standing motionless in the doorway. He'd just barged in without knocking or calling out, and now he was staring slack-jawed at me and his daughter. He had most assuredly gotten an eyeful already, and I still hadn't bothered to take my hands off Selene's ass cheeks.

"Anna was right. She said she saw a girl come in here, but she wasn't sure if it was you. I guess..." he said, his voice uncertain, and only then did I decide to move away from Babygirl, hoping that would help Matt process the situation. He turned his dark eyes on me and looked at me with such hate that anyone else in my shoes probably would have been afraid.

"You really don't have any shame, do you, Neil? You keep on making the same mistakes," he said in a wrathful hiss while a frightened Selene inched closer to me, grasping my arm nervously. Her nails dug into my bare flesh. I glanced quickly at her and saw that she was scared. I couldn't stand seeing her like that. I pulled back from her touch, and she looked lost, so I rested a reassuring arm around her shoulders. Tinkerbell rested her head on my chest, holding me tight.

"I keep on wanting your daughter. What of it? This shouldn't come as a surprise," I admitted, sounding indifferent, and Selene sucked in a breath. She obviously hadn't expected that kind of statement from me and certainly not in front of Matt, who let out a bitter laugh.

"The way you want her is sick!" he shouted. "You've even turned her against me!" he added accusingly.

Did he seriously believe all the blame for this situation could be laid at my feet? I had come between them, yes, even if that was never what I wanted, but I was hardly the only problem the two of them had. He needed to stop being such a coward and quit blaming me exclusively.

He should have just focused on fixing the already damaged relationship he had with his daughter instead of obsessing over who she was seeing or screwing.

"Selene, I called. I went out to Detroit. You refused to talk to me. Your mother and I are both worried about you." He turned to Selene, his affect changing completely. He moved closer to his daughter at a cautious pace, ignoring me entirely. I struggled to hold back my laughter because Matt Anderson really knew how to make an ass of himself. Still, Babygirl was holding tightly to me, a tacit plea that I not let her go.

I wasn't going to. Not right then, at least.

"Look at you," Matt said, scrutinizing her from head to toe. "You've lost weight. You look exhausted..." he went on, frowning as he looked at her throat. I knew what he was frowning at—the marks I'd left on her with my excessive passion in bed. When it came to Tinkerbell, I couldn't control myself. That was what my sexual partners liked about me—how I pushed the boundaries. I was confident that Selene, likewise, appreciated my more intense nature, but it was different for a parent. I would never be the guy anyone brought home to Mom and Dad.

"He is draining the life out of you, Selene. He's going to keep doing it for as long as he can, as long as you continue to let him. He did it before with Scarlett, and now it's your turn."

That goddamned name was enough to cloud my reason. I squeezed Babygirl closer to me and stared Matt down, bristling to fight back. But Matt was, in addition to being my mother's partner, the father of the woman who had somehow managed to worm her way into my soul. For her sake, I restrained myself. It wasn't easy, though.

"You can't understand. No one can understand why this is so important to me," Selene answered, speaking for the first time since Matt had barged into the pool house. "Maybe I sound like a crazy kid with my head in the clouds. But I would rather take the risk and follow my heart because I know that it will be worth it," she added, sounding even more determined. My gaze softened, and for just a moment, I wondered what I had done to deserve someone like her.

I had always thought of my life as a cursed pendulum that swung between pain and pleasure. Tinkerbell seemed to want to stop that pendulum, boot the Boy out on his ass, and force me into a better reality.

"He's brainwashed you. You're addicted to him. Maybe only sexually... but that's what it is." The sound of Matt's voice pulled me from my thoughts.

Had he really just said that?

I burst into laughter.

If anything, it was the other way around: I was the one who was sexually dependent on his daughter, especially in recent days.

Selene looked up at me, puzzled, while her father glowered at me. He would have happily murdered me.

"Trust me, Matt, you don't know shit," I answered, brushing off the remnants of my inopportune laughing fit.

"So you say," he scoffed indignantly at me. "But we both know you've got problems. There's no reasoning or communicating with you. You steamroll your way through the world like we all owe you something. I know you're probably treating my daughter like a doll, like some servile doormat who exists just for your pleasure!" he lashed out at me. "You're twisted, and just the thought of you putting your hands on her makes me sick!" he yelled with all the breath in his lungs. Selene clutched me tighter. She hated it when people raised their voices and trembled when she felt like she was in danger. It was insane that I now had to protect her from her father when I really should have been protecting her from me first.

Matt wasn't wrong about everything: I was twisted.

"It's okay," I said in a low, reassuring tone. I felt the sudden urge to comfort her and to make her understand that even though I was a mess, disturbed, and all mixed up, she could trust me. I used two fingers to tilt her chin up and force her to look into my eyes. The ocean in hers was tumultuous. She was confused. Instinctively, I kissed her lips, more chaste but no less intense than the ones I typically gave her. Her eyes slipped closed in abandon, as though I were now her entire world.

I smiled against her mouth before turning to look at Matt, who was staring at us like he'd caught us fucking raw rather than exchanging a fairly ordinary consoling gesture.

"You don't love her," he murmured wretchedly, probing the shadows behind my eyes. "You haven't changed. I can see it. And I know you're not going to change," he went on, sounding agonized. I licked my lip, tasting his daughter's sweetness again, and stared at him with a look of satisfaction as well as challenge.

"I don't need to tell you shit," I answered, neither confirming nor denying anything. "But one thing I do know for certain—there's nothing you can do to stop me," I concluded with a hint of masculine pride that I knew a man like him would surely understand. Matt Anderson did, in fact, take the hit and staggered back miserably, staring at me in shock.

Selene continued to cling to me like I was the only thing anchoring her in place. She tracked her father's movements as he walked with shoulders slumped out the door. He looked wrecked as he accepted the bitter truth that he had lost his daughter.

Possibly forever.

14

*"He doesn't need a woman, Selene,
he needs a goddamned psychiatrist."*

SELENE

Agonized.

That was how I felt when Matt left the pool house, so disappointed to have caught me with Neil once again. He hadn't seen what went on the night before, but I'm sure he got the idea.

I sighed and sipped my unsweetened coffee, which I never used to drink.

I'd been spending too much time with Mr. Disaster—I was picking up his habits.

I was alone in the kitchen after Neil had fled to the bathroom for another shower. His brief absence allowed me to think clearly for once and reflect on what had just happened.

I needed to have a conversation with Matt.

I tortured myself with mental images of him wallowing in misery in one of the sumptuous rooms of his mansion until my stomach cramped up. Abruptly, I gulped down my last bitter sip of coffee before leaving the mug on the kitchen island.

I got off my stool and walked to the hallway to let Neil know I was leaving.

I couldn't hear the roar of the running water, so I figured he was out of the shower. But when I poked my head past the half-opened door, I froze in astonishment.

Neil stood there, facing the mirror, unmoving. He wore just a towel around his hips, and his wet hair dripped down the back of his neck. His body was stiff with tension. At first, I thought he was just looking at himself in the mirror the way anyone might, but when I looked closer, I saw his vacant stare.

His golden eyes were wide open but hazy, locked on his reflection. He didn't so much as blink, lost in some unknowable world. He was experiencing a disconnect from reality; he was dissociating.

For the first time, I felt afraid.

It was a type of fear that I didn't know how to manage: primordial, intense, and draining.

I was on high alert; fleeing or defending myself were the only options my lizard brain suggested.

The more seconds went by, the more palpably dangerous the situation became.

My anxiety became unbearable, and I let out the breath I hadn't realized I'd been holding. That short but intense exhalation captured Neil's attention, and he turned sharply in my direction.

Caught gawking at him, I stepped back a few paces and tried to flee. Neil was too quick, though, and he caught me by the wrist.

I whirled around to face him, and my back slammed up against the wall outside the bathroom door. I stared at the rise and fall of his chest as he panted.

His smell was so intense, and he held me with strength but without violence.

The distance between us was negligible.

I tracked the journey of a water droplet that ran down his neck to wet the defined muscles of his chest. I heard him sigh and got up the nerve to raise my head and meet his eyes.

Neil watched me with a furrowed brow; his bright eyes were glassy and obscured by dark thoughts. His full lips flattened into a grim expression, and his jaw was tight.

"I'm sorry," I whispered, reassuring him that no matter what I witnessed, I wasn't going to judge him. "I just wanted to let you know that I'm going to go talk to Matt," I informed him, my voice shaking. He took note of it and bent down until our faces were level with each other. He studied me closely, looking for any hint of fear. I wasn't as skilled at hiding my emotions as he was; he could probably see that I was frightened. He didn't say anything in response and just inched closer to me until his torso was flush with my chest. I found myself caught between him and the hardness of the wall, squeezed between them with no escape route.

"The Boy is jealous of you," he murmured, a hot breath against my ear. "But I've got him under control. You have nothing to be afraid of," he continued, his voice low and unsettling.

"And what would he do to me if you didn't have him under control?" I managed, sounding calm even as my legs began to tremble.

Neil grazed my neck with the tip of his nose and placed his elbows on either side of my head, leaning his whole body into mine.

"He'd destroy you," he answered, and my blood ran cold. I didn't say anything out of fear that I might trigger some irrational reaction. Instead, I just tried to keep from crying as Neil backed off a bit to look at my forehead. For a second, I didn't know what he was looking at, but then I realized it: my scar. He stared at it with absent eyes, the pupils so shrunken that they almost appeared entirely golden. I could hardly recognize him. Something inside told me that this was not the man I loved.

It was a chilling, unsettling sensation, and it raised goosebumps all over me. It felt like I was watching someone else try to seize control of Neil's mind, and Neil was fighting back. The sight of him, so lost and confused, hit me like a stab of pain to the chest.

"They're called alters..." he murmured. He wanted to talk, to open up to me. There was something dark, though, that was holding him captive. I could see it in the incredible effort it cost him just to manage those few weak words.

"Who are?" I raised a hand to touch him, but he stepped back. My heart felt like it cracked in two when he shot me a severe look, warning me not to lay a hand on him.

"The people who live inside me..." he answered flatly.

"Are they dangerous?" I managed, sounding uncertain.

"Are you afraid?" He dodged my question, and I held my breath, incapable of admitting that I was. He felt it nevertheless, and it grieved him. Then he blinked rapidly. He had exposed more of himself than he wanted to and obviously felt like he needed to change the subject to avoid showing even more vulnerability.

"Matt's your father; you can go talk to him whenever you want. You don't have to run it by me or anything," he said frostily, his tone even but remote, like he wasn't really there. He turned then, not waiting for my answer, and returned to the bathroom at a leisurely pace.

The rigid posture, the straight back, the sedate pace...

I cocked my head to one side to get a better look at him: That wasn't Neil.

He was a robot, devoid of human emotion, not my Disaster.

I watched him, astonished, as he went back to the bathroom and shut the door behind him.

I sighed and stood still for a few seconds.

It was happening more and more often. Neil was having these periods of blackout or confusion where he couldn't even recognize me. I should have been growing accustomed to it, but instead I grew more and more troubled every time it happened.

I shook my head to clear it and headed out to find Matt.

I rubbed my arms as I hurried around the house to the front door, where I rang the doorbell. I wasn't sure if my father was still inside—it wasn't like him to hang out at home when he could have been at the hospital—and I didn't want to surprise anyone by sneaking in through the kitchen.

After a few moments, Anna opened the door, looking slightly confused.

"Hi, Ms. Anna. Can I come in?" was all I said, giving her a small, friendly smile. When her moment of shock wore off, the older woman stepped aside to allow me in.

"Miss Selene. I saw someone going into the pool house last night, and I thought it was you, but I couldn't be certain," she told me, looking me up and down with an expression of concern on her face. "You've lost weight..." she elaborated uncertainly.

I had been going through a lot of difficult things recently, and the toll it took on me was obvious.

I had lost a few pounds, but it wasn't as serious as everyone seemed to believe.

"Yup, it's me. In the flesh," I joked to ease some of the awkwardness between us. "Is my father around?"

Anna didn't even have time to answer before Matt, who had been sitting on the living room sofa, got to his feet and looked miserably at me.

"Selene." He seemed at first almost awed by my presence, but his face quickly hardened into the severe expression of a disappointed father. All of his muscles tensed under his fancy blazer.

"I wanted to..." I moved toward him, chafing my hands together because they were still cold. "I wanted to talk to you," I finished, closing the distance between us. Matt furrowed his brow and then stepped toward me looking agitated. He cupped my face in his hands and stared at me, unspoken hurt clear in every line on his face.

"I am... trying to protect you," he said before I could say anything more. He stared into my eyes. "You are my daughter. And you've completely fallen for a guy who is only going to bring you pain. Maybe he already is," he added wretchedly. "I knew you two were still seeing each other, but I was in denial. He's never here, and it worried Mia at first. She thought he'd gotten caught up in another one of his messes, but then, thanks to Logan, we found out he'd actually been going to Detroit all the time to see you..." he said bitterly.

"I've always made my own decisions when it comes to my life. And you haven't really been a part of my life for the past twenty-one years, so you can't just come in and play the concerned father now," I shot back irritably, pulling myself away from his touch. Matt kept his hands suspended in the air, shocked at my response.

"I can't stay out of this, Selene. Not when my daughter gave her virginity to my partner's son. Not when my daughter continued to sleep with him under my roof, completely betraying the trust I'd placed in her. Not when my daughter is choosing to destroy her own life chasing after a seriously disturbed boy with mental problems. You don't know him, Selene." Matt's whole affect changed, and he started raising his voice, one hand clenching into an angry fist. Surprised by this sudden shift, I took a few steps back.

"I know everything. I know about Kim, about the abuse, about the psychiatric treatment—"

"Did you know he abruptly stopped treatment three years ago against Dr. Lively's advice?" Matt cut in. "Did you know that he's supposed to be on medication but refuses to take it? Did you know that his psychiatrist is in constant contact with Mia, asking her to get her son under control before he hurts himself or someone else? Did you know about all of that?" he burst out furiously.

His words froze me where I stood. I felt like I was going to cry, my throat tightening around a knot of emotion, but I worked hard to breathe through it and keep a clear head.

"And do you know what he does when you're not around? You've known him for how long? A few months, Selene? I've known him for a good four years now!" he said firmly. "And I can assure you—I know a lot more about him than you do." He looked at me, his eyes oil-dark as he hammered in his point. I was struck silent again, confused and stunned by what I was hearing.

Matt saw that and took the opportunity to pile on.

"When I look at you, I see Scarlett all over again," he said softly. "That girl cared so much for him, and at first, Neil liked her a lot..." And there she was again, the famous Scarlett Scott, daughter of officer Roger Scott. The one who was still a mystery to me, though apparently not to anyone around me.

"That girl followed him around like a puppy for a year. She put up with everything, accepting anything Neil threw at her. He would undoubtedly tell you she was crazy, but he's the one who made her that way."

I looked Matt solidly in the eye as I swallowed that bitter pill.

"Neil isn't evil, but his brain doesn't work the way others do. His reality isn't the same as ours, Selene. He sees Kim in every woman he meets because she's always in his head. He does to women what Kim did to him. He manipulates them, he brainwashes them, he uses them, and then he throws them away. Not out of malice, but because there's something broken inside him, a trauma that he hasn't resolved. Mia has gotten so many calls from Dr. Lively. He's worried because Neil hasn't made any progress in years. The whole situation is very delicate, and his ability to manipulate others has only grown. He should be on consistent medication to help him control his outbursts, his impulsive behavior, and his unstable personality. Neil isn't like Jared; he isn't like any other guy you've ever known. I only want what's best for you. And the best thing for you is to get far away from him." Matt placed his hands on my shoulders as my head spun. I swallowed painfully, like my throat was full of thorns. It wasn't anything new to me, but hearing it from my father was different somehow.

"Did he...love Scarlett?" I ventured.

"No, definitely not." Matt shook his head as though what I'd said was patently ridiculous. "He's never loved any woman; I don't think he's even capable of it. What I do know is that he feels a powerful physical attraction toward his lovers, especially the blonds. He certainly felt that for Scarlett. Neil hates talking about her because he knew he made some serious mistakes with her. He tries to justify what he did by blaming her, saying she was obsessed and too in love with him. But when she would come over here and go up to his room, he definitely didn't have any problems..." he trailed off, suddenly uncomfortable.

"Sleeping with her," I finished for him, staring into the middle distance.

"Yes." Matt nodded. "He never turned her down. She always thought it meant that there might be a future for them, and she started going to more and more extreme lengths because of it. Sometimes, she'd wait outside the front door all night while he was out with his friends or lovers. Other times, she'd even..." He sighed, licking his lips uncomfortably. "She'd self-harm in the hopes of receiving just a little bit of love from him, like he'd led her to believe..."

I felt like I was taking gut punch after gut punch, and I didn't have the capacity—or the will—to fight back.

These details were new to me. Neil had never told me.

"This is all just a game to him, Selene. Please don't put your trust in him," Matt went on. "Please don't let him draw you in and trap you, or eventually, the same thing that happened to that poor girl will happen to you. You could lose yourself completely in him, and he'll just move on to the next girl. First it was Scarlett, who tried and failed to save him. Now, there's you, and after you, there'll be another girl and another one and on and on..." he said with a sigh of exhaustion.

I looked at him uncertainly. I wriggled away from his hands that had been holding my shoulders so tightly, feeling like I might be sick at any moment.

"Neil..." I managed. "Neil...is sincere with me. He's himself with me," I said in a bewildered whisper. Who was I really trying to convince, my father, who was staring at me like I'd lost my mind, or myself?

Maybe I *had* lost my mind.

"He is *not* himself when he's with you, and that's exactly the problem," Matt said softly. "Think about it, Selene. How did this so-called relationship of yours start?" He looked deeply into my eyes, probing for doubts. "It was a way for him to amuse himself. He lured you in, and you got rid of Jared. Not because you wanted the relationship to end, but because Neil made you do it. I know that he got in your head and convinced you to give him what he wanted, no matter how dirty or wrong it felt. Isn't that right?" he asked, troubled. I took another step back, shaking my head no. "And what happened after you dumped Jared? Did Neil quit sleeping with other women? Did he enter into a real relationship with you? No," he said tightly, while I just stood there motionless, listening. "He's never going to do it, Selene. He's never going to start something real with you. He'll just keep you dangling on a string until the day he inevitably cuts it. And he will cut it, Selene. Then you'll fall, devastated and still in love with him, and he'll move on to the next Scarlett so he can play another round of his game. And that will keep happening over and over again until he actually heals, until he gets help for his problems. He doesn't need a woman, Selene; he needs a goddamned psychiatrist to assess him. He needs medication; he needs treatment. He doesn't need romantic love. You have to understand that. I need you to understand." He raised his voice, taking me by the shoulders again and giving me a shake. By that point, I was in a fugue state.

I felt like I'd been transported to a bewildering, undefined other world.

Matt might have been right, or he might have been a skillful manipulator who was using his knowledge of Neil's past to freak me out. He wanted to inject doubt into what I thought I knew; he wanted to taint it with his own disparaging beliefs about Neil.

At the end of the day, I had never been able to completely trust my father before, and this wasn't going to be the one time that I did.

"I... I gotta go..." I muttered, turning toward the door. I rubbed my forehead, which was throbbing. I felt a tremendous migraine coming on, and I didn't even have my pain meds with me. My doctor told me that I was recovered and that the headaches would become more and more infrequent, except when I was experiencing anxiety and stress. Lately, that felt like all I was experiencing.

"Selene!" Matt called after me.

I walked out of the house and strode over to the pool house. It was insane to want to seek refuge in the arms of the same person everyone was warning me off from because he was apparently so dangerous. And, of course, Neil's instability sometimes made me afraid, but I knew that he would never hurt me. Not if he could help it. And I couldn't abandon him now when he'd finally started opening up to me and allowing me to support him a little. He was slowly putting more trust in me, giving me a little bit more of his soul.

I pounded on the door, upset, as I waited for Neil to answer. As soon as he did, I swept inside, dragging a hand through my hair.

I wanted to pretend like I'd sorted everything out with Matt, but I was no good at hiding what I was feeling. And, in that moment, I was visibly shaken.

"Let me guess..." Neil let the door close with a thud. He was dressed now in a gray sweater, and I could see from the raised veins on the backs of his hands that he was uncomfortable. "He told you I'm a whack job. Some kind of psychopath who needs treatment and that you ought to get far away from me, right?" A cruel smile twisted his lips. They were still pink and swollen from the passionate kissing we'd indulged in all night long.

Neil truly was addictive, and what if...

What if Matt was right?

What if I was so addicted to him that I couldn't see the truth?

"Chill out, we're just playing," he had told me during one of our first encounters.

"How are we playing? What does this game consist of?" I had asked him in return.

"If I told you, what fun would that be?" he'd answered cryptically.

Every sentence of that conversation seemed to bore into my temples. All the little certainties I'd built up in the last few days began to crumble in the face of questions that required answers.

"You're thinking too hard," Neil noted, stepping toward me. I took one step back. I knew I couldn't think straight when he got too close to me. Maintaining a reasonable distance from him was the only way I could keep my thoughts in order. But the brief flicker of hurt on his face when he saw my hesitation killed me. I didn't want to push him away or treat him like a monster the way almost everyone else did, but I needed to process what Matt had just told me.

"We need to talk about Scarlett. You were with her for a long time, right? I need to know everything that happened with you two," I told him firmly. Neil wrinkled up his forehead and turned inward for a moment, staring at the open air behind me before eventually turning his attention back to me with a sigh.

"This again?" His lips curled into a sneer.

"You've never actually told me about her. You always dodge my questions," I retorted.

"What did your dad say to you? Fucker...instead of fixing his issues with you, he just talks shit about me. Incredible." He gave a scornful shake of his head at Matt's audacity. I remained impassive, waiting for him to actually respond to me. Neil took note of that and ran his tongue nervously over his lips before touching his hair. It was difficult, ignoring that destabilizing charm of his.

"I need to know, Neil. I was all yours last night, so now I want something in return," I insisted, clinging to our old deal. He shot me a glance, lightning quick, like he wasn't sure whether to kick me out of the pool house or finally spill everything. Eventually, his shoulders slumped and he relented.

"What exactly do you want to know?" he asked, his face turning as unmovable as ever.

"All of it. Start from the beginning," I said. I followed him with my eyes as he moved toward the kitchen island and leaned against it. He narrowed his eyes at me, assessing whether I was actually ready to listen.

I gave him a look of certainty, and he began to speak.

"I met Scarlett at a club. I was there with the Krew; she was there with some friend of hers. I took note of her right away. It would have been hard not to, a girl like that—tall, blond, sexy. I went up to her and started a conversation with the sole purpose of getting her into bed. I made it clear to her that I wasn't the type to make any commitments, and she accepted my conditions. So we started seeing each other, but I never talked about myself with her. I just took what I wanted from her. I enjoyed it at first. I enjoyed being with her, and I found her extremely physically attractive. But I didn't change my mind. I still didn't want a relationship." He looked attentively at me, searching my face for some emotion. I tried to remain cool and conceal the jealousy that devoured my insides at the thought of him with someone else.

"And then?" I cleared my throat, prompting him.

"And then Scarlett convinced herself that she could have some grand love story with me, that I could change. She started acting like a girlfriend. She'd follow me everywhere. She'd throw a jealous fit every time she found me with someone else…" His voice was low and measured, like he was flashing back on all those memories in his mind. "She'd do anything to get my attention. She'd go on these intense crying jags to show me how desperate she was, and she had insane overreactions to everything. She thought she could make me pity her enough, or maybe be so afraid of her hurting herself, that I'd do anything she wanted. And she was partially right. I didn't want her to do anything crazy, so I tried to let her have her way. When we'd go out or she'd come over, I tried my best to feel the old attraction to her, but that attraction had been fading for a while. I'd fuck her and think about Kim the whole time, but in her mind, we were making love, and that was enough for her to consider us in a relationship." He sighed nervously, looking both genuine and tortured. It was a tremendous effort for him to tell me about her, and I appreciated him for that, though I still had my doubts about his story.

"Is that why it lasted a year, then? You couldn't figure out how to extricate yourself? And you never gave her any reason to believe she might have something more with you? Was this poor girl just building castles in the air all by herself?" I took a deliberately accusatory tone; something about all this just didn't sit right with me. I really wanted to nail down his culpability in all of this because it seemed patently ridiculous to me that Scarlett had just turned into a lunatic obsessed with him out of nowhere.

"Are you suggesting that I led her on?" he asked immediately, stiffening. "Was it leading her on to make it clear from the jump that there would only ever be sex between us? Was it leading her on to tell her straight out that I wasn't a relationship guy? Was it leading her on to tell her bluntly that I was fucking other people? Then, sure. If all that is leading her on, then I led her on big time." He spread his arms wide before letting them fall back to his sides.

"Then why was she so convinced? Why did she refuse to give up? Is it really possible that you bear no responsibility?" I took a step toward him as he swallowed thickly. I decided not to mention what Xavier had told me about Officer Scott's vendetta. The man hated Neil so much he was constantly looking for a reason to throw him in jail.

But why?

"I have no idea what the fuck was going on in her head. I became a kind of fixation for her. The only thing I did wrong was trying to manipulate her. I started messing with her head when I realized that my threats couldn't keep her away from me. I tried every way I could think of to show her that she wasn't going to get any love or affection from me, but the only thing that ever worked was pretending to go along with it, playing her game..." he said in exasperation, scrubbing a hand over his face as I continued staring at him.

"And with me?" I whispered, pulling his eyes to mine like a magnet. "Is it like that with me? Am I just the latest Scarlett?" I echoed my father's words. The corners of my eyes were tingling, but I held myself back. Neil could sense how discouraged I was, and he drew himself up straighter. His long legs would bear the burden of our conversation, while I could see in the set of his shoulders the same intransigence that he brought to every situation. He moved toward me one step at a time, and my heart skipped a beat.

"There is no comparison between you and her," he said irritably, and then he touched my cheek while I stared stupidly into his golden eyes. They looked even brighter, reflecting the sunlight that filtered in through the big windows. "You're not a Scarlett, and you never will be because you are something entirely different. You are *more*, Tinkerbell," he answered mysteriously, looking me right in the eye as he traversed the edge of my lower lip with his thumb. I tried to look down to escape his gaze, but he didn't appreciate the coy gesture and tilted my chin back up until I was forced to look at him.

"Are you afraid of me?" he murmured, sounding disappointed. "You are. I can see it in your eyes..." He shook his head and sighed. "I never slept all night next to Scarlett. I never shared my personal space with her. I never touched her and thought about how she was mine alone. I never broke any of my numerous rules with her. I never thought of her as a precious pearl that I needed to protect. I never wanted to feel her body with no condom between us. I never told her about what happened to me or Kimberly. Is that enough to convince you that you are not her?" He smiled, brushing the tip of his nose against mine. I felt his breath against my mouth as he stroked my stomach before flattening his palm over my breast and giving it a squeeze. "Is that enough for you?" He grazed my lips with a brief, chaste kiss. He didn't wait for me to answer but instead dipped down to my neck and got to work seducing me. My skin burned, immediately recognizing the touch of the man I loved, and a blistering desire bloomed between my thighs. I put my hands on his waist and tried to push him away, but my attempt was so feeble that Neil just gave a self-satisfied chuckle.

"You use me like..." I tried to say as I felt his lips on my throat. He nibbled and sucked the flesh there, pulling a gasp from me. Meanwhile, his powerful, masculine hands traversed my hips and ass, pressing me against him.

"Like I want you more than anything," he finished for me. Then he shifted against my lower abdomen so I could feel the arousal burning in his body, the tremendous erection tenting his jeans, and the relentless desire he had to make me his again. Immediately.

"No..." I gulped. My mind screamed to push him away while my heart was pounding so wildly that I thought it would never slow down again.

"Yes," he answered arrogantly. "Always, Tinkerbell. I want you always..." He cupped the back of my head in one hand and pressed my face to his. He didn't stop when he felt me stiffen; instead, he slid his tongue between my lips, and there was nothing for me to do but surrender. His carved-marble stomach brushed up against my breasts underneath my thin sweater, and I shivered. My nipples stiffened, greedy for his attention, while he coaxed an ardent response from me with his tongue. His burning fingers ran all over me: hips, thighs, and ass.

It felt like Neil was trying to absorb me into himself, like he wanted to erase my identity and instead merge the two of us together. He cradled my face in his hand and deepened the kiss, inching me back until I hit the wall. I kissed him back with the same intensity, trying to extract every rotten, broken thing inside him, trying to make him feel safe and sweep away his misery. I moaned as my back butted up against the wall, and Neil continued to lay claim to me with a wild possessiveness that mocked my fears of not being enough for him.

Abruptly, the doorbell rang and halted the momentum.

Neil broke off the kiss and rested his forehead against mine, eyes nearly closed in satisfaction. Meanwhile, I couldn't catch my breath.

We were both panting. My lungs burned just like my lips, which had been chafed by our devouring kisses.

"Who the fuck is it now?" he asked grumpily.

"Maybe you should...open it and find out?" I whispered, brushing aside the lock of chestnut hair that had fallen over his left eye.

"Maybe I should just leave whoever it is out there while I rail you up against this wall like I've been imagining?" he offered with an impish expression that made me feel warm all over. I shut my eyes for a second to gather myself and opened them again. The chemistry between us was way too strong.

Our bodies were drawn and locked together like magnets.

"Come on, get the door." I nudged him gently away from me, though I would have happily indulged his desires. If we hadn't been interrupted, we surely would have made love again to express our hidden feelings and the words we couldn't say with the only means of communication that always worked perfectly for us.

Neil gave a huff but went to the door.

As he did so, I straightened my sweater and patted down my hair, tousled from our kiss.

"Miss Anna," I heard him say. The housekeeper appeared in the doorway with a rectangular box wrapped in black paper with a red bow around it.

"I hope I'm not disturbing you, but this package arrived for you," she told him, offering it to him.

Neil looked down at the box, frozen in place for a few seconds. Then, he grabbed the package and thanked Anna before watching her leave.

He kicked the door closed with his heel and sat down on the couch, placing the package on the low table in front of him.

A strange disquiet swirled all around us; the air itself felt inexplicably tense.

Neil lifted his face to look at me.

We realized that we were both thinking the same thing: This package contained nothing good, and it had undoubtedly been sent by *him*.

The only opponent in this game.

Player 2511.

15

"Really? No one wants to tell the sad tale of
Scarlett Scott for the brat?"

SELENE

I sat down beside Neil, trying to give him the support he needed to face the situation.

He had unwrapped the box, and bits of black paper were now strewn all over the floor.

Inside, however, was nothing too macabre, just a laptop.

Neil had powered it on, and a login screen with an empty password field immediately appeared.

A goddamned password that we didn't know. There was a Post-it Note stuck to the keyboard, however, that said:

Have fun.

Player 2511

"Try to stay calm," I said softly, stroking his thigh. I could feel the tension in his muscles and how ragged his breathing had become. That email Player had sent me, blackmailing me over the things he'd recorded using my webcam, was etched into both of our minds. Since then, I hadn't touched anything with an internet connection. Neil had forbidden me from going anywhere near social media. He took my cell phone, and I had to buy another one, a dumb phone that explicitly did not have a camera. My laptop had been completely destroyed when he threw it against my wall.

I understood where he was coming from with that: his rage at being spied on during such an intimate moment had set him off so completely that he just lost it.

"How? How am I supposed to stay calm?" Neil leaped to his feet, digging a hand into his hair.

I understood what he was feeling. The worst part was the feeling of impotence. We couldn't fight back; we had no way of defending ourselves. All we could do was continue taking the hits as they came while trying to figure out who was hiding under Player's mask.

"If we lose our heads now, we'll never get to the bottom of this," I murmured cautiously, still trying to support him. But Neil just looked so on edge. His gaze was cutting, his jaw tight with anger, and his shoulders rigid; every inch of him gave off an impression of banked power that was as dark as it was dauntless.

"I'm not used to just sitting around doing nothing while some asshole in a mask fucks with me!" He raised his voice and began stalking back and forth across the living room with one hand on his hip, the other rubbing his forehead intently.

"I understand that. But we can't give in to panic or rage. We just have to figure out who he is. The law can take it from there," I told him, fully confident that the system would be on our side and send that psychopath up the river.

"The law…" Neil repeated. He stopped and looked derisively at me. "The law isn't gonna do shit about this. And I'm not going to wait around for this maniac to hurt you or my family again!"

He gestured at the window, through which the house was clearly visible, and I sighed.

Neil felt responsible for everything that had happened up until that point, all of the threats that had been going on for months. Logan's accident and then mine. Everyone's life was at risk, and that was too great a burden for even someone as tenacious as Neil to bear on his own.

"After Chloe, he's shifted his focus to the two of us," he said wretchedly.

My forehead creased in a frown. Did something happen to his sister? He spotted my obvious confusion and bit his lip, regretting letting that information slip.

"Chloe? What—" I started to say, but he beat me to it.

"Remember after I spent the night in Detroit? How I left first thing the next morning because Logan called and asked me to get back to New York as soon as I could?" he asked, and I nodded.

He took a deep breath and went on. "That night, Chloe had vanished after going to a party with her friend Madison and the Krew. Apparently Luke is dating Madison, which I didn't know," he explained. "Player called me and told me a riddle over the phone. I memorized it, and Xavier, Logan, Alyssa, and I tried to solve it. There was a time limit; we had to go fast," he said, clearly reliving memories of a terrible day I'd never even known he experienced. "We found her a little while later. She was locked in the trunk of a broken-down car in a motel parking lot. The car was rigged to explode. If we hadn't gotten her out of there in time, my sister would be gone," he finished, swallowing with difficulty.

I got up from the couch then and went to him, teary-eyed.

I could feel his silent pain, which his pride would never allow him to openly show. I had never seen him cry, not even during Logan's hospital stay. I had caught glimpses of so much of him: his fears, his insecurities, his doubts...but rarely his softer feelings.

Those he secreted away, experiencing them all alone and never sharing them with anyone.

"Why didn't you tell me?" I asked thickly, trying to ignore the lump in my throat. He looked at me, ashamed, and I felt my heart clench, urging me forward until I could touch his jaw. His clean smell tormented me once again, just like the desire to love him that swelled inescapably in my chest.

I didn't want him to feel guilty.

Neil was a victim just like the rest of us, not the architect of the whole clusterfuck.

"I didn't want to scare you. I was going to tell you when the time was right," he answered before inclining his head slightly to press a kiss into the center of my palm. A simple, ordinary move that nevertheless warmed me.

"Don't think about what might have happened. Chloe is okay," I said, trying to reassure him, but he turned gloomy again. He turned away from my touch, and I could see that he was still silently castigating himself for everything. He opened his mouth as if to say something but closed it again with a furious growl. Then he went back to pacing with his hands in his hair. It was clearly one of those moments when he was dying to smash something or go a few rounds with his punching bag.

I kept silent for a few moments, making space for his intense, uncomfortable feelings before asking my next question.

"Do you have any theories about who Player might be? Have you gotten any other clues that could help us figure it out?" I asked. Neil frowned at me, considering the question.

"No. Xavier thinks it might be some ex of mine, but I doubt that," he answered skeptically. It was a logical theory: Player very well could be a former lover with a grudge.

"So what are you going to do with the laptop?" I asked. Neil regarded the laptop on the table thoughtfully for a few moments.

"Luke will be able to access it. He knows a lot more about that stuff than I do. I'll text him to meet up." He pulled his phone out of his jeans and hastily tapped out a message to his friend.

"I'll go with you," I suggested.

"No," he answered immediately, keeping his head bent over the phone screen.

"I'm going. I'm not going to let you face this mess all by yourself," I said, digging in my heels. Neil looked at me then, irritated by my persistence. I didn't allow myself to look intimidated and crossed my arms over my chest instead, daring him to argue with me. He slid his phone back into his pocket and advanced on me slowly, like a predator approaching his prey.

"Why…" he began, bending his head until our gazes were level, "do you always have to be so fucking pigheaded? Huh?" he whispered, his warm breath brushing against my lips. His placid tone clashed with his obvious attempt to cow me. I shivered a little but didn't back down.

"And why do you always have to make decisions for the both of us?" I shot back at him. I stared hard at the expanse of his throat left exposed by his sweater and considered pressing a kiss to it. He certainly enjoyed it when I paid attention to that area; maybe I could relax him a little bit. But then he cleared his throat to get my attention, and I looked back at his face, noting his smug smile.

"Okay…" he conceded with a deep breath. "Come with me. But I'm warning you—no chatting with Luke. In fact, ignore him completely. Don't even look at him," he ordered sternly, brushing past me to grab his coat and throw it on.

Half an hour later, we were standing outside Luke's apartment door.

I chafed my hands together to warm them while Neil rang the doorbell incessantly, waiting for his friend to open the door for us.

"I'm coming!" We heard his voice through the door, which he quickly pulled open with an annoyed huff. When he saw Neil's irritated glare boring into him, he arranged his face into a serious expression. "You trying to break the doorbell or what?" he chided Neil sarcastically.

"Should have been quicker, Luke. I don't have time to waste," Neil snapped, brushing past him with a shoulder-check. As he did so, I took note of the several inches Neil had on his friend. Then I looked at Luke, who had just then noticed my presence.

"Hey, Selene. This prick didn't tell me you were coming too. How are you doing?" he asked, looking me up and down. I did the same right back at him. I wasn't attracted to him, just ordinarily curious. He was dressed in all black, highlighting his lean body, chiseled and well-balanced. His blue eyes stood out against his pale skin, while his blond hair looked a little shorter than I remembered.

"I'm good. And yourself?" I answered quickly, trying not to show how stressed and anxiety-ridden I actually was. There was no need to add weight to this already tense atmosphere.

"Parker," Neil barked out behind him. "You wanna get your ass over here and help me?" Luke rolled his eyes skyward and moved to let me inside.

"Someone's in a hurry. We can catch up another time, maybe just the two of us," he winked. I gave him the smallest possible smile and didn't say anything. I could feel Neil's burning eyes on me. His eyebrows were arched into a resolute expression, and he appeared to be clenching his jaw deliberately.

I turned my attention to the modern luxury decor of the apartment. I recalled that Luke's dad was a lawyer and his mother a celebrated journalist. I moved toward the giant leather sectional in the living room and paused in front of a framed photo on the wall there. It was Luke with his parents and a little girl who looked about ten years old, probably his sister.

"That's Gwen," Luke said, coming over to me when he spotted me looking at the lovely little girl.

"You two could be twins," I observed.

"Everybody says that," he chuckled.

"Are you done?" Neil cut in from behind us. I turned to find him waiting impatiently for us to finish our exchange. He alternated his gaze between us, giving me a look of such pure anger that it gave me goosebumps. "Maybe the two of you can go out one of these evenings and really deepen your acquaintance," he continued bitterly. "But right now, Parker, I came here for an important reason, and I need your undivided attention," he said reprovingly. Luke turned away from me and snapped to attention like a little toy soldier.

"I was just trying to be polite," he said defensively before sitting down on the couch with a heavy sigh. I remained standing, keeping my distance from both of them.

"Sure you were. And I know exactly why," my Disaster shot back, sounding anything but calm.

"What are you talking about? You're the one who always has ulterior motives with women, not me," Luke defended himself, growing more belligerent.

"Oh, my apologies. You're a fucking saint, I forgot. Xavier is so right about you." A faint, mocking smile spread across Neil's face, but before Luke could say anything in response, someone else rang the doorbell. He stood up and went to get the door, shooting Neil a dirty look as he did so.

I was grateful to whoever it was for breaking up their tiff.

I was afraid they might have actually come to blows otherwise.

"Please try to stay calm. How many times do I have to say that to you today?" I took advantage of Luke's absence to chide Neil, but he just narrowed his eyes at me in an angry glower.

"You shut up," he snapped, making me flinch. I tugged my coat around me more tightly and practically plastered myself against the wall in discomfort. I hated it when he talked to me like that.

"Ah, there you are. Luke said you all were meeting up about some problem. What's up, dickhead?" Xavier came into the living room with his typical swagger, flanked by his faithful partners in crime: Alexia, the blue unicorn, and Oops! All Curves Barbie. Goddamned Jennifer.

If I was merely discontented before, I became truly irritated with their presence.

"Hey, Babydoll. What a surprise, finding you here," the dark-haired boy added, shamelessly checking me out. Fortunately, I was buttoned up to my neck; otherwise, his dark, perverted eyes would have made me feel even more uncomfortable than I already was.

"Looks like the brat forgot the way back to Detroit," Jennifer commented as she moved briskly toward Neil, who was standing in the center of the room. He watched her warily as she inched over to drop a kiss against his collar. It would have taken just the smallest tilt of his head, and he could have met her lips with his own, but instead he held still, looking bewildered by the blond's bold advances. Not happy with this, Jennifer placed her hand ostentatiously on the waistband of his jeans, and Neil immediately took a step back to prevent her from actually touching his dick through his pants.

All the while, I was holding my breath.

This pathetic little scene of Jennifer begging for a kiss from him made me sick to my stomach.

What was her next move? Get on her knees and get him good and hard in front of everyone?

If she did, though, it would have been on par with the Krew's usual activities. Certainly nothing out of the ordinary.

Had I not been completely paralyzed with jealousy, I would have grabbed her by the stupid little braids and given her a swift kick in the ass.

"What? You don't even want my greetings now?" she asked him in a sultry tone.

"I don't even remember the last time we greeted each other," Neil shot back.

And that was enough for me. I stalked over to them, determined to mark my territory and show this bitch she needed to go back to her kennel. I took Neil's forearm and pulled him against me, determined not to give up an inch of what I had so painstakingly conquered.

"Wow, the kid's pissed off," Alexia noted as she sat down on the sofa next to Xavier. Jennifer simply narrowed her eyes at me in a defiant glare.

"Afraid, princess?" she taunted me.

"Of you? Never," I answered cheekily.

Jennifer regarded both Neil and me with a malicious smile before walking off to join Alexia. My fingers tightened on Neil's arm as I leaned in to whisper in his ear.

"If you don't want me talking to Luke, then you keep away from that poodle in heat," I said in a low tone, pulling back just far enough to look him in the eye. He quirked a corner of his mouth, amused by my dire warning, and I got lost in his golden eyes.

I completely forgot that I was standing in the middle of an enormous living room under the watchful eyes of the entire Krew.

Instead, it was just the two of us.

Then, all at once, I showed everyone exactly how jealous and possessive I was.

I leaned in to give him a kiss, and certainly not on the collar. After he got over his momentary surprise, Neil parted his lips and returned my impulsive gesture. His tongue tangled savagely with mine, and he moved voraciously, leaving me breathless.

Instinctively, I pressed my chest more brazenly against his, grinding myself against him. Neil didn't let out a moan, but I thrilled when

I felt his body react, growing hard from the erotic tension between us. He let one hand drift down to my backside and gave it a squeeze, making me gasp. I was forced to break the kiss briefly to get some oxygen, and he took the opportunity to gently bite my lower lip.

"You done putting on a show?" he murmured against my mouth.

"From what I recall, you're the exhibitionist," I shot back.

"True, I wouldn't mind screwing you right in front of that blond fuck you've been smiling at. However, we are here to solve a problem," he reminded me, continuing to hold me close.

"Your blond's the one who keeps shooting her shot because she can't get it through her head that you belong to me," I said bluntly.

Goddamn, I hated her.

"So possessive, Babygirl," he said, sounding highly entertained.

"A little bit, maybe," I admitted with a shrug.

After one last amused glance, Neil let me go. We both turned serious as we faced the Krew.

They were all sitting on the sofa, staring at us like they'd seen a couple of ghosts. All at once, my face flushed as I realized how shamelessly I'd just behaved, and all out of jealousy.

"My friends, you're so hot for each other I'm gonna get hard over here. Babydoll knows what she's doing." Xavier was the first to break the silence with a sarcastic round of applause. Luke just cocked an eyebrow, and the two girls seemed focused on Neil, who remained as impassive as ever. "If you're ever looking to share her someday, holler at me," Xavier went on. I went rigid at his deranged proposal and immediately recalled all of Neil's vices, which he still had. I felt a wave of anguish thinking about those times in the past when I'd seen him doing sketchy things with multiple women.

My mood visibly deflated, and Neil raised my chin with two fingers and bent to give me a tender kiss.

"Don't listen to that asshole," he whispered. "No one's going to lay a hand on you as long as I'm around," he finished firmly. He'd never said anything like that to me before. I smiled at him and nodded gently, and he refocused on the problem of Player with renewed energy.

"Back to this," he sighed, gesturing to the laptop he'd put on the coffee table. "Today I got a package from Player with this computer inside. It requires a password to log in, and I have no idea what that password might be," he informed Luke, who had meanwhile opened the laptop. He rested his elbows on his knees as he examined the display with its locked login screen.

"Okay...we could probably brute force it, but it would take some time," Luke observed. "I suspect Player probably gave you some clue about the password..."

"Because why would he give you a laptop you can't access?" Xavier said, finishing Luke's sentence. Neil began to pace anxiously, rubbing his chin.

"Maybe think about previous puzzles or, I don't know, maybe about—" Before Luke could finish what he was saying, Neil stopped and gave him a eureka look.

"Hard candy," he said immediately. I frowned, not understanding what he meant. Meanwhile, Luke had already typed it in and was smiling at the screen in satisfaction.

"Yeah...hot damn, that's it," he said excitedly.

"So the son of a bitch shattered your windshield with a rock just to give you a password?" Xavier asked.

I stiffened at the realization that there were still more things about the Player situation I did not know. I looked over at Neil to find him looking guilty and apprehensive. He moved closer to me as if to calm me down and tried to take my face in his hands, but I tossed my head.

"After the incident with Chloe, he took another shot at me. I was going to tell you..." he attempted to explain himself, but I just took a disappointed step away from him.

More secrets. More things he'd kept from me.

"When? When, exactly, were you going to tell me all of this?" I burst out.

"When the opportunity arose. But now isn't the time to talk about it," he scolded me with an authoritative tone. He didn't want to be contradicted or condescended to in front of his friends.

I was about to tear a strip off him anyway, but then Luke called out and distracted me.

"Everyone...look at this," he said, sounding disturbed.

I decided to table my discussion with Neil for later, and we both walked around the coffee table to get a look at the laptop screen.

"The desktop only has one icon on it; some app called *Dark Show*." Luke pointed a finger at it and gave Neil a curious look. "So we should open it, right?"

"No. Hold on," Neil answered. "Put some tape over the webcam lens." He stepped back, walking away from the computer. He suddenly seemed disoriented as he began breathing heavily and broke out into a cold sweat.

Something wasn't right.

I knew he was probably flashing back to when Kim tried to film him, triggering his fear of being captured by a camera, a phone, a computer—anything with a lens.

"Why?" Xavier asked, stretching out on the couch.

"Because..." Neil swallowed hard. I could tell from the grim expression on his face that he didn't want to explain himself. It was hard for him to talk about that kind of thing. He gave me a searching look, and I smiled, trying to beam to him the knowledge that I was right there with him. "Because it screws with my head," he murmured, going pale. His pupils were so blown they'd almost swallowed the molten gold of his irises. I was afraid that he might melt down at any moment, but he just squeezed his eyes shut and opened them again, pushing away the dark thoughts that had shadowed his face.

"You're right. This thing is probably loaded with malware, and Player could be using it to spy on us." Luke got up and vanished into another room in search of black tape. He returned, tearing a piece off with his teeth, and stuck a square of it right over the webcam.

I glanced at Neil and watched him let out a sigh of relief. Now that the danger had passed, he could lock his phobia back up in the drawer where he kept it separate from the rest of himself.

"Okay, I'm opening it. Get ready," Luke informed us. He hovered over the icon and shot a look at Neil. When he nodded in assent, Luke clicked.

Immediately, a chat preview popped up, though it didn't look like any messenger service I'd ever seen.

Jennifer and Alexia leaned in to get a better look at what was going on.

"The fuck is this..." Luke muttered in astonishment. "It's requires a username to proceed." He looked up at Neil, who was standing over him.

"Dark Knight," I suggested before he could say anything.

Both of them turned to look at me in surprise. Neil's stare was, as always, sultry and stormy. Meanwhile, Luke just entered the username I'd suggested into the name field and added a password consisting of apparently random numbers before clicking "Register."

Then, the actual chat window opened, and there was already one other person online.

The only person who could possibly want to talk with us.

Player 2511: Good job. You did it.

The new message notification made everyone jump. Apparently, the psycho had been waiting for us.

Luke gulped, looking unsure of what to do. Neil shook his head in surprise and rubbed a hand over his face.

"Answer him. Ask him who the fuck he is and what the fuck he wants," he said in a furious rush. Luke immediately did so.

Dark Knight: Who are you?

Player 2511: Nah, that would make it too easy. This game doesn't end until I say it does.

Neil growled impatiently and gestured for Luke to move.

"Let me talk to him," he demanded, taking Luke's seat between Xavier and Jennifer. Luke then moved to stand next to me.

Dark Knight: Tell me what you want.

Player 2511: I want lots of things.

Dark Knight: Tell me one of them.

Player 2511: Take the tape off the camera and strip.

Neil stared dumbfounded at the message, and I stared right along with him.

So Luke had been right: Player obviously had control of the webcam and could use it to spy on us. I felt a burst of disquiet in my chest at the knowledge that, in addition to being a strategist, a hacker, and a crazy person, Player was also a goddamned creep.

"No!" I blurted out unthinkingly. Neil lifted his face to look at me and immediately saw the terror in my eyes. "This is about your personal autonomy. Yours was already trampled on once before; I won't let it happen again." The fury in my words made it crystal clear that there was no way I was going to allow him to submit to that lunatic's demands. Neil looked steadily at me for a few moments, locked in his unknowable inner world, before typing once again.

Dark Knight: What do I get in return?

Player 2511: Your little slut's privacy. I won't release the video.

Neil held perfectly still, his fingers hovering over the keyboard. I went white.

Our tormentor was playing dirty: He was using me to force Neil's hand.

And the blackmail material he had provided was the perfect weapon.

I moved closer to my Disaster and slipped a hand into his soft hair, forcing him to look at me. Then I crouched down and met his eyes, strengthening the emotional connection between us.

"Please don't do it," I whispered.

He was shaken. He didn't seem to be processing anything around him. His golden eyes stayed fixed on me while Alexia and Jennifer began to offer more theories about what was going on.

"This is a woman, just like I thought from the start. Why else would she want you naked?" Xavier cut in, the blood draining from his face.

"Don't be an idiot, Xavier; it could be a woman or a man," Luke said, rolling his eyes.

Neil was still in shock, staring blankly. I gently traced the contours of his lips with my thumb, trying to sooth him.

This nightmare would be over soon.

"Hey..." I said softly.

"It's my fault. You weren't supposed to get caught up in this..." he answered, sounding tortured.

"Well, I'm in it now, and I'm not leaving you alone." I leaned in to give him a comforting kiss, but he rejected it, pulling back. I was briefly hurt but regrouped and moved closer to him. "Don't give in to him. Please," I begged.

Neil had already gone through more than enough hell for one lifetime; I wasn't about to let this lunatic damage his psyche and wound his soul even further.

"I couldn't give less of a fuck about myself. But you..." he hissed through clenched teeth. Abruptly, he cupped my face in his hands and moved closer to me. His grip was so powerful it made me flinch, and his eyes pierced me like he was trying to tattoo his thoughts into my skin. "You matter to me, and I am not going to let this asshole destroy your life. Not now, not ever." He released me suddenly, as though he'd been burned.

Neil went back to typing, even more furiously than before.

Dark Knight: Why are you doing all this?

Player 2511: Because I enjoy humiliating you.

Dark Knight: What did I do to you?

Player 2511: Think about it...how much pain have you brought to how many people?

Dark Knight: Don't answer my question with another question.

Player 2511: You turned my life into a tragedy. But now it's my turn to decide how the story ends. Clock's ticking...

I looked away from the screen as Neil got abruptly to his feet. He pulled a hand through his hair with a growl of rage.

"I have an idea," Luke cut in. "Ask him to send the video of you and Selene together."

Neil turned on him. "What the fuck? Are you nuts?"

"No, I'm not. I want to make sure this person actually has a video and that it's not just a trick he's using to manipulate you," Luke answered, and we all fell silent, thinking.

"That could actually be a good move," Xavier joined in, agreeing with Luke. "We need to level the playing field. This asshole has to know he's fucking with the wrong people..."

"Hey!" Alexia shouted, drawing our attention back to the laptop. Instinctively, I clutched Neil's arm.

Another window had popped up on the left side of the screen with an incoming video call, waiting for us to accept.

I was shocked. Was Player actually going to show himself?

Neil didn't waste any more time, reaching out to click accept on the video.

For a few seconds, we waited.

They seemed to pass so slowly that it ratcheted up our fears all out of proportion. Then, a woman appeared, sitting in a chair. She wore a white mask that completely obscured her face with just two slits for eyeholes. Her long blond hair fell over her breasts, and she wore a tight leather top with thin straps.

She was sitting in a bedroom. I caught just a glimpse of a round bed covered in black sheets surrounded by LED light strips that constantly cycled through colors. On the wall above the upholstered headboard was a fire-red light emitting a soft glow that gave the whole room a potent, disquieting vibe.

"Fuck!" Xavier blurted out. "I fucking told you it was a woman!"

"Neil...do you recognize her?" Luke put in. Then he turned to look at Neil, who stood frozen, staring at the laptop. I squeezed my fingers around his stiffened arm to show him that I was right there, but he remained blank, his cloudy eyes fixed on the woman on the screen.

He shook his head slightly but said nothing.

"How's he supposed to recognize her? With all the chicks he's fucked, I'd have trouble picking out one specific one too!" Xavier joked. Luke elbowed him.

"If you don't shut your fucking mouth, Xavier, I'm putting my fist in it," Neil threatened, surfacing from his fugue. His look of menace was enough to get Xavier to perk up into a battle-ready stance.

"Sure, you wanna punch me so you can feel better about your own bullshit? Be my guest, but it's not going to solve your problems." He stepped to Neil without fear, but Luke stuck out an arm to push him back.

"Not the time, Hudson. Give it a rest," the blond boy said reprovingly. Xavier grumbled something unintelligible while Alexia moved over to calm him down. Luke turned back to the woman on the screen. Unlike us, she apparently couldn't see or hear anything from our end, but she didn't seem bothered by that.

"So what do we do now? Can I ask if she has the video?" Luke turned to Neil, who tensed up for a minute; I could see it in the way the fabric of his coat suddenly stretched against his muscles. Then, he nodded. Luke turned back to the keyboard and began to type.

Dark Knight: I'll take my clothes off for you if you show me the video.

Then we watched in real time as Player answered us. I took the opportunity to scrutinize her more closely. Her hair didn't look natural to me—maybe she was wearing a wig?—and her skin was almost transparent, pale as a porcelain doll. Her firm breasts were packed tightly into her top. Both her fingers and her nails were long, the tips painted with dark polish.

She read the question but made no move to answer it. Instead, she sat still and stared into her screen. Luke shot a weighted glance at Neil and then typed some more.

Dark Knight: Have I ever had sex with you?

Neil's breath caught. He pursed his lips as if to object but apparently thought better of it and remained silent.

"Jesus, if this girl went to all this trouble just because Neil hit it and quit it, imagine what I'd do to him if I went off the deep end. They'd never find the body," Jennifer joked, twirling one of her braids around her index finger. She sat on the arm of the couch, one leg crossed over the other to expose an expanse of thigh in her tight little skirt. She noticed me watching her and gave me a fake smile.

But then there was another new message alert, and my blood ran cold as I read:

Player 2511: Yes...

I turned automatically away from Neil, caught in a flare of jealousy. He must have noticed because he turned to face me, looking first confused and then ashamed.

Was it really true? Were my life and Logan's and Chloe's lives all at risk all because some woman wanted revenge for the fantasy of a love that Neil had never given her?

I sat rigid, watching him in a disbelieving haze. He didn't have the guts to hold my gaze for more than a few seconds, though, so he let his shoulders slump and turned back to the computer.

"Okay, let's try another question..." Luke murmured, typing again.

Dark Knight: Are you Player, then? Did you think up all the puzzles and carry out all the attacks?

The woman on the screen stretched her fingers out over the keyboard as if to respond, but then she appeared to have second thoughts.

She stopped and sat back, leaning easily against the back of the chair. She stared intensely into her camera lens, like she wanted to pass through the screen and join us. I flattened a hand against my chest.

Despite not being able to see him, the woman appeared to have zeroed in on Neil, and she stared right at him, making no moves to answer that last question.

Suddenly, she raised her hand and slowly fluttered her fingers in a sardonic little wave before cutting the feed.

The chat app closed itself, and the computer began to shut down without any of us doing a thing.

Luke jumped and stared at the blank computer screen like it was possessed.

"Yeah, she's got full remote control of this fucking thing. We need to get rid of it," he said, sounding shaken.

We all fell silent for what felt like endless minutes. No one knew what to say, except...

"Well, well, well... I'm expecting apologies out of every one of you now. You all thought my theory was bullshit, but what do you know? Player is a woman after all," Xavier said loudly, stroking Alexia's arm as she clung to his side. His ability to shift moods on a dime was possibly even more dramatic than Neil's. Several times, I'd seen him dissipate the tension in a room by cracking a joke or saying something absurd, but just then, a circus full of clowns couldn't have eased the bitterness inside me.

"We don't know for certain that the woman really was Player. She didn't answer any of our questions," Luke shot back. "We also didn't get any confirmation that she actually has a video of Selene." He looked at me with a smile of reassurance. I didn't have the wherewithal to smile back.

"Who the hell was she then?" Alexia asked.

"Maybe Scarlett? Because of the shit that went down on spring break?" Jennifer dandled her crossed leg and looked hard at me and then at Neil as though trying to communicate something to him. The idea that they might have some private, special understanding bothered me, so I turned to look at him in the hopes of catching his reaction. There wasn't one. Neil's face remained blank as though there were no untoward implications in what she'd said at all.

The silence of the rest of the Krew as they exchanged guilty looks with one another only heightened my suspicions.

"What...what happened on spring break?" I asked, but every one of them looked away, feigning indifference. "What the hell happened on spring break?" I asked again, raising my voice.

"Oh, I'm sorry...did your man not tell you?" Jennifer was the only one to answer me, but she certainly wasn't doing me any favors. She made an exaggerated remorseful face before grinning with self-satisfaction.

"Really? No one wants to tell the sad tale of Scarlett Scott for the brat?" She looked around at her friends, who kept their faces carefully blank. No volunteers there. Then she shot a gleeful look at Neil and stood up with all the grace of a big cat, walking across the room to loom over me. "As you can tell, nobody really likes thinking about what happened on that infamous vacation. Guess I'm the only one who cares enough, princess, to clear these things up for you..."

"Get to the point," I snapped at her. She was no friend of mine, and she wasn't doing me a solid. These preliminaries were pointless.

"Jennifer," Neil interjected in a menacing tone, but she just raised her hand and tsk'd her index finger back and forth.

"I'm going to tell her either way, sweetheart. So let me talk." She winked at him, and he took a deep breath, like he was trying to keep himself under control. Then he let that breath out, apparently surrendering to what was about to happen.

"Would you believe that your man isn't the upstanding citizen he pretends to be?" Jennifer shot him a malicious look. "Three years ago, he started seeing Scarlett on the regular. At the same time, he continued to fuck me, Alexia, and anyone else he could get his paws on." She gave me a humorless grin. "Then for some insane reason, he decided he was gonna take his little girlfriend on spring break with him. Can't say why, though it for sure wasn't to give her a Miami vacation. My guess? He wanted to introduce her to his real self." She paused for effect and then went on. "We all stayed at a hotel near Crandon Beach for the week. Neil enjoyed the... *festive* atmosphere just as much as the rest of us. He got high, he got drunk, he partied every night, and..." Jennifer advanced on me, shrinking the distance between us until the fruity smell of her perfume made my nose itch. "Honestly, I couldn't tell you how many women he fucked in that one week, but I do know he'd regularly do it right in front of Scarlett just to show her how little she meant to him. Wait... that's kind of like what he did to you, isn't it?" she continued softly, staring deep into my eyes. Painful memories rose up in my mind of that Halloween party where Neil had done just that, using Jennifer specifically because he knew it would hurt me the most. But I swallowed down my feelings. I wasn't going to give her the satisfaction of watching me crumble right in front of her.

"One crazy night—one of many crazy nights that week—people started playing what they called the 'Spring Break Games.' You know, like the Olympic Games? Anyway, one of them involved kids jumping off the hotel balcony's railing and landing in the pool..."

she went on, and a disquieted feeling in my chest made me stagger back. I wanted to turn and look at Neil's face, to gauge his expression, but my body refused to move.

"All messed up after a week of watching her boyfriend nail other girls right in front of her face, Scarlett got wasted and decided she was going to play too…"

I clapped a hand over my mouth to muffle a cry. Silence pressed in all around me; the only thing I could hear was the beating of my own heart.

"She jumped from the third story, and she made it into the pool, but she hit her head on impact. And Scarlett's life was never the same after that. She was in the hospital for months, relearning how to walk and feed herself. She tried to come back to school even though her brain still wasn't right. Unfortunately, everybody knew by then what she'd done and why she'd done it. A few assholes even filmed it with their phones, and the video was all over campus. People were assholes to her, making fun of her for throwing herself off a building for a guy who didn't even love her. Scarlett, after all, was supposed to be a good girl. She was smart and responsible; she would never do something so crazy. And she wouldn't have if Neil hadn't been putting her through emotional torture for so long. He did everything he could to convince her that he didn't want her; he showed her the worst parts of himself and told her she ought to get far away from him. But Scarlett was too deep in love, so Neil had to give her the coup de grâce. A few months after she tried to go back to school, Scarlett vanished without a trace. Just up and left her friends, her family, and even her dad," Jennifer finished, shifting her gaze to Neil.

I was frozen, absorbing her words, which struck like lightning bolt after lightning bolt into my soul.

"Do you really believe he won't do the same to you? Do you think he's going to change for you? I guess you don't know him as well as you thought you did," she needled me with a sardonic smile.

I recoiled when I felt Neil's hand lightly touch my shoulder. I sucked in a breath and stepped back.

"Don't touch me," I demanded, trying to push past him so I could get out of there.

"Selene..." He took me by the forearm and forced me to halt. Even the sorrow I saw in his face wasn't enough to convince me to stay in that room.

"I begged her not to do it. Not to jump. She told me it was going to be her gesture of love for me, her way of showing me that she'd do anything for me. She wasn't in her right mind. I...I...pleaded with her not to do anything stupid, but she was wasted and blind with jealousy and so goddamn angry that she wasn't listening to me..." he murmured wretchedly.

His suffering eyes made my knees go weak. But I reminded myself that those eyes were also cursed and cruel with a dangerous capacity for doing harm. There was a darkness in them that would never fade. "It's burned into my mind, that moment when she stepped up on that railing. She turned at the last second to look at me before she jumped. She was crying, and I tried... I tried to stop her, but..." He hung his head, his grip on me growing more possessive. "That was another reason I wanted to push you away from me. I didn't want you to get dragged into my shit. I know better than anyone that I've made so many mistakes, just like I know I'm not the right person for you..." He looked down at his fingers, tightened around my arm, and slowly released me. My skin felt burned in the spot where his hand had been, and I automatically massaged the area with my other hand.

"I want to leave." I raced toward the door, not caring that Jennifer and the rest of the Krew were watching me run away.

I waited impatiently for the elevator, and when the doors opened, I darted inside, only narrowly evading Neil, who was hot on my heels.

It was freezing when I walked out of the building, and I turned down a random sidewalk, fumbling for my phone so I could call a taxi.

The problem was, I didn't know any numbers for a taxi service, and my new phone deliberately didn't have any apps, so I couldn't order a ride either.

"Motherfucker!" I blurted out. It wasn't the kind of thing I usually said, but I was trying very hard not to cry, and anger seemed like the most effective way to hold back those tears.

"Selene..." After a few interminable moments, I heard Neil's voice calling out from behind me. I just leaned over the curb, hoping to get lucky.

Now would be the perfect time for a taxi to just happen to be passing by so I could make my escape.

"I want to go back to Detroit," I told him, still not turning around. I could hear his heavy breathing, a sure sign he'd had to run to catch up with me. Then he was grabbing my elbow and spinning me around until our eyes locked. Perhaps for the first time, I saw in those eyes a genuine fear of losing me. They were brilliant and so goddamned wounded that I couldn't help but soften slightly.

"All of that is in the past," he said. "I..."

"Are you going to hurt me like that the next time you want to push me away?" I asked challengingly, my lip trembling.

Damn, did I want to cry. Neil could sense what I was feeling, and he looked at me like he wanted to pull all the suffering from me and take it on himself. His voice dwindled into a plea, and the sound of it made me let go of all those tears I'd been holding back. "You don't have to be afraid of me, not ever. Jennifer just wants to win. She's jealous of you. You know it, and I know it. Don't let her win." He tried to stroke my cheek, but I jerked away from his touch. "I hate seeing you cry," he said in a helpless murmur.

"I can't look at you the same..." I tilted my face down, tears running down my chin as I tried to wipe them away with the back of my hand.

"Selene, I stripped away everything for you. I bared my body and my soul. You know everything there is to know about me. There are no more secrets. And I've always told you the truth. If I didn't tell you everything about every time in my life, it was because even I was ashamed of it. I wanted to protect you from everything. Even from me..." He seized my face in his hands, and I went rigid. I was afraid he'd be able to sense the love I felt for him.

Because Neil had worked his way inside me. Even knowing that we'd never be a fairy tale and never get our happily ever after, my heart would always be his.

"You care for me, Tinkerbell. Don't let things that happened with other people cancel out your feelings for me. Not when I've just started to trust you..." He pressed his forehead to mine and gently rubbed the sides of my face with his thumbs.

"I should go..." I said again in low tones, fighting with myself.

"You don't want to go. I know you don't. I'll give you time to process all of this, but please just stay here with me," he whispered against my lips.

"I don't know. Every time I turn around, I'm finding out something new about you, Neil, and..." And my heart was shattered into a thousand pieces. I could see them, falling at my feet once again. I was being ground down by him, by the mysteries that surrounded him and by all the things I didn't know.

"You don't fucking get it!" There it was, that thing he did best. He pulled away from me and looked at me with so much disdain, like I was no longer Selene. Like I was just an enemy to him. "You grew up in a glass bubble, in a normal family with normal parents. You hate your father so much just because he stepped out on your mom, just because he was away at work a lot... While I was raped and subjugated and humiliated by a psychopath years older than me.

William beat me basically from birth because he thought I was a bad seed, no son of his. He never wanted me, and he took out all his rage and disgust on me. That tattoo you like so much," he gestured to his right arm. "I got it to cover the scars from where he would use me as a human ashtray. I've got the same ones on my left arm; you've seen them. I left those uncovered because I need to see them and remember what kind of man raised me. I told you right from the start that I'm not like other people, that I've got issues I'm working on, and that I'm not perfect. And I did that because I wasn't just fucking you, Selene. I told you about myself, I confided in you, and I trusted you implicitly. All of my wrongs are a direct result of the things that happened to me. It's sheer luck that I'm not locked up in fucking prison or hooked on drugs because people like me, people with the kind of history I've got? They don't get to live real lives. You have no idea how many times I've thought about ending it all for good. You have no idea how many times I've hoped that goddamned stalker would just take me out already; then we'd both have fulfilled our purposes!" He vented all the sickness that was inside him, and he did it with the rage of a man who had been suppressing his hurt for far too long and had reached the limits of what a man could endure.

Neil wobbled, almost collapsing in on himself, and he looked so tired. Tired of everything.

His strength was dwindling; he'd been fighting his whole life to no avail.

"If you're so sure, just do it. Go away and disappear. I won't chase you—I don't chase anyone, Selene. You know that better than anyone. I won't even accept any change of heart from you. God may forgive, but I don't...remember that." He turned his back to me, rubbing his temples. His right hand had started to shake, and I realized how on edge he actually was.

After everything I'd gone through for him, I couldn't allow something that happened in his past to scare me away. I couldn't let fear destroy me, not after Neil had actually opened all of himself to me.

I didn't know Scarlett. I didn't know the Neil of three years before. I didn't know what they actually experienced in their relationship. I didn't know if she'd become overinvested in something that, right from the start, never involved love. Neil had made that clear to her, but Scarlett, determined and in love, decided to risk it all.

She'd jumped off that balcony of her own accord, not because Neil forced her, though it was clear to me that he was hardly blameless.

He could have chosen not to hurt her, not to choose others over her, or not to flaunt his most twisted impulses on that vacation. He could have chosen not to use his typical dominating methods, the kind that could make anyone a stranger to themselves.

But the most serious mistake was now mine. I was judging him the way everyone else did.

So how could I expect Neil to open up and tell me everything about himself?

"I'm sorry..." I whispered. I advanced on him slowly and embraced him from behind, resting my cheek against his rigid back. "I didn't mean to judge you. I would never do that," I murmured. He held still and let me get it all out. I wept like a child in the depths of despair, making us both shake with my sobs. After what felt like forever, Neil turned around to wipe the tears from my cheeks.

I looked up at him through wet, clinging eyelashes, and he bent to drop a comforting kiss on the tip of my nose.

"Shh...that's enough now, Babygirl. You know I don't know what to do when you start bawling," he said softly, with a hint of irony that made me smile sadly. Then he stroked my face with both hands and bent down toward my lips. I immediately stretched up to seize that kiss, which tasted of bitterness, suffering, and words unspoken. Neil kissed me softly, as though seeking permission. The same man who always took whatever he wanted with perfect confidence was now attempting to reassure me in his own way.

It was a delicate kiss, yet so powerful that it unleashed a ferocious storm of feeling between us.

So kiss me now.
Now, when it's possible.
Now, when it's our life and our time.
Now, when it's just the two of us.
Kiss me always.
Build a delirium inside me.
Pass your madness on to me.
Invent a new kind of kiss just for me.
Give me the gift of your fiery passion.
Destroy me and then create me once again.
Hold me and crush me against you.
Put your arms around me and never let go.

I grinned against his mouth.

When I realized that he had no intention of stopping, however, I went back to following the languid movements of his tongue and shut my eyes as the taste of him flooded me.

He tasted good, like man and strength, protection and chaos. Like him.

Just him.

I groaned as he sucked my lips between his playfully. He was trying to soothe the storm inside and restore some harmony between the two of us. Goosebumps rose up uncontrollably all over my skin beneath my clothes, and I trembled against his chest.

"Want to go?" he whispered before pulling back slightly, and I panted like I'd just run a marathon. I gripped his coat and nodded, too overwhelmed to speak.

Neil stared intensely at me before draping his arm around my shoulders and guiding me toward the car with him.

Half an hour later we were back at the house.

Neither of us said anything in the car.

Neil had gone silent again, and I took the time to reflect on everything that had happened.

Player was a woman, or so we believed, and we had no idea what else she might have in store for us or who her next target would be.

We also still didn't know her true identity. Maybe it was Scarlett, or maybe it was someone else. As for me, I still needed to stay away from anything online because Player might still be trying to monitor or record me. That threat, however, felt a bit distant compared to the knowledge that, for all I knew, she could be lurking in my basement right now, waiting to hurt me.

If Player really was one of Neil's former flames, she would see me as a threat and might be acting out against me due to jealousy or some sick obsessive compulsion.

The more I thought about it, the worse my headache became, so I made a concerted effort to clear my mind as we got out of the car and walked up the driveway in silence.

The air was freezing cold, and I paused for a moment to watch my breath condense in the air with each exhalation.

Meanwhile, Neil had lit another cigarette—he'd already smoked three on the drive back—and was staring into the middle distance.

I waited for him to unlock the pool house's door, wanting nothing more than to shower and rest a little bit. But he just stood there, breathing in the smoke from his Winston and keeping his eyes fixed on me.

"What now?" I asked him. I didn't like the look on his face one bit. He was uncomfortable and agitated again, almost like my very presence irritated him.

"I don't know what the fuck I'm doing with you either," he

scowled, still sucking down his nicotine to soothe the turmoil within.

"What are you talking about?" I asked with a frown.

"I..." he said in an uncomfortable murmur. "I want to be straight with you..." He took another drag, and the cigarette trembled between the fingers of his right hand. "I'm not in love with you, Selene," he said softly, his ice-cold eyes boring into me. There was nothing in those eyes. "But..." He moved closer to me, and with the same hand that held the Winston, he tucked a bit of hair behind my ear. He tracked the movement with his eyes. I tilted my head back to get a better look at him, lingering on the short scruff that had so often grazed my cheek, giving me goosebumps when he kissed me. "It was never just sex with you," he continued. Those words hit me right in the pit of my stomach; I felt them carve themselves into my heart, the place Neil had wounded most of all.

"Which means...?" I prompted him, staring at his velvet lips clamped around the cigarette's filter.

"Almost everything I have in this life has been taken from me at one point or another, but there was always one precious thing that I held on to. One thing I guarded jealously. Something I don't give away to anyone, especially not to women because too many of them are cruel, and I would never give them another weapon to use against me..." He exhaled his smoke upward for my sake before returning his gaze to me.

"I don't understand," I admitted.

"You were the first person—the only person—to ever see all of my soul, and it'll probably stay that way," he said softly, putting out the cigarette after one last drag. I smiled because I heard the encouraging truth beneath his words, but he remained grave, like he still considered it a misstep, giving himself to me. I moved closer to him and slid my hands underneath his coat to wrap around his warm, sweater-clad waist.

He didn't pull away; he allowed himself to be touched without complaint.

"So what?" I looked up at him—if I'd been a bit taller, I could have reached his lips and shut him up with a kiss.

"Do you know why I've always thought of you as my Neverland?" he asked, tucking both hands into the pockets of his coat as my arms continued to encircle him. I leaned against him fully, and the feeling of his hard body pressing up against mine was thrilling.

"Why?" I answered. He smiled, but then his stare turned cold. Neil was emotionally withdrawing to cope with the things he felt when we were together.

"Because you're someplace far away... far away from the world that we live in. Pure, free, untainted. You are the most beautiful... refuge I've ever had." He smiled tragically at me. The tone of his voice was so soothing that I relaxed against him, feeling protected.

"That's a good thing," I murmured affectionately.

"Not when it's happening to someone like me. Someone who can only watch the moon rise high in the sky, admiring it there amongst the stars, without ever being able to reach for it..." he stroked my hair, taking a deep breath.

"But I'll keep on admiring you from down here on the ground. Your light will make it through the rubble in little slivers, and I'll still get to see it. Even if I can't follow it. When I see that light, I'll think of you. It will remind me that you were here, that I once met you and experienced you." His knuckles were rough as he stroked my cheek. "You are just like the moon. The most I could aspire to is to dream of wandering amongst the stars while you remain fixed there, resolute against the darkness... You're like an untouchable queen, Babygirl. And I am not your king." He pressed a kiss to my forehead and another to my lips. "Not your prince, not your savior, not your man..." he murmured against my mouth, his smoke-scented breath rolling over me.

In his lightless eyes, I saw regret, disillusionment, and broken dreams. I saw loneliness and fear so powerful that I couldn't fight back against them.

The true monster inside him wasn't Kimberly but the fallout from her abuse. It had been with him so long that he didn't even believe it was possible to live without it.

And, in all likelihood, he never would.

What could I do, in that case, to salvage our relationship?

I had to leave it up to chance.

"How about a trade?" I suggested, apropos of nothing, and he frowned. I slipped a hand into my coat and extracted two hard candies. One was coconut flavored, the other honey. I'd picked them up for later snacking at the clinic's café a few days ago while Neil was talking to John. "Pick one. Consider it an invitation to pass into my kingdom amongst the stars," I continued in a tone of reverence that made his lips creep up into an amused smile.

"A candy?" he asked skeptically.

"Yup. Which one do you want?"

Inside my head, I played a silly little game with myself: If he chose the coconut candy, then that would mean that there might be a chance for us, that Neil might agree to continue to walk by the light of the moon, even if he never changed otherwise. If he chose the honey candy, it would mean that he was going to remain alone, fighting endlessly against the past without ever finding a way forward.

Neil raised his hand to pick a candy, and I closed one eye in anticipation, afraid to see what choice he'd make. My heart raced, and when I saw the one he'd taken, it was as though a swarm of butterflies took flight inside me.

Neil had chosen the coconut candy.

The broad smile that spread across my face made him blink in bewilderment.

"Good job! Excellent choice!" I enthused, closing my fist around the remaining honey candy—the one that symbolized Neil as he was—Kimberly, the wounds left open, the hurt, the shame, everything I wanted to sweep away to give him a second chance.

"What now?" he asked, turning the candy over in his fingers, examining it like a curious child.

"Now you fly with me, Peter Pan," I said, and then I stole a kiss from his lips.

All I wanted was him and me.
A couple packets of pistachios.
Two candies.
Our mess.
All I wanted was something simple.
No love stories.
No changes.
No Prince Charming.
All I wanted was this undefined "us."
Any kind of story as long as he was in it with me.
I knew we didn't have a future together.
I knew that Neil wouldn't stick around.
That one day he would leave for who knew where...
My common sense screamed it to me constantly.
But I didn't care what was going to happen in the future.
I wanted our relationship to be meaningful.
To leave a mark on his soul.
And, right then, all I wanted to do was fly...

16

"Not answering wasn't lying; it was just omitting details that I'd address later at the appropriate time."

NEIL

It had been a month since the candy "trade."

I'd picked the coconut one without giving it much thought, and when Babygirl told me I was going to fly with her, I didn't immediately understand what she meant. But I indulged her anyway to keep from disappointing her.

The things she did sometimes struck me as childish, weird, or beyond my understanding, but they brought a smile to my face, nonetheless.

Tinkerbell had been living with me since then, and we were constantly doing what she called "making love," whereas I thought of it as "fucking her wherever and whenever I wanted." She made me agree not to screw anyone else by promising to meet all of my needs.

And so she had.

I didn't even think about other women anymore.

I ignored the blonds who crossed my path and instead imagined having her soft little body pressed up against mine.

I still continued to tell her that we were not in a relationship, though. At least I could be honest about that. I wouldn't call us a couple or give her any false words of love.

Selfish as I was, I was committed to enjoying whatever it was between us to the maximum before I had to honor the underhanded deal I'd made with her mother.

Selene had no idea our coupling had a hard end date—an unfortunately imminent one.

As soon as I started my internship, I'd be gone. And she probably wouldn't understand my decision at first. She would hate me, maybe even think I was a fucking liar, but I knew that, with time and clarity, she would one day stop thinking of me as the man of her dreams and see why I made the choice to let her go.

Her happiness was more important than mine, and that's all there was to say about it.

"I like the way you scream my name..." I gasped out from behind her. I clutched her hips possessively, so hard that I left imprints from my fingers on her snowy skin.

I watched her ass as it rhythmically struck my pubic area. I watched the curve of her back, glistening with sweat...because she was perfect.

Her slim shoulders and narrow hips were perfect. The line of her spine was perfect. The back dimples that I brushed with my thumbs were perfect...my Tinkerbell was perfect, especially when she whispered how much she cared about me, that it wasn't just physical pleasure, and that she gave me what I needed because she loved to feel me truly engage with her.

"Tell me you're mine. Only mine." She turned her face slightly to look back over one shoulder, her small hands fisting the sheets beneath us as I continued to move forcefully. I stared fixedly at the place where we were joined together, the place that was so soft and warm as I vigorously rocked in and out of it that I felt like it had a supernatural power to make me feel less wrong.

I had always been hers.

Ever since the first time Tinkerbell had fluttered her wings and alighted upon my heart.

"I'm only yours, Babygirl..." I bit her shoulder and licked along her spine, picking up the beads of sweat that gleamed on her pale skin.

Her taste was good. Her smell was good; everything about her was good.

I thought constantly about new things to do with her because she brought out my most insane fantasies about all the emotions I'd never been able to indulge in before.

I did nothing but fuck her, kiss her, hold her, and want her every hour of every day—every fucking minute—and still, whenever I wasn't right in front of her, I was thinking of nothing but ripping those panties off and getting back between her thighs.

She had become my drug. My obsession.

Babygirl had staked her claim. She had taken up her rightful place inside me.

All I'd done was strip off her clothes, while she had stripped me down to my soul.

Lately, even my nightmares of Kim were being replaced with erotic dreams about her or the two of us together, to the point where I'd get hard in my sleep like a teenager with out-of-control hormones.

"Keep going...you have no idea how incredible your ass looks from here..." I slapped her right ass cheek, and she jolted forward in surprise. I admired the reddening handprint I'd made there. The more I looked at it, the more I felt like she belonged to me. Like she was entirely mine, and that if anyone tried to deprive me of my Neverland in the brief period of time I had left with her, I'd kill them with my bare hands.

"Neil...please," she begged me for some respite because I'd already dragged out this savage bout of lovemaking long enough, but whenever I withdrew from her body, I felt empty again. Incomplete. I felt myself again, the little boy who needed attention and could no longer accept the loneliness because he had gotten a glimpse of how beautiful it could be to share his days with someone else.

My breathing was ragged, and my muscles were rigid.

I was sweating hard and still all revved up as I felt her slim body being pushed to its limits by my deep strokes, exhausted by my stamina.

I withdrew until I lost contact with her heat before plunging back into the hilt because I knew that she would take me.

I was big and painfully aroused, but I knew that she wouldn't shut me out. She had accepted every side of me, even that one.

I muttered a curse, not caring about the sound of the headboard slamming against the wall. Her back bowed deeper and deeper until she collapsed, helpless, on the sheets. One side of her face was pressed against the mattress, and her knees trembled as they propped up her ass, leaving it exposed and vulnerable to all my twisted desires.

I stretched out over her, propping up my weight on my forearms, which inched forward with every thrust. I could penetrate her from a different angle in that position, gliding more easily and taking full possession of her, way down into the depths of her soul. And Babygirl raised her pretty little ass to let me do it.

The position only intensified her experience, and she groaned as I pushed deeper, determined to drive the last bit of clear thinking right out of her head.

My hungry mouth laved ferociously at her soft skin. I kissed her shoulder and the nape of her neck; all over I licked and nibbled.

I was marking her, making her feel that I had been there. Making her feel how much I wanted her, and not just physically but with all of me, with all the frenzy I could muster.

I wanted to get inside her, inside her head, underneath her skin.

I wanted to stake a claim in her as well—a spot that would continue to belong to me even after I was gone.

Even when it was someone else flying to my Neverland.

Even when this absurd "us" we had created melted into nothingness.

I would remain inside of her.

Like a brand, a tattoo, an indelible mark, a bleeding wound.

She screamed out my name, but still I didn't stop.

I realized she was close, and it was time for me to really make her lose it, so I withdrew slightly to begin a series of short, powerful thrusts. I dragged one hand from her stomach to her clit and teased it with ruthless intensity that had her gasping for breath.

Her pussy tightened around me. She released me slightly only to suck me back in as she approached orgasm.

Burning hot, soaking wet, tipping over the edge...

I squeezed my eyes shut, my head full of clouds.

Colors, lights, words, thoughts... none of it made a fucking lick of sense to me.

I swore, and with a bestial growl, I exploded inside her. Hot, unstoppable spurts that I forced all the way inside her with one last vigorous thrust.

With my lungs sapped of oxygen and my head feeling much lighter, I collapsed in exhaustion on top of her body.

"Babygirl..." I gasped out next to her ear as my expanse of muscles completely obscured her slim frame. She didn't say a word, made no movement, and appeared completely inert underneath me. "Selene..." I said again, more concerned this time, and frowned as I propped myself up on my elbows to make sure she was okay. The idea that I'd gone overboard and been too rough with her was disturbing.

"I'm alive," she managed, her lush mouth and cheek half-buried in the mattress.

Her ocean eyes were closed in exhaustion, and her breathing was ragged but deep. I sighed in relief that she was okay and pressed a kiss to the bend of her neck. I knew that I was insatiable, an unstoppable machine, and that she struggled to keep up with me, but that was the price of sexual exclusivity with me.

She had taken on the responsibility of keeping me fed all by herself, so she couldn't really complain if the beast wanted to eat all the time.

"Remember that time I told you that being with me wouldn't be anything like being with Jareth?" I whispered, amused. "Well, I guess now you know what I was talking about..." With a twist of my hips, I pulled myself out of her warm pussy and rolled over next to her, my back flat against the wrinkled sheets.

I stared up at the ceiling.

Her smell was in the air.

That fucking coconut smell that made me want to go another round already. But after turning to look at her, I banished the idea of suggesting such a thing to her. Her eyelids were heavy with fatigue, and there were numerous marks all over her body, some of them pink, some of them darker. All of them left behind by my rough fingers and greedy lips. I'd worn her out, and even when I promised myself that I was going to be gentle with her, I always wound up mercilessly dominating her instead.

"You sure you're okay?" I rolled onto my side and looked into her eyes. I wanted to hide the distress I was feeling in that moment, but I knew she'd sensed it already. Instinctively, I reached out and grabbed her wrist. I turned it over, pressing my lips to the underside, and lingered there for a few moments, trying to focus on her pulse.

It was strong and regular. It pleased me just to feel it.

"I'm always okay with you," she said in a small whisper.

"You can tell me if you're not," I insisted, moving closer to plant a kiss on her shoulder. After a few moments, I pulled back to give her what was undoubtedly a distant look.

I couldn't do much better than that.

I'd always hated cuddles, soft caresses, and all that bullshit. I couldn't give her those things, but I did feel the urge to let her know that I cared about her in my own way.

Selene, like most women, required at least some minor show of affection, especially after sex. But as bad as I was with words, I was somehow even worse with romantic gestures.

I just hoped she could understand some of what I was trying to tell her through the few means I understood and had at my disposal.

I stroked the curve of her slightly arched spine with my fingertips. Her ocean eyes were pointed at me, glittering just like the sea. I'd been drowning in them since the very first moment I saw her. Her crimson lips were parted just a bit, exhausted by my kisses. Her hair was disheveled and spread out in disorderly waves all over the sheets. Her nose scrunched up adorably as she smiled at me.

"I really am okay. I don't want to change you, you know. I like you—all of you," she whispered, soft, sweet, and weary. She was beautiful in her simplicity, though I had never told her that. I wasn't accustomed to giving compliments; I didn't like exposing myself in that way. I didn't want my Babygirl to see too much of what was going on inside me. "What are you staring at?" She shifted slightly under my fingers as I continued to stroke her skin, watching her face raptly as though I'd been hypnotized.

"You're even cuter after sex." I let slip a bit of sincerity, biting my lower lip in delight at the funny little forehead crease that had just appeared between her eyebrows.

"Cute..." she repeated thoughtfully before pursing her lips in a disappointed expression. Apparently, she didn't appreciate that descriptor either.

"Yeah, you look...really *nice*." I grazed her neck with the tip of my nose, and she shivered when my beard scruff made contact with her delicate skin, and damn it if I wasn't feeling the urge to fuck her again.

My cock was in complete agreement.

"Neil..." she said in a lazy grumble, making it clear that I shouldn't even think about starting anything up again.

"Uh huh?" I answered in a low murmur, slowly rubbing my erection against her thigh. I knew she couldn't resist me.

"Don't try that innocent act on me. I need a break and a shower." She jerked away from my burning touch, and I shivered at the sudden cold absence. She sat up on the edge of the bed, offering me a view of her back and her butt cheeks, still red from my smacks.

Was she really turning me down?

I huffed in irritation and rolled over to stare at the white ceiling.

"Yeah, yeah, okay... Go on and take your shower..." I muttered irritably. If I'd been with Jennifer or one of my other blonds, she would have been begging me to give her a little more attention. Selene, however, wanted to put my mind through its paces rather than content herself with my naked body next to her.

Abruptly, my lucubrations disappeared as I felt her hands on me, her small body climbing astride me like a savage tigress. Her long hair fell over her breasts and stiff, pink nipples peeked between the auburn locks.

I stared at them, swallowing hard and longing to suck them.

"Are you upset?" she asked, positioning herself right on top of my erection.

I narrowed my eyes, forcing myself not to touch her. I folded one arm up underneath my head and let the other rest on the sheet.

"No," I answered way too quickly. She giggled.

"You took me twice last night. And you woke up this morning wanting more of the same. You have to give me some time to get used to all of this; you really are quite demanding..." She leaned down and began to pepper light kisses on my neck, just where I liked them. She sucked a patch of skin there slowly, delicately, like she was afraid of hurting me, and pressed her breasts against my pectorals. My cock stiffened, and when Selene felt it twitch between her legs, she reddened.

Instead, I squeezed my eyes shut and opened them slowly, breathing deep.

Fortunately, I'd had a lot of practice resisting sexual urges, or else I would have had her right back on her hands and knees again.

I seized her hips roughly and yanked her off me, depositing her on the mattress.

"What...what's the matter now?" she asked, confused.

I turned my back to her and swung my legs over the side of the bed. I sucked in a breath when my feet hit the cold hardwood floor.

What time was it? More importantly, how long had we been locked in the pool house's bedroom? We'd gone out last night for dinner, after which I'd brought her right back here and promptly lost all track of time.

I ran a hand through my sweat-slicked hair, and my eyes landed on the pack of Winstons on my nightstand.

The problem was, I was getting far too used to Selene's presence, and that was going to make her absence much more difficult.

Our time was running out.

I'd finished my studies, and in the spring I'd be starting my internship in Chicago.

I'd been working hard to get everything together before then, though Selene had been a constant distraction.

"Nothing," I answered her after a long silence.

"I really am sore, Neil. You weren't gentle. I'd never reject you. It's just that..." she trailed off. After taking a drag from my cigarette, I got to my feet and turned to look at her. She was sitting with her knees drawn up to her chest, clutching the sheet against her breasts.

Watching my naked body, she grew steadily more uncomfortable. Her gaze dropped down to her knees, but then she appeared to gather her nerve and looked back up at my face.

"Is it about graduation? Are you stressed about the next step?"

"No," I interrupted her. "I don't give a shit about that." I blew the cigarette smoke out my nose.

I should have thought of graduating from college as an accomplishment, but instead it only stressed me out, as did the idea of leaving for my internship. I'd only sent my confirmation email to Professor Robinson a week earlier, making him, Logan, and Megan the only people who knew about my decision. Megan had texted me the same day, saying, "Congrats, colleague."

Selene was still in the dark about all of it.

She continued to stick by my side, to support me and try to be the right woman for me, unaware of what I was planning.

I told myself I wasn't just enjoying these last moments with her; I was also protecting her even if Player had apparently disappeared into thin air once again.

We'd seen no further signs of the woman from the video chat. There were no more puzzles or threats or attacks, and though we'd checked multiple times, there was no sign of any videos or pictures of Selene being sent to people or posted anywhere.

Had she finally given up?

Nothing about it added up for me, though.

The woman on the video hadn't revealed her identity, and in general she had seemed way too innocuous and accommodating.

I'd purchased a new laptop for Selene, but I still wanted her to keep her socials deactivated and made her change all her passwords, just to be safe. I also told her to tape up the webcam like I did with my own MacBook.

"Neil..." Babygirl broke me from my reverie—I'd been standing there staring vaguely at the bed with the cigarette still dangling from my lips. I turned my gaze to her only to find that she was standing right in front of me, naked. "Will you stop being patronizing and shutting me out of your world?" she said, resting her hands on my hips. I gasped. Her fingers were cold, and she was trembling. She pressed a kiss to my stomach before moving up to my chest, pinning my eyes with hers.

"You've taken it over completely," I said in a confused murmur. "My world," I continued, taking another drag. I narrowed my eyes as curls of smoke wafted up while she smiled in satisfaction.

"Well, that's nice to hear, considering all the effort I put into getting in there," she said slyly.

"Not so much for me," I answered brusquely. Babygirl rubbed the base of my spine and pressed herself against me. I tried to take shallow breaths to avoid succumbing to the temptation of her lovely tits against my abdomen. She must have been able to feel it because she gave me a wicked look. She walked her fingers along my abdomen, which contracted with her touch, before continuing up my chest worshipfully, as though she had gotten the chance to closely examine something surreal and fascinating. "What are you doing?" I asked her warily.

The cigarette was still burning between my lips as I let my arms relax while Selene grazed my shoulders and biceps with her fingernails. She used her index finger to trace the lines of my toki while the other hand did the same on my pikorua. I let out a guttural groan. I wouldn't have minded if she'd just moved those fingers over a few inches so they could wrap around my cock. She could have given me a moment of pleasure to wipe away all the angst, but that apparently wasn't her intention.

Instead, she wanted to talk.

Talk, talk, and more talk...

"I never told anyone that before, you know?" she whispered, wrapping her hands around my waist again and clinging to me.

Pinching the cigarette between my fingers, I leaned sideways to stub it out in the ashtray before focusing on her.

"Told anyone what?" I asked, blowing out the last lungful of smoke away from her face.

"What I was going to tell you that night in Detroit. Do you remember?" Her eyes probed mine, and I hesitated, just observing her ocean stare.

How could I have forgotten? It had been unbearable, knowing I was about to hear those soul-eroding words from her mouth. An "I love you" only conjured up the verbal abuse, the harassment, and the sexual assault I had suffered at the hands of Kimberly.

I didn't answer at first and went rigid instead. I thought about pushing her hands away, but instead I held still and stared at her.

"Not even to Jareth?" I asked, suddenly eager to know.

"Not even to *Jared*," she said pointedly, though she should have known by then that I didn't give a shit what that dude's name was.

"Good. Someday you can tell the right person."

Selene must not have liked that answer because she curled her lip and gave me an annoyed look.

Her brilliant gaze dimmed, and then her hands fell away from me. The abrupt detachment was alarming.

"I know your heart, Selene. You don't need those useless words to make me understand. Just keep showing me with your actions, with your choices and with your bravery. I have no use for banal declarations of love. I can see how you feel about me..." I tucked a strand of hair behind her ear and smiled slightly. Babygirl blinked slowly at me, her face taking on a curious expression.

"Why do you hate to hear a woman tell you she loves you?" she asked me. I had known this moment would come. But still it wasn't remotely easy, holding back the anger and the memories those words awoke in me. Selene didn't know any of that, though. She was just honestly curious.

"Because Kim used to whisper it while she was raping me," I admitted with disarming coolness.

Selene gasped and pressed a hand to her mouth.

"I...I'm sorry. I didn't know..." she babbled, mortified. She moved closer, silently asking permission to hug me. I did not object. I welcomed her warmth as she clung to me, resting her head against my torso. I breathed in the good smell of her hair and wrapped an arm around her waist, letting my hand rest on her ass, which I gave a good grope. Even in a moment like that, I couldn't just be a normal man who was content giving her soft touches and tender affection. Instead, I remained the pervert who wanted nothing more than to stick his tongue between her thighs, like I'd done the night before.

And let her moans drown out my tedious thoughts.

Let her thighs squeeze all the misery out of my head.

Let her scream my name with all the romance inside her to tell me in a different way about this thing that bound us together. This cursed thing I refused to define...

....

After spilling another part of my history to Selene, I took a long shower before joining her in the kitchen. The last time I'd seen her in front of a stove, she was charring a grilled cheese sandwich that I had eaten only out of extreme hunger.

I sat without commenting for a few moments on a stool, my chin balanced on my palm as I watched her attentively. She moved gracefully around my space, like it had now become hers as well.

"I know you're already done and you don't have to, but have you thought about walking in the spring with the rest of your graduating class?" she asked cheerfully. The smell of scrambled eggs was in the air. Selene was undoubtedly cooking because, according to her, breakfast for someone my size should consist of more than just a cup of coffee.

As usual, I ignored her questions in favor of feasting my eyes on her tight ass. Sooner or later, I'd have that too.

How many asses had I seen in my life?

Still, hers seemed like the best one I'd ever encountered.

"Neil, are you listening to me?" Tinkerbell shot me a look. I didn't answer because, by then, my attention had shifted to her bare legs, left exposed underneath one of my sweatshirts. It was enormous on her. She didn't even bother asking my permission to wear them anymore; she just knew that she could and that she was the only woman besides my sister who'd ever had that privilege.

"No. You know, trying to have a conversation with me while half-naked is never going to be productive." I continued to size her up like a predator lying in wait. She shook her head in amusement, and her auburn hair swayed back and forth at the base of her spine. I was reminded of the moment last night when I wrapped that hair around my fist as I thrust into her from behind. I shifted on the stool, irritated.

A giant hard-on in tight jeans was one of the worst inconveniences that could befall a man.

"I was talking about graduation. Don't you think you should do something to mark the occasion? Maybe a party? And what about after that? Do you have plans?" Selene looked radiant, sounding like she was the one who had graduated instead of me. She was prouder of me than my own mother was.

She grabbed two plates and deposited the scrambled eggs on them before picking out some clean silverware and walking over to me.

"You must be hungry, Tigress. Guess fucking really takes it out of you," I said, trying to redirect the conversation to something more comfortable. I didn't want to talk about the future with her. I didn't like lying to her so the only thing I could do was refuse to answer. Not answering wasn't lying; it was just omitting details that I'd address later at the appropriate time.

"Why do I get the feeling you're trying to dodge my questions?" she asked suspiciously, handing me one of the plates. Selene had gotten eerily good at understanding me even when I didn't say a word. All she had to do was look deep into my eyes and read the silent language of my body, and I'd find myself absolutely fucked.

"You get that feeling because I don't really want to think about that stuff yet," I said. It was a plausible enough excuse. Selene just cocked a doubtful eyebrow.

"Neil, we both know you're not just going to hang around the pool house indefinitely. Don't try to tell me you haven't got plans." She went over to the refrigerator and pulled out a carton of orange juice before bringing it back to me.

"Then let's just say I want to firm them up a little before I talk about them." I ceded some ground, trying to silence the voice of my conscience that urged me to just tell her about the internship in Chicago and Megan.

"What about that guy? Professor Robbins or something?" She bounced on her stool like a little kid, and as I stared at her, I couldn't help but think about how funny she was sometimes.

"Robinson. Professor Robinson," I answered, and she nodded as she poured the orange juice into glasses for us.

"Yeah, him. You said he wanted to meet with you about something. What was it?" she asked, and fortunately I hadn't put any eggs in my mouth by that point, or I would have choked on them.

Over the course of our "relationship," I had told Selene some details about my studies, including my final project with Robinson and our meeting. At one point, I'd even gotten quite close to telling her the truth about my conversations with Judith, but I pulled back because I knew Selene. She had a stubborn streak and could be rebellious, and I didn't want her fighting with her mother. Ms. Martin agreed to accept our quasi-relationship only because she knew it was temporary and that I would keep my word.

"It was nothing," I said, underplaying it. "He just wanted to compliment me on being one of the best students in the course," I lied. Well, it wasn't a total lie, but neither was it what Professor Robinson and I had actually talked about the last time I saw him in person. On that occasion, he'd shaken my hand and told me that I'd made the right decision accepting the internship.

"Wow, I didn't know you were such a nerd…" Selene teased me as she scooped up her first forkful of eggs.

"Because I'm not," I shot back, giving her a dirty look.

"Okay, don't get your panties in a twist, Mr. Disaster." She gave me a sweet smile, which I did not return. I forked up a little bit of eggs and tasted them, hoping they were more edible than the charred toast. Selene watched me uncomfortably the whole time I chewed.

"Uh…how do you like it?" she asked. I looked deep into her eyes, and Babygirl chewed her lip uncertainly. In that moment, it occurred to me just how vitally important my judgment was to her because, when it came to me, she valued everything.

"They're edible… I've known for a while now that you're not exactly a chef," I answered easily with typical nonchalance, but I tamped down a smile of amusement, hoping to bug her a little. She arranged her lips into a pout and then cleared her throat awkwardly and immediately poured more OJ into her glass.

"Always gotta be an asshole," she grumbled under her breath, but I still heard her loud and clear. Then she turned back to her eggs and ignored me with a miffed look on her face.

And that was adorable too.

"Come here." I patted my knee invitingly. She raised her eyes up from her plate and looked hesitantly at me, thinking it over. "Come on, Tinkerbell. You know I hate to wait," I chided her, and she got slowly to her feet, dabbing her lips with a paper towel. She walked around the kitchen island and perched on my leg. Automatically, I rested a hand on her exposed thigh and kissed her neck, feeling her quiver against me. Like always, she smelled of coconut. I held still and breathed in her smell, trying to banish all the dark thoughts from my head. "Eggs are fine, but I'd rather have my breakfast between your legs," I said in a seductive whisper as I felt her move against my thigh, wriggling.

"You should..." She swallowed and cleared her throat, trying to maintain some composure. Oh, did she think I was joking?

"Yeah, I really should, Babygirl..." I grabbed her hips abruptly and sat her down on the kitchen island. She let out a surprised gasp. I swept the plates off the island and urged her to lie back. I didn't give her any time to process what was happening before I'd flung up her sweatshirt and yanked down her panties. She let out a little excited cry when I threw them onto the floor behind us. I slipped my head between her thighs and began licking her little by little, just as I had fantasized about before.

She arched her back and pressed her knees together to hold me more tightly against her. I found her already slick and puffy. Babygirl was just as turned on as I was. I focused on winding her up, circling her clit with my tongue before moving down to ratchet up the shocking sensations that had her trembling uncontrollably.

She moaned my name repeatedly, lost in a whirlwind of pleasure.

She clung to me like we were one being.

I was her drug.

I could make her come undone, despite all her prudishness.

And knowing that made me feel like one smug bastard.

Perhaps there were important words that she would have rather heard from me, but I wouldn't have been me if I could have given them to her.

Physicality was the only medium I could use to communicate, and my desire for her was the only certainty I could offer.

I fixed the fly of my jeans where my erection had begun to pulse with yearning to simply *get on with it* already, but my goal with this was to take her over the edge without demanding anything from her in return.

I paused for a moment to nibble on her inner thigh and glanced up at her through my lashes.

Selene was breathless, cheeks red, and mouth open. Her breasts rose and fell convulsively with the rhythm of her breath. She groaned in irritation and squeezed her knees together, urging me to pick up where I'd left off.

I smirked as I went back to tormenting her until someone banged on the door.

Abruptly, I raised myself up and whipped my head around to see who the idiot with the shitty timing was.

"Oh God!" Selene muttered, leaping off the kitchen island. She pulled down the sweatshirt to cover herself before clutching me, apparently experiencing a moment of lightheadedness. Before I even had the chance to figure out who the interloper was—and punch him in the face—the door swung open. Logan, wearing a huge, oblivious grin, walked in with a tray in his hands. He stopped abruptly when he registered the state of the kitchen—and of us.

"What the fuck..."

"Are we doing?" I finished for him. Logan stared down at the eggs all over the floor and the puddle of juice, which had spread out considerably next to it. Selene, meanwhile, was red with embarrassment as she clung to my sweater.

"'What happened' is what I was going to say," my brother said, looking first at Babygirl, wearing just my wrinkled sweatshirt, and then at me. He lingered briefly on the crotch of my pants, and I knew he had to be seeing my hard-on. There was no hiding it, really.

I gave him a cheerful grin, and he cocked an eyebrow back at me.

"You were clearly...uh..." he mumbled, trying not to laugh.

"Having breakfast," Selene supplied, clearing her throat loudly.

Logan obviously knew exactly what we'd been doing, and he knew me well enough that the truth wouldn't be surprising or embarrassing. But I respected Selene and her sense of modesty. She would have been extremely uncomfortable if I'd started joking around with Logan about what we'd gotten up to.

"Sure. Of course. And I see you did not like the eggs..." He chuckled, jerking his chin at the mess. Selene tucked a bit of hair behind her ears while I just rakishly licked my lower lip, still savoring the taste of her.

"No! I mean...the...uh..." Tinkerbell had no idea what to say. Her cheeks were burning; it made me soften toward her. Instinctively, I sat down on a stool and pulled her onto my lap.

"I wanted something else for breakfast." I wrapped an arm around her waist, pulling her closer reassuringly. She looked over her shoulder at me, and I smiled to let her know everything was okay.

"Okay..." Logan said, adopting an expression of total indifference. "Anyway, Selene, someone had Miss Anna fix this up for you." He put the tray down on the kitchen island and lifted the colorful lid to show Babygirl what was underneath.

Her eyes went wide, and she leaned in to get a closer look.

"But...that's toast with cherry jam," she said softly.

Immediately, she turned to look at me. I'd let her have her fun in the kitchen, but I'd known full well that she wasn't going to want those eggs either.

"You did this, didn't you?" Her gaze moved to my lips and lingered there for a few moments.

"Maybe..." I shrugged. She stared at me with shocked adoration.

"Whoa, tigers. I'm right here, remember? Try to keep your lusts at bay," Logan cut in before I could give her another one of my breathtaking kisses. Selene shook herself and stood up, catching sight of something on the floor near Logan. The blood drained from her face as she crouched down to scoop up her torn panties, which she immediately hid behind her back.

Once again, I had to hold back my laughter.

"Thank you so much, Logan, and…uh… Please thank Miss Anna for me as well. I'm just going to go get dressed. I…I'll be right back," she said clumsily, fleeing into the bedroom. I took the opportunity to scope out her ass again, and the realization that she'd been sitting on my lap with no panties on was terribly thrilling. I could have slid my hand between her legs and finished what I'd started, but instead…

"You and I need to talk," Logan said, giving me a disappointed look. Naturally, my every erotic fantasy evaporated in the face of my brother's scowl.

"About what?" I asked flatly.

"You know I think it's great that you've been seeing Selene exclusively. Chloe and I both support this relationship of yours, even if the rest of the family doesn't. I'll always support you, Neil. But you can't just keep her trapped in the bedroom all the time. I'd like to hang out with her, and our friends want to see her too. The gang's been asking about her ever since they found out she's in town, and they want to know why she never comes out with us," he said chidingly. Ever since he became single again, Logan had been going out every night to various clubs and bars with his group of friends. It wasn't the first time he'd asked me to share Selene with him and the others, but I'd never agreed to it.

My time with Babygirl was limited; I couldn't afford to waste it.

"She's here for me," I said roughly, like the overbearing asshole I was. I had no right to keep her isolated from the world, but she'd be back to her normal life soon enough when I left her.

For now, she had to stay with me.

"And that makes it right? You could go with her, you know. Let's all go out together. Are you really so selfish that you're fine with keeping her locked up in here like your sex slave?" he scolded me darkly.

"That's not how it is. We have conversations and—" I attempted to defend myself, but Logan spoke over me.

"Oh yeah, totally. I bet you even let her have a break when she's on her period if she asks. You're a real prince, Neil," he said with pointed sarcasm. I fumed at him, a look of annoyance on my face, but he just shook his head.

"She's so crazy about you that even the landscaping can tell." He gestured at the view out the window as if to illustrate his point. "And, meanwhile, what are you doing? Have you even told her about the internship yet?" he demanded. My prolonged silence and indifferent posture gave him all the answers he needed. "For fuck's sake, Neil!" he blurted out.

"Don't yell," I said menacingly, getting to my feet. Logan, however, was one of the few people who wasn't scared when I tried to use my size to intimidate him.

He knew that, no matter what he said or did, I was never going to lay a finger on him.

"You're making a mistake. She needs to know that all of this is just a...last hurrah before you go. You don't have to tell her about her mother if you don't want them to fight, but she deserves to know about the rest of it." He waved his hands through the air, tired of saying the same thing to me over and over, as he'd been doing for the last month. I rubbed my face in frustration and turned away, looking instead at the mess I'd made tossing my breakfast all over the floor.

"Not once in my life have I ever focused exclusively on just one woman. I've never wanted to share my space with someone else," I admitted, thinking about how nice it was that Selene just liked being with me and liked taking care of me even more. In the evenings, she ordered my favorites for dinner and made sure I ate. In the mornings, she attempted breakfasts, and at night she comforted me when I was unsettled by another nightmare about Kim. When I got mad and went off on her because of my mood swings, she knew no resentment or anger; even after the most heated argument, she'd come running into my arms the moment I asked.

"I know," Logan murmured behind my back. "And you know it's going to break her heart, but you're going on ahead anyway," he scolded me. I turned to see the sadness creeping over his face.

"She asked to be with me," I said defensively.

"Neil, we both know you're smarter than that. Selene didn't sign up to be with you for just a few weeks while you fuck her all you want and let her think she's your girlfriend," he answered shortly. Described in those words, the whole thing made me sound like a son of a bitch.

"She's knows that she's not my girlfriend. That there is no fucking relationship," I corrected him before glancing at the closed bedroom door to make sure Selene wasn't about to rejoin us. "I never promised her anything, never declared any nonexistent feelings. You know what I'm like," I pressed, stepping toward him.

"No, Neil. I don't. Not anymore. I would have said you weren't a liar." He gave me a disappointed look, his jaw tight.

"I'm not lying to her. I just held back one detail," I snapped back.

"You're hiding an important part of your future. If you start working in Chicago, you're not going to come back here. Have you actually thought about that? Plus, you'll be sharing an apartment with another woman," he went on, and I grimaced.

"What is wrong with you?" I dragged a hand over my face. "I have zero interest in Megan, and I never fucking will. That would be completely out of bounds." I shook my head, disturbed at just the thought of the two of us in bed together.

To me, she would always be that little girl in the basement. I hadn't touched her when I was ten years old, and I wasn't going to touch her now at twenty-five.

"You don't know what might happen. You're going to be living together, and whether you want to or not, you'll be spending a lot of time with her."

"That doesn't mean I'll sleep with her," I said confidently. Megan was a beautiful woman, compelling and sexy, but I'd never go there, no matter what she tried.

I had always been stronger than her and her games.

Logan would undoubtedly see that for himself soon, and then he'd apologize to me for insinuating something so insane.

"We'll see," he said challengingly before looking away thoughtfully. "As far as Selene goes...try to act like a man. Not just someone who wants to fuck her." With that said, he started to leave, shoulder-checking me on his way to the door.

17

"Why don't you go fly into someone else's heart, Tinkerbell?"

NEIL

It was eight o'clock at night, and I had no idea what the hell I was doing.

Logan had never come back, but his words were still bouncing around inside my head.

Selene and I had lunch together, and then she spent a few hours with Matt. I had no idea where they went or what they talked about, but I knew it was right for her to have some time with her father. Judging by her eyes when she came back, though, things between them had gone poorly yet again.

I leaned against the doorframe and watched as she stood in the bedroom, painstakingly fastening her bra.

She'd just taken a shower.

Her scent hung in the air, commingling with my own.

I looked her slowly from bottom to top, appreciating every detail. I began with her tapering feet, her defined calves, and her tight thighs. I craned my neck slightly to better admire the curve of her ass and gave a groan of approval.

She was perfect.

I moved my eyes up over her flat stomach to the bounty of her.

Her tits would look even better, though, if they were being cradled in my hands or mouth. That was where they belonged.

She hadn't realized I was there, and she gasped when she turned around and caught a glimpse of my shadowy figure in the doorway. She quit doing up her bra to stare intensely at me.

"Did..." she swallowed. "Did you want to get dressed?" she asked timidly.

"No, you go ahead..." I answered, remaining motionless in that same arrogant stance. She watched me with passionate longing, and I knew she wanted me to say something else to her, but I was determined to keep my desires in check.

"What, don't you want me anymore?" she needled me with a sly smile.

So Tinkerbell liked to play games with me.

And, standing there all sweet-smelling in her underwear, she would pose a serious challenge to any red-blooded man.

In answer to her question, I took her delicately by the wrist and pressed her open palm to my hard cock.

She sucked in a breath but didn't resist. She'd asked if I wanted her anymore... Well, I'd answer her question in my own special way.

I let her feel my full length before pushing her hand down to my balls. I narrowed my eyes, delighting in her light, timid touch while she held her breath. I moved closer to steal that breath right out of her lungs.

Again...more...always more. I could never get enough.

"I'd say the answer is pretty clear," I whispered before giving her a deliberately brief kiss to leave her wanting more. Selene shut her eyes, anticipating more intense contact, but I just laughed merrily. She took a step back, realizing I was baiting her.

"Want to go out tonight?" I asked her abruptly, thinking again of what Logan had said. He was right—I couldn't let her think she was my whole world here in this pool house and then just rip that away from her without warning. She deserved to have some fun, to be with her friends and to live something like a normal life.

"What do you mean?" she murmured in surprise, pushing her bangs to one side and dazzling me with her big eyes, luminous like the sea at sunrise.

"It's Saturday night. We could go out. Logan's going clubbing with his friends, and he said they'd like to see you. I'll go with you." I shrugged, and her expression shifted from stunned to thrilled. For a second, I was annoyed at the idea that she was so happy to lose time going out to some shitty club with her friends instead of staying home with me, but I reined in my instinctive selfishness and forced myself to think. It was just a night out; what mattered was that we were together. It didn't matter where we were or who else we were with.

"And the Krew? Don't you want to see them?" She bent down to dig a pair of high-waisted jeans and a very short skirt out of her bag. I frowned, looking at the second garment, and she stared at me, waiting for a response.

"I see them plenty when I'm on my own," I told her.

"So Jennifer can come on to you unimpeded, right?" She lifted up the skirt and peered at it as though debating whether or not to wear it. She also got her little sly shots in, showing me just how jealous and possessive of me she really was, despite the fact that I'd told her repeatedly that I wouldn't tolerate her attaching any strings or restrictions to us.

"Whatever Jennifer does or doesn't do, it shouldn't mean a thing to you. I haven't slept with her in months, if that's what you were thinking," I told her, entirely honestly. I hadn't even felt the need to seek out other attention since before Selene even moved in. At that moment in time, Tinkerbell was the only one my body wanted.

It would have been pointless to fuck any other women when I wouldn't even be able to come with them.

She let the skirt drop and hurled herself at me, flinging her arms around my neck. I went rigid, like I always did when she came at me like that, full of sweet, effusive affection.

"Wow, is Neil Miller being faithful to me?" Her hand sank into my hair, stroking my scalp. I swallowed as her breasts brushed against my abdomen. A fire ignited in my chest that would have burned us both if I didn't keep it under control.

"Yes," I admitted, and she smiled, delighted like I had never seen her before. She stood up on her tiptoes, pressing her still-half-naked body against me, to give me a kiss. I opened my lips, responding with identical passion. I slid a hand through her silken hair before cupping the nape of her neck and using it to pull her closer to me. I was going to take everything she had to give. I devoured her, feeding on her feminine power, her feeling, and her sickly sweetness as I stole a little bit more of her dreams. Finally, she broke away from me, panting.

"Take it easy, Mr. Disaster. You know I need to breathe." She rested her forehead on my chest, and I rubbed her head soothingly.

"Get dressed, Babygirl. And don't wear anything too short or flashy," I ordered her, and I regretted it the moment I said it. Even I didn't know why I'd made such a ridiculous request—I didn't have any right to tell her how to dress. But the idea of watching her walk into the club and seeing all the men drool over her ass bothered me. A lot.

She looked up at me, her brow creasing.

"What?" she asked.

"I just meant..." I scrambled, "I like the way you dress. You know how to be sexy in your own way." I stroked her cheek, and she smiled while I tried not to reveal the strange, unsettled feeling that was tying my stomach in knots.

I headed back to the main house, partly to give her some time to get ready and partly to get away from her before I changed my mind and decided to keep her locked up in the pool house with me. I found Logan and let him know we were coming out with him before taking yet another shower.

I had hoped that the hot water would soothe my anxieties and help me reorder my thoughts, but I was still on edge, still troubled about what was going on inside me.

I couldn't recognize myself.

I was getting more and more mixed up by the day.

Selene's proximity created disorder, confounding my reality and staining the darkness that surrounded me with so many irritating colors.

I huffed anxiously and stepped out of the shower to dry my hair. Then I tended to my beard, careful not to cut myself because my right hand had started shaking once again.

"Fuck," I blurted out. I needed to calm down.

Selene was just one girl among many others, and very soon she was going to disappear out of my life and out of my head. And I would be who I was before.

The me I recognized, the one who lived in a manageable amount of chaos without too much needless worry.

I went straight to my walk-in closet, glancing at the clock along the way. It had only been an hour since I left Babygirl in the pool house, and already I wanted to see her again.

I put on a dark pair of jeans and a sweater—the black-on-black look suited my mood.

I could have dressed a little nicer, but the truth was, I didn't actually want to go out.

The only thing I wanted to do was to stay with Selene, preferably naked and bathing in her heat with her thighs locked around me and her heels digging into my ass cheeks, spurring me to dominate her harder with every thrust.

But for once, I was trying not to think only of myself.

"Meet me outside in thirty. Let's take your car," Logan demanded, walking past my open door. He'd just gotten out of the shower as well, and he had a towel wrapped around his waist and an open box of cereal in one hand. I rolled my eyes.

Only my brother pregamed on Saturday night with handfuls of dry Lucky Charms.

"Don't be late; I'm not waiting for you," I warned. Then I hurried down the stairs and out the back door.

The icy air clawed at my face like a metal pincer as I walked quickly across the yard to the pool house. When I walked in and didn't see Selene, I was immediately alarmed.

Nervous, I went to the bedroom and only calmed down when I found her there rearranging some clothing in her suitcase. She turned to look at me, and her eyes were full of such all-encompassing heat that they activated a suffocating lust inside me.

"I'm ready," she announced before I could say anything. She knew that I hated to wait.

I stood in the doorway and looked her up and down. She wore black pumps with four-inch heels, a pair of skinny jeans that were definitely too tight and displayed every single curve, and a gold top cut dangerously low over her breasts under a short winter coat. She looked great, but apparently I hadn't been clear enough earlier when I told her *nothing flashy*.

Again, I felt that strange burning sensation in my chest, so intense that I had to rub the area with one hand.

"You don't like it?" she asked, chucking a lipstick into her purse.

What did she need that for? She already had on too much lipstick; it made her lips look even more plush. I lingered over the shadowy makeup surrounding her azure eyes, making them even more brilliant. Her long eyelashes, made even more noticeable by mascara, opened like fans around that crystalline blue. I stepped closer to get a better look at her, and she gulped, feeling the intensity of my presence.

"You're back to the leather jacket? No elegant coat tonight?" she teased me.

I grinned seductively and stepped closer to her.

"I like to change it up," I answered absently. I was focused on her cleavage, which I felt was entirely too sexual for the occasion. Tinkerbell was sexy, and not just a little bit either. The thought of other people seeing that and wanting her bothered me. Selene watched me the whole time with palpable lust. Apparently she would also prefer to strip down and fuck rather than go out.

"You look incredible no matter what you wear," she told me adoringly. I didn't say anything but just circled her, getting a good 360-degree look at her.

Her ass caught me and held me—those jeans were way too powerful. Shit.

Selene didn't move, allowing herself to be admired. She could probably feel my eyes burning into her back and that dream ass, but she didn't say a word.

I closed the distance between us as though her body were magnetized and surrounded her, pressing my chest to her back. Selene let out a little gasp.

"I don't want to break any noses tonight, Babygirl," I whispered into her ear, touching a lock of hair that had fallen over her shoulder. She swallowed hard, going stiff when I pressed my hips against her, showing her exactly where she belonged. "Stay close and be good," I warned her ominously.

Half an hour later, the two of us, along with Logan, pulled up outside the club.

Tinkerbell had chatted with my brother the whole way while I focused on driving and only took furtive looks at her in the rearview mirror.

She'd often looked tense and like her mind was somewhere else. Several times, I'd wondered what she was thinking about. The not-knowing made me apprehensive.

Plus, the idea of spending a Saturday night with her friends was not exactly thrilling me. Selene seemed happy to see them, though. She threw herself into Julie's arms when she spotted the girl in front of the club's entrance. Then she doled out hugs to Adam, Jake, Cory, and Kyle, the musician who, for some inexplicable reason, pissed me off just by existing.

"Don't make me look bad. No picking fights tonight," Logan admonished from beside me. I was visibly on edge because I got the sense that my Babygirl was just a piece of meat dangled in front of so many hungry lions.

And I would have killed every one of those fuckers if they dared step over the line.

"If no one fucks with me, I won't fuck with them. You know me—I'm all about cause and effect," I answered drily, spinning my car keys around on my index finger. I glanced up at the blue LED sign for *The Blarney*. I made a skeptical face. I'd never been to this particular place, but I doubted it had much more to offer than Blanco did.

Already bored, I turned my attention back to Babygirl, who was hugging herself against the cold. She felt my eyes on her and moved to me like I'd called for her, reaching out to take my hand in hers in such a genuine way that I shivered.

Why would she do a thing like that?

She'd done it before, but I didn't want her making a habit of it.

I looked at her tightly and flinched out of her grasp.

Too intimate.

All of this was too intimate.

I felt a stab of pain in my chest when she gave me a disappointed look, but I tried not to let any of that show on my face.

"Fuck, this place is the bomb. Come on, let's go." Logan draped an arm around her shoulders and gently urged her forward.

Maybe I was an asshole for shooting her down like that, and maybe Babygirl wouldn't talk to me for the rest of the night, but I didn't like pretending.

I was just myself.

She'd said she could accept that—accept me—and I hoped she realized that I wasn't going to change.

After a moment, I went after her and tried to get in on her conversation with her friends. I was clearly no longer the first thing on her mind. The sadness I'd seen on her face earlier was gone.

"When Logan told us you were coming out tonight, we literally cheered, doll," Cory told her. I wrinkled my nose at the nickname—I didn't like the idea of anyone else having a special name for her—but I forced myself to shut up and let her enjoy her evening.

"Yeah, you jerk. You completely forgot about us." The one teasing her that time was Jake with the tattoos and blond hair. He pulled her into an affectionate hug, and I immediately spotted his hands resting at the base of Selene's spine. I sincerely hoped he didn't move them lower.

For his sake.

"I have to agree. We need to have another meeting of the Nabokov book club..." Next it was Kyle Lucky's (or whatever the hell his name was) turn. The musician really rubbed me the wrong way. He had his long hair pulled back in a ponytail, and his frosty blue eyes looked sly, not at all friendly. He stared at Babygirl and lingered on her cleavage.

That was when my instincts forced me to get closer until I could put my arm around her and pull her tightly against me.

Selene went stiff and craned her neck back to look at me.

She was pissed, and I couldn't blame her. One minute I was refusing to hold her hand, the next I was acting like a possessive freak.

The rest of the group looked at me fearfully. Several of them took a step back, and they all exchanged quizzical looks. No need to tell me; I could see from their tight faces that they weren't loving my presence there in the club.

"Good evening," I said, smiling. I could almost taste their fear on my tongue. Each one of them knew that I wasn't anything like Logan, that I ran with the Krew, and the kind of reputation I had. They all just stood there stiffly, watching me.

"Neil's with us tonight," Logan announced firmly, and their expressions went from confused to alarmed in a nanosecond.

I laughed like the fucking asshole I was.

"Are you two…um…together?" asked Julie, a girl I always used to spot holed up in the library. She was cute but anonymous, someone I never would have taken note of if she hadn't been a friend of Logan's. She looked curiously from me to Selene.

"We're hanging out," I answered vaguely, and Babygirl peeled my arm off her, even more annoyed.

What was her issue now? She knew perfectly well how things were, and I wasn't going to give her any illusions to the contrary.

"Hanging out?" she repeated sharply, her frosty gaze boring into me. She shook her head, compressing her lips into a bitter line. "You're such a jackass," she fumed and tried to pull away, but I reached out and grabbed her wrist before she could escape.

"You need to get your head right instead of putting on airs for your little friends," I whispered into her ear, making sure she knew not to cross the line. I was unsettled by how outraged she was, especially with Kyle right there watching every move we made. I had no desire to put on a show for him or to lose my cool in front of the rest of them.

"And you need to not be an asshole for once in your life," she shot back at me.

Then, with juvenile obstinance, she smiled at Julie and walked into the club with her, completely ignoring me.

"Keep calm and just...hang out." Logan said as he patted me on the back, prompting me to move inside the club along with the rest of them. Reluctantly, I followed him, and we all moved through the doors past a powerful man who checked our IDs before letting us inside.

The club was just another spot.

It wasn't anything new or different from all the other clubs I used to hit up with the Krew.

Lusty women, guys looking to score, irritating music, and the reek of alcohol and smoke in the air.

My eyes scanned the room for Tinkerbell, already annoyed, but all I saw were some square tables, the flash of colored lights, and some indistinct figures. My girl seemed to have disappeared into thin air.

She'd checked her coat at the door and then walked into the crowd without looking back.

"Fuck," I snapped in frustration. After a wary look, I headed over to the bar, which was lit up with alternating red and blue lights. I propped my elbow up on the empty surface and continued scanning the room, trying to spot Selene. My one consolation was that the musician was not far away, talking with Adam, so I at least knew he wasn't with her.

"Quit worrying. Since when are you so jumpy anyway?" Logan, meanwhile, had positioned himself right next to me exclusively to bust my balls. I rolled my eyes at him.

"I didn't realize you'd taken us to such a sketchy place," I answered when I noticed the girls slinking amongst the tables. They were all over the customers as they took their orders.

They were shameless and crude, the kind of women I'd usually love to spend a few hours with.

"Afraid you won't be able to be a good boy with Selene here?" Logan teased as he also watched the young waitresses prance around on their high heels, shaking their asses.

"Fuck you and your advice," I shot back. He just laughed. He had no idea how much I'd rather be at home alone with Babygirl than doing any of this shit. I liked it when she opened those incredible eyes wide and watched me ecstatically as I moved inside her. I liked it when she whispered to me that I was the only man she wanted in all the world. I liked it when she finally lost control and gave herself over to me completely, scratching up my back and sides.

I liked it when she fell asleep right next to me, one leg tucked between mine.

Knowing that one day soon all of that was going to drift away, however, was upsetting me.

Someone else was going to take her plush lips and kiss away all her doubts and fears and insecurities.

Someone else was going to make love to her divine body, even though "making love" was nothing more than a deceptive phrase that Babygirl liked to use.

Imagining her happy and satisfied with someone else made me want to start smashing in faces, but I knew that letting her go was still the best choice.

Every day, I was more and more convinced of that.

My dependence on Kim wasn't like drugs or alcohol or any other addiction.

It was not an evil that I had taken on from the outside; it was an evil that was deeply rooted in my own head.

An evil that had invaded me so completely and refused to leave despite the war I constantly waged against it.

It was an evil that lived inside me. An evil that *was* me.

"Look who's here..." Logan said in a singsong voice that told me he was uncomfortable. I looked to see what had caught his attention and spotted the Wayne sisters, Alyssa and Megan, dancing in the middle of the crowd. The former grinned at a friend and tossed her hair without a care in the world. She didn't look at all like a girl who'd just been dumped after cheating on her boyfriend. Beside her, Megan danced sensually. I checked her out, unable to stop myself. She had a black shirt tied off high on her abdomen. It left her flat stomach exposed while simultaneously emphasizing her abundant breasts. The leather pants she wore hugged her ass so tightly that I could see the outline of the thong she had on underneath.

I turned my gaze to my brother, worried about how he'd react to seeing his ex.

"And how do you feel about that?" I asked when I caught him staring at Alyssa. It was clear he hadn't gotten over her. I wished I knew what was going on inside his head.

Feelings were deadly weapons.

And love was the worst of them...a human being's greatest source of suffering.

After being betrayed similarly by Amber, Logan should have taken it slow and been even more cautious with women.

"I don't feel like I'd ever get back together with her. But I would give it to her good one last time. Just to really show her how pissed I am," he said tautly.

"You'll find someone better. Those Wayne bitches are best kept at arm's length..." I told him. I looked for Megan, and to my surprise, I found her green eyes fixed on me.

I stared back at her impassively. Her black hair, clipped up into a high ponytail, swayed in time with her hips. Her full lips broke into a mischievous smile as she registered my inquisitive gaze on her body.

She was telling me something, but I didn't have the same unspoken understanding with her as I did with Selene.

Babygirl was an open book to me; Megan was not.

All at once, the thought of Tinkerbell gave me a terrible stab of pain in my chest. I leaned over to speak directly in Logan's ear so he could hear me over the music and asked, "Have you seen Selene anywhere? I lost track of her a while ago." His gaze shifted, looking at something over my shoulder, and then his forehead wrinkled in surprise.

I turned around to see what—or who—was so shocking.

What the fuck?

I found Selene dancing with Julie in a provocative, sensual fashion. Too provocative. Too sensual.

Her friend was cycling through a series of erotic movements that made her look very different from the shy girl I'd seen in the library.

But I didn't give a shit about her.

My eyes immediately locked on what was mine, on the five feet and six inches of curves designed to set off an uncontrollable desire between my legs. I watched Selene, enchanted. She looked like the sexiest fucking angel, halfway to drunk. She was wild and divine.

Her ass swaying back and forth was turning me inside out, while her long hair fluttered in the air like auburn ribbons with every movement of her hips. There were guys watching her—just her—and they were practically foaming at the mouth.

They were watching my goddamned Neverland. My Tinkerbell.

The problem was that not only did Selene have a truly mind-blowing body but also such a perfect little face that she inevitably cast a spell over anyone passing by.

"Has she been drinking?" Logan asked, giving me a sideways look. I hoped she hadn't; that wasn't like her at all. The last time she'd drunk too much at a club, she wound up losing her virginity. To me.

I continued to watch her warily.

I could tell from looking at her sad little smile that something wasn't right.

Babygirl was upset, dwelling on something.

I wanted to go to her and ask her what had her so troubled. I wanted to kiss her and take her home, but instead I held still and kept leaning against that fucking bar to prove to myself that she didn't have any power over me. She had no power as she danced, and some asshole rubbed the fly of his jeans in excitement. She had no power as she pretended I didn't exist while she had fun with her little friend. She had no power as she let Kyle put his hands on her hips and chase her audacious movements. She had no power as he plastered himself against her, grinding his crotch against her ass.

She had no power…

She was completely free to do whatever she wanted with whomever she wanted, in fact…

Suddenly, I pounded my fist down on the bar as an indescribable madness began to pulse in my veins. I fought against myself and my instinctive urge to break the musician's nose. I fought against my fear of losing Selene.

I fought my anxiety, my possessiveness, and the fear that, deep down, I simply wasn't enough for her.

What the fuck were these human emotions burning up my chest?

They hurt; I felt like I was suffocating.

"Neil?" my brother called out behind me, alarmed, but by that point, my vision had already gone blurry from rage.

I stalked rapidly over to her, shoving aside anyone in my way. I never once took my eyes off Selene and Lucky, whom I was already picturing laid out on a stretcher, breathing through a tube.

Babygirl immediately spotted me striding menacingly through the crowd, and her eyes went wide as she abruptly stopped dancing. He, meanwhile, just made a confused face. I shoved Kyle aside violently as soon as I reached them. He stumbled back, and I stabbed a finger at him.

"Walk away from her now, or I'll put you in the hospital. Your choice, dickhead," I threatened him, totally unconcerned with the attention I was attracting. Fortunately, the loud music kept my wrathful voice from carrying too far. Kyle looked me up and down with disgust plain on his face. He looked at me like I was an insect, human garbage, a psycho he'd cross the street to avoid. But I ignored his looks and seized Selene by the wrist and pulled her savagely against me. She trembled even as she glared defiantly at me. Lucky retreated like the coward he was.

"Did you like having someone else's cock rubbing up on you?" I burst out, just a short distance from Selene's face. I hated letting that part of me out; I hated the mindless beast I turned into when I lost my head. But Selene had a unique power to drive me insane, and not just in bed. "Is mine not enough for you?" I pressed.

"Your vulgarity is embarrassing," she hissed at me, and my eyebrows shot up in surprise. I couldn't stand it when she got all condescending, and I hated it even more when she did it in front of people.

"Oh, that bothers you now?" I said tauntingly. "Yet when I'm fucking you and I whisper all that filthy shit into your ear, you turn into a fucking faucet." I went on, visibly infuriating her.

"What do you even want with me? Why don't you go find Megan?" she shot back. I was thrown for a moment, but I realized that she must have noticed my appraisal of the dark-haired girl and had misunderstood. "You obviously like her even though you try to deny it. It's pathetic," she said, taking another shot. My hold on her wrist tightened until she bared her teeth in a snarl.

"So this was payback, huh?" For a fleeting moment, I wanted to bite the surly little moue right off her mouth. I should have been even angrier, but instead I just laughed. Selene was getting up to ever more childish antics, and all it did was show how much she cared about me. I was just about to explain how I didn't give two shits about Megan when the musician came back over to butt in unnecessarily.

"Let her go. You're hurting her," he told me, jerking his chin at my fingers wrapped around my Babygirl's slight wrist.

My Babygirl. *Mine*. Maybe that wasn't clear to him.

I turned my gaze on him and gave him a fulminating sneer. I could have decked him, but I decided that it was my duty to teach him a valuable life lesson in a classier way.

I refocused on Selene and took her face in my hands. Then I bent to meet her lips, catching her off guard. But there was nowhere to escape. I held the back of her neck and thrust my tongue aggressively into her mouth, forcing her to give in to me. I was not at all surprised when she went rigid in my arms and pressed her hands to my chest like she was going to push me away.

But I knew she'd surrender soon enough. I knew my Tinkerbell, and she never could resist me. I pressed myself against her, enveloping her completely. I made her feel all the muscled planes of my body and chased her tongue with mine until she gave in.

I claimed her ferociously, hotly, and so intensely that she couldn't keep up.

Her coconut scent was all around me; the delicate taste of her mingled with my own, which I knew to be mostly smoke, anger, and possessiveness. We became an unstoppable whirlwind of passion. She clutched my shoulders, trying to stop the assault of passion, and I knew she needed to catch her breath, but I didn't care. I had a greater purpose; I was sending a clear message to anyone watching us at that moment.

I'd always been better with actions than with words.

A profoundly feminine moan from her throat got me even harder. My heartbeat was pounding in my ears, my body pumping desire out through every vein. I groped one of her breasts roughly, pulling a gasp from her. Then, I shot a sideways glance at Kyle, who was standing there motionless, just watching us.

Shocked and impotent.

I grinned into Selene's mouth like a son of a bitch.

There was no need to hit him; he knew his place now. And, more importantly, he knew mine.

I groaned with arousal, and he flinched away, embarrassed.

Pride crowed in my chest, and I finally pulled back from Babygirl, licking my lips with a masculine self-satisfaction that the asshole couldn't fail to see.

"You're going home with me now. We tried this night out with friends shit, and it didn't work," I ordered her in a tone that brooked no argument. Selene was panting, and her cheeks were flushed. She looked a little out of it, not quite processing what had just happened. "And I'm going to fuck you however I want," I added menacingly. But, instead of being cowed, Selene grinned wickedly at me like I'd just whispered some sweet nothing to her.

I grabbed her by the hand like she'd tried to do to me an hour earlier and dragged her toward the exit, stopping only to let Logan know that we were leaving.

As soon as we got outside, Selene clutched me, and I wrapped an arm around her shoulders to let her know that I would now accept—that I now needed—her closeness.

"You're such a prick. You were staring at her like you wanted to do her right there on the dance floor. Megan is hot and..." she began, sounding rather unlike herself. Usually my fairy wasn't so explicit.

"She is, but that doesn't mean I'm interested," I argued, exasperated. Somehow, she and Logan appeared to have reached consensus on that stupid fucking subject.

"You can't understand. After everything I've been through for us, I am so afraid of losing you," she raised her voice, dodging my arm. I stopped in front of the car and turned to look at her. Selene was on the edge of tears. My heart felt like it was being squeezed in a vise at the knowledge that she *would* inevitably lose me, even if she wasn't emotionally ready to know that yet.

Would she ever be?

I was used to suffering; I would be able to get over our separation, but I wasn't sure that she could. I was afraid of causing her pain, but it was too late to pull back now.

We were both too invested.

"Babygirl..." I moved closer and cupped her face in my hand, forcing her to look at me. She lifted her lashes slowly, and for the first time, I felt like I could see myself in the depths of her eyes, the same way I could in the eyes of my siblings. "If the day ever comes that you lose me, it won't be because of Megan..." I admitted.

"Then because of who?" she said in a tragic whisper. I hoped she wasn't going to start crying because every tear she shed seemed to take a piece of me with it.

Me...because of me, was what I should have said.

Instead...

"You're such a mess. A mistake. A giant disaster," I told her shortly.

And you are also the best thing that ever happened to me.

If I could, I would ask you to stay with me forever.

To never leave.

I'd walk you home and make sure your bed stays warm through all these cold winter nights.

I would try my hardest to make love to you, just the way you want, and then we'd fall asleep together.

I'd like you to lie on top of me because I'd want you close by. No—I'd want you on me all the time.

I would still have nightmares, and maybe I'd have those forever, but when I woke up from them and opened my eyes, I would know that my real life was better than any dream I could have. And the nightmares wouldn't hurt so much.

We'd have breakfast together, and I'd get Miss Anna to make you a cherry pie because I know you love it.

Then I'd steal a kiss from you, all sweet.
Actually, no.
That I would do with my usual presumption because I've discovered that your kisses fill me up. I can't say with what, but they do fill me...
But all of that is beyond my abilities.
And I'm sorry if I can't make it into your light.
I'm sorry that I can't stop listening to the other part of me, the part you think is twisted and wrong.
I'm sorry that I keep obeying my pride, my thoughts, and my...fears.
But I can't get to you.
It hurts too much.

I caressed her soft cheeks.

"Excuse me, you are the dictionary definition of a human disaster. You do realize that, right?" she answered irritably.

Ah...the girl was truly adorable. How was I ever going to let her go?

"Why don't you go fly into someone else's heart, Tinkerbell?" I asked her wryly, breathing in her feminine scent. She frowned thoughtfully for a few moments. My hands wouldn't move from her face; hers moved down to claw at my hips.

"Because yours is the only one I've ever wanted to land on," she confessed, her eyes brimming with hope and feelings unvoiced.

"You're going to meet your Peter Pan, and he'll accept you just as you are. You won't need to change because you're already perfect. Dorky and occasionally childish, sometimes awkward or shy. Smart but naive. You should stand out proudly from the crowd and never think of your kindness as a flaw. Keep dreaming and try to love those who are capable of giving that love back to you, of giving you everything you deserve. Because God knows you've suffered enough, and between the two of us, I'm the one always causing problems. Smile again and enjoy life the way you did before you met me because, as far as I can tell, I've taken everything from you, including that smile. You'll move on from this with your head held high, knowing that you've dealt with worse before. Whatever happens between us, you'll overcome it. I know you will. Never feel bad about yourself just because a dumbass like me gives up on you. Know that I'll have my reasons for doing it, and also know that... wherever you go, you'll always keep a part of me with you."

"Why are you telling me all this?" A single tear rolled down her cheek, and I immediately caught it with my thumb as I continued to stare at her.

"Because life's nothing but a con. It tricked me already, and I don't want it to trick you too."

Selene had power over me.

Her eyes scrambled my brains. Her smile drove me wild. She had captured my soul, and now she was in the driver's seat.

But none of that changed who I was.

I couldn't return her fantasy of love. I couldn't condemn her to a life with me. A life with a crazy person who belonged with the other crazies.

I wasn't sure exactly what I felt for her, but I knew for absolute certain that her happiness mattered more than mine. So, I would let her go.

Even if the voices inside me spoke of nothing but her...

18

*"I'd been dragged out into an ocean of troubles,
and I was drowning there."*

SELENE

Neil and I were not together.

Still, for me, his choosing the coconut candy had marked the start of something. Although exactly what that something was, I could not say.

"Why did I agree to do this crazy thing with you?" I said in an anxious whine as the powerful rumble of his Maserati cut through the air like it was trying to shake the sky itself.

"Because you're just as crazy as I am." Neil adjusted the rearview mirror and glided his hands along the steering wheel as though it were the contours of a female body.

"Will you quit telling me that?" I grumped, observing the perfection of his sharp profile. I stretched out my arm and dug a hand into the longer hair on top of his head until those honey-colored eyes shifted to look at me.

"Buckle up, scaredy cat." He winked at me.

"Please don't go overboard," I sighed, grabbing the seatbelt to fasten it and adjusting myself in the passenger seat. We were going to the clinic—I had persuaded Neil to consider therapy again, and John had invited him to come to the clinic.

"Keep whining and I won't fuck you for a month," he threatened firmly, stepping on the accelerator to make the engine howl again.

"Bull crap. You can't go a month without sex," I answered confidently, a defiant smile spreading across my face.

"True." His deep chuckle made me shiver. "But I just said I wouldn't fuck *you* for a month. I could always get it from someone else." His lips twisted into a canny, sensual smile that immediately killed any desire I had to joke around. He knew his other lovers were still a sensitive issue for me. He may have stopped sleeping with Jennifer and the rest of them, but he hadn't stopped thinking about Kim and his need to get revenge on her.

Every time some blond gave him an appreciative look, he gave one right back.

I could feel how difficult it was for him to maintain his self-control in those situations. He was holding back for my sake so he wouldn't hurt me.

"Don't even joke about that." I punched his bicep, which just made him break out into laughter. I quietly pulled back my hand, nursing my now-sore knuckles.

"You're ridiculous, and you're gonna hurt yourself someday doing shit like that. You can't just punch a mass of muscle like me." He took my hand with his larger, masculine one and pressed a gentle kiss to the tingling knuckles. "Is that better?" He grinned at me, but I didn't know how to answer, too drunk on simply looking at him.

"Now quit talking. I want to show you how you handle a panther," he winked again, and I rolled my eyes at him.

"Okay. If I die, tell my mother I loved her," I grumbled, settling down in the seat. Then, his hand was grasping my leg, sliding up my inner thigh and drawing perilously close to my most sensitive spot.

"I care too much about your safety to risk your life, Babygirl. I mean...who would suck me off so nicely if you died?" His voice was just a rasping, sensual whisper as he grazed his fingers across my jeans-covered pussy.

I automatically clamped my thighs together, feeling his hand stuck fast against that part of me that only he could awaken. I knew that, in his mind, he had just said something romantic to me.

Any other woman probably would have taken offense if a man talked to her like that, but I loved it.

I had habituated to Neil and his concept of *true romance*.

"Now let's get back to our high-speed trip." He pulled his hand away, abrupt and unsatisfying, and put it back on the steering wheel. He rested the other on the shifter.

"Alright, I'm ready," I said, biting my lip at the blatant lie. I hadn't had time to prepare myself psychologically when we took off like a rocket, the acceleration slamming me into the back of the seat. "Neil!" I yelled indignantly.

He just laughed and rolled down the windows to let the wind blow in and rearrange our hair. My heart leaped into my throat before dropping back down into my stomach, making me nauseous.

"Relax, Tinkerbell." He shot me an amused sidelong glance and hit the gas even harder, sending the speedometer off the charts.

"Sure, yeah. Of course I'm relaxed right now!" I had to shout so he could hear me over the wind and the sound of "Scary Love" by The Neighbourhood, which he kept using the controls on either side of the wheel to turn up. "I love this song," I added, grinning at him and trying to enjoy the insanity that I only allowed myself to experience when I was with him.

"Me too..." He returned the smile but didn't look back at me, keeping his eyes on the road.

He looked carefree, peaceful, and so beautiful in this moment of lightness.

The cold wind caressed my skin and rucked up my bangs. I

reached up with one hand, trying in vain to fix it, and he shot me a quick look before shaking his head in amusement.

I'd never seen him smile so much.

For the first time since I'd met him, he looked like a normal man who'd had a normal childhood.

Free from his monsters.

Free from his past.

Neil had lowered his walls at least a little bit during that month together. Even if he did go out of his way to constantly remind me that he did not love me and we weren't a couple.

Still, I'd seen an obvious growth in his feelings toward me.

Neil had been infuriated when he saw me dancing with Kyle at the club that night. I could still recall the shock on his face as I moved in that sensual way.

The shimmering gleam in his eye had lit a fire in my belly from across the room as he stared at me, inhaling slowly. Every breath he sucked in took mine as well.

It had been useless trying to pretend that I was enjoying myself with anyone else when all Neil had to do was envelope me in that golden gaze, and I went weak at the knees.

My heart did nothing but chase after his in a race that had no end.

I hummed along with the song on the radio, tilting my head slightly when I felt him throwing furtive, curious glances at me.

"No distractions," I scolded him with a beaming grin. I rested a hand on his thigh, and he stiffened slightly like he always did, but he didn't reject my touch. I stretched my other arm out the window and opened my hand as if to catch the air.

"See, that wasn't so bad, was it?" he asked when he was forced to slow down as we hit traffic. I'd barely noticed the thrill ride was over, so lost in the whipping wind and the boy I loved so madly.

"I still say we're lucky not to have gotten in a wreck. I was really afraid for a few minutes there," I teased with a mocking smile, which he frowned at. The truth was, I had faith in Neil. I trusted him completely, in fact.

When I was with him, all my fears disappeared.

"Were you doubting my skills?" He turned abruptly onto a less-traveled street, and just a few moments later, he pulled into the clinic's large parking lot.

"Which skills are you referring to?" I needled him impishly. Neil turned to look at me, and it was like a curtain of shadow had passed over him, extinguishing his easy joy and leaving his face dark and cold. I squeezed his thigh, trying to show him my support, and he gave me a sad smile.

"Today's going to be a clusterfuck," he said, undoubtedly referring to Dr. Keller's invitation for him to sit in on a bibliotherapy session. "You should have picked the surprise I have for you instead of going to this fucking clinic," he added. Several times now Neil had mentioned having some sort of "surprise" for me, and I could already imagine what it might be. "And it's not about sex, if that's what you were thinking," he clarified. "Though we will do that after the surprise," he went on, and I made a face. He was stoking my curiosity to make me regret telling him to accept John's invitation.

"You can show it to me when we get back home." I moved closer to give him a peck, but Neil leaned out of my reach. That was nothing new—whenever he was feeling pressured, confused, or exposed, he would reject my affection.

As we got out of the car and I followed him into the clinic, I didn't even bother trying to hold his hand or take his arm because I knew he wouldn't let me. He still wasn't used to me making those kinds of fond gestures, which would have been so simple and normal for any other couple.

He thought of them as infringements on his independence.

Almost as soon as we entered the clinic, Dr. Lively was there to meet us.

"Welcome, you two," he said, greeting us with a polite smile. Beside me, Neil remained cool and only gave him the smallest nod. I responded with considerably more enthusiasm.

"Hi, Dr. Lively," I smiled at him.

"I'm glad you both came. Neil, if I could have a word with you?"

Instinctively, I took a step back, and Neil turned to look at me.

"Can you give me a few minutes?" he asked considerately. I just nodded and watched him follow the doctor toward his office.

Left alone in the waiting room, I glanced around briefly. The furniture perfectly matched the antiseptic walls, and the only spots of color were provided by a few paintings and a couple of plants.

The place was so impersonal and pristine that I couldn't get comfortable there.

I shot a glance at the woman behind the reception desk. She was talking on the phone, occasionally pausing to type something into her computer. A couple of people who looked like employees passed through the corridor, chatting amongst themselves. None of them seemed to have taken note of my presence.

"So you're telling me this is normal for you?"

A man's voice resounded off the walls of an office near Dr. Lively's; the door cracked slightly open. I ignored it at first, well aware that it was none of my business who was getting mad in what was presumably a therapy session. But then I heard another furious growl, and my curiosity got the better of me. I walked down the brief stretch of hallway to the office and approached the open door slowly. I rested my hand on the doorframe and peered inside.

It was John, having an animated argument with someone I couldn't see.

"Exactly. And you can't expect to just barge into his life now!" The voice that argued back at him was female and a bit familiar. I narrowed my eyes, searching for a glimpse of her face or body.

"You think I don't know that?" he shot back, tossing some papers down on his desk. "I know how to behave; I don't need your advice on the matter. Christ!" he blurted out, reaching the limits of his patience.

A derisive feminine laugh was all he received in return, and he shot a furious, reproving look at the woman.

"You haven't changed a bit, I see. Your biggest flaw is still that temper. All those herbal teas aren't doing it, I guess…" Then the woman finally passed into my field of vision as she moved closer to him. A sophisticated suit hugged her slinky form; her blond hair was pulled into a neat bun, and her high heels gave her a certain classy bearing. The woman was very familiar indeed.

She was Mia Lindhom.

What the hell was she doing there? And, more importantly, why was she having a fight with Dr. Keller?

"I have always been there whenever you needed me. You are the one who forced me to live in the shadows, Mia, but you cannot forbid me from making my own choices now," he said firmly with an odd sort of sorrow in his voice.

"It's not the time, John," she answered anxiously. I still couldn't figure out what exactly they were talking about. It was surprising to me that they knew each other at all, but perhaps Neil's years as a patient at the clinic could explain that?

"Mia… whether you like it or not, he is as much my son as he is yours. And he deserves to know."

I gasped and clapped a hand over my mouth.

My blood ran cold. I exhaled roughly as though someone had just punched me in the gut.

I staggered back, trying to get as far as humanly possible from the scene I'd just witnessed. I only stopped when I bumped up against a hard chest. I turned around, still distressed, and met Neil's eyes. They were fixed on mine, watching me like always.

He examined me thoroughly, trying to figure out what was wrong.

A rivulet of cold sweat made its way down my back.

"What happened, Babygirl?" he asked, making me gulp. I wasn't sure about anything. My brain had somehow committed every word of Mia and John's argument to memory without deriving any conclusions from it. Only questions. Enormous questions.

"Selene." Neil cupped my face in his hands, freaked out by my silence, and forced me to look up at him. I'm sure my eyes must have been wide with shock. He furrowed his brow and looked over my shoulder at the partially opened door. Afraid that he might actually figure out what had me so shaken, I grabbed him by the hand and pulled him back into the waiting room. "Will you tell me what the fuck's wrong with you?" he snapped, but he followed me without complaint.

I stopped abruptly and hurled myself at him for a kiss. Neil went rigid against me, but he didn't push me back. He welcomed the kiss, which I kept sweet and brief to hide my bitter feelings. Before I could deepen it, however, he took my face in his hands and pulled us apart so he could look me in the eye. No amount of flirty behavior was going to distract him; he was too sharp. Maybe if we'd been in a bedroom, it would have been a bit easier.

"I don't know what's going on with you, Selene but I'm not an idiot. Tell me what's wrong," he insisted, more firmly this time. I scrounged up all my courage and deployed the only weapon I knew he was weak against. I grasped his hips and pulled him against me to kiss his neck, then along his jaw, and finally brushed my mouth over his beard scruff. Neil tracked my every movement through heavily lidded eyes.

He was suspicious; I needed to make something up quick before those suspicions grew.

"This place stresses me out. It makes me think about what

happened to you and the stories I heard from the other people in the group... Let's get out of here. I don't want to see the bibliotherapy. You can apologize to Dr. Keller for both of us, and we'll come back to see him some other time," I told him in what I thought was a pretty convincing way. His stare softened as he felt the sincerity in my words.

I was honestly stressed out even if it wasn't for the reason I'd stated. He gave me a small, melancholy smile and nodded his head.

"You're the one who said I should come here; I would rather have given you your surprise," he chided me. He tucked a strand of hair behind my ear and shuffled me along toward the exit. I walked quickly, eager to get out of there as fast as possible. I didn't even want to think about what would have happened if Neil had been the one to overhear the conversation between Dr. Keller and his mother. I myself was struggling to process it, and I couldn't tell him something so potentially earth-shattering until I was absolutely certain about what I'd heard.

Did Mia really have a son with John?

And was that son Neil?

The idea itself was insane.

I wholeheartedly hoped I had somehow misunderstood.

Finding out a truth like that would only be more trauma heaped upon Neil.

I almost broke down and told him everything when we stopped beside the car. He held his shoulders taut as he watched me warily, and I could see the old fears surfacing in his mind. He opened his mouth as if to say something but closed it again, silently, and got into the car.

He was running away, like always.

I knew that outburst of distress was making him insecure about our relationship again. Neil undoubtedly thought I was judging him—judging his past—and recoiling from it like a coward when, instead, I was grappling with a different but equally grave discovery.

I was afraid that this might be how I lost him for good.

This was a situation that couldn't be fixed with a heated discussion and a peaceful compromise.

Neil was going to hate his mother for lying to him.

He was going to hate John for not being there for him.

He was going to hate William for taking out his anger on an innocent child. The scars on Neil's arms, the years of abuse he'd suffered from that man, and the years of barely suppressed hostility—all of it would take on a new meaning.

"What's on your mind?" he asked, one hand on the steering wheel. He shot me a dubious look, and I shivered. "And don't try to bullshit me, Selene. I'm not a fucking idiot," he added irritably.

Apparently I hadn't been sufficiently convincing after all. Neil just knew me too well—I couldn't lie to him. "Nothing, really. It's just that sometimes you say things that make me think..." I said, offering yet another real thing that had occupied my mind at one point in the hopes of diverting him from what was actually bothering me at the moment.

"What do you mean?" he pressed, clenching his jaw.

"You make love to me, and then you tell me the weirdest things. Like that I'm going to find my real Peter Pan, that I'll tell another man I love him, and that I'm perfect, but—"

"You think what we do is making love?" he interrupted, focusing only on the first thing I said.

He just couldn't tolerate that word.

"I make love to you, Neil," I said again, more firmly. I knew that we had different ways of experiencing sex: For me, it was an exchange of affection and emotion, while, for Neil, it was pleasure, eroticism, passion, chemistry, and ownership—nothing that involved the softer emotions. "Isn't that how it is for you?" I asked him pointedly. I didn't really want to get into a fight, but I was relieved to have redirected him so completely.

"You want to change me," he said accusingly, pushing back an unruly lock of hair that had fallen over his forehead. As usual, he didn't give me a direct answer. But having a conversation with Neil Miller was a massive undertaking that always required a great deal of mental effort.

"That's not true, and you know it. I accept you as you are," I said in my defense. "You're the one who can't accept me," I insisted. "Is this a new tactic to push me away? Are you trying to go back to the way things were? When you went out of your way to screw random blonds you don't give a crap about just to hurt me?" I tried to keep my voice calm even as jealousy bloomed in my stomach and chest.

Neil's lips twisted into a cryptic smile, and he gave a satisfied grunt.

"You give the best advice, Babygirl," he answered, sounding amused as he kept his eyes on the road.

"Or maybe you should switch to dark-haired girls. You could start with Megan," I snapped back. But that wasn't really right, was it? Megan was the only woman who *did* mean something to him, more so than Jennifer, Alexia, or any of the other women who had enjoyed Neil's body in the past.

He became serious and gave me an ominous look.

"Megan was involved in the dark web incident. Ryan Von Doom, Kimberly's boss, was her guitar teacher. He and Kim ran the website together, making their money selling videos to pedophiles online," he confessed all at once, leaving me speechless.

It occurred to me that receiving so many shocks in one day couldn't possibly be good for me.

"Is that how you two know each other?" My temples were pounding; my head ached so bad that I had to squint.

"Yeah. Kimberly wanted to film Megan and me acting out a perverted version of the *Peter Pan* movie. She took us down to the basement and made us take our clothes off. I knew what she wanted right away, and I managed to avoid the worst of it. I never touched Megan. I would never do that…" He swallowed hard, gripping the steering wheel with both hands while showing no emotion at all on his face.

It was as cold and impassive as a sheet of metal.

He could have been telling me about his most recent exam in school, rather than the brutal psychological violence he'd experienced.

"How…how can you talk about it like that?" I asked hesitantly, shocked at his casual, cynical tone.

"I've got hell locked inside me, Selene. I've been living with the memories for so long that they don't have the power to upset me anymore," he answered, reaching up to open the big house's electronic gate. I looked out at the long driveway.

A deafening silence fell over us as Neil parked in his usual spot. He shut off the car and leaned back against the seats, still staring fixedly in front of him.

"Still think I'd fuck her?" he demanded. He turned to look at me, angry this time.

"I am so sorry that happened to you…" I took his hand in mine and kissed his knuckles. I felt guilty for having spoken so dismissively to him. "I didn't realize. I'm sorry," I said in a shamed whisper as I looked into his eyes. He allowed me to touch him, but his face was still impassive as he stared at me.

"Does…does Alyssa know about this?" I asked softly.

She had tried to get in touch with me several times after everything went down with Neil, but I was ghosting her. I wasn't ready to have a relationship with her, and not just because she'd kissed the man I loved. I couldn't forgive the way she'd lied to me and taken advantage of my trusting nature.

"No," he answered. "Megan never told her sister about it. Even her parents just pretended nothing happened. They were in shock, so she had to deal with it all on her own. I actually admire her for that, you know? She went through the same therapy I did and came out the other side stronger," he admitted. Clearly, this woman was an important part of his past. They had walked through hell together and come out alive, hand in hand.

"And the two of you..." I wasn't sure how to ask him if there'd ever been a deeper interest or special connection.

Neil sighed and looked down at where I still held his hand in mine, stroking the back of it with my thumb. "There was never anything between us," he finished my thought. "Except one kiss. We were teenagers, and we did it for some stupid game; it didn't mean anything to me," he went on. I didn't say anything, but truthfully, even the idea of them only sharing a kiss made me jealous. Neil must have seen it on my face, though, because he leaned in and kissed me. It was gentle and innocent, but no less intense than the rough, passionate claiming kisses he usually gave me.

"It's cold out here. Shall we go in?" he said quietly against my mouth, his voice softening. I just nodded and followed him back to the pool house; I needed to rest and clear my head.

When we got there, I took off my coat and threw it on the sofa, tugging the sleeves of my sweater over my fingers. I slumped down into the armchair and stared at the fireplace Neil had just activated. A terrible feeling of impending doom pressed down on my chest again like a boulder. I wanted to tell Neil everything I'd heard at the clinic, to have him talk to his mother and figure out what the hell John had to do with either of them. But I didn't have the guts to do that.

Neil peeled off his leather jacket and hung it up, giving me a questioning look. I pasted a reassuring smile on my face.

"I'm going to shower. Eat if you're hungry," he informed me.

And then I was alone, left to wallow in my thoughts. Immediately, the frustration inside burst forth in the form of tears. Who did I have to talk to about this? Matt hated me, and my mother was just hoping that I'd wake up from the twisted fairy tale my life had become over the last few months. Alyssa wasn't my friend anymore. Bailey was really only concerned with Tyler. Janel couldn't stand Neil, and I couldn't stand hearing her run him down. When I really got down to it, I was alone. I'd been dragged out into an ocean of troubles, and I was drowning there. I screamed for help, but no one could hear me.

Neil was the most important person in my life; my heart was bound to his. I knew that I was going to live through this upcoming misery along with him.

I didn't even want to think about how much he was going to hurt.

His world would come crashing down on him all over again.

He'd find out he'd been living a lie his whole life, that the man who beat him was not his biological father.

That his mother knew it all along.

That his real father knew it.

That I knew it...

And he'd probably never smile at me again.

He'd never touch me again.

He wouldn't let me sleep next to him anymore.

Or kiss his lips.

Or touch his body.

But I would do everything I could not to lose him.

I would keep fighting.

For him.

For us.

I curled up into an agonized ball on the armchair, trying to warm myself before the fireplace. The exhaustion of the day made my muscles ache even as the throbbing in my head slowly eased. I shut my eyes slowly, and then...

I had no idea how long I'd slept.

I wasn't as cold as I had been, though, and a pleasant torpor made me moan sleepily as a hand gently stroked my hair. I cracked my eyes open to see a pair of golden ones staring at me. They were so luminous, I had to take a moment just to stare at them.

"I thought you might join me in the shower, instead you fell asleep. Can't keep up, huh?" Neil's deep voice sent shivers down my spine, and I shifted slightly, feeling the numbness in my bones from sitting too long in an awkward position.

"I'm sorry," I mumbled, and he gave a slight frown of confusion.

"You can make it up to me tonight, Tinkerbell," he whispered lewdly.

I sat up slightly to get a better look at him: He was crouched down next to me wearing just a pair of gray sweatpants, and he smelled strongly of bath gel. His chestnut hair was still wet, and one renegade lock of hair had fallen over his eyebrow. I avidly watched the appealing movements of his arms and chest as he lifted a hand to fix it. "Do you want to sleep out here or with me?" he asked, touching my cheek. What a stupid question.

With him. Always with him.

"With you," I answered immediately. He smiled and held out his hands to help me up. I leaned against his body for support, sucking in a breath when I felt his bare chest pressed against my sweater. I wished that I was also naked and could soak in his warmth skin-to-skin. I looped my arms around his neck and planted a kiss on his jaw.

"How many times do I have to tell you—you are sickeningly sweet." He wrinkled his nose, making an annoyed face, and I moved further down his throat.

"You seem to like my sweeter aspects," I said in an arch murmur.

"No, I like it when you scream my name while I'm hitting it from the back," he whispered wickedly. Then he slapped my ass, and I jerked forward.

"Asshole," I grumbled, trying to catch my breath. Neil just bit his lip to hide his amusement. Then he surprised me, whirling me around so my back was to him and my ass hit his pelvis. He reached up and covered my eyes with one hand. "Neil!" I called out in surprise, but he just leaned down to my ear and kissed my throat.

"Shh..." he said in a coaxing whisper, pushing me to walk sightlessly forward. At first I moved slowly, afraid I was going to crash into something. But his arms around me and the marble-hard body at my back gave me a feeling of security and made me feel protected. I let my head fall back to rest on his chest and let him guide me.

"Walk straight ahead. Now turn right."

I obeyed, walking blindly at Neil's urging until my thighs hit something soft.

"Lie down," he instructed as I felt the soft top of the mattress with my hand. He uncovered my eyes once I was on the bed, but I still couldn't see anything because the room was pitch black. I laid back, my heart racing. My quickened breath cut through the air—the only sound. I looked over and tried to find Neil next to me; although I blinked several times to acclimate to the darkness, I still couldn't make out anything. Not even the outline of his body.

Suddenly, I felt his weight on top of me. He climbed over me gingerly, his chest pressing against mine, and slotted his hips between my thighs, which parted obligingly for him.

"What a romantic way to get me into a bed," I snarked.

His deep, masculine laugh shook both of us. Then he began kissing my neck, and I gasped at the feeling of his hot mouth against my skin. He moved down my throat, and I moaned, writhing underneath him.

I stroked along his spine, tight and powerful. My hands drifted down to squeeze his glutes, appreciating the honed musculature. Just touching him seemed to shut down the darker turn of my thoughts and banish everything that had happened during the day.

I pressed my palm to his crotch and found him already stiff and upright. He emitted a heated groan when I grasped it, and internally, I crowed with pride. I wanted him to peel off my clothes and satisfy me the way only he could, but instead Neil held still above me, his head fitting into the curve of my neck.

For a moment, he felt fragile as I clutched him close to me.

"Remember the time you once told me that there is a star for everyone, far enough away that our mistakes cannot tarnish it?" he said in a thoughtful murmur.

"Sure. It's from Bobin, the French poet," I answered, sinking one hand into his hair while continuing to stroke his firm back. Neil pushed himself off me, and I was alarmed to no longer feel his warmth. I groped for him wildly, like I would die without him. My heart rate sped up, afraid I'd done something wrong. I could never tell with Neil; it was impossible to predict how he might react to things. Then I heard a switch being flicked.

I was blinded by a dazzling light.

A sky filled with stars and celestial bodies stretched as if by magic across the entire ceiling, lighting up the room.

Neil had a small planetarium on the bedside table, and he used it to project this incredible vault of heaven before lying back down beside me to appreciate it.

"Whenever you're sad, stretch out on the bed and look up at the stars. There are about fifty thousand of them up there right now. I think that should be enough to obscure any pain..." he said heartbreakingly, and I turned to look at him.

"Should a cynic like yourself really be rhapsodizing about the stars?" I asked him wryly, watching the light bounce off his face. He turned to me and gave me a tiny smile.

"I don't know, should a girl who dreams of Prince Charming be spending so much time with the dark knight?" he said in a familiar needling way.

I rolled onto my side and inched closer to him, resting a hand on his naked chest. His skin there was cold, so I wrapped my arms around his chest to warm him. I tilted my face up until our breaths commingled.

"Why do I get the feeling that you're trying to prepare me for an injury that you're probably going to be the one to inflict?" I murmured with a sick feeling in my stomach that all of this was not an innocently sweet gesture from Neil.

He was trying to get me to understand something.

He wanted me to read his silent language.

"Because you're smart, Tinkerbell. And you know that this thing between the two of us is impossible," was his cold response. "I still have my past hanging on to me. It's like this long cloak of shadows that just keeps surrounding and suffocating everyone who gets close to me..."

Neil had a fiercely independent soul, wounded and untamed. I loved him as he was—as all that he was. I loved him because of his differences. I knew, though, that love wasn't enough to cure him. We both knew it. His words hurt, yes, but I could also feel the truth in them. It was raw, but it was true.

If, one day, he chose to exercise his freedom away from me, I would have still kept on loving the rebellious, tortured beast within him.

There was no cure for me, either.

"Neil—" I began to say, but he silenced me with a kiss that halted my words in midair.

He thought words were useless. He'd always rather turn me inside out, ignite my feelings with the same passion that always brought us together.

"Use me, Selene. Do it while you still can..." he said, before capturing my lips once again. He slid over top of me, pulling off the rest of my clothes with unsentimental efficiency. He took what he wanted, like always. He opened my thighs wide for him and joined us together with all the ferocity inside of him. He thrust his fears into me, the broken hopes, the frustration, the misery, and all the hurt he was feeling. It was a punishment, an attempt to make me see that there was no future for us, that we were both destined to lose this ceaseless war between us.

That, even as we sought refuge, we sought it from a land of never. Never was, never will be.

19

> "I was going to close my circle,
> I was going to complete my game,
> and I was going to destroy my opponent
> utterly."

PLAYER 2511

I got out a cigarette and tucked it between my lips.

Rage wound through me, making me shake.

The need for revenge had long ago dragged me down into this chasm of hatred and loathing, and I wanted to escape.

"Don't you think that move with the webcam exposed us a little too much?" His voice echoed around my living room, and the sound of his anxious pacing was getting annoying, but I refused to lose focus.

Smoke framed my face before floating up toward the ceiling in thick spirals as I leaned forward, digging my nails into the leather armrest of my chair.

"No," I said confidently.

"No? What if he figures out our identities?"

"He hasn't figured out shit about our identities. More importantly, he has no idea what my next move is going to be." I offered a sneering grin to go with my sharp words.

"What are you thinking? What's fucking next?" he asked, an expression of concern passing over his face while my face showed nothing but weightless, untroubled ease.

"We're going to lay a trap for him. The little fish will come in for a nibble, and then we can finally hit him." I leaned forward and scooped up some of the darts I so enjoyed playing with. I stood up and faced the photos affixed to the wall. "We already took a shot at Logan." I hurled the first dart at baby bro's face, an odd shiver of excitement running down my spine. "Then we went after that little slut he's been screwing." I threw the second dart at little sis. "Finally, it was Chloe's turn." I shut one eye, took careful aim, and fired the last dart right into Selene's angelic little face.

"So? Who's up next? His mother?" He huffed impatiently, and I shot him a smile as I turned the last dart over in my hands. I caressed it slowly for a moment before hurling it at the image of my next target.

Him.

"Fuck no. There's no point hurting the mother; they have a bad relationship. We went after the people he cared about the most to hurt him through them, but we've toyed with him for long enough. Now..." I paused with my tongue between my teeth and a feeling of self-satisfaction.

"Now what?" he prompted me and folded his arms over his chest, all curiosity.

"Now I'm going to create my final puzzle..." I said, my eyes on the dart lodged in the center of Neil's image. It was still vibrating slightly, stuck fast in his chest, right about where his heart would be.

"Remember, I have a score to settle with him too. I want to be in the room when we kill him," he blurted out wrathfully, though he knew perfectly well that I didn't tolerate demands. I shot him an icy look and lifted my jacket with deliberate slowness, just far enough to reveal the glock holstered there. My message was clear.

"And I'll get one of those too, right?" His eyes lit up at the prospect. I fixed my jacket so it covered my weapon and gave him a mysterious smile.

"Not if you keep holding it sideways, you won't. This isn't an action movie. I don't need ridiculous stunts and stupid tricks. I need people with training." I waved a dismissive hand and turned my back on him.

"I've been learning how to shoot and—"

"Go away," I ordered flatly, walking over to my office. As soon as I went inside, it was quiet as the grave all around me once more. I walked around the imposing desk and seated myself comfortably in the chair behind it.

I opened my schematic and regarded the labyrinth I had created with satisfaction.

The crow signaled the first round of the game and demonstrated my purpose up front: revenge. I traced my finger along the old diagram I'd drawn, my fingertips catching against the rough paper and making a pleasant rasping sound.

I got to the second round: the music box that was connected to the legend of the little girl whose father punished her for her disobedience. I smiled mockingly as I continued to drag my fingers along the others.

Number three... Fuck, that one was my favorite.

The pictures of his whole family except for Neil and the acrostic that spelled out Logan's name, revealing my intention to attack him right from the start.

The fourth round was the personification of death, a skeleton on his white horse in Gustave Doré's famous painting.

Round five, I'd used a Rubik's cube to hint at where I'd hidden Chloe in a car alongside a bomb. If her little brother hadn't found her in time, the blond girl would have been blown sky-high.

"Fuck...you won almost every round," I grumbled, sliding

my finger down to the sixth round, which was connected to Hard Candy and malware I'd used to spy on his little slut and make a video to blackmail her.

I still had that video in my possession, but I had a different goal: I wanted to see my last target bleed.

"Only the seventh one left to go…" I chewed thoughtfully on the inside of my cheek and pulled a pencil out of the glass holder, tapping it against the paper.

It wasn't easy, thinking up a puzzle, but it was exciting. I could feel the adrenaline pumping through my veins.

I had spent so many years wondering what my purpose was and now I knew it: I was meant to do evil, to keep myself afloat in this shitsack world.

I allowed my madness to take form on the paper.

I moved my hand, drawing lines, words, and scribbles, generating my final masterpiece, my last riddle, the seventh level.

It was no accident that this game had seven rounds. I had always had a special love for the number seven.

In Pythagorean philosophy the number seven was associated with a perfect union of the material and the spiritual. In sacred geometry, the number is linked to the circle, and that was precisely why I'd chosen it. I was going to close my circle. I was going to complete my game, and I was going to destroy my opponent utterly.

I was interrupted then by the squeak of the door opening.

She moved slowly into the room, and I watched her shapely legs as she did. I set down my pencil, and for a moment, just appreciated her feminine shape.

"Are you working without me?" she asked, giving me a sly smile. I stared deep into her eyes as I leaned back in my chair, arrogantly folding my hands over my abdomen.

"You've already done your part," I answered bluntly. She moved closer and put her hands on the desk. She stroked the surface of it with her long fingers as though it were my body. Then she leaned forward to give me a better look down her shirt at her firm tits.

"I still want to help," she said in a naughty whisper.

"How? By acting like a slut?" I sneered, and she recoiled. I could smell her fear, and it excited me. "You're children, all of you. I'm the one who makes the rules around here," I said pointedly. "Now get out of here and wait for me in the bedroom," I ordered, gesturing to the door with a jerk of my head. I would absolutely fuck her later; at the moment I had more important things to deal with.

I turned back to my puzzle.

My prey was going to take the bait, and then I'd have him in my clutches, and I would butcher him.

I wanted to hear his cries of pain, taste his blood on my tongue... Fuck, my hands were trembling just thinking about it.

He would never make it out of my labyrinth alive, and I would be right there, listening to the very last beat of his heart. Watching him crawling to me, pleading for mercy like the disgusting worm that he was.

"I'm going to watch your face as you take your last breath." I turned the pencil over in my fingers, thinking about that moment when our eyes would meet. Then, I opened the desk drawer and slipped out the mask that I would wear.

One last time.

20

"Neil had never known the sweet smell of a rose because all he had gotten, his whole life long, were the painful punctures of the thorns."

SELENE

It was May third.

Neil's birthday. And that wasn't the only thing that made the day special...

I thought back on how all of this had started, purely by chance. I would never have believed back then that Neil and I could come this far together.

For the past few months, we had decided to put our problems on pause and had simply spent time together, getting to really know each other. And now, after supporting each other through all the fears and worries, we were here together on Neil's graduation day.

Who would have guessed?

My hands were shaking with suppressed joy for Neil. He was achieving such an important goal, and he, more than anyone else, deserved this moment. He deserved to have this, to feel accomplished and satisfied and proud of himself.

"He's nervous..." Logan whispered into my ear. Never for a moment did my eyes leave Neil's powerful body. He was wearing an elegant gray suit for the first time since I'd known him and a graduation robe over it.

He was simply beautiful.

His hair was neatly arranged, except for that eternally unruly piece over his forehead, and his beard was cut short and tight. His profile was perfect, and his lips were red because he kept nibbling them nervously.

I shifted in my seat. I'd worn a black pencil skirt with a seductive slit up one thigh and a white blouse that tied in a bow around the collar. My feet ached in my Louboutins, and my heart was racing in my chest.

The rector had already yielded the floor to the big cultural figure who'd been invited to do the commencement address.

Next, they began announcing names, and with Neil's came his list of honors.

Logan, the rest of the family, and I immediately leaped to our feet to give him the standing ovation he deserved. Tears poured down my cheeks, though I had promised myself I wouldn't cry. The emotions were just too powerful; I couldn't hold them back. Logan gave me a tight hug; Chloe and Mia clung to each other. It was a magical moment for all of us.

This boy...

This boy whose childhood had been destroyed by human cruelty, who had spent so much time nursing his wounds alone in the corner of his room.

This boy who had been set apart from everyone else because he was considered so dangerous.

This damaged boy with the broken heart...

He'd done it.

He had become an accomplished man.

A great man, whom I loved.

The only man I loved.

I wiped away my tears with the backs of my hands just in time for another wave of emotion to get me right in the heart at the cap throw.

I smiled up into a sky punctuated by so many spots of black, which then rained back down like confetti. The air was festive, and the love I felt for Neil was so overpowering that it made me light-headed. I pulled away from Logan then and went to find him, seeking him out like oxygen. I quickly picked him out from the crowd of people. He was laughing with some fellow students, sans robe.

And when he turned the full power of that golden gaze on me, I wavered a little on my high heels.

Immediately, he quit paying attention to the other people, abandoned whatever conversation he'd been having, and came to me with that confident stride and that agile body, which was only enhanced by the suit.

I nearly swooned when he wrapped his arm around my waist and gave me a sensual kiss.

"Congratulations, Mr. Future Architect. And it's your birthday today, too. You're all grown up now," I said cheerfully, coaxing a small smile from him. I smoothed the lapels of his suit, gathering my courage before telling him, "I'm proud of you. I couldn't be prouder, Neil. And you should be proud too." He watched every line of my face as I spoke. He grazed a thumb along my cheek, and I pressed a worshipful kiss to the palm of his hand.

"I'm already brainstorming my present," he whispered wickedly and kissed me again, this time just below my ear. I flushed and watched him step back curiously so he could get a better look at me. He examined my outfit, which I had selected to be chic and sensual but not at all vulgar, and I watched as a strange light flared in his eyes. "You're beautiful, Tinkerbell," he told me for the first time.

My eyes went wide as I marveled at him, and I was very glad that I'd worn something a little more stylish for him. I wanted to be attractive and to impress him, at least on this one occasion, and maybe I had succeeded.

"I'm happy you like it—" I began before someone grabbed him by the arm, interrupting our intimate moment. The other new graduates were all clustered together, taking pictures, laughing, and chatting. Neil would never agree to have his picture taken, but he deserved to celebrate like anyone else, so I gave him his space. But I immediately regretted that when I spotted some girls congratulating him a little too effusively with lingering cheek kisses.

"Looking a little green there, Selene."

I startled when Logan, accompanied by Chloe, came over and elbowed me in the ribs.

"They're giving him such fuck-me eyes," I said in a burst of outrage. I rarely employed that kind of language, but I just couldn't stand to watch some little blond sexily bat her eyelashes at Neil, desperate for his attention.

"Maybe. But you're the only one he fucks," Logan answered. I turned automatically to look at him. I didn't care if it made me look insecure, seeking assurance from him like that. I *was* insecure when it came to whether Neil truly desired me exclusively. "You're the one he wants, Selene. He can't admit that to you, but he does have feelings in his own way." Logan turned back to watch Neil some more, his eyes shining with admiration and affection.

"Shall we go, then? I've planned a party for Neil." Mia joined us looking every bit as composed and elegant as always with Matt by her side. I blanched as I thought back on the argument I'd overheard between her and Dr. Keller. I watched her warily as she rubbed my father's back. I wondered if he knew about the connection between his partner and the psychiatrist.

Meanwhile, Neil had returned and stood beside me. He slid his arm around my waist right there in front of our parents with zero shame.

I turned red in visible discomfort.

I knew that my father would never approve of our relationship, and I could feel his dark eyes on me, burning with resentment.

"Sorry for leaving you on your own," Neil whispered in a voice so warm it gave me chills. He smirked at me, taking note of my reaction.

"Congratulations," my father said to him. He stared first at the intimate way we touched each other before his eyes moved up to Neil's face. He proffered his hand seriously, grimly. Neil went rigid; I could feel his fingers digging harder into my side. I held my breath, but, fortunately, he simply reciprocated the gesture after a moment's hesitation, giving my father's hand a firm squeeze.

"Thank you," he said coolly, his voice firm and composed. Mia looked admiringly at her son, though it seemed to me that there was also some guilt in her eyes.

"I'm proud of you." She moved closer to him until she could drop a kiss on his cheek.

Neil tensed up but did not otherwise react. He permitted the gesture, trying hard to accept it. He wasn't used to receiving that kind of affection, and he still saw it as a danger. In truth, he considered all human contact damaging. He sometimes struggled even with me, though I tried to be understanding and patient. I wanted to show him that the world didn't just contain monsters and child-eating witches but also good and worthy people.

How could I blame him for feeling as he did? Neil had never known the sweet smell of a rose because all he had gotten, his whole life long, were the painful punctures of the thorns.

An hour later we were back at Matt and Mia's home. The enormous living room was already all set up. In the middle was a long table covered in an array of dishes accompanied by crystal glasses and silver cutlery. Everything was done in shades of ivory and cream to add a touch of refinement to the ambiance.

No bright colors, no balloons or streamers. That wouldn't have been to Neil's taste anyway.

Mia had designed it all to the hilt.

Anna moved amongst the crowd of friends and colleagues as they stood around sipping champagne and nibbling on appetizers with the bored, superior attitude typical of high society. I quickly gave up on making conversation with anyone and just watched Neil stand next to his mother and hoped he'd turn his attention to me.

I was pathetic... I often felt like I was living in Neil's shadow, unable to reach him.

"Yes, I'm so glad you could come. This is Neil," Mia was introducing him to one of her work acquaintances. The first thing I noticed about her was her artfully styled red hair and the showy jewelry that proclaimed her wealth. The second thing I noticed was the young woman about my age she had with her. The latter was blond and swathed in a bright pink dress that left little to the imagination. She stared stupefied at Neil while he reluctantly pretended to be interested in what the older woman had to say. My heart lurched, however, when he took note of the girl's alluring stare and checked her out more carefully, lingering on the deep neckline of her curve-hugging dress. He lifted the champagne flute to his full lips and took a small sip from it. Slowly, sensually, staring directly at the enthralled blond.

He liked making girls succumb, making them dizzy with a desire that he undoubtedly would have satisfied had I not been in the way.

Would he ever stop trying to mete out his revenge on Kimberly through these women who reminded him of her?

Would he ever exorcise the ghost of that monstrous blond?

I sometimes even felt a stab of jealousy toward her, toward the babysitter I had never met nor seen but who seemed to be omnipresent in our relationship. I felt like, despite all the years that had passed since her abuse of Neil, she could destroy us at any moment.

"I don't think I can do this," I murmured to myself, feeling breathless. I stroked my hair anxiously and headed out into the backyard, trying not to trip in my high heels.

The bow at my collar seemed suffocating all of a sudden, and there was a constricted feeling inside me tighter than the pencil skirt's waistband.

Goddamned jealousy.

I stalked down the walkway and sat down in a chaise lounge beside the pool. The sun had set by then, and the lights below the pool's waterline alternated colors in a pleasing display.

My first kiss with Neil had been in a pool.

So much had changed since then—*I* had changed since then.

"What are you doing out here by yourself?" I started at the sound of his baritone in real life.

I looked up and first spotted a pair of shiny black shoes before my eyes slowly moved up his firm legs. He had one hand tucked into the pocket of his fancy suit pants while he held a champagne flute in the other.

How long had it been since I'd furiously hurled myself out the kitchen door?

It couldn't have been more than a few minutes; Neil must have followed me pretty much immediately after I left.

"I needed to get some air," I said sharply.

His soft chuckle of amusement only made me more uncomfortable, so I turned my eyes back to the crystalline water of the pool and ignored him.

"What am I going to do with you, Tinkerbell?" Neil crouched down and rested his elbows on his knees until his beautiful face was level with mine. I finally relented and gave him my attention again. Though I did frown at him. "I told you from the start that I can't change…"

He sure had. In fact, he never missed an opportunity to remind me of that fact, as though I weren't already aware…

"Yes, and no one is asking you to," I shot back, a sullen look on my face.

"But it still bothers you when I look at other women," he said with a smile so crafty that it made me want to slap it right off his face. I took a deep breath and looked back at the pool lights, which had shifted to blue and violet.

"You look mainly at the blonds," I said, my voice soft but filled with bitterness. Neil inhaled sharply and put his glass down on the little table next to us before reaching out to rub my knee. I shivered when his fingers made contact with my bare skin, exposed by the skirt's slit, but I told myself to stay calm. Stay clear. He was trying to seduce me, but I wasn't going to let him.

"Sure, I look at them. And then I forget their names the next moment. These days, I only have room in my head for you. I want you every day. I don't know what exactly you've done to me, but you continue to be my Neverland," he murmured hoarsely.

I probed his gaze slowly, and in his eyes, I saw his sincerity as well as his lust and his longing…

Longing for me.

He licked his lips, staring at my mouth before moving down to the place where my tight shirt stretched to reveal the shape of my breasts. Then he abruptly grabbed my hips and pulled me to my feet until my chest bumped against his.

The sudden contact made me rock back on my heels. His masculine scent went to my head, while his strong hands went to my ass, gripping it possessively until I was flattened against him.

"Feel what you do to me, Selene. Only you. No one else," he whispered into my ear. He licked down the curve of my throat as he ground his erection against my lower abdomen. I let out a rough, involuntary moan and clutched his wide shoulders as if to keep from falling. "You're my new addiction. You need to quit being paranoid. Concentrate on kissing me instead," he growled angrily before crashing his mouth over mine.

He palmed one of my breasts and rubbed his hardness between my thighs and tore an embarrassing whine from me.

I had to put a halt to this quickly, or I wouldn't be able to stop at all. I bit his lower lip and held it sensuously between my teeth.

Neil groaned, his eyes falling half-closed in arousal.

"I have a present for you," I whispered into his mouth. His eyes lit up, a flicker of wicked perversion. I grinned and shook my head to nip lewd fantasies in the bud. "I'm not talking about sex. We can do that after..." I moved his greedy hands off my body and bent down to retrieve a small blue velvet box from my purse.

Neil cocked his head to one side with a look of confusion as I stood back up.

"Are you about to propose?" he teased with a smug smile before sitting back down on the chaise and pulling me with him until I was perched on his lap. He began to stroke my naked thighs and wriggled in agitation underneath me. "Babygirl...you aren't easy to resist..." he said in a provocative whisper, breathing heavily against my shoulder.

"Think about opening this instead," I instructed, trying not to look too embarrassed. I'd never given him anything so important before, and I hoped he would like it. I hoped he would think of me whenever he looked at it. Neil took the box, his face becoming serious again. Slowly, he opened it and peered inside. I knew what he would see there: a silver bracelet with a small charm on it shaped like a clam.

You are my shell was engraved on the back of the charm.

Once, Neil had drawn a shell with a pearl inside on my skin with a marker. He told me a story about it and instructed me to draw the same thing whenever I felt lonely.

I didn't understand how much that really meant to him until the day I left Detroit, when he snuck a glass cube with a pearl inside into my pocket. I had associated that talisman with my survival in the car wreck that had followed right after. I kept my hand around that cube the whole time, even after I was rendered unconscious by the collision.

"Wear it when you're feeling lonely, so that even if we're far apart, I can still be with you." I looked at Neil's face and found him astonished. For a second, I was afraid he'd reject my gift, but then he stretched out his arm and tugged the cuff of his shirt up slightly, inviting me to put the bracelet on him. I rushed to do up the clasp, admiring the way the polished silver shone against his amber skin.

"I'll be forced to think of you." He stroked it with a delicate touch that was entirely unlike him, like it was the most precious thing in all the world. He looked lost in thought, and his face grew shadowed. The moment between us was heavy with feeling.

"Pardon me..." Miss Anna approached then, and we both got to our feet. Neil kept one arm around my waist to keep me from running off.

"What is it, Miss Anna?" he asked, pushing a hand through his hair, clearly annoyed at having been interrupted.

"There's a man in the living room asking for you," she told him.

Intrigued by this, we both went back inside and quickly spotted the energetic figure of John Keller wearing a particularly distinguished suit. I froze immediately when I saw that he was talking to Mia in an isolated corner. They looked as though they might be arguing again.

"John, you finally showed!" Neil went over to him and clapped him on the back.

I was surprised; I hadn't realized Neil invited him, though I probably should have expected it. Their relationship had deepened in recent days. They saw each other regularly at the clinic, and John was trying to convince Neil to come back to therapy or participate in follow-up sessions with the group. Neil was still working on trusting him, though.

I stepped closer and watched Dr. Keller giving Neil an abashed smile. Mia sighed anxiously as she rubbed a hand across her throat, visibly unsettled.

"We're going to have dinner shortly; would you like to stay?" Neil asked, apparently thrilled with the presence of this man who had been making inroads to his life, little by little. This man who still had so many secrets.

"Is Dr. Lively coming too?" Neil went on.

"Krug asked me to pass along his apologies for missing the party. He intended to come, but his son just got in from Boston, and he needed to spend some time with him. I'd be happy to stay in his place," John answered.

"Oh, you don't need to do that..." Mia attempted to dissuade him, but her son lifted a hand to stop her.

"What's your problem, Mom? You got to invite anyone you wanted to this party—*my* party—now you can let me decide whether Dr. Keller stays for dinner," he said in his usual high-handed manner. Mia swallowed awkwardly but decided not to fight him.

Ten minutes later, we were all seated around the table.

The air was thick with tension. I had a bad feeling, and it made my skin crawl. I couldn't help but think about what I'd overheard between John and Mia. Neil sat right next to me; beneath the table he rested a hand on my thigh. Dr. Keller was on his other side, with Mia and Matt directly across from us. The rest of the seats were filled with other guests. My stomach was in knots; overpowering anxiety made my throat tight, and my heart was battering against my ribs. I concentrated on breathing. I pretended to ignore my father's resentful looks at Neil and me, pretended to enjoy the cracker smeared with caviar I raised to my lips.

I pretended and pretended and pretended…

"If you don't like it, you don't have to eat it." Neil's hot breath touched my cheek, and he gave my leg a squeeze to get my attention.

"How did you know?" I whispered, trying to keep anyone from overhearing us.

He gave me a very amused look. "Because you're wrinkling your nose in disgust," he answered. "I'm not crazy about caviar myself. I'd much rather be eating you, maybe upstairs in my room, just like the good old days?" He had moved dangerously high on my inner thigh. I slammed my legs together, blushing.

"Neil…" I cautioned him. I shooed his hand away, already feeling the burn that only his hot touch could create. I rubbed my thighs together, seeking some small relief.

My core did not stop throbbing.

It felt like my heart was beating right between my legs, and the sensation was becoming unbearable.

"Careful, Babygirl, you'll get drenched," he whispered, which only made the situation worse. He cast a surreptitious glance at my clenched thighs and gave a smug chuckle.

Before I could say anything back to him, however, Matt had turned his attention to John, addressing him with an unusual icy intensity.

"So, Dr. Keller, how long have you been working with Krug?" he asked, interlacing his fingers and resting his chin on his hands. Mia's eyelid twitched as she fingered the pearl necklace she wore.

"For about three years, but I've known Dr. Lively for much longer…" John answered, elegantly dabbing his mouth with a cloth napkin. Matt cocked an eyebrow, like what John said was somehow sketchy or unbelievable. I didn't know what was wrong with him.

Was Matt jealous? Did he know about John's history with Mia and was this all some dumb male rivalry thing?

"And have you always worked here in New York?" Matt pressed, biting into a breadstick. John placidly took a sip of his water before putting the glass back down on the table.

Apparently he, like Neil, had the ability to confront these special situations with the utmost self-confidence.

"Yes. I have traveled a lot, though, and—"

"Do you have children? A wife?" Matt interrupted before John could finish his sentence. I was unnerved by the ways Matt seemed to be putting the screws to him without even giving him a chance to respond.

John sighed and shot a brief glance at Mia. There seemed to be some kind of unspoken connection between the two of them, a kind of mutual understanding that they could never reveal to anyone else.

"No. I've only had one significant relationship in my life. I was young at the time, too young. After that, I focused on my education and then on my career..." John waved a dismissive hand. He clearly didn't want to talk about his private life, but my father obviously wasn't satisfied with that.

"You should stop interrogating Dr. Keller, Matt. It's annoying," I interjected, feeling heated. Neil coughed—apparently some caviar went down the wrong pipe—and I immediately slapped his back until he recovered.

"Selene! Where are your manners?" my father scolded me as though I were still five years old. Mia whispered something into his ear, maybe urging him to calm down. Meanwhile, I just watched him steadily so he could see the indifference on my face.

"Tinkerbell, I like it when you get aggressive, but now isn't really the time. Save that energy for later..." Neil murmured, causing a flare of pleasure in the bottom of my stomach.

"It gets on my nerves when he does that overbearing asshole thing," I answered under my breath.

"We both know how he is. Ignore him. Now's not the time to make a scene..." he advised me.

"I'd say we'd better start eating down this mountain of food. Anyone want more caviar?" Logan cut in, serving Chloe a portion as she nodded enthusiastically. I smiled when her big gray eyes met mine and an odd warmth spread through my chest. The baby of the family had actually accepted me, and she told me she genuinely hoped that Neil could have a real relationship with me. Though, she added, she was well aware of how weird he was, so she wasn't getting her hopes up.

She told me her brother would need time to bond with me, and I was trying to give that to him. I had no intention of giving up on him.

"I need a smoke. You want to come with?" Neil wiped his mouth and tossed his napkin down beside his plate before standing up. I raised my head to watch appreciatively as his muscles moved beneath his button-down and elegant suit jacket.

I was so proud of him and proud of the man I knew he'd one day become. He had the makings of a successful architect. I could practically see it now; he'd be respected by his colleagues and, of course, still adored by women.

Could he not see how much potential he had?

"I'd better not..." I said, clearing my throat. I knew that if I went with him, we'd shut ourselves up in the pool house and wouldn't come out again. He seemed to know what I was thinking because he narrowed his eyes and fixed me with a stare of such overwhelming roguishness that it took my breath away. But he didn't insist and instead just headed out the glass doors into the backyard.

"Thank you, Selene." John leaned toward me, and I frowned, not immediately understanding what I was being thanked for. Then I remembered: I'd saved him from the Matt Anderson Inquisition.

"You're welcome," I answered reassuringly. I would have defended him as a matter of course. I knew my father well, and I would never have allowed him to screw with someone like Dr. Keller.

He didn't deserve to get raked over the coals by Matt for no good reason.

"Ahem, ladies, gentlemen, pardon me." Anna poked her head into the dining room with her hands clasped in front of her. She looked hesitantly at Mia. "Ms. Lindhom, I'm so sorry to bother you during dinner, but there is another visitor here for your son." She cleared her throat, and Mia turned her full attention on Anna, waiting to see who the visitor was. Mia's eyes went wide when a tall, imposing man with glacial eyes and a disturbing kind of charisma walked in—William Miller.

"Good evening," he smiled politely at everyone but especially at his ex-wife, whom he immediately moved toward. "I wanted to congratulate Ne..." His confident stride halted abruptly when he caught sight of John's petrified stare.

"John?" William's lips barely moved as he said it. He looked like he'd seen a ghost. John just clenched one hand into a fist, clearly trying to get a handle on himself.

"William," he answered shortly, never looking away from the other man's metallic stare.

"What...what are you doing here?" Mia attempted to insert herself between them, but the hatred, the bitterness, and the competition running between the two men was obvious.

They had a score to settle with each other.

"And how do you two know each other?" Matt pointed at them, asking a useful question for once. Logan and Chloe also seemed confused yet curious about the situation.

I was simply scared.

I felt that fear creep down my spine and wrap around me in an eerie embrace that made my skin crawl.

"Where is my son?" William asked with a seemingly benevolent smile that nonetheless boded no good, and under the table, my legs began to tremble.

Mia shook her head and got abruptly to her feet, drawing everyone's eyes to her.

"Whatever you have in mind, William, he isn't part of your conflict." She attempted to put a hand on his shoulder, but the man backed away from her, still staring John down with a smile so sinister it would have given the devil himself chills.

I was glowering at him, trying to figure out what exactly he intended to do, when Neil came back into the room. He walked back over to the chair beside me and bent to scoop up the lighter that had slipped out of his pocket and fallen on the floor.

The moment he registered his father's presence, however, he straightened up.

William smiled widely and approached Neil, like he'd been waiting to do it all day.

"What are you doing here? Who invited you? Fuck off." Neil stepped back in disgust and gestured to the front door. William just shook his head and gave an amused chuckle.

"You know, I really didn't appreciate that little stunt your friend Xavier pulled with my car. I could have had him arrested for that; you should be thanking me. Don't I even get a hug for being such a great dad?" he taunted, opening his arms wide.

"William!" Mia scolded him, but he silenced her with one raised hand, determined to finish what he'd started.

"This is an important day for you, my dear boy. And so, I'm going to give you the best gift you've ever received," he went on in a soft, cruel voice, looking back at Neil.

Next to me, John glared at William, the agony visible on his face.

"What the fuck are you talking about? I told you to leave!" Neil's voice got louder, and everyone at the table flinched.

"Are you ready to tell your son the truth, Mia? Or would you like me to do it?" William seemed overcome by hatred. John's presence had stoked his bitterness, his memories of the past, and, more than anything else, his desire for revenge. He turned his glacial stare on Dr. Keller and smiled.

Neil stepped back and looked around for me.

It was as though we were joined by an invisible thread, his eyes locked on mine.

I could immediately sense that he needed me beside him, so I got up and joined him.

I stood close to him, grasped his arm, and gave it a squeeze. It felt like I was gripping a rock shot through with dark tension.

"Isn't it funny, Neil? That I'm going to be the one to finally give you the answers to those questions you have? All those whys that have filled up your head since you were little?" William began to speak, his voice rough and cold. "Once upon a time, there was beautiful woman who believed in great love..." he continued, soft and derisive, as he stared Neil right in the eyes. The only soundtrack to this scene was broody silence and our anxiously bated breaths. "She loved one man but was forced by her father to marry another. She couldn't accept this other man, so she decided to continue both relationships at the same time." He began to move through the room, circling the table under the rapt gazes of the guests. "She fell pregnant by her great love, and she knew very well that she had to keep the truth from the other man who, by that time, had become her husband."

Neil was unmoving, fixated on that evil man's little tale. Mia's shoulders slumped, and she hung her head in surrender as William went on.

"During those nine months of pregnancy, I thought of you as my son, Neil. I thought it was my little baby growing bigger every day inside my wife's womb. Then you were born, and it was the most beautiful moment of my life. You were strong and sturdy. I still remember exactly how it felt that first time to hold you in my arms." He formed a cradle with his arms, pretending to rock an invisible infant.

"I had imagined you'd look just like me. Maybe you'd have my blue eyes or a head full of black hair. I thought that, at the very least, you'd have one of my features to make it clear that the blood flowing in your little veins was the same as in mine. But there was nothing. The bigger you got, the more unlike me you looked. Your eyes began to take on that gold color; your nose was small and straight, your mouth was too fleshy, and you had that wild cloud of brown hair. I thought all the time about the differences between us, how far apart you felt…"

Neil kept his eyes on William as the older man came slowly back around the table. He began to circle Neil, then, looking him from head to toe as though observing a specimen.

Tears began to pour down my cheeks.

The confusion that clouded Neil's face hurt so much it was hard to catch my breath.

"Your mother made the decision to keep hiding it from me for a decade, the fact that you were another man's son. I only found out because I overheard an argument between her and your father. Your real father. After that, my anger only grew every time I looked at you. Every time I saw you make another face or gesture that was unmistakably *him*. I no longer considered you a son of mine. I hated you because you were a bastard, born from betrayal, from an extramarital affair. From an illicit fuck between your mother and her lover." William's voice grew louder, and the tone shifted as he took heavy strides over to Neil, who remained motionless. "You are and always have been an unwanted child, Neil, a cuckoo in the nest. As far as I'm concerned, you're not a Miller, and you never were. My family—my real family—consists of my wife and my two children,

Logan and Chloe. You were always just excess baggage!" he shouted, full of wrath, and everyone cringed. Mia burst into tears, Logan and Chloe jumped to their feet in shock, and John's eyes went wide. But Neil looked as though he'd been petrified in place. He didn't even blink. He looked vacant, abandoned, and deep in shock.

"Your father is John Keller, the man sitting here at your fucking table. There's the truth you wanted—you have been ruining my life for over twenty years!" he screamed furiously, right up close to Neil's shocked face.

His heart was shattered. I knew it, because I had felt mine break at exactly the same moment.

He didn't deserve this.

John stood up then, walking around the table to give William's back a hard shove.

"You don't get near him! You don't scream at him like that, and you don't even think about putting your hands on him again!" John howled like a beast. The veins in his neck were popping, and his breath came in ragged pants. He faced William without a trace of fear, and the latter backed away a few steps. Then he smoothed down his expensive suit jacket, pleased with the turmoil he'd just unleashed.

Mia sobbed and watched as Matt then stood up slowly, letting the napkin that had been in his lap fall to the floor. I followed the fabric's trajectory, watching as it landed and lay motionless on the floor.

"Well, I'm heading out. Have a lovely evening," William said, the only one with the audacity to break the anguished silence in the room.

"Oh, and Neil? Happy birthday!" he said at last, a little hint of irony mixed in with all the malice. Then he vanished out the front door, slamming it behind him. I sucked in a breath at the loud sound before slowly turning my attention to Logan, who was holding

Chloe and staring at their mother in shock. Neil still stood next to me, but his eyes were staring out into the void.

His gaze was fixed but sightless, like someone had switched him off.

He didn't blink. He didn't give a single sign of life.

There was nothing in him.

"Neil...I...I'm sorry." John kept his distance, but his eyes were glittering with pain. He wanted to touch his son, to hug him, but he knew the risks. Neil wasn't just another young man; he was *special...different*.

"Don't get any closer, Dr. Keller," Logan whispered. He'd let go of Chloe and was approaching his brother at a slow pace. Neil didn't move a muscle. His breathing was shallow, his eyes devoid of emotion, and his face a mask of rage and incredulity.

Time continued to pass, but the rest of us had stopped.

Tick...tock...tick...tock...

Only the sound of the grandfather clock's pendulum swinging back and forth filled the room.

After what felt like an eternity, Neil turned his icy stare on Mia and blinked, the only sign of life he'd shown thus far.

"Neil, I can explain what happened," his mother murmured through her tears, stepping hesitantly toward him. I could sense her fear from where I stood, but I admired the courage she had, facing him like that. "I was afraid of losing you; that's why I never told you. That's why...you have to believe me..." Neil remained frozen, staring at her, his hands tightened into fists. His eyes had become unrecognizable, two murky pools of hatred.

"You...you're..." he said in a low voice, as though it were a struggle to get the words out, as though there was something heavy bearing down on his chest or his throat. Then, abruptly, he shot out an arm to push his mother violently away. "A whore!" he shouted furiously. He clenched his jaw and ground his teeth together while

Mia lost her footing and fell to the floor. John's eyes went wide as he moved to help her up, Chloe clutched Logan fearfully, and my father watched the whole scene unfold in shock.

Mia began to weep, and Neil just looked at her without so much as a flicker of human compassion on his face.

My heart began to beat frenetically, pulsing in my throat before falling back into my chest like I was on a roller coaster. I couldn't speak.

Mechanically, I turned my eyes to John, where he was helping Mia up.

I had never seen her look so destroyed, so grief-stricken.

All at once, it felt like there was a fire blazing all over me, and I turned to find Neil staring at me. I blinked, tears clinging to my eyelashes, and I tried to understand what he was thinking. He moved to me, his footsteps sure. Then he stopped and scrutinized me carefully.

I wanted to run away, but I was so shaken by everything that I couldn't move.

His hot breath hit my cheek.

He touched me gently, tracing the line of my jaw with his index finger. What was he trying to say to me?

The suffering in his eyes tore my chest open.

I could have offered him comfort. Maybe he was looking for me to have to his back, to support him, but I couldn't bring myself to lie to him. And that was when I made my fatal error.

"I knew..." I admitted, trying not to burst into tears. Neil stopped touching me, his eyebrows flying upward in surprise. "I knew," I repeated guiltily. The blood drained from his face while he fought to keep his anger under his control and waited for me to go on. "I overheard a conversation between Mia and John at the clinic. You were busy talking to Dr. Lively. I wanted to tell you about it, but I didn't know anything for sure..." I exhaled forcefully. "I had suspicions but no proof, and I didn't want to freak you out for nothing. I'm sorry...I—" I didn't even get to finish my useless attempt at a justification before I watched him pulling away from me. I saw it all over his face as he growled in frustration and dragged his hands through his hair. "Please, forgive me..." I begged.

Neil looked at me, his pupils blown, and I gasped.

There was nothing to be seen in those eyes.

Not him, not me, not everything we had been building together.

The only things I saw in there were sharp edges and jagged points, and they stabbed into me. He gave me a disgusted look, and then he turned his back on me, not just with his body, but with all that he was.

He shook his head dazedly and stared at John, full of fury.

"The legend of the pearl...all that bullshit you were constantly telling me..." he began. His voice was thin and sharp as a needle. "You approached me with the sole purpose of getting to know me without telling me who you really were. You got me to talk to you. You got me to confide in you about my history. But you weren't a doctor who wanted to help me. You were a filthy fucking liar who was trying to gain my trust with his lies..." he spoke in a low mutter, breathing erratically. John tried to answer him, but Neil held up a hand to stop him. "I will not forgive you. Never. Not you and not your whore."

His eyes were alight with hate, his voice deep and colored with a rage that he still tried to fight, though I could see it rising up, wreathed in flames to drag him back into hell.

Neil had gone through so much in his life. No matter how much fate tested him and tried to destroy and demolish him, he had come out victorious. He managed to stay standing, even when he had to carry a burden that would have crushed another man.

But now the shadows seemed to close in around him like a long black cloak.

"Please let me explain—" John began, but he didn't get to finish before Neil turned to the table.

With a bone-rattling howl, he grabbed the edge of the table and flipped it over.

"Get out! Leave! All of you!" he thundered. He tore his jacket off wrathfully, as though it had been choking him, and hurled it to the ground. Then he began to grab bottles, crystal glassware, plates—whatever he could get—and hurled them against the wall.

A beast.

His every move and cry was like some animal that had just been rudely awakened from a deep sleep. Sweat beaded on his forehead, and his shirt strained with every movement like it was going to tear. His breathing grew heavy, so heavy that it clawed at me. For a second—just an instant—he met my terrified eyes, but he did not recognize me.

There was no pity, no feeling.

There was nothing. Just rage and darkness. Disillusionment and anguish. A lie over twenty years in the making that was now killing him.

"Out!" he shouted again before continuing to smash everything still intact. The room was soon unrecognizable; there were shards of crystal everywhere, dents and smears all over the walls, and the floor was covered in discarded food and broken bottles. No one dared to stop him; no one even dared to get close to him. Not even Logan, who had pressed himself into a corner with his sister, holding his hands over her ears to shut out the sounds of destruction.

Neil's destruction.

"You have to get out! All of you, get out of my life!" he continued to shout in the grips of his fury.

John stared at him, stunned—he had never seen this part of his son before.

"Get out...you have to get out..." Neil repeated under his breath.

He rubbed his temples like a madman. Veins stuck out starkly from his tensed neck, and he was covered in sweat. He paced back and forth over the shards of glass, which crackled underneath his shoes.

"Go away…" he muttered to himself over and over again. Then, as if he'd had some bizarre epiphany, he turned around and ran up the stairs, taking them two at a time. Driven by foolish bravery and a determination not to lose him, I ran after him. I found him in his room, somehow even more furious. He flung open drawers and closets, tearing out his belongings and stuffing them in an open bag on the bed.

"What's going on, Neil? What are you trying to do?" I said as I walked into his room. I had abandoned healthy fear, common sense, basic logic—everything.

He could have turned his anger on me, but I didn't care about that in the moment.

I wasn't just going to stand there and watch him walk out of my life.

"Get out," he said in a furious mutter. He looked shell-shocked, incapable of reason, and destroyed. Completely destroyed.

"Do you really want to leave?" I said to his back, murmuring through my tears.

How could I ever accept the idea of only seeing him in my dreams? Of feeling him only through my memories? There was no amount of distance that could keep me away from him.

I drew in breath through his mouth.

It was my heart that beat in his chest.

How could I let him go?

Without even glancing at me, Neil grabbed his car keys, slung his bag over one shoulder and shoved me aside roughly as he passed. My hip hit a sharp corner of his desk, and I gritted my teeth against the pain, but I recovered quickly.

I raced out of the room after him. Neil was fast and determined, I had to run to catch up to him. He went thundering down the stairs, his feet pounding the floor like he wanted to destroy every part of that house. He threw the front door wide open with a sharp, decisive movement.

"Please, no! Wait! Think about this!" I clutched one powerful arm, trying to hold him back, but he jerked himself free, sending me tumbling to the floor. I felt a sharp shock to my shoulder when I landed, and I gasped in pain. My breath was ragged with fear that I would not be able to keep him there, with me. I looked up at him, searching for recognition, trying to create some kind of connection with that honey gaze that now watched me intently from above.

But he had fallen deep into the dark.

All my pleas would be wasted.

"Quit looking at me like that; it's over. This was always going to happen anyway. Ask your mother about it if you want to know more..." He smiled a cruel smile, all icy calm. I sucked in a breath as though he'd just put a blade through my chest. And he didn't say anything else before walking out the door and slamming it behind him so hard that the walls shook.

Those were the last words I'd ever hear from his lips.

"Where did he go? He shouldn't drive like that," said Logan, from behind me. He helped me up to my feet, but I wasn't processing anything.

My vision was blurry with tears; my whole body was trembling...

A piece of my soul had been torn away. Neil had cruelly ripped it out of me and taken it along with him.

"He's gone," I said in an incredulous whisper.

Neil had left...and he wouldn't come back.

21

*"Peter Pan had taught me that only those with
happy thoughts have the ability to fly."*

SELENE

The brisk late-November wind caressed my face and rustled the campus trees while I drew absently on a piece of paper.

I'd been sitting on the same bench for at least ten minutes. My class had been finished for a while, but I didn't feel like going straight home. I stared down at my notebook, tracing the sharp outlines of what I'd just created.

"Every time you feel alone, draw a pearl inside a shell."

I could still hear his sultry voice inside my head and feel his scent all around me. I searched for him constantly, like a dying woman searching for water in the desert.

And I wondered if his life had changed for the better, if he'd been able to process the pain of discovering such a life-altering secret.

I wondered if he was okay, if he was working.

I wondered if he had another woman or maybe more than one. Just the thought of it made my stomach tighten until I felt like vomiting.

And then I did.

I crouched down beside the bench and expelled the four cups of coffee I'd had that morning. My lungs burned, my chest shook, and my cheeks were wet with tears. Tears that did nothing to ease my soul or free me from the feelings inside.

I felt the chill on my skin and in my heart, which now felt like it was wrapped in barbed wire. I was in a constant storm of bleak anguish. Whenever I thought of Neil, it was devastating.

I couldn't breathe.

I dragged myself through each day in my now-hollow world, surrounded by people I couldn't bring myself to care about. I pretended that I still wanted to live, but in truth, my life had crumbled into nothing on that May day.

I had lost a part of myself.

And I still couldn't get Neil out of my head.

"Shit, Selene. Were you sick again?" I felt two strong hands around my waist as someone helped me stand up and steady myself. My head was spinning; I couldn't remember the last time I'd had solid food.

"Selene, can you hear me? Hey?" I recognized the soothing sound of Ivan's voice as my chest bumped into his. I blinked, trying to clear my head and focused on him. There was his black hair, his green eyes with the bright flecks, the dimple in his right cheek, and that sensual mouth curved into a sweet smile. "I just got out of practice. Are you alright?" he asked, brushing a bit of hair away from my face.

"Captain…" I managed in a croak. He stroked my cheek and pulled me in for a tight hug, allowing my tears to soak his team hoodie. He stroked my hair, nuzzling his face against my head, and somehow managed to soothe my anguish and calm me down until I could stop crying.

Ivan had become my constant; his presence was a necessity for me. I would not have survived losing Neil without him, his sister Janel, and Bailey. They were my best friends.

"I'll take you home with me. Let your mother know. When did you last eat?" He held my face in his hands and looked into my weary eyes. "You can't live on coffee *and* be constantly throwing up that coffee. It's no good... You're losing too much weight," he chided me, a bit of severity in his tone. He stooped to pick up my notebook and pencil and remained hunched over the drawing, the same one that I now reproduced night and day whenever I got the chance. He sighed heavily and closed the notebook before straightening back up. "You need to stop thinking about him. It's only hurting you..." He handed me the notebook, and I slipped it into my bag. Then he abruptly wrapped an arm around my shoulders and urged me to follow him to the white Porsche he'd parked nearby.

He was right.

I was only hurting myself, but I couldn't help but think about Neil.

Six months had passed, and I still dreamed every night about that terrible day.

"Quit looking at me like that, it's over. This was always going to happen anyway. Ask your mother about it if you want to know more..."

I had done just that.

My mother told me about how Neil admitted to her that he had accepted Professor Robinson's internship in Chicago and that he didn't think it was possible for us to have a relationship. So he had promised her that he would leave me behind, that there would never be a place for me in his life.

I couldn't believe Neil had kept such important news from me, and, even worse, that he didn't tell me he was supposed to share an apartment with Megan Wayne.

I couldn't handle the idea of him out there in Chicago with her; my brain simply refused to process that truth. I pretended it wasn't the truth so I didn't fall apart completely—so I could keep on surviving.

On one hand, I hoped he was with her because it would mean he'd moved on and was doing well. On the other hand, I couldn't bring myself to imagine the two of them actually together.

I was jealous.

I slipped miserably into the passenger seat of Ivan's car, curling in on myself and resting the side of my head against the window. I stared out blankly into the void.

"Ms. Martin..." I looked over at Ivan, who had his phone in one hand and the other on the steering wheel. He'd asked me to tell her but, in the end, he'd had to do it himself. By that point, my friends were well-practiced at getting in touch with my mother for everything as well as supporting me every day and worrying about me constantly. "She's at work, right? Okay...that's what I figured. No, no, I'm not leaving her daughter alone; don't worry about that. She just got sick again today. Yeah...I thought I'd just take her back with me. Of course, thanks for the vote of confidence. You can call me or Janel if there's an emergency." He hung up and slid his iPhone back into the pocket of his jeans. When he raised his hips to do so, I took an involuntary glance at his tensed abdomen before quickly looking back at his face. "You're staying with me," he said gently, never taking his eyes off the road.

I didn't say anything in response.

Every day, Neil was there, invading and occupying my thoughts. I convinced myself I saw him in every face, in every moment, in every breath.

I imagined I could smell him everywhere I went, even in Ivan's car.

I let our drive wash over me.

I watched the tall buildings looming over us until we drove into a private garage. I got out of the car and followed Ivan over to the elevator that would take us up to his apartment.

"Are you feeling better?" He smiled at me as we entered the enclosed space of the elevator, where his cologne was overpowering.

I just nodded, watching as the buttons lit up with each floor we ascended.

I'd been spending more and more time with Ivan, and I'd told him everything that happened with Neil. He understood what I was going through as well as feeling sorry for me.

"First things first, I'm getting you something to eat." He held the apartment door open for me, and I went inside. Immediately, I was hit by the clean, pleasant smell of the place. The living room was exactly as I remembered it: spacious and luxurious with a large leather sofa and tasteful decor. The multiple windows offered an incredible view of the city.

"Make yourself at home; I don't have any other practice or anything today. We can hang out for the rest of the day." He unzipped his hoodie, exposing the T-shirt he wore underneath. It hugged his muscular torso like a second skin, and I quickly looked away, embarrassed.

I knew Ivan; he'd never been sketchy or disrespectful toward me, but he was still a young man and his proximity was occasionally unsettling.

"Where's Janel?" I asked. "She wasn't on campus today, and I texted her but she didn't answer," I told him, still standing motionless in the living room.

"She's with our dad. You do remember that our parents are separated, right?" He gave me an incredulous look, and I nodded, feeling like a dummy.

Janel regularly went to Dearborn to spend time with her father, who was living there. She had, in fact, told me she'd be there today, and I'd forgotten because, as usual, I was lost in my own head.

"I hate being a burden on you all." I sat down on the leather sofa and tracked his lean frame as he went into the kitchen. He rolled up his sleeves to the elbow, a move I found especially hot. His jeans were tight against the hard muscle of his butt, and his legs were long and powerful. He was a little shorter than Neil but no less fit and cut.

"You're not," he said, grinning at me before he began fixing something to eat. Unlike a lot of young guys, Ivan seemed at ease in the kitchen.

"Should I call you Chef instead of Captain?" I got up from the sofa and left my coat behind with my purse and my phone, and then I followed him into the kitchen.

"I don't cook all the time, but I don't mind doing it," he answered congenially. His back was to me as I sat down on a stool at the kitchen island, the perfect opportunity to closely observe his wide, basketball-player shoulders. His back muscles shifted slightly with every movement of his hands, and, bizarrely enough, I found myself considering his masculine appeal. Maybe I was just trying to drive out the honey-colored eyes that had been haunting my dreams for months.

"Why didn't you go to Dearborn with your sister?" I propped my elbow up on the island and balanced my chin on my palm. Ivan appeared to stiffen up, and I hoped I wasn't being nosy.

"Because I don't really get along with my father." He looked over his shoulder at me and sighed. "He really wanted me to go to med school and become a doctor like him. But I went my own way. I chose sports. He's never accepted that. He's never even been to see one of my games," he said in a low, hurt voice.

"If playing basketball is what makes you happy, then, sooner or later, he's going to see that you made the right decision," I answered with a warm smile, and he nodded, seemingly bolstered by the confidence of my words.

Abruptly, a ringtone sounded from the living room.

We exchanged looks, but I immediately had a feeling it was mine. I scrambled down from the stool and ran to retrieve it from my bag. Every time I got a call, the thought crossed my mind that it might be from Neil. Though, by then, the hope of ever hearing from him was steadily fading.

"Hello?"

"Selene." Hearing Logan's voice made a chill run through me.

"Logan, what happened? Is everything okay? Did you hear something?" I demanded anxiously.

"No, nothing yet. I've been asking the Krew about him, but they haven't heard anything either. I'm thinking that my only option now is Alyssa..." he said, his tone changing as he said her name.

"Why would you ask her?" I frowned.

"Megan's her sister; she might have said something to her," he pointed out.

"Are you sure you want to do that?" I bit my lip. I knew how difficult it would be to get back in contact with his ex or possibly even have to see her. Logan had just as much pride as Neil did, and he didn't tolerate disrespect or pathological liars. He'd had plenty of times to talk to her in the last six months if he'd wanted to, but he never had.

"Yes. You know I'm with Janel now; Alyssa's in the past," he told me calmly. I was the one who had introduced him to Janel when he came to see me in Detroit one weekend. It was love at first sight with the two of them. They didn't get to see each other very often because of the distance, but they talked and texted every day. The relationship was still in its early stages—they'd only gone out on a couple of dates and shared just one kiss. I was hopeful, though, that something serious would develop between them.

They both deserved it.

"Alright. Remember to keep me posted," I told him. Logan texted and called fairly often, so there was really no need to remind him, but I was too anxious to do otherwise.

Logan knew how I was; he would understand.

"Of course. Take care of yourself, and don't forget to eat. Hopefully, I can come for a visit soon," he said before hanging up, and I heaved a sigh.

I walked back to the kitchen, tucking my phone into my jeans, and slumped back down on the stool, more troubled than when I'd left.

"Logan?" he guessed, continuing to devote himself to food prep like an ideal househusband.

"Yeah. No news," I admitted miserably.

"You should forget about his brother." He turned to look at me, his jaw tightened. "I still remember that time he sucker punched me in the face. I didn't fight back because I knew I'd have to explain it to my coach the next day, and I didn't want to risk getting kicked off the team. But that dude is insane; he's violent. He's lucky I walked away that night." He waved a hand in the air and leaned back against the counter to watch me more closely.

He knew it bothered me whenever someone said something bad about Neil. I could not be reasonable or impartial when it came to him—an insult to him was an insult to me.

"He's not as bad as he seems. I know him really well, and he's had some truly terrible experiences. Neil's been through hell, and I can't cast judgment on him. I won't. I'm sorry." I shook my head and stared down at my knees. I'd been wearing the same pair of jeans for days. I needed to get myself sorted out and cleaned up and start taking care of myself the way I used to do.

But I didn't have the strength.

"Because you're in love with him. Obviously," Ivan sighed. I blushed darkly, and he cocked an amused eyebrow. "Oh, come on, don't be scared. You know you can tell me anything. You can trust me," he said reassuringly.

"I do trust you, but that still doesn't make it easy to talk about…" I relaxed slowly, trying to suppress my discomfort. "He changed me. I wasn't weak or irrational like this before. I have never been so vulnerable with someone. I was always afraid of love, but then I met Neil…" I paused, trying in vain to get a handle on the emotions that threatened to spill out all over. "I gave him all of me, and now I feel like I'm losing my mind without him," I admitted in an embarrassed whisper.

"Chalk it up to a learning experience. Something that helped you figure out what you want and what kind of person deserves to be with you..." he said thoughtfully. "That you slept with him, that you gave him more than you thought you would, that you let him hurt you so often just to stay with him—none of that matters. It's not important, Selene." Ivan moved closer, walking around the kitchen island to take my hand and gently stroke it. "Just stow Neil away with the rest of the baggage from your life experiences, and try to move on. Do you have any idea how many other assholes you're going to meet?" he murmured, rubbing the back of my hand.

I smiled at the kind gesture.

"Are you one of those assholes, Captain?" I teased him.

"Maybe," he laughed softly, showing me his dimple. I turned my eyes to that adorable little detail on his cheek and reached out to touch it lightly with one finger.

"This dimple is diabolical," I said.

He watched me smugly, and I could see his ego swelling in real time. "Yeah, that's what all the ladies tell me," he answered proudly.

"Don't let it go to your head," I huffed, and he narrowed his eyes challengingly at me.

"Oh, you go to my head, alright." He winked at me, and I went red when I got the innuendo. I was used to that kind of thing from Neil but not from other guys. I got embarrassed and blushed too easily. I sat up straighter on the stool, putting some appropriate distance between us. Ivan could see that my mood had shifted, and he moved back to the stove, realizing he'd overstepped his bounds.

"Uh, would you go and..." he muttered, suddenly awkward. Then he looked at me in that sweet, knowing way of his. "Set the table?" he suggested calmly, ignoring my timid reaction just before. I silently thanked him for understanding why I was uncomfortable and gave him a firm nod. Then I moved around the kitchen, following his instructions as I set the kitchen island with plates, glasses, and cutlery for two. Ivan continued to cook, concentrating hard.

"That should be it..." he muttered to himself, peering into the oven to see if the baked chicken and potatoes were done. It was a simple enough recipe, but Ivan seemed to find it more complicated than that.

"Wait, let me check." I went over to the oven and examined the dish, glancing at the clock on the wall. "It needs five more minutes," I said, smiling at him. An odd feeling of warmth spread down my spine when I met his green eyes, already staring intently at me.

Immediately, I felt guilty.

Was it selfish of me to spend an afternoon just thinking about myself? Was it wrong to enjoy being with someone other than Neil? Was it crazy to seek some peace after so many months of misery? By any sort of logic? No. By the heart? Yes.

I was saved by the oven's timer, and I scooped our portions onto plates, finding myself excited once again at the prospect of having lunch with Ivan.

He seemed just as comfortable with me, telling me all about his teammates, his passion for sports, and his relationship with Janel. He also asked me about Logan, trying to determine whether he really was different than Neil. If not, he wouldn't have approved of his sister dating him.

"So you like to ski too?" I asked, drying the last dish. I insisted upon at least doing the dishes to repay some of his kindness and hospitality.

"Yeah. It relaxes me so much on bye weeks. I love getting out into nature." He sat down on the sofa, and I followed suit, making sure to keep a respectable distance between our bodies.

"You devoured it all; good work," Ivan murmured in satisfaction, staring at the hand I had rested over my pouched-out stomach. The sensation of a full belly had become novel to me. Lately, I was just eating alone at home, and I wasn't eating much.

I regularly skipped meals and took advantage of my mother's absence to call a glass of juice or a cup of yogurt a "meal."

I missed Neil so powerfully that I'd stopped taking care of myself. I just...didn't feel the need anymore. Eating, drinking, sleeping... they'd all become pointless activities.

"Yeah. You'll have to roll me out of here," I said lightly and looked away as he laughed. I wondered what sort of feelings I could possibly provoke in a person like Ivan: Was it curiosity, compassion, pity, or something else?

We were friends, sure, but I didn't understand why he was so concerned about me.

I wasn't sure if he was attracted to me or liked me as a friend in my own right or simply saw me as Janel's bestie who needed help because she was in a bad way.

He was good at concealing his thoughts and intentions.

Then again, Ivan was the golden boy; he'd probably have no idea what to do with a girl who was depressed and constantly on edge.

"I feel so awfully guilty when you take care of me like I'm your helpless little sister. You have friends and practices—you shouldn't have to neglect your commitments for me," I said apropos of nothing, just musing on the time and attention he reserved for me. Too much of it.

"Don't worry about it. I like spending time with you," he answered easily. His voice was so peaceful; it calmed my nerves. I smiled and made myself more comfortable on the couch, turning my attention to the plasma screen in front of us where there was a documentary about big cats that Ivan seemed to be really into.

"Did you know that lions have barbed penises?" he asked

seriously. I shot him a look and found him focused on the screen, apparently rapt.

"I did know that, yes. But I always wondered if that posed any sort of risk to the lionesses. What do you think?" I almost laughed at the absurdity of our discussion.

Ivan was funny and undoubtedly a handsome guy. He had his own kind of appeal, seductive and mysterious but never dangerous or dark, never wild or rough.

"Huh…I suppose it must not," he said, his mouth contorting into a skeptical expression.

Then Ivan cleared his throat and situated himself on the couch; I turned away to avoid getting caught staring at him. I drowned out those thoughts with memories of another man, the only man I loved. I curled up tightly on the sofa, watching that big cat documentary until I began to relax. I let my eyes—too heavy and exhausted by sleepless nights—close as I surrendered to the lure of sleep…

I opened my eyes slowly, as images from my dream swirled around in my head. A dream more real than I could possibly have imagined.

I dreamed that I'd decided to let Neil go. That I realized that love was not possession and it did not involve suffering. Love was freedom.

To set someone free is the greatest gift you can give the one you love.

It is the grandest demonstration of love, especially when it involves a great sacrifice.

I thought I heard his baritone whisper: *"Wherever you roam, my Pearl, no matter how vast the ocean, you will always find your Shell again. Whenever you feel lonesome, I will be with you. Remember that."*

But I knew that was just another illusion conjured up by my spirit as it struggled to cope with his absence.

I sat up slowly, stretching out my arm muscles, and felt a warm hand touch my cheek and a thumb smear something wet from my skin.

"You were crying in your sleep," Ivan said in a desolate whisper. He was crouched in front of me with a look of worry on his face.

I blinked rapidly and sat up all the way. I glanced around, disoriented. "What time is it? Did I... I fall asleep? Oh God. I'm sorry," I winced. I didn't tell him what my dream had been about. It hadn't exactly been a nightmare, but, for all that, it had hurt like needles stabbing between my ribs.

Had I seriously been crying?

I didn't know anything by that point; all I felt was a vast confusion swirling around in my head.

The truth was, I was afraid.

Afraid of Neil's decisions.

Had he gone back to sleeping with random blond women all the time like he did before? I was afraid he'd fallen back into his old, bad habits. I was afraid that finding out about his biological father had destroyed him so thoroughly that he'd go back to harming himself.

"Selene... Hey... Are you okay?" Ivan stroked my hair.

I blinked, trying to push the pain down lest it tear me in two like a dagger to the gut.

My eyes found his, and I nodded, lying.

"It is nine o'clock, though. I chose to let you sleep. You needed it; you were exhausted." He tucked a lock of hair behind my ear like a big brother looking after his sister.

I felt a terrible stab of pain in my chest.

"Ivan," I cried out. He watched me attentively, waiting for me to speak. "How do you forget someone who can make you hurt so much even from far away?" I said in a tortured whisper, thinking about how completely shattered my world was without Neil in it. I had warned him: I'd told him that I would lose my mind if he wasn't in my life, and I meant it, but he didn't care.

He didn't believe I was serious.

"You can't. You just have to give it time until, eventually, your heart gets used to the absence," he added, sounding devastated as he stroked my hair.

He balanced his elbows on his flexed thighs and continued watching me steadily.

Instinctively, I just kept talking.

"My mother told me that Neil was always going to leave my anyway. That he didn't want to warp my life. He didn't want to drag me into his problems. He never thought he was the right man for me. He didn't want to become the center of my world; he didn't want me to abandon my friends, my mother, or my college career. He made the choice for the both of us. He didn't even give me a chance to decide what was right for me, you know? He was so selfish!" I exploded furiously.

More and more, I found myself flip-flopping between moments of despondency and moments when I really wanted to hate him. Sometimes, I even convinced myself I really did hate him, but then I always came back around to loving him even more somehow.

It was too much. Too draining, this thing I felt for him.

There was no explaining my love for Neil. Just like no one could explain why the shore continued to welcome the sea's embrace when its wild flood always went away again and always took with it a few more grains of sand.

"He wasn't being selfish. Selfish would have been forcing you to follow him. I can't stand the guy, but I do believe he let you go because he was thinking of your happiness," Ivan said thoughtfully, applying some logical reasoning to the peculiarities of that human disaster. He was probably right.

I just shrugged and let the conversation die until Ivan drew my attention back to him.

"Selene..." he said, looking deeply into my eyes. I knew he could see all the suffering there. "I think I know one good way to forget about your troubles. At least for tonight," he said in a whisper, like there was someone else in the room with us who shouldn't overhear.

I said nothing. Even worse, I did nothing as he leaned forward until I could feel his hot breath on my face. I did not object when he cupped my cheek or nuzzled my nose with his. I did not object when his soft lips settled over mine, feather-light, nor when he began to move them, urging me to share in the kiss. To create this completely new and unexpected joining. His hand moved from my cheek to the back of my neck, sliding into my hair as he thrust his tongue into my mouth. We both leaped to our feet the moment his tongue met mine. He flattened his other hand against my back, pressing our bodies closer together until they collided, heated but still a bit cautious.

"You did tell me I shouldn't ask for permission," he murmured against my mouth. "Now you can say I'm very rude." He smiled and then resumed kissing me with more longing, more intensity. He tilted his head, pressing more deeply into me and stealing my breath away. He tasted like mint, like something good and right, as he continued to delight me with his passion and sensuality.

"Ivan..." I babbled out his name, confused. I had no idea what I was doing. My brain seemed to have powered down. I rested my hands on his chest, and guilt bore down on my long-shattered heart.

I wanted to stop thinking about Neil. To do that, I would need to find someone who wasn't like Neil, someone who was whole. Someone like I used to be. So why did it feel wrong to kiss Ivan but right to suffer for Neil?

Why did it feel wrong for me to accept another man's interest but right for Neil to share another woman's bed?

But, more importantly, was it right, what I was doing at that moment?

Was it going to make me happy?

I gasped when, in one wild movement, Ivan scooped me up into his arms without ever breaking the kiss. My legs wrapped around his waist, and his hands tightened on my ass. He carried me swiftly down the hallway and into the bedroom, shutting the door with a careless kick. He laid me out slowly on the enormous bed and positioned himself on top of me, between my legs, balancing his weight on his elbows.

We were both breathing hard, our chests trembling, our bodies burning up.

But I didn't want...didn't want...

"Are you okay?" he asked, staring into my eyes. I could feel his erection between my legs, and it was neither surprising nor arousing.

No visceral desire bloomed inside me, no urge to be dominated, and no need to give him pleasure.

I stared at him in a daze.

I'd unintentionally messed up his hair, and his lips were wet from our kisses.

No, I was not okay. That was obvious from my vulnerable, irrational behavior.

The real Selene would not have acted on impulse like this.

And it was for that very reason that I did something I would come to regret, my biggest screw-up: I kissed him again.

His tongue tangled ardently with mine.

One hand moved from my waist to my ribs before fondling one breast and beginning to unbutton my shirt.

I kept my eyes closed. I let him do it, but I didn't look.

I didn't *want* to look.

I imagined that his fresh taste turned bitter and smoky, that his cologne was replaced with the odor of musk, and that his lean, athletic body was instead a powerful, virile one, heavy and sharp-edged.

I imagined him pressing down on me unsparingly like an overbearing god.

Just as Tinkerbell would have done, I spread my wings and flew far away.

But, then again, Peter Pan had taught me that only those with happy thoughts have the ability to fly.

I felt my body tense up with the pulsating need to have Neil inside me.

My stiffened nipples pressed against my bra, seeking his lush lips.

My cheeks were wet again. Another tear slid down my face and vanished into the sheets.

"You smell like coconut..." Ivan licked my neck and groped one breast that had been exposed by my now completely unbuttoned shirt.

And I recalled that day after our first night together. Neil sat on the couch with me, kissed me, and breathed in the scent of my skin.

"My bed smelled like coconut this morning," he had told me. We both longed to relive that moment, starving for each other.

We were right there.

Just me and him.

A bowl of popcorn.

And that mess of ours, which was starting to take shape in my head.

And in my heart.

I smiled at the thought, lost in the past, lost in that insane film of us, which could be called anything but a love story. Then I stroked along Ivan's hoodie. I slid my hands underneath the fabric and felt his smooth, soft skin; the muscles there were tensed and defined. I moved around to the front, glancing along his tight abs and finally reaching his hard pecs. With my eyes still closed, the only thing I felt was his mouth coaxing mine to kiss him again and again until I was consumed. Until I consumed myself...

22

> "I wished I could kick-start my own heart
> and make the emotions turn over."

NEIL

People say that life is like a rainbow, each color corresponding to a specific phase, a time span.

Mine has always been characterized by darkness. It was certainly no accident that the liar who gave birth to me called me Neil.

And then, to make matters worse, she'd added on the fucking surname of a man who wasn't my father.

A man who beat me and treated me like a cuckoo in the nest, a slimy insect. A man who thought I was some insane freak and never showed me an ounce of human empathy.

And now I knew why.

"Fuck you!" That was my new daily mantra against life, against my mother, against William, against John, and against Judith. Even against Selene, whom I'd had to let go so she could be happy far away from me.

I'd stopped giving a shit about other people. Stopped putting my family first and stopped privileging their problems over my own. I'd stopped trying to be better, to sand down my rough edges for the benefit of others. For the benefit of Selene. I'd stopped chasing after people, seeking their acceptance.

I quit chasing the world, and, yes, that meant I stayed behind. But it also meant I stayed myself.

My life was a prison from which no one could free me.

I'd quit believing in anything beautiful. I'd snuffed out my last little lights of hope the same day I was supposed to snuff out my birthday candles.

Was I angry? Probably always would be.

Was I disillusioned? No, I was worse.

I was embittered and disgusted.

The heavy bag swung back and forth with my violent blows. I'd gotten back into training, and I did it constantly. Every morning I got up with the sun and worked out my tension that way. The chains tensed as they supported the weight of the relentlessly jerking bag. I alternated hooks, uppercuts, and jabs, fast and sure.

Drops of sweat slid down my neck to my bare chest; all my muscles were tensed and burning.

Adrenaline pulsed in my veins, swamping my brain, making it impossible to think clearly.

My black sweatpants were plastered to my legs, my hair kept irritatingly sticking to my forehead, and my knuckles were on fire because I hadn't worn gloves. Just white elastic wraps that were now stained from the deep tears I was putting in the skin there.

I could smell the sharp scent of the blood, and I liked it.

It made me feel alive, dirty, and satisfied.

"Is it normal for you to make this kind of racket first thing in the morning every morning, Miller?" Megan's drowsy voice made me stop. I steadied the bag with both hands and turned to look calmly at her. I looked first at her long, bare legs and then at her bountiful breasts protruding from under my white sweatshirt, which barely covered her crotch.

Her fuchsia thong was visible.

"I don't know. Is it normal for you to wear my fucking sweater when you know damn well I don't want you to?" I snapped irritably, glaring at her sleepy face, her swollen lips, and her still half-closed green eyes.

"I didn't get a chance to do laundry yesterday, and your sweater was clean and smelled like... Whatever, I wore it. Don't get your panties in a twist." She shrugged and walked past me to the kitchen with a familiar arrogant sway to that little ass.

"Take it off, Megan, before you piss me off!" I threatened her sternly. She sat down on a stool, letting the fabric of the sweater ride up on her hips and showing me that scrap of panties again. I swallowed hard.

"Get as pissed as you want. I'm not scared of you," she grumbled indifferently before taking a bite of Nutella toast. I still hadn't figured out how she could eat that crap and still have that body.

It is a fuckable body, I thought.

That was exactly the word for it: fuckable.

The thought of sharing an apartment with Megan no longer bothered me the way it had six months before. It was now just a part of my daily life, like seeing her wander around half-naked and having indecent thoughts about her. Still, I had set certain boundaries for myself that I wasn't going to cross.

Those were still firmly in place, and they weren't going anywhere.

"Oh yeah? You want me to come over there and tear it off you?" I began unwrapping my hands slowly, still holding eye contact with her. My wicked gaze locked on hers, and I was pleased to see the effect I was having on her. She wriggled on the stool, tightening her thighs together before gulping down her mouthful of toast and blinking rapidly at me.

I had been learning how to read the female body and sense its wants since I was a child.

And, right now, I was sensing her want in a major way.

"Don't even try it. I can defend myself, as you well know," she shot back immediately. She'd given up on eating and assumed a ready posture. But I always got what I wanted, and if I wanted my sweater back, I would take it.

"I can put you on your back whenever I want." I adopted a menacing expression as I stalked toward her with slow, determined steps like a hunter closing in on his prey.

Megan's eyes opened wide. Sensing the danger, she leaped off the stool.

"Don't you start!" She began to cackle as she darted around the kitchen island to escape me. She failed miserably, though, because I managed to snatch her easily and shoved her down on our living room couch.

"Fuck, hold still!"

She laughed against me and the sound of it rebounded off the walls around us, her disheveled hair fanned out beneath her. I lifted her arms up over her head, holding her wrists, and settled myself over her slender body, putting my weight on her. I felt her breath catch when my bare chest grazed her nipples. They were hard beneath my sweatshirt, and I knew she was ashamed. I knew she wanted me, though she still refused to admit it. She was in denial because she could not show herself to be vulnerable. She could not let her instincts get the better of her good sense.

"I know you want to fuck me." I leaned forward until my nose brushed along hers. It wasn't because I was attracted to her or found myself drawn to her beauty; it was because I was an asshole, and I liked to make her squirm.

I breathed in her pleasant orange blossom scent, the same as it was when we were children sitting out in the yard and she tried to teach me Spanish. To me, she was forever that little girl with the white bow in her hair. It felt simultaneously as though it had been both a blink and a lifetime since that moment.

"And what makes you think that? A little too sure of yourself, I think," she answered, sounding annoyed. She hated it when I tried to tame her. She was a fighter, a brave warrior who would never let a man dominate her. She wriggled under me, twisting her wrists in an attempt to get out of my iron grip. I smiled smugly as she huffed in frustration.

"Do you think I'm stupid?" I answered lazily. "Do you think I haven't noticed the way you've been looking at me ever since we started living in this apartment together? You can deny it to yourself but not to me," I breathed against her lips, staring at the tiny mole beside her cupid's bow. She licked her lips, and her breathing turned heavy, her nipples straining more and more against the white fabric that covered them.

"I don't—" she began to say, but then we were interrupted by the sounds of someone else's footsteps in the living room.

Both of our heads snapped to the woman who was watching the scene before her with an expression that was both thoughtful and bewildered. Who knew what was going through her head, finding me in a compromising position with Head Case's half-naked body spread out underneath me?

"You really do have a type, huh? Blue-eyed brunettes," Megan noted as I got up, freeing her from my grasp. I stood up, watching the woman in our living room.

She was in her early twenties.

Pale skin with sharp, delicate features. She was undoubtedly hot but very angelic looking.

I scrutinized her more closely, searching for a pair of full, pouty lips that I would not find. My gaze roved over her slim but not upturned nose before delving into her blue eyes.

An ordinary blue like all the others, not the ocean I had been immersed in just a few months before.

Still, she bore a *slight* resemblance to Tinkerbell the night before. Now, though, she looked nothing like her.

"I...um...left my number for you in the room," she stammered, twitchy and timid. They were qualities I deliberately sought out in my women these days, despite the fact that they all turned into fierce lionesses in the sack and made it clear that their alleged shy reserve was just another strategic front.

What was this particular girl's name? I didn't even remember.

I usually didn't, and I had to cover for it with some banal nickname.

Her gaze swept longingly down my body, lingering on my crotch.

"I don't give a shit where you leave your number, sweetheart. I'm not going to call you anyway," I said, cold and clear. She winced at my stormy face.

Why did they all make the same mistake?

These women thought I was going to chase after them just because they'd deigned to give me a fuck that was about as pleasurable as a walk in the park.

"But, I thought—"

I stopped her before she could get on some bullshit. Or worse, start crying.

Shit, I hated having to go through this whole pointless dance the morning after.

I took a few steps closer, looming over her petite frame, and stared down at her indifferently like nothing had happened between us the night before. Like *she* was nothing.

"Listen, little girl..." I began to recite the same script, going through the same motions in front of the same audience: Megan, who had settled in happily to watch the show. "I fucked you, and you enjoyed it." I reached out slowly and touched her lower lip with my thumb, remembering the lewd way that beautiful mouth had wrapped around my cock. I felt her shiver with arousal and smiled. "You did good. I've got to hand it to you. A real slut in training. I'm sure you'll improve with practice, but you won't get it with me," I said in a sultry murmur, all crude, calculated sweetness. She glared at me and swatted my hand away clumsily. I gave her a thin, fake smile and went on, "I don't give a shit about what you feel or think or want. Get out of this apartment and forget about me. Do not get your hopes up; there won't be a second time." I didn't raise my voice—I didn't need to. My haughty, arrogant tone was enough to break her. I watched her scatter into pieces on the floor like so much confetti.

Used and then discarded.

Exactly what had been done to me.

Exactly what Kim did and called it love.

If that was love then, fuck, I'd loved them all.

I was a true romantic.

At least I, unlike Kim, insisted on always having consent from my partners.

"You're a…a real…"

"Asshole?" Megan offered from back over in the kitchen. "Girls call him all sorts of things: perv, bastard, fuckboy, sociopath… The field's wide open, really. For the record, I'm on your side, babe." She raised a hand in the air as if to ratify her support, but the woman was so freaked out that she couldn't respond. She retreated a few steps away from me and clutched her purse to her body like I was a monster she was going to have to outrun.

I laughed heartily, as cruel and malicious as I could make it, and bit my lower lip to put on my false face—a face that had been increasingly fucked up for months now—while I waited for the insults to start.

They all did it; I was used to it by then.

"Can you make it to the elevator, or do you need a push?" I

sneered, and she shook her head, horrified. Her eyes glazed over, and I could tell she was willing herself not to cry. I felt nothing about that.

I hadn't felt pity for anyone in a long time.

"Piss off, you know where the door is." I gestured to it with my chin. She turned her back to me and ran out, slamming the door so hard behind her that Megan flinched.

"Damn, that's one way to get rid of a girl. You need to get some new material, though. You can't keep putting on the same show every morning," she said through a mouthful of toast, sitting on the stool once again. She was still wearing my sweatshirt.

"Keep your nose out of my business," I snapped.

My moods were shifting even more abruptly than normal; my personality was in constant flux. Sometimes vulnerable, sometimes nonchalant, and sometimes irascible and irrational. I was trying to fight everything I felt inside, trying to stuff it deep, deep down, but I couldn't quite manage it.

Because there was nothing left in my life.

There was no family, no siblings, no hope, no ocean eyes to lose myself in, and no smell of coconut.

Nothing.

Except the nightmares.

And the two packs of Winstons I smoked every day.

The occasional fuck.

Work.

And the darkness.

"You're just mad…" Megan stopped focusing on the jar of Nutella and looked at me, trying to get a bead on me. The word *mad* sank into my chest, arousing a feeling of anguish.

I wasn't mad. I was *enraged*.

I stalked over to the kitchen island and grabbed her toast to give me some time to think up a response. I took a bite and chewed it anxiously.

There was a time when my Babygirl's smile was enough to light up my bleakest thoughts.

She was my safe place, the only one that I could trust. My Neverland.

"You better get ready quick if you want a ride to work, otherwise you're taking your bike." I tossed the unfinished toast into the trash. Thinking about Tinkerbell made my stomach clench up. I already knew I was going to need uncountable cups of coffee to get through the rest of the day.

I walked to my room. Fortunately, the apartment was big enough for each of us to have our own rooms and bathrooms. I could not have handled sharing intimate spaces with her. I threw the door open, and immediately my nose wrinkled with disgust. I could smell sex and some undefined feminine fragrance. The bedsheets were still all rucked up and dirty, and I wasn't about to sleep on them without first washing off any remnants of some girl I didn't know. I yanked them off the bed and wadded them into a ball on the floor. A small piece of paper fell out as I did so.

I grinned and then bent down to grab it, taking it with me into the bathroom.

Naturally, I immediately flushed it down the toilet without bothering to read it.

Did that girl seriously think I was going to call her?

"Pathetic..." I said in a flat mutter as I got into the shower and began scrubbing myself with a large quantity of body wash. I wanted to erase the hands and mouths that crawled all over me, even if I did allow them to do it. I was doing whatever I could to drive away the memory of Babygirl's ocean eyes by finding them in the face of another, along with her radiant smile and those plush lips I constantly longed to feel wrapped around me...

I glanced down to where my cock seemed to have had a reaction to my reminiscing. I felt a jolt of electricity run down my spine, making me gasp. I pressed my forehead to the shower wall and heaved a sigh. I focused on stifling any dirty thoughts: I was not going to jerk off in the shower to thoughts of her.

It wasn't happening.

I would always be stronger than my desire for her.

I went back to soaping myself as the tepid water slid down my worked, swollen muscles. Since I had started working out harder every day, my body had changed. I felt even sturdier, more toned, and more defined.

I had forgotten how it felt, being desirable to others, during those months when I was solely focused on Selene.

But it didn't make me feel the way it had before—satisfied and proud. Instead, it was just irritating and boring because sex was nothing but a way to keep from going completely out of my mind.

The Boy wasn't happy with the situation either; we were both struggling just to survive.

I washed one more time and contentedly breathed in the new, clean smell that had replaced the odor of that girl. Then I got out of the shower and slicked back my dripping hair before wrapping a towel around my hips and padding over to my room.

"Neil, would you get a fucking move on?" Megan threw open my bedroom door and froze, staring almost drunkenly at my damp body. I had to marvel at her sometimes when she reacted to my body like that. I raised the corner of my mouth in amusement and ignored her, instead opening a drawer to pull out a pair of clean boxers.

"Need something, Head Case?" I gave her a bland look; her breath caught, and she cleared her throat, blinking several times. She was all ready for work in a black blazer and skirt that looked sexy as hell, clinging perfectly to her well-balanced curves.

"No," she shook herself, holding tightly to the doorknob. "I just wanted to see how far along you were. We can't be late." Megan was struggling to keep her emotions under control. The electric attraction between the two of us was palpable; it had been hard to handle for the first couple of months, but I'd learned how to live with it without ever crossing the line.

"I realize that. Give me ten minutes." I held the boxers in one hand and used the other to loosen my towel. I could have dropped it entirely and given her a real eyeful, but I preferred to tease her a little first. I watched her artfully made-up face as I gave her a warning look. She took a wary step back and immediately covered her eyes as I let the skimpy towel fall to the floor and stood there, completely naked.

"Oh, you motherfucker! You're disgusting!" she shouted like a lunatic and slammed the door behind her as she fled the room. I burst out laughing because even Megan had her moments of naivety. She always presented herself as so tough, but she was soft too, in her own way. She often blushed when I walked around the apartment half-naked, and her face went up in flames when those green eyes of hers glanced between my legs.

I quickly finished dressing in a neat blue suit and white button-down. I dried my hair and combed it back so it wasn't as disheveled as usual. I rubbed my bristly jaw, where I had the beginnings of a beard, before grabbing my pack of Winstons and car keys off the desk. My gaze snagged, though, on something shiny and silver with a little shell dangling off it.

Her bracelet.

I'd quit wearing it, but I hadn't thrown it out. I'd never be able to bring myself to get rid of it. I decided to take it off one night after it had gotten caught in the blond hair of some girl who was sucking me off.

It had suddenly hit me how sick the whole situation was—how sick I made myself—and I couldn't wear it after that.

"Neil! Let's go!" Megan hollered from the other side of my closed door. I ignored her, turning my attention from the bracelet to my phone. I grabbed it and after dabbing some cologne on my throat, walked out of the room.

"Get off my ass. I'm ready," I said huffily, brushing past her. We took the elevator down, and I leaned back against the mirrored wall, taking the opportunity to check my emails and texts.

The most recent one was from Logan. My heart lurched when I read it:

I thought about our pinky promise today. And, last night, I dreamed of her... Do you remember the promise you would always make to me when we were little? I need that promise.

I need you to keep your promise.

My promise... I used to tell him that I would come back to him, that he meant everything to me, and that he was a part of me.

And he still was, as was Chloe, but I wasn't ready to allow them back into my life.

I was alone, and I was strong in that loneliness with my shattered soul.

I wasn't ready to look into Chloe's gray eyes, just like I wasn't ready to look at Logan and think about the fact that I didn't really have anything to do with him or with his family. William called me a cuckoo in the nest, and those words had given me invisible wounds.

"You wanna move, playboy?" Megan stood in front of me, her head cocked to one side. Her eyes searched me, trying to figure out what was wrong. Mine landed instead on her lush mouth. I hadn't even noticed I was still standing in the open elevator while people waited to get inside.

"I can already tell I'm not going to be able to stand you today," I grumbled irritably, tucking my iPhone back into my pocket as I pulled out my keys. I was lost in thought as we walked to the parking garage, the click-clack of Megan's dizzying heels hammering in my head. Her walking in front of me, however, did afford me the opportunity to check out her ass, wrapped up tight in the pencil skirt she wore.

"You're not looking at my ass back there, are you?" she said, throwing a sharp look over her shoulder. I gave her a sly smile and slapped her butt when we got to my Maserati.

She jumped slightly and scowled menacingly at me.

"Of course, I'm looking at your ass. Professional looks good on you," I admitted easily as I opened the door and slid into the driver's seat. Megan followed suit, getting into the passenger seat and buckling her seat belt. As she did it, her skirt rode up high on her thighs, revealing a generous expanse of skin. I could see the edge of her thigh-highs, and I squeezed my eyes shut, feeling a strange heat in the bottom of my stomach.

My body's reaction was instantly frustrating, and I turned my gaze out the windshield instead.

I couldn't accept the fact that Head Case had any kind of power over me at all, not when my head was full of Babygirl. Selene had become my addiction, and even though I had moved on, I would always keep a part of her deep down inside me.

"That's why I wear leather pants instead of these stupid suits because you men are all dogs." Megan had noticed my vacant stare, and so she was chattering to help me out. She knew better than to ask questions; I hated talking about what had happened before. So, instead she would just go on about nothing to distract me from my darker thoughts.

"You look sexy in anything. I've always said that. And you look especially sexy in office wear. Trust me." I didn't look at her, concentrating on the road instead as I merged into Chicago traffic. It was one of the largest cities in the United States, and I'd already seen most of its famous spots with Head Case. I liked the bold architecture on display throughout the city.

"That's not true. I'm not sexy." Megan lit up a Chesterfield and blew smoke out the open window as she watched the buildings towering all around us. I'd never asked her why she had so little confidence herself in that way, but I'd always presumed it had something to do with Ryan. The monster probably tore her down and insulted her while he was abusing her.

My psychiatrist called them *cognitive distortions,* incorrect beliefs that a victim of violence carries with them into adulthood. Especially victims of the kind of thing that happened to Megan and me.

"Yes, you are," I told her seriously, then I pulled the cigarette from her lips and brought it to mine.

"The fuck are you doing? You can't light one of your own?" she snapped irritably. I sometimes thought that Megan was too much like me and that was why we couldn't really get along.

"I'm busy driving. Be nice for once." I shrugged and took a drag, tasting her lipstick mixed with the harsh bite of nicotine.

It didn't drive me wild, but it didn't disgust me either.

Parking beneath the huge skyscraper that housed our firm's offices, I followed Megan up to the entrance. Automatic doors opened to welcome us into the monochrome lobby, luxurious but impersonal. Head Case immediately said hello to one of the receptionists while I ignored everyone and headed directly for my floor.

"You could stand to be a little more polite to your coworkers, you know," Megan muttered as we stepped into the elevator going up to the twentieth floor.

I'd taken more elevators in the past six months than I had in my life up until that point.

"I do what I want with who I want," I answered grimly before putting on my best mask for the occasion as the doors slid open on our floor. Before us stood my mentor, Daniel Moore. He was a man in his mid-fifties, confident with a calculating smile.

"Okay. See you later, then. Try not to kill anyone." Megan bid me farewell with a cheeky smirk before walking on to the office of her mentor, a pretentious, superior woman who would have driven me up a wall.

"Neil, I've been waiting for you." Moore slapped me on the back as I drew even with him in the hallway. Before I had the chance to say anything, he started telling me about a project. One of mine, actually. "Your notes on the theater revamp were nothing short of perfection. Researched down to the smallest detail. You have potential. A-plus work!" We entered his office, and he took a seat behind his desk while I remained standing, allowing my problems to fade into the background.

Work was the only thing that could really keep my mind occupied and force me to be productive.

"I'm glad you liked it. It took me three nights because I had a number of other projects to review. I was worried it wouldn't be up to your standards," I answered with a small half-smile. I'd gotten very good at bullshitting in Chicago. I made myself look friendly as I held Moore's gaze. I was just an intern, but I'd already earned his respect and that of everyone else on the team. My coworkers didn't know me. They didn't know about my mental health problems, about my struggles to control my anger, or about my conversations with the Boy. I acted like a normal man at work. Maybe a bit prickly sometimes and taciturn, but ultimately a reasonable sort of person.

All of it was a performance designed to allow me to maintain my position and win the favor of the asshole seated in front of me.

"You're really doing top-shelf work here. You're honestly more capable than many of my colleagues," he mused.

"I don't feel like I'm better than anyone," I answered humbly. It was true—I *knew* I was better. "I'm just striving to improve." Architecture really was my field, my dream, and I found that it was oddly fulfilling to dive into a new project. I enjoyed it; it was perhaps the only true satisfaction that life had ever given me, and I hoped it wouldn't be snatched away from me.

"I'm going to be swamped today. There are a couple of projects I'm responsible for that I'd like to put in your hands. I want to you to get your take on the plans." He pointed at a thick stack of papers to his right, and I blanched. Immediately, I wanted a cigarette. That stack of papers was about eight inches high, and this idiot was entrusting them all to me?

"Are you sure about that? I mean, these are important projects, your clients, and..." I played the newbie card, like I wasn't sure I could really pull this off. In this new world of mine, it wasn't ever a good idea to demonstrate too much confidence. People would start to think of me as the enemy, and then they'd try to compete and try to undercut me, and that would only stunt my professional growth.

"I'm sure, Neil. I don't even need to review your work. When you finish this internship and get your license, you are going to be a great architect. Professor Robinson is my brother-in-law, you know, and he's been singing your praises for a while. Now I see why." He got up out of his chair, glancing at his phone, which had begun to ring incessantly. "I've got a meeting in ten. Get to work, Neil." He slapped me on the back again and sped out of his office, snapping at whoever was on the other end of the call.

"Fuck's sake..." I paused, holding back more expletives in case some dickhead came along to chide me about it. "Cool, fantastic," I muttered to myself instead. I wasn't going to get home before eight o'clock. I kicked the door shut and walked over to my desk. I took off my jacket and hung it up on the coatrack before sitting down in the swivel chair. With a deep sigh, I rolled my shirt up to the elbows and started looking through the various projects I was supposed to deal with.

Some I just checked over; others I modified. I gave my ideas free rein, just like he'd asked me to do, though I always thoroughly evaluated whether they were actually the best ideas.

Hours later, I was still hard at work in the office all by myself with a mug of coffee steaming next to me.

I hadn't stopped to eat anything. I was forcing myself to finish all the projects so I didn't have to hear about it from Mr. Moore. I knew I wouldn't have been able to keep my cool if he tried to lecture me, so I tried not to give him any reasons to bust my balls. Weary, I cracked my neck and rubbed my shoulder. There was a strange needles and pins sensation along my arm and the fingers on that hand were numb.

I glanced at the clock—it was almost four o'clock, and I hadn't seen Megan at all. I was pretty sure she probably also had important projects to work on, so we would undoubtedly be driving home together.

Just then, someone knocked on the door, and I immediately assumed it was the Head Case herself. I didn't say anything, just watched as the door opened wide to reveal…

Logan?

I blinked in shock, afraid I was having some sort of hallucination.

I did not feel particularly thrilled or delighted by his presence. Instead, I was mostly surprised and confused.

I leaped to my feet and stood motionless, watching him. My heart began to pound in my chest, my breath catching in my throat.

"Hi…" my brother murmured. The sound of his voice made me really feel that he was there—this was no dream. How long had it been since we'd seen each other? How much had our relationship changed? He walked in slowly, clearly wanting to wrap me up in a fraternal embrace. But he restrained himself.

"Neil!" An enthusiastic female voice called out, echoing off the office walls. Chloe rushed past Logan, and I moved instinctively, rounding the desk to meet her. She hurled herself into my arms with teary eyes. She threw her arms around me and pressed her cheek to my chest, and I went rigid. I tried to hug her in return, but my arms just remained stubbornly frozen in midair. Without conscious thought, I took her by the shoulders and pushed her back, away from me. Chloe stared at me in confusion and used the back of her hand to wipe away the tears that kept flooding down her face. Once again, I felt nothing at the sight of those tears. I wished I could kick-start my own heart and make the emotions turn over.

I couldn't even feel them, let alone express them.

What the hell had happened to me? Where had my love for them gone?

"What...what are you doing here?" I asked coldly. I didn't even recognize my own voice.

"After six months, that's all you have to say to us? Our lives have ground to a halt...and you want to know what we're doing here?" Logan answered, shocked by my apathy. Honestly, even I couldn't understand it.

"We needed to see you and talk to you." Dr. Keller appeared from behind Logan and moved to stand next to him.

I clenched one hand into a fist as I felt anger boiling under my skin. My siblings had brought the man who claimed to be my father to see me. But he was nothing to me. No one brought me up; no one was there for me. I'd never had a male figure I could rely on and confide in, except for Dr. Lively.

Wait—had Dr. Lively known? Did he betray me too? Just the idea of it made my brain hazy.

"Talk to me? I'm busy, John. I'm working. We can't all spend our days fucking with our patients," I sneered at him. "You had over twenty years to talk to me, but no...you preferred to lie to me. It was more entertaining that way, right?" I didn't raise my voice but just leaned easily against the desk and folded my arms over my chest in an arrogant, superior manner. Chloe stepped back a bit, shocked at my indifference. John just sighed heavily, trying to be patient.

"I've been trying to reach you..." It was Logan who spoke then, and I turned my attention to him. "I emailed you constantly. I texted and called every day, but you never answered. I thought something had happened to you. I thought you might be sick or—" But I interrupted him, finishing his thought with a cruel smile.

"That I might be high off my ass in some club? That I was spending my nights shit-faced, fucking whatever easy pussy happened along?" I couldn't seem to express myself in anything but the most vulgar way, despite the fact that Chloe was standing right there. Normally, I was much more considerate of her. My sister sucked in a breath at my harsh words and moved to stand by Logan, visibly disturbed and afraid.

"What happened to you? Why are you treating us this way?" Logan couldn't conceal the profound disappointment mixed with sadness in his tone.

I let my arms fall loose to my sides and straightened up before striding over to them.

"You want to know what happened to me, Logan?" I stopped in front of him, close enough for him to feel my breath on his face. "I collapsed. I became a dead man walking. A dead man who couldn't make sense of his shitty life. I wanted to end it all, maybe crash my car or something. But then someone rescued me. Someone talked some sense into me, and I was able to move on," I confessed explosively.

"I'm done with New York, with my family and my old friends and my old life. Because of your father…and mine." I threw John a disdainful glance. He didn't wince but only stared probingly into me like he was trying to see into my soul. Trying to see if there was something other than anger and bitterness in there.

"I was wrong, and I know that. I had planned to talk to you when it was all said and done. I decided that, after you graduated, I was going to sit you down and explain everything. I was afraid of how you'd react, Neil. You have your issues; your mental health is fragile.

Introducing traumatic information like that was always going to be risky and—" John attempted to move closer to me. He was talking to me like I was his patient. I raised a hand to silence him.

"I trusted you," I said, raising my voice. Chloe flinched and grabbed Logan's arm. John just stared at me, though, ashamed but not afraid of my outburst. "I told you about myself. About my past. I told you about Selene. I thought you were different. I thought you were sincere, a man who was committed and who had good values. But, instead, I find out that you're just the asshole who fucked my mother and left her alone and pregnant in the clutches of someone else. You disgust me." My mouth twisted into a bitter scowl, and I looked disdainfully at him. I stepped back a few paces—I couldn't bear to stand next to him.

"That's not how it was," he snapped back. "I did not *fuck* your mother. I *loved* her. That's very different," he went on, advancing fearlessly on me. His strength and determination were commendable; I was not at all safe to approach at that moment. "I loved Mia with all that I was, but we could not be together. Her father forced her to marry William. I knew that she was pregnant with you, and right from the start, I wanted you. She was afraid and wasn't sure she could go through with the pregnancy, and I was the one who encouraged her to keep the baby!" His eyes turned glassy. Every word was full of feeling and pain. I could feel it even if I couldn't define it. "I thought about you every moment of the day. I asked Mia about you, about everything in your world. My life stopped making sense after the third of May..." He undid the cufflink of the button-down he wore underneath his suit and rolled up the cuff to show me something. "I got this tattoo to honor your birth. It's your initials." He turned his wrist over, showing me letters inscribed there, and I felt the blood drain from my face. I remembered it. I'd spotted it one time when we ran into each other at a bar. I'd even suggested he go and get the faded ink touched up.

I attempted to feign indifference as I looked back at his face. In the worried creases around his eyes and mouth, I saw the desperation of the father who didn't know how to chisel through the concrete encasing his son's heart. "I tattooed this on my body so that I could feel close to you every minute of every day. Every second. I wanted you to know how important you are to me, that my love for you is always there; it has never gone away. My blood runs in your veins; we are one and the same, Neil, and I can't tell you how bitterly I regret not being there for you when William was hurting you, when Kimberly..."

I shook my head to stop him. I breathed raggedly, trying to control my rage. If John had been there, maybe I wouldn't have been abused by that woman or beaten by my mother's husband. I threw out one arm as if to break my fall. Logan instinctively reached to steady me, but he'd barely touched me before I stood up straight and stiff again.

"Don't touch me. Get out of here. Leave," I said, barely whispering. My head was starting to get fuzzy, and I was afraid I was going to explode. I couldn't deal with my reality. Chloe and Logan's presence only reminded me that William wasn't really my father. John only made me think about the years I'd been fed lies.

My brain wasn't ready to process it all. I was still too fragile—too broken.

"Neil, we came all the way to Chicago for you. Please. Chloe and I don't deserve this treatment; all of this had nothing to do with us. We are still your brother and sister. We always will be." Logan tried to reach for me again, but I pulled away and showed him my back, dragging my hands over my face and through my hair. I was on the edge of another meltdown, and with a bestial growl, I seized the pen holder from the desk and hurled it at the wall. I roared in fury.

"Get out!" I shouted with an anger that felt powerful enough to make the building shake. The tendons in my neck stuck out; my eyes were feverishly wide.

And all I felt inside was emptiness.

None of them could understand what it was like, watching your life fall to pieces and not being able to do a single thing about it.

My right hand shook, and I realized I was approaching the edge. I moved away from them and turned to stare out the big windows looking out on the adjacent skyscrapers.

"Get out," I repeated, my voice rough from my recent outburst. I touched my forehead and found it slick with sweat. The pain was bad enough to break me in two, but I was stronger than it and I fought. Otherwise, I'd never be able to come back to life.

Eventually, the three of them did as I demanded.

I didn't watch them go. I stood motionless, surrounded on all sides by my darkness, and listened to their footsteps recede further and further into the distance.

Finding out about John had been a trauma that I could not get over.

Maybe someday my love for my family—for my siblings—will rise up again but, for now...

I was in the dark.

Trapped in a prison of my own hate and repressed rage, and all I wanted to do was suffer there in silence.

23

"I am always here for you the way you have always been there for me."

MEGAN

Jace the coffee boy was surprisingly incapable of making a drinkable cup of coffee.

Irritated, I got up and marched briskly out of my office. These high heels were super uncomfortable, but they did force me to adopt a different, more feminine posture.

I couldn't wait to get home and sack out on the sofa.

I walked into the little break room where they kept the coffee machine—I needed a real cup, one that didn't taste like dirt water. I nodded hello to a few coworkers who were there for the same purpose and began fixing myself a cup.

"Yeah, he is breathtakingly gorgeous," one of the PAs giggled to her colleagues, tossing her thick blond hair over one shoulder.

I had never been the type to engage in water-cooler talk like that, at least not when I was on the clock.

"Oh yeah, he can absolutely get it. Have you seen all those muscles? He'd blow your back out..." another one put in, and I grimaced at the crude comment. I took a sip of my coffee and tried to look uninterested as the girl went on.

"Whenever I see him in the halls, I always sneak a little peek at that peach, and I know you do too..." she said in a naughty half-whisper. I glared at her then and gave an exaggerated cough, disturbing them. All three turned to look at me, eyebrows cocked haughtily. Women's minds were sometimes just as filthy as men's.

"Apparently he's from New York. He's not everyone's cup of tea, though. I heard he has a really bad temper. Annie took a run at him, but he dropped her after a little bit of mouth stuff," a third woman cut in, a pocket-sized brunette with a very interesting set of tits.

I assessed them curiously; they might have even been bigger than mine.

"Yeah, she told me about that too. But she also told me that he's gifted...extremely gifted..." the blond answered with a mischievous click of her tongue.

"Meaning?" the brunette asked eagerly, her eyes lighting up with lust.

"The New Yorker is well above average size..." the other woman clarified. I shook my head, bored with this superficial exchange. They clearly didn't know how to look any further than skin deep if that was how they talked about Neil. I'd been living with him for six months, and I knew that he wasn't just a good-looking body to ogle or a fantasy lay. He was so much more than that.

I enjoyed listening to him talk. He had a surprising breadth of knowledge, and I always learned something from our conversations.

At one point, he had pretty much hated me. Couldn't stand to be around me. But after I saved him and convinced him to give himself another chance, something had changed.

I had found him wasted outside of Blanco the night he found out John was his biological father. He was sitting on the ground just outside of the club, leaning against the crumbling wall and feeling sorry for himself. I couldn't leave him alone in that condition. So I suggested he go to Chicago with me right away. Professor Robinson had demonstrated enormous confidence in Neil, and he could use that to his advantage. It had been difficult to convince him at first. Eventually, I had to get him up and drag him back to my apartment, where I spent hours getting him to see reason.

If I had left him there in an angry fugue, maybe in the hands of the Krew, he would have self-destructed. He would have kept on drinking, and given the kinds of friends he ran with, maybe even started using drugs. He could have turned down a dark path and been lost forever.

Since then he had not magically transformed into some nice, friendly guy, but he had been willing to have me in his life.

I was thoughtful as I finished my coffee and tossed the paper cup into the trash. The chattering all around me had ceased, and all three women were staring at me, annoyed.

Oh, they *hated* me.

They knew I shared an apartment with the guy who had been the object of their collective desires for months, and they were envious. They assumed we were sleeping with each other, and that made them feel like I was competition. They were trying to challenge me, thinking they could turn his head with a little workplace flirtation.

Little did they know, Neil hated it when a woman came on too strong, and especially when one approached him shamelessly at work.

He was drawn to a challenge, to women who were intelligent and classy, like little Selene. The others were never going to get anything more than a one-time fuck from him.

I cleared my throat and walked over to the machine for another cup of coffee. Not for me but for my "gifted" roommate. I drummed my fingers on the counter as I waited for it to be ready. Finally, I grabbed the mug and went to the door, tossing a sultry glance over my shoulder at the trio as I left.

"Have a good one, fellow professionals," I said with a puffed-up smile. I was flaunting my ability to approach Neil whenever I wanted, and they knew it.

I strode confidently toward his office but froze mid-step when I spotted Logan, Chloe, and Dr. Keller walking away from his door looking abashed. I tried to flag them down, but by then they'd already made it to the elevators.

Sighing heavily, I knocked on the door and waited a couple seconds for Neil to tell me to come in. When I got no response, I pushed my way inside to make sure he was okay.

Neil was alone, sitting in his chair and staring out the big windows in consternation. Looking at him, I got the same topsy-turvy feeling in the pit of my stomach I had been getting every time I saw him these days. I tried to ignore it.

"Brought you some coffee." I moved efficiently over to him and couldn't help but look at his lush mouth.

I inhaled deeply, taking in the pleasant smell of his cologne. Neil got up out of his chair, his face shadowed with sadness. He rounded the desk and began to pace around the office anxiously. His elegant pants broke perfectly against his long legs and highlighted his firm ass.

I snorted to myself, forced to admit that my coworkers' raptures over his looks weren't exactly wrong.

"I just kicked them out. My brother, my sister, and..." He scrubbed a hand over his face, his white button-down stretching against his pumped biceps. I didn't understand what was happening to me—I couldn't quit staring at him. "John," he added in the barest whisper, like it cost him a great deal of effort.

I sat down on the edge of his desk and crossed my legs, giving him my undivided attention.

"You already know what I think about that. I've said all along that you shouldn't have cut them out of your life. William's a piece of shit, and he was trying to hurt you. The way you've reacted is only giving him what he wants." I tracked his masculine body stalking back and forth in front of me. One hand on his hip and the other massaging his anguished head. Neil loved his siblings; they were everything to him, but finding out about his biological father had made him surly and distrustful even with them.

He needed to work through that trauma if he ever wanted to open his heart to his family again.

"And what am I supposed to do?" He pinned my gaze with his luminous eyes. "Go back to my old life? Back to New York? Back to that house? I can't. Everything there would just be a reminder of what I was, who I've been for years, and all the shit I've been through, and…fuck! I just don't want to! I'm stable now. I'm doing better. I can't reconcile that past with the life I have now." He heaved a sigh, his chest rising and falling raggedly.

"You could try just giving your father a second chance and maybe let your siblings be a part of your new life? You can keep the past locked away but at least try to be open to the people you love," I answered cautiously. Neil watched me closely, and I melted when his eyes dropped to scrutinize my mouth.

"Why are you doing this?" he asked in a low voice. His tone was deep and pleasing to the ear. Devastatingly attractive. He took a few steps closer, looming over me.

"Doing what?" I lifted my face to look at him and took a moment to appreciate the lines of his face. They were finely drawn but also strong. His bright, piercing eyes gave me an unsettled feeling.

He was an angel with an ominous allure.

A demon of ethereal beauty.

"Helping me. You've been doing it right from the start, ever since you found me shit-faced outside that club…" He stopped himself at my genuine smile, which nevertheless made him cock his head to one side in confusion.

"Do you remember that kiss when we were kids?" I asked him.

"Of course, I remember," he answered seriously, giving me a tortured look. Once again, I had the almost painful urge to touch him, but I chose not to. If I had a little less self-control, I would have given him a hug.

"I do too. You were the person who showed me that I didn't have to be afraid to kiss someone. You showed me that a kiss was supposed to be an exchange of affection, not force or violation." For a moment, I was hypnotized by his lips and wondered what it would be like to feel them on me—to taste them again—after so long. But I knew that wasn't right. Neil had drawn a very clear boundary in his mind when it came to me, and he wasn't going to cross it. "We always avoided each other because of what we went through together, but I think we've also always supported each other too. I could kiss you because I knew that you were like me, so I wasn't ashamed. There was never any discomfort or embarrassment with you; I always felt like there was this thing that connected us. The terrible thing that happened to us also meant that we were... bonded," I said softly. Neil's face turned stormy. He didn't like hearing me talk like that, undoubtedly afraid that I'd develop some sort of emotional involvement with him. But if I did, I would have been able to deal with it myself.

He didn't say anything in answer. He just tossed his head like he was trying to shake off his worries. Then he gave me a hint of a tender smile.

Our lives had always been distinct, and after the incident, mostly separate, but it sometimes felt to me that our trajectories were two undulating lines that would never straighten out. Two lines that originated from the same point and were heading in the same direction.

"So don't ask me why I'm doing it, Neil. I am always here for you the way you have always been there for me. When we were children, when we were teenagers, and now that we're adults." I allowed myself to stroke the back of his hand, and he didn't reject my touch. I had never been much given to physical displays of affection, but this gesture was instinctive, impulsive, and, most of all, honest.

His skin was mostly smooth, rougher on his knuckles, and for all that his veins protruded in a show of strength, his fingers were long and slender. They were attractive hands, large and manly. The kind of hands that made you want them on your body, leaving their imprint in bruises and blushes.

"I should..." Neil cleared his throat and broke our contact, stepping back. "I should finish my work." He rubbed his eyebrow with his thumb and sighed uncomfortably. He seemed to be wrestling with something. He licked his lower lip and let out a sigh of frustration.

I stood motionless, staring at him, unable to move. My lower abdomen pulsed, and desire was starting to overtake my rational mind.

Shit.

I had to get out of that office.

I needed to get away from him as fast as humanly possible. ASAP.

I should have been able to retain at least a modicum of logical thought, but it was so hard when I saw how his eyes were locked on my thighs, which had been exposed by my position on the desk.

I held perfectly still, waiting to see what he'd do.

I didn't understand what was going on any more than he did. His stare heated, those golden eyes seeming to glow even brighter, and his breathing sped up slightly.

He looked at me carefully: at my hips and then up to my breasts and then my mouth, where he stopped. I held my breath; his stare felt like a touch.

Breathe. Breathe, Megan, I ordered myself.

Never before had I been so weak.

This was not the place to indulge in my desires. He was not the man to help me act out my lusty fantasies. I felt like a fool. A total idiot.

And all at once, I came back to myself.

"Yes... I also have to finish up a project." I hopped off the desk, the movement clumsy, and I was lucky that my wobbly legs held me up.

"Perfect, we can ride home together," he confirmed the way he always did, but this time, there was something different in his voice. Something dark and extremely erotic. I couldn't stand being so close to him a moment longer—my body was going up in flames.

I nodded with a strained smile and hurried awkwardly out of his office.

I spent the next few hours reviewing and editing projects for my mentor. Yet I had a feeling I'd not had in a long time, a disquieting heat, especially intense between my thighs.

How long had it been since I'd been sexually attracted to a man?

I didn't say a single word on the ride home. I didn't even look at Neil and tried to avoid getting drawn into any pervy banter with him. I also continued to muse on what it was about him that was so different from other men, about why I found myself so drawn to him.

Maybe I was just tired. Stressed out from work. A long, hot bath would probably take care of all my problems.

Yes, that was it. No need to worry.

"I'm wiped," I said as I walked into our apartment while Neil slipped off his nice coat and hung it up on the rack. Then he went straight for the refrigerator while I kicked off my heels by the door before collapsing into the soft cushions of the living room sofa. My butt really appreciated the cushy surface after sitting in an uncomfortable chair for hours on end.

"Want some wine?" His voice pulled me out of my considerations about my butt's workday, and I turned to give him a thumbs-up.

"Man, my ass is sore," I muttered as he handed me a wineglass. I sipped it with a contented sigh. Neil sat down next to me, his legs slightly splayed in his usual casually arrogant posture.

Sexy posture. Because every move he made was so incredibly fucking sexy.

"Women tell me I give a good massage. Want one?" he asked slyly, and I was relieved he could get back to joking after that visit from his family. He smiled mischievously at me, but I politely declined. Instead, I stood up and stretched my muscles before putting the empty wine glass back down on the coffee table in front of us.

"My butt requires a long bath and more comfortable clothes, not your groping hands, you perv." I walked away, confident that he would check out my ass the way he did every time I walked in front of him and went to my room for some fresh clothes and a little pampering.

After a relaxing hour in the tub, I wandered back into the living room wearing a T-shirt sans bra and my fuchsia thong. Neil wasn't there.

The heater in our apartment was broken, and our temperature choices were either sweltering or no heat at all, so Neil was now used to seeing me walk around the place half-naked. Just as I had gotten used to seeing his chiseled physique covered only by a pair of boxers. I went into the kitchen and pulled open the fridge to grab a bottle of water, already thinking about the book I was going to read in my downtime.

"You should really wear a bra." I jumped in surprise when I heard his voice right behind me. The bottle of water I was just about to drink from fell into the sink with a thud. I turned to look at him, though I would rather not have.

His golden eyes seemed to glow in the gloom of the kitchen.

I languidly appraised his body. The gleaming amber skin, broad shoulders, the half-moons of his pectorals, and his flat stomach that led into an inverted triangle shape that vanished into his black boxers. I dwelled for a moment on a tattoo decorating his left hip, thinking that I'd seen it on some other occasion.

He must have known what I was thinking because he gave me a smug smile that spoke directly to my pussy.

Shit.

"What are you looking at?" he asked, a hint of delight in his tone, and then he reached down with one hand to touch himself between his thighs. He cupped the bulge of his manhood underneath the black fabric. I gasped at the blatant move, realizing immediately he was trying to mess with me. He'd done it frequently in the last six months, but this time I wasn't sure that it was just a joke.

Neil was calculating, twisted, and an asshole.

A magnificent asshole with an angel's face and the devil's eyes. I'd always shut him down before, telling myself that I wasn't really attracted to him.

I could feel desire for men, but when I did and I tried to act on it, thoughts of Ryan often filled up my head.

"Would you rather it was one of your girlfriends standing here right now?" Neil went on, letting go of himself. He leaned back against the counter and watched me curiously. His self-confidence was overpowering. I totally got why girls couldn't resist him.

"Maybe..." I said, adopting a confident demeanor of my own. I wasn't going to allow myself to be cowed by him. I met and held his gaze, feeling an odd warmth spreading through my chest. "But you know I love anything that's got a soul," I reminded him, narrowing my eyes.

"And you think that I have a soul?" he asked. I could feel the sensuality rolling off him. Neil didn't even know how inherently erotic he was, and I liked that aspect of him. I liked it, and my body liked it too, so much so that I involuntarily arched my breasts forward, the nipples stiff and ready to be sucked.

"You saved me in that basement. I've always known you have a soul. A good, scrappy one, too," I confessed.

Something shifted in his eyes. Neil went stiff, and I could see the memories filling up his head. There was no longer any trace of teasing on his face.

Before he ran the way he usually did, I moved toward him. Neil stood up straight and tried to go, but I grabbed him by the forearm. He looked at me, bewildered, but I didn't know what I was doing any better than he did. I just wanted him to stop blaming himself.

"You didn't hurt me. I'm grateful to you; you stopped the worst of it," I whispered, rubbing his arm. Neil stared fixedly at the motion of my fingers, which slowly crept downward toward his wrist. I took his hand and brought it to my heart. He sucked in a breath when his palm came into contact with my breast, grazing my nipple.

"Megan…" he cautioned, but I just kept following my instincts. Covering his hand with mine, I guided him down to my stomach, but before I could get him to the place where I wanted him the most, he flinched away from me and stepped back in shock. "No. Fuck. No!" he exploded, looking at me like I wasn't even a person. "You know I like to mess with you; I do it all the time. That doesn't mean I'm actually going to screw you." He passed a hand over his face and stared at me in horror. "Were you… Were you actually going for it?" He cocked his head to one side.

"I was actually kinda trying to get you to go for it…" I chuckled, but he apparently didn't see the humor in the situation because he just scowled in annoyance.

"This isn't funny," he growled. "None of it is funny!"

I looked down then and saw beneath his boxers an erection the likes of which I'd rarely seen before.

Correction: had *never* seen before.

He looked in the direction of my stare, and when he saw his own body's reaction, he blanched. Instead of taking the opportunity to brag about his obvious endowment, Neil Miller seemed ashamed of it. Or like he was about to be sick.

"Looks like someone disagrees with you," I said teasingly, tapping my finger against my chin. The look he gave me was so cold that I actually shivered.

"What the hell is wrong with you?" he exploded in anger. "You want to get fucked? Go find someone else. I'm not going to do the job for you. That would be totally fucking insane," he added, a little more hesitantly. He took another step back and shook his head as if to clear it. "You're not even my type," he sneered, though the flickers of heat in his eyes suggested otherwise.

Neil was working hard to keep his impulses under control.

"Why are you still letting Kimberly make decisions for you?" I asked challengingly. "Nothing happened that day in the basement. We were children, and nothing happened because you saved us. We're both adults now. If you want to touch me, if you want to kiss me, if you want to fuck me, you can!" I opened my arms wide, egging him on. Neil furrowed his brow in confusion. "If you can tell me no because you honestly don't want me, then I won't say a thing." I advanced on him, and he stepped back until he hit the edge of the kitchen counter behind him. "So reject me, Neil. Tell me you aren't attracted to me. But don't lie to yourself; don't give in to Kim. Don't let her have that power over you." I lifted my face to look up at him finding him bewildered, to say the least. There was a lost look in his eyes, and his mouth had fallen slightly open. He was panting.

"No," he whispered, grasping on to the edge of the counter behind him like he needed some sort of anchor to resist me and suppress everything he was feeling. "I said no," he repeated in exasperation.

"Yes, Neil. Yes. For fuck's sake. Free yourself from this senseless, poisonous belief you have about me. I am just a woman who has experienced the same kind of thing that you have, that's all. I hate it when you look at me like I'm some other kind of *thing*, like I'm something wrong. I hate it when you connect me with Kimberly and your memories. And I hate it when you call me Head Case because it's not crazy to see reality for what it is. And the truth is, we—" But before I could say aloud that we were drawn to each other, Neil fell upon my mouth with unstoppable force. His tongue urged me to open my lips to him, and as he invaded me completely, I felt his clean flavor mixed with smoke on my tongue. It was so intensely erotic that I groaned. His hands cupped my breasts, which had grown heavy with want, and he fondled them as he continued kissing me.

It was earth-shaking.

We staggered back against the kitchen island. It wasn't just a kiss; it was pure sex.

He rubbed my hips and moved down to my ass cheeks, squeezing them hard as he ground his erection against my lower abdomen.

I felt the most marvelous chill run down my spine.

I let out a whine of pleasure, and Neil pulled away abruptly, leaving my mouth swollen and sore.

He stared at me in shock.

"Don't tell me you're still thinking about it," I panted. "Stop giving that woman more power over you. I'm not proposing marriage here; this will just be sex for me too," I reassured him, my smile genuine.

We both wanted the same thing: to fuck each other.

Something ignited inside him, his body champing at the bit to let loose the desire that burned inside him.

He was still trying to fight it, to push it down, but then his shoulders slumped and he surrendered fully.

"I'm not the gentle type," he warned, resting his hands to either side of my hips on the kitchen counter.

"And I don't like being underneath anyone," I shot back, my tone amused. He frowned slightly as he gave my curves a long, lewd look.

"Me neither," he admitted. "So?" he asked, and the register of his voice only whipped up the storm inside me further. All at once, I used my forearms to lift myself up and sat on the kitchen island and wrapped my legs around his hips, pulling him into me. I hissed when I felt his massive dick between my thighs.

"So we compromise. Find a position that's comfortable for both of us. Equal height, equal decision-making power. I don't like being submissive," I told him clearly, leaning forward to kiss his neck. "So don't even think about it," I added, sucking his earlobe into my mouth. The vibration of his deep chuckle spread through my chest.

"Whatever you say, Head Case. But we're not doing it here." He gathered me into his arms and lifted me up. I let out a cry of surprise as he walked us briskly toward my room. I moved against him with every step, my nipples rubbing up against his chest, drawing the tension inside me unbearably tight.

"How many men have you been with?" he asked as he kicked the door open.

"Not many, just two. After Ryan," I admitted easily. I didn't have a high body count for someone my age, not with men or women, because, despite what my current circumstances would suggest, I wasn't promiscuous.

"And how long has it been since you fucked a man?" he went on.

"About a year," I answered. The memories of Ryan and what he'd done to me had limited me. I was limited by my fears, by my inability to trust, and by the pain that I still felt deep in my chest. The same pain that had me tossing and turning through the night with terrible nightmares. For all those reasons, I couldn't bring myself to have sex with just anyone.

"Good," was all he said as he slowly laid me out on the bed. I'd just told him I didn't like being in a submissive position, but Neil was clearly used to something different. So before he could stretch out above me, I pushed him over until his shoulders hit the mattress. He gave me a look of surprise but didn't have time to object before I was clambering on top of him. I peeled off my shirt as I straddled him, tossing it onto the floor. His stare turned hungry as he looked at my bare breasts and the tattoo right between them along my sternum.

He lifted a curious hand to stroke it and mapped the lines with his fingers.

"It's a black butterfly," I said, anticipating his question. "It symbolizes phobias, insecurities. Things we can't control. Things we'll never be free from." I leaned down to pepper his jaw with kisses. He wasn't fully relaxed; his head was still somewhere else. I began to move against him, stoking his desire. His breathing sped up, but he was still too controlled. He put his hands on my hips, and I couldn't tell if it was a weak attempt to stop me or a silent request to keep going.

"I want you now..." I whispered, stopping for just a moment to slide his boxers down his legs and throw them off the bed.

When I was finally able to admire his nude body in full, it took my breath away.

I dazedly stroked his neck, his pectorals, and down his abs, my hungry eyes locked on the large cock standing tall between us. I panted as I glided my hand over him, making sure it wasn't some sort of dream. His body reacted to my touch; the tip of his penis became moist, and his balls contracted, giving me a little burst of pleasure.

"Satisfied?" he murmured as he sat up to pull me against him. He stroked my back and then squeezed my ass, urging me to move. I couldn't speak—for the first time, it was really hitting me what was about to happen, and the brief flicker of insecurity made me falter.

I would have preferred a little foreplay to cut the tension, but

Neil apparently didn't like to waste time. He bent his head over my breasts and gently bit my nipple before sucking it to soothe the burn as I arched into him. He was aggressive, wild. He wasn't going to stop.

I had started this, and now he was making it clear to me that there was no backing down.

And I longed for it. I had forgotten the euphoria that came with sharing this kind of intimacy with another person.

With him, I wasn't thinking about Ryan. I wasn't thinking about the torn and tattered little girl who lived in my memories.

I stopped thinking entirely the moment his tongue moved along the contours of my tattoo before circling languidly around my areola. I dug a hand into his hair and pressed him harder against my chest. He pushed my thong to one side until he could feel on his fingertips how aroused I was. I had never felt so engaged with a man; my body seemed to accept him without reservation.

Without revulsion, without nausea.

Pleasurable shivers ran down my spine as he slipped two fingers inside me and moved them with practiced wickedness. I squeezed my eyes shut and gave myself over to him, moaning weakly.

Then, he stopped touching me and took advantage of my sudden physical weakness to reverse our positions. I found myself with my back against the mattress and him above me, his hips slotted in between my thighs.

"I told you—"

"I'm not letting you be on top. You can dominate other guys, but not me." The smell of his shower gel made me feel drunk, and for some reason it made me want to lick his warm, smooth skin.

I caressed his back, moving down to his rock-hard butt cheeks. I groaned in approval, and he smirked, kissing every inch of skin he could find. He started with my throat and moved down between my breasts before sinking all the way to my stomach. He brushed against my navel, and I waited impatiently for him to get to the out-of-control fire that was blazing just below, but instead he stopped. He held still, staring at the thong I was still wearing, and I had no idea what the hell he was thinking about.

I was fighting for my life while Neil seemed entirely too cool and rational.

"What's going on?" I gasped out.

Was he seriously going to leave me frustrated, dying to feel his tongue in the place I needed it the most?

I let out a whine of disappointment, and Neil blinked rapidly before parting my knees and pulling my panties off with an angry growl.

He stared at me—stared at all of me—and I swallowed hard, a little embarrassed. I wasn't the blushing kind, but the way he was looking at me was uncomfortable. There was conflict in his eyes, desire and anger as well.

All at once, his thoughtful expression vanished, and he lowered himself onto me.

I would have liked to feel his tongue between my thighs, but Neil made up for it by rubbing his tip against my clit in slow, intense movements.

Feeling him so big and hard against me was brain-scrambling.

"I don't know if I can come," he muttered into my ear, but I was too dazed to speak. His face was awe-inspiring; I couldn't stop looking at it. His lips were wet, his eyes gleaming with want. I was ready, eager to welcome him inside. He could feel it, and as I grasped his hips, he bit down on my neck and plunged into me with one strong, hard thrust.

I screamed with all my might.

For a second, I was afraid my flesh had torn, and I let out a groan of commingled pain and pleasure. Unconsciously, I lifted my pelvis to make it easier for him to get deeper in. I had thought I was prepared for his size, but I absolutely was not. He filled me so completely, and I struggled for air.

Tensing up only would have made things more difficult, so I forced myself to relax against the mattress.

"Fuck, you're tight..." he whispered as I felt my body struggle to accommodate his invading presence. My head fell back and my nails dug into his sides.

He let out a groan full of some weird animal satisfaction.

Then he paused when he felt my breath catch and looked me in the eye to see if I was okay. I could feel my inner muscles burning, but I was perfectly alright. The last thing I wanted him to do was stop before I got mine.

"Still sure?" he asked hesitantly, and by way of response, I seized his mouth and kissed him emphatically, with passion and longing, and moved my body experimentally beneath him, trying to figure out what he liked.

I wanted to know whether he liked it slow and intense or wild and hard.

I had my doubts because Neil was pretty silent, rarely moaning or making any sound at all.

He let out a roar, however, when I moved more boldly, when I bit down on his shoulder or scraped my nails down his back.

I groped his ass, urging him to move faster, and got a particularly satisfying rough moan of approval for my trouble.

He was also trying to read my reactions to see how far he could go with me.

"Yes, like that... Don't hold back...you're magnificent," I slurred, scraping my nails against his shoulders. He would have some pretty obvious marks the next morning. He began thrusting harder, angling himself so he hit my clit with each stroke. His powerful back contracted with each thrust of his hips.

And I worshipped him with my whole self, touched him with all the passion that I had, and whispered to him that I trusted him.

I trusted Neil as I'd never trusted anyone else before.

"I didn't put a condom on," he murmured, his strokes speeding up. I had noticed that as well as the fact that it appeared to be unusual. He always had a full pack of condoms in his room and on his person, so I figured he always used them.

"Don't worry, I'm on the pill," I managed to gasp out.

"But I didn't ask you." He paused. He was struggling to think clearly and looked at me in confusion. "I didn't ask you. I got carried away, and that's not like me. I always wear them with everyone except..." His pupils dilated. His thoughts raced away from the room, chasing some other woman.

Something had changed. Neil was closing in on himself again.

He remained suspended with his weight on his elbows. His hard cock was still inside me, still aroused, but the emotion wasn't there anymore. I rubbed his shoulders reassuringly as he gasped for breath. Then I bucked up against him, feeling a stab of pleasure in the bottom of my stomach.

But Neil just continued staring seriously at me, lost in thought, no longer concerned about picking up where he'd left off.

I wasn't going to be able to stand it much longer.

I couldn't stay unaffected with his chest pressing down on me and my thighs compressing his hips.

"So now it's not Kim but Selene that you're allowing to rule you? You don't have a choice, Neil. Either you fight your torments or you lose your mind." I caressed his jaw, and he went stiff. I breathed in the smell of him that had mixed with my own and sucked in a breath when, in one decisive movement of his hips, he pushed himself back inside me. Slowly, he penetrated me fully, squeezing his eyes shut to drink in my moan of pleasure. Then he put his hot mouth against my ear and inhaled.

"Use me. I want you to enjoy this, Megan. Let this be something completely different from what you went through with Ryan..." he whispered, his voice almost yearning.

He began to move again, and this time, he seemed determined not to stop. I was fully in his power, and I had never felt more naked.

It felt like my soul had been stripped. Of everything, even my fears. I cried out as he pounded me ferociously. A burst of heat lit my skin aflame, my back bowed upward, and my knees trembled as they struggled to hold up against the brutal impacts of his pelvis.

He'd quit holding back, just as I'd asked him to do.

It was a forbidden connection that we had, filled with transgression and the unspoken weight of memories.

The visual of him sweating, his muscles flexing, and his skin gleaming left me speechless.

"Neil..." I was going to come if he continued at that pace, and he just pounded relentlessly, strategically into me, fully aware of how aroused I was. I grew wetter and wetter, rocked with profound shivers, my throat ragged from screams of delight.

Neil was about to shatter me into a thousand pieces but also to reinvent me, to rearrange me, to remake me, and to put all my pain to rest.

"This is sex, Megan. Not what those sick fucks forced on us..." he whispered as I let loose another uncontrollable cry. Tears stung my eyes. I blinked them away and smiled at him. Neil watched me intently, trying to read my reaction, and I ended our exchange of stares with a kiss.

I wanted more from him. An emotional connection that made words unnecessary.

I knew Neil was the right man for this and knew that he would understand me.

He kissed me back, breathing hard through his nose, and I grabbed his hair, pulling him against me. I was no longer in control of my body; I couldn't stop wanting him.

When he moved even faster, my mind went hazy with pleasure,

fully subsumed by our all-consuming madness. And then, with a liberating shout, I exploded beneath him.

He continued delving into me, and I could feel him laughing into the bend of my neck, delighted to have given me an orgasm.

The first one I'd ever had with a male partner.

That realization gave way to an almost suffocating joy that I expressed with an involuntary sob. I covered my face with both hands, embarrassed by the unexpected tears, and Neil hovered over me, panting and sweating.

"Everything okay?" he asked in concern. I just nodded, trying to hide my weakness from him. But he was suspicious, pulling my hands away from my face to look closely and make sure. His eyes softened, and he wiped a tear from my cheek with his thumb, fully aware that he was the source of these new and wonderful emotions.

"Have you never climaxed with the other men?" he guessed. My heart was pounding in my chest. I wasn't accustomed to spilling my secrets, but I had lowered all my defenses to him.

I shook my head. It had never happened with the others because I hadn't been able to trust them. I never felt entirely safe when I was with a man before, nor did I feel certain of their good souls.

Just before we started, I'd told him that I love anything with a soul, but I'd forgotten to specify that the soul also had to be a pure, honest, and noble one.

Like his.

It occurred to me then that he'd made sure I was fulfilled but hadn't worried about his own pleasure. I knew that Neil hadn't come yet, and I wanted to give him that. I didn't say anything, just moved my pelvis, urging him to continue.

He watched me first in confusion, then with understanding as he began to drive more powerfully into me.

I gave myself over to his storm, letting myself be struck by his lightning. He caressed my thigh with one hand, and I squeezed him between my knees to show him that it was all okay. He could take from me what he'd already given.

I was worn-out from his strong, powerful thrusts when I finally heard that long, profoundly male groan of release. He was right at the edge.

All at once, he pulled out of me and orgasmed on me, painting my stomach with long, hot streams.

I'd thought he might come inside me, but I supposed he wasn't quite ready to share that kind of intimacy. For someone like him, it would have been a massive show of trust, and, knowing how guarded he was, I knew he would need time before he could let go like that.

He collapsed on me and pressed his forehead against the pillow as he tried to catch his breath. I could feel his heart pounding as I was crushed beneath his weight, unable to move or breathe. I felt like I'd been split in two, completely shattered, and yet it was the best experience I'd ever had with a man in my entire life.

"Thanks," I murmured, incredulous, exhausted, and satiated. A mild numbness spread throughout my muscles, and my eyelids drooped. My body had just released an enormous amount of the suffering, fear, and pain that had kept me tied down for far too long. Neil rolled over next to me, and I felt the cold as he put distance between us. I turned my head to look at him. He laid completely still, staring up at the ceiling. His plush lips were red; droplets of sweat had collected between his pecs. His cock was still stiff and reddened.

All scrambled up and more than a bit wild.

"Thanks for what?" he asked abruptly, his voice lazy, his muscles relaxed.

"For making me reevaluate sex with men." I smiled. He turned, his eyebrows drawn together. "Relax, I'm not going to ask you to be my boyfriend," I reassured him. Neil did not look at all peaceful, though. There was still something on his mind.

"You've always kept me at arm's length these last six months. What made you decide to give in today?" He aimed his golden eyes at me. The thin light filtering in through the window highlighted the layer of sweat on his forehead and cheekbones. I wanted to touch him again and seek out some of his warmth, but I didn't want to make him uncomfortable.

"Because I realized that I could trust you. It was never easy being with a man after the assault I endured," I admitted plainly. I was still reckoning with the psychological fallout from that cursed time with Ryan, which had cut so deeply into my soul. I'd built a suit of steel armor around myself to protect me from everyone else.

I had always thought of myself as a strong, brave person, but like every human being, I had my vulnerabilities and my fears. I hadn't thought I was capable of feeling new emotions. My heart had been worn-out and drained for so long that I thought it would be impossible for me to experience true physical and emotional understanding with another person, man or woman.

"You trust me?" Neil repeated, sounding skeptical. I trusted him completely. He was the one who saved me when I was a child. Because of him, I'd never been filmed by Kim. Because of him, the police arrested her and Ryan and put a stop to their cruelty.

"Yes. You're the only person I've ever completely trusted," I whispered.

His eyes were still locked on mine. It seemed to me that the gold of his eyes always turned more liquid when he was disbelieving or amazed by something. Neil wasn't much of a talker and not given to expressing his emotions, but I knew he felt things deeply. Even if he did keep them a secret from everyone, himself included.

"I need to... I have to go back to my room." He stood up, proudly and gloriously naked, and I admired the way his ass muscles contracted with every step as he made his way to the door.

"Miller," I called out after him. He turned and gave me a look. "You have an outstanding ass. And the front's not bad either. But aren't you forgetting something?" Neil frowned, confused, and I pointed at his boxers abandoned on the floor. He rolled his eyes at me.

"Afraid you won't be able to resist the urge to jump my bones?" He shot me an enigmatic smile as he clutched his boxers in one hand, still continuing to display his entire body with all its power and allure.

"Well, I am now that I'm aware of your enormous...*potential*," I admitted with a shrug. "By the way, congrats on the royal scepter, your majesty."

He shook his head and went back to the door.

"Thanks, Head Case. You can check out its magnificence any time you like." He winked before exiting the room and leaving me alone.

I hadn't expected him to stay and sleep through the night with me, nor did he seem like the type to cuddle in the afterglow.

That wasn't Neil.

I collapsed back on my pillow, thinking about what had just happened.

I could smell both of us on the rumpled blankets, his warmth and mine, his clean smell mixed with my own. But the little half-smile faded from my lips when I thought back on the moment when Neil's face had darkened at hearing Selene's name.

I never asked him about her. We never spoke of her because every time I'd so much as alluded to her, he'd broken something. I wasn't entirely sure that he wasn't thinking about her during sex. In fact, I was sure that's what he was doing with the other girls. Why else would they all look like photocopies of Selene?

I didn't look like her, though.

I mused on that for a long time: I bore no resemblance to the girl.

Did that mean that he hadn't been thinking of her when he was with me?

I huffed and decided to go to sleep. Thinking too much would only get me keyed up and anxious. I pulled the sheet over myself, putting off showering until the morning. Oddly enough, it didn't bother me to have a man's smell on my skin or even traces of his semen on my stomach.

Unsettled by the new things I apparently accepted now, I shut my eyes and drifted off to sleep.

....

The sun's rays filtered through the room's large windows to touch my skin. I opened my eyes slowly, remembering what had happened the night before. The experience felt almost dreamlike, but when I looked down at my naked body and caught a whiff of Neil's scent still on me, I knew it had all been real.

I got out of bed slowly, lowering my feet to the floor and grimacing in pain when I felt the ghost of his presence between my legs.

I dragged myself to the bathroom like a plane crash survivor and skipped right by my reflection in favor of a relaxing shower.

My muscles were sore. Even some I hadn't known I had.

I babied my body, gently massaging all the aching parts.

I spent about half an hour under the warm spray of the shower, hoping to claw back some of my physical strength and mental clarity, which Neil had apparently completely drained from me in one night. I hadn't realized getting it on with him would be such a singular experience. My stomach tightened and my legs went wobbly at the memory of having him, even if it was only once. I'd held out against his charm, his predator's smile, his ruthless seduction, and his teasing moves for months, but finally, I succumbed. And I couldn't find it in me to regret it.

After my shower, I put on a pair of black leggings and a matching top and went to the kitchen. My heart did a little flip and landed in my stomach when I saw him there. He was sitting at the kitchen island in just his sweatpants, smoking a cigarette.

His golden eyes, which had been immersed in the phone he had clasped in one hand, looked up to scrutinize my face. The grim glint in his eye took my breath away. He looked confused but also furious. The flickers of rage I saw in his gaze cut into my like fiery blades.

"What's up?" I asked, moving toward him. "As you can see, I'm not wearing any of your clothes today, so no need to bust my chops about it," I offered.

"Sit down," he demanded, exhaling cigarette smoke. His voice had never sounded so hard or intense as it did in that moment. I'd seen him raging and furious before and though I had always been a strong woman, the feeling of impending danger put me on my guard.

"Are you freaking out? Is this about last night? Look, nothing happened for me, it was just—" He chuckled low, searing me with his gaze. Truthfully, it hadn't been just sex for me; it had been a lot more. But I couldn't tell him that.

"You're still in touch with Dr. Keller, apparently. I'd like to know why he's asking you about me, and, more importantly..." He paused, forcibly grinding out his butt in the black ashtray on the kitchen island. Then he stood up, revealing himself in all his glory, and my breath caught. "How long has he been ordering you to manipulate me?" he asked with a derisive sneer. Neil looked deep into my eyes, like he was trying to probe my soul and draw forth all my insecurities. A chill ran down my spine.

Shit.

"Di-did you read my text messages? That's a violation of my privacy, you know?" was all I could manage; I couldn't think clearly. Neil stalked toward me, and my body went up in flames; I trembled with every step he took.

"Don't give me that bullshit. You left your phone here in the kitchen, and he called you this morning. I didn't answer, but, yeah, I looked at your messages. And, what do you know? All of them are about me." He slapped the phone into my open palm as I watched, dismayed. The screen was open to a long text chain between me and my psychiatrist. "Why the fuck did he ask you to get close to me and keep tabs on me? Did you also know all along that liar was my father?" he raged, and I stared at his face, twisted in anger.

"I didn't know Dr. Keller was your father until you told me. He just asked me to be there for you and to encourage you to go back to therapy because he thinks you're a good kid." I stared into his eyes, trying to show him how sincere I was.

"Is that why you were always showing up? The pool house, the clinic, at school...because he asked you to do it?" he guessed, and I was hit with a wave of his hot breath, smelling of smoke and coffee. "You were lying to me too. Just like everyone else..." He grabbed my arm impulsively, and in his rage, he pulled me painfully toward him.

I put a hand on his wrist, trying to claw his hand away.

"Neil, you're hurting me. Let go." I tried to twist away, but his shadowed gaze kept me pinned to the spot, and I felt a stab of fear in the pit of my stomach.

"I don't fucking trust anyone anymore. You were the only person I shared any part of my life with for these past few months, and you...you agreed to keep an eye on me for him? Was that the deal?" he went on wrathfully, his naked chest heaving with his ragged breath. I needed to find some way to calm him down before it was too late.

"I didn't know he was your father. You have to believe me," I said again, chagrined. "He just wanted me to support you as a friend. That's it. I thought it was kind of a weird request too, but John has always been good to me and kind, and he's a great therapist. I had no idea that he was keeping a secret like that," I explained. His eyes narrowed to slits as he evaluated my answer.

"Megan, if you are lying to me..." he tightened his fingers around my arm for emphasis.

"I'm not lying to you. I swear it." Neil was the last person I'd ever lie to. For six fucking months, I'd been suppressing feelings and nullifying my emotions, but everything had changed in one night. It hurt to think of him not trusting me. "Honestly. I wouldn't do that." I exhaled against his full lips.

We were so close; all I'd have to do was lean forward a little, and I'd be kissing him.

That was, in fact, what my body had been screaming at me to do for the past few minutes.

Neil released me with an anguished sigh.

"I would never hurt you. Whatever your relationship with John, that has nothing to do with me," I went on. I rubbed my arm where it had been crushed in his grip and inched closer to him. Neil stood motionless, staring at me. At my every movement and facial expression. He was studying me, scrutinizing me thoroughly, and a shiver of apprehension ran down my spine, raising goosebumps all over my skin. Neil noticed it, his eyes moving over my bare arms.

"Megan," he said, and I raised my head to look at him. I locked eyes with him, hoping to reassure him, but he remained unmoved. "I hope for your sake that you aren't lying to me. Because, if you are, you're out of my life for good," he said firmly, his gaze unyielding. His eyes had an unsettling gleam, and there was no more anger in his face, just a dangerous sort of determination.

I chewed my lower lip, feeling weak. I felt like I couldn't trust my body anymore. It went up in flames whenever he got near me.

I should have been afraid, should have run away, but instead I chose to follow my instincts. The same instincts that had been tormenting me internally since I spotted him sitting on that stool.

"Neil…" My voice was warm, hoarse, and frustratingly aroused. He frowned. I broke the unbearable tension between us by standing up on my tiptoes to kiss him.

I expected him to do something, to shove me away or yell at me, but none of that happened.

For a man who valued control so much, Neil seemed, for once, unable to keep a lid on his emotions. He was becoming vulnerable, yielding with me. I used my tongue to urge him to indulge me and groaned when he, unable to pull away from my kiss, bit down hard on my lip. I refused to give up and boldly demanded his reciprocity.

Eventually he let his instincts take the lead and surrendered.

Kissing him was unlike anything I'd ever experienced before—I couldn't help myself.

I stroked his hard chest and clasped him around the waist to pull him closer to me, to feel his hard-on exactly where I wanted it. He growled in frustration as he gave in to the kiss, but his body told me clearly that he wanted me.

The desire grew overwhelming, and I pushed him down onto the sofa. I situated myself astride his lap and looped my arms around his neck. I ran my hands through his hair, so soft under my fingertips. My nipples were so stiff that they made just the right kind of friction against my tank top. His clean smell overwhelmed me.

"You really are a bitch." He reached down to grope my ass cheeks. I gasped for breath as he gave me more rough kisses.

He had taken control once again.

"Never said I wasn't," I answered, my voice contorted with longing. I was already so wet for him, eager to belong to him again. "And you want me just as much as I want you. I see that now, Miller." A guttural moan of profound pleasure rose up from his throat, my pussy clenched, and I dug my nails into him desperately. It was a move that drove him wild. He sucked in a breath and bit my lower lip until it bled, tearing my tank top roughly from my body. He stripped me of everything, not just my clothes but also my reason and common sense.

Why was he the only one who affected me like this?

Why did my arousal go through the roof with him?
Why had I never really been drawn to anyone like him before?
Why did I thrill at the idea of being his again?
All my inhibitions were gone; I was no longer myself.
I became a different woman.
And, as scary and illogical as it was, I knew we both needed what was happening.
We were profoundly troubled. Wounded.
Stained.
Alike…
But, above all, inexplicably entwined.

24

"Tinkerbell's soul had wandered deep inside me."

NEIL

There are two kinds of filth: the kind that other people hurl at you and the kind that grows inside you.

The second kind is the one that doesn't wash away.

It's something you bear on your skin; it stays with you for your whole life long.

It stays in your soul.

It flows in your blood.

The only time I ever felt clean was with Tinkerbell.

Never with anyone else.

No other embrace had the same warmth. No other kiss had the same sweetness.

Now more than ever, I was confident that no one else would have the same power she did.

Tinkerbell's soul had wandered deep inside me, and no amount of time or other pairs of blue eyes or any sort of fucking could have erased what Babygirl was to me.

And now I'd proved that by hitting rock bottom and succumbing to the one woman I swore I'd never touch: Megan.

I didn't know whether to feel like more of a piece of shit for using her up and tossing her aside or for deluding myself for the past six months.

Yes, the biggest ass-kicking was the one I'd delivered to myself.

Everything had been so clean and clear when I'd fallen into temptation with my roommate. I did everything I could to relive the past, to shrink the distance between me and Babygirl's ocean eyes. I had tried as hard as I could to imagine Selene's body beneath me instead of Megan's.

I tried to replace her orange blossom scent with one of coconut.

That's why I'd gone even further.

That's why I'd forgotten the condom.

That was why it felt so tight, why I liked it so much, why I... why I...

For her.

Only for my Babygirl, who I imagined when I could not touch her. Who I saw over and over again in each one of them.

Who I could sense all around me but would flee the moment I tried to grasp her with my hands.

I'd always thought it would feel different with Megan because we were tied together so deeply by our cursed past and the cruelties of fate. But, though I definitely felt an undeniable connection with her, it wasn't comparable to what I felt with Selene.

No, it didn't stretch that high. Didn't tunnel so far in or dive down that deep.

It didn't hurt as much. It wasn't all-consuming.

It didn't plumb the void I wanted to fill with kisses from Tinkerbell's magnificent lips.

It did not achieve the sensual delights of her small, delectable hands, which I longed to feel on me again. They were the only ones capable of washing away the filth and of touching my soul.

"Shit!" I snapped in frustration as I struggled to work on a project I wasn't processing the first fucking thing about. Everything fell apart after I gave in to Megan. I had been fine at first; I'd been screwing anonymous strangers, and it had been going great. Then, because of her, I found myself in the eye of a bewildering storm.

I'd almost done it again, though, right there on the couch the next morning after we had an argument. But then one fateful slip-up saved me from making the same mistake again.

I'd whispered a name. It wasn't hers...

I'd thought it would never happen. That name that I always kept on the tip of my tongue had wriggled its way to freedom on a whisper. It was a whisper that had been waiting too long to burst forth into the world because the other women were not enough. I needed Babygirl's color, the shape of her, her words, and her feelings.

I needed my Tinkerbell to fly me away from reality.

"Coffee?" The sound of Megan's voice drew my attention to her smiling face. I had no idea how she could be so good-humored after what we'd done. She shut the door to my mentor's office and walked briskly toward me. Her black outfit was sleek and sophisticated, but her prominent curves no longer had the same effect upon me. I'd sated myself on them, and my hunger had vanished, like it had done with all the other women.

Except for Selene.

The more I tasted her skin, the more I craved her.

The more I kissed her, the hungrier I became.

The more I pushed inside her, the more I wanted to stay there.

Because that was where I belonged—my Neverland.

Did I have to fuck Megan to figure that out? Maybe.

I convinced myself that I only thought about Selene when I was in the others because we lacked an intellectual connection. But that was something that I had with Megan, and so, like the asshole that I was, I decided to test myself with her. I wanted to see if it was possible that I was deluding myself about the feelings I'd shared with Babygirl, but I was wrong. Even the woman I'd thought of as such an imposing presence that she would obliterate the memory of Babygirl had come to nothing.

It didn't have anything to do with physical attraction or intellectual understanding. It wasn't about shared history or the abuse we'd both suffered. I simply needed my Pearl to find myself.

"Thanks," I answered, trying to make the moment less uncomfortable.

Megan set the steaming mug down on my desk, licked her lips nervously, and sighed as she tucked a bit of black hair behind her ear. It had been just as much of a mistake for her as it had been for me.

I could read her; her green eyes couldn't hide anything from me.

We shared an apartment; there was no way to go on like nothing had happened, but at the same time, she could feel me growing distant. I didn't touch her anymore or tease her with sexual innuendos or dirty jokes.

"No problem. Still working? How's it going?" Her voice was even.

"Not great. I don't get a fucking thing about this," I admitted with a snort. I sat up from the suddenly uncomfortable desk chair and grabbed my coffee, walking over to the big glass windows that offered a panoramic view of Chicago.

All I ever did was fall on my ass and get back on my feet only to stumble once again. I never got it right.

I felt like a ship adrift at sea with no compass.

I didn't know what choices to make. I didn't know where to go or who I could talk to—who I could trust.

"You need to stop blaming yourself about stuff that's not your fault." Megan broke the silence, moving closer to me. I could smell her perfume, and it was pleasant, but it didn't stir me like it had before. "What happened between us was something that I let happen," she went on. She looked calm, but I knew that she wasn't really. She'd been walking around with a wounded look lately and getting lost in thought. Proof that she'd been hurt by my careless attitude. After all, I was the prick who fucked her and called her by another woman's name and thereby ruined everything, our friendship most of all. If "friendship" was, indeed, what it could be called.

"I never wanted to use you. I know you don't deserve that. I know what you've been through." I squeezed the coffee cup tightly before tossing it intact into the trash can. I was still nauseated by the same poison that had been killing me for days.

"Look, I already told you what I think, Neil," she murmured. I stared blankly out the window at the sky. It was a sky I didn't even recognize anymore, like I didn't belong on this world beneath it. "I really think you should try again with your siblings. And with John and with..." Her long fingers grazed my shoulder, and I sucked in a breath. Just a few days before, her nails had been digging passionately into my flesh like she was trying to tear my back open. Yet now I flinched, bothered by her touch. She drew back her arm and cleared her throat before continuing. "And with her too. With Selene. You're not going to be able to replace her with someone else. And, if having sex with me was another test to see if you could... well, then I guess it served a purpose, at least. Forget about what her mother said; forget about the right thing to do. Let her make the choice about what's best for her..." I turned abruptly, expecting to be hit with Megan's disdain, but instead, I was surprised to find her smiling. It was a slightly strained smile but a genuine one, the first I'd gotten after days of the frosty emotional distance I'd selfishly shown her.

"You don't know her. Selene can't think clearly about me. She's completely incapable of making sensible choices because she's blinded by—"

"By love," she supplied. "She's just in love. That's it." She smiled again, and I stiffened up. I wasn't sure what made me more uncomfortable: Selene's corrosive feelings for me or this tender behavior from Megan.

"I don't deserve your smiles. There's no use trying to bullshit about us. I know you're disappointed. I know you feel used. I could apologize to you and tell you how sorry I am, but it wouldn't fix anything, and we both know that." I stared down into her eyes, using my height to loom over her. Despite her sky-high heels, she still had to look up at me, blinking thoughtfully. I looked at her sensuous mouth, but I didn't feel that shiver of arousal that I'd been feeling for the past six months. All I'd really felt for her was fucking curiosity. I wanted to see if I could move on with someone like her. I wanted to see what it felt like to be with someone so similar to myself. Megan wasn't like the other women, and she never had been, but she wasn't my Babygirl either.

I had used her to figure out what kind of connection we had and if it could possibly be stronger than the memory of Selene. If it could make me forget about the smell of coconut and a pair of crystalline eyes.

Because she was the only one who ever felt like mine.

And I had always felt like hers.

Megan's eyes were full of things unspoken, hidden questions, and shattered dreams. I was so good at fooling and hurting any person who got close to my twisted, chaotic brain.

"An apology is not what I want from you. I just want to go back to the way we were before. I never asked for any feelings from you or a relationship. I never wanted to be anyone's replacement. You have enough problems, Miller. I don't want you beating yourself up over this on top of everything else." She breathed in deep and moved closer to me. She should have hated me—she should have slapped me in the face—but she didn't look like she intended to do any of that. "We're adults, and we're responsible for our own choices. I take full responsibility for my actions. I just want you to be okay. I want you to be happy with the people you love."

Her maturity was shocking, as were her green eyes staring steadily up at me like I'd never touched her while picturing someone else. Like I hadn't come on to her for months specifically to make her crazy over me. Like I'd never used her to learn about myself and analyze the depthless hell I'd fallen into.

"I have work to do," I muttered.

I really didn't want to talk to her about what I'd felt after sending my siblings away or when John had shown me his tattoo. I didn't want to admit to her my longing to go back in time to the day before graduation when I was with Babygirl. Her little body clinging to me, one leg entwined with mine, her small nose pressed close to my chest.

I liked that inexplicable *us*.

The moment when I was inside her and she was also inside me and the whole world became nothing more than a sheet of paper that we crumpled up and tossed away from our Neverland.

"I'm going back to work too. You know where to find me if you need." Megan headed for the door, and my mind crashed back into the real world.

"Let's ride home together..." I told her the way I always did. I could move on if she could, and we could put what happened to us to rest. We still had to live together, and our internships lasted another six months. I couldn't keep behaving like an asshole, ignoring her, and refusing to even meet her eyes.

"Yeah." She gave me one last brief smile and walked out of the office, leaving the door half-open. For a second, I thought there might be someone out there, perhaps a client waiting to come in, but when no one came in, I snorted and went back to staring at the papers in front of me.

Someone stepped through the doorway and cleared his throat. I whirled around and met a pair of bright eyes, identical to my own. I'd seen them on so many other occasions without ever clocking the incredible similarity. It was ridiculous how only now did I spot that kind of detail.

Because he was right there: John Keller, the liar.

"What the fuck are you doing here?" Every nerve flared to life, and I crushed my pen between my fingers. My eyes remained locked on him as he slowly moved toward me. After shutting the door behind him, John looked around the office with polite curiosity and ignored my question.

"I want to have a talk with you." He tucked his hands into his pockets and observed me without fear or apprehension but rather with a profound determination. It was unnerving.

"We already had a talk. I don't have anything to say to you," I muttered, shuffling some of the papers to avoid his insistent, probing gaze.

"Then let's have another talk," he answered with a hint of irony that I found as bothersome as his confidence. Since when did Dr. Keller act like that? Did he think that just because he was my biological father, he had the upper hand? He didn't know shit about me.

"What about what I said before was unclear to you? Do you just like confronting me? I'm not changing my mind. I don't have any room in my life for liars." I slapped my hands palms down on the desk. He took note of the wild gesture but didn't look surprised. He held still and continued to study me, like he was holding one of his sessions with a patient.

"You're the one who isn't seeing this situation clearly, son. And, because of how obstinate you are, I have no choice but to impose myself in a more forceful way." He shrugged so arrogantly that I shook with anger. He just kept staring at me. With a growl of rage, I stalked over to him.

"What the fuck are you after, huh? You can't just drop in here anytime you want because you happen to know where I work. I don't want to see you. I don't want to have anything to do with you. You've been absent my entire life; it's too late to show up now... John." I said his name slowly, with emphasis, to make sure he knew that I'd never call him anything else. His bright eyes went dark, a sure sign I'd wounded his pride. I grinned at him, and his jaw ticked.

"Are you trying to hurt me? You know, kid, for a son of mine, I was expecting a little bit more. A cleverer play." He gave me a mocking smile, and I took a step back from him.

"Don't test me, you asshole," I warned.

"Oh no? What would you do if I did? Hit your father?" he pressed. By then, my right hand had started to shake, and my breath was coming in rapid pants, and I couldn't stop blinking.

"Stop," I hissed through my teeth, but his gaze only grew sharper as he quirked one corner of his mouth in an insouciant half-smile.

"Come on, show me what you've got. Be a man. You want to feel like a man, don't you? Would you feel more like one if you hit your father? Huh? Would it make you happier if you hurt me?" he insisted, and I didn't think any more. I clenched my hand into a fist and tensed my arm to put power behind it, power that would make him bitterly regret this move.

I took a swing at him, trying to indulge his insane demand, but John crouched slightly to dodge and stepped back lightly.

Before I even had time to process what happened, he was inside my guard. He palmed the back of my head with one hand and pulled me to him, slamming me against his chest.

He was hugging me.

It was my first paternal hug.

The only one, in fact, that I'd ever received.

"That man you believed to be your father taught you that a man is someone who hits. The man who is your father is teaching you that a real man loves and forgives," he whispered into my ear, wrapping his other arm around me like I was some small, helpless child. Like I was *his* child who had been lost to him for so long, and now he had finally found me again. I held perfectly still, processing this strange, novel, and unexpected contact.

I could feel his heart beating in his chest.

Inside *my* chest.

His breathing was ragged. His hand clutched more tightly at the nape of my neck while the other rubbed my back. He smelled clean, pure. Familiar. I felt new, destabilizing emotions coursing through me, sending tremors through the iceberg that had long ago replaced my heart.

And I became a little less Neil and a little more his son.

"You abandoned me..." I whispered. My arms remained flat against my sides. I wasn't reciprocating his embrace, but I didn't cringe away from it the way I feared I might.

"Never by choice. The Lindhoms were a powerful family. Your grandfather even set his goons on me. If I'd gotten too close to your mother, they would have had me taken care of." He cupped my face in his hands and stared deeply into my eyes, searching for some sort of connection, some relationship, anything that might keep his hope alive.

"I loved Mia. You were not the result of a mistake or a one-night stand. You came from love. I felt joy when I found out about you. I was excited for you to come. But fate was cruel to me, as it also was to you." He shook me slightly as though trying to force the words into my head. He could sense my mistrust, my fear, and my misery. "You have to believe me, Neil. I will never leave you again. You can count on me. I will always be there for you. Always. You aren't alone anymore. Please, just give me a chance..." He was on the verge of tears. I continued to stare at him as he touched my hair and cheeks as though I weren't quite real, as though he were trying to convince himself that I was really there, flesh and blood, standing right in front of him.

"I don't... I don't know..." I said in a confused mutter. I didn't have the strength to reject him, but I wasn't ready to forgive him either.

He continued to hold my face as he leaned in and pressed a kiss to my forehead. He lingered there for a moment, as if to hold me to him for as long as possible.

"I'm here. I'll give you all the time you need to get to know me and accept me. I understand how upsetting this all is, but please allow me to remain a part of your life." His voice broke.

I thought.

I thought for a long time about what I should do.

I had a lot of confusion but also a great sense of relief in knowing that William had never really been my father. That man and I didn't share anything except a last name, and there was nothing tying me to him, save our mutual hatred and disgust.

I gave John a nod; that was all he was going to get from me for the time being. I'd never been good with words anyway.

"Could we talk for a minute?" he asked tentatively. I could sense that he feared my rejection, which, in a move that surprised even me, didn't come. I leaned back against the edge of the desk and gestured at the chair near him. He gave me an incredulous look before smiling and sitting down with a heavy sigh. I wasn't sure why I'd given in, but for some reason, I felt like I needed to face him and hear him out even if I wasn't yet ready to forgive his years of absence.

"What do you want to talk about?" I asked, wishing I could light up a cigarette.

"I'd like to know how you are. How the internship's going..." I knew that wasn't what he really wanted to ask, but I played along anyway.

"I'm not great... I do like my work, though," I interrupted bluntly.

"Not great? You miss your siblings, don't you?" he pressed.

I didn't say anything, but the memory of how I'd driven them away knocked the air out of me. My godforsaken pride had trapped me in this corrosive hatred that I couldn't help but vent on everyone around me, even the people who didn't have a fucking thing to do with it.

"They weren't involved in any of this, Neil. William was a son of a bitch, telling you like that, but they had nothing to do with it. You are all still bonded by the good, loving relationship you've cultivated with them all their lives. Don't let that man shape anything else about your life," John said urgently. He knew that, deep down, I loved them. My love for my siblings and theirs for me was the only kind of love that I actually believed in. Still, there was something inside me, some dark power that urged me to give them up, crushing the smaller, more human part of me.

I heaved a frustrated sigh and stared unwaveringly at him. It had always been easier for me to pretend to be inscrutable rather than showing myself fragile and miserable.

"I'm perfectly capable of managing my life and my relationships with my siblings. I don't need advice from you," I said scornfully.

"That goes for Selene too..." He hesitated slightly. "She doesn't have anything to do with it either, Neil. I've heard from her a few times in the past six months, and she told me that you were the one who made the choice to end it between the two of you. She knows about her mother and what you two talked about, and still she doesn't accept your decision," he said, soft and disappointed. And then the anger, that anger that turned me into nothing but a beast, got the upper hand. I let my arms fall to my sides and stood up straight, instantly demonstrating the power Babygirl still held over me. Even from so far away. Even though there was no longer an "us."

"She needs to live her life, John, and she needs to get away from me to do it. Her mother was fucking right. Why can't anyone understand where I'm coming from? Do you know how much easier it would have been to bring her to Chicago with me? To take her and use her up at my leisure? She's the only person I've ever shown my soul to. I made the right choice for both of us." My voice got louder and louder before faltering.

It was a bitter taste that I'd experienced twice before: the first time when I was a child and the second at in my early twenties.

And that was why I went to war internally. I wasn't going to drive Babygirl crazy.

She wasn't going to live this cursed life and have this dreamless future because of me.

"I'm afraid it's not only up to you to make that decision. You should have told her about Chicago and let her decide what she was going to do. She accepted you, Neil. She never would have abandoned you..." John stood up to face me.

I gave him a sardonic smile. All I wanted for Selene was a better life. Why was that so hard to understand?

"I've forgotten her already anyway. I've moved on..." I finished tersely. I needed to shut him up and shut down this line of inquiry and get back to work.

"You've forgotten about her?" John lifted his eyebrows like I'd just said the most ridiculous thing he'd ever heard. "Typically, one's pearl isn't so easily forgotten," he continued. "I did hear she was seeing someone, though." He tucked his hands into his pockets and scrutinized my face, probing for reactions, for emotional shifts. I wasn't surprised to hear that about Selene. I'd figured she'd eventually go out with someone.

Apparently that love she was always talking about really was just a lie after all.

I'd always known that. It just took her a little longer to realize.

"So she's got a boyfriend now?" I blurted out, feeling a strange, acidic feeling rising from my stomach into my throat. John smiled a smug little half-smile, and I scrubbed a hand over my face.

Just the thought of it made me feel on edge.

"So what if she does?" he answered pointedly with an amused undertone to his voice. My eyes bugged slightly—so what? So, I didn't want to think about some guy's lips on her; I didn't want to think about him rubbing his slimy mitts all over her.

She had only ever been mine.

I was the one who took her virginity. I was the one who had given her her first orgasm. I had tasted every part of her, touched her everywhere, and possessed her in every possible way. I was the first man to ever see her naked, the only person she'd explored sexuality with in her entire life.

I couldn't deal with the idea that she'd now shared those same things with someone else.

"It's her life. If she's happy, I'm happy." I shrugged and tried to look indifferent, but I almost puked as I said it. I knew I couldn't blame her for anything. After all, I'd also let other hands and mouths kiss and touch me. Though none of them got *in* me, to the place where only she had been. The place where I still kept her.

I tried to quell some of my possessiveness and think clearly: She had moved on just like I had told her to, and I couldn't judge her for that. I had no right to get all pissy about it. It was tough to admit it, but it was true: finding out she had a boyfriend put me off my game.

I shook my head and smiled ruefully.

I had been right all along: pleasure was real, and so were orgasms and the loneliness that made people cling to one another just to believe in something.

But love was just a big lie, and Selene's was no different.

This was only confirmation of that.

"You know, Neil, we often feel haunted by our best memories because our souls long to return to the people and places that allowed us to feel our best," John answered. He seemed concerned by my exhausted silence.

That was true enough: Selene was the only good memory I had. Which, I supposed, meant she'd never stop haunting me. Babygirl had cast a fucking spell on me; nothing else explained this turmoil.

"I'm good right now. I have everything I need," I said, trying to make him—and even more so myself—buy my bullshit.

In reality, I was like a desperate man walking through the endless desert.

I was looking for my path.

But it wasn't there; I couldn't find it.

I looked up at the sky, but it always looked the same, one uniform color without hues.

I looked at the ground beneath my feet, and that was always the same as well: barren, devoid of anything that bloomed.

"You have everything you need, except the things you really want..." John met my gaze, but I immediately lowered my eyes to conceal my weakness. I didn't know what I really wanted.

I had gotten used to surviving on my own, and sometimes I thought I didn't want anyone by my side. Other times, I wondered why I couldn't be like any other normal human being, capable of developing healthy relationships and nurturing them over time.

"People like me don't get better, John. We're fucked up, and we stay fucked up," I said sadly. "I need to get back to work now. You should leave." I pointed at the door.

He didn't answer but just watched me closely for a few seconds, assessing my sudden coldness. Then he sighed heavily before giving me a knowing look.

"Don't be afraid of life, Neil. She is not our enemy." He strolled over to the door with his hands still in his pockets, and with one last quick glance, walked out and left me alone to fill the void with even more emptiness.

I knew that it was just fear.

Fear of loving.

Fear of being loved.

Fear of forgiving only to suffer again.

Fear of trusting.

Fear of offering myself up again.

Fear of the world.

Fear of me—of what I was.

I wasn't going to seek out Selene. I wasn't going backward.

I would keep my Babygirl safe and sound deep down in my soul.

And as the soul was immortal, so too would be my Tinkerbell.

25

"It hurt, but what had I been expecting?"

SELENE

New York was just as I remembered it, yet every time I walked into Matt's house, it felt different.

"You were crazy to come here with a fever," Logan said, handing me a mug of hot cocoa, and I sneezed again. The big house was completely silent since Anna was the only other person there besides the two of us.

"Like a little cold was going to stop me." In reality, I was running a fever, one so high that my white sweater did nothing to prevent the chills that moved down my arms and back. But nothing would have stopped me from flying out to New York and, potentially, seeing Neil again.

Logan had called me a few weeks before and explained what happened when he, Chloe, and John went to find my human disaster out in Chicago. He was there, sure enough, and living with Megan.

It hurt, but what had I been expecting? That he'd be sitting in a corner, wallowing in his misery? Maybe he had been at one point, but then Megan had been there to pick him back up. She was with him, in the place I should have been, doing what I should have been doing.

I was angry both with Neil and with myself because I should have done more on the day of his graduation. I should have kept him from walking out that door and going off on his own.

"It should have stopped you. You're obviously unwell." Logan laid a hand on my forehead and cocked an eyebrow. "In my opinion, your temperature's way too high." He took me gently by the arm and guided me down to sit on the couch. I left my luggage where I'd dropped it next to the door. "There will be other holidays, you know," he chided me.

But we both knew it wasn't the prospect of celebrating an early Christmas with Matt's family that had brought me out from Detroit. It was the tentative, begrudging promise Logan had extracted from his brother that Neil would at least try to see his siblings over the holidays. If there was even a chance Neil would be there, I had to go.

My wavy, disheveled hair fell into my eyes, and Logan lifted a hand to arrange it over my shoulder. As he did so, I studied his weary face and frowned.

"Okay, what's wrong?" I could tell that something was bothering him beyond just my fever.

"Nothing…" he sighed. He balanced his elbows on his knees. His gaze was absent, a preoccupied expression that exposed his obvious worry.

"Logan," I said more firmly. He looked at me, upset as he chewed his lip before finally giving in.

"We got another riddle this morning," he admitted, all in one breath, and my eyes went wide with horror.

We'd all stopped thinking about Player after Neil's graduation and the revelations about John. I suppose we were all foolish enough to imagine that he'd stopped thinking about us as well, and his sudden reemergence was alarming. Looking anxious, Logan stood up to pull a note out of his jeans pocket.

"Here…" He handed it to me, and I took it hesitantly as he sat back down beside me. "He sent this along with a bouquet of black roses that I've already thrown away." His jaw clenched as he passed a hand over his face. I opened the folded piece of paper and ran my eyes along the printed lines:

Photo
Mosaic
The missing piece
Game over

Player 2511

I stared at him, dumbfounded, and let the paper drop to the floor as though it were a superheated piece of metal. I rubbed my temples, and I could no longer tell if my awful headache was from the fever or simple exhaustion with everything that was happening.

"Have you talked to your brother about this? He needs to know, Logan." I lifted my head to look at the boy who was now on his feet in front of me, nervously pacing the living room.

"After the way he booted us out of his office, I doubt he cares that much about what happens to us," he snapped with uncharacteristic abrasiveness. He was still angry and disappointed about Neil's behavior, and I couldn't blame him.

"Try him. I can't believe he'd truly be indifferent to this," I continued, trying to ignore the headache that was steadily worsening and the weakness in my muscles.

"I've already texted him," Logan admitted. "He said we'll talk about it when he gets here."

So he *was* coming. I hadn't been sure before, and the knowledge made me uneasy. I had no idea how I was going to react when I saw him again. What, if anything, would he say to me? Did he still have any feelings for me?

I had no idea how his life had changed in the last six months. I didn't know if there was someone else in his heart now or if that person was Megan.

I tried to stifle the thought of her; I didn't want to believe things would have progressed that far between them.

Would he really be capable of having sex with the woman who'd gone through a nightmare with him?

I'd always felt jealous over Neil and all the women he had eating out of his hand, but I considered Megan much more of a threat. He allowed himself to let go with me in a way he never did with his casual lovers. He made love with me the way he'd never done with anyone else before.

But what did he do with her?

I clung to the memories that I'd been living off for the past few months. I clung to hope and to the sheer instinct that made me believe that he valued me more than he'd ever been willing to show.

"I'm going to go get cleaned up, then," I said, getting up from the couch. I climbed the stairs slowly and moved into the bathroom. I scrutinized myself in the mirror. I had lost some weight, and the fever only made me look even more bedraggled.

My eyes were only half-open and glassy, my cheeks were red, and my lips were chapped and puffy. My hair was a long, wavy tangle.

I had lost all desire to take care of myself.

"You look awful," I muttered to myself before turning on the faucet and cupping my hands below it. I rinsed my face with the cold water. Chills passed through every part of me, and I swayed on legs weakened by muscle aches.

I should have just gotten into bed and rested, but I wanted to wait for Neil. I wanted to see him, no matter how uncomfortable I was. I sighed and pushed open the bathroom door only to startle when I found Anna standing there.

"Selene, are you okay?" She frowned at my drawn face. I smiled and gave her an insincere nod.

"Sure am. Do you think you could find some fever medication when you get a chance? I think my temperature might be going up." I didn't just think it; I was positive. I was basically on fire, but my obstinate brain made me keep fighting it. Anna cocked her head to one side suspiciously, undoubtedly aware that I was lying through my teeth. Fortunately, she didn't push the issue, so I just walked around her and slowly made my way back down the stairs, my vision both blurring and tunneling.

"Oh hey, you're already here!" I heard Logan's voice from deep in the living room, and like I was equipped with invisible sensors attuned to his presence, I scented Neil before I even saw him.

I slowed down even more. I wasn't sure if I could remain steady on my feet with him right there in front of me. Close to me.

How long had it been since I'd last seen him? An eternity.

"Yeah, I bumped up my flight," he answered, and I shivered. His voice was as masculine and penetrating as ever, and it still seemed to wrap itself around me, as though his body were already covering mine.

I clenched my fingers around the stair railing to keep from swooning as I stood motionless on the bottom step of the staircase.

And there he was, also unmoving. My stomach was in knots. I shivered down to my bones when I saw him.

Finally.

That was when Neil lifted his head up and spotted me. His unknowable gaze drew me in and broke me down completely, making me forget even my own name.

I held my breath—it felt like all my air had been pulled into that virile body just a few feet away from me. His wild hair was a little bit longer than the last time I'd seen him. His shoulders under his black leather jacket looked a bit wider, and his legs, displayed beautifully in a pair of sweatpants, looked thicker and more toned. Clearly he'd been working out again.

I wanted to cry, but I resisted the urge so I wouldn't look like the hopelessly enamored girl that I was.

"We wanted to get here as soon as possible." And then there was another voice that broke the spell, shattering the connection between us. A feminine voice. Familiar. It was Megan, whose dark head emerged from behind Neil's back. What was she doing here? With him?

A cloud immediately moved over me, and I exhaled sharply.

"Oh, hey, Megan. I wasn't expecting you to come." Logan looked as bewildered as I felt. I had already been picturing how I'd take the opportunity to get Neil one-on-one, to talk to him and clear the air. But Megan's presence complicated that.

"Yeah, she's with me. I told her about everything," he answered firmly. He'd quit looking at me and was moving into the living room along with the sexy brunette who had instantly obliterated my self-esteem.

"Show me the letter," Neil said, getting straight to the point. Clearly he wasn't interested in anything but Player.

I gathered my courage and forced myself down the last few steps to meet them. Megan's emerald green eyes immediately turned to me, and I couldn't help but think about how gorgeous she was, how well she suited him.

"Hi, Selene." She gave me a tight smile, looking uncomfortable. She tucked her hands into the pockets of her leather jacket and chewed her lower lip nervously.

"Hi...Megan," I answered in a shaky voice. Then, like a doofus, I sniffled, sneezed, and had a brief coughing fit, which, naturally, drew everyone's eyes to me. Even Neil's.

Expressionless, he searched my face. I was the one blushing like an idiot because apparently I'd turned into my most awkward self, just accumulating faux pas. I stared back at him for what felt like forever. I didn't dare to blink because I was too afraid that, if I did, he'd vanish, turning out to be just another of my dreams.

Just the thought of it made my eyes burn.

I tried to be strong, tried to hold back the tears that I'd been spilling daily since he left.

I should have been screaming at him about all the suffering he'd caused me already, about how I tore myself to pieces every night imagining his breath against my skin, his hands on my body. But I couldn't bring myself to do that because I was weak when it came to him, bending to his will, twisted back and forth by those devilish eyes.

"Selene, are you sure you're okay? Did you actually take your temperature?" Logan put a hand on my shoulder, and I flinched at the unexpected contact, all my thoughts melting away. I sneezed again before nodding firmly, convinced that an actual child would be a more convincing liar. And, in fact, Logan did twist his mouth into a skeptical expression and gave me a quietly reproving look.

"I'm fine. I'll just hang out with you all for a little bit, and then I'll go upstairs and lie down, okay?" I said, offering what I thought was a reasonable compromise. He smiled wryly at me and shook his head.

"Perfect, I'll ask Anna to bring you some medicine, then. You need to rest," he told me sternly before turning his focus back to his brother, who hadn't stopped staring at me even for a moment. His golden eyes picked at my skin like so many tiny pins and needles.

I felt naked, like my white sweater and jeans had been peeled away and my every fear and insecurity was exposed for him to do with as he wished.

"Here's the riddle Player sent this morning. There was also a bouquet of black roses that I threw out." Logan handed over the paper, and Neil snatched it from him, turning his attention abruptly from me to the note. He sat down on the sofa, legs spread wide, and studied it closely. Megan sat down beside him and rested a hand on his knee.

I watched them in silence, feeling like a third wheel. I sensed too much intimacy and too much understanding between the two of them, and it hurt. I should have been the one sitting by his side. It should have been my hand on his body.

"I have no idea what he's trying to say," Neil muttered, passing a hand through his messy hair. Seeing him right there in front of me and being unable to touch him was unending torture.

I felt breathless, rocking back and forth on my heels to keep myself from going straight to him the way I wanted to.

"Me neither. I don't get what 'photo' has to do with 'mosaic' or any of the rest..." Logan folded his arms over his chest and gave a heavy, thoughtful sigh. Megan's eyes were riveted to the note, and she looked absorbed, trying to figure out what it meant.

"I'm going to take it back to Chicago with me and try to figure it out there." Neil got to his feet, the note still clutched in one hand. He pulled a pack of Winstons out of his pants pocket, and without giving me so much as a look, walked right past me. The smell of musk washed over me, and it felt like I'd been punched in the stomach. Megan got up and followed him, and I watched the two of them walk through the kitchen, heading outside to the yard.

"Stop thinking those ugly thoughts, Selene." Logan came over to me, smiling as he laid a hand on my forehead. I cocked an eyebrow at him and snorted.

"What ugly thoughts? That he wants Megan?" I asked him, sounding notably nasally.

"You don't see the way he looks at you, do you? You're the only person he sees, Selene. It's been like that for a while." He tucked a strand of my hair back and searched my sorrowful eyes for any glimmer of hope. I didn't say anything because I had not observed anything of the sort from Neil. I had looked him eye to eye several times, and on each occasion, he'd only seemed indifferent. "Don't let her occupy your place. Go to Neil and talk to him," he urged me with conviction, giving my shoulders an encouraging squeeze.

I didn't know what I should do; I felt too vulnerable.

Too afraid.

I was afraid that he might hurt me. Or rather, that he would cut me to ribbons with his cruel words. Neil knew how to land a blow, and he was an expert at the kind of psychological torture that kept me at a distance.

I'd been waiting to see him again for months, and now that I finally had the opportunity to talk to him, I was shying away like the rankest coward.

"Go on, you can do this." Logan pushed me gently in the direction of the kitchen. I allowed myself to be pushed, moving with difficulty not only because of my physical exhaustion but also because I was too overwhelmed by all the feelings Hurricane Neil had stirred up.

I sighed and slowly rounded the kitchen island. My heart beat faster and the chills intensified. I felt like a child preparing to face down the fearsome giant who had already shattered her heart once before.

I reached the glass doors and froze when I spotted Neil and Megan outside, standing close together as they talked. Too close. He still had the riddle in one hand, and he held a cigarette in the other. His face was dark and pensive as he looked out over the lawn. She touched his face, bolstering him, petting him, but the worst was yet to come. She stood up on her tiptoes and dropped a kiss on his lips.

My breath caught.

Neil took a step back, breaking the contact and looking annoyed, but that wasn't enough to soothe me.

I staggered back, aggrieved, and every fear I had, every insecurity, rose up to remind me that my instincts had always been right: He was attracted to her.

As I stood there in shambles, I couldn't suppress another loud sneeze, and the two of them turned to look at me.

I was caught in the act.

Caught spying on them.

I couldn't even look at them; I just turned on my heel and ran away. I sped out of the kitchen and immediately ran into Logan, who managed to catch my arm as I hurried past him.

"So? Did you talk to him?"

I scowled at him. For a moment, I thought about making up some lie, but I immediately realized there would be no point. I shook my head as tears filled my eyes. I knew Logan could see how much pain I was in.

"I don't feel good, Logan. You were right. I need to rest. I'm going upstairs to my old room." I pulled myself out of his grasp and climbed the stairs as fast as I could, using up the small amount of strength I had left.

I threw the door open, and immediately, memories flooded me, shredded me, and devastated me. This was the room where we'd had our first "real" time together. The first time when we were both fully aware of what we were doing together because we were incapable of pulling free from the desire, the twisted, unhealthy connection that had drawn tight around us like a confining rope.

Miserable, I laid down on the four-poster bed and curled up into the fetal position, not even bothering to pull the covers over me.

I could feel the ache in my head pulsing, the cold sensation running up and down my body, my broken heart beating, and my tears slipping down my cheeks.

Now that I was there, I allowed myself to cry.

No one would see me there; no one would judge me.

I was alone.

I had finally lost Neil for good, and I had lost myself as well because I no longer had the strength to keep on fighting.

I closed my eyes and fell asleep with my chills for a blanket, my shivers for a caress, and my pain for a constant companion.

I slept for a long time until I felt a hand touching my forehead and stroking my hair.

I mumbled out a shaky "thanks, Logan." I assumed he was playing nursemaid and looking after me. I was confused, then, when I felt his lips settle, soft and warm, against my cheek before slowly moving down to my throat. I let out a little involuntary sigh of pleasure, and a warm sensation spread through every part of me.

It was weird of Logan to be touching me in such an intimate and, frankly, carnal way.

But maybe...

I opened my eyes and turned my head and thought I was hallucinating when I met Neil's grave, intense stare, fixed on me.

He'd been sitting on the side of my bed for who knows how long.

My blood began to boil in my veins: I wasn't sure if I was outraged or thrilled by his presence.

"What are you doing here?" I asked him, my voice dry as I tried to sit up. I couldn't, though; my muscles were still too weak. I clearly wasn't any better for my rest.

He didn't answer but just watched me closely with both sadness and apprehension on his face.

Was he worried about me? More importantly—how long had he been there?

"You're still running a temperature..." he noted, his voice deep and austere, and he stopped stroking my hair. I watched his full lips flatten into a line and had the urge to kiss him. My cheeks burned at the lecherous idea.

His shadowy aura made me feel even smaller than I actually was.

In that moment, I wished I could be like Megan—strong, sure, confident—but I wasn't. I wasn't surprised Neil had chosen her instead.

"You shouldn't be here; go back to your girl. I get it, you know? You don't have to explain anything to me." My headache was throbbing, but that didn't stop me from venting my anger.

An immature girl.

That was what I acted like, but I didn't care. Neil didn't know what was going on inside me; he had no idea what I'd gone through in the last six months.

There is no pearl without her shell.

How was I supposed to live now that he'd chosen someone else?

"I don't think you do get it. I don't think you can." He stretched out an arm and tucked a bit of hair behind my ear. I wanted to dodge him, to shove his hand away and avoid his touch, but I couldn't. His fingers brushed my soul and touched my heart, and I loved to feel them on me.

"What do I not get? That you're with her now? That you've been living with her for the last six months? That, in those same six months, you've completely ghosted me, never answering a single call or text? What am I failing to get, Neil? Because, to me, the conclusion is so obvious only a total idiot wouldn't get it." A sob escaped my lips, and I finally found the inner strength required to push his hand away. I scooted backward until I was plastered against the headboard, trying to escape his eyes.

"It's not what it looks like..." Neil looked down at my hands and reached out to touch me again. He stroked my hands with his fingers, and the heat of him began to burn through every part of me again.

I could sense a bizarre need on his part to have some sort of physical contact with me. I knew it was the only way he knew how to communicate, but I wasn't going to give in. The fire that he could stoke between my thighs wouldn't be enough to distract me this time.

"Oh no? Then tell me you haven't had sex with Megan or anyone else in these past few months. Tell me that you've been thinking about nothing but me and that goddamned day in May because that is what I've thought about every moment since then and I am *ruined*. I have been completely ruined by you!" My voice rose a couple octaves as I again pulled away from the touch of his hand. The heat of his flesh was replaced by chill, and my head was pounding again.

I really had been ruined. I'd tried to forget him by kissing Ivan; I'd even tried to make love with him, but it hadn't worked. I put a stop to it before we could even get started because, just as he was about to pull off my jeans, I realized that I didn't really want him.

I only wanted Neil inside me.

Only him inside my soul.

"We've both had sex since then. We've moved on; it's the right thing to do." His voice changed, becoming brittle and stern, a clear sign that I was right once again. Something had happened between him and Megan, and he didn't have the guts to admit it. In fact, he thought I was just like him, that I would be just as thoughtless.

I almost laughed in his face.

"Both of us?" I sneered at him. "I'm not like you. I have never been like you. I couldn't just replace you with a snap of my fingers. I haven't been with anyone else, I haven't..." I hesitated.

He was scowling at me. His eyes burned with undiluted rage that he seemed prepared to spew at me like a dragon.

"Seriously? I'd lay bets right now that you have a boyfriend and that boyfriend is your beloved captain of the basketball team. You already admitted to me that you liked him. Have you really not fucked him once in all these months?" he asked sharply, giving me a look full of disdain. "You can't bullshit me with that little angel face, Selene. You've finally figured out what I knew all along—that whatever you felt for me was an illusion. So don't try to lie to me!" He leaped to his feet, every muscle tensed beneath his clothes. The loud, biting sound of his voice seemed to stab into my ears and pulsed in my head. I automatically began to rub my temples, wincing in pain. I was in no condition to sit through one of his outbursts. Neil appeared to realize that he'd gone overboard and looked at me ashamed, like he wanted to apologize. But he didn't.

"Look, I don't want to fight with you." He sighed miserably and sat back down on the bed, the springs whining underneath his weight. He shot me a guilty look, and I refused to meet his eyes because I knew that, if I did, I'd drown in those golden depths all over again.

"I didn't sleep with Ivan. We just kissed, and that's the truth." I kept my eyes down, self-conscious about my confession. I couldn't stuff down my feelings and pretend I didn't still love him.

"I tried... I tried to go further with Ivan, but I couldn't do it," I went on, embarrassed.

I raised my head to check his reaction, and what I found was disconcerting: Neil was astonished.

His eyebrows were raised, his lips parted in surprise, and there was a strange gleam in his eyes. I couldn't be sure, but I strongly suspected that he was relieved that no one else had touched me the way that he had. All at once, though, his expression shifted, and he turned inscrutable, retreating behind his wall of ice to keep me from seeing too deeply into him.

"It's your life. Whatever you've done, you don't have explain yourself to me." He licked his lower lip, an unconscious gesture of anxiety, and lowered his eyes. For the first time, I didn't believe a single word that was coming out of his mouth.

"You'd rather pretend you don't care than admit your mistakes to yourself, wouldn't you?" I said provokingly. "You always believed my feelings were fake, and now that you see they weren't, you don't have the guts to come to terms with the choices you made. You refuse to admit that you were the one who was in the wrong." I struggled to my feet, the muscles in my legs threatening to go out at any moment, but my single-minded determination gave me the strength to face him down.

"You refused to tell me about Chicago. You hid the truth from me. You told my mother you were going to leave me, and you made that decision without ever asking me. You never asked what I wanted; you didn't even consider making an attempt at long-distance. When you found out about your biological father, you cut everyone out of your life. Even me, the person who had only ever supported you and stood beside you even when you humiliated me with other women, even when you trampled on whatever pride I had left, even when you pushed me out in the cold. You made a new life for yourself while destroying mine. I thought about you day and night, and while I was doing that, where were you, Neil? In bed with Megan or other women? How many were there while I was grieving you? While I was crying all the time and not being able to eat? How many? And look at me, for God's sake, Neil!" My voice grew louder and louder as I spoke, and I felt powerful in a way I'd never felt before. Finally, Neil lifted his eyes to look at me. I froze when his stare landed on my lips.

"Is that what you think? That this was easy for me?" He jumped up, towering over me with all that dangerous power. "You think I didn't go to shit? The first few months, all I wanted to do was take the easy way out, and the only reason I am standing in front of you right now, safe and sound, is Megan. She is the reason I survived, and I have no idea where the fuck I'd be without her. I fucked other women to hurt myself the way I've always done. And yes, I slept with Megan too, and I regret that bitterly. So what are you going to do now? Judge me? Tell me that I disgust you? I didn't disgust you so much when you were underneath me having a great time!" he yelled, close to my face. By then, I was no longer capable of reason, and so I simply slapped him full in the face.

I poured all my frustration into that slap, all my disillusionment and suffering, but also my love.

Insanely enough, there was love in my pain.

Neil kept perfectly still, not uttering a single word even as his cheek began to turn red. He looked at me, unhappy but not particularly surprised by my actions. He looked like he was trying to figure out whether I was serious or not.

"Get out," I muttered. All at once, I was inundated with thoughts of other women touching him, and it made me nauseous. I'd always suspected it, of course, but having it confirmed beyond a shadow of a doubt was infinitely worse. My head spun. My brief moment of triumph gave way to the feverish exhaustion. I staggered back, fuzzy-headed.

"No," he answered. "You haven't even heard the best part yet." He moved closer, wrapping his arms around my waist for support. Instinctively, I pressed my hands to his chest and my body trembled as I stroked his flexed muscles. I looked up into those bright eyes that wouldn't stop staring at my pallid face. "I thought about you every time." He leaned down to get his lips close to my ear, and his stubbly jaw grazed my cheek. The proximity made me flash back to when I was his and he was mine and nothing else existed for us.

"I would think about you to get myself hard. I'd imagine your coconut scent, your soft skin, your ocean eyes, your button nose, and your perfect mouth to push myself over the edge, but I couldn't orgasm with any of them, except for Megan. I always picked brunettes with blue eyes, and they always looked so much like you at night, but in the morning, they were completely different," he whispered, tightening his arms around me until it was hard to breathe. He lifted one hand to stroke my hair, and I held my breath. I was trapped in his strong arms, lost in his words. "I became a director who only made the same movie over and over again. The same plot but different actresses... similar to you, but never actually *you*. And maybe I do disgust you now. You'd have every reason to feel that way. But at least I've told you the truth; the whole truth," he concluded.

He buried his face in the bend of my neck and breathed in my smell. I almost groaned from the pain of his crushing grip as I fought with myself, fought the part of me that wanted to give in. I didn't want to do it, not now; it would be too humiliating after what he'd just told me, after everything he'd done.

I wanted to be better than I was before. Stronger. I needed to learn how to love myself as well. But then a tear rolled down my cheek, and the urge to kiss him, to taste his lips, began to build inside me.

No, dammit.

I didn't have to do it. I *couldn't* do it.

"Outside, Megan kissed you. I saw it," I said brokenly, pulling away from him. Neil stared intensely at me, his hands still clinging to my body, digging in like claws that wanted to keep marking me.

"It's not what you're thinking. We have this connection that I can't explain, but that's it," he answered uncertainly, as though searching for the right words. I stepped back; I would have rather heard that she was just another fling for him, but I'd known all along that wasn't the case.

"Are you in love with her?" I asked him directly. His eyebrows shot up in surprise, like I'd said the most ridiculous thing in the world to him.

"Fuck no! Absolutely not!" he blurted out immediately, not even thinking about it. There wasn't an ounce of hesitation in him, and that did reassure me a bit.

Then, his eyes drifted back down to my mouth, and I realized what he was about to do.

Did he seriously have the balls to kiss me after all of that?

Neil clearly wasn't interested in wasting any more time, though, because he bent his head and grazed my lips with his own. When he felt my tacit agreement, he kissed me fully.

He did it so slowly, so delicately, that it actually hurt me. A pain I couldn't name or describe suffused my chest as if to remind me how it had been without him and how I'd never be able to forget him.

My fingers splayed out on his chest, creeping down to his abdomen. He clasped the nape of my neck possessively to pull me closer to him, but he didn't go overboard. He wasn't demanding anything.

It was a gentle kiss but a powerful one as well.

Neil had become my whole world.

I breathed through him; I fed myself on him.

His absence had made me sick and nearly drove me insane. There was no cure for the devastating kind of love I had for him.

"You should rest," he said firmly after a little while, breaking the kiss. I immediately felt the loss of his lips. He was surely stifling his own desires because I was hurting, but if he'd tried to make love with me right then, I would have given in. I would have let him peel away every reasonable thought I had and sink down deep into my soul once again. But my body was in no shape to keep up with him.

Fortunately, he had some common sense even if I didn't.

"Yeah..." was all I said, my cheeks aflame. I felt like I was burning up, and I wasn't at all sure it was just the fever. Neil slowly guided me back down on to the bed. I kicked off my shoes this time and slipped beneath the blankets to cover myself.

He sat down beside me.

He arranged the blankets over me, revealing a sweetness that I hadn't seen in him before except with his siblings.

"You worried about me now? Surprising..." I bit my tongue, but it was too late; his eyes moved from the blankets back to my face, and I was embarrassed by the dumb comment. He just gave me a small yet head-spinning smile and didn't say another word. Then his stare turned blatant, delighted by my spreading blush. I held his gaze, sucking in a breath when he laid a hand across my forehead.

"You're sick. I'll stay with you until the fever breaks."

An odd warmth spread through my chest at all the attention he was giving me. It was a kind of tenderness he'd never shown me before. His big hand felt cool against my overheated skin, immediately soothing.

"Tomorrow you'll have a fever too if you stay close to me. You just kissed me," I mumbled, blushing again when he gave me a cheeky smile.

"Don't care. I'd die for a kiss from you," he answered sincerely, and there wasn't even a flicker of mockery in his eyes.

My heart did somersaults in surprise.

Did he really just say that?

Or had the fever started burning off brain cells?

I didn't say anything in response, just snuggled down under the blankets and rested my head on the pillow, seeking some sort of respite for my worn-out body.

The clean softness of the material all around me had my eyelids drooping.

I tried to ignore the chills that made me shiver constantly.

I fell asleep once again, but nightmares troubled me, made me mumble nonsensically.

I woke up a few hours later and looked around for Neil, but I couldn't find him.

Did he leave already?

The room had been swallowed up by darkness, with only a hint of light coming in through the window. It was enough, however, to see that I was alone. I didn't move; I held still and tried to endure the throbbing pain in my head.

"Neil?" I called out in distress after a few moments. I calmed down when I heard footsteps heading toward me and then the sound of blankets being pulled aside as someone got into the bed with me. I felt his breath on my face and his hard chest pressed against me. He wrapped an arm around my waist and drew me to him.

"I'm right there, Tinkerbell," he said in a gentle whisper. He held my icy hand in his to warm it up.

"I'm...going to die..." My head hurt so bad, and my eyes were struggling to perceive the world correctly, so I narrowed them as I curled up against him. My body shook all over, and Neil wrapped me in a tight, protective hold.

"No, Babygirl, you're not going to die. You just have a very high fever," he answered in a soothing tone, but I still wasn't completely sure he wasn't a figment of my imagination.

Did he really stay with me? Or was I still dreaming?

"But what if I am dying, though?" I said in a barely lucid mumble as I relaxed against his powerful body.

"Then I'd die with you," he answered immediately, a strange certitude in his voice.

"Like Romeo and Juliet?" I insisted. I was genuinely delirious at that point, and he was patiently indulging my nonsensical rambling.

"Yeah, just like them," he answered, sounding amused.

"But..." I closed my eyes completely, trying to string a thought together. "No, dammit...we're Tinkerbell and Peter Pan. I finished the book, you know. Peter chooses Wendy in the end," I went on, making myself sad. I might have started crying again.

Neil drew his nose along my neck and gave a satisfied grunt as he breathed in my scent. There was no ulterior motive in the movement. He was just cuddling with me, holding me in his arms. I tried to relax and enjoy the little zaps of pleasure I felt all down my spine. His stubble was almost ticklish against my skin.

"Mhm...so Peter was a real asshole, then? What happened to Tinkerbell?" he whispered in my ear before nibbling on the lobe and slowly laving it with his tongue. He wouldn't have been Neil if he didn't try to slip in a little seduction even in a moment like that.

"I... I don't know..." I said, trying to remember. Even with the human disaster right there next to me, I found my eyelids shutting once again as sleep overtook me.

I spent the night like that, grasping on to him as I was tossed between overwhelming heat and icy chills. My heart raced, and it got hard to separate my sleeping world from the waking one.

I was babbling all kinds of nonsense, most frequently Neil's name. My breathing was rapid, and I groaned constantly at the ache in my head that wouldn't go away. I tossed and turned, kicking aside the covers before plastering myself against him. I clutched his chest when I dreamed that he was leaving with Megan and was only able to relax when he spoke to me soothingly, assuring me that he was still there and wasn't going anywhere else.

"Neil...no...no..." I babbled at one point, my body jerking but my eyes still closed. I clasped his arm in my sweaty grasp, seeking his protection.

"I'm right here. I brought you some medicine. Take it and your fever should start to go down. You're going to feel better." His voice sounded far away, but I could still hear it. His face was semi-obscured in the dim half-light of the room, but I could see just enough to know that he was beside me, trying to soothe me. He dropped a delicate kiss on my forehead, then the tip of my nose, and then my lips. "You're going to feel better, Babygirl," he repeated against my mouth. I smiled, but it was so small he probably couldn't make it out in the darkness. Nevertheless, he smothered it in a possessive kiss. His lips were cold or maybe mine were just so hot—either way, it was the best feeling in the world, having his mouth on mine again.

He pulled back way too soon, and I grunted out a protest. His mouth was a temptation that I couldn't resist, not even when I was sick. I told him that and heard him chuckle.

"Still the same Babygirl." He pushed my hair aside and gently rubbed the back of my neck, trying to relieve some of the soreness in my body, the exhaustion that had seeped into my muscles and bones. His touch apparently had magical properties because I sighed, contented, and inched closer to him. This time, I buried my nose in his chest and breathed in his masculine, sensual smell. Maybe I told him that because he answered me with, "Now's not the time to be thinking about that, Tigress. Be good..."

Neil Miller telling me to be less horny? I laughed until I fell asleep in his arms.

When I woke up, I finally felt better.

I was still a bit sweaty, and I reached up to feel my forehead; it was still warm but no longer hot. I sat up and looked blearily around. Beside me, I could make out the impression of Neil amongst the blankets. I ran my hand over it and found it still warm, a sign that he'd only recently moved.

Was he gone?

Had he returned to Chicago with Megan?

"How are you feeling?" I jumped as the door swung open and the man himself appeared, a glass of milk in one hand and a plate in the other. His hoodie was unzipped, and he wore a white T-shirt underneath that emphasized his abdominal muscles. After so many agonizing months, I knew that the sight of him like this, looking casual and rumpled first thing in the morning, would be ingrained in my memory forever.

He was as lovely as a painting, and I'd be admiring him all my life.

I gulped. What I really wanted to do was tear off those clothes and show him that I could do more for him than all his other useless lovers put together. We used to communicate so well between the sheets, and I missed that intimacy, especially because Neil was often at his most vulnerable during those times. It was when he'd give another little piece of himself.

"A lot better, thanks. Did you stay here all night?" I adjusted the pillows behind my back and made myself comfortable against the headboard. Neil sat down beside me and checked my forehead, unconsciously licking his lips. I held perfectly still, just staring at him in a daze.

"Yes. Fortunately, your temperature's gone down. I had to get your father to write a prescription for you. You were very sick. He and my mother are downstairs. They wanted to see you, but I asked if I could be alone with you for a little while," he added hastily, seeming uncomfortable. It surely wasn't easy for him, seeing his mother again after everything that had happened and knowing how she'd lied to him for years. I wanted to ask if he'd given her a chance to try to explain herself, but, knowing him, he'd just thrown up an impassable wall of pride.

Neil gave me a watchful look, and I gave him a small smile, trying to wordlessly express my gratitude to him. "I also took off your clothes because you got really overheated and sweated a lot." He glanced quickly at my legs, and I grimaced. I blushed violently at the thought of the horrible white panties I was wearing with the dumb little pink heart in the middle. Neil set my breakfast down on the bedside table and stared deep into my eyes.

"You shouldn't be embarrassed about me seeing you in your underwear. Your captain did too, didn't he?" he needled. I had already been more than clear about what happened with Ivan, but Neil continued to poke at it because he thought I was lying to him. He couldn't wrap his head around me staying faithful to him even when we were no longer together.

"He didn't see my underwear. I already told you—nothing happened," I said again.

Still, I felt so small and impotent beneath his glowering, scrutinizing stare. His jaw clenched and his eyes darkened. I began to wonder if Neil was incapable of coping with me having any contact at all with another boy, no matter how relatively minor.

"So he didn't touch you?" He looked away from me so I couldn't read his emotions on his face and handed me the glass of milk. I took it just to humor him, but I didn't actually feel like drinking it so I simply held it in my hands.

"He didn't touch me *there*, if that's what you're getting at," I clarified.

"And did you touch him?" he pressed. I stared at him in horror.

"No! Oh my God!" I burst out. "No," I said again, embarrassed. He heaved a sigh of relief, like I'd just lifted an enormous boulder off his chest. Then he gave me a lascivious smile.

"Good job, Babygirl." He shrugged in his usual careless way and pointed at the still-full glass of milk. I shook my head and his gaze turned ominous. If I didn't obey him, we were going to have a fight, and so, with a huff of irritation, I brought it to my lips and took a sip.

"I do have some self-respect. The things I've been feeling ever since I met you are real, not the delusions you pretend they are. I couldn't just slot someone else into your place. But you did…" I felt like I might puke just thinking about it, jealousy tightening my stomach. I immediately moved the glass away from my lips as they twisted in disgust. Neil spotted it and shot me a miserable look.

"I brought you some breakfast…" He changed the subject, grabbing the plate and offering it to me. Up close, I could see that it was a slice of cherry pie. Where did he get that? My heart swelled with emotion. "I asked Anna to make it for you," he told me, sounding almost awkward. I took the plate from him and examined the slice—it looked so good my mouth began to water.

"Thank you…" I answered, marveling at him.

Five minutes later, I'd drunk all the milk, finished all the pie, and was licking my lips delightedly. Neil gave me a satisfied smile.

"Good stuff?" he asked mischievously when he noticed me staring slack-jawed at him. I went tomato-red as I tried to get a grip on myself.

"Yes, very good," I babbled.

"I'm glad." He leaned forward, pressing an unexpected kiss to my forehead. Then he stared at my lips, and I knew what he was trying to tell me without words: He wanted me just as much as I wanted him. He slowly drew his thumb along the contours of my mouth as though trying to memorize it. He gathered a few crumbs as he went and then licked them sensually from his thumb.

I gulped and shifted uncomfortably. Then, all at once, I remembered that he had slept with Megan, and I looked up at him, anguished. The torment on my face must have been obvious, much like the misery that had been grinding me down for months.

"Whatever you're thinking right now, I want a full reset." Neil used two fingers to lift up my chin until our eyes met again. Then, he stretched out over me, forcing me to lie back on the bed. My back hit the mattress as he hovered above. He held himself there, palms on either side of my head. I had no idea what he was going to do next, and the tension only ratcheted up along with my fear that I would succumb to him again.

If he made a move, I knew I wouldn't have the strength to reject him.

Abruptly, Neil wrathfully tore back the blankets that separated us and studied my bare legs. I opened them to make room for his body between them, and he settled down on me. I could feel his erection, hard and insistent between my thighs, and my longing for him exploded in my chest.

My head spun, my body temperature spiked again, and my knees went weak. One of his typically savage sex sessions probably would have killed me at that point.

So I tried—I tried as hard as I could—to resist him.

"Please...no..." I put my hands against his hips, and he could feel how anguished I was. My soul was already shattered; I would feel so used if he took something from me without being able to give me any reassurances in return.

I could no longer tolerate that kind of behavior from him.

"It's okay. I don't want to do that. Not with you, not like this." He dropped a tender kiss on my forehead, and I was surprised at his reaction. For a brief, stupid moment, I wondered if his attraction to me had faded and he didn't want me at all anymore. Maybe he preferred Megan? "There's something else I want." He ran the tip of his nose over my cheek and then down to my throat, breathing me in deep like he'd missed the smell, like it was the most incredible perfume he'd ever encountered. His wild hair tickled my skin, and his stubble rubbed against me, drawing shivers of pleasure.

"What do you want?" I asked shakily. I rubbed his strong back and squeezed my legs more tightly around him, letting him know that I was there for him and I always would be.

"I want you to make me some promises." Neil stared intensely into my eyes. He looked like he was about to ask for something extreme, something important.

"Okay..." I looked at his lips, where I'd left a trace of myself. Where I'd given all of myself.

"Promise me..." Neil propped himself up on his elbows and played with my hair with one hand. "Promise me that...you'll always have faith in yourself, even when people try to hurt you. Promise me that you'll keep making mistakes, but that you'll learn from them. Promise me that you'll become the person you want to be and do everything in your power to make your dreams come true."

He gave me a small but earnest smile, and it made my heart beat faster. "Promise me that you'll always keep those ocean eyes so deep and luminous, that you will live your life to the fullest. Promise me that you will stay good and sweet because it's the world that's wrong, not you, Selene..." He squeezed his eyes shut as though trying to capture the moment and take it away with him to wherever he went next. Then he opened his eyes again and they rested on me: hot, intense, and gleaming.

"Promise me that you won't be afraid of anything, but that you'll stay away from deadly things and guard yourself like a precious jewel, because that is what you are. You are the most beautiful thing God ever made." He smiled as he rested his forehead against mine, and I wrapped my legs possessively around him. I could feel him pulling away again, this time for good. "Promise me that if you ever meet another man who is anything like me, you'll stay far away from him. Because people like me can't change, and you deserve so much more." He sighed deeply and gave me a silently reproving look, but I would never undo any part of us. I would do it all again in a heartbeat because he was where my life truly began. He was the reason I felt alive, that I figured out who I was and who I wanted to become.

"Promise me that you'll make love like you've always wanted with someone who is not me and is not like me. Promise me that you'll love again, someone other than me. Promise me that you'll allow yourself to have another chance, that you'll become a loving wife and mother, and that you'll allow only the right man to take his place beside you. Promise me you'll fly high because that's why fairies have wings: to get away from evil and all the people who want to hurt them. Promise me that this time in your life will be a lesson and that you'll learn it well. That you'll understand in the future that the damned cannot be saved. We might need an angel, but we can never be like them. Promise me that you'll see that I'm telling you the truth, no matter how much I wish it were different. No matter how much I wish it could be some other way for us. Promise me that you'll keep on believing in love and that you'll give your whole heart to the ones who deserve it because your heart is so precious. It's worth so much more than you think, Tinkerbell." He brushed his lips across my own and shut his eyes, holding back the urge to kiss me.

But, Mr. Disaster, I can't make those promises to you. I won't.
Never.

Instead, I promise that I'll never stop loving you.

I promise I'll never stop belonging to you.

I promise that you will always be there; no matter how far you go, you will remain with me. Inside me.

You will forever be a part of me.

I wanted to tell him all of that, but instead I just shook my head.

"Kiss me." It wasn't a request. I grabbed his head and seized his mouth, and I infused that kiss with every promise I would not keep.

"Selene." Neil pulled back, staring at me in shock, his mouth swollen and glistening from the passionate kiss I'd stolen from him. We were both struggling to catch our breaths, our cheeks red, our eyes bright with desire, and our bodies aflame. I could feel what he felt—something strong, powerful, incontrovertible. His body was motionless against mine, our hearts beating as one. The connection between us was real and profound. It was silent, but it was true.

I found myself in his eyes.

I found security in his arms.

I found home in his scent.

We were bound together.

We were a mess of contradictions.

We were want, dangerous energy, and vivacity.

A calamitous love.

Unstable magic that had created something awe-inspiring.

"I always thought you were made to push my madness beyond all boundaries, Tinkerbell," he murmured, a look of sorrow passing over his face. "But I can't follow you…" He sighed, fighting himself. "I'm heading back to Chicago tomorrow." He moved to get up, trying to avoid looking at me.

"Wait." I restrained him with my legs, pressing my heels hard into his butt. I wrapped my arms around his back, the same back that so many other women had stroked and clawed in the months we'd been apart. But none of them had been able to lay a finger on his soul. It wasn't an easy thing to get to. It was hard, clawing through the armor that Neil used to protect himself from the world. And I knew that better than anyone.

"Please, Selene. Just let me go..." he begged, squeezing his eyes shut and breathing heavily. He wanted to stay with me on this bed. He probably even wanted to make love the way he always did, with all the fiery longing inside him. I could feel him between my legs, his torso pressing down on my breasts, his hips grinding slowly against me, but he was trying not to lose control. "I am fucking begging you... and never in my life have I ever begged anyone for anything." He clenched his hands into fists on either side of my head. His breathing grew labored, and he chewed his lower lip, continuing to fight his own instincts.

"I know you don't want to go. I can feel it," I insisted. I touched his face and stared deeply into his eyes, trying to remind him of what we were until six months before. "You want to run away because you're afraid of what you're feeling right now and of what you might feel if you let yourself go with me right now on this bed. Am I right?" I whispered gently against his lips. I moved to kiss him properly, but he turned his face aside.

"Have you ever trusted someone else as much as you trust me? Have you ever made love to a woman like you did to me? Have you ever allowed yourself to let go completely? Have you looked any of the others in the eye the whole time? Have you slept beside any of them through the night? Did you ever hold them? Tell them about yourself? Did you do all of that with anyone else?" I demanded. Neil gave me a thoughtful look. He rested his forehead against mine and shook his head. "You were making love to me in your own way all along, without realizing it. Maybe these months of separation have helped you see that. And that's the truth." Neil closed his eyes, and I felt his body shivering, softening slowly, and with a sigh of frustration, he allowed himself to rest atop me.

The last bit of his resistance melted away as he laid his cheek on my chest, right where my heart was.

I slid my fingers into his hair and held him, cuddling him close to me, because there was no need to do anything else. He was already inside of me, just like I was already inside of him.

....

Megan had gone over to her parents' place while I was sick. I didn't ask if she was going back to Chicago with Neil.

Instead, I stayed in my room, in bed.

According to my father, I was still too weak to get up.

I'd reluctantly let him come see me, and it had been strange talking to him again. He was never going to accept my relationship with Neil, and just like he always did, he made that clear again with cutting words.

We all ate lunch together, though, like we were a happy family in a holiday commercial. Despite the fact that there was nothing joyful about us at all.

Neil wouldn't even sit at the table—he couldn't bear to be that close to his mother.

Fortunately, Logan and Chloe were there to keep the mood up.

Neil seemed to be back to his old self with them.

When I'd come down for lunch, I'd seen the three of them in the living room talking, but I'd given them their privacy. I had no idea what they were saying to one another, but my heart swelled with joy when Neil pulled them both into an affectionate hug.

Maybe he was finally realizing that even though they had different fathers, they were still siblings, connected by a bond so durable that nothing and no one could ever destroy it. Not even William Miller, that total bastard.

After lunch, I returned to my bed. My temperature hadn't spiked, but I still had a very bad headache, and my body felt weak.

When I was feeling a bit stronger, I took a shower to scrub off some of the sweat from the previous night. I got dressed then in a heavy sweater and jeans because I was still cold.

"Sure you're not hungry? You skipped dinner."

I gasped when Neil walked into the room without knocking or asking for permission, as usual.

"No, I had plenty at lunch. I feel like a beached whale," I said, giving him a fond look.

Neil burst out laughing in response. He shut the door behind him and leaned back against it, folding his arms over his chest.

"You've lost weight, actually. But at least you kept that ass plump and sexy," he noted, narrowing his eyes.

"Apparently you never miss an opportunity to check in on it," I shot back.

"I'd love to do a lot more than that with your ass, Tinkerbell," he said in an impish whisper. The room felt like it was filled with him, inundated with his powerful scent, a little, inescapable cage for me. I sat down on the side of the bed and planted my feet firmly on the floor.

"I'm in the mood for..." I paused, looking him carefully up and down. He watched me curiously, waiting to hear what I was going to say. His hand tightened on the opposite bicep, and he swallowed hard, and I could see what he wanted now that I was feeling better.

"Pop Rocks," I finished with a big grin. Neil made a face and cocked his head to one side in confusion. A lock of chestnut hair fell over his eyebrow. He was so beautiful even when he was blinking in befuddlement.

I got up and grabbed my coat, moving purposefully toward the door.

"What are you doing?" he demanded.

"I want to go buy some." I shrugged as I grabbed my purse and slung it over my shoulder. "I haven't had them since..." I froze to avoid saying Jared's name. The last time I'd had Pop Rocks was when my ex had shown up at my house in Detroit and given me a package of them along with an apology bouquet.

I shook my head, shoving that memory back down. I didn't want to talk to Neil about him; it wasn't right.

"What the hell are Pop Rocks?" Neil pushed off the door abruptly and advanced on me, still looking confused.

How could he not have heard of Pop Rocks?

"They're my favorite candy. They taste like candy floss. You should really try them; they're—"

"We can't go out. You're sick," he scolded, adopting the autocratic tone that I despised. I snorted, and with what I believed to be an uncharacteristic boldness, I walked right over to him.

I stopped right in front of him and tilted my face up to look into his eyes.

God, his eyes...

"I'm not asking for permission," I answered insolently, suppressing the urge to just kiss him.

He gave an annoyed sigh and raised a hand to cup my cheek. I sucked in a breath at the motion, which felt somehow both affectionate and dominating.

Just then, Neil could have pushed me down on the bed and swallowed me up, demonstrated all of his possessive power over me and shown me how badly he wanted to reassert his place after months apart. But he did none of that and instead just gave me a merry little smile that warmed my heart.

"So spoiled... Come on, let's go buy you some fucking Pop Rocks," he grumbled irritably, and I did a little happy dance. I was about to throw my arms around him, but he raised a hand in protest and shook his head at me. "No, do not latch on. You know I can't stand it when you're so—"

"Sickly sweet," I finished for him with a huff.

Half an hour later, we were in Logan's Audi R8.

I'd asked Neil to call for a ride, but he insisted on pestering his brother until Logan lent us the car. He'd finally agreed, only telling Neil not to smoke like he usually did inside the car for the sake of the leather seats.

Neil drove with easy mastery, one hand on the steering wheel, the other on the shifter, and his gaze pointed out the windshield.

The idea that he was going to leave for Chicago the next day was deeply troubling.

What would become of us? Would we stay in contact? Would he even give me the chance to make a choice about whether or not I wanted to be with him this time or would he continue to do what my mother had asked and ignore what I wanted?

He stopped for a red light on a lonely street illuminated only by a few streetlamps and the signs on the closed stores. It was late and close to Christmas, so we still hadn't found a place open that would have my candy. I leaned back in my seat and looked at the billboard out the window.

"Think it was worth it?" Neil asked abruptly, and I turned to him. He was drumming his index finger on the steering wheel as he stared blankly at the traffic light.

His face was so impassive that, for a second, I thought I'd imagined him speaking to me.

"What are you referring to?" I asked.

"This *thing* that has been going on with us since we first met," he answered tersely. I remained silent, the song on the radio an accompaniment to my thoughts until, finally, I spoke. "Do you mean was it worth the risk, the pain, and you putting me through the wringer all just to experience what we've shared?" I asked, perhaps a little too bluntly, because he shot me a look and just nodded coolly.

"Of course, it was. If I had it to do all over again the only thing I would change is maybe slapping you a few more times. I was way too lenient with you, honestly..." I answered sincerely. He laughed out loud, but I wasn't joking.

What if he got bored of me? What if he thought of me as just a friend he'd sought comfort from in the past?

I was pulled from those morose thoughts when Neil grabbed my hand and brought it to his lips for a gentlemanly kiss. Then he met my eyes and smiled at me.

"After Kim, I couldn't feel joy. All I could see was darkness and evil all around me. But you were the one joyful moment life allowed me. Brief but intense. My Neverland. And that's what you'll always be, Tinkerbell," he said in a tragic murmur. I was stunned by his confession; it hit me straight in the heart. He released my hand, and I just barely managed not to cry. He could sense that and began to put more emotional distance between us again, turning his attention to the stoplight. He didn't wait to hear what I had to say; he didn't want to hear it. He wasn't asking me for anything in return; he was merely opening his heart to me for a single, brief moment. He'd given me a glimpse of his marvelous soul, the one I'd fallen in love with so long ago.

The light turned green, and he hit the gas, driving through the intersection.

I sat back in my seat and turned to look at him. I wanted to tell him that he didn't have to leave me behind, that I would always be with him, but I didn't have time to speak.

A pair of blazing headlights blinded me.

My eyes went wide.

A van was barreling down on us, about to crash into the car.

I screamed and clutched Neil's arm.

He turned and saw the approaching lights, getting closer with every second.

But it was already too late.

A collision.

A crash so powerful that I could feel my bones break. My head smashed against the passenger window.

A stab of pain shot down my spine.

My heart stuttered.

I lost feeling in my body.

I was cold…too cold…

26

"Neil was so still that I immediately knew he was unconscious."

SELENE

How ephemeral was the barrier between life and death?

I knew for certain that I touched it—I saw Death's face.

But while life did take a little break, she did not abandon me altogether. She came right back to me.

I could feel the beat of my heart; it was slow, but it was there.

I was lying on the ground, my cheek pressed to the cold ground, the taste of blood heavy on my tongue.

How had I gotten out of the car?

More importantly—where was I?

I flexed the fingers of one hand to make sure I was really still alive, but they immediately fell limp, too weak to do anything.

Warily, I moved my head slightly to try to figure out what was happening around me.

I was in a building of some sort. Old with bare concrete walls, it was dirty and poorly maintained. There were dust and pieces of rubble everywhere.

It seemed like a warehouse or something like that.

And then I spotted the three figures standing nearby.

They all were dressed in black, their faces covered with colorful masks. Two of them were dragging Neil's body, holding him by the ankles like he was some animal carcass. Neil was so still that I immediately knew he was unconscious at the very least, and it felt like my heart was being squeezed in a vise.

"Tie the asshole up before he comes to. We're fucked if he does," one of them ordered. It was a menacing, decidedly male voice. I tried again to move, but my muscles wouldn't obey me. I fought, focusing on them, but the pain was too intense.

I could feel my heart beating slowly in my chest, my breath scraping at my lungs, leaking out in small, pained gasps.

"Neil..." I mumbled.

"Is she alive?" another one of them asked.

"Yeah."

I didn't recognize the voices; it was hard to distinguish one from another.

I couldn't feel my body; my brain was sending out signals that my muscles simply weren't receiving.

"Deal with her, Gregory," the first man who had spoken ordered. Slowly, I shifted my eyes to him. His mask was white, and it covered his face completely with just two small slits for his eyes, allowing their cruelty to show.

Was this Player?

I couldn't be sure, but the mask reminded me a lot of the one I'd seen the person in the Jeep wearing just before my taxi crashed.

"The rest of you, over here," he continued impatiently.

I fought my body's weakness as even my eyes struggled to remain open, but I needed to see who these bastards were. Suddenly, hands wrapped around my wrists and pulled me up. I screamed with every breath of air I had left in my lungs until I found myself upright with an unfamiliar torso at my back. My legs weren't strong enough to support me, so the man behind me put an arm around me to keep me from crumpling back down to the ground.

"Up and at 'em, girly. We want you to watch," he whispered into my ear. I could feel his slimy breath on my skin, and vomit rose up in the back of my throat. He used one hand to grab my jaw and force me to look at the group of masked men who had surrounded Neil. They'd tied his hands with ropes to keep him from moving, even while semiconscious.

A rivulet of blood leaked from one corner of his mouth and another from a wound on his temple.

"Neil!" I screamed, but the man behind me pulled me tight against himself to silence me.

"Don't bother yelling, you little slut," he threatened. "No one's around to hear you anyway. Be patient—we'll have our fun with you later. Right now, it's his turn." He ground himself against my ass, and I tried in vain to wriggle away from his body touching mine.

"Who are you?" I demanded.

"Boss, kitten here wants to know who we are," the guy behind me said, loud and mocking, and the one in the white mask who appeared to be giving orders turned to look at us. I shivered. He stood up straight and walked toward me; I felt like I was crumpling into myself with every step he took, like a discarded piece of paper in his fist. He stopped right in front of me and cocked his head to one side.

I thought I could make out a pair of light-colored eyes, but I wasn't sure.

His collar-length blond hair, however, was visible. He raised his hand, and I cringed, turning my face away to try to avoid his touch. His whole torso vibrated with a guttural laugh.

This was fun for him. All just a game.

"You are sick in the head!" I spat at him, ignoring the terror that I could feel churning in the bottom of my stomach.

"Oh, but you remember me...don't you, Selene?" he whispered, honey-sweet, and I knew then that this was him. I was looking at Player in the flesh.

"No...don't touch her..." Neil's voice echoed off the walls of the place, sending a jolt of warmth straight to my heart. Player and I both turned to look at him.

Neil was trying to get up using just his legs, despite his injuries.

He was panting for breath, and after several tries, he managed to get shakily to his feet. His cold gaze was unyielding.

He was prepared to fight anyone who tried to lay a hand on me.

"People, what the fuck are you doing? Bring him to his knees," Player ordered. One of the masked men punched him in the stomach, and Neil doubled over. Then his knees hit the concrete, just like that bastard wanted.

"No! Leave him alone!" I screamed again, swamped by terror. I tried to wriggle and flail, but the stranger behind me was strong enough to hold me still.

"Do you think you scare me? You're a bunch of assholes in masks! Why don't you grow a pair and show your real faces?" Neil exploded, tightening his abdomen against another stab of pain.

He raised his face to look directly at Player, who began to laugh robustly in response.

"I know that I'm the one you want," Neil went on. "So take me and leave her," he added through his gritted teeth. Player jerked his chin at one of the men, and my heart began to pound, my knees getting even weaker.

"No! Please! Don't hurt him!"

No one paid me any mind. One of the men grabbed Neil's arm and dragged him to his feet. The man held him from behind, pushing Neil forward like a human sacrifice for the other man who let out an evil laugh.

I screamed and struggled even harder. My throat burned, my lungs ached, and my heart cracked open in my chest.

"No! Don't hurt him! Please!" I insisted in a rush of desperate tears.

"Please!" I sobbed again. The man behind gave me a sharp shake and swore at me, telling me to shut up.

"You don't scare me, you sons of bitches," Neil hissed between his teeth with terrifying determination. It was a determination that would cost him dearly because he had no way of defending himself with his hands tied behind his back. And, sure enough, the guy in front of him buried his fist in Neil's abdomen again.

I felt a stab of pain in my own stomach, like I'd been punched along with him.

Tears blurred my already hazy vision, but I could still see, I could still hear... It was all too clear what was happening.

More blows followed, one after another.

Neil didn't scream; he didn't make a sound. He just absorbed the hits, squeezing his eyes shut with each swing, gritting his teeth at each burst of pain, and tightening his abdominal muscles to mitigate some of the outrageous violence.

I shut my eyes because I wasn't strong enough to keep watching. I wasn't brave enough.

Each strike seemed to hit me as well.

I could feel them against my flesh. I could feel the pain.

It was like a hammer swinging forward unstoppably to shatter his bones, and it was breaking me too.

I wanted to cover my ears so I wouldn't hear the wrathful grunts of the bastard who was beating the hell out of Neil, but my own wrists were still pinned behind my back by the asshole holding me.

"Stop it! Please, just stop it!" I pleaded under Player's icy gaze. He was watching the scene unfold before him without a hint of pity or even basic human compassion. His arms were loose at his sides, his face turned toward Neil, and his posture stiff and confident.

"That's enough for now," he said finally. The man immediately stopped hitting Neil and took a step back.

I tracked Neil's body with my eyes as the second guy dropped him. My chest grew unbearably tight when I watched him hit the ground, covered in sweat, weak, and suffering. His lower lip was split, and blood was streaming from deep wounds on his face. His chest rose and fell rapidly, and his eyes were closed, but he was still there. I could hear him panting, trying to stay in the world.

"Neil!" I called out desperately, and surprisingly, the asshole behind me actually let me go. I pulled myself across the floor until I could kneel beside him. I could smell the metallic odor of blood in the air. Neil had curled into the fetal position, trying to protect his wounded torso. He coughed wetly. "Hey..." I said in the gentlest whisper, rubbing my nose along his sweat-slick cheek. I stroked his hair, all covered in dirt and dust and forgot about everything else.

I even forgot about the men standing all around us. The men who deserved to die slow, painful deaths for what they'd done to him. I curled up against him as if to transmit my warmth to him.

If they wanted to hit him, now they'd have to hit me too.

I laid down over Neil, showing those monsters my back. I was trying to protect him, to shield him, even though my body was far too small to cover his.

His eyes were still closed and puffy, his equally swollen lips slightly parted.

"Neil...I'm right here, Neil. Tell me you're okay." My voice shook with fear that he wasn't going to open his eyes, making me spiral. If he didn't come back to me, I... I...

My fear, which prevented me from even forming clear thoughts, fell away as those golden eyes opened to rest dazedly on my face. I smiled in relief and pressed my forehead to his. "Nothing's going to happen to you; I swear on my life. You have to stay with me," I told him, whispering so softly that only he and I could hear. Neil tried to move, but he immediately winced in pain and groaned.

"Selene..." he muttered under his breath. "Quit fucking around... get back." His breathing was labored; he struggled just to string together a few words. I had no intention of leaving him alone to face all of this, to absorb a punishment he didn't deserve, or to be destroyed by these psychopaths and their madness. But one of the men grabbed me by the forearm and lifted my unwilling body and tossed me aside like a rag doll. I crumpled to the ground right on top of a pair of women's shoes. I looked up at her and immediately recoiled in fear. How had I failed to notice that there was a woman?

She had blond hair and a red mask.

"Get away from him! What do you want from us? What do you want?" I burst out.

They had completely surrounded us. There was no escape route.

There were so many of them; they were cruel and much stronger than us, especially when we were still nursing our wounds from the car wreck.

My eyes locked on Player and the men flanking him.

Another man moved to stand behind Neil, watching his every move. The others appeared to be simply awaiting instructions.

"That was just a taste, Neil." Player advanced on him slowly. Then he gave Neil's arm the slightest nudge with the toe of his shoe. Neil tried again to get up on his feet, but he couldn't do it. He struggled into a kneeling position instead and glared up at Player. His coat was open and bedraggled, and there was blood all over his white sweater. Player snapped his fingers, and, as one, everyone around us brought their hands to their faces and began to remove their masks.

They tossed them on the ground one by one, all of them except for Player. He alone kept his face concealed. I gasped when I recognized two of the faces, and a chill passed through me.

"So lovely to see you again, angel..." Bryan Nelson burst into a laugh so diabolical that it gave me goosebumps. I remembered him; I'd met him once at the first party I'd ever gone to with Logan, just after I arrived in New York. He was the host, and he'd tried to pick me up, but I'd shot him down immediately.

His brother was Carter Nelson, the boy Neil had beaten up for trying to rape Chloe. How had I not thought about the Nelson brothers before?

"Wait—how do you know her?" the blond girl, her red mask dangling from her hand, moved over to him and allowed me to get a better look at her. It was Britney. The girl Neil had used to get under my skin that night in the pool house with the Krew. The same one we'd seen later in the club with Megan.

What did she have to do with this? What could she possibly want from us?

She moved closer to Bryan and blinked curiously at him as he draped an arm around her shoulders, whispering something into her ear.

"Gregory, Lex, Dallas, Dean..." Neil muttered, his eyes going wide. "Seriously, Nelson?" He turned to look at the blond woman, his jaw clenching. "You set your teammates and some whore I fucked on me? Why?" Neil demanded.

"Why? Are you actually asking me that?" Bryan raged. He made a fist with one hand, ready to hit Neil again, but Player raised a hand, cowing him into stillness. Bryan gave a growl of rage and began to speak again. "You beat the hell out of my brother. He was in a coma—he almost died because of you, you motherfucker. Did you think you'd just get away with it? When this guy came looking for me..." he gestured to Player standing motionless next to him, "and asked if I wanted to get back at you, I agreed. I agreed and cut a deal with him because we both had the same goal: to see you fucking dead. I got my friends to help keep an eye on you. Britney let you pick her up just to see what kind of relationship you had with Selene. Then she posed as Player in that fucking video chat. We wanted to throw you off the scent, making you think Player was a woman. We were fucking with you, Miller," he explained.

"So you're the one who thought up all the puzzles and carried out all the attacks?" Neil asked, in shock. Bryan shook his head with an evil grin.

"Nah, I just helped out a bit. Logan's wreck and your skank's and the one with Chloe, the rock through your windshield, all of that..." He paused, a malicious gleam in his eyes. "I helped Player carry it out. But I didn't make up the riddles..." He turned to look at the only man still wearing a mask.

The masked man raised both arms, making the dark fabric of his sweatshirt stretch over his biceps as he uncovered his face with an agonizing slowness.

Little by little, I watched his sharp features emerge: a short beard, a square jaw, thin lips, hair the color of wheat, and gleaming eyes, such a light blue that they were almost white. He tossed his mask at Neil, and I watched Neil's face to see if there was any recognition there, but all I saw was bewilderment.

"I used to see you out in the yard when I'd come to get Megan. You were always alone out there, just playing by yourself with this old basketball. A snot-nosed little outcast. I actually felt sorry for you..." Player said, and Neil narrowed his eyes. A flare of understanding ignited there.

Neil knew exactly who this man was.

"Ryan..." he murmured, sounding stupefied. The man lifted one side of his mouth in a sinister smile. "You're supposed to be in prison..." Neil continued, horrified. All at once, the air turned icy, and time seemed to stand still as a rivulet of cold sweat made its way down my temple. Player was Ryan Von Doom.

Neil had told me all about him: He had used his position as a guitar teacher to abuse children, specifically Megan. But his real career had been as the owner and operator of an illegal dark website, trafficking videos and images of that same abuse for other pedophiles online. He had been the one pulling Kimberly Bennett's strings.

"You're right, I should be," he shot back cheerfully. "But you know, Neil, there are just so many loopholes in the legal system…" He laughed with gusto, sounding delighted. "I was operating my network, building my business, giving all sorts of people a place where they could discover themselves and explore their sexual fantasies. You probably didn't know this, but there were plenty of important people using my site: judges, lawyers, doctors, law enforcement, politicians… The dark web is the blackest part of the internet's soul. On my end, I could verify who had accessed the site and track my users' data. I got email addresses, phone numbers, home addresses, everything I needed to threaten whoever tried to get in my way."

He grinned in that delighted way again, like he was proud of what a slimy bastard he was. "I held their careers, their public images, in the palm of my hand, and they knew it. So I played a few cards to reduce my charges. I wound up doing a few years behind bars, took a rehabilitation course here and there, and, of course, spent a little time in a psychiatric facility." He drew perilously close to Neil and circled him slowly, smiling that unceasing smile. He was so puffed up with sick satisfaction at having wriggled out of his rightful sentence. "Sure, I maybe have escaped doing real time in the end, but I didn't want to spend *any* time in prison, Neil. And, if it weren't for you, I never would have. I had a good thing going, and then your call to the police blew it all to hell. You are the reason the cops came looking for me after they arrested Kim. It was your pigheaded rebelliousness that ruined everything. When Kim told me that you were uncontrollable and unsuited to our needs, I doubted her. I thought you would change. That, with time, you'd learn how to obey like the other little shits. But you never did. Instead, you destroyed everything we'd built. You destroyed all of our lives." Ryan's eyes had turned cloudy with twisted evil.

"I have been in hell ever since the day that you..." he stabbed a finger at Neil with all the rage he could summon up, "ruined everything! I was arrested; I was threatened and attacked when my so-called crimes were spread across the front pages of every paper in the city. Meanwhile you...everyone thought you were some superhero, saving all the little bastards like you from big, bad criminals like us." He stopped in front of Neil, daring him to respond.

"You're a deranged lunatic. I did the right thing!" Neil blurted out fearlessly. He was sweating from the pain, purpling bruises spread over his face, and his eyes had emptied of all emotion, replaced instead by two pits of fire.

"When I was in prison, all I thought about was how to get back at you. After I attacked a few of my fellow inmates and attempted suicide a couple times, a judge allowed me to be transferred to a psychiatric facility. I had realized pretty quickly that it would be a lot easier to get out of there than a maximum security prison. I pretended I was crazy just to get out and find you so I could end you." He laughed, smugly pleased with himself, and I shuddered.

"You weren't pretending, you crazy son of a bitch!" Neil shot back. By then, he'd managed to stagger back up on his feet, but Bryan pounced on him, grabbing him by the shoulders and holding him still so Ryan could take the opportunity to backhand Neil so hard the corner of his mouth began to bleed. I sucked in a breath at the sudden violence and then screamed. With a strength I didn't know I had, I stood up, but Britney immediately elbowed me in the stomach, sending me back down to my knees. She knocked the wind out of me, and I curled forward in pain.

"Quiet, skank," she said menacingly. She positioned herself right next to me so she could keep an eye on me. I shot her a glare filled with undiluted hatred before turning my attention back to Neil, who was looking at me.

"Don't touch her, you cunt!" he shouted furiously at the blond girl. He twisted madly against the rope, but two of the other guys came up to stop him.

"Fucking hold him," Ryan cut in, impatiently watching his lackeys struggle to pin Neil, despite the fact that he was still tied up. One of them aimed a kick at the base of his spine, and Neil contorted in pain but did not cry out. He wasn't going to give them the satisfaction.

He landed on the floor, gasping for air.

"Neil!" I cried, but he just spat a glob of blood at Ryan's shoes and lifted his face to glare at him.

Neil's eyes were alight with rage. I was afraid that he wasn't going to be able to stop himself from provoking that madman and that we would never get out of that warehouse alive.

"You know, Ryan, you and I do have something in common—our incredibly fucked-up brains. So you must know that you can hit me all you want, torture me, kill me... but I'll never let you break me. You don't scare me, and you never will." He grinned, all defiance, but then he fell into a coughing spasm. He was obviously in bad shape, and I wanted nothing more than to run to him and hold him in my arms, to try to bolster him in some way. But Britney was on top of me, preventing me from getting up.

"I suggest you quit trying to irritate me," Ryan said menacingly. Neil just laughed in his face. It was a tense laugh because I could see that Neil desperately wanted to hit him, but he couldn't, and that rage was spreading like a poison inside him, a corrosive acid that ate away at his reason.

"No! Don't hurt him anymore! Please." Despair filled my voice, and tears rolled down my face at my own helplessness. There was nothing I could do to save Neil, nothing I could do to end this insane situation. Ryan turned to look at me, and his eyes narrowed in consideration. For a moment, I even managed to delude myself into thinking that he might actually listen to me. Then he turned his attention back to Neil, kneeling before him, and his stare turned spiteful.

"I know how tough you are, Neil, and I know that you're not afraid of anything. That's why I've had to plan all of this down to the smallest detail," he said in a deep, unsettling voice. "I had Bryan watching you at the university. He was my spy. He noticed that you'd often sketch pentagrams in your notebooks during classes. Did you know that Kim had one tattooed right on her back?" he asked, squatting down on his heels. He bored those frozen eyes of his deep into Neil's, who just stared back wrathfully, saying nothing. "You might not remember, but I bet your subconscious does," Ryan continued. Neil's eyebrows rose as he struggled to keep a clear head. I knew how much it hurt him to recall that woman at all, so I figured he was trying to fight the memories back down and not show any weakness. His gaze flickered to me, and for a moment it softened.

But then he abruptly cut our eye contact and turned his attention back to Ryan, his gaze dripping with disgust.

"Why 2511? What does it mean?" he hissed through gritted teeth.

Ryan slowly got to his feet, taking his time, straightening his pants before he answered.

"I've always been fascinated by numerology and esoteric symbology. I used it to twist your mind into whatever shapes I desired. The riddles themselves were intended to confuse you, but they also contained messages that would have revealed everything if you'd only figured out how to read them. 2511 was just another riddle that you failed to solve. All you needed to do was understand what each number meant. The number two can symbolize separation, like the kind you forced upon Kim and me when you decided to play hero. You did know that we were lovers, right?" Ryan cocked his head to one side and feigned a sorrowful sigh. "The number five is associated with Mercury and thus with cleverness...my puzzles were rather *clever* if I do say so myself. Don't you agree?" he asked mockingly.

Neil tried again to pull away from the men pinning him, but they held him fast. Ryan went on without pause. "Finally, eleven is a profoundly powerful number. It symbolizes divine justice. I was taking justice into my own hands. I needed to get my revenge on you. Attacking your loved ones was only ever a way to drive you out of your mind, to make you afraid, but you stayed strong. You remained stupidly brave right up to the end. I closed the circle perfectly with the final riddle, number seven: photo, mosaic, missing piece. Remember my puzzle with Logan's acrostic inside it? I sent it along with *photos* of everyone in your family, except you. You, therefore, were the *missing piece* of my *mosaic*. The true target." In one swift, sure motion, Ryan pulled a gun out of the back of his waistband. I was completely petrified as he aimed the gleaming metal barrel right at Neil's forehead. The psycho handled it with obvious skill, his outstretched arm steady, his index finger hovering over the trigger, ready to fire without a moment's hesitation.

Neil swallowed hard, but he showed no sign of shock or terror. He just alternated his gaze between Ryan and the weapon, watching. I could see the beast inside of him: the unstoppable, dangerous, and uncontrollable one.

"Well, I'll be fucked... Nobody told me this was the where the party's at."

Just then, an unexpected voice bounced off the walls of the warehouse. I turned to find Xavier, flanked by the rest of the Krew as they walked toward us. Ryan turned to see who the intruders were, and while he was momentarily distracted, Neil seized the opportunity to elbow one of the guys holding him in the crotch and then head-butt the other. The two of them hit the ground immediately, and Neil aimed a disarming kick at Ryan's wrist. The gun tumbled out of his grasp, and Neil quickly kicked it away.

"Who the fuck are you?" Ryan seemed disoriented. He looked around, trying to see where the gun had gone, and then turned back to Xavier, who continued to swagger through the warehouse.

"The Krew. Haven't you heard of us?" The black-haired boy grinned before whistling nonchalantly.

The basketball players, Bryan included, all backed away fearfully. I realized why when I saw Luke draw even with Xavier, pulling a knife out of his leather jacket. Meanwhile, Jennifer and Alexia swung baseball bats with a challenging ease.

Xavier came to a stop right in front of Ryan, and before the latter could speak, he pressed an index finger to his mouth. I had no idea what the hell Xavier was doing, but I did know that he was crazy and had no limits. He immediately spotted the gun that Neil kicked right at him and stooped to grab it before anyone else could. Then, he immediately pulled one of his own from his jacket.

Now, he held one gun on Bryan, who immediately lifted his hands in surrender, and the other on Player, who blanched but remained motionless, staring at him.

"We followed you after you tossed Neil and Selene into your shitty van. You should have paid a little more attention. All you had to do was look in the rearview mirror once. We were right on your ass the whole way here," Xavier explained, his voice low and menacing. "Now, none of you dumbfucks move, or I'll shoot you and anyone who tries to stop me." He jerked his chin, signaling us to move over to him. Neil drew closer to me, and I gasped as I felt his breath wrap around me like a warm blanket. My head was spinning, and my body was weak, but just being near him gave me the strength I needed to keep fighting.

"Are you okay?" he asked me, concerned. As always, his intense voice reached down to touch the deepest part of me. I didn't answer him. Instead, I just reached out and touched his split lip. "I'm right here with you, Babygirl. You don't have to be afraid. Nothing's going to happen to you—not on my life." He tried to reassure me, and I smiled sadly at him. He inched closer, getting down on his knees until he could kiss the tip of my nose. "I'm right here," he said again, fiercely. I took his face in my hands and kissed him. I knew he needed physical contact, even if it was hardly the most opportune moment.

A second, all I needed was a second...

My tongue slid into his mouth and sought his desperately. I could taste the blood filling his mouth and more tears fell down my face. I didn't want to cry, but I couldn't help it. I wished I had the power to absorb all that physical and mental pain for him. I tried to tell him that with my eyes, and he seemed to understand because he gave me another kiss, this one innocent and brief. A kiss of reassurance. A kiss to say for him too it was enough to simply be in my presence to be "okay." He urged me to get up, and my legs shook as I wrapped my arms around his waist. He was unsteady on his feet, his wrists still bound with ropes, but he was trying not to put too much of his weight on me. Together, we made our way over to Xavier under the defeated stares of the lunatics who had ambushed us.

"Luke, cut Neil free. Jennifer and Alexia, get Selene out of here," Xavier ordered, his weapons still pointed at Player and Bryan. Before I knew it, the two girls had pulled me away from Neil while Luke held onto him so he wouldn't go tumbling to the floor.

"No!" I cried. I couldn't leave that place without him. I stretched out my arms, trying to grab on to him. His mouth curved into a smile that contained pain as well as bravery and gave me a look that said "everything's going to be okay."

"Go, Babygirl. I'll come back to you, I promise," he said in a low murmur. I couldn't quit staring at him, like I might never see him again, like those bastards might start hurting him again. Just thinking about it made more tears spill from my eyes.

"Go, go, hurry up," Xavier prompted us. Without another word, Jennifer dragged me toward the exit with Alexia following closely behind.

Outside, we were surrounded by darkness. Only the warehouse in front of us produced any sort of light.

We walked a few feet away and stopped in front of Xavier's Cadillac, parked in a dirt clearing.

Exhausted, I leaned on the hood and tried to catch my breath.

"Police should be here any minute," Alexia told Jennifer.

It occurred to me then that had the Krew not come in when they did, Ryan would have shot Neil. They may not have had a moral code or much compassion for anyone outside their circle, but they had shown for sure how much they did value and respect Neil.

"Thank you for...for doing what you did." I turned to face the girls so they could see the gratitude in my face, and they both scowled like I'd said something wrong. Jennifer ran a nervous hand over her braid and gave me a mocking smile.

"We didn't do it for you, brat. We did it for Neil," she said haughtily.

"We all know how much you mean to him. There was nothing else we could do," Alexia added, her expression considerably softer. I was just about to answer her when the sound of screams from inside the warehouse made me jump. I assumed the worst and moved to go back inside, but Jennifer automatically stopped me with a hand to my chest.

"Just wait here. It's probably just Luke and Xavier beating the shit out of someone," she said in an attempt at reassurance that did nothing to calm me down.

The noises coming from the warehouse, which sounded more like animal growls of rage, made my skin crawl.

Neil was still in there, and I would die if he didn't come back safe to me.

I stared at the warehouse's entrance the whole time, fear bubbling up to throttle me.

I began to weep with frustration and mentally counted the minutes that passed way too slowly. But then, at last, I spotted Luke and Xavier making their way toward us with Neil between them. He was exhausted and hurt, his head drooping, and the moment I saw him, my heart began to beat again.

Suddenly, he raised his head and his eyes locked on mine.

In all that chaos, Neil was searching for *our* chaos.

Bright and colorful, joyous and pure.

Cobbled together from candy and fortune cookies, secret smiles and chills of delight, and long kisses.

Made of *us*.

"I'm here," I said to him, and his gaze softened. On his face, I saw the guilt he felt over everything: his past, Ryan's insane revenge plot, the eager complicity of Bryan and his friends...all the things that had spilled over onto his loved ones. I shook my head; it wasn't his fault.

He was a victim just like the rest of us.

I began to run toward him; I couldn't wait a moment longer to have him in my arms.

Meanwhile, I heard the sound of police sirens in the distance.

"It's really over," I murmured to myself as I raced toward Neil, and it felt for a moment like the world had been freed from all evil. Suddenly, a dark silhouette lurched into view behind them. I slowed involuntarily as my eyes fixed on the blond head of Ryan, who was at that very moment lifting his arm to aim a gun right at the three men. "Neil!" I screamed and began running again, even faster now with my heart throbbing in my throat.

Xavier frowned, the first to process my warning. He immediately pulled his own gun out of his pants and whirled around to face Ryan.

Everything happened very fast.

Too fast. Two gunshots rang out, making us all tremble. I stopped abruptly and watched as Ryan slowly hit his knees, the gun falling from his limp fingers.

He'd been shot in the abdomen, but his cold eyes looked past Xavier to stare intensely at me. His swollen lips mouthed an almost imperceptible "game over" at me.

What...what was he talking about?

"Neil!" It was Luke's shout that made me understand that the game was, indeed, over. And we had lost.

I stared at Neil's body, his wounded face, his eyes still locked on me.

I ran to him just as his legs were giving out and grabbed him around the waist as he sagged against me.

A viscous moisture spread in the place where our bodies were plastered together. I glanced down and saw a red stain growing across the front of his white sweater.

That was where Ryan's bullet had struck him: right in the chest.

"Neil," I mumbled as he stared deeply into my eyes, a silent farewell. His body collapsed, drained of all strength, and slowly, gently, I lowered him to the ground. I knelt down next to him and cradled his head in my lap. "Neil..." I said again. He was still there with me, I could tell because he blinked and his eyes roved over my face.

"My love...can you hear me? Stay awake. Talk to me. Do anything, but just please don't go to sleep." I stroked his cheek. He looked dazedly into the darkness of the sky and swallowed weakly. His breathing was slow, his gaze absent as though searching inwardly for more strength. But all of his had been swallowed up by the curse that was his life.

There was no one around us then. Just me and Neil, marooned in our Neverland.

I touched his face and his injured mouth, and he groaned in pain. I gave him an apologetic look.

"Neil, you can't pull any dirty tricks on me now, understand?" I murmured around the knot in my throat. "I can't do this without you. You know that I..." I stopped myself before I could say "I love you." Small, simple words that he refused to hear from me because they reminded him of Kim and what she'd done to him.

But I do. I love you. I love you not just for the person that you are but for the person that I become when I am with you.

I wanted to tell him all of it, but I resisted the urge once again because I knew he couldn't take it.

"Selene..." he said in a soft whisper as I continued stroking his cheek. Tears began to pour down my cheekbones, the ocean in my eyes draining away with every labored breath he took. "I know... how you feel. No need to say it." He understood me; he had always understood me, and he was the only one. "*Ya pihi irakema,*" he went on, and my brow furrowed in confusion. I had no idea what he meant—it sounded like he was speaking another language. "The...Yanomami people...that's what they say when...when... it means, 'I have been contaminated by your being.'" A coughing fit forced him to stop, and I stroked his hair soothingly, and he gulped before continuing. "It means...that a part of you is with me forever. It lives and grows inside me," he managed. His chest was heaving, but slowly, so slowly, and there was nothing I could to do to stop the terrible thing that was happening to him except cling to the thin hope that a miracle might occur.

Neil's eyelids drooped, as though he were about to sleep, and I touched him gently, trying to keep him with me.

"Don't go to sleep. Help is coming, okay? We're going to be okay. You're going to be okay." I kept touching his face all over, trying to transmit my love to him through the skin. His skin was still warm. His heart was still beating. He was still right there with me, just like the stars watching us from above and the moon that held court over the entire world. Even the unfair parts. Even the cruel parts.

"I always told you that I never...say I'm sorry, but I guess... now's the time to do that. I'm so sorry for...everything I've put you through." He gave me a weak smile and another groan of pain. "Don't cry, Tinkerbell...it's not over yet. Remember..." he went on in a small, almost inaudible whisper. "The planetarium?" My vision was starting to blur as I floated in a sea of misery, trying not to drown. Salty tears dripped down and fell from my chin. He lifted his arm and used his index finger to gather them up, collecting them as if to take them with him.

Wherever he decided to go.

"Yes, I remember." I couldn't stop crying. The pain was a tearing, wrenching thing, a cord pulled tight around my throat.

I was choking. I was drowning. *I was dying.*

"Promise me that you'll keep watching the stars. That you'll fight against the pain and not let anything block your dreams..." he whispered. I squeezed his hand, and he wove his fingers into mine, forever. We were forever, etched high in the sky. We were immortal because love is an immortal thing. "That you'll...draw a shell with its pearl when you feel lonely. That you'll forgive me because...if I could do it again, I wouldn't make the same mistakes." His golden eyes turned glassy, the impenetrable wall of pride collapsing right in front of me.

The knight had laid down his shield at my feet. He stood before me, still gleaming, and offered up the little golden chest in which he had always hidden all his feelings.

"Promise me that...you'll let me live inside you too. Think of me when you eat pistachios or find a shell on the beach or open a fortune cookie..." He grinned again, and his breath grew fainter and fainter. He was fighting hard to keep breathing and to keep his eyes open, and I touched him encouragingly again. I knew that he was strong. I knew he could do it.

He had to do it.

"Neil, keep talking to me. Stay right here. Don't close your eyes." I kissed his sweat-slick forehead and held him close to me. My heart pounded against my ribs, and the unceasing tears continued to flow. I blinked hard so I could see his face—his beautiful face—clearly again.

An angel—that's what he was.

But he'd never known that about himself.

If only he could have looked through my eyes. He would have seen himself clearly and the universe he contained within.

"Remember..." he spoke again, and I thanked God that I could still hear his voice. "When I asked...how it ends...for the princess and the dark knight? You deserve...a princess ending...be safe...that would make me happiest." He squeezed my hand in his large, warm palm, but his fingers were already cold and moved stiffly. He coughed again and a look of such intense pain moved over his face that I would have given anything to erase it.

The angels began to gather around him.

I couldn't see them, but I could sense them.

I could feel the little gusts of wind made by the beating of their wings. They were preparing to take him away with them. Away from me to an unknown—unknowable—place.

Maybe there was a better world to go to. Or a distant star.

Our star.

"You can't go. What about me? I can't stand it...you should have a second chance, Neil. You deserve a second chance. You deserve to have it with me." My lips trembled as I clutched him to me.

"I'll never leave you, Babygirl," he whispered again. "I'll be in the wind...the sun...your dreams. I'll be in the perfume of a flower, in a book you read; I'll be in your memory. Wherever your hands or your eyes rest, that's where I'll be. Always with you." He slowly kissed the back of my hand where it rested in his, where it was at home.

"I can't say what love is, Selene." Neil stared up at the sky and gave a long, slow blink. His breathing was getting even slower, and each inhalation was more of a struggle. "Don't think...I could ever believe an 'I love you,' but...if I had to say what love was...to me...I'd say, tell John he was right. Love comes in...many forms. It has ocean eyes and smells like...coconut. Love is the sound of your voice...the feel of your skin, the taste...of your lips...your hands... your words... For me, love wears...your face..." He smiled again, a smile that seemed to sing of all the lovely things the world had to offer. It sang of the little yellow flowers that bloomed in the fields and meadows, of the sweet shade of a sheltering tree, of the wind, and of the sea. It sang in harmony with me.

"The ambulance! It's here!" Xavier shouted as the ambulance came to a stop a few feet away from us.

I hadn't been registering anything that was happening around the two of us. It was as though the entire world had stopped. But I was relieved now to see that help was here. He was going to get the medical attention he needed and go right back to upending my life. I beamed down at Neil, whose head was still balanced on my legs, his bright eyes locked on mine. But something wasn't right.

Slowly, silently, those eyes closed, like the curtain falling after the actors gave their final bows. His hand slipped out of mine, and the sound of his labored breathing ceased, making the silence seem to echo.

"Neil." I touched him gently, the lump in my throat making it hard to get words out. "Neil...you said you wouldn't go..." I choked out.

The honey-colored light in his eyes had gone out. I clutched him to me as tightly as I could, as though I could meld our bodies together and become one with him.

I stared down at him, his eyes closed in eternal sleep. A droplet landed on his face, and almost immediately, another one landed on mine.

Then there was another and another.

I tilted my face up and watched the rain begin to fall hard, like tiny silver pins coming to prick my skin.

Even the heavens were weeping as I did over the cruelties of fate. For the life that was handed to an innocent child, one who did nothing wrong but still suffered such evil at the hands of humanity's worst monsters.

The heavy clouds made it impossible to pick out any stars, save one. I narrowed my eyes.

Yes, there was a single star up there.

Right above us.

It remained there, quiet but unbowed. Shamelessly commanding our attention, heedless of the existence of evil, of misery, like there was nothing in all creation that could cast a shadow over *it*.

It could even force the clouds to move aside so it might look down and illuminate us.

Next to the moon, it shone with a light all its own. They hung there together.

Together in the night sky.

Together amidst the storm.

Together…in the darkness.

The sky had one new star, one beloved by the moon.

Sometimes it would look silver, sometimes gold. And it would show itself every night.

Everyone would see.

It would be outstanding, noble, majestic, and beautiful.

But, more than anything else, it would be far, far away from any sort of pain…

27

*"How impolite, this sun.
How unjust, this life."*

SELENE

I strolled down the tree-lined street.

The sun delicately caressed my skin.

The air was brisk and sweet-smelling all around me.

Maybe I should have gotten a bouquet of flowers for the occasion? But no, Neil wouldn't have liked that.

That kind of mushy stuff wasn't for him; he would always rather have a pack of pistachios.

"Hi, Mr. Disaster..." I knelt down. "How are you? See, I came again to see you today. Did you think I'd forgotten about you? How could I?" I smiled at him.

I wondered if he could see or hear me. I liked to think that he could, that there was some sort of other world where souls had a different kind of life.

"I took my final exam today. Pretty soon, I'll be graduating myself, and you'll be right there with me, won't you?" I stroked the marble tombstone that bore his picture. It was cold to the touch.

"I brought you some pistachios..." I showed him the package

with a sorrowful smile before resting it on the warm ground in front of him, amongst the fresh flowers. I traced the image of him with my fingertips. My eyes ached and my heart hurt; a tear streaked slowly down my face to settle on my lips, where I could still taste him. It was a taste I guarded jealously because it was the most precious one in all the world.

"I still hear you whispering my name at night when I'm trying to sleep. At school, in class, I feel your hands touching me. I still feel your kisses on my body, your honey-colored eyes all over me. It wasn't supposed to be like this. You were hurt so much in life, and you deserved to have a second chance. But life is cruel, you know. It takes from those who don't have anything to give. And sometimes it gives to those who don't deserve it." I imagined that I was touching him as I knelt on the earth while the sun eavesdropped on our conversation from high up in the sky.

How impolite, this sun.

How unjust, this life.

"Who would have guessed that you with all your chaos would be the one to make your way inside my heart? You're a complete weirdo. A total disaster. Way too complicated and unmanageable. And I miss you like I'd miss a limb. I miss watching you draw in your notebook with a cigarette between your lips. I miss your intellect that you tried to hide because you didn't want the world to see how deep you were, how different from your outward appearance. I miss being able to nag you about smoking too much. I miss your dirty jokes that made me turn bright red and how you'd kiss the tip of my nose. It was so unexpected and so sweet.

"Sometimes, I give my mother a kiss like that, and I think of you. Remember when you called her Ms. Calvin? You were always terrible with names." I smiled wistfully and wiped my cheek with the back of my hand.

"There are so many beautiful memories of you that I treasure.

Every one of them is a part of me. I had never needed grand declarations. All you had to do was look at me and I felt you with me. Your golden eyes could crumble and disintegrate me like a powerful wave crashing down a castle made of sand." I smiled. I smiled as I clung to that part of my life—the story of us that I would never forget. "*Ya pihi irakema*... You contaminated me too, Mr. Disaster, and there's no cure for this disease, you know. There's no..." my voice broke, and I was incapable of continuing to speak through my sobs.

It wasn't a life anymore, what I had. It was a *prison sentence*.

"You asked me to make all those promises to you...and I never said I would, but you left anyway. And that was unfair...that was so incredibly unfair of you." I wiped my nose with the back of my hand, tears blurring my vision. I struggled for air, my heart aching. I felt like I was being torn in two. I was a cracked and broken pearl who had lost all of my luster because what was a pearl without its shell?

Without Neil, there was no *me*...

....

A hand was stroking my hair tenderly.

I opened my eyes slowly and gave a little yawn. The first thing I saw was the colorless wall in front of me, followed by the machine that monitored vital signs and finally the bed where I'd been resting my head and arms after falling asleep in an extremely uncomfortable chair.

"Was it the same nightmare again?"

I heard a voice—warm, deep, *his*—and my eyes immediately moved toward him. I kept my eyes opened wide just in case this Neil was also a dream. I didn't want to blink and have him disappear.

"Neil..." I said softly.

If I'd thought I was cried out, I was sorely mistaken. Just seeing him safe and sound was enough to churn up all the things I'd felt when Ryan shot him.

Neil could see it, the misery and the joy, and he just kept on stroking my hair.

His face was beautiful, even with the now-fading bruises and healing cuts all over it. He still had that shadowy aura that had drawn me in from the very first moment I met him. His plush mouth curved into a fond smile, and his bright eyes enveloped me.

He had a white bandage wrapped around his chest. There was an assortment of pillows behind him that allowed him to sit up comfortably, and a blanket lay over his hips.

"Come here," Neil said, raising his left arm and inviting me to nestle underneath it.

"It was a really bad one. You were dead, and I was talking to you, but it wasn't really you—I mean, it was you, but you were..." I muttered, sniffling as I clambered onto the bed next to him. I embraced him and rested my head on his chest, on the area that wasn't wounded. The place where I could feel his heart beating, strong and sure.

"Relax, Babygirl."

The surgery had been tricky, and the area was still painful, despite the doctor's assurances that he would be able to remove the stitches soon. I grazed the warm, bare skin of his neck with my nose and breathed in his smell, clean and all-encompassing just like it always was. I didn't stop crying, and Neil continued to hold me gently, like a baby.

His Babygirl.

"I'm right here, and I'm still alive, Selene. Shake off the bad dreams; you know I hate to see you cry," he chided me with just a hint of severity. His voice was like a pair of hands, stroking my most secret places, touching the depths of my soul. I reddened at my own thoughts: I wanted him. For better or worse, I wanted all of him: his strengths and his weaknesses, the finest parts of him, and the most awful.

I accepted him completely, and that, for me, was love.

"I know. But it was traumatic, going through all of that. Watching your eyes close and your breathing stop…"

Neil pressed his fingers to his lips to silence me. His skin was warm and soft. I pressed a chaste kiss to them, then another and another. I moved down his smooth palm worshipfully. I tried to imbue each kiss with all the love I had for him, because it was there and it was strong.

Even stronger than before.

"Let's talk about something else. I was just thinking that this is one of the few times you've been in bed with me fully clothed, and that's terrible." He gave me a tiny smile that told me exactly what he was thinking about. Even after having gone through such a tragic situation, Neil could still find it in himself to be cheeky. I shook my head and gave him an amused look.

"Now is not the time to be thinking about…" He moved his hand over my breast with his usual proprietary ease and gave it a squeeze through my sweater. I gasped.

"Fucking?" he offered in a low whisper, and I couldn't help but stare at his chest. My Disaster was half-naked, his torso almost completely on display and all the dizzying angles of his upper body exposed.

He didn't even need to get undressed.

It was almost like we were already making love.

My body went heavy with longing because, in a very real way, Neil was already inside me. He stared into me as I stared into him. I was burning up not just with embarrassment at his total lack of shame but also from the lusty, carnal feelings coursing through me.

"I was going to say 'that kind of thing.' Now is not the time to be thinking about that kind of thing," I said throatily. "But I'm glad to see your pervy instincts are also fully recovered; I was starting to worry," I teased as I gently caressed his stomach. I loved to touch him, and I knew he loved my touch as well. I knew exactly what kind of attention Neil required.

And, indeed, his breathing became unsteady, and I could practically feel the sexual tension pulsing in his swollen veins.

"Move that hand a few inches lower, Tinkerbell, and we'll be in business. There's someone down there who could really use a little touch from you..." he murmured into my ear. His breath was warm against my cheek, and I shivered. Memories of our intimate times together stole the air from my lungs.

It had been more than seven months since we'd last been together. Long months in which I had no physical comfort or relief because I was too busy torturing myself over Neil. He, on the other hand, had spent that time sleeping with an unknown number of women, Megan included.

It still hurt whenever I thought about them together.

What hurt even more was the uncertainty: What was going to become of us? What paths would our lives follow?

Neil had been different when he came out of surgery.

He still had cheeky little comments for me, and he'd touch me like he owned me, but he never said a thing about us having any kind of relationship. He hadn't even kissed me.

"Sorry, lovebirds, are we interrupting something?" Logan poked his head into the room, followed by Janel and Chloe. I automatically climbed out of the bed and stood up, smoothing my hair and sweater nervously.

"Neil..." After pressing a brief kiss to my cheek, Chloe came over to her brother, grinning joyfully at him.

"Hey, kiddo, I've been waiting for you. You usually come at the same time every day; what happened?" Neil was finally back to being sweet and affectionate with his siblings. After the trauma he'd experienced, everyone was worried that he might experience a breakdown, so Dr. Lively came to the hospital to talk to him every day since he woke up. He was a vital source of support who kept Neil from falling back into the void, especially because he had refused to say anything about Kim or Ryan. His mental state was still fragile, and his troubles were very much present.

"Hey... how are you doing?" Logan rested a hand on my shoulder, pulling me from my private thoughts. I smiled at him, trying to hide my fears, but I'd never been a very good liar. Then Janel rushed over to wrap me in an affectionate hug before moving back beside Logan, whom she'd been seeing for several months at that point.

"I don't know, Logan." I sighed. "I'm worried about what happens next. Neil hasn't said anything about us or his intentions when he gets discharged. He hasn't given me any indication of what the future holds or what direction our relationship will take. And, frankly, our relationship ended months ago, and he's never actually said anything about starting it back up," I murmured unhappily.

Neil had opened his heart to me and said so many incredible things after he'd been shot, but once he'd gotten out of surgery, he didn't mention a single one of them again. He had comforted me like earlier when I had nightmares, but he didn't renew any of his sentiments from outside the warehouse.

"What do you mean?" Logan gave me a bewildered look. I grabbed his arm and pulled him deeper into a corner while Neil was occupied with Chloe. Janel followed us, looking concerned about my frustrated face.

"Logan, he hasn't kissed me. Not even once," I hissed. "Not since he woke up after the surgery. He hasn't expressed any feelings to me. He treats me like a friend who he gives the occasional hug or dirty joke. Have you noticed that?" I continued. Janel's lips parted, but she just shook her head while Logan's eyebrows flew up in befuddlement.

"Okay, so, that is weird. It's not like him to hold back with you, but try to put yourself in his position. He nearly died; he was confronted with Ryan again after all these years. All of that put a lot of strain on him. Plus, he was terrified for you, too. Dr. Lively says he'll probably have PTSD from all of this, so it might take him a little while to get back to the Neil he was before," Logan said consolingly. He was trying to soothe me, but my instincts told me that there was something more.

The conflict between us and Player may have been over, but the one between Neil and me wasn't.

"I think he's trying to send you a message, Selene. Something like, 'Hey, don't get your hopes up. We're not going to be together because I'm not the one for you,'" Janel offered. She still disliked Neil and continued to believe that he was a danger to me.

And what if she was right?

After all, wasn't there a small, distant part of me that thought the same thing?

"Fuck, Janel, are you trying to give the poor girl a heart attack or what? Jesus," Logan cut in before turning to face me again. "Listen, Selene," he said, resting his hands on my shoulders and looking deep into my eyes. "Neil is unusual. You know that as well as I do. Just give him some time; you'll see. He's going to come to you himself and talk things out. Just trust him and try to be hopeful for once." He gave me a small squeeze, urging me not to keep beating myself up and smiled as he waited for me to respond. But all I could do was nod. There was a suffocating heaviness in my chest that made it impossible to speak.

I had always been an anxious girl, in need of reassurance and certainty, and that need had only intensified when it came to Neil.

This impasse of ours, him being so ambiguous when it came to me, made it impossible for me to ever feel comfortable.

If he left me again, if he ran away from this, I wouldn't have been capable of moving on.

"Is this a bad time?" Mia's voice interrupted our conversation.

I turned to watch her enter the room with a cardboard box in her hands. She moved uncertainly, obviously afraid of her son's reaction. I'd never seen her look so upset, nor so thin. She was just as elegant and turned out as ever, but her blue eyes looked weary and dull.

"Hey, Mom," Logan said.

Neil, by contrast, abruptly stopped talking to Chloe, his face turning grave and ominous. His lips turned down slowly into a hard, angry line as he stared defiantly at his mother.

"What the fuck do you want? I don't want to see you. How many times do I have to tell you that?" he barked, making everyone jump. Mia had come to the hospital every single day, but that still wasn't enough, as far as Neil was concerned, to make up for her years of lies.

"I wanted to see how you were doing. I also brought you a treat, your favorite—chocolate and pistachio." Mia approached him slowly and handed him the box. Neil's face twisted into a disgusted scowl.

"Do you think a dessert is enough to make up for what you did? You lied to me for years, whored it up with your lover, kept me away from my real father, and allowed the asshole you married to beat me. Do you think I'm just going to forgive you?" He smiled bitterly at her. "Never! It's never going to happen!" he shouted. His hands clenched hatefully into fists, the tendons in his neck tightened, and his eyes became two slits of fire.

Mia staggered back until she bumped into someone else: John Keller.

"Oh, that's just perfect! Now the whole lying family is complete." Neil shook his head, smiling derisively as he looked between his mother and father. He was the kind of angry that made him lash out mercilessly at whoever was around, but John was not afraid. He just looked earnestly at Neil until the latter stopped smiling.

"This is not mature behavior, Neil. You have every right in the world to be angry with me or with your mother. Trust me, I've been angry with her for a long time too." Dr. Keller stepped closer to Neil while Mia gave him a look of silent surprise. "But I don't think berating her like that is going to make you feel any better. You don't have to be like that, Neil. I've gotten to know you; we've had several good talks, and I know that you can rise above hatred and anger. She is still your mother," he said calmly as he moved over to the bed. He gave Logan and me a polite wave as he walked past us before grabbing a chair and pulling it up to Neil's bedside. Then he sat down and crossed one leg over the other in a show of defiance, as if to say *I'm going to sit right here whether you like it or not.*

Like father, like son.

The more I saw of John, the more I realized how similar the two of them really were. They had the same confidence bordering on arrogance, the same certitude. Even the same unflappable, invincible demeanor.

"Who told you I wanted to see you?" Neil shot back at him after a lengthy observation of the other man's brazen attitude. Logan and I exchanged a furtive glance, and then he went over to put his arm around his mother's shoulders and offer her some gentle comfort.

"I told myself that. Are you trying to keep me from checking in on my son's condition? I've visited you every day you've been in the hospital so far, and I'm not going to stop now." John threaded his fingers together and rested them on his stomach, with the small hint of a victorious smile on his face.

Neil sighed irritably, but before he could say anything in return, the doctor breezed in, clipboard in hand.

"Good morning, everyone," he said politely, glancing around at Neil and all his relatives. He gave them a reassuring smile before glancing down at his paperwork. "You, sir, are one lucky young man. As you already know, the surgery was a success. We've kept you here since then for observation and to ensure that no complications arose, but, fortunately, the bullet did not pass through any vital organs, not even the heart, which we had feared. But," and he lifted one finger, and I couldn't help but flinch. "It was a very close thing. Someone up there must really like you. We're going to discharge you today, and I've prescribed a course of painkillers for you to take home with you." The doctor smiled warmly as Neil's brow furrowed. John got up immediately to clasp the man's hand.

"Thank you so much for everything, doctor. Are you sure he's going to be okay?" he asked, looking every inch the father worried about his son. Mia also approached the doctor, flanked by Logan and Chloe.

"Yes, he will. Obviously, he'll need to be careful with physical activity and keep a close eye on the surgical site, and he should take his prescribed medication whenever he experiences pain, but he'll have a follow-up office visit next week," he explained. Then he shook hands with Neil, wished him a swift recovery, and excused himself.

John was grinning, but his son still looked angry despite the positive news.

"Great. Now I can get back to my fucking life where I get to have some say over which of you I see," Neil muttered to himself, and his words sparked a strange anxiety in me.

What if I was one of those people he planned not to see anymore?

"Oh, I plan to come bother you no matter where you end up. Including Chicago, in case you were wondering," John shot back at him. "I'm going to get a coffee," he continued, tousling Neil's hair affectionately while Neil grumbled out a low "fuck off" that went totally unacknowledged by his father. Mia followed John out of the room, and Logan took Janel and Chloe along with them. As he left, he shot me a meaningful glance, and I knew that he was giving me an opportunity to talk to his brother one-on-one, just like he'd advised.

But the moment we were alone, I began to feel antsy. I'd been waiting so long to have this conversation, but now that the moment had arrived, I was scared. I was scared of what he'd say, scared he'd push me away again.

"Could you grab me a cigarette?" he asked, and I jumped, like it was the first time I'd ever heard his voice before. Neil tilted his head to one side, undoubtedly wondering why I was reacting so oddly, but he didn't say anything. I scrambled around for the pack of Winstons before spotting it on the roll-away table. I couldn't help but sigh as I reached for it: I would much rather he asked me to stay with him, to start all over again and begin our journey together. Instead, he asked me for a pack of smokes.

"Here," a voice broke in. Before I could even fulfill Neil's request, Megan scooped up the cigarettes and tossed them carelessly at him. My mouth dropped open at her presence—she looked amazing as usual in a pair of skinny jeans and a simple red sweater that only highlighted her incredible body. She wore her dark hair up in a high ponytail, her lips were appealingly pouty, and her eyes seemed especially green.

"What are you doing here, Head Case?" Neil looked her up and down, his eyes narrowing slightly at the shape of her breasts, barely concealed by the leather jacket she wore.

Seeing his eyes on her like that was a punch to the gut, especially now that I knew for sure what had happened between them.

I didn't breathe again until Neil looked away from her. He pulled a cigarette from the pack and stuck it between his lips. He knew he couldn't smoke in the hospital, but he liked to hold there it, unlit. It was soothing for him.

"I came to see you," she answered, not acknowledging me. Was she seriously just going to pretend I wasn't there? This bitch...

"Have you been tracking the papers?" she continued, moving closer like she had every right to push herself right up into his space. "Bryan Nelson, that Britney chick, and all the basketball players were arrested, and they're in jail. That prick Ryan, though, he offed himself in his cell the first night. Guess he couldn't face the idea of spending the rest of his life in jail. The cops think he launched another dark website selling child porn videos. They're doing this big investigation trying to trace all the people who bought his videos and get their identities. Apparently it's going to be a huge bust. The scope of the whole thing is still blowing my mind..." she told him incredulously, while Neil stared at her like he had no interest at all in what she was telling him.

But I knew that was just a front. The things that happened to him hurt him so deeply that he couldn't even bring himself to talk about it. He had yet to express himself about any of it, but I strongly suspected that, inside, he was being rocked by strong emotions.

"Fucker should have lived so he could suffer, rotting in prison," he answered darkly. "How are you feeling, knowing that he's dead?" he asked Megan. She stood next to his bed, her arms folded tightly and her shoulders tense.

"He's been dead to me for years," she answered, cold and sharp. Then, very unexpectedly, she reached out to brush back a curl that had fallen down over his forehead. Neil's eyes immediately shot to me, and he could see the hurt expression on my face. He blinked and cleared his throat before sitting back stiffly to duck Megan's touch.

"I didn't say you could touch me," he scolded her firmly, and my heart leaped. I was well aware that Megan surely found Neil's particular amalgamation of beauty and charm to be irresistible, but I was the one who fought so hard to know him, to dig down into his soul and show him that he wasn't a monster. I was the one who had my pride trampled over as I struggled to support him without judging.

I was the one who accepted him. I was the one who loved him.

She couldn't take that away from me.

"Dr. Keller told me the doctor was going to discharge you," Megan went on, and my rage only grew sharper. For a second, I imagined stalking over to her and grabbing her by the hair. I could have exposed the jealous, possessive creature that I was inside, but I didn't want to give her the satisfaction. If I showed her my insecurities, that would only bolster her own opinion of herself, and I didn't want that. So, despite the fact that my blood was boiling, I fought to keep myself under control and think rationally about what to do.

"Yeah, I'm heading back to Chicago," Neil answered, and my breath caught. My mind got stuck on that one single word: *Chicago*.

"Okay... I think I'll probably head back soon too. Let me know what your plans are. You can come with me if you want," she offered, and that was when I snapped like a wild animal. I couldn't take one more second of her presence.

"Excuse me, Wayne," I called out to her and finally she turned to look at me. "Are you going to give us a minute alone, or do I need to kick your ass out of here? Because, believe me, I can do it." I gave her an insouciant half-smile, and Megan's eyebrows flew up in surprise.

I had dedicated a year of my life to Neil.

I had given him all of me; he couldn't just walk away like nothing had happened.

I needed explanations, and this chick had to get out of here. Immediately.

"Oh, hey Selene. Guess you finally grew a pair, huh? Congrats. I'll give you two some privacy," she answered with a combative air before leaving the room—and Neil—to me.

I refused to waste any more time. "Want to explain to me what the hell is going on in your head?" I snapped at Neil, and, of course, he just kept silent the way he always did when I tried to have a conversation with him. Instead, he just got out of the bed and pulled himself up to his full height. For a moment, I felt like the wind had been knocked out of me.

"What exactly is unclear to you? I have to finish my internship, and I still have another six months to go before I can try for my license." He walked over to the small closet space where a few articles of clothing were hung up. He grabbed a white hoodie and began pulling it on using only his left hand. He could have asked me for help, but he didn't.

Even then, a swelling of pure love urged me to go to him and hug him and show him that I'd never let him leave me again. But the last, final bit of my pride that I guarded so jealously would not allow me to do that.

"Are you going back to Chicago? When? Tomorrow? Today? Couldn't you stay here a little longer with your family?" My voice came out as a wheeze. I could have said it better, could have sounded more determined, but the pain was too strong to be ignored. Just talking calmly to him was exhausting.

"My family?" he echoed, not looking at me. He grabbed a bag out of the closet and put it on the bed, stuffing the rest of his things inside. "I don't have a family. I'm not going to forgive my mother. I can't go back to living with her and Matt. My siblings can come see me any time they want, though." His unzipped hoodie left his chest exposed, and I examined the bandage there. Neil's motions were too quick and sharp; he was ignoring the doctor's warnings. If he continued acting like an idiot, he was going to tear his stitches.

"And what about me? What about us? Are we back to the same old thing, Neil? Are you going to dump me because my mother has filled your head with her fears?" I moved closer to him, drawing from deep inside myself to find the strength to face him.

"There hasn't been an us since the day I graduated. Sure, your mother was part of it, but it would have happened either way. You know that because I've been telling you right from the beginning. Did you think I was lying? I can't give you the things you want. A person like me with the issues that I have... I can't give you a normal relationship." His right hand shook as he zipped up the bag. He glanced around, searching for his cigarettes and phone. As soon as he spotted them, he tucked them into his pants pockets. He was doing everything he could to avoid meeting my eyes. Why? Was he that afraid to show me a moment of vulnerability? Was he afraid that I would dig down deep inside him and make him see that this choice was the wrong one for both of us?

"Oh really? So there is no us, then? Shall I remind you that you told me that I am what you think of when you think of love? Do you think I'm stupid, Neil? Do you think I haven't figured out that you also have strong feelings for me? I saw it that night I was so sick and again when everything went down with Ryan. Goddammit, look at me when I'm talking to you!" I shouted, reaching the limits of my patience.

When he finally turned to look me in the eye, all my noble intentions of not showing any weakness and standing strong against him faltered.

My knees threatened to give way as he stepped toward me, eventually stopping right in front of me. I lifted my face to look at him, and he stroked my cheek.

"It's done now, Selene. And you're free. When you were lying in that hospital bed after Ryan nearly killed you, I swore to you that I'd always protect you and that I'd always be there for you, even if it couldn't be in the way you wanted most. My life is somewhere else now, and yours is in Detroit. It's with your mom and your friends and your studies. When I'm gone, you'll finally be able to have some peace again." His stare was so powerful and so intense that it made me tremble. "And I remember everything I said but I thought I was dying, Selene. I thought I was never going to see you again, and it was my last chance to tell you how important you were to me...how important you still are to me." He continued gently cupping my face, and I just couldn't understand him. His words said he didn't want me in his life, but his eyes were screaming that he loved me. He bit down on his lower lip, obviously fighting back the urge to kiss me.

He wanted to do it, and I wanted him to do it, but still, something inside held him back.

Neil did not believe himself capable of being with me. He was too afraid of letting me down. He still believed I couldn't possibly want to make a life with him, despite the fact that I knew about his problems and accepted him. I'd even talked with him about maybe getting back on medication to help control them. I would have stayed by his side, though, even if he decided to never go back to therapy, but he couldn't stomach the thought of making me a part of his everyday life. For him, it was freakish, wrong, and shameful to do so.

I closed my eyes, savoring his affectionate touch.

"If you choose to go back to Chicago, I will interpret that as you choosing Megan as well. You're going to go back there and live with her, and she's going to try to get with you like she already did once before, and I can't take it." I broke the spell of his touch, shoving his hand away. His face remained serious and unmoved, like nothing could rattle him. "I can't deal with you living with her for another six months and coming back to me whenever you feel like it. So, if you walk out that door, if you decide to leave, then I'll end this thing between us myself. Because I deserve better. After everything I've been through with you, I deserve a second chance too, and if you don't want to give that to me, then I'll have to say goodbye and move on." My heart cracked a little more with every word.

I would never forget him; I would never be able to move on. His absence would be a wound that I carry with me for the rest of my life. But I had no other choice; I couldn't keep chasing after someone who only wanted to get away from me.

Neil remained silent, and I stared up at him in mute distress.

The space between us felt heavy with unexpressed feelings and desires that neither of us had the courage to name.

Because loving required a great deal of courage, and I was finally understanding that Neil had none.

"Good luck, Selene," was all he said. He grabbed his bag and brushed past me, refusing to even glance at me. He couldn't face reality and the huge mistake he was making.

I knew he would regret this one day, but by then, it would be too late.

I squeezed my eyes shut and dug my fingernails into my palms in an attempt to hold still, but in the end, I had to speak.

"Please—rethink this," I said, reaching out to clutch his arm.

"Selene, don't." He jerked out of my grasp and once again avoided my eyes. I knew he was refusing to look at me because he too knew that he was making a stupid, wrong decision. I knew that we could tackle his fears together; all he had to do was accept what he felt for me and understand that he couldn't run from love. The fabric of his hoodie slid through my fingers as he walked out the door, leaving me alone with nothing but his smell to fill a vast emptiness that I knew would be inside me for a long, long time.

There was nothing for me to do but let him go. I stood there in that room, ruminating over our conversation for several minutes, until I heard footsteps and looked over to see Megan's tall boots. I didn't look into her triumphant face. Neil was not the spoils of war or some trinket to be fought over.

Honestly, since she was so perfect, she should have known better than to stand there and rub her happiness in my face.

I lifted my head to show her that I wasn't afraid of her either, but in complete contrast to my imaginings, there was no smug satisfaction on her face. Just a quiet understanding that had me stunned. I realized that perhaps I could take this moment to actually talk to her, woman to woman.

"Okay, listen to me Megan. And please do it without interrupting," I said, and she narrowed her eyes warily at me. She didn't urge me to go on but neither did she seem uninterested in what I had to say. "Neil loves pistachios," I began. "He'll eat them any time, except first thing in the morning. It's a good idea to always have some around. His favorite colors are black and cobalt blue. If you give him clothes in those colors, he might actually wear them. He loves The Neighbourhood—just hearing one of their songs puts him in a better mood. He sketches to relax, and he keeps his drawings in a notebook that he never lets anyone see. He hides it among the rest of his books like a little kid, but you shouldn't touch it without asking, because he'll probably get mad at you. He loves it when you play with his hair and goes wild when you kiss his neck. These things make him happier and calmer. Try to be patient when he has an outburst and when he spends a really long time in the shower and definitely when his right hand gets shaky. He smokes way too much. Get him to quit if you can or at least get him to cut back. He loves literature and philosophy, especially Bukowski and Schopenhauer. He needs something physical, usually boxing, to help him deal with the nightmares, so don't be surprised if he gets up and trains early in the morning. You have to learn how to read his eyes. He's not good at expressing himself verbally, but if you look in his eyes, you'll find all the answers he can't give in words. Love him as he is because that is what he needs more than anything: to be loved. Hold on to him because he's a special person and deeper than anyone knows, and when you're..." I choked, feeling nauseous at the thought of what I was about to say. But I took a deep breath and continued. "When you're in bed together, try not to be on top of him. He hates that position because it reminds him too much of Kim. Just...take good care of him, Megan." I swiped the back of my hand across one cheek while she stared at me in shock. I inhaled shakily, trying not to collapse on the spot. Not in front of her.

I didn't wait to hear what she had to say. I didn't need to.

Instead, with all the feigned confidence I could muster, I walked out of the room and out of the hospital, and a few hours later, I got on the first flight back to Detroit.

28

> "I could have held on to anger at her over what happened with Neil, but I knew that she wasn't really to blame."

SELENE

It was a week later, and I was taking my life back. Or, at the very least, I was trying to do that.

Back in Detroit, there was snow on the ground, and more fell each day. I loved being the first to walk down a sidewalk and watch my tracks appear behind me.

My grandmother used to say that when the snow fell, it kissed the trees and the earth and then tucked them all in under a soft, white blanket.

The roofs of the cars in the parking lots were completely white, as were the tree branches, the benches, and the roofs. Everything.

All of it white and clean.

All of it marvelous and new.

And still the snow fell, slow and gentle and soft, but also...sad, somehow.

As a child, I'd loved the snow. I loved to make snowmen as tall as I was and dress them up in Dad's scarf or Mom's sunglasses. It was a nice childhood memory from a normal, everyday childhood. Happy, carefree, bright. So different from Neil's.

Did you ever play in the snow?

Did you make a snowman and watch him melt in the sun?

Did you ever laugh in the midst of a snowball fight?

Did you ever watch the snowflakes fall and think about how each one was slightly different from all the others?

I supposed I'd probably never know.

When I got back home, I dropped my bag on the floor and hung up my coat on the rack. I caught a whiff of something sweet in the air and smiled involuntarily.

"I'm back," I called out before heading into the kitchen to look for my mother. The first thing I saw was a cherry pie on the table with a candle shaped like the number twenty stuck in it, and then my mother burst into the room brandishing an air horn. It made a sound so loud it practically burst my eardrums as she danced and cheered like a delighted child.

"Happy birthday, my love." She pulled me into a warmly maternal hug, and I reciprocated, still a little dazed. I did take the opportunity to sneak the air horn out of her hand before she could cause permanent hearing damage.

"I'm sorry, sweetheart. I didn't know what kind of party favors to get. The woman at the store recommend this, and..." I cut her off with a fond shake of my head. As determined and serious as my mother could be, she could also be a ridiculous weirdo.

I could have held on to anger at her over what happened with Neil, but I knew that she wasn't really to blame.

All she'd really done was show Neil the anxieties any normal mother would have. It was Neil's job to reassure her that he wanted what was best for me—and to actually follow through on that. Instead, he was too scared of his own feelings and too distrustful of the concept of relationships in general.

So I couldn't blame my mother, and I couldn't blame Matt or Megan for the fear that Neil had displayed from the very beginning of our acquaintance. Sure, they may have further discouraged him or added fuel to his belief that he was not capable of having a real relationship with someone, but fundamentally, Neil had always believed that the only thing he had to give to a woman was his body.

"Mom, just the birthday song would have been fine…" I rubbed my ear, and before we sat down to have some pie, I grabbed her hand. We exchanged a knowing look and a pair of big grins. We both knew what had to happen when it snowed on my birthday.

"Wait, let me get on my coat and gloves," she said, and a few minutes later we were out on the lawn in front of the house, ready to build our traditional birthday snowman. Together, we found the perfect flat area and piled up a useful heap of snow. I knelt down and began shaping it and patting it down so it could form the base of our snowman. From time to time, I'd lob a snowball at my mother, who tried to use her red winter hat with its cute little pom-poms to shield herself.

Sometimes I wondered which one of us was really the kid and which the grown-up.

"Perfect." I smiled in satisfaction as I admired the three large balls of snow stacked on top of one another. That was when my mother produced two round stones and a carrot so I could give our snowman a face. I dug through the snow until I could find a handful of pebbles to use for his sullen mouth.

"He's kind of grumpy, this snowman," my mother noted, standing before him with her hands on her hips and her head cocked to one side.

"I need a leather jacket, Mom," I said, grabbing two serviceable sticks and sticking them into the snow to create arms. My mother watched me thoughtfully before making a skeptical face and heading into the house. A few minutes later, she came back with a leather jacket that had red studs on the shoulders. I took it from her and wrapped it around the snowman, sliding the sticks into the armholes.

"There. Since Neil couldn't be here, I've made a snowman version of him. Of course, the real Neil is a little taller and broader, but it's a pretty good likeness, isn't it?" I turned to my mother, who was staring at me like I'd completely lost my mind. She broke into peals of laughter, and I cocked an eyebrow at her.

What was so weird about it?

"You even got the scary pout." She moved closer and slung an arm around my shoulder. At the same time, the streetlamp came flickering on, driving away the evening gloaming. We stood there, examining our crappy Snow-Neil. As I stared intently at him, I realized that I had missed a few details. I arranged another pebble in the corner of his mouth.

See there, I've found a way to have you with me on my birthday.

And, naturally, the traitorous tear I'd been trying to hold back for too long slid down my cheek. I swiped it away immediately. I didn't want my mother to see me hurting.

"Let's go inside, Selene. It's getting colder." As we walked up the drive, my eyes continued to sting.

"Go upstairs and have a nice hot bath before dinner," my mother instructed, and I obeyed her. Maybe a relaxing soak would ease some of the melancholy that hovered over my days.

I walked into my bedroom and stopped short when I saw something bizarre.

I walked forward numbly until my legs hit the edge of the bed, staring down at the...bouquet of candy?

I studied it for a long moment, afraid I was having a very bizarre hallucination.

But now...there really was a bouquet of candy wrapped in a red bow.

Next to it was a small box, and I instinctively looked over my shoulder for any observers before picking it up. There was a small pink tag on the box that said "Happy Birthday," and my hands shook as I breathed deep and sat down the bed to slowly open it.

Immediately, I saw something shiny. A bracelet.

It was silver with a single gleaming pearl suspended from it. Tears welled up in my eyes, and I felt hope beginning to unfurl in my chest. But I didn't want to delude myself because I couldn't take another disappointment.

No, Neil was in Chicago.

I was dreaming.

I squeezed my eyes shut and gave my arm a pinch. I waited a few heartbeats before cracking one eye open and looking around the room.

Nothing had changed.

It was still my room; I was still on the bed with the pearl bracelet in my hands.

"Not dreaming, then," I whispered as I tried to delicately clasp it around my wrist without dropping it. I ran my fingers over the assorted candy; some were honey-flavored, others coconut. Nestled in amongst them was a fortune cookie.

I picked it up, cradling it in my hands as though it were a precious jewel before breaking it. I pulled out the slip and read: *"Don't kiss me like you love me. Kiss me because you love me, and because I'm ready to love you back. Come outside."*

I pressed my hand to my lips and glanced around in disbelief—he was here?

Flustered, I pulled on the first pair of shoes I could find and raced out of my room. I hurried down the stairs, tripping on the last few steps. My heart was in my throat, and my legs were trembling. Before I could get to the front door, my mother appeared and handed me my winter coat. She didn't have any of her usual questions for me, and I looked up at her, wide-eyed.

"I'll probably regret this," she sighed. "But I couldn't keep watching you be miserable..."

She smiled and opened the door for me. I ran down the porch steps, and then I saw him.

He was leaning on the Maserati he'd parked right in front of our house, and every muscle in my body felt frozen. My arms fell uselessly to my sides as my eyes locked on his.

How many hours did it take him to drive here?

Why didn't he just fly?

But I didn't really care about that. Neil was right there with his golden eyes, just as angelically beautiful and irresistibly sexy as ever.

I felt like my soul had been drawn out of my body toward him, but when I recovered from my trancelike state, I ran down the driveway, stumbling clumsily in my eagerness.

He shook his head and smiled, and I blushed.

Hope bloomed again, love burst forth, and the snowy city suddenly had every bit of the charm it had for me as a child as I got closer and closer.

I leaped into his arms and hugged him tight, dissolving into tears again. Only this time, they were tears of joy.

I wrapped my arms around his neck and my legs around his hips. Neil lifted me and held me tight against him.

I could feel his heart beating.

His urgent breaths.

His soul softening and merging with my own.

My tears dripped down the bend in his neck, the same place where I'd found comfort in so many times of suffering but also in moments of ecstasy.

"You're an asshole and...completely crazy!" I sobbed against him. Neither of us wanted the enchanted moment to end.

"Yeah...crazy about you, Tinkerbell," he whispered into my ear, clasping me even tighter like he didn't want to let me go. I slid along his body until my feet were resting on the snow but didn't move away from him. I remained in his arms, surrounded by his blazing heat and his musk-and-tobacco scent.

I stared deep into his eyes and saw everything that he was feeling—I felt it too.

It was a painful, all-encompassing feeling, so powerful that it actually hurt. My head throbbed, and I couldn't stop tearing up.

What would I have ever done without his madness, which had become my madness too?

Neil was the beginning and the end for me.

"I'm sorry, Babygirl. I'm so sorry. I was scared to admit to myself that I couldn't be without you. I don't know what changes you made inside me…" he cupped my face in his big hands and stroked my cheeks with the pads of his thumbs, "But I can't let you go. I won't. What would the shell do without the pearl? They were made for each other." He smiled at me, and his eyes were so bright they looked like polished gold.

And then he kissed me. His lips, warm and soft, were gentle against mine. Our tongues danced in the darkness, in the falling snow, and in the glow of the streetlamp.

"Promise me you won't run again. That you'll stay with me," I whispered against his lips. It was the only promise I ever wanted from him.

"I promise, Babygirl." He kissed the tip of my nose and then my cheeks, my forehead, my chin, and my throat. He kissed me everywhere—kissed me completely—and stared at me with those glorious eyes so that I would know that this was real. We were finally together.

"But what about Chicago? Megan? Your job?" Reality crashed back in on me far too soon, but he immediately reassured me with a sweet smile.

"I'll deal with that later. I spent this whole week in my apartment;

I didn't even go to work. I didn't have the strength. The thought of not seeing you again was agonizing. I was sick. I couldn't sleep. I couldn't eat, and then, finally, I understood. I understood everything..." He kissed me again, this one rougher, more passionate, and more carnal.

It was one of his true kisses, neither sweet nor gentle but intense and devastating, the only way Neil Miller knew how to be.

He continued to contaminate me even though he had already invaded my heart and every other part of me. I tickled his neck, and he spun me around, backing me against the car door.

After so much suffering, our mutual desire and eagerness to be together was exploding. I could tell by his panting breath and the way his chest pressed into me.

We might have started making love right there in the street on his car, but fortunately for us both, my Disaster broke the kiss and pressed his forehead to mine. For once, he was gulping air just as much as I was.

I smiled at him, passing my hand over the manicured stubble that only made him look more handsome and masculine, before dropping another chaste kiss on his lips.

"Have you ever made a snowman?" I asked him. He gave me a confused look.

"No. Why?" he answered. I took his hand and pulled him over the snowman version of him. "Hey, that thing kinda looks like..." he muttered as he took a good look at my masterpiece. I gave him a cheesy grin.

"Like you! Look, he's even doing the pout," I said, pointing at the hard line of the snowman's mouth. I was still holding his hand in mine, and, for once, he wasn't pulling away from the gesture. He gave me a look so heavy with feeling that my heart leaped in my chest. Then, he reached into his jacket pocket and raised an eyebrow as he pulled out...a package of pistachios.

"There, now he's more like me," he said, tucking it into the twigs on one "arm" and smiling. While he was concentrating on perfecting my snowman, I stooped and gathered up some snow. I silently packed it into a ball and then lobbed it right at his head.

"What the fuck?" he blurted out in his usual curmudgeonly manner before turning to me and giving me a menacing look that immediately shut me up.

He narrowed his eyes challengingly, and one corner of his mouth lifted up slightly as he squatted down to prepare enough ammo for a veritable snowball war. Except that his were way too big and thrown with way too much force.

"Enough! You're terrible at this!" I zig-zagged across the lawn, trying to outrun his missiles. One hit me in the face, another in my back, and one right on my left butt cheek—that one stung.

"Never should have challenged me, Tinkerbell!" Another snowball to the leg took me down. I burst into laughter as I collapsed in the soft, white expanse. I rolled over onto my back, trying to catch my breath as I stared up at the night sky, dotted with the occasional star. Then my view was obscured by an even lovelier sight.

Neil stretched out on top of me, covering me with his huge body. He propped himself up with his elbows on either side of my head, and I noticed that the tip of his nose was red along with his cheeks and lips. I touched his face and found it freezing, so I peppered him with warm kisses wherever his skin felt clammy.

"Selene," Neil whispered against my lips. "Come with me. Let's get out of here." I stared up at him, blinking in surprise.

"How? I can't. School, my mom… I can't…"

Neil shook his head and kissed me again before grinning at me.

"I already spoke to your mother. She knows everything, and she's okay with it. We'll go away for a few months. I'm not sure how long. All I know is that I want to be with you. I want to experience life with you, far away from everyone and everything else. I want to live the way I never really have before. My life has been more like a prison for me. I want to be free, and I want you to be free with me. Will you fly off to Neverland with me?" he asked, a hopeful glint in his eyes.

Was he worried I might say no?

That I might leave him?

Never.

We were each other's future. I never could have lived without Neil.

"Yes, I will. Let's do this crazy thing together, Mr. Disaster. I'll follow you anywhere you want to go," I said softly before capturing his lower lip between my teeth and pulling gently on it. He let out a rough groan. I preened internally at my ability to exert this kind of power over him. Neil belonged to me. He was as much mine as I was his, and it wasn't about ownership.

It was about union, about sharing and understanding and emotional connection.

Neil got up and held out his hands. I grabbed them, and he pulled me to my feet and leaned against his chest, blushing. He gave me an amused smile, but then my mother interrupted our intimate moment by walking out onto the porch with the candy bouquet in one hand and my red wheelie suitcase in the other.

"Everything's been arranged," she explained, shooting a sly smile at the boy I loved before immediately turning stern again. "Now, I have your word that you will take care of my baby and keep me posted every time you move. Do not make me regret placing my trust in you." My mother lifted her index finger in the air like she was giving a lecture in one of her classes, and Neil just smiled at her, pulling me closer.

I wondered what he could have said to her to convince her to let me leave with him. I knew that Neil had a way with women, but worming his way into my mother's heart was still quite a coup for him.

"Don't worry, Ms. Martin. I would lay down my life for your

daughter," he said, his words full of meaning and love. The unspoken love that Neil would never be able to put into words.

He was giving me all of him, and that was enough for me.

He smiled and dropped a kiss on my forehead before grabbing the handle of my suitcase and gesturing for me to follow him.

I grabbed the candy bouquet and hugged my mother, thanking her for giving us a chance.

I stowed my bag in his trunk, and we both got in. Immediately, we looked at each other and locked eyes.

Neil was staring at me like he was seeing me for the very first time, and I felt a flicker of the old fear. Was he thinking about backing out? Was he no longer ready to take on this crazy journey together?

"Neil?" I murmured, pressing a hand to my pounding heart. We were going to be alone together for a long time. We'd be able to really get to know each other, warts and all. I was going to have to learn how to deal with a man like him.

I was filled with joy but also with tension.

He was mine.

Finally, there was an us.

"What are your intentions with me?" He stared seriously at me and bit his lip nervously, and for a second, I genuinely thought he was going to end things again, and I was going to end up as completely destroyed as I'd been before he showed up. But then, his grave face turned excited, and he gave me a sexy smile.

"Only the worst, Tinkerbell..." he said and gave my thighs a fevered look.

"So...can I officially call myself your girlfriend?" I teased, and he just took my hand and lifted it to his mouth for a gentle kiss.

"You're a lot more than that, Babygirl. You're my Pearl."

Then, his fingers still interlaced with mine, he started the car and pulled up, picking up speed like the madman that he was.

I watched him, hopelessly in love, and he looked back at me, heavy with expectation, and I realized a fundamental truth: in every one of his smiles, I was there.

I was the one who made him smile.

Like a boy who had been fighting monsters for a long time and would continue fighting them, but with me by his side.

I would never understand why fate had thrown us together.

I couldn't explain why my heart had chosen him of all people.

Neil was the messiest, most flawed person in the world; someone I should have steered clear of, but for some crazy reason, he had me under his spell.

He turned my life upside-down, gave me wings, and showed me how to fly to another land.

Neil and I were the result of a chance meeting, like when the moon first met the darkness.

We were surprising and inexplicable.

A coming together destined to last a lifetime and to astonish anyone who witnessed us.

And that was called love.

Neil and I, we were in love.

The chaos we made together—it was *love*.

I had fought for him, and I would do it again a million times over. I had listened to my feelings. Some might say I was too forgiving or too naive, but despite being just a regular girl with her whole life ahead of her and an empty bag waiting to be filled with new experiences, I'd managed to overcome all of my fears, every bit of common sense, and all limitations to capture the heart of a man I'd once thought unobtainable.

I had been strong and tenacious because I had always known that it was deep within those honey-colored eyes that my future lay.

29

"I had my family and a genuine bombshell waiting at home for me."

NEIL

I opened my desk drawer and slid out the pack of Winstons.

I'd made a deal with Babygirl that I'd only smoke three a day, but I was already on my fifth.

I've heard it said that men change with time as they grow and mature, but as far as I'm concerned, that's bullshit. Ten years later, I definitely considered myself a better man—a little bit better—but I wasn't a different one.

"Fuck," I muttered as I glared at plans for the theater I was renovating. I was exacting, especially when it came to work, and I was never satisfied until I'd achieved the highest possible level of perfection in anything I designed. "I'm not convinced. I think we need to redo it," I told my colleague, Sharon Smith. She was about my age, bleach-blond and slender with a pair of absolutely sinful lips. She was the kind of woman I could pick out from a distance: dangerous, seductive, and dead set on getting whatever she wanted.

In the past, I might have tried to get her into bed, but I was working to control my obsession with blond women.

"Right now?" Sharon asked in confusion. She put her hands on her slim hips, which were covered in a knee-length pencil skirt that only highlighted the curve of her ass.

And it was a nice ass, for sure.

Standing between us, however, was my large desk and my even larger loyalty to my woman.

Yes, loyalty.

Despite the fact that she often gave me sly little glances or innuendos, I had never for a second considered fucking Sharon. I had my family and a genuine bombshell waiting at home for me.

My Babygirl was a potent combination of incomparable beauty and intelligence.

Never in a million years could I have replaced her with someone else.

"Yes, but I think I can manage it. You can go home if you're tired," I said gruffly. It was only six p.m., and I imagined she wasn't at all tired, but I did hope she'd take me up on my offer because working alone with her was uncomfortable.

There had been a time when I worried that I'd lose my appeal as I aged and become less desirable for women, but instead the exact opposite had happened.

In my ten years with Selene, I frequently had to rein in my hedonistic impulses because the women had not let up, especially at work. They vied for my attention, longing for even one night of sexual objectification from yours truly.

Some of the fault lay with me and the excessive attention I paid to my body. I'd never given up the gym or my daily training. My body was still vigorous and virile, and though I hated to admit it, a part of me delighted in being physically attractive.

"No, that's okay." Sharon shrugged. I stubbed out the cigarette in the ashtray and got up, tucking my hands into the pockets of my slacks. "I can stay," she added with a smile, obviously pleased to be spending more time with me.

I resisted the urge to roll my eyes so I wouldn't appear rude and walked over to her, turning the project plans so she could read them as well.

"We need to fix the stairs. I don't think this positioning is the best option, and this room needs to be larger," I explained, pointing out each element I thought needed work. She leaned forward as though looking closer and rested a hand on my lower back, over the white button-down that I wore. Her delicate fingers slid up and down in a heated caress. I gave her a severe look, and she recoiled.

"Sharon..." I said her name so sternly that she actually stepped back a few paces. "Don't take liberties I haven't granted you." I wanted to add that I wasn't a kid anymore, and a pussy in heat had no effect on me, but I knew I shouldn't outright insult her.

I was already well-known around the office for my rough edges. People thought I was an asshole because I didn't chat or make small talk. I spoke to people only when necessary, and some found that condescending.

I was taciturn by nature, though. That was another thing that hadn't changed.

"It's not like you're married. You don't wear a ring..." Sharon gave my hand an inquisitive glance. I didn't immediately see what that observation had to do with my rejecting her advances. No, I wasn't married, and I never would be, and Babygirl had accepted that. We had talked about it at length, and I explained how I felt—that we didn't need a ritual or paperwork to know how we felt about each other. There were certain conventional things that I just didn't believe in, nor did I find them useful at all.

"Just because I'm unmarried doesn't mean I'll have sex with my coworkers," I answered, scowling.

This conversation was getting on my nerves, stoking the anger that was my old friend and had never left me. I was beginning to think that I needed to be more explicit with this woman. I moved confidently toward her. "And, just to clear up any doubts you may have, Sharon—there's only one woman I fuck. My woman," I said quietly, and she let out a gasp. "Forgive me for the vulgar language, but sometimes a guy has to resort to that kind of thing when he's setting things straight," I added with a smile of satisfaction. She gave me an affronted look but then cleared her throat and went back to looking at the plans as though she were suddenly extremely interested in them.

"Uh...I agree with you on the stairs. I think we should..." she went on, beginning to draw up a list of changes that we should consider.

We worked until the clock said 9:30 p.m., an hour when I should have already been home to cuddle with my daughter and eat dinner with Selene. Usually dessert consisted of my tongue between her legs or a hard fuck on the kitchen table because we often had to take immediate advantage of Nicole's sleep to sneak a little moment for ourselves.

Selene had gotten used to my ways, and now she loved them.

Outside of the office, I was no different than I used to be. The same confident, perverted Neil. Only with my daughter did I show my sweeter, more affectionate side because that was, apparently, a side I had now because of her.

It felt like my own heart was beating inside her tiny body. The feeling was completely novel and unexpected...incredible.

When Selene told me she was pregnant, she thought I was going to cut and run. That I was going to abandon the both of them, not realizing that I already knew she'd gone off the pill.

When I got home from work that day, I found her sitting on our bed and crying. I could still see her blue eyes blurry with tears, the skin around them puffy from crying about how I might react. I thought she was sick, that something was seriously wrong with her, so my heart was in my throat as I sat down next to her. Ideas of what she might say ran through my head, each more horrifying than the last. But then she just handed me a pregnancy test with two pink lines. Positive.

I froze, staring at her, wondering if I was dreaming. In that moment, the Boy's bitter, pitiless words came back to me: *"Today, you abuse yourself. What if, one day, you abuse your daughter?"*

And the fear rushed over me, dredging up every dark moment of my life.

What I had been.

What I'd been subjected to.

The harm I had done to others. To Selene.

I questioned whether I really deserved such a gift, if I could ever live up to the responsibility of being a good father.

But I knew that I had a fairy by my side, the same fairy who was about to give me the greatest gift in all the world.

Our child would be wanted fiercely—first and foremost by me.

I could make Selene's dream of getting married come true, but I could fulfill her dream of being a mother and my own of being a better man for my twin pearls.

For my family.

My loved ones.

Because this, too, was love.

Another kind of love I'd come to believe in.

"That's good for tonight. I'll take care of the finishing touches in the morning." I dropped my pencil on the sheet of sketch paper, drawing my colleague's impeccably made-up eyes to me. She let out a yawn and stretched, her back likely complaining after hours in an uncomfortable chair.

"I'll head out in a few minutes," she said, sounding flatter and noticeably cooler than normal.

"Suit yourself." I didn't argue with her. Setting aside her occasional inappropriate advance, Sharon was an intelligent architect and as serious about her work as I was.

I took a break to check my phone and found just what I suspected I would—a text from Tinkerbell. I'd somehow forgotten to tell her I'd be staying later, despite the fact that she was constantly on my mind.

Every damned second of the day.

The little one and I were waiting on you for dinner. Mama even had a surprise of her own for you...

I hurried to tap out a reply like a teenager hanging on his crush's every word: **Sorry, Tinkerbell, I had to go over a project. I miss you so much. What kind of surprise are we talking about?**

I rested my elbow on the armrest of my chair and stroked my lower lip with my index finger. I could already taste my evening meal. Selene had a devastating power over me—just imagining her feminine voice saying the words on the screen was getting me hard.

Completely, painfully hard.

The message notification chimed again:

Nicole's already down, so I thought I'd wait up for you. Naked. You could have eaten your dessert off me. Too bad...

If there was anything Babygirl had learned in her years of living with me it was exactly how to provoke me.

I glanced up at Sharon and caught her looking thoughtfully at me. I adjusted myself in my chair to try to keep my insistent erection under control.

Fortunately, I had a sacrosanct desk to block me.

I snorted in frustration and wrote back to her:

Well, now my dick's hard while my colleague is four feet away. Low blow, Babygirl.

I could envision her in my head: her cheeks pink with jealousy and her ocean eyes animated by anger as she spat out curses and threats. Another thing that hadn't changed was Selene's jealous streak. If Selene could have tied me to the bed to keep me from encountering other women, she would have happily done so.

My phone buzzed again.

The blond one? I will cut your balls off if you so much as look at her!

I laughed aloud, drawing Sharon's attention. All of Babygirl's claws came out when she got jealous, and her potty mouth did too.

She was adorable.

Oh, you should see her. She's wearing this skirt today that's so tight I can see the outline of her thong...

I chuckled to myself as I impishly typed out the first thing that came to mind. I enjoyed bringing out this blind fury in her. Sometimes she'd chuck a slipper at my head when I pretended to give other women the eye—especially the blond ones.

In reality, it often felt like my body only reacted to her ocean eyes, but Selene didn't know that. I didn't want her to be too secure, so I regularly provoked her.

Another message alert:

You nasty pervert. You'll pay for that one!

I laughed before trying to become serious and determined once again. I was in my office, after all. I couldn't be unprofessional. I glanced up at Sharon and saw her staring at me, probably trying to figure out what had me so delighted.

The answer was simple: It was Selene. She was my joy.

She was my moon, and my daughter was my brightest star, and there was no room for anyone else in my dark sky.

"I think I'm done." Sharon got up from her chair huffily. Maybe she was annoyed at how little attention I'd paid her, but my family would always come first, and at that moment, my head was already back home. All I wanted to do was snuggle with Nicole, and then it would be her mother's turn. I wanted to lay her down on our bed and spread her legs wide for me and just lose myself in her heat. Just the thought of it made my body tense up and my throat tighten. I undid a button at my collar in an effort to get some more air.

"Okay, go ahead," I answered in a rasping voice. It was the same seductive tone I used when Selene and I were fucking, and that was not okay. Sharon's breath hitched, and I watched her fall prey to my charms, just as I'd feared she might. I had to fix it. "See you on Monday," I added, hasty and awkward, before looking meaningfully at the door. I didn't stand up to show her out. I couldn't.

She told me goodbye, and I watched her leave the office, obviously on edge, but I didn't give a shit.

Once I was alone, I palmed the fly of my pants, trying to soothe my hard-on. I heaved a frustrated sigh before angrily snatching up my phone again.

Great. Now I can't work because of you. Prepare yourself; I want you naked when I get home... And I'm not going easy on you.

I tossed the phone down on the desk and began putting away the project I no longer cared about. I stood up and stretched my legs as I waited for Selene's reply, which was very prompt:

Counteroffer: I have a really fun game for you to play. It's called "Oh No, My Balls Fell off Because I Ogled Another Woman's Thong..." I'll be waiting at home for you, love...

And, in spite of the threat, I only grew more aroused because Babygirl turned into a genuine tigress in the sack when she was truly pissed off.

I loved provoking that jealousy, making her abandon all her inhibitions and dragging her with me past all boundaries. She became this dizzying whirlwind of beauty, heart-stopping curves, and flushed cheeks.

A knock at the door roused me from those thoughts. Apparently the building wasn't as empty as I'd thought.

"Come in," I groused. I had hoped I could finish up and get home and dedicate myself to my Pearls, but now I'd have to stay and deal with whatever this new dickhead needed.

"Am I disturbing you, Mr. Keller?"

I let my phone fall to the desk, and my eyes locked on her, on that body that I could have picked out of a crowd. Blindfolded. Warmth spread through my chest as I looked at her, and my heart pounded faster, hot blood pumping through my veins.

She was so fucking gorgeous, my Tinkerbell.

It had been six months since she gave birth, and she had only blossomed like a flower, still with all her purity and angelic delicacy.

Her breasts were fuller and showed to their best advantage in the high-necked pink blouse she wore, just as clean and elegant as she was. Her round, perfect hips were encased in a sophisticated pencil skirt, and she showed off her long legs in a pair of high heels that she wore with masterful ease.

She had everything required to be the perfect woman—*my* perfect woman. She was earnest, intelligent, and beautiful, and she had the biggest heart. I had discovered over the years just how jealous I felt when men undressed her with their eyes. I regularly had to stifle the urge to break some noses.

If I had ever lost Selene, I would have lost myself.

"Ms. Anderson, what are you doing here? I don't see clients at this hour..." I leaned arrogantly against the desk and clasped my hands to fight back the omnipresent urge to simply jump her.

"Well, I definitely didn't come here to talk business." My Tigress locked the door behind her with an impish look, and I stared deep into her eyes to show her just how much I appreciated this surprise of hers and how richly I planned to reward her.

I watched her waver for just a moment on those heels. My devouring stare always had the same effect on her.

I was fucking her before I even touched her.

"And why did you come to see me, Ms. Anderson?" I smirked as I watched her move closer to me, slow and graceful. Never vulgar or overtly sexual, but she had every bit of my attention in that moment.

The electric spark between us hadn't dimmed in the slightest. In fact, it had grown, as had our knowledge of each other, our understanding, and our physical attraction.

Selene understood that sex was much more than a simple biological need for me.

I still had issues with my mental health, and I knew that I experienced sexuality in my own unique way, but I was no longer ashamed of it.

She had accepted me.

"Did you try to work with your colleague in that condition?" Her ocean eyes dipped to the crotch of my pants bowed obviously outward. Her cheeks instantly flamed up, and a troubled twitch of her jaw told me she was about to start raging at me.

"This is all your fault, Tinkerbell. You and your text messages. Sharon didn't see anything. I was sitting down the whole time," I explained, sounding amused but firm. Then I pushed myself off the desk and stalked toward her like a big cat who had just laid eyes on a lovely gazelle.

She froze in the middle of my office, her breathing becoming erratic. I could see her arousal in the way her breasts heaved and pressed against the demure shirt. The way her knees trembled and how she rubbed her sweaty palms on her skirt.

I sniffed the air like an animal might, and she gulped.

"Where's our Little Pearl?" I asked her with a lascivious edge as I circled her. I stopped right behind her and slowly leaned against her back. Her wavy auburn hair tickled my face, and the scent of coconut surrounded me. There was nothing better than the scent of the woman who had pulled my soul out of my body.

"My mother is with her; she's staying over tonight. Tomorrow we're having the barbecue with everyone, remember? I told her I was just going to come over here and see how things were going..." She stopped talking when I gave her hips a possessive squeeze. I pressed my hips against her ass and dragged the tip of my nose along the curve of her neck.

"I can't wait to get home to her." I missed my daughter. I missed holding her when I had to spend so many hours in the office. I'd often have Selene send me pictures or videos of her doing weird stuff like chomping on her little feet. "Just don't say anything more about your mother or it'll all go to shit down there."

"Oh, I think everything's going really well down there. The corporal is saluting. He's so polite, you know..." Selene had given my cock a nickname after Nicole was born. She was trying to eliminate any sort of vulgar language from her vocabulary because she didn't want Nicole to pick it up.

"This weird kink you have of addressing my cock by his rank is disturbing," I murmured into her ear. She giggled and ground her ass against me. I let out a rough moan and licked her neck until her head fell back against my chest. Right where it belonged.

Where it would always be.

"Take your clothes off, Babygirl," I said in a low voice before retreating to the desk and leaning comfortably against it as I waited for her to do as I said. A flare of desire lit up her blue eyes, and I grinned smugly at the effect I still had on her.

Her hands moved up to the collar of her shirt, and she began to gently undo each of the buttons.

"Ready to play, Mr. Keller?" Her sweet, sensual voice was sufficient to shake my self-control. I drummed my fingers on the wooden surface of the desk as I tracked her every movement. Every curve, every line.

Selene let her shirt fall to the floor before moving on to her skirt.

She slid the side zipper down, and I watched as the black fabric skimmed her long legs on its way down.

Now, she wore just her lingerie and a pair of high heels, and I couldn't catch my breath.

A matching set in white lace with a pair of thigh-highs in the same color. That was all that stood between her flesh and my hungry desires.

Her bra barely contained her flourishing curves, and only a microscopic triangle of fabric concealed her smooth pussy from me.

Every part of me longed to touch, lick, and suck every inch of her body.

How many times had I fucked her?

How often had I seen that body naked?

I knew her by heart, every inch, and yet I stared at her nipples beneath the snow-white fabric like I'd never encountered tits before.

She was perfect.

A priceless pearl, luminous and lovingly shaped as any sculpture.

"You're a work of art," I blurted out. It wasn't the first time I'd thought something like that, but it was the first time I'd said it aloud to her. My compliments to her were usually confined to the occasional "you're so pretty" or "beautiful." Nothing more.

But there was no adjective that was truly worthy of her and her perfection.

"Not true," she said, taking on an embarrassed stance. Her cheeks were as red as two cherries, and she pressed her legs together shyly.

I loved this about her, when she would get all awkward and shy. I loved everything about her.

"It's the truest thing I've ever thought or said, Tinkerbell," I whispered, getting lost again in the warm, depthless ocean of her eyes. I felt cradled there, like a child. Like I could peel away all of my weapons, all my defenses, and simply allow myself to be what I was.

A man who had been thoroughly contaminated by a woman.

I never told her that I loved her, and she had quit expecting it from me. She knew how those cursed words hurt me and how I refused to soil our pure, singular, honest relationship with them.

Besides, I had other ways of communicating my feelings to her.

"Well, thank you, Mr. Keller. I'm flattered." She moved a few steps closer to me, still looking embarrassed. As usual, I took the initiative and grabbed her around the waist and pulled her against me.

Her perfect body molded itself immediately to mine.

I grabbed her ass, giving it a rough grope. She jumped, putting her hands on my shoulders.

"I want to fuck you, Babygirl." I kissed her neck, breathing in her smell. "Right now. Can't wait any more."

I kissed her hungrily—a powerful, rough, carnal kiss.

I whispered to her that she was my everything.

That she and our daughter were my world.

I whispered that my soul was hers and there was no reason for a shell to exist without a pearl to protect.

And now, I had two precious pearls to keep safe.

I guided her to the leather couch I kept in my office. Not for clients, as I led people to believe, but for exactly this kind of fuck session with my woman. I laid her out beneath me, continuing to devour her mouth as I positioned myself between her thighs. I spread them wide until I could access that special spot, my heaven.

It was a funny thing, a devil like me spending so much time trying to get into heaven.

I squeezed one of her breasts and pinched her nipple, swallowing her gasps. My hands touched her everywhere, down her stomach and further to her mons before pulling her panties aside.

When I stroked her between her legs, I found her sweetly wet and ready for me.

"How many times today have you thought about me doing this to you?" I pushed my fingers ungently into her and there she was, her flesh slick and boiling. She arched beneath me and shifted her pelvis to accommodate my movements. She looked deep into my eyes, mouth opened, to let out those moans that were music to ears. She hooked her legs around one another against my ass and clawed my back, still covered by my shirt.

"Always. I always want you. I think about you all the time," she murmured breathlessly. I wanted to hear that from her every day. I loved hearing how often she thought of me, how much she cared about me, and how deeply she desired me, how it was just the same for her as it had been that first day we met.

I loved to hear that she couldn't live without me because I couldn't live without her either.

"That's how it is for me, too. I'm constantly thinking about you two when I'm not with you. You are my life," I admitted. Selene had always had the key to the dark, hidden treasure chest that contained my heart.

"And you're ours," she answered between moans as I tore off her panties. I had no problem letting her go home without them. She was going home when I did anyway. And I would surely fuck her again when we got there.

I undid my leather belt, undid the button on my pants, and lowered my zipper before letting her take over.

She didn't strip me, she just wrapped her hand around my erection, and I groaned as she began to firmly stroke it.

I kissed her, licking and nibbling greedily like I was drawing sustenance from her lips.

Then, with a harsh jerk of my hips, I was inside her.

My version of romance merged with her purity, her nobility, her ocean, and her *love*.

That fucking word again. Perhaps, in the end, I'd fallen victim to it myself.

I squeezed my eyes shut and reveled in the hot sensation of

invading her, of becoming a man who, despite the past that still clung to him, was living a better future.

I shivered because it was always a little surreal to me to realize that I really had been lucky enough to find my Neverland.

She really existed, and she was right there with me.

Her eyes locked on mine, her hands clasping my tense biceps as I moved urgently against her. She gasped, and I gave her a harder thrust until she let out a high-pitched cry that she muffled against the bend of my neck. I pounded deeply into her, impulsive and implacable.

I felt a visceral need to lose myself in her.

To get outside myself.

To push beyond my boundaries.

Once, she had looked to me like another line I couldn't cross, but instead she turned out to be my horizon.

"You're the horizon," I admitted to her as I set off on a relentless race for the pleasure I'd been craving for hours, minutes, and interminable seconds.

"Love..." she whispered, peppering my throat with kisses.

I pulled the cups of her bra down and sucked her stiff nipples.

Selene sucked in a breath and locked eyes with me again because she never wanted me to merely touch her body—she wanted me to touch her heart, her soul, everything.

She took urgent possession of my mouth as she writhed like a goddess beneath me.

Her sweet taste washed over me, awakening every inch of me.

It was overwhelming...so powerful it hurt.

"I belong...inside you..." I continued to mutter dazedly. Selene always said that sex was when I confided my true thoughts in her. She said it was the time when I was most comfortable talking, perhaps because I was never entirely clearheaded. I was not fully conscious of my thoughts, so I opened myself up, lowered my walls, and allowed my emotions to speak.

She must have been thinking the same thing because she smiled at me, and that's when time stopped.

The world ceased around us because she was so vast, so infinite that it was terrifying.

What kind of fairy magic was this?

Selene grazed her nose against mine then bit into my lower lip and sucked it with a groan of delight.

I thrust into her more eagerly, more roughly.

I felt her shudder beneath me, and I knew that she was close. I clutched the sofa's armrest on either side of her head, trying to hold on to my composure. My fingertips turned white where they gripped the leather, and my muscles flexed underneath the shirt I longed to rip off along with my pants.

Her nails dug into my back as she arched into my powerful, violent thrusts.

Our ragged breathing bounced off the office walls, and our scents mingled to create a new one that was an aphrodisiac all on its own.

"You belong inside me..." she whispered, her eyes shut tight before giving herself over to a devastating orgasm that had her screaming aloud.

Then, she smiled up at me, her lower lip bloody from where I'd bitten it a little too hard without even realizing it. I licked it gently to ease the pain—a silent apology. I let my head fall into the hollow of her throat and its coconut smell.

She gripped my hair in her hands, and at the same moment, I exploded as well.

Inside her, in my home, my refuge. In the place where I belonged.

Because I too had found my place in the world after traveling for so long down a path of pain.

The Boy who locked himself in his room to get away from the monster was a persistent memory, but it hurt less.

The memory lived inside me but was locked away in a drawer with the rest of my past.

My present was right here with Selene and our daughter.

"Fuck," I collapsed on top of her, breathless. Our bodies were still locked together, sweaty, exhausted, and still humming with adrenaline. My shirt stuck to my back, my half-undone pants pulling against my thighs. My ass was exposed, and that was exactly where Babygirl's hands came to rest.

"You like grabbing my ass, huh? You've become a little freak," I teased her. She blushed, but her blue eyes shone with tiredness.

She was exhausted.

Not just because of the demanding amount of sex I required to ease my mental conditions, but also because of everything else she had to deal with: the pregnancy, all the changes, the new rhythms of our lives, and a daily routine that now revolved around Nicole.

"You were perfect, like always. Sometimes I wonder if I can really be enough for you." She sighed, giving me a sorrowful look. She rubbed my back gently, smiling a little half-smile that hinted at much deeper emotions.

"I wonder the same thing. Sometimes, I ask myself what I possibly could have done to deserve someone like you," I said honestly. It was inconceivable that she was the one who felt herself inferior to me. She had no idea how attractive she was to men, nor how much other women envied her.

"You won't cheat on me, right? You'll stay with me? You won't abandon Nicole and me?"

And there it was: the paranoia. About a secretary, a blond coworker, women I'd had in the past, and women who worked with me or even just near me.

It hadn't been easy for her to stick by me these last ten years of our relationship.

We'd been through a number of dark periods, had full-on crises, and I had pulled a lot of shit.

There were times when I disappeared for days because of my stupid pride, and it caused so much suffering for her. We would fight and start yelling at each other, and I'd have to pull back to get some perspective on the relationship.

I know she wondered then if I was out having sex with other women.

Maybe she still suspected I had.

And, if I was being completely honest, there were women I found tempting, and there still are. But I'm different now.

I had a daughter, and I needed to be a model for her of what a partner was and what a serious and responsible father was. I couldn't make the mistakes of my past when I let my knee-jerk reactions and my demons take the wheel.

But even though I'd had a child with her—a sure signal of how invested I was in us as a family—Selene still got lost in those old fears. I never would have made a decision like that unless I was absolutely certain of how I felt.

"Never, Babygirl. I could never do that you. I wouldn't do any of that shit; just put it out of your mind because you are the only one for me." I dragged myself out of her and watched my cum slip down between her legs. I continued to stare as I stood up before shooting her a heated glare and leaning down to press a gentle kiss to her mons. And then another, a little further down. Where she liked me best.

I traced her with my tongue and licked her ardently. I could taste our commingled fluids, and she trembled beneath me.

This profane gesture was, in my silent lexicon, a message of my absolute devotion to her. My reliance on the bond between us, the ever-growing attraction I felt for her, and the deep importance she had for me.

Tinkerbell understood this because she smiled and gave me a little nod, as though I'd just spilled my deepest thoughts to her.

"Promise?" she whispered, looking deep into my eyes.

She was beautiful like that, so soft and sweet. She was a woman now, but she was also still the girl I'd met ten years before.

The girl who fought for me, who stood by me no matter what. Who had given everything to me, body and soul.

The girl who had crawled inside me and taken up her rightful place.

A place that would always belong to her, no matter what happened.

"I'm crazy about you, Selene. Can't you see that? Who knows what spell you used…" I grumbled because sometimes it did still bother me the tremendous power she had over me.

I was absolutely fucked, and that knowledge frightened me. If Selene ever decided to leave me, I'd die.

So I spent every day trying to show her how much she meant to me. Maybe not with words or bouquets of dying flowers, but with my heart, which she held in her hands. It had been broken, badly damaged by the past, and she would have been well within her rights to throw it away. Instead, she had guarded it and cared for it and pieced it back together into something new. My heart was not unlike a mosaic: a collection of shards that came together to create something original.

"Shall we go home?" I stood up and reached out to help her up. Completely naked, as delicately lovely as a butterfly, she rose up to meet me and smiled, full of love.

"Let's go home." She kissed my lips, and I slid a hand into her hair, deepening the kiss until I could steal every last bit of her breath.

Because I didn't just want to lose myself in her body, I also wanted to fight for us.

Sunday came, the day of the family barbecue.

No one would have thought I'd one day be capable of this kind of life, that I'd be able to put the abused boy back in his corner and move forward as someone ready to live for real.

No one...except Tinkerbell.

I would always be grateful to her for that.

After taking a shower (and using up an entire bottle of body wash), I dressed and went downstairs.

We'd gone back to New York after our trip. Selene finished her degree and graduated with honors while I launched my career.

I was now an established architect, but even when it came to that, she was special. She was the one who believed in me and encouraged me back when I was scribbling designs in a notebook that I hid on my bookshelf.

It felt like an eternity since those days.

I shook the memories off as I descended the large marble staircase that led to our main floor. I had designed our home myself. I wanted a one-of-a-kind place that would make my girls feel like real princesses.

I found my woman on the big leather sofa in the living room, nursing our little one. I leaned against the doorway and watched them in awe, like always.

Selene delicately cradled Nicole against her and murmured tender things to her like, "Mama and Daddy love you. You're everything to us. You're our Little Pearl..."

They were the most beautiful thing I'd ever seen.

To say they were merely a part of me would be reductive. They were the two halves that made up my soul. Without either one of them, I would have been nothing.

I stepped into the room, unable to resist the urge to go to them. Selene spotted me immediately and gave me a brilliant smile. I crouched down to plant a kiss on it. Then I turned to our little one and kissed her gently on her forehead, taking the opportunity to breathe in her baby-powder scent.

"Good morning to my girls. I knew I'd find you both here." I leaned back, watching as Nicole turned her attention from her mother to me.

It was incredible how she immediately recognized my voice and incredible how all it took was one look from those ocean eyes flecked with honey to reduce to me to a puddle of goo.

"Yeah, you know you're Daddy's Little Pearl, don't you?" I whispered, and she batted her long brown eyelashes at me before giving me a tender little smile that made her chubby cheeks look even plumper.

She was adorable, and I was already so possessive of her.

I could barely stand it when other people held her or kissed her or gave her cuddles.

I could deal with Judith babysitting, but only because I would never entrust my daughter to a stranger. Still, I missed her so much every time I had to go to work and wanted nothing more than to get back to her.

"Good morning to you. We were waiting for you, like always." Selene kissed the tiny tip of Nicole's nose while I continued to gaze at our little one, enamored.

She was a true masterpiece, a wonder of nature.

Her lips were very pink and had the same shape as mine; she had a mass of chestnut hair, and her nose was small and delicate.

Nicole was a living symbol of our victory over evil, over the dark side of the world that Tinkerbell and I had defeated together. She was a perfect combination of Selene and me and a more beautiful gift we could not have asked for.

"Here, take her," Selene said, giving me a long look. As usual, my face shuttered, and I felt a stab of fear in my stomach. The Boy's voice still echoed in my head, warning that one day everything that happened to me might spill out onto Nicole. The damned part of my soul piped up to remind me that I was, deep down, still the same disturbed man, and I had only managed to create the appearance of normalcy around me.

"Neil, stop whatever dark thoughts you're thinking right now and take her," Selene insisted, her face sorrowful yet determined, like she was ready to go to war. She knew about the things that were broken inside me, about the monsters who constantly tried to invade my life.

We had won many battles but never the war.

I took a deep breath before hesitantly stretching out my arms as Selene passed Nicole to me. I clasped my daughter to my chest and stood up. I always felt so helpless when that tiny being looked right into my eyes.

I stood in awe of her.

I bent down, grazing the tip of her nose with mine before dropping a small kiss on it, and she grinned. I automatically smiled back. She loved nose kisses, just like her mother. Nicole wriggled her plump arms and legs, expressing her delight at being with me.

"Happy to be with Daddy?" I asked her.

I had broken all my patterns for my little girl. I quit smoking first thing in the morning so she didn't have to breathe in the noxious smell. I kept my face clean-shaven because I didn't want to irritate her skin, and I tried to be present for all her feedings, especially the morning and evening ones. My low, warm voice conveyed all the love I felt for her, all of the protection I would give her. For her, I would kill with my bare hands. I would give my own life to protect hers. The bond I had with Nicole was too strong—it was an emotion I'd always tried to ignore the existence of.

"You know, you are always gorgeous, but you look especially good with her in your arms. There's nothing to be afraid of, Neil. You are not a danger to your daughter," Tinkerbell said, her voice warm and sensual in my ear. My eyes met hers in an explosion of feeling, and I couldn't help but smile.

I felt fortunate every day to have met her.

I was the only man who existed for her. I knew it from the way she looked at me and touched me. The love that she showered on me with every single move and gesture. I had never seen Selene so much as glance at another man. I'd never seen her blush with someone else the way she was doing right then, for me.

She told me over and over again how I was perfect to her, even with my many flaws. She told me how appealing I was and how jealous she got when women threw their heated looks my way. But what my Tigress didn't realize was that she outshone them all and erased anyone who had ever come before.

"Good morning, Neil." Judith poked her head into the living room and walked over, her eyes already on my daughter.

But no one, not even my mother-in-law, dared to take my Little Pearl from my arms without asking permission first.

I greeted Judith, cooed at Little Pearl for a few more minutes, and kissed her little face all over. Then and only then was I prepared to step back and let my mother-in-law hold her, giving her a look of warning as I did so.

"Don't worry, I am familiar with babies," she reassured me, taking Nicole in her arms and giving her a good cuddle. Judith was an available and attentive grandmother. She was always there at Selene's side whenever she needed help or support, and she had been overjoyed when she found out Selene was pregnant.

Which had surprised me.

My relationship with Judith was odd. There was a definite wariness between us but also a great deal of mutual respect.

I watched her as she left the living room, taking my little one with her, and I already felt the deep hollow in my chest that meant I was missing her.

"So...seems like somebody forgot about something?" Selene approached me with a little extra sway in her hips. I looked her up and down like a creep, already imagining her naked underneath me. She wore a knee-length white dress speckled with little blue flowers, and it highlighted all her curves. She'd put her long hair up into a chignon, and I imagined taking it all down and wrapping it around my fist like a rope as I took her from behind.

"You forgot something first, Tinkerbell. We went from morning blowjobs to morning feedings in a matter of weeks," I admitted.

Once upon a time, Selene's first wake-up call was for me. Now, though, we'd altered that habit as well to make room for someone more important.

"Oh my God, Neil! My mother is right there!" Selene scolded, shooting a look over her shoulder to make sure that Judith was far enough away that she couldn't overhear my usual filthy mouth.

"Don't try to tell me you don't miss sucking me off every morning. Quit being such a little goody-two-shoes." I grabbed her ass a little too aggressively, and Babygirl came crashing into me. Her cheeks were pink as ever, and I peppered them with kisses.

"And what am I supposed to tell my mother about this?" She looped her arm around my neck and used her other hand to point out the bite mark I'd left on her lower lip. I gave her a self-satisfied smile.

I loved to see my marks of possession on her...

Her eyes went wide like she was about to swoon because my version of romance was having a devastating fucking effect on her. So I decided to keep going. "Tell her that your man is insatiable and he fucks you like an animal, even in his office. And he's so crazy about you that, sometimes, he just has to take a bite out of you," I shrugged. "And then you could tell her about how I love to bend you over my desk and how I completely lose my mind when you let me take your a—" She slapped a hand over my mouth, breathing heavily.

It wasn't angry breathing, though.

It was the ragged breathing of a woman who was just as turned on as I was.

But just then, we were interrupted by my cell phone.

"Work's not supposed to call on Sunday; you answer it," I told her seriously. I needed to get some distance from her and try to temper some of the arousal pumping in my veins. I adjusted my pants, looking down at the vulgar bulge that I would not have been able to hide if Judith had appeared wearing one of her arch, dangerous expressions.

I was just about to make good my escape when the doorbell rang as well. I cursed, thinking that someone must have arranged all this specifically to annoy me, and as Selene went into the kitchen in search of my phone, I went to open the door.

Behind it, I found five dazzling smiles: Logan and Janel, Chloe holding tightly onto her boyfriend Simon's hand, and John, bringing up the rear with a tray of sweet treats.

"Did you just get up? You have a pissed-off face on." My brother, like always, wasted no time before giving me shit. I snorted. I couldn't exactly say I was annoyed about the hard-on that I now had to try to hide with my polo shirt. Instead, I gave him a sarcastic smile and a slap upside the back of his head.

"How about just this once you just come inside without shooting the shit for thirty minutes?" I said fondly. "Hey Janel, come make yourself comfortable," I added to his girlfriend. She greeted me with a cheek kiss as she rubbed her baby bump, which was even more swollen than the last time I'd seen her.

"Oh, don't fuss," she said. "I'm still pretty spry, despite my resemblance to a whale," she said, gesturing to the little guy in her stomach who was due out in about two months.

"No, you don't look like a whale. You just look extremely...uh... pregnant." I bit my lip, hoping that passed for polite conversation. I still wasn't good at that kind of thing. My brother wrapped an arm around her hips and whispered that that had been Neil-speak for "you're glowing."

Cool, we could go with that.

"Never change, big brother." Chloe launched herself at me and smacked a kiss on my cheek, clinging to me like a koala—my Little Koala. No matter how old she got, Chloe was still my kid sister.

"Hey, kiddo. I thought you were coming by yourself." I shot a wary look at Simon Lively, who extended his hand in greeting.

The young blond man was the son of my doctor, Krug Lively. It turned out, in addition to helping her process what Carter Nelson did to her, bringing Chloe in for therapy sessions with Dr. Lively had led her to the love of her life. Not that I had known a thing about him until just a year before.

"I'd say that your face looks more like that of a man who was interrupted in the midst of indulging himself with the woman he loves." John stepped up and greeted me with a shoulder pat before shutting the door behind him. I sighed and gave him a speaking look. My father understood me better than almost anyone else.

Our relationship had changed a lot, and fortunately, it has improved. It wasn't easy moving past the traumatic discoveries I made on the day of my graduation. I still hadn't been able to forgive my mother for lying for so long.

I probably never would.

Mia was still with Matt, and they lived in the same ostentatious mansion, and despite the poor relationship I had with her, I hadn't stopped her from being a grandmother to Nicole. She was free to visit Nicole whenever she wanted, though I usually tried to be at work when she came, and we rarely encountered each other.

Selene was the one who convinced me to let Mia have a chance to know her granddaughter. Only she was able to get me to put aside my pride like that—if it had been up to me, my mother would never have gotten near Nicole.

As for Matt, he was still an asshole. His relationships with me and Selene hadn't really changed. He was an involved enough grandparent, though his prestigious career still took first place in his list of priorities.

"You're here already! It's so nice to see you…" Selene greeted the guests with a hint of strain in her face that did not escape my notice.

She said hello to everyone with her usual graciousness and touched Janel's baby bump admiringly. The two of them immediately started talking about onesies, diapers, and all the other baby minutiae I didn't care much about.

What I did care about was the way she stood so stiffly and refused to meet my eyes, even incidentally.

That wasn't like her.

We communicated as much with our eyes as we did with our words—probably more, in fact. The disquiet I read in her expression worried me.

Something was wrong.

An hour later, the women were laying out the table in the backyard while the men, predictably, all gathered around the grill. My father and Logan were usually in charge of cooking the sausages and hot dogs, though my brother often ended up cussing himself out as he overcooked them.

While we waited for the sausages, John watched me carefully like he was gearing up to give me another one of his irritating speeches.

"Son, is everything okay with Selene?" he asked finally. The question also caught Logan's attention. I anxiously lit up a Winston and shot Selene a curious glance. She was hovering around the table with the women, holding Nicole in her arms. Finally, after ignoring me for so long, she looked at me. Her ocean eyes shimmered, crystalline in the reflected sunlight, but I didn't like what I read in them: They were a storm-tossed sea.

Those eyes were screaming that she was disappointed and angry.

But why? What had I done?

Maybe she was upset that I was smoking?

"Sure, why do you ask?" I turned my attention back to my father, pretending that all was well, but he and Logan just gave me skeptical looks. Apparently they had also noticed that Selene had barely said a word to me.

Usually, Babygirl would be all over me. Cuddling me, sitting on my lap, and giving me kisses without the slightest concern for who might be looking. Today, however, she ignored me completely, save for the occasional disdainful glance.

"I think you should go and have a chat with her. She's obviously upset about something, and I'm sure that confronting you will do her a lot of good." My father pulled the cigarette out from between my lips and snuffed it out in an ashtray. "And this crap isn't helping," he muttered with a displeased expression. I knew that he was right, but I was an awfully proud man. It was a personality defect that I'd been carrying around with me my entire life, and it frequently caused misunderstandings with Selene.

I always waited for her to talk to me or open a discussion. I hated interpersonal problems. I had too many of them already, and arguing was the part of our relationship that irritated me the most.

We did have a lot of long conversations, but that was all due to Selene. I remained the same close-mouthed man I'd always been. The same Boy who preferred to close himself off in a world of his own and protect himself with a wall of silence rather than show any vulnerability.

Despite the renewal I had experienced since Nicole, I was still afraid of breaking into pieces or completely self-destructing.

"Look, Selene is the sweetest woman I know," Logan interjected, placing the cooked sausages on a platter. "And you two are an incredible couple, but you can be a real shit. Talk to her; try to figure out what's wrong. Sure, you might get into an argument, but at least you'll have a chance to get rid of her worries. You two have faced so many obstacles; there's nothing left that could possibly destroy your relationship. All you can do is make it better." I was amazed by the pup's wisdom. Logan had grown so much; he was now a well-respected IT manager who handled the entire technical infrastructure of a company, and soon he would be a father himself. Unlike me, he was planning to marry Janel shortly, and I knew that had made Selene a bit sad.

I had seen the faraway look on Selene's face when Janel talked about dresses and flowers, and every time I wondered again why I couldn't bring myself to give that to Selene.

Maybe that was the reason for her sudden bad mood?

"Yeah, I'll go talk to her." I looked over to where she had been and saw that she'd passed Nicole to Judith while she went back into the house, probably to grab another dish from the kitchen. It was the perfect opportunity to talk to her alone.

When I went through the glass doors, I found her standing with her back to me, focused on getting two cartons of orange juice out of the refrigerator.

"So now everyone has noticed you avoiding me. Wanna keep putting on a show for them or, would you like to tell me why?" My firm tone made her jump and whirl around. Luminous eyes scrutinized me furiously as wisps of coppery hair framed her face. She looked like one wrong move from me would make her erupt.

"You want to know why?" She set the juice down on the marble countertop and advanced upon me angrily. "It was your colleague Sharon on the phone. She asked for you and then she called me *Mrs. Keller*. Now, I'd like to know why your coworker would call looking for you on a Sunday and why she would call me that when she knows very well that I am not your wife. I can't help but think it was a little derisive, Neil." Her voice grew louder as she spoke, and she looked at me with the kind of disappointment I never wanted to make her feel. "Oh, and she wanted me to tell you that she *really enjoyed herself* working with you this week. What the hell does that mean?" Her voice turned suspicious. Her frustrating jealousy had only intensified, and it was all because of me, because of the shit I pulled when we were younger. I usually tried to be understanding when this kind of argument came up because I knew how hard it was being with me.

I moved closer to her until I could cup her face in my hands. Selene tried to jerk away from me, but I wouldn't let her.

"It doesn't mean anything. It means she wants to get under your skin. When are you going to stop falling for this stuff? When are you going to understand that I..." I paused, my chest tight with anguish. I still couldn't just tell her how I felt; I never had, and it remained a huge stumbling block for me.

Those words seemed to get caught in my throat, never making their way out into the air between us.

We could gaze into each other, we could get lost in the intensity of the other's eyes, forming an intimacy so profound it felt like making love, but still, I could not say the words. I could not verbally express my deepest feelings—the ones she most needed to hear about in these moments of insecurity.

"You know that I...that I'm crazy about you," I managed at last. I gave her a kiss, trying to show her the truth of what I was telling her. I didn't like feeling far away from her. I didn't like arguing or having these stupid unresolved misunderstandings between us. I didn't like seeing her run from me as she was preparing to do just then. She pulled back from my touch, not allowing me to deepen the kiss.

I let out a wounded animal groan at her rejection.

"You can't fix everything like that, Neil. You can't use sex as a weapon to steamroll me—I don't trust that woman, and I'm not going to let you change the sub—" I didn't let her finish the sentence before I was the one taking a step back.

"Change the subject? So you want to fight this out right now?" I gave her a mocking smile, and my right hand began to shake. I ran my hands over my face and into my hair, let out a growl of irritation. After ten years of being together, I could not understand how she still didn't trust me even a little bit. "Christ, Selene!" I exploded, and I saw in Babygirl's face that she knew what was happening. She was well aware of what one of my episodes looked like. "I don't look at anyone but you. I take my work seriously, and I give it my all. The only woman I have ever fucked in my office is you. Not a colleague; not a secretary—you!" I jabbed a finger at her, and every muscle I had shook with rage. She could see how close to the edge I was and drew closer to me, alarmed. She took my hand in both of hers and kissed the back of it, and, little by little, the storm inside my head began to subside. Her touch always had the power to bring me back to myself and put to bed the monsters when they threatened to resurface.

"I'm sorry... I didn't mean to suggest that. It's just that... I get so jealous over you being surrounded by these bitches who I know would have zero problems destroying a family if it meant one night with you. You know that it's true," she said with a careworn sigh.

I looked down at her coldly, and she blinked miserably at me and squeezed my hand more tightly in hers. I knew she didn't really want to question my fidelity, but her jealousy was her worst enemy, and it often made her impulsive.

Selene was a mother who wanted to protect her family from all outside threats. I understood where her fears were coming from.

"You know, I have learned a few things from being an asshole for so long. I know how to spot these women you think are so dangerous and how to keep them away." I grabbed her around the waist and pulled her into me until she settled into my arms, where she so often took refuge.

"She's blond..." she said in a fearful murmur. She feared that my fixation on blond women might reemerge, as had happened a few years prior. She was afraid that I would once again start feeling the need to reenact my abuse, raping myself all over again.

It was Dr. Lively who told us we should be prepared for the possibility.

"That hasn't happened in a long time," I said softly. I always felt guilty when Selene had to confront the realities of who I was.

"But what if it does?" She was on the verge of tears, and I stroked her cheeks with my thumbs.

I did not want to see her miserable. Especially not because of me.

"Then, I hope you would still be able to accept me and that you wouldn't leave me." I pressed my forehead to hers, breathing in her scent. "I would never purposely let anyone divide us or destroy what we have together, but I can't predict the future, Babygirl. I still have the same conditions, you know..." I stroked her hair as she nestled deeper into my chest. I let her feel the thumping of my heart, a heart whose every pulse and tremor belonged to her. "I've decided I'm going to step back from the theater project. It's not really important to me, and I don't give a shit about working with that woman. I have other things I can work on, and it's more important for me to know that you have peace of mind," I said firmly.

Avoiding more uncomfortable situations with Sharon would be good for me as well.

I was strong, but I did still have periods of emotional instability when I was reminded of Kim and what she did to me, and it did sometimes feel like the only way to avoid falling into the void was to go back to my old habits. There were times when I had to force myself to take a step back and control the sick urge to punish myself again because I knew that, if I ever did make such a mistake, I would lose my Pearls, the most precious parts of my life.

Selene lifted her chin and gave me a probing look. She seemed confused by what I'd said.

"And no objections from you; I've already made my decision." Before she could reply, I kissed her soundly, pouring all the repressed passion of the day into her.

As usual, I was knocked off kilter by the sweet taste of her. Her kisses could gentle even the worst of me.

Because she had accepted all of it.

She had picked me for all that I was.

She would have had every right in the world to go out and find a better man, but she wanted me.

Only me.

....

After we'd hashed it out, the Sunday proceeded like normal. Babygirl was once again buzzing around me, and I monopolized my Little Pearl, holding her close to my chest and entertaining her all day.

"Could I at least say goodbye to my little star?" John grumbled, standing in the doorway while Nicole blew raspberries and flailed her tiny limbs as I gave her kisses.

"Your little star? She's your granddaughter, Dad. That's it."

Beside me, Selene chuckled, prepared to watch the two of us bicker yet again. I couldn't stand it when anyone else gave Nicole a nickname.

"Okay. So can I say goodbye to my granddaughter, Grandpa's little star?" John said in the almost eerie baby voice he used when he talked to my daughter.

Fortunately, for all that I loved her with all of my heart, I was not quite that addlepated.

"Actually, I also call her little star, and I will warn you, Dr.

Keller—grandmas get priority," Judith interjected, strutting into the room. She'd put on her elegant coat and was adjusting her shoulder-length hair. My father gave her a heated look, and she blushed before clearing her throat.

"You know, Ms. Martin, I'm always fascinated by your pointedly precise interjections. I believe there's a lot that you could teach me, if you'd only accept my invitation to have dinner..." He winked at her, and Judith pulled herself up, straight and wary. I'd never really understood their dynamic, and I didn't even know for sure whether they liked or disliked each other. But ever since Judith had gotten out of her long-term relationship with Professor Coleman, my father had started taking every opportunity to poke at her.

"Keep me posted on any developments with the little guy. We'll see you next Sunday." Selene gave Janel a hug, and then the other woman sagged against my brother. She was clearly exhausted after the full day she'd just had. I had no idea what it felt like for a woman to shoulder the burdens of a pregnancy, but I had been there for all nine months of Selene's thrills and miseries, so I could imagine how Janel was feeling then.

"Be good, Pup. You've caused enough trouble already," I told Logan, gesturing to his fiancée's round belly. Then I ruffled his hair, and he griped out an irritable "fuck off." Then, I gave Chloe a hug and politely suggested that Simon keep his hands off my sister until after the wedding. Selene cut in then to lay a calming hand on my shoulder.

When it was just the three of us at last, we went upstairs to our bedroom where Little Pearl's crib was also located.

Selene went into the bathroom to change while I settled into the leather armchair in front of the window and continued to hold my daughter in my arms. The full moon outside lit up her innocent little face. Her ocean eyes were dotted with gold and fixed attentively on me, delightedly roving over every inch of my face. Her little hand patted my chest and grasped my shirt in a tiny fist.

"Here we are again, Nicole. Time for our nightly chat…" I touched her little hand, and it vanished into mine. Her skin was milk-white, so different from mine, but it was my blood pumping in her veins. I was in awe at the power of nature and of a God who had given me such a miracle. "You know, Daddy gets afraid sometimes of watching you grow up in this messed-up world. Afraid you might meet evil people, people who might do mean things. Things I'd never want you to experience or even know about. Never." I breathed in her smell: baby powder and innocence and *mine*, and she kicked her plump legs, landing small blows on my thigh. "Your life and Mama's life are everything to me. The only things that really matter. And I'll always protect you. You know, before you, I didn't want to have a daughter because I was afraid. And then you were born, and I'm still so scared. I'm not a perfect man, but I do want to be a good father for you." She wrapped her small hand around my index finger as if to show me how she was clinging to me—how she needed me. "The first time you smiled at me, I knew that you were my second chance. Daddy promises to never let you down.

"I'll always be there for you. I'll tell you everything, all about Mama and me. I'll tell you about Grandpa John and Grandma Judith. I'll explain why Uncle Logan is a puppy and Aunt Chloe is a koala.

"I'll tell you all about my life, a life that began the day I met Tinkerbell and led up to the joy of your birth." I stood up, my peaceful, sleepy girl nestled in my arms. Her lips parted in a minuscule yawn as she snuggled closer to me. I kissed her forehead and hugged her gently, trying to banish the fear of not living up to her expectations.

Would she be proud of me one day?

"Asleep?"

I turned to find Selene leaning against the bathroom doorframe and watching me fondly. A silky blue-green nightie was the only thing covering her curvy body. Her nipples pressed against the fabric that caressed her soft body just like my hands were about to do.

I glanced down at our Little Pearl and found her eyes closed. Nicole was sleeping sweetly in my arms, as she often did.

My voice was the only lullaby sure to make her fall asleep quickly.

"She has as much hair as you do." Selene moved closer and began rubbing my shoulders. I shivered. Her touch was pure fire.

"Yeah, she's pretty like Daddy," I answered smugly. Selene rolled her eyes, took the baby, and moved over to the crib.

"Let's try to be quiet until she gets into deeper sleep." Selene returned to me, and I grabbed her hand, guiding her to the leather armchair in front of the window. The room was dark, save for the glow of a small table lamp.

I sat down and pulled her onto my lap, maneuvering her until she was straddling my hips. When she opened her eyes indulgently, the contact gave me goosebumps all over like a teenager. My eyes ate up her bare legs, and my hands followed, touching them possessively all the way up to her ass.

"You are the most beautiful thing I've ever had," I whispered breathlessly as I slipped my fingers beneath the straps of her nightgown and kissed the hollow of her throat. Her throat, her jaw, all the way up to her lush lips.

"Thank you," I whispered in her ear, my voice unsteady; it was as though our souls had briefly touched, and it left me shaken.

"For what?" she murmured. I smoothed down her long hair and then traced down and down the curve of her spine.

"Thank you for choosing me. Thank you for continuing to be my Neverland and for giving me the greatest gift: our Little Pearl," I admitted uncomfortably. I still wasn't used to exposing myself like that.

Her eyes gleamed with love, and I knew she was about to cry.

"No, Babygirl, don't do that," I muttered gruffly.

She broke into laughter instead and rested her head in the crook of my neck, holding on tight to me.

I wanted to keep kissing her and take off the rest of her clothes, but I was distracted by a small figure staring at us.

The Boy stood just a few feet away in his familiar Oklahoma City jersey and dirty shorts with an insolent smile on his face.

I was not surprised. I often encountered him around the house or even at my office.

He was always there, and he probably always would be.

I had not abandoned him—I could never.

I still had nightmares about Kimberly, but every time I did, Selene was always there to touch me and hold me close and remind me that dreams existed also. I had gone back on the medication that I'd stopped against Dr. Lively's advice all those years ago, and I acknowledged that I would likely have to take it for the rest of my life because the things that troubled me were not the kind of things you cured.

The best I could do was keep them under control, but even in that, I had brave Selene by my side to help me manage my impulses and to soften my rough edges. I still went to group sessions at Dr. Lively's office at least twice a month, and Selene went with me, holding my hand tight to remind me that everything we went through, we went through together.

I gestured for the Boy to get out because this was for sure not the moment to talk to me, and he chuckled as he ran over to the window. He climbed up onto the sill, and before opening it, he turned to look at me.

Over time, the two souls in my body had reached a state of compromise. They were no longer at war; neither was a winner nor a loser.

There would always be an Adult Neil just as there would always be the Boy, who now threw open the window and took flight, vanishing into the starry sky.

I knew that he would be back, just not to hurt me this time.

"What are you looking at?" Selene said. I looked away from the window to her ocean eyes and reached out to touch her lips. All was well; the Boy had simply learned how to fly away from the pain, and I had accepted his presence inside myself.

"Nothing, Tinkerbell." I shrugged and slid my hand into her hair, cupping the back of her head and drawing her to me. I made only one request of her, the only one I'd ever really needed: "Kiss me..."

She stared at me, maybe wondering when I had been contaminated by her.

From the very first moment I met her.

I did not consider myself a perfect man, and I knew I never would be. Maybe that was all love really was: accepting yourself and all your imperfections.

There are no fairy tales, just stories with love in them—love in all its forms.

Once, in a grocery store, I told Selene a story about her future.

I told her how she'd have two beautiful children—a girl and a boy. How she'd have a beautiful home and a husband who adored her. I told her that she would be an independent, appealing, elegant woman and how her daughter would have her ocean eyes and her son her tenacity.

I told her about the parties she'd have with music and barbecue and how she'd be an exemplary mother, a dream wife, and the perfect woman.

I even told her that her husband would be a lucky man.

But I'd gotten one thing wrong. I told her that I would be far away from all of it, traveling aimlessly across the world.

Instead, I would be the man at her side, the father of her children, and she would be my future, along with the chaos that always circled around me, the issues I would always have, and the ever-present ghosts of my past. And we had made our peace with that.

There was lots that was imperfect about us, but that's what made us unique. Who wanted another charming prince and a princess?

Instead, I would always be a dark knight with torments deep inside, and my Babygirl would always be the greatest of warriors.

And now you who have gotten to know me and come this far, having read my story and heard all about the chaos surrounding me, tell me the truth: How often did you want to smack me?

You might have thought my way of being impossible to understand, my nature terrible, my mind twisted, but if I've lingered in your heart at least a little bit…

Never think that you can't do it.

Never think that the light does not exist or that not everyone is meant for the sun.

That life is a tunnel with no exit.

Do not forget that the sky is vast enough to offer opportunity to everyone.

Do not think that you are alone or that you aren't strong enough to face this life.

Never believe that you are fundamentally wrong.

No one ever said it was easy, but no one ever said it was impossible.

Be happy.

Seek happiness everywhere.

Love and accept yourself.

Fight your monsters and slay them.

Grab your past by the hair and toss it away from you.

Seek out your Neverland.

They hide, but I can tell you that they do exist.

It manifests in different ways and takes on all sorts of disguises, but it's there, and it's close.

Look around; it likes to play hide-and-seek, but I'm confident you'll find it.

Look for a star—or fifty thousand of them—up in the sky, and let it obscure your troubles.

Have a piece of candy or a slice of cherry pie and savor the sweet parts of life.

Or open up a bag of pistachios and think of me as though I were right there, your hand in mine.

Fly high over the obstacles in your path the way that Peter Pan and Tinkerbell would.

Keep smiling.

There is a second chance for everyone; there's one for you too.

You are not a monster.

The ones who hurt you are.

Rest a hand on your chest and close your eyes.

You can feel your heart beating, can't you?

That means Life is on your side.

So live and do it to the fullest.

Fuck what other people think.

That's what I did.

I moved on, and finally… I won.

And now it's us: Neil, Selene, and Nicole.

Two Pearls and their Shell.

…For all victims of violence and sexual abuse.

**WONDERING HOW IT ALL BEGAN?
READ ON FOR A QUICK LOOK AT
LET THE *GAME* BEGIN.**

1

SELENE

They say in life we have to make the right choices, but we don't always have the ability to recognize them. Who establishes right and wrong? Does the right thing really make us happy?

I was lying comfortably on my bed and surfing on my laptop. I was supposed to leave for New York that morning, though I wasn't enthusiastic about it. I lived with my mother in an apartment in Indian Village, a residential neighborhood of Detroit. At least that's where I *had* lived until my mother had the bright idea to turn my life upside down overnight.

I hooked one ankle around the other and kept on scrolling through the gossip blogs about one of the most famous surgeons in New York, Matt Anderson, and especially about his partner, Mia Lindhom, the high-profile director of an important fashion house.

I carefully examined the photos of her taken at various moments in her day. She was all sophisticated beauty: tall, with a refined, slender frame. Her hair was the color of gold, her eyes a luminous gentian blue.

"He chose well," I commented to no one as I chewed on my index fingernail.

Yes, Matt Anderson (also known as my father) had, after a series of affairs, finally decided to leave my mother for a younger, more beautiful and more famous woman.

I wondered if she had children too, but there was no information on the subject.

"Selene! Don't pretend you can't hear me!" My mother came into the room, huffy after shouting my name for several minutes. Still, I didn't pull my gaze away from the pictures of Matt and Mia looking happy and carefree together.

"Since when does he like blonds?" I asked, scowling seriously as she walked around my room, gathering up the clothes scattered here and there. I wasn't a neat freak like her.

"Since he met Mia, probably? Anyway, I have your suitcase packed downstairs," she reminded me, though it was hardly necessary. I knew full well that my flight was scheduled for ten o'clock. I had already bathed and dressed, albeit reluctantly. I didn't want to repair any relationship with Matt, much less become part of his life after he had been so completely uninterested in mine for so long. So, I kept opening random web pages, just to keep my mind occupied even as I could feel the anguish rising inside me.

Parents rarely understand how much their actions affect their children's emotional state. My adolescence was marred by fighting and my father's constant affairs. Indelible memories that I tried to fight against every day in vain. Going to live with him was a terrible punishment for me that was probably going to bring all sorts of unhealed wounds to the surface.

"Selene..." Mom sighed, sitting down on the bed beside me. She closed my laptop gently and smiled at me, finally getting my attention. "I just want you to try," she said in an indulgent murmur.

Sure, she wanted me to *try* to accept a man who had long since ceased to be my father.

Four years had now passed since he left us to live with his current partner. Four years in which he had tried to call and talk to me but got no response. Four years in which, every time he tried to see me, I locked myself in my room and waited for him to leave. I sighed at those nagging memories and tilted my chin down to hide my pain from the only person I truly loved.

"I can't do it..." Memories of her weeping and raving over the lack of respect shown by the man she'd married were embedded too deeply in my mind.

Matt had started off by sleeping with a nurse ten years his junior. One lover became two, three, four...until I lost count. Or rather, until Mia came along and took him away from us for good.

"Sure you can do it. You're a bright girl..." She stroked the back of my hand and gazed lovingly at me. She believed in me, and I never wanted to let her down. Never.

"I don't want anything to do with Matt," I muttered like a wayward child. I needed to act like a woman, put on the mask of acceptance and display a certain maturity, but it was nearly impossible to act rationally when anger had taken me over inside.

"Selene, I know it's not going to be easy. I don't expect the two of you to get along right away, but I at least want you to give it a chance... You've refused to speak to him for too long." She looked at me with the pained expression that inevitably corralled my pride. She was fully aware that her big blue eyes—identical to my own— had the power to make me surrender. Still, I tried to make my case.

"Mom, that man doesn't deserve my respect. *You* know..." I answered, scowling, and it was the truth. After everything she and I had gone through *by ourselves*, my mother knew very well how much it cost me to go along with her request that I live with a "father" who was nothing of the sort.

"I get it, sweetheart. But I've forgiven him for what he did. You should, too."

I stared silently into her eyes. My mother had the enormous fortitude required to forgive that man's wrongdoings, but I wasn't like her. I didn't have her strength.

ACKNOWLEDGMENTS

For the third time, I find myself sitting before a blank page, trying to find the words to express my immense gratitude toward all the people who have chosen to go on this incredible journey with me.

Where do I begin?

I'll start by saying that, since I was a child, I have dreamed of writing a novel. A novel that depicted reality in all its facets, the negative and the positive. I chose the theme of sexual abuse to highlight a social issue that is a persistent problem to this day. A problem with psychological and emotional consequences, which I have tried to explore respectfully with real-life victims in mind. I hope I have been able to convey to you the importance of accepting loved ones without making them feel that something is wrong with them and the importance of going beyond judgments or prejudices. And, of course, the importance of powerful feelings like love, which often flexes its power silently, taking on unexpected and extraordinary forms.

I very much want to thank my readers, my fearless Tigers who believed that Neil and Selene were special right from the start and that, despite their craziness, their messy relationship deserved to be seen.

There are so many of you, and each one has contributed to the development of this project, which was born in my early twenties when I still believed that my passion was a pipe dream and I was too afraid to come out of my shell. Back when the thought of presenting these two disasters to the world was totally out of the question.

I was so afraid, but I've realized since then that fear is so often what keeps us from flying, and we are all strong enough to overcome it.

I'd like to thank my family, who support and encourage me every day to get better, to grow, and to never give up even when it gets difficult.

Thanks to my publishing house Sperling and Kupfer, which I have always called Selene's "Mama" because they've believed so much in me and in the creation of this series.

And last but certainly not least, I want to thank my editor Elena Paganelli, who, right from the first, took me by the hand and guided me on this extraordinary adventure. She swept away all my worries and fears. She allowed me to explore my inner self through my writing, through collaborative work, and through understanding, dialogue, professionalism, and mutual respect. I will forever be grateful to her not only as an editor but also as a dear friend on this long journey.

I adore you all.

Kira Shell

ABOUT THE AUTHOR

Kira Shell is a bestselling Italian author with over 600,000 copies of her dark romances sold. She began writing the Kiss Me Like You Love Me series in 2017. The series has over six million Wattpad reads. Kira is a law graduate and lives in Italy.

Instagram: @kira_shell_
TikTok: @kirashell